Get connected power of the Internet

McDougal Littell's online resources for students and parents provide motivating instruction, practice, and learning support.

Visit classzone.com for eEdition Plus Online purchasing information and a free demo

eEdition Plus ONLINE

This online version of the text encourages students to explore geography through interactive features.

- Animated maps and infographics
- Onscreen notetaking
- Links to online test practice

classzone.com

With a click of the mouse, students gain immediate access to this companion Web site to *World Cultures and Geography*.

- Links correlated to the text
- Web Research Guide
- Demographic data updates
- Self-scoring quizzes
- Interactive games and activities
- Links to current events
- Test practice

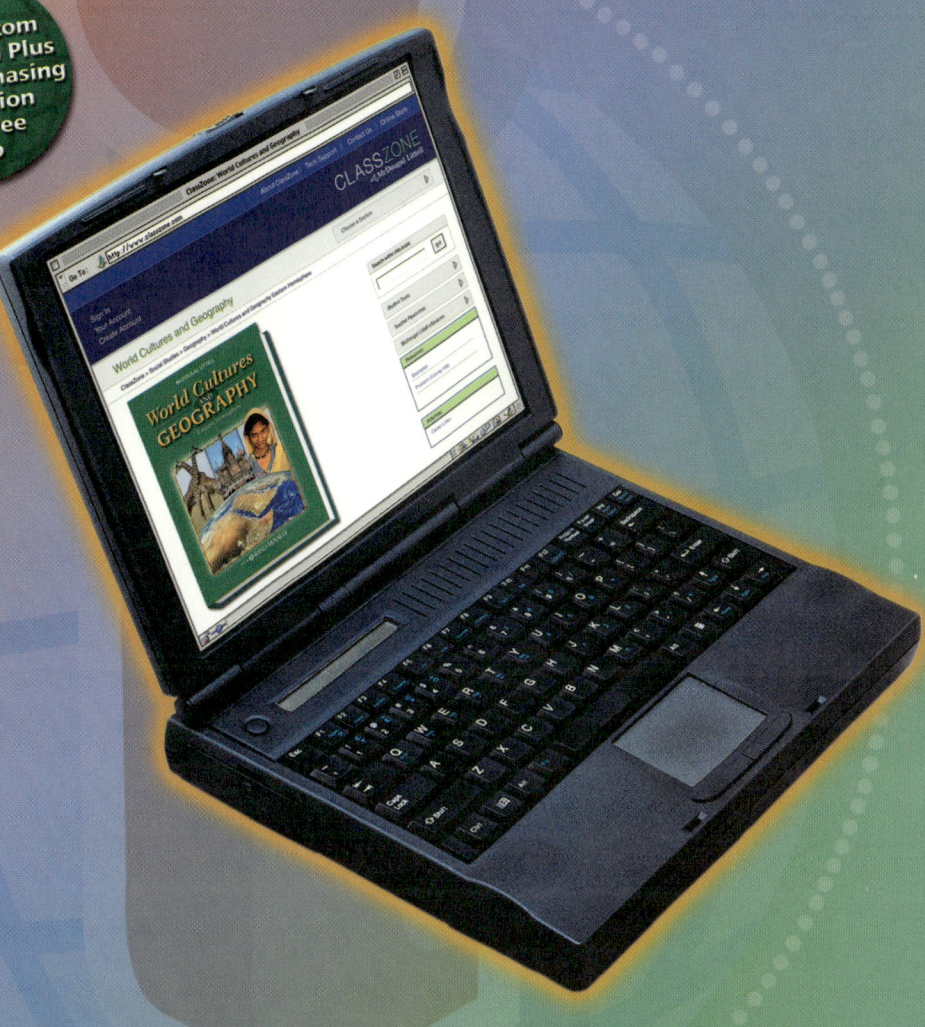

Now it all clicks!™

McDougal Littell

World Cultures AND GEOGRAPHY

Eastern Hemisphere

McDOUGAL LITTELL

McDOUGAL LITTELL

World Cultures AND GEOGRAPHY

Eastern Hemisphere

Sarah Witham Bednarz

Inés M. Miyares

Mark C. Schug

Charles S. White

McDougal Littell
A DIVISION OF HOUGHTON MIFFLIN COMPANY

Senior Consultants

Sarah Witham Bednarz is associate professor of geography at Texas A&M University, where she has taught since 1988. She earned a Ph.D. in educational curriculum and instruction in 1992 from Texas A&M University and has written extensively about geography literacy and education. Dr. Bednarz was an author of *Geography for Life: National Geography Standards,* 1994. In 1997 she received the International Excellence Award from the Texas A&M University International Programs Office.

Inés M. Miyares is associate professor of geography at Hunter College–City University of New York. Born in Havana, Cuba, and fluent in Spanish, Dr. Miyares has focused much of her scholarship on Latin America, immigration and refugee policy, and urban ethnic geography. She holds a Ph.D. in geography from Arizona State University. In 1999 Dr. Miyares was the recipient of the Hunter College Performance Excellence Award for excellence in teaching, research, scholarly writing, and service.

Mark C. Schug is director of the University of Wisconsin–Milwaukee Center for Economic Education. A 30-year veteran of middle school, high school, and university classrooms, Dr. Schug has been cited for excellence in teaching by the University of Wisconsin–Milwaukee and the Minnesota Council on Economic Education. In addition to coauthoring eight national economics curriculum programs, Dr. Schug has spoken on economic issues to audiences throughout the world. Dr. Schug edited *The Senior Economist* for the National Council for Economics Education from 1986 to 1996.

Charles S. White is associate professor in the School of Education at Boston University, where he teaches methods of instruction in social studies. Dr. White has written and spoken extensively on the role of technology in social studies education. He has received numerous awards for his scholarship, including the 1995 Federal Design Achievement Award from the National Endowment for the Arts, for the Teaching with Historic Places project. In 1997, Dr. White taught his Models of Teaching doctoral course at the Universidad San Francisco de Quito, Ecuador.

Copyright © 2005 by McDougal Littell, a division of Houghton Mifflin Company. All rights reserved.

Maps on pages A1–A37 © Rand McNally & Company. All rights reserved.

Warning: No part of this work may be reproduced or transmitted in any form or by any means, electronic or mechanical, including photocopying and recording, or by any information storage or retrieval system without the prior written permission of McDougal Littell unless such copying is expressly permitted by federal copyright law. With the exception of not-for-profit transcription in Braille, McDougal Littell is not authorized to grant permission for further uses of copyrighted selections reprinted in this text without the permission of their owners. Permission must be obtained from the individual copyright owners as identified herein. Address inquiries to Supervisor, Rights and Permissions, McDougal Littell, P.O. Box 1667, Evanston, IL 60204.

Acknowledgments begin on page R60.

ISBN 0-618-37741-7

Printed in the United States of America

X 2 3 4 5 6 7 8 9 – VJM – 07 06 05 04

Consultants and Reviewers

Content Consultants

Charmarie Blaisdell
Department of History
Northeastern University
Boston, Massachusetts

David Buck, Ph.D.
Department of History
University of Wisconsin–Milwaukee
Milwaukee, Wisconsin

Erich Gruen, Ph.D.
Departments of Classics and History
University of California, Berkeley
Berkeley, California

Charles Haynes, Ph.D.
Senior Scholar for Religious Freedom
The Freedom Forum First
  Amendment Center
Arlington, Virginia

Alusine Jalloh, Ph.D.
The Africa Program
University of Texas at Arlington
Arlington, Texas

Shabbir Mansuri
Council on Islamic Education
Fountain Valley, California

Michelle Maskiell, Ph.D.
Department of History
Montana State University
Bozeman, Montana

Vasudha Narayanan, Ph.D.
Department of Religion
University of Florida
Gainesville, Florida

Amanda Porterfield, Ph.D.
Department of Religious Studies
University of Wyoming
Laramie, Wyoming

Mark Wasserman, Ph.D.
Department of History
Rutgers University
New Brunswick, New Jersey

Multicultural Advisory Board

Dr. Munir Bashshur
Education Department
American University of Beirut
Beirut, Lebanon

Stephen Fugita
Ethnic Studies Program
Santa Clara University
Santa Clara, California

Sharon Harley
Afro-American Studies Program
University of Maryland at
  College Park
College Park, Maryland

Doug Monroy
Department of Southwest Studies
Colorado College
Colorado Springs, Colorado

Cliff Trafzer
Departments of History and
  Ethnic Studies
University of California, Riverside
Riverside, California

v

Some scientists believe the continents were once joined, page 35.

A variety of people inhabit the world, page 14.

UNIT 1

Introduction to World Cultures and Geography

STUDENT GUIDE TO THE SUNSHINE STATE STANDARDS	xix
STRATEGIES FOR TAKING THE FCAT	S1
PART 1 Introducing the FCAT	S2
PART 2 FCAT Strategies and Practice	S6
RAND MCNALLY ATLAS	A1
FLORIDA STATE ALMANAC	A38
GEOGRAPHY SKILLS HANDBOOK	4

Chapter 1 Welcome to the World   14

FOCUS ON GEOGRAPHY	15
READING SOCIAL STUDIES	16
1 The World at Your Fingertips	17
Citizenship in Action	21
Interdisciplinary Challenge Investigate Your World	22
2 Many Regions, Many Cultures	24
SKILLBUILDER Reading a Time Zone Map	27
Literature Connections "The Giant Kuafu Chases the Sun"	
CHINESE FOLK TALE	28

Chapter 2 The Geographer's World   32

FOCUS ON GEOGRAPHY	33
READING SOCIAL STUDIES	34
1 The Five Themes of Geography	35
Citizenship in Action	39
SKILLBUILDER Reading Latitude and Longitude	41
Linking Past and Present The Legacy of World Exploration	42
Technology: 2004 A Map of Earth in 3-D	44
2 The Geographer's Tools	45

Satellite photographs of Earth, pages 2–3

UNIT 2

Europe, Russia, and the Independent Republics

UNIT ATLAS   54

Chapter 3 Western Europe: Its Land and Early History   64
- FOCUS ON GEOGRAPHY   65
- READING SOCIAL STUDIES   66
- **1** A Land of Varied Riches   67
- **2** Ancient Greece   72
  - SKILLBUILDER Making a Generalization   77
- **3** Ancient Rome   78
- **4** Time of Change: The Middle Ages   84

Chapter 4 The Growth of New Ideas   92
- FOCUS ON GEOGRAPHY   93
- READING SOCIAL STUDIES   94
- **1** Renaissance Connections   95
- **2** Traders, Explorers, and Colonists   101
  - SKILLBUILDER Researching Topics on the Internet   106
- **3** The Age of Revolution   107
- **4** The Russian Empire   112
  - **Technology:** 1781 James Watt's Double-Action Steam Engine   117

Chapter 5 Europe: War and Change   120
- FOCUS ON GEOGRAPHY   121
- READING SOCIAL STUDIES   122
- **1** European Empires   123
- **2** Europe at War   127
  - SKILLBUILDER Reading a Political Cartoon   133
  - **Literature Connections** "Fionn Mac Cumhail and the Giant's Causeway," retold by Una Leavy **IRISH LEGEND**   134
- **3** The Soviet Union   136

A stained-glass window from the Middle Ages, page 88

A wealthy merchant family built this Renaissance palace, page 97.

These dogs helped fight World War I, page 129.

J.K. Rowling wrote the popular Harry Potter books, page 177.

UNIT 2 continued from page vii

Chapter 6 Modern Europe — 144
FOCUS ON GEOGRAPHY — 145
READING SOCIAL STUDIES — 146
  1 Eastern Europe Under Communism — 147
    SKILLBUILDER Using an Electronic Card Catalog — 153
  2 Eastern Europe and Russia — 154
  3 The European Union — 161
    Linking Past and Present The Legacy of Europe — 166

Chapter 7 Europe Today — 170
FOCUS ON GEOGRAPHY — 171
READING SOCIAL STUDIES — 172
  1 The United Kingdom — 173
  2 Sweden — 178
    Interdisciplinary Challenge Spend a Day in Renaissance Florence — 182
  3 France — 184
  4 Germany — 188
    SKILLBUILDER Making an Outline — 192
  5 Poland — 193

The Brandenburg Gate in Berlin, page 141

A high-speed train rushes across France, pages 144–145.

UNIT 3
North Africa and Southwest Asia

UNIT ATLAS — 202

Church of the Holy Selpulcher in Jerusalem, page 231

Chapter 8 North Africa and Southwest Asia: Place and Times — 210
- **FOCUS ON GEOGRAPHY** — 211
- **READING SOCIAL STUDIES** — 212
- **1** Physical Geography — 213
- **2** Ancient Mesopotamia and the Fertile Crescent — 217
  - SKILLBUILDER Comparing Climate and Vegetation Maps — 222
- **3** Ancient Egypt — 223
  - Citizenship in Action — 225
  - Technology: 3500 B.C. The Potter's Wheel — 228
- **4** Birthplace of Three Religions — 229
- **5** Muslim Empires — 234

Chapter 9 North Africa and Southwest Asia Today — 240
- **FOCUS ON GEOGRAPHY** — 241
- **READING SOCIAL STUDIES** — 242
- **1** A Troubled Century — 243
  - SKILLBUILDER Reading a Historical Map — 248
- **2** Resources and Religion — 249
  - Interdisciplinary Challenge Explain the Pyramids of Ancient Egypt — 254
- **3** Egypt Today — 256
  - Literature Connections "Thread by Thread" by Bracha Serri YEMENITE POETRY — 262
- **4** Israel Today — 264
  - Linking Past and Present The Legacy of North Africa and Southwest Asia — 268
- **5** Turkey Today — 270

Nefertiti, queen of Egypt, page 268

The Blue Mosque in Istanbul, pages 200–201

ix

UNIT 4

Africa South of the Sahara

UNIT ATLAS 278

Mount Kenya, page 292

Chapter 10 Africa South of the Sahara: Geography and History   288
FOCUS ON GEOGRAPHY   289
READING SOCIAL STUDIES   290
1 The Geography of Africa South of the Sahara   291
    Citizenship in Action   294
2 African Cultures and Empires   296
3 The Impact of Colonialism on African Life   301
    SKILLBUILDER Interpreting a Chart   306
4 The Road to Independence   307
    Technology: 1100 House of Stone   311

Chapter 11 Western and Central Africa   314
FOCUS ON GEOGRAPHY   315
READING SOCIAL STUDIES   316
1 History and Political Change   317
    Citizenship in Action   320
    Linking Past and Present The Legacy of Africa South of the Sahara   322
2 Economies and Cultures   324
    SKILLBUILDER Drawing Conclusions   329
3 Nigeria Today   330

A Bantu woman, page 296

Chapter 12 Eastern and Southern Africa   336
FOCUS ON GEOGRAPHY   337
READING SOCIAL STUDIES   338
1 History and Governments   339
    Interdisciplinary Challenge Discover the Source of the Nile   344
2 Economies and Cultures   346
    SKILLBUILDER Reading a Satellite Image   351
    Literature Connections "My Father's Farm," by Isaac Olaleye NIGERIAN POETRY   352
3 South Africa Today   354
4 Kenya Today   358

A cheetah in Serengeti National Park, page 303

UNIT 5

Southern Asia

UNIT ATLAS — 366

Chapter 13 Southern Asia: Place and Times — 374
FOCUS ON GEOGRAPHY — 375
READING SOCIAL STUDIES — 376
1 Physical Geography — 377
2 Ancient India — 385
   SKILLBUILDER Reading an Elevation Map — 391
3 Ancient Crossroads — 392

Chapter 14 India and Its Neighbors — 400
FOCUS ON GEOGRAPHY — 401
READING SOCIAL STUDIES — 402
1 History — 403
   Technology: 750 B.C. Qanats — 408
2 Governments — 409
   Interdisciplinary Challenge Tour the Ganges River — 414
3 Economies — 416
4 The Culture of India — 420
   SKILLBUILDER Understanding Point of View — 424
5 Pakistan — 425
   Literature Connections "The Sandstorm," from Shabanu: Daughter of the Wind by Suzanne Fisher Staples
   REALISTIC FICTION — 432

Chapter 15 Southeast Asia Today — 434
FOCUS ON GEOGRAPHY — 435
READING SOCIAL STUDIES — 436
1 History and Governments — 437
   Citizenship in Action — 441
   Linking Past and Present The Legacy of Southern Asia — 442
2 Economies and Cultures — 444
   SKILLBUILDER Distinguishing Fact from Opinion — 448
3 Vietnam Today — 449

A farmer in Afghanistan plows a field, page 417.

Mount Merapi in Indonesia, page 381

An Indian woman

Ancient statues stand on Easter Island, page 529.

Tokyo, the capital of Japan, page 488

The kangaroo lives only in Australia, page 473.

East Asia, Australia, Oceania, and Antarctica

UNIT ATLAS   458

Chapter 16 East Asia, Australia, and Oceania: Land and History   466
FOCUS ON GEOGRAPHY   467
READING SOCIAL STUDIES   468
1 Physical Geography   469
2 Ancient China   475
    SKILLBUILDER Creating a Database   481
    Literature Connections "War Wounds," from *Echoes of the White Giraffe* by Sook Nyul Choi REALISTIC FICTION   482
3 Ancient Japan   484
    Citizenship in Action   485
    Technology: 2009 Three Gorges Dam   489

Chapter 17 China and Its Neighbors   492
FOCUS ON GEOGRAPHY   493
READING SOCIAL STUDIES   494
1 Establishing Modern China   495
    Interdisciplinary Challenge Visit the Forbidden City   500
2 The Governments of East Asia   502
3 The Economies of East Asia   506
4 The Cultures of East Asia   510
5 Establishing Modern Japan   516
    SKILLBUILDER Reading a Population Density Map   521

Dancers perform in Papua New Guinea, page 533.

Chapter 18 Australia, New Zealand, Oceania, and Antarctica   524

FOCUS ON GEOGRAPHY   525
READING SOCIAL STUDIES   526

1 History and Governments   527
2 Economies and Cultures   531
    SKILLBUILDER Using Primary Sources   535
3 Antarctica   536
    Linking Past and Present The Legacy of East Asia, Australia, and Oceania   540

SPECIAL REPORT Terrorism and the War in Iraq   544

SKILLBUILDER HANDBOOK   R2
ENGLISH GLOSSARY   R24
SPANISH GLOSSARY   R35
INDEX   R47

Mount Uluru in Australia is the largest free-standing rock in the world, pages 466–467.

xiii

Features

Interdisciplinary Challenge

Investigate Your World 22
Spend a Day in Renaissance Florence 182
Explain the Pyramids of Ancient Egypt 254
Discover the Source of the Nile 344
Tour the Ganges River 414
Visit the Forbidden City 500

Infographics, Time Lines, and Cartoons

Technology: 2004—A Map of Earth in 3-D 44
Technology: 1781—James Watt's
   Double-Action Steam Engine 117
Political Cartoon: World War I 128
Political Cartoon: Versailles Treaty 133
Political Cartoon: World War II 143
Infographic: The Houses of Parliament 175
Technology: 3500 B.C.—The Potter's Wheel 228
Infographic: Why Camels Are Well Adapted
   to Desert Travel 298
Technology: 1100—House of Stone 311
Technology: 750 B.C.—Qanats 408
Technology: 2009—Three Gorges Dam 489
Infographic: Bunraku Puppetry 513

Literature Connections

"The Giant Kuafu Chases the Sun" 28
"Fionn Mac Cumhail and the Giant's Causeway," from
   Irish Fairy Tales & Legends by Una Leavy .. 134
"Thread by Thread" by Bracha Serri 262
"My Father's Farm," from *The Distant Talking
   Drum* by Isaac Olaleye 352
"The Sandstorm," from *Shabanu: Daughter of
   the Wind* by Suzanne Fisher Staples 432
"War Wounds," from *Echoes of the White Giraffe*
   by Sook Nyul Choi 482

Linking Past and Present

The Legacy of World Exploration 42
The Legacy of Europe 166
The Legacy of North Africa and Southwest Asia .. 268
The Legacy of Africa South of the Sahara 322
The Legacy of Southern Asia 442
The Legacy of East Asia, Australia, and
   Oceania 540

DATELINE

San Francisco, U.S.A., June 26, 1945 17
Lucknow, India, May 10, 1857 24
Frankfurt, Germany, January 6, 1912 35
Babylonia, about 600 B.C. 45
London, England, May 6, 1994 67
Athens, Greece, February 2, 1997 72
Rome, 295 B.C. 78
Rome, A.D. 476 84
Paris, France, 1269 95
Sagres, Portugal, 1421 101
Leipzig, Germany, April 1839 107
Moscow, Russia, 1560 112
Norway, September 1905 123
Sarajevo, Bosnia-Herzegovina, June 28, 1914 127
Warsaw, Poland, May 14, 1955 136
The Kremlin, Moscow, April 12, 1961 147
The Kremlin, Moscow, 1988 154
Western Europe, December 2001 161
Barcelona, Spain, May 30, 1999 173
Stockholm, Sweden, December 4, 2001 178
Paris, France, August 26, 1944 184
Berlin, Germany, October 3, 1990 188

xiv

Gdańsk, Poland, 1980 193	Mauryan Empire, 232 B.C. 385
Mesopotamia, 3000 B.C. 213	The rain forests of Cambodia, 1861 392
Babylon, Hammurabi's Empire, 1750 B.C. 217	Ramnurger, near Benares on the Ganges River, April 19, 1796 403
Cairo, Egypt, 1458 B.C. 223	
Jerusalem, June 10, 1967 229	New Delhi, India, August 15, 1947 409
Mecca, Arabia, 9th day of Dhul Hiijah, A.D. 622 234	Manthini, India, July 1999 416
Sèvres, France, August 10, 1920 243	Agra, northern India, 1643 420
Khuzistan province, Persia (Iran), 1908 249	Pakistan, August 14, 1947 425
Cairo, Egypt, November 17, 1869 456	Burma, 1274 437
Tel Aviv, Palestine, July 14, 1921 264	Surin, Thailand, November 17, 2001 444
Ankara, Turkey, November 25, 1925 270	Saigon, South Vietnam, April 30, 1975 449
Bamako, Mali, March 8, 2000 291	Yokohama, Japan, September 1, 1923 469
Southern Africa, A.D. 500 296	The Imperial Palace, China, 2640 B.C. 475
The Royal Palace, Kongo, July 6, 1526 301	The coast of Japan, A.D. 1281 484
Nairobi, Kenya, December 12, 1963 307	The Forbidden City, Beijing, China, February 12, 1912 495
Berlin, Germany, February 26, 1885 317	
Yaounde, Cameroon, October 1, 2000 324	Seoul, South Korea, December 10, 2000 502
Zazzua, Hausaland, ancient Nigeria, 1566 330	Baku, Azerbaijan, September 1998 506
Hadar, Ethiopia, November 1974 339	Beijing, China, July 12, 2001 510
Ethiopia, 1985 346	Tokyo, Japan, May 3, 1947 516
Witwatersrand Main Reef, South Africa, 1896 354	Waitangi, New Zealand, 1940 527
Kenya, 1999 358	Sydney, Australia, September 15, 2000 531
Nepal, Southern Asia, May 29, 1953 377	South Pole, Antarctica, December 14, 1911 536

SKILLBUILDER

Reading a Time Zone Map 27	Interpreting a Chart 306
Reading Latitude and Longitude 41	Drawing Conclusions 329
Making a Generalization 77	Reading a Satellite Image 351
Researching Topics on the Internet 106	Reading an Elevation Map 391
Reading a Political Cartoon 133	Understanding Point of View 424
Using an Electronic Card Catalog 153	Distinguishing Fact from Opinion 448
Making an Outline 192	Creating a Database 481
Comparing Climate and Vegetation Maps 222	Reading a Population Density Map 521
Reading a Historical Map 248	Using Primary Sources 535

Citizenship IN ACTION

High-Tech for the Developing World 21	Aid for Children 320
Saving Special Places 39	Aung San Suu Kyi 441
Recording the Past 225	Tokyo National Research Institute for Cultural Properties 485
Helping the Hungry 294	

Strange but TRUE

Pictures to Words 25	The Fish That Did Not Die 295
Spartan Soldiers 74	Floating Seeds 341
Roman Law 79	The World's Most Destructive Volcano 382
Rasputin 116	Dragons of Komodo 439
War Dogs 129	The Tomb of Shih Huang-ti 476
Space Dogs 148	Mysterious Stone Statues 529
The Dead Sea 215	Gondwana the Supercontinent 539

Connections To...

Science: Digging into the Past 18
Math: Measuring Earth 46
Language: Metropolis 73
History: The Bayeux Tapestry 86–87
Economics: The Middle Class 88
Math: Perspective 98
Science: New Ships 103
Science: Pollution 157
Language: The Russian Language 159

Economics: Tourism 163
History: Lascaux Cave Paintings 185
Citizenship: Neve Shalom/Wahat al-Salem 266
Literature: Looking for Troy 272
Science: Disappearing Tusks 325
History: Ancient Churches 350
Technology: Drawbacks to Dams 428
Technology: Gunpowder 478
Technology: TV in Tuvalu 532

Spotlight on Culture

Mercator Map 47
Architecture 82
The Printing Press 99
The Hermitage Museum 115
The Ballets Russes 125
Soviet Film 140
Solzhenitsyn 150
Easter in Ukraine 156
The Development of Cuneiform 220

Persian Carpets 252
Yam Festivals 309
Seats of Art 327
The Beat Goes On 348
The *Mahabharata* 422
Wayang Kulit 446
Fine Protection 487
The Martial Arts 514
Maori Carvings 528

Biography

Amartya Sen 20
Aristotle 76
The Medici Family 97
Anne Frank 131
Beethoven 190
Hatshepsut 226
Anwar Sadat 258

Wole Soyinka 332
Nelson Mandela 355
Ashoka 389
Mohandas Gandhi 406
Sun Yat-sen 497
Charlie Perkins 533
Robert Falcon Scott 538

Focus on Geography

How have geographic features influenced
    settlement patterns? 15
How has new technology increased our
    knowledge of Earth? 33
How does the Gulf Stream affect the climate
    of Europe? 65
How can trade spread disease? 93
How has Europe's small landmass affected its history? . . 121
How are the new republics of Eastern Europe using
    natural resources to build their economies? 145
Why is it important for Europeans to protect
    their seas? 171
How have sheep contributed to the spread
    of deserts in North Africa? 211
How have rich oil deposits affected Southwest
    Asia and the world? 241

Who owns a country? 289
How can an entire town move across a country? 315
How might a country's wealth lead to its poverty? . . . 337
How did rivers contribute to the development
    of civilizations? 375
How has a sudden increase in population
    affected South Asia? 401
How has migration influenced Southeast Asia's
    culture? 435
Does land area have any influence on population? . . . 467
How does exchanging ideas affect a region's
    development? 493
How can people affect a region's environment? 525

The World's Heritage

Sagarmatha National Park 36	The Pyramids and the Great Sphinx 260
Ancient Greek Architecture 75	A Wealth of Animals 303
The Scientific Method 108	Life in Mohenjo-Daro 386
Russian Icons 158	Nonviolence 412
The Houses of Parliament 175	Cambodia's Temple Treasures 438
The Plow 214	The Longest Wall 480

VOICES FROM . . .

Today: David McCullough 18	**Africa:** Pan-African Congress, 1945 308
Ancient Greece: Heraclitus 75	**Ghana:** Kofi Annan 320
Sumeria: A student scribe 221	**China:** Confucius 477
Israel: David Ben-Gurion 265	**Australia:** Barbara Marie Brewster 534

MAPS

UNIT 1
Culture Regions of the World 25
World Time Zones 27
African Time Zones 31
Pangaea 35
Australia Today 36
Human Migration 39
Latitudes and Longitudes of the World 41
Road Map of North Island, New Zealand 46
Mercator Projection 47
Robinson Projection 47
World Population and Life Expectancy, 2000 48
Latitudes and Longitudes of Australia 51

UNIT 2
The Channel Tunnel 67
Land Use in Europe Today 71
Greek Colonization, 800 B.C. 73
Extent of Roman Control, 509 B.C. to 146 B.C. 80
The Roman Empire, A.D. 14 81
The Gulf Stream 91
Italian City-States, c. 1350 96
Routes of Portuguese Explorers, 1400s 102
Routes of Columbus, Cabot, and Magellan,
    1492–1522 105
The Expansion of Russia, 1584–1796 114
Spread of Black Death in Europe 119
European Colonial Possessions, 1914 124
Austria-Hungary, 1900 126
Europe After World War I 129
Europe After World War II 132
The Iron Curtain and the Warsaw Pact
    Nations, 1955 138–139
Population Density in Europe Today 143
Ethnic and Cultural Groups of the Soviet
    Union, c. 1950 149
Former Soviet Republics and Warsaw
    Pact Members, 2001 155
The Balkan States, 1991 and 2001 157

Russia's Natural Resources Today 159
Land Use and Resources in Selected Eastern
    European Nations 169
The United Kingdom Today 174
Sweden Today 179
France Today 185
Germany Today 189
Poland Today 194
Transportation in Selected European Countries 199

UNIT 3
Turkey: Vegetation Map 216
Turkey: Climate Map 216
The Fertile Crescent 218
Morocco: Climate Map 222
Morocco: Vegetation Map 222
Jerusalem's Old City 229
Holy Places of Three Religions 233
Vegetation and Precipitation in Algeria,
    Libya, and Egypt 239
Desertification in North Africa 239
Changing Boundaries in Palestine, 1947–1949 245
The Arab-Israeli Wars, 1967 and 1973 245
The Ottoman Empire, 1807–1924 248
Products of Southwest Asia and
    North Africa, 2000 250
The Suez Canal 256
The Nile River and the Aswan High Dam, 2001 257
Population Distribution in Egypt, 1998 259
Vegetation in Egypt, 1998 259
The Location of Istanbul 273
Iran-Iraq and Persian Gulf Wars 275
Oil Reserves in North Africa and Southwest Asia 275

UNIT 4
Deserts in Africa 291
2000 Years of Bantu Migration 297
African Slave Trade, 1520–1860 302
European Colonies in Africa, 1912 304

xvii

African Political Systems, 2001 308
European Colonies in Africa, 1886 313
The Congo Basin, 2001 318
The Arms Trade in Western Africa, 2001 326
Ethnic Groups of Nigeria, 2001 331
Transportation in Liberia 335
Aksum Trade Routes, c. A.D. 350 340
Political Boundaries of Eastern Africa, 2001 347
Provinces of South Africa, 2001 356
Kenya, 2001 360
Land Use in Eastern and Southern Africa 363

UNIT 5
Elevations of South Asia 378
India and Its Neighbors, 2001 384
Indus River Valley Civilization, 1700 B.C. 387
The Gupta Empire 390
Elevations of Pakistan 391
Trade Routes in Ancient Southern Asia 393
The Spread of Hinduism and Buddhism,
    500 B.C.–A.D. 600 396
Elevations of India 399
Physical Features of India 399
The Mughal Empire, 1524–1707 405
South Asia Economic Activities and
    Resources, 2000 419
The Languages of India 421
Pakistan, 2000 427
Population Density in India 431
Southeast Asia, 2000 440
Vietnam Divided, 1973 451
Vietnam, 1960s 455
Kingdoms in Southeast Asia 455

UNIT 6
Physical Features of East Asia 470
The Ring of Fire 472
Physical Features of Australia 473
The Route of the Ancient Silk Road 479
Population Density in Australia 491
The Long March, 1934 498
North and South Korea, 2001 504
Industry in East Asia, 2000 509
Cultural Exchange with East Asia
    Throughout History 512
Population Density of Japan, 2001 519
Population Density of North Korea, South Korea,
    and Japan, 2001 521
Population Density in China 523
Spread of Buddhism in South and East Asia 523
The Island Groups of the Pacific 529
Products of Australia, 2001 532
Antarctica 537
Risk of Desertification in Australia 543

ATLAS
Europe, Russia, and the Independent Republics 54
North Africa and Southwest Asia 202
Africa South of the Sahara 278
Southern Asia 366
East Asia, Australia, and Oceania 458

SPECIAL REPORT: TERRORISM AND THE WAR IN IRAQ
Flight Path of the Hijacked Airliners,
    September 11, 2001 544

CHARTS, DIAGRAMS, AND GRAPHS

Natural Regions of the World 38
Estimated World Population, 2000, by Continent .. 49
World Population Growth: 1600–Present 49
Population Growth in European Cities, 1800–1890 .. 109
World War I Alliances (1914–1918) 128
World War II Alliances (1939–1945) 130
Members of the European Union, 2001 162
Nuclear Energy Generation, 1999 186
The Five Pillars of Islam 235
Independence Days in Southwest Asia and
    North Africa 244
Africa's Deserts 294
Communication in Western Africa and the
    United States 306
Major Lakes of Africa South of the Sahara 313
Endangered Animals in Western and
    Central Africa 335
GDP of Southern African Nations, 2000 348
South Africans Today 356
The Four Noble Truths and the Eightfold Path .. 395
Literacy Rate and GDP in Sri Lanka, India,
    and Afghanistan 431
Languages of Southeast Asia, 2002 445
The Dynasties of China 476
Terrorism: A Global Problem 546

Student Guide to the Grade 6–8 Sunshine State Standards

At the beginning of every section in this book, you will see a listing that contains combinations of numbers and letters (such as A.1.3.1). These combinations are codes that refer to standards and benchmarks developed by the state of Florida for its public schools. These standards and benchmarks describe the knowledge and skills you are expected to have learned by the end of specific grades.

Standards labeled with "SS" are specific skills related to the study of social studies. Benchmarks labeled with "FCAT" are specific skills tested on the Florida Comprehensive Assessment Test.

The following chart contains the complete wording of these standards and benchmarks. When you see a list of codes at the start of a new section, you can use this chart to find out which skills you will be studying as you work through the chapter. In this way, you will be able to keep track of what you learn throughout the year.

SOCIAL STUDIES

Time, Continuity, and Change [History]

Standard 1	The student understands historical chronology and the historical perspective. (SS.A.1.3)
SS.A.1.3.1	The student understands how patterns, chronology, sequencing (including cause and effect), and the identification of historical periods are influenced by frames of reference.
SS.A.1.3.2	The student knows the relative value of primary and secondary sources and uses this information to draw conclusions from historical sources such as data in charts, tables, graphs.
SS.A.1.3.3	The student knows how to impose temporal structure on historical narratives.
Standard 2	The student understands the world from its beginnings to the time of the Renaissance. (SS.A.2.3)
SS.A.2.3.1	The student understands how language, ideas, and institutions of one culture can influence other cultures (e.g., through trade, exploration, and immigration).
SS.A.2.3.2	The student knows how major historical developments have had an impact on the development of civilizations.
SS.A.2.3.3	The student understands important technological developments and how they influenced human society.
SS.A.2.3.4	The student understands the impact of geographical factors on the historical development of civilizations.
SS.A.2.3.5	The student knows significant historical leaders who shaped the development of early cultures (e.g., military, political, and religious leaders in various civilizations).
SS.A.2.3.6	The student knows the major events that shaped the development of various cultures (e.g., the spread of agrarian societies, population movements, technological and cultural innovation, and the emergence of new population centers).

SS.A.2.3.7	The student knows significant achievements in art and architecture in various urban areas and communities to the time of the Renaissance (e.g., the Hanging Gardens of Babylon, pyramids in Egypt, temples in ancient Greece, bridges and aqueducts in ancient Rome, changes in European art and architecture between the Middle Ages and the High Renaissance).	
SS.A.2.3.8	The student knows the political, social, and economic institutions that characterized the significant aspects of Eastern and Western civilizations	

Standard 3	The student understands Western and Eastern civilization since the Renaissance. (SS.A.3.3)
SS.A.3.3.1	The student understands ways in which cultural characteristics have been transmitted from one society to another (e.g., through art, architecture, language, other artifacts, traditions, beliefs, values, and behaviors).
SS.A.3.3.2	The student understands the historical events that have shaped the development of cultures throughout the world.
SS.A.3.3.3	The student knows how physical and human geographic factors have influenced major historical events and movements.
SS.A.3.3.4	The student knows significant historical leaders who have influenced the course of events in Eastern and Western civilizations since the Renaissance.
SS.A.3.3.5	The student understands the differences between institutions of Eastern and Western civilizations (e.g., differences in governments, social traditions and customs, economic systems and religious institutions).

Standard 4	The student understands U.S. history to 1880. (SS.A.4.3)
SS.A.4.3.1	The student knows the factors involved in the development of cities and industries (e.g., religious needs, the need for military protection, the need for a marketplace, changing spatial patterns, and geographical factors for location such as transportation and food supply).
SS.A.4.3.2	The student knows the role of physical and cultural geography in shaping events in the United States (e.g., environmental and climatic influences on settlement of the colonies, the American Revolution, and the Civil War).
SS.A.4.3.3	The student understands the impact of significant people and ideas on the development of values and traditions in the United States prior to 1880.
SS.A.4.3.4	The student understands how state and federal policy influenced various Native American tribes (e.g., the Cherokee and Choctaw removals, the loss of Native American homelands, the Black Hawk War, and removal policies in the Old Northwest).

Standard 5	The student understands U.S. history from 1880 to the present day. (SS.A.5.3)
SS.A.5.3.1	The student understands the role of physical and cultural geography in shaping events in the United States since 1880 (e.g., western settlement, immigration patterns, and urbanization).
SS.A.5.3.2	The student understands ways that significant individuals and events influenced economic, social, and political systems in the United States after 1880.
SS.A.5.3.3	The student knows the causes and consequences of urbanization that occurred in the United States after 1880 (e.g., causes such as industrialization; consequences such as poor living conditions in cities and employment conditions).

▶ **Standard 6**	The student understands the history of Florida and its people. **(SS.A.6.3)**
SS.A.6.3.1	The student understands how immigration and settlement patterns have shaped the history of Florida.
SS.A.6.3.2	The student knows the unique geographic and demographic characteristics that define Florida as a region.
SS.A.6.3.3	The student knows how the environment of Florida has been modified by the values, traditions, and actions of various groups who have inhabited the state.
SS.A.6.3.4	The student understands how the interactions of societies and cultures have influenced Florida's history.
SS.A.6.3.5	The student understands how Florida has allocated and used resources and the consequences of those economic decisions.

People, Places, and Environments [Geography]

▶ **Standard 1**	The student understands the world in spatial terms. **(SS.B.1.3)**
SS.B.1.3.1	The student uses various map forms (including thematic maps) and other geographic representations, tools, and technologies to acquire, process, and report geographic information including patterns of land use, connections between places, and patterns and processes of migration and diffusion.
SS.B.1.3.2	The student uses mental maps to organize information about people, places, and environments.
SS.B.1.3.3	The student knows the social, political, and economic divisions on Earth's surface.
SS.B.1.3.4	The student understands how factors such as culture and technology influence the perception of places and regions.
SS.B.1.3.5	The student knows ways in which the spatial organization of a society changes over time.
SS.B.1.3.6	The student understands ways in which regional systems are interconnected.
SS.B.1.3.7	The student understands the spatial aspects of communication and transportation systems.

▶ **Standard 2**	The student understands the interactions of people and the physical environment. **(SS.B.2.3)**
SS.B.2.3.1	The student understands the patterns and processes of migration and diffusion throughout the world.
SS.B.2.3.2	The student knows the human and physical characteristics of different places in the world and how these characteristics change over time.
SS.B.2.3.3	The student understands how cultures differ in their use of similar environments and resources.
SS.B.2.3.4	The student understands how the landscape and society change as a consequence of shifting from a dispersed to a concentrated settlement form.
SS.B.2.3.5	The student understands the geographical factors that affect the cohesiveness and integration of countries.
SS.B.2.3.6	The student understands the environmental consequences of people changing the physical environment in various world locations.

SS.B.2.3.7	The student knows how various human systems throughout the world have developed in response to conditions in the physical environment.	
SS.B.2.3.8	The student knows world patterns of resource distribution and utilization.	
SS.B.2.3.9	The student understands how the interaction between physical and human systems affects current conditions on Earth.	

Government and the Citizen [Civics and Government]

Standard 1	The student understands the structure, functions, and purposes of government and how the principles and values of American democracy are reflected in American constitutional government. **(SS.C.1.3)**	
SS.C.1.3.1	The student knows the essential ideas of American constitutional government that are expressed in the Declaration of Independence, the Constitution, the Federalist Papers, and other writings.	
SS.C.1.3.2	The student understands major ideas about why government is necessary and the purposes government should serve.	
SS.C.1.3.3	The student understands how the legislative, executive, and judicial branches share power and responsibilities (e.g., each branch has varying degrees of legislative, executive, and judicial powers and responsibilities).	
SS.C.1.3.4	The student knows the major parts of the federal system including the national government, state governments, and other governmental units (e.g., District of Columbia, American tribal governments, and the Virgin Islands).	
SS.C.1.3.5	The student knows the major responsibilities of his or her state and local governments and understands the organization of his or her state and local governments.	
SS.C.1.3.6	The student understands the importance of the rule of law in establishing limits on both those who govern and the governed, protecting individual rights, and promoting the common good.	
Standard 2	The student understands the role of the citizen in American democracy. **(SS.C.2.3)**	
SS.C.2.3.1	The student understands the history of the rights, liberties, and obligations of citizenship in the United States.	
SS.C.2.3.2	The student understands that citizenship is legally recognized full membership in a self-governing community that confers equal rights under the law; is not dependent on inherited, involuntary groupings; and confers certain rights and privileges (e.g., the right to vote, to hold public office, and to serve on juries).	
SS.C.2.3.3	The student understands the argument that all rights have limits and knows the criteria commonly used in determining when and why limits should be placed on rights (e.g., whether a clear and present danger exists and whether national security is at risk).	
SS.C.2.3.4	The student understands what constitutes personal, political, and economic rights and the major documentary sources of these rights.	
SS.C.2.3.5	The student understands how he or she can contact his or her representatives and why it is important to do so and knows which level of government he or she should contact to express his or her opinions or to get help on a specific problem.	

SS.C.2.3.6	The student understands the importance of participation in community service, civic improvement, and political activities.	
SS.C.2.3.7	The student understands current issues involving rights that affect local, national, or international political, social, and economic systems.	

Economics

Standard 1	The student understands how scarcity requires individuals and institutions to make choices about how to use resources. **(SS.D.1.3)**
SS.D.1.3.1	The student knows the options and resources that are available for consumer protection.
SS.D.1.3.2	The student understands the advantages and disadvantages of various kinds of credit (e.g., credit cards, bank loans, or financing with no payment for six months).
SS.D.1.3.3	The student understands the variety of factors necessary to consider when making wise consumer decisions.
Standard 2	The student understands the characteristics of different economic systems and institutions. **(SS.D.2.3)**
SS.D.2.3.1	The student understands how production and distribution decisions are determined in the United States economy and how these decisions compare to those made in market, tradition-based, command, and mixed economic systems.
SS.D.2.3.2	The student understands that relative prices and how they affect people's decisions are the means by which a market system provides answers to the three basic economic questions: What goods and services will be produced? How will they be produced? Who will buy them?
SS.D.2.3.3	The student knows the various kinds of specialized institutions that exist in market economies (e.g., corporations, labor unions, banks, and the stock market).

FCAT — Florida Comprehensive Achievement Test
Language Arts

Grade 6–8 Reading Benchmarks

LA.A.1.3.2	The student uses a variety of strategies to analyze words and text, draw conclusions, use context and word structure clues, and recognize organizational patterns.
LA.A.2.2.7	The student recognizes the use of comparison and contrast in a text.
LA.A.2.3.1	The student determines the main idea or essential message in a text and identifies relevant details and facts and patterns of organization.
LA.A.2.3.2	The student identifies the author's purpose and/or point of view in a variety of texts and uses the information to construct meaning. (Includes **LA.A.2.2.2** The student identifies the author's purpose in a simple text, and **LA.A.2.2.3** The student recognizes when a text is primarily intended to persuade.)
LA.A.2.3.5	The student locates, organizes, and interprets written information for a variety of purposes, including classroom research, collaborative decision making, and performing a school or real-world task. (Includes **LA.A.2.3.6** The student uses a variety of reference materials, including indexes, magazines, newspapers, and journals; and tools, including card catalogs and computer catalogs, to gather information for research projects, and **LA.A.2.3.7** The student synthesizes and separates collected information into useful components using a variety of techniques, such as source cards, note cards, spreadsheets, and outlines.)
LA.A.2.3.8	The student checks the validity and accuracy of information obtained from research in such ways as differentiating fact and opinion, identifying strong vs. weak arguments, recognizing that personal values influence the conclusions an author draws.
LA.E.2.2.1	The student recognizes cause-and-effect relationships in literary texts. [Applies to fiction, nonfiction, poetry, and drama.]
LA.E.2.3.1	The student understands how character and plot development, point of view, and tone are used in various selections to support a central conflict or story line. (Includes **LA.E.1.3.2** The student recognizes complex elements of plot, including setting, character developments, conflicts, and resolutions.)

Grade 8 Writing Benchmarks

LA.B.1.3.1 The student organizes information before writing according to the type and purpose of writing.

LA.B.1.3.2 The student drafts and revises writing that
- is focused, purposeful, and reflects insight into the writing situation
- conveys a sense of completeness and wholeness with adherence to the main idea
- has an organizational pattern that provides for a logical progression of ideas
- has support that is substantial, specific, relevant, concrete, and/or illustrative
- demonstrates a commitment to and an involvement with the subject
- has clarity in presentation of ideas
- uses creative writing strategies appropriate to the purpose of the paper
- demonstrates a command of language (word choice) with freshness of expression
- has varied sentence structure and sentences that are complete except when fragments are used purposefully
- has few, if any, convention errors in mechanics, usage, and punctuation

LA.B.1.3.3 The studetnt produces final documents that have been edited for
- correct spelling
- correct punctuation, including commas, colons, and semicolons
- correct capitalization
- effective sentence structure
- correct common usage, including subject/verb agreement, common noun/pronoun agreement, common possessive forms, and with a variety of sentence structures, including parallel structure
- correct formatting

SUNSHINE STATE STANDARDS

Strategies for Taking the FCAT

This section of the textbook helps you develop and practice the skills you need to take the reading and writing sections of the Florida Comprehensive Assessment Test (FCAT). **Part 1, Introducing the FCAT**, provides some basic information on the FCAT and describes the types of questions you will find on the reading and writing tests.

Part 2, FCAT Strategies and Practice, offers specific strategies for tackling the skills that are tested on the reading section of the FCAT. You will find a list of these skills on page S2. Strategies on how to handle the Writing FCAT are also provided. Each strategy is followed by a set of questions that you can use for practice.

CONTENTS

Part 1: Introducing the FCAT	**S2**
Part 2: FCAT Strategies and Practice	**S6**
Analyzing Word Structure and Context Clues	S6
Comparing and Contrasting	S8
Determining the Main Idea	S10
Identifying the Author's Purpose and Point of View	S12
Locating, Organizing, and Interpreting Information	S16
Using Reference and Research Materials	S18
Synthesizing and Separating Information	S20
Checking Validity and Accuracy of Information	S22
Recognizing Cause and Effect	S26
Understanding Character and Plot Development	S28
The Writing FCAT	S32

Introducing the FCAT

FCAT, or the Florida Comprehensive Assessment Test, measures your achievement in reading, writing, mathematics, and science against official benchmarks. These benchmarks, part of the Sunshine State Standards, outline the skills you are expected to know and perform at particular grade levels. The following pages provide you with further information on the reading and writing sections of the FCAT.

The Reading FCAT

The Reading FCAT takes an hour to complete and consists of 6 to 7 reading passages. Each passage runs between 200 and 1,000 words in length and is accompanied by 8 to 12 questions. These questions are designed to test your mastery of the skills listed in the table below.

Grade 6 Benchmarks	
LA.A.1.3.2	Uses a variety of strategies to analyze words and text, draw conclusions, use context clues and word structure clues, and recognize organizational patterns.
LA.A.2.2.7	Recognizes the use of comparison and contrast in a text.
LA.A.2.3.1	Determines the main idea or essential message in the text and identifies relevant details and facts and patterns of organization.
LA.A.2.3.2	Identifies the author's purpose and/or point of view in a variety of texts and uses the information to construct meaning. (Includes **LA.A.2.2.2** Identifies the author's purpose in a simple text and **LA.A.2.2.3** Recognizes when a text is primarily intended to persuade.)
LA.A.2.3.5	Locates, organizes, and interprets written information for a variety of purposes, including classroom research, collaborative decision-making, and performing a school or real-world task. (Includes **LA.A.2.3.6** Uses a variety of reference materials, including indexes, magazines, newspapers, and journals; and tools, including card catalogs and computer catalogs, to gather information for research projects and **LA.A. 2.3.7** Synthesizes and separates collected information into useful components using a variety of techniques. such as source cards, note cards, spreadsheets, and outlines.)
LA.A.2.3.8	Checks the validity and accuracy of information obtained from research, in such ways as differentiating fact from opinion, identifying strong vs. weak arguments, recognizing that personal values influence the conclusions and author draws.
LA.E.2.2.1	Recognizes cause-and-effect relationships in literary texts. [Applies to fiction, nonfiction, poetry, and drama.]
LA.E.2.3.1	Understands how character and plot development, point of view, and tone are used in various selections to support a central conflict of story line. (Includes **LA.E.1.3.2** Recognizes complex elements of plot, including setting, character developments, conflicts, and resolutions.)

Types of Questions on the FCAT

All of the questions on the Reading FCAT for Grade 6 are in a format called multiple-choice. At some other grades, however, questions called performance tasks also appear on the test.

Multiple-Choice Questions

A multiple-choice question consists of a stem and a set of four choices labeled A, B, C, D or F, G, H, I. The stem usually is in the form of a question or an incomplete sentence. One of the choices correctly answers the question or completes the sentence. Correct answers to multiple-choice questions receive 1 point; incorrect answers receive 0. The following are some strategies for answering multiple-choice questions:

- Read the stem carefully and try to answer the question or complete the sentence before reviewing the alternatives.
- Read each alternative with the stem. Don't make your final decision on the correct answer until you have read all of the alternatives.
- Eliminate alternatives that you know are wrong.
- Do not waste time struggling with questions that appear too difficult. Proceed to other questions. When you have finished those questions, go back to the ones you missed.

Performance Tasks

Performance tasks require you to respond to test questions in your own words. There are two types of performance tasks:

Short-Response Questions are identified by the following symbol:

A short response should take from three to five minutes to complete. Short responses are scored from 2 to 0 based on the following rubric:

Rubric for Short-Response Questions	
2 points	– Shows a complete understanding of the reading concept. – Response is accurate and complete. – Necessary supporting examples are included. – Information is clearly based on the text.
1 point	– Shows a partial understanding of the reading concept. – Includes information that is correct and based on the text but is too general or too simplistic. – Some of the supporting examples are incomplete or omitted.
0 Points	– Response is inaccurate. – Response is confused or irrelevant. – No response is given.

Extended-Response Questions are identified by the following symbol:

Extended-response questions require more thought and longer answers than short-response questions. Extended responses should take from 10 to 15 minutes to complete. Extended responses are scored from 4 to 0 based on the following rubric:

Rubric for Extended-Response Questions	
4 points	– Shows a complete understanding of the reading concept. – Response is accurate and complete. – Necessary supporting examples are included. – Information is clearly based on the text.
3 points	– Shows an understanding of the reading concept. – Response is accurate. – Supporting examples are not complete. – Supporting examples are not clearly based on the text.
2 points	– Shows a partial understanding of the reading concept. – Includes information that is essentially correct or based on the text but is too general or too simplistic. – Some supporting examples are incomplete or omitted.
1 point	– Shows a very limited understanding of the reading concept. – Response is incomplete and flawed. – Response may not address all the requirements of the task.
0 points	– Response is inaccurate. – Response is confused or irrelevant. – No response is given.

The following are some strategies for completing performance tasks:
- Read the question carefully. Look for key words that will help you write your answer.
- Sometimes a question may have two or more parts. Ensure that you answer every part.
- Include information from the passage in your answer.
- Write your answers on the writing lines provided.
- Do not skip any questions. Incomplete answers earn partial credit.

The Writing FCAT

At grades 4, 8, and 10, Florida students take the Writing FCAT. This writing test consists of a short writing assignment, called a prompt. The prompt involves one of two kinds of writing: **expository writing,** which requires you to explain a topic, or **persuasive writing**, which requires you to convince someone of something. You will not be told the prompt beforehand, but you should be able to write a response based on your own opinions and experience. You will have 45 minutes to plan and write your response.

The following are some strategies for answering writing prompts:
- Read the prompt carefully and focus your answer on what it asks.
- Plan your time. You will have 45 minutes to complete your writing. Allow yourself time for planning, writing, *and* proofreading.
- Jot down an outline to organize your writing before you start.
- Provide details that support your main ideas effectively.
- Conclude your response by summing up the main points of your explanation or the main reasons for the course of action you suggest.

Writing test responses are scored from 6 to 1 based on the following rubric:

Rubric for Writing Assessment Responses	
6 points	– **Focus:** clear, appropriate, and well maintained – **Organization:** logical and clear, with a beginning, a middle, and an end and good use of transitions – **Supporting details:** precise, related to the topic, and effective – **Conventions:** sophisticated vocabulary, mostly error-free standard English, and varied sentence structures
5 points	– **Focus:** clear and appropriate – **Organization:** sensible and obvious, with a beginning, a middle, and an end; some deviation from the logical progression of ideas; few transitions – **Supporting details:** generally appropriate and effectively expressed – **Conventions:** standard English and varied sentence structures
4 points	– **Focus:** basically clear despite some vaguely related material – **Organization:** occasional deviation from the logical progression of ideas – **Supporting details:** adequate but uneven – **Conventions:** some errors in grammar, usage, and mechanics; little variation in sentence structure
3 points	– **Focus:** appropriate but obscured by unrelated material – **Organization:** some unclear relationships between ideas – **Supporting details:** inadequate to support the topic – **Conventions:** errors in grammar, usage, and mechanics; little variation in sentence structure
2 points	– **Focus:** minimally related to the topic – **Organization:** little evidence of organizational planning – **Supporting details:** few, if any, logical details – **Conventions:** errors in grammar, usage, and mechanics; limited variation in sentence structure
1 point	– **Focus:** only minimally appropriate – **Organization:** little if any, evidence of organization – **Supporting details:** minimal or illogical details – **Conventions:** many errors; limited variation in sentence structure
Unscorable	A response may be considered unscorable for any of the following reasons: it is off topic; it is only a restatement of the prompt; it contains too little writing to be evaluated; it is in a foreign language; it is plagiarized; it is illegible; no response was written.

STRATEGIES

Analyzing Word Structure and Context Clues (LA.A.1.3.2)

Word structure and context clues are used to help the reader understand words and phrases in passages and graphics. Descriptions and explanations often appear near unfamiliar words and phrases to give the readers clues to their meanings.

1 Skim the document to get an idea of what it is about.

2 Use active reading strategies. As you read, look for words or phrases that are unfamiliar to you.

3 Use context clues to help you understand an unfamiliar phrase or word. Use the descriptions and explanations near the phrase or word to help you understand what they mean. (Here, for example, the sentence after the word *archaeologists* explains what the word means. The context of the sentence in which *submerged* appears indicates that it means "gone underwater.")

4 Before re-reading the passage, skim the questions. Previewing the questions will remind you to look for context clues to understand the meaning of unfamiliar phrases and words.

answers: 1 (D), 2 (G)

How Archaeologists Work

Geographers have learned about ancient culture groups with the help of archaeologists. These scientists study sites that the groups used to inhabit. They look at ruins of buildings, bones, and other evidence left by the people. Archaeologists study artifacts to learn about people's culture and history. They study pots, tools, artworks, and even food remains. They use their knowledge about the place and people they are studying to figure out how the artifacts were used. Using special techniques and equipment, archaeologists carefully remove artifacts from aboveground, underground, or underwater. Underwater artifacts may include entire towns that have been submerged because of changes in the ocean's water levels. Underwater artifacts can also include sunken ships. Archaeologists maintain accurate records of their work. They photograph and map the sites they are investigating because arechaeological research often destroys portions of the sites.

> Here the key words are "nearly opposite." Make sure the alternative you select is an antonym or means almost the opposite of the word given.

1 Which two words from the passage are MOST opposite?

  A. investigating, studying
  B. equipment, tools
  C. place, site
  D. destroys, maintain

2 Read this sentence from the passage.

  These scientists study sites that the groups used to inhabit.

  What does the word *inhabit* mean?

  F. destroy
  G. live in
  H. explore
  I. leave behind

PRACTICE

Read this passage about prehistoric cave paintings before answering Numbers 1 through 3.

Prehistoric Cave Paintings

Prehistoric people left no written records. However, archaeologists have learned about some prehistoric people by examining the cave paintings they left behind. Archaeologists are not sure exactly what the purpose of these paintings was. Some scientists do believe that the paintings are more than vivid scenes from daily life. They believe that the paintings may have represented religious beliefs. The early artists may have believed that the pictures they painted had magical powers that would bring good luck to the hunters. Some of the paintings may have been a kind of textbook to help young hunters identify various animals. The use of pictures to communicate information represents an important first step in the later development of writing. Prehistoric artists made their paint from natural sources. They used three basic colors—yellow, black, and red—that they obtained from clay, charcoal, and minerals such as iron. The artists often chose natural protrusions on the cave walls on which to paint animals. Drawing the pictures on places in the cave where the wall extended out made the pictures look three-dimensional.

1 Read this sentence from the passage.

Some scientists do believe that the paintings are more than vivid scenes from daily life.

The word *vivid* comes from the Latin word *vivere*, meaning "to live." What does *vivid* mean?

A. alive

B. dull or unclear

C. active or lively

D. artistic

2 When the author states "the paintings may have been a kind of textbook to help young hunters," he means that the paintings were

F. a way to teach young people to hunt.

G. written directions about how to hunt.

H. a kind of book about art.

I. a kind of book about animals.

3 The passage talks about *prehistoric* people. What does the word *prehistoric* mean? What details from the passage point to the definition?

STRATEGIES

Comparing and Contrasting (LA.A.2.2.7)

To better understand a topic, historians and geographers often compare and contrast information. Comparing involves looking at how two or more things are the same and how they are different. Contrasting means examining only the differences.

1 Skim the passage to get an idea of what it is about.

2 As you read the passage, look for clue words that show that two things are alike. Clue words include *both, all, like, as, likewise,* and *similar to.* (Here, the words *similar to* tell you that the Atlantic Coastal Plain and the East Gulf Coastal Plain are alike.)

3 Look for features that two things have in common.

4 Look for clue words that show how two things differ. Clue words include *different, differ, unlike, by contrast, however,* and *on the other hand.*

5 Look for ways in which two things are different. (For example, this sentence shows that Florida has a longer coastline than any other mainland state.)

6 Before re-reading the passage, skim the questions. Previewing the questions will help you focus your readings.

answers: 1 (D), 2 (F)

Florida's Land and Water

3 Florida is part of a land region called the Atlantic-Gulf Coastal Plain, which stretches along the coast from New Jersey to southern Texas. Florida itself has three main land regions. The eastern part of Florida is made up of the Atlantic Coastal Plain region. It is a level plain about 30 to 100 miles wide along the Atlantic Ocean. The East Gulf Coastal Plain is Florida's second land region. Located along the Gulf of Mexico, the East Gulf Coastal Plain is (similar) to the Atlantic Coastal **2** **1** Plain. Both regions include islands located along their coastlines and swamps farther inland. The Florida Uplands is the third main land **4** region of Florida. This region (differs) from the other two in that it has a higher elevation.

5 Florida has a longer coastline than any other state in the mainland United States. The Atlantic coast has 580 miles of coastline. The Gulf coast has 770 miles. The largest river in Florida is the St. Johns River. Lake Okeechobee is the largest lake in Florida.

1 The Florida Uplands region is different from the other two regions in that

  A. it has a longer coastline.
  B. the land includes islands.
  C. the land elevation is lower there.
  D. the land elevation is higher there.

2 In what way are the Atlantic Coastal Plain and the East Gulf Coastal Plain regions similar?

  F. They have swamps farther inland.
  G. They have high elevations.
  H. They have short coastlines.
  I. They have no coastlines.

PRACTICE

Read this passage about the early people who inhabited Florida before answering Numbers 1 through 3.

Early Inhabitants of Florida

Before Europeans explored Florida, several culture groups were already living there. Three of the groups were the Calusa, the Tequesta, and the Apalachee. The Calusa lived along the southwest coast of Florida. The Tequesta lived near the area that is now Miami. The Apalachee lived in northwestern Florida.

The Calusa lived in villages in houses made of wood and built on piles. Unlike many other culture groups in Florida, the Calusa depended on the sea for their food rather than on farming. They made tools from seashells and fish bones. The Calusa were fierce fighters and expert navigators. They most likely traveled to Cuba and other islands in the Caribbean. The Tequesta, like the Calusa, also made a living from the sea. However, they were a more peaceful people than the Calusa. The Tequesta lived in wigwams, which they made by bending poles, tying them in the center and covering them with palm leaves. Unlike the Calusa and the Tequesta, the Apalachee depended on farming for a living. They grew corn, squash, and oranges. They were similar to the Calusa in that they lived in villages and were fierce fighters.

1 Which word or words in the passage gives you a clue that the Apalachee had a different way of making a living?

   A. unlike
   B. like
   C. however
   D. most likely

2 In what part of Florida did the Apalachee live?

   F. the southern part
   G. near Miami
   H. the northwestern part
   I. the southwestern part

3 The passage discusses early culture groups in Florida. Write a short paragraph that compares and contrasts where they lived and how they made a living.

STRATEGIES

Determining the Main Idea
(LA.A.2.3.1)

The main idea is a statement that summarizes the most important point of a paragraph, a section of a book, an article, or a speech. The main idea of a paragraph is often stated in the first or last sentence. If it is the first sentence, it is followed by sentences that support the main idea. If it is the last sentence, the details build up to the main idea.

❶ Skim the article to get an idea of what it is about.

❷ Identify the topic by first looking at the title or subtitle. (Here, the title tells you what the passage is about.)

❸ Identify what you think may be the stated main idea. Check the first and last sentences of the paragraph to see if either could be the stated main idea.

❹ Identify details that support that idea. Some details explain the main idea. Others give examples of what is stated in the main idea.

❺ Before re-reading the passage, skim the questions. Previewing the questions will remind you to look for the main idea in each paragraph and the details that support each main idea.

answers: 1 (D), 2 (F)

❷ Immigrants Affect American Society

❸ Immigration to the United States in the late 1900s helped to make the United States more diverse. Most of the immigrants who arrived in the United States during its early history came from Europe. However, nearly 85 percent of the arrivals since 1981 came from either Latin America or Asia. The Census Bureau predicts that the U.S. Hispanic population will increase from 11 percent to 16 percent by 2020. The Asian population will climb from 3 percent to nearly 6 percent by then.

Several factors contributed to the recent surge in immigration. One cause is the Immigration and Nationality Act of 1965. It allowed people from a greater variety of countries to enter the United States. The lure of America also played a role. As with earlier immigrants, many of the newcomers came to the United States seeking economic opportunity and, in some cases, political freedom.

❶ What is the main idea of the first paragraph?

   A. The Asian population increased in the late 1900s.
   B. The Hispanic population in the United States will most likely grow by 2020.
   C. The Immigration and Nationality Act of 1965 brought more immigrants to the United States.
   D. Immigration added to diversity in the United States.

❷ If the passage needed a new title, which would be best?

   F. "Immigrants Provide Diversity"
   G. "Early Immigration"
   H. "Obstacles to Immigration"
   I. "Laws Promoting Immigration"

Here the key word "main idea." Mak the statement you choose summarize most important po the paragraph.

PRACTICE

Read this passage about immigrants before answering Numbers 1 through 3.

> **Talented Immigrants**
>
> Recent immigrants have brought, and continue to bring, many talents to the United States. The National Science Foundation estimates that 23 percent of all U.S. residents with doctorate degrees in engineering and science are foreign-born. High-tech industries, such as those located in Silicon Valley, California, have benefited from their skills.
>
> In addition, immigrants are an important source of labor. Some studies indicate that without immigrants, the workforce might actually begin to shrink by 2015. In other words, U.S. businesses wouldn't be able to hire enough people to maintain their productivity. . . .
>
> Many immigrants enrich American arts and culture. Latin music, for example, has become very popular. . . . in addition, immigrants, and their sons and daughters, are acting in a greater number of movies.
>
> —Jesus Garcia *et al. Creating America* (2002)

1 What is the main idea of this passage?

  A. Many immigrants have doctorate degrees.

  B. By 2015 the workforce in the United States will begin to shrink.

  C. The talents of many immigrants have benefited the United States.

  D. Many immigrants are successful authors.

2 Which is the BEST new title for the passage?

  F. "Immigrants Arrive in the United States"

  G. "Immigrant Contributions"

  H. "The Immigrant Workforce"

  I. "Workers in the United States"

3 Which sentence would also support the main idea of the passage?

  A. Several immigrants have become successful authors.

  B. Early immigrants arrived from European countries.

  C. Many immigrants today settle in cities, where there are more jobs.

  D. The number of immigrants to the United States has increased dramatically.

STRATEGIES

Identifying the Author's Purpose and Point of View (L.A.A.2.2.2, L.A.A.2.2.3, LA.A.2.3.2)

An author's purpose is the reason he or she has for writing something. The purpose might be to entertain, to inform, or to persuade. An author's point of view refers to opinions or beliefs that the author holds. A person's religion, education, and life experiences can all influence his or her point of view. Identifying a point of view helps to understand an author's thoughts and opinions about a topic.

❶ Skim the passage to get an idea of what it is about.

❷ Do the author's background or beliefs affect his or her point of view? (Here, for example, the author is clearly of the opinion that the Aboriginal people provided knowledge about their environment that is still useful to us today.)

❸ Look for statements that show the author's views on a subject. Are there words that show a positive or negative view? (Here, for example, the word *resourceful* shows that the author has a positive view of Aboriginal people.)

❹ Before re-reading the passage, skim the questions. Previewing the questions will help you focus on how to determine the author's point of view.

Aboriginal[1] Peoples and Their Heritage

When Europeans first came to North America, they learned a lot of things from Aboriginal peoples. And a lot of that knowledge is still being shared today.

First Nations[2] and Inuit[3] have lived in North America for thousands of years. Their ancestors had to be very resourceful to thrive in this ❸ territory with its varied landscape and its often harsh climate

In the Arctic, where living conditions are severe and there are no trees, Inuit's ancestors used snow's insulating qualities to invent the igloo. They also perfected the kayak, a boat adapted to icy waters. For instance, if a kayak capsizes, the kayaker can quickly put the boat upright without getting out. Also, kayakers can easily thread their way through ice floes.

Eastern North America is covered with dense forest and a great many waterways. By inventing bark canoes, Aboriginal peoples of this region used these waterways to penetrate the forests!

❶ Aboriginal peoples living in the Prairies were nomads who hunted buffalo, a migratory animal. They perfected a lightweight, solid dwelling that was easy to move from place to place: the teepee. This dwelling is made of poles arranged in a cone shape and covered with animal skins.

On the Pacific Coast, Aboriginal peoples built dams to catch fish. They lived in permanent villages and developed a tradition of sculpture.

Over the centuries, Aboriginal peoples have acquired knowledge, invented technology and developed a way of life adapted to their specific environment. They have depended on nature for their survival and have had a special relationship with it. For them, the Earth is sacred, something to be respected. In fact, they consider themselves a part of the Earth.

Aboriginal peoples transmitted a great deal of very useful knowledge to the first Europeans who arrived in North America (sometime around 1500).

[1]**Aboriginal**: native

[2]**First Nations**: native groups officially recognized by the Canadian government

[3]**Inuit**: native peoples who live in the Canadian Arctic, Alaska, and Greenland

PRACTICE

For more test practice online...
TEST PRACTICE CLASSZONE.COM

For example, Aboriginal peoples introduced Europeans to new plants. Some were used for food and others for medicine. Today, many of the items we find in our medicine cabinets come from traditional Aboriginal healing methods and remedies.

It would have taken Europeans much longer to establish themselves in North America without the contribution of Aboriginal peoples. And today, life would be very different!

—From the Indian and Northern Affairs Canada Website

1 What was the author's purpose in writing this passage?

  A. to explain how Europeans taught the Aboriginal people new ways of using the environment

  B. to demonstrate that Aboriginal people taught Europeans how to use the environment of North America to survive

  C. to show the resourcefulness of Aboriginal people

  D. to persuade people to learn more about Aboriginal people

> Here the key words are "author's purpose." The question is asking you to explain why the author wrote the passage

2 With which statement would the author agree MOST strongly?

  F. The Aboriginal people benefited from the Europeans.

  G. The Aboriginal people learned survival skills from the Europeans.

  H. Europeans would never have settled in North America without help from the Aboriginal people.

  I. The Aboriginal people respected their environment.

3 Which statement supports the author's point of view?

  A. Aboriginal people prevented the European settlement of North America.

  B. Some medicines today are made from ingredients imported from South America.

  C. Aboriginal people helped the Europeans settle of North America.

  D. Most medicines today are made from foreign ingredients.

answers: 1 (B), 2 (I), 3 (C)

PRACTICE

Read this passage about technology and change before answering Numbers 1 through 4.

Technology and Daily Life

The Internet is a worldwide computer network linking tens of millions of government, education, business, and personal computers. When the Internet was first introduced, it was used largely for e-mail, bulletin boards, and newsgroups. In the 1990s, the World Wide Web, the Internet information retrieval service, made it possible for ordinary users to move quickly and easily from one Internet site to another.

As the 20th Century drew to a close, thousands of institutions, from hospitals to airports to banks, relied on computers to perform essential tasks. Computer use also grew in homes and schools. By 2001, more than half of all U.S. households had a personal computer. And from 1985 to 1998, the number of computers in classrooms leaped from 630,000 to more than 8 million.

Computers and the Internet revolutionized communication and research. Using the Internet, a person can track down information on nearly any subject. Internet users can also send and receive electronic messages called e-mail. In addition, they can shop at on-line stores.

Other forms of new technology have also transformed American life. One popular example is the battery-powered cellular telephone. People can carry these phones with them anywhere. Between 1990 and 2001, the number of cellular phone subscribers in the United States grew dramatically from 5.3 million to more than 110 million. . . . It took 20 years to sell the first 1 million TV sets, but only $4 \frac{1}{2}$ years to sell 1 million cellular telephones. Today, Americans seem quite willing to use all kinds of high-tech products, such as fax machines and CD players. The microwave oven gained rapid acceptance. Almost unknown in the 1970s, microwaves could be found in three out of four American homes by the late 1980s. . . .

In the last decades of the 20th century, the world of medicine saw many breakthroughs. Engineers developed smaller, more precise surgical instruments. These and new technologies such as lasers allowed doctors to perform surgery through tiny incisions in the body, which heal more quickly than large cuts. New tests helped doctors to make better diagnoses.

—Jesus Garcia et al. *Creating America* (2002)

1 What was the author's MAIN purpose in writing this passage?

　A. to persuade people to limit their use of technology

　B. to inform people about how the Internet works

　C. to help people decide what new appliances to buy

　D. to describe how technology has benefited people

2 Which statement would support the author's point of view?

　F. The use of computers has led to the loss of jobs for many workers.

　G. Computers today make it possible for ordinary people to use the latest technology.

　H. Technology will make daily life more complicated for most people.

　I. Technology limits the kind of information that is available.

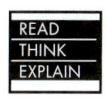

3 The author talks about the changes brought about by technology. Write a statement describing what the author thinks about these changes. Use two examples from the passage to support your statement.

4 Which headline best describes the author's point of view in this passage?

　A. "Technology Must Be Stopped"

　B. "Technology Improves People's Way of Life"

　C. "What's Next for Technology?"

　D. "Technology Reduces People's Creativity"

STRATEGIES

Locating, Organizing and Interpreting Information
(LA.A.2.3.5)

When you do research, you first locate sources and identify the information you need. You then interpret the information, analyze the facts, and organize the information to meet your needs.

1 Skim the passage to find specific information you need. Then go back and read that information carefully.

2 Evaluate the information. Consider whether the source is reliable. If you are looking for facts, be sure there is no confusion between facts and opinions.

3 Assess the information given. For example, this paragraph clearly establishes the topic, which is described later in the passage.

4 Ask yourself questions about the text. Is the information consistent with what you already know? Does the text give reasons why the Inca roads were impressive?

5 Before rereading the passage, skim the questions to identify the information you need to find.

answers: 1 (C), 2 (I)

The Grandest Roads in the World

Were the Inca roads more impressive than those built by the Romans? Here's how Cieza de León, a soldier who traveled the Inca roads in 1547, described them.

"The Incas constructed the grandest road that there is in the world as well as the longest. . . . this road. . . . passes over deep valleys and lofty mountains, . . . over falls of water. . . ."

The Incas built two roads the length of the country. The Royal Road went through the highlands for a distance of 3,250 miles, while the Coastal Road followed the seacoast for 2,520 miles.

These roads provided a vital communication link, and kept the empire united. . . .

Impressive bridges spanned the rivers. One of the most famous . . . . was 40 feet wide and 148 feet long. Travelers crossing it swayed 118 dizzying feet above the river. Twisted rope cables as thick as a person's body held up the walkway, which was made of woven lianas (tropical vines) covered with branches . . .

—Carolyn Gard, from *Calliope*, March 2000

1 Which statement BEST summarizes why the roads built by the Incas are considered so impressive?

   A. The roads passed through amazing scenery.
   B. Many people used the roads for travel.
   C. The long roads were built across a harsh landscape.
   D. The Incas built two sets of roads.

2 Which of these statements from the passage represents an opinion?

   F. "The Incas built two roads the length of the country."
   G. "Twisted rope cables as thick as a person's body held up the walkway, which was made of woven lianas (tropical vines) covered with branches…."
   H. "Impressive bridges spanned the rivers."
   I. "'The Incas constructed the grandest road that there is in the world….'"

PRACTICE

Read this passage about the Berlin before answering Numbers 1 and 2.

Berlin: Capital of Unified Germany

My first visit to Berlin was in 1985. West Berlin was the western world's outpost in the center of East Germany. I arrived by night train from Munich, traveling through East Germany. During the night, an East German border guard shining a flashlight in my face suddenly awakened me. He demanded brusquely to see my passport and examined it closely. This was my introduction to the east.

West Berlin did not seem very different from what I knew: a prosperous city with attractive stores and restaurants and neon signs and ads.

Of course, I had to visit the Berlin Wall. It went on and on—decorated with all forms of graffiti, including art projects and political messages.

I was warned by friends in West Berlin to be careful in East Berlin. I decided that I must visit. I took the S-Bahn (the urban rail lines) to the east. It passed through some empty stations, and a few minutes later I arrived in a very different place. East Berlin was mainly shades of gray. There was little advertising. The people dressed very simply and fairly uniformly. There were rows of large, plain apartment building blocks and some areas of the city that looked like the war had only recently ended.

I visited Berlin again in 1991. This time there were no border guards, and pieces of the wall were being sold as souvenirs. . . . Berlin's role in the reunified Germany was still not clear, but there was a sense of exhilaration. Germans were elated to be able to stroll through Brandenburg Gate, . . . or to contemplate the open spaces where the Wall had been.

—Beryl Goldberg, from *Faces*, March, 2002

1 In what way was West Berlin different from East Berlin?

  A. East Berlin was in East Germany; West Berlin was not.

  B. West Berlin had train service; East Berlin did not.

  C. West Berlin was a wealthy city; East Berlin was not.

  D. East Berlin had the Berlin Wall; West Berlin did not.

2 Which of the following statements from the passage is an opinion?

  F. "During the night, an East German border guard shining a flashlight in my face suddenly awakened me."

  G. "It [the Berlin Wall] went on and on—decorated with all forms of graffiti . . ."

  H. "It [the urban rail line] passed through some empty stations . . ."

  I. "Germans were elated to be able to stroll through Brandenburg Gate, . . . or to contemplate the open spaces where the Wall had been."

STRATEGIES

Using Reference and Research Materials (LA.A.2.3.6)

When you write a paper, you need to research information about your particular topic. To find sources of information, you may use an electronic card catalog. This is a computerized search that lists books, periodicals, or other resources found in the library. These resources are listed by title, by author, by subject, and by keyword.

❶ Decide whether you want to search the electronic card catalog by subject, title, author, or keyword.

❷ The catalog lists the records that match that subject. Choose one of the listed records to find out the details of that resource.

❸ The catalog will display a screen, similar to the one shown here. The screen provides details such as the author and title of the resource, information about its publication date, and the resource's availability.

❹ Look for any special features in the book. For example, this book is illustrated and includes maps and an index.

❺ Note the book's call number. This number tells you where the book will be located in the library.

❻ Skim the questions. Previewing the questions will help you focus on certain sections of the electronic card catalog screen.

answers: 1 (D), 2 (H)

France

❶ Title:	France / Brian Sookram
Author:	Sookram, Brian
❷ Published:	New York: Chelsea House, c1999.
❸ Subject:	France
Series:	Places and peoples of the world
Material:	128 p.: col.ill., maps; 21 cm
Note:	Includes index.
	❹ Surveys the history, geography, economy, government, people, and culture of France
LC Card no:	89015694 / AC
ISBN:	0791047385
Other ID no:	lmcarc / AMP-3536 / STRINGFELLOW
System ID no:	ACF-5525
Holdings:	Children's Dept.
❺ Call Number:	x944 Sookr.B -- Juv. Book -- Out

If you have a library card, you may place a hold on this title for pickup at the library.

❶ Which would be the BEST way to search for other resources about France?

   A. by series
   B. by author
   C. by ISBN
   D. by keyword

❷ Which topic is the person using the information from this electronic card catalog MOST likely researching?

   F. ways of pronouncing French words
   G. recipes for French meals
   H. the landforms found in France
   I. good hotel rates for vacations in France

S18

PRACTICE

For more test practice online...
TEST PRACTICE CLASSZONE.COM

Study this entry from an electronic card catalog before answering Numbers 1 and 2.

Ancient Rome

Title:	Ancient Rome / Don Nardo
Author:	Nardo, Don
Published:	San Diego, CA: Kidhaven Press, c2002.
Subject:	Rome -- Social Life and customs.
Series:	Daily life
Material:	48 p.: col.ill., col. maps; 24 cm.
Note:	Includes bibliographical references (p. 43-44) and index. Discusses the daily life of ancient Romans including their families, homes, occupations, education, and methods of worship.
LC Card no:	2001002248
ISBN:	0737706120
System ID no:	ACT-8541
Holdings:	Children's Dept.
Call Number:	x937 Nardo.D -- Juv. Book -- Available

If you have a library card, you may place a hold on this title for pickup at the library.

1 What topic is the person using this electronic card catalog most likely researching?

   A. the government of the Roman Empire
   B. the road system in ancient Rome
   C. how Romans celebrated holidays
   D. who the famous rulers of Rome were

2 The special features of this book include bibliographical references, an index, and

   F. a CD-ROM.
   G. maps.
   H. glossaries.
   I. sound recordings.

STRATEGIES

Synthesizing and Separating Information (LA.A.2.3.7)

Synthesizing information involves putting together clues, information, and ideas to form an overall picture of an event. A synthesis is often stated as a generalization, or broad summary statement.

❶ Skim the document to get an idea of what it is about.

❷ Consider what you already know that could apply. (Your general knowledge will probably lead you to accept this statement as reasonable.)

❸ Read carefully to understand the facts. (Facts such as these help you to base your interpretations on evidence.)

❹ Look for explanations that link the facts together. (This statement is based on the evidence mentioned in the sentences that follow.)

❺ Bring together the information you have about a subject. (This interpretation brings together different kinds of information to arrive at a new understanding of the subject.)

❻ Before re-reading the passage, skim the questions. Previewing the questions will help you synthesize the information in the passage.

answers: 1 (C), 2 (I)

Wheeling into the Future

❷ For the people of Mesopotamia, the Tigris and Euphrates rivers were essential to their existence. Farmers used the rivers to supply a system of irrigation that had ditches carry water to the crops. Traders traveled these rivers to reach the lands around the Persian Gulf. . . . **❸**

❹ Travel overland, however, remained unchanged for centuries. It was either on foot or by pack animal. People had learned that it was easier to drag heavy objects along on pieces of animal skin or tree bark. Gradually, this idea led to the development of sleds. By adding runners to the bottom of a platform, the ancients were able to reduce friction from the ground, thus making the load even easier to pull.

❶ Yet it was the invention of the wheel that revolutionized transportation. **❺** The wheel has been called the greatest mechanical creation of all time. With wheels and an axle, a wagon pulled by a pack animal could transport a far heavier load. The earliest wheeled vehicle was probably a Sumerian sled to which four wheels were added. By 3500 B.C., the Sumerians were building roads to ease their movements and encourage trade between one city and another.

—Karen E. Hong, from *Calliope*, November 2000

❶ In addition to providing transportation, the rivers in Mesopotamia

    A. were important for fishing.

    B. prevented war.

    C. were important to agriculture.

    D. prevented trade.

❷ Read this sentence from the passage.

Yet it was the invention of the wheel that revolutionized transportation.

Which sentence from the passage supports this statement?

    F. "Traders traveled these rivers to reach the lands around the Persian Gulf."

    G. "Travel overland, however, remained unchanged for centuries."

    H. "Gradually, this idea led to the development of sleds."

    I. "With wheels and an axle, a wagon pulled by a pack animal could transport a far heavier load."

PRACTICE

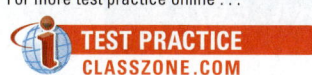

Read this passage about Iran's resources before answering Numbers 1 through 3.

Iran's Resources

Iran has always had substantial mineral wealth and natural resources. These have attracted invaders throughout the ages. In the past, its rich deposits of iron, copper, and lapis lazuli[1] attracted bands of invading nomads and warriors, including Assyrian raiders. [More recently, countries such as Russia, Turkey, Britain, Germany, and the United States have fought over Iranian oil or have interfered with affairs in Iran in other ways.] Equally important, Iran's mineral wealth encouraged trade with the outside world.

　　Today, huge reserves of oil lie beneath the surface of Iran. Various foreign powers compete for these rich oil fields. The Iranian government awards contracts to companies to develop oil fields in Iran and the Persian Gulf. Iran's economy relies heavily on revenue from its oil reserves.

—Roger B. Beck et al., *World History* (2003)

1 Why have various groups of people invaded Iran throughout history?

  A. Iran's geography made it easy to invade.

  B. They wanted to govern Iran.

  C. They wanted to open businesses in Iran.

  D. They wanted Iran's mineral resources.

2 Which of the following headings best synthesizes the information in this passage?

  F. Oil—Helpful and Harmful

  G. The Oil Curse

  H. Iran and the World

  I. The Search for Oil

3 Which statement best summarizes the information from the passage?

  A. "Iran's economy relies heavily on revenue from its oil reserves."

  B. "Today, huge reserves of oil lie beneath the surface of Iran."

  C. "Various foreign powers compete for these rich oil fields."

  D. "These have attracted invaders throughout the ages."

[1]**lapis lazuli**: a bluish, semiprecious gemstone

STRATEGIES

Checking Validity and Accuracy of Information (LA.A.2.3.8)

When you read a passage, it is important to question the validity and accuracy of the information it contains. One way to do this is to distinguish between fact and opinion. A fact is a piece of information that can be proved to be true. Statements, statistics, and dates may be facts. An opinion, on the other hand, is a belief, feeling, or judgment expressed by someone. An opinion cannot be proved to be true. Being able to distinguish facts from opinions is part of thinking critically. It helps you know whether to trust an argument or to change your own opinion when someone is trying to influence you.

❶ Skim the passage to get an idea of what it is about.

❷ Identify the facts and opinions expressed in the passage. Look for statements that express a person's opinion, judgment, or feelings. (This sentence expresses a person's judgment about a decision.)

❸ Think about how the facts in the passage could be checked for accuracy. Where might you look to see if they are true? (For example, the statistics in this sentence can be proved to be true.)

❹ Identify arguments in the passage that are weak. (For example, this sentence does not give a strong argument against poaching.)

The Poaching Problem

❶ Many African countries today are working to make sure their endangered species will survive. During the 1980s, a large demand for ivory led to the destruction of many elephants. In Africa, poaching, or the illegal killing, of elephants caused the number of elephants there to be cut by half. The elephants were killed for their valuable ivory tusks. Because elephants in Africa's savannahs, or grasslands, have the largest tusks, they took the worst hit. But as soon as the elephants in the grasslands began to vanish, hunters began killing the smaller elephants in Africa's forests. <u>In 1977, there were about 1.3 million elephants in Africa. About twenty years later, there were only 600,000 elephants.</u> ❸

In 1990, the Convention on International Trade in Endangered Species (CITES), an international agreement between governments, banned the sale of ivory. This ban helped to keep the elephant population stable. However, in the late 1990s, CITES decided to lift ❶ part of the ban. It allowed some countries to sell ivory to Japan. There is a big market for ivory in Japan. <u>This was a very bad decision, and many people believed it encouraged the poaching of elephants in</u> ❷ <u>Africa.</u>

Even though it is against the law to kill elephants in Africa, people continue to do so. Most of the time the animals are killed for their tusks. Sometimes, however, these animals are killed for revenge. In some parts of Africa, roaming elephant herds come in conflict with the increasing number of people in the region. Farmers there fence their land to keep the roaming animals out. However, when the elephants move onto their land, trampling the farmers' crops and endangering their lives, the farmers get angry. In their anger, they sometimes hunt down the elephants and kill them.

Scientists are working to help the situation. They have invented a pepper spray to use on the elephants. The spray hurts the elephants' sensitive eyes. The elephants recover, but they also learn to stay off the farmers' land.

Elephant poaching continues to be a problem in Africa. Beautiful animals such as the elephant should be protected against such killing. In the mid-1990s, an elephant researcher from the Wildlife Conservation Society was flying a small airplane over a part of a forest in the northern part of the Congo. There he saw a bunch of elephant carcasses, or remains. The researcher returned to the area and found more than 300 dead elephants. All had their tusks cut off. Two months later, the researcher found more than 1,000 dead elephants in the same area. The researcher was so angry that he chased the poachers out of the forests by destroying their camps. For a while, his actions helped to stop the poaching of elephants in this region.

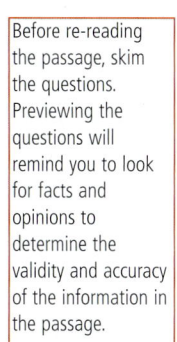

> Before re-reading the passage, skim the questions. Previewing the questions will remind you to look for facts and opinions to determine the validity and accuracy of the information in the passage.

1 The information in this passage could best be used for a research project on

　A. the grasslands of Africa.

　B. protecting endangered animals.

　C. the animals of the Congo.

　D. the work of conservationists.

2 Which of the following statements best supports the idea that poaching is a practice that should be stopped?

　F. Animals as beautiful as elephants should be allowed to roam freely.

　G. Herds of elephants destroy farmers' fields in Africa.

　H. During a twenty-year period, more than half the elephant population in Africa was destroyed through poaching.

　I. Poaching provides ivory to many parts of the world.

answers: 1 (B), 2 (H)

PRACTICE

Read this passage about Africa before answering Numbers 1 through 4.

The Spread of African Deserts

In Africa, desert climates are found in the Sahara to the north, and the Namib and Kalahari to the south. These areas have very little rainfall, high temperatures, and few plants and animals. The Namib experiences temperatures of over 100°F and receives 0.5 to 2.0 inches of rain each year. The Kalahari has temperatures as high as 115°F and receives less than 5 inches of rain each year.

South of the Sahara is a semiarid region known as the Sahel. This area is experiencing desertification, a process by which a desert spreads. One cause of desertification is drought—a lack of rain. The lack of rain causes fewer plants to grow. Without plants, soil blows away, leaving behind dry land. Overgrazing and overuse of the land for farming also cause desertification. The lack of land for farming leads to hunger, which is widespread in many African countries.

Several organizations are working to solve the problem of hunger. Since 1977, a global volunteer organization called the Hunger Project has been working to end hunger in developing nations. In Africa, where poverty and hunger are widespread, the Hunger Project is sponsoring the African Woman Food Farmer Initiative.

The organization sponsors the program because south of the Sahara women grow 80 percent of Africa's food. Each of the 100 million rural African women produces more than 3 metric tons of food each year. African women are involved in storing and transporting food and in bringing the food to market. However, they have little control over the money that the food brings in. African women have an unfair situation.

In addition to their work as farmers, African women are responsible for tasks at home. They prepare, cook, and serve their family's food. They are responsible for collecting water and making sure it is purified for drinking. Women are in charge of keeping their houses clean and making any needed repairs. Women have to gather fuel for cooking and for keeping their houses warm. They are also responsible for raising their children.

So far, the African Woman Food Farmer Initiative has loaned money to more than 14,000 women farmers in eight countries. The program has also provided health, nutrition, and literacy training for 9,000 women who farm.

1 The information in the passage could best be used

  A. to obtain support and donations for the African Woman Food Farmer Initiative.

  B. to stop the problem of hunger in Africa.

  C. for a research project on the spread of the desert in Africa south of the Sahara.

  D. as reasons to visit Africa south of the Sahara.

2 What does the author use to support the purpose for the African Woman Food Farmer Initiative?

  F. statistics about the temperatures and rainfall in Africa south of the Sahara

  G. facts about the role of women as farmers in Africa

  H. an explanation of desertification

  I. the involvement of the Hunger Project

3 How does the geography of Africa south of the Sahara contribute to the problem of hunger in Africa?

4 Which of the following statements from the passage is not a fact that can be proved?

  A. "Each of the 100 million rural African women produces more than 3 metric tons of food each year."

  B. "In Africa, desert climates are found in the Sahara to the north, and the Namib and Kalahari to the south."

  C. "So far, the African Woman Food Farmer Initiative has loaned money to more than 14,000 women farmers in eight countries."

  D. "African women have an unfair situation."

STRATEGIES

Recognizing Cause and Effect
(LA.E.2.2.1)

A cause is an action or event that makes something happen. An effect is the event that is the result of the cause. A single event may have several causes. It is also possible for one cause to result in several effects. Examining cause-and-effect relationships will help you see how events are related and why they took place.

1 Determine why an action took place. Ask yourself a question about the title and topic sentence. (For example, "What were the problems after independence?")

2 Look for results or consequences. Ask yourself "What happened?" (the effect). Then ask, "Why did it happen?" (the cause). (For example, "Why did people in East Pakistan rebel?")

3 Look for clue words that show cause, such as *because*, *due to*, and *since*.

4 Look for clue words that show effects, such as *brought about*, *led to*, *as a result*, and *consequently*.

5 Before re-reading the passage, skim the questions. Previewing the questions will remind you to look for words that signal a cause and those that signal an effect.

answers: 1 (B), 2 (F)

❶ Problems in Pakistan after Independence

When Pakistan became independent, it was a divided nation. Its east and west regions were separated by more than 1,000 miles of territory that was part of India. East Pakistan lay to the northeast of India. West Pakistan lay to the northwest. These two regions were different in language, history, and ethnic background. They were alike in that Islam was the main religion. The people in East Pakistan felt that the government of West Pakistan was neglecting them. This brought about a rebellion by the **❷** people in East Pakistan in April 1971. In December of that year, India sent its army to help the people of East Pakistan. As a result, the army of West Pakistan, which had occupied East Pakistan, withdrew. A new nation, Bangladesh, was formed from East Pakistan.

Shortly after Pakistan became independent, its new leader died. Since Pakistan was left without strong leadership, the country went through a series of military takeovers. After several leaders had failed to stay in power, Benazir Bhutto was elected prime minister. However, because of months of disorder in the country, she was removed from office in 1996. Nawaz Sharif was then elected prime minister in 1997.

❶ The people in East Pakistan rebelled against West Pakistan because

  A. they were upset about being a divided nation.
  B. they believed that the government of West Pakistan was neglecting them.
  C. there were too many military takeovers by the government of West Pakistan.
  D. India sent its army to help West Pakistan.

❷ Why did West Pakistan withdraw from East Pakistan in December 1971?

  F. because India sent its army to help East Pakistan
  G. because there were many military takeovers
  H. because it was a divided nation
  I. because West Pakistan's leader died

Read this passage about monsoons in South Asia before answering Numbers 1 through 3.

Monsoons

A monsoon is a wind that blows over the northern part of the Indian Ocean and most of the surrounding lands. The time from June through September marks the coming of the monsoon winds and the rainy season. From April through October, the monsoon blows from the southwest, causing moisture to build up over the ocean and heavy rains to fall on South Asia and Southeast Asia. From November through March, the monsoon blows from the northeast.

In South Asia, heavy monsoon rains fall from June through October. Because March through late May is hot and humid, the monsoon rains in June bring great relief. In India, children start school in June, after the rains begin. They take their vacation during the spring, when it is too hot to study. In Southeast Asia, the summer monsoons last from April to September.

Farming in the region depends on the timing of the monsoons. Monsoons that come too early can mean that farmers don't have enough time to plant their seeds. Rains that arrive too late can result in crop failure. Severe flooding can bring about ruined crops, damaged property, and danger to the people living in the region.

1 What causes heavy rains to fall on South Asia from April through October?

    A. the monsoon winds that blow from the northeast

    B. the very hot temperatures

    C. the monsoon winds that blow from the southwest

    D. the very dry winds

2 Why do students in India start school in June?

    F. That month starts the dry season in India.

    G. It is cooler when the rains stop in June.

    H. The students help farm the land before then.

    I. It is too hot before the rains fall in June.

3 Read this sentence from the passage.

Farming in the region depends on the timing of the monsoons.

Why does farming in South and Southeast Asia depend on the monsoons? Use information from the passage to support your answer.

STRATEGIES

Understanding Character and Plot Development (LA.E.2.3.1)

When you read a story, it is important to recognize its characters and its setting. It is also important to understand how the characters and plot are used to develop a story line or conflict.

❶ Skim the story to get an idea of what it is about.

❷ Identify the main characters in the story.

❸ Identify the setting of the story. Where and when did the story take place? (This story takes place after the bombing of Seoul, the capital of Korea.)

❹ A story's plot consists of its sequence of events. Generally, each event is caused by an event that came before it. The last part of the plot is the resolution. This is where any loose ends of a story are tied up.

❺ Identify the conflict. The struggle that a character faces is generally the conflict in the story. The conflict can be between the characters in the story. The conflict can also be between a character and other forces.

❻ Before re-reading the story, skim the questions. Previewing the questions will remind you to pay attention to the characters, setting, and plot of the story.

War Wounds

"Is that a picture of your dog?" Junho asked, looking at the pencil sketch of Luxy that rested on top of the bookcase. "You must miss it very much. . . ."

"Oh that," I said, flustered and surprised. "Yes, that's my boxer, Luxy." I missed my dog, but I hadn't talked about her with anyone since we left Seoul. . . . I frequently thought of how Luxy used to wait eagerly at the top of the stone steps in front of our house for me to come home from school. . . . But I never talked of Luxy, for I was afraid that people might think I was childish and insensitive to mourn the loss of my dog when so many people were dead or missing. Junho was different, though . . . sharing my sadness. . . . I stared at Luxy's picture, and I imagined how scared she must have felt when we all abandoned her. . . . I shook my head and swallowed hard. . . .

"What is it, Sookan? What are you thinking about?" Junho said, looking very concerned.

"Oh, Junho, I was remembering the first bombing of Seoul. It was horrible. . . . All I could do was stand by the window and watch the bombs explode. Hyunchun, my third brother, came rushing into my room, shouting, '. . . Come on. Those planes will be right on top of us next. Let's go.'"

"Did you all get out safely?" Junho asked anxiously. . . .

"Oh, yes. We put thick blankets over our heads and joined the throngs of people headed up Namsan Mountain. We stayed up on the mountain all night and watched the bombs erupt into flames in the city below. . . . As we were sitting there, I realized that my brother Jaechun was holding a large bundle in his arms, which he rocked back and forth like a baby. I instantly realized it was Luxy wrapped in that bundle. . . .

"The bombing finally stopped at dawn and we began making our way back home. We found our house half bombed . . . . We . . . started to unwrap poor Luxy. When we uncovered her, she gave such a loud, joyous bark. . . . She made us laugh and forget that we were sitting in the middle of a bombed city."

Junho's face brightened. . . . "Luxy was lucky to be so well loved and cared for."

"Well, . . . Things got worse. About six months after that, we had to leave Seoul. I left her all alone. I don't know what happened to her. . . . "…Each time I see a dog or hear a dog bark, I feel guilty that I did not love Luxy enough to save her; she, my dog, who depended on me. I had thought only of myself. . . ."

—From *Echoes of the White Giraffe* (1993) by Sook Nyul Choi

❶ Who is both the narrator and a main character in this story?
- **A.** Junho
- **B.** Sookan
- **C.** Luxy
- **D.** Jaechun

❷ Which pair of words best describe Junho?
- **F.** impatient and likable
- **G.** friendly and understanding
- **H.** determined and popular
- **I.** suspicious and outgoing

❸ Sookan feels guilty because she
- **A.** ignored her friend.
- **B.** did not leave with her family.
- **C.** did not save her brother.
- **D.** did not save her dog.

answers: 1 (B), 2 (G), 3 (D)

Read this passage about how two mountains were formed before answering Numbers 1 through 3.

The Story of the Two Brothers

Two large mountains face each other across Pago Pago . . . Harbor on the island of Tutuila . . . in American Samoa. They are known as the Two Brothers: Matafao . . . and Pioa. . . . The story of how they came to be is told and retold to children throughout the islands. It contains an important message.

Long ago, a man had two sons. He loved both children dearly, as fathers will. One he called Matafao; the other, Pioa. As small boys, they fought constantly. As they grew to manhood, their fights became ever fiercer and more frequent.

Time passed. The father grew gray and old. Tired of listening to his sons fight with each other, he began to despair. He knew the time was drawing near when he would leave them. What would become of his angry children?

The day came when he called Pioa and Matafao to him. This is what he told them, "My heart is heavy inside me. It seems you cannot love each other as brothers should. In fact, you cannot be together without one of you starting a fight. The only solution I can see is to separate you forever. Therefore, from this day forward, you will live apart from each other. Pioa, you shall live in the east," he said. "Matafao, you will live in the west. Perhaps the sea will be wide enough to keep you from fighting when I could not."

And then he added, "Should either of you manage to start a fight, you will be turned into stone on the spot where you stand."

Soon, the old man died.

Although the two brothers could not seem to love each other, they both loved their father. Their grief for him was great. In fact, they found they were unable to eat. Had their sadness continued, they surely would have sickened and died, too.

With the passage of time, grief lessens. So, it was with them. The two brothers found themselves happy again. They decided to host a feast. They would roast a whole pig and many chickens. They would . . . bake a cake with so many tiers, it would be fine enough for the finest Samoan wedding.

Matafao and Pioa ate well at their feast. In fact, Matafao may have eaten a little too well. He decided to climb a cliff, and look over his lush green island.

At that moment, high above their heads, a seabird picked up a rock and, raising his great wings, took to the skies. When a wind sprang up, the rock slipped from his claws. Hurling down the cliff, it struck Pioa on the top of his head.

Pioa looked up. Being so quick to anger, he blamed his brother, not the seabird or the wind.

"It is your fault, Matafao!" Pioa screamed. "You threw the rock!" With that, he picked up a stone and threw it at his brother.

At those angry and unjust words, Matafao also got angry and threw some rocks. One knocked off Pioa's top. It fell into the sea with a giant splash, and lies there to this day, a small, rocky island.

As when a volcano erupts, rocks began to fly between the brothers. Only then did they remember their father's warning: Whoever starts another fight will be turned into stone.

Too late, they found their father's words were true. Their lower limbs had hardened and turned to stone.

Matafao realized then that fighting with his brother was wrong. He stopped and begged his brother to stop as well. Pioa's rage was too great and he refused and continued to fight.

"Stop, Brother. I beg you," Matafao pleaded again. When he realized his words were ignored, he fought back.

It was at that moment that Pioa and Matafao became the mountains known as the Two Brothers. Pioa, humbled by his own wrongdoings, stands the smaller of the two. The dark cloud that hovers over his head brings rain to the islands and remains as a reminder to Samoan children to love one another.

❶ How would you describe the father in the story?

- **A.** sad and discouraged
- **B.** mean and upset
- **C.** smart and content
- **D.** happy and determined

❷ What does the story try to explain?

- **F.** why the two brothers fought each other
- **G.** how two large mountains in American Samoa came to be
- **H.** how the two brothers, Matafao and Pioa, got their names
- **I.** how the seabird came to be

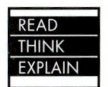

❸ In the story the father says "My heart is heavy inside me." Why does the father feel this way? Use details and information from the story to support your answer.

STRATEGIES

The Writing FCAT

During the writing FCAT, you will be given 45 minutes to plan and write a detailed response to a prompt. The first part of the prompt gives you the writing situation. The second part gives you more specific directions for writing. The writing test may feature an expository prompt (that asks you to explain something) or a persuasive prompt (that asks you to convince someone of something).

① You have only 45 minutes, so manage your time well. Make sure that you assign enough time for all of the tasks involved in writing—jotting down ideas, developing an outline, writing the response, and proofreading.

② Read the Writing Situation to get an idea of topic.

③ Then read the Writing Directions carefully. Look for cue words. Are you being asked to explain or define something or to persuade or convince someone? Also, identify the audience to whom you must write your response. Use an appropriate tone and language.

④ Jot down ideas on a separate sheet of paper. Use these ideas to develop an outline for your response. (In the actual test, you will receive a separate booklet in which to plan your response.)

Carefully read the information below. Then write your response on a separate sheet of paper. Make sure to use correct spelling, grammar, and punctuation.

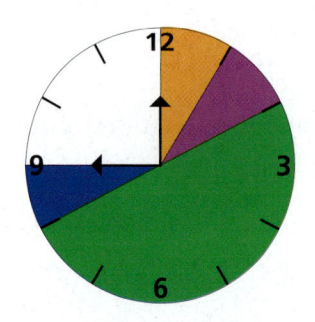

This clock shows about how much time you should spend on each part of the writing process

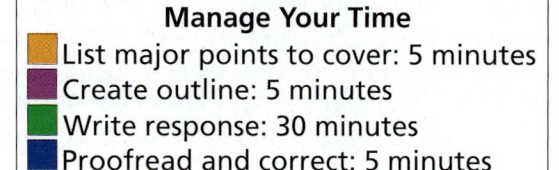

Manage Your Time
- List major points to cover: 5 minutes
- Create outline: 5 minutes
- Write response: 30 minutes
- Proofread and correct: 5 minutes

② **Writing Situation:** You are given the opportunity to visit any region of the world you would like.

Directions for Writing: Think about the region you would like to visit.

③ Now explain to your reader which region you would choose and why.

A top-scoring response will include the following elements:

- clear statement of which region you would like to visit.
- information explaining why you chose that region, including specific details and logical development
- restatement of why you would choose to visit a particular region
- grammatical, legible presentation of your ideas

You will be graded on spelling, grammar, and punctuation. So, after you finish writing, proofread.

PRACTICE

For more test practice online...

TEST PRACTICE CLASSZONE.COM

Carefully read the information below. Then write your response on a separate sheet of paper. Make sure to use correct spelling, grammar, and punctuation.

Writing Situation: The superintendent of your school district has announced a plan for students in all elementary grades to study a foreign language.

Directions for Writing: Think about how taking a foreign language would affect students.

Now write to convince your superintendent to accept your point of veiw on the plan.

RAND M°NALLY
World Atlas

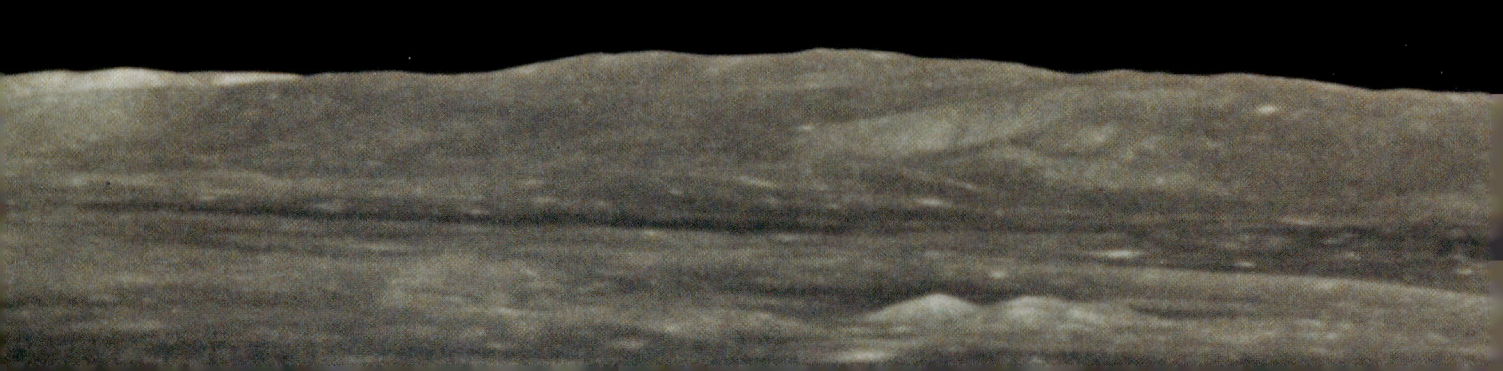

Contents

World: Physical A2	North America: Political A23
World: Political A4	South America: Physical A24
World: Climate A6	South America: Political A25
World: Environments A8	Europe: Physical A26
World: Population A10	Europe: Political A28
World: Economies A12	Africa: Physical A30
Plate Tectonics A14	Africa: Political A31
World: Time Zones A16	Asia: Physical A32
United States: Physical A18	Asia: Political A34
United States: Political A20	Australia and Oceania A36
North America: Physical A22	North and South Pole A37

Complete Legend for Physical and Political Maps

Symbols

- Lake
- Salt Lake
- Seasonal Lake
- River
- Waterfall
- Canal
- △ Mountain Peak
- ▲ Highest Mountain Peak

Cities

- ■ Los Angeles — City over 1,000,000 population
- ▣ Calgary — City of 250,000 to 1,000,000 population
- • Haifa — City under 250,000 population
- ✲ Paris — National Capital
- ★ Vancouver — Secondary Capital (State, Province, or Territory)

Type Styles Used to Name Features

- **CHINA** — Country
- ONTARIO — State, Province, or Territory
- **PUERTO RICO (U.S.)** — Possession
- ATLANTIC OCEAN — Ocean or Sea
- *Alps* — Physical Feature
- *Borneo* — Island

Boundaries

- International Boundary
- Secondary Boundary

Land Elevation and Water Depths

Land Elevation

Meters	Feet
3,000 and over	9,840 and over
2,000 - 3,000	6,560 - 9,840
500 - 2,000	1,640 - 6,560
200 - 500	656 - 1,640
0 - 200	0 - 656

Water Depth

Less than 200	Less than 656
200 - 2,000	656 - 6,560
Over 2,000	Over 6,560

World: Physical

World: Physical

World: Political

World: Political

World: Climate

TROPICAL
- Hot with Rain All Year
- Hot with Seasonal Rain

DRY
- Desert
- Some Rain

MODERATE (RAINY WINTER)
- Hot, Dry Summer
- Hot, Humid Summer
- Mild, Rainy Summer

CONTINENTAL (SNOWY WINTER)
- Long, Warm, Humid Summer
- Short, Cool, Humid Summer
- Very Short, Cool, Humid Summer

POLAR
- Tundra – Very Cold and Dry
- Ice Cap

HIGHLANDS
- Varies with Altitude

0 1000 2000 Miles
0 1000 2000 3000 Kilometers

Copyright by Rand McNally & Co.
Robinson Projection

RAND MCNALLY

A6

World: Climate

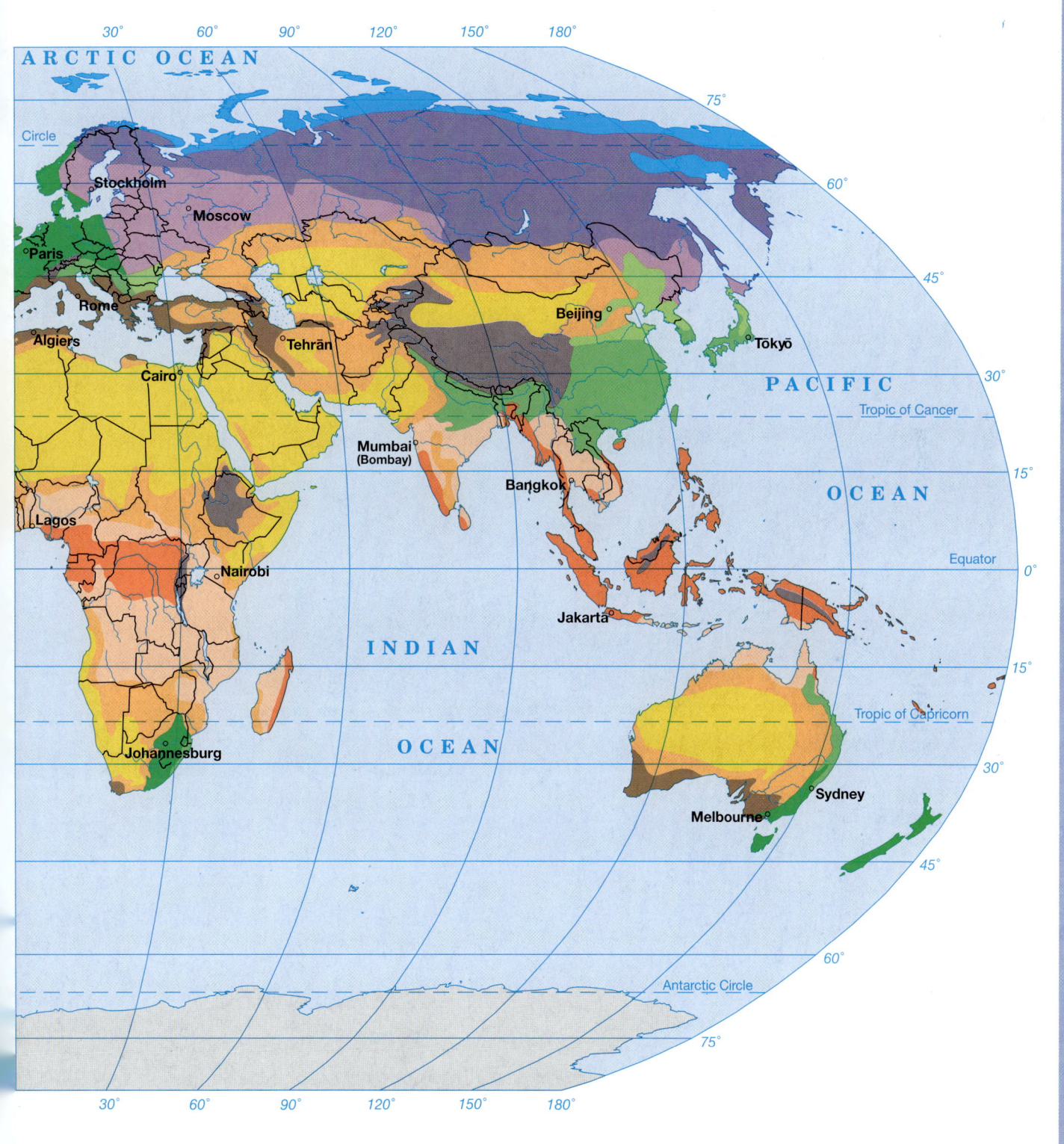

A7

World: Environments

Legend:
- Forest
- Swamp
- Crop and Woodland
- Cropland
- Crop and Grazing Land
- Grassland
- Desert
- Tundra
- Barren
- Urban

Copyright by Rand McNally & Co.
Robinson Projection

A8

World: Environments

World: Population

Per square mile *(per square kilometer)*
- Under 2 *(Under 1)*
- 2-60 *(1-25)*
- 60-125 *(25-50)*
- 125-250 *(50-100)*
- Over 250 *(Over 100)*

Copyright by Rand McNally & Co.
Robinson Projection

Rand McNally

A10

World: Population

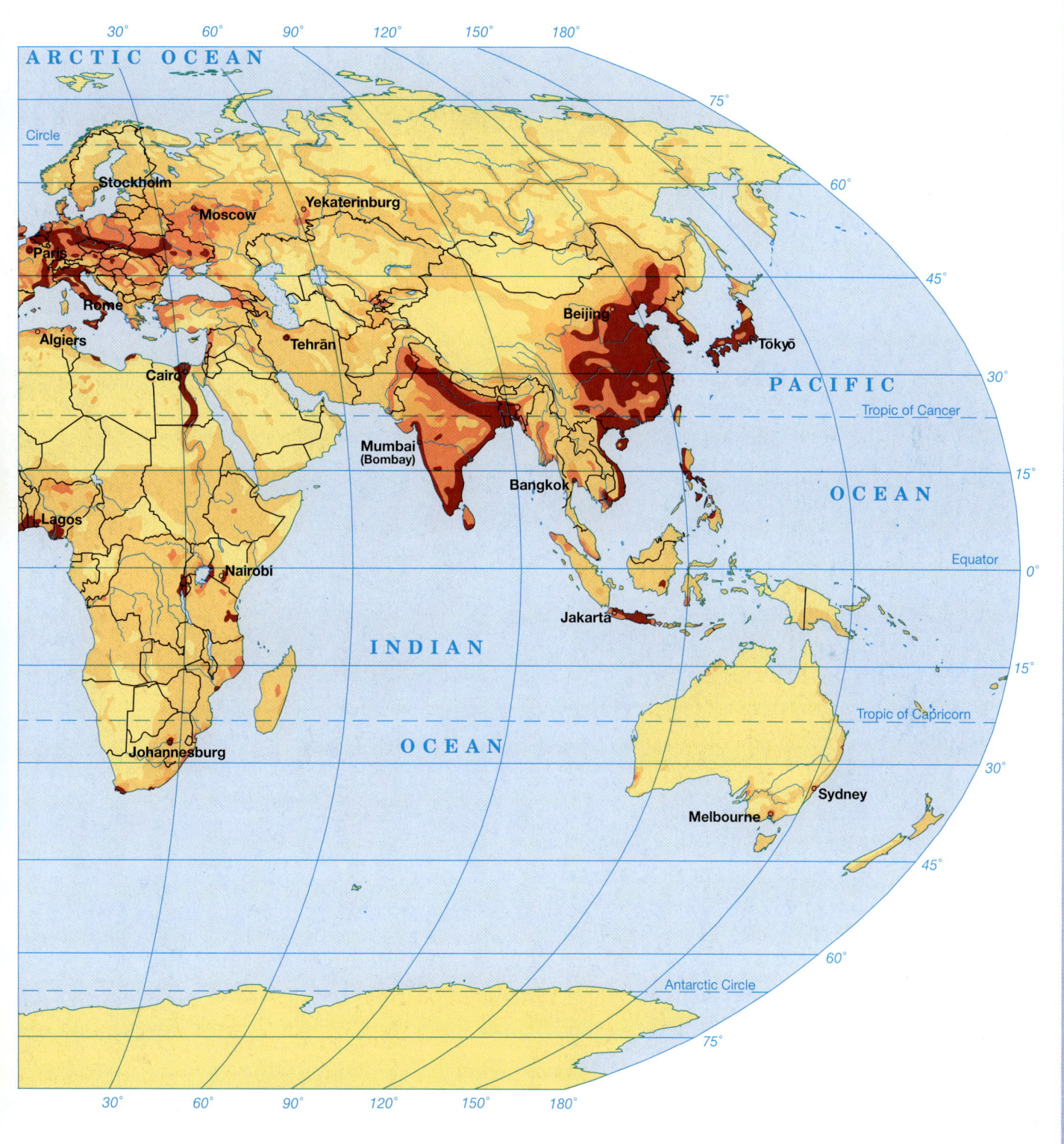

A11

World: Economies

Legend:
- Little or no activity
- Nomadic Herding
- Hunting, Forestry, Subsistence Farming
- Forestry
- Agriculture
- Stock Raising
- Manufacturing, Commerce
- Fishing

Copyright by Rand McNally & Co.
Robinson Projection

A12

World: Economies

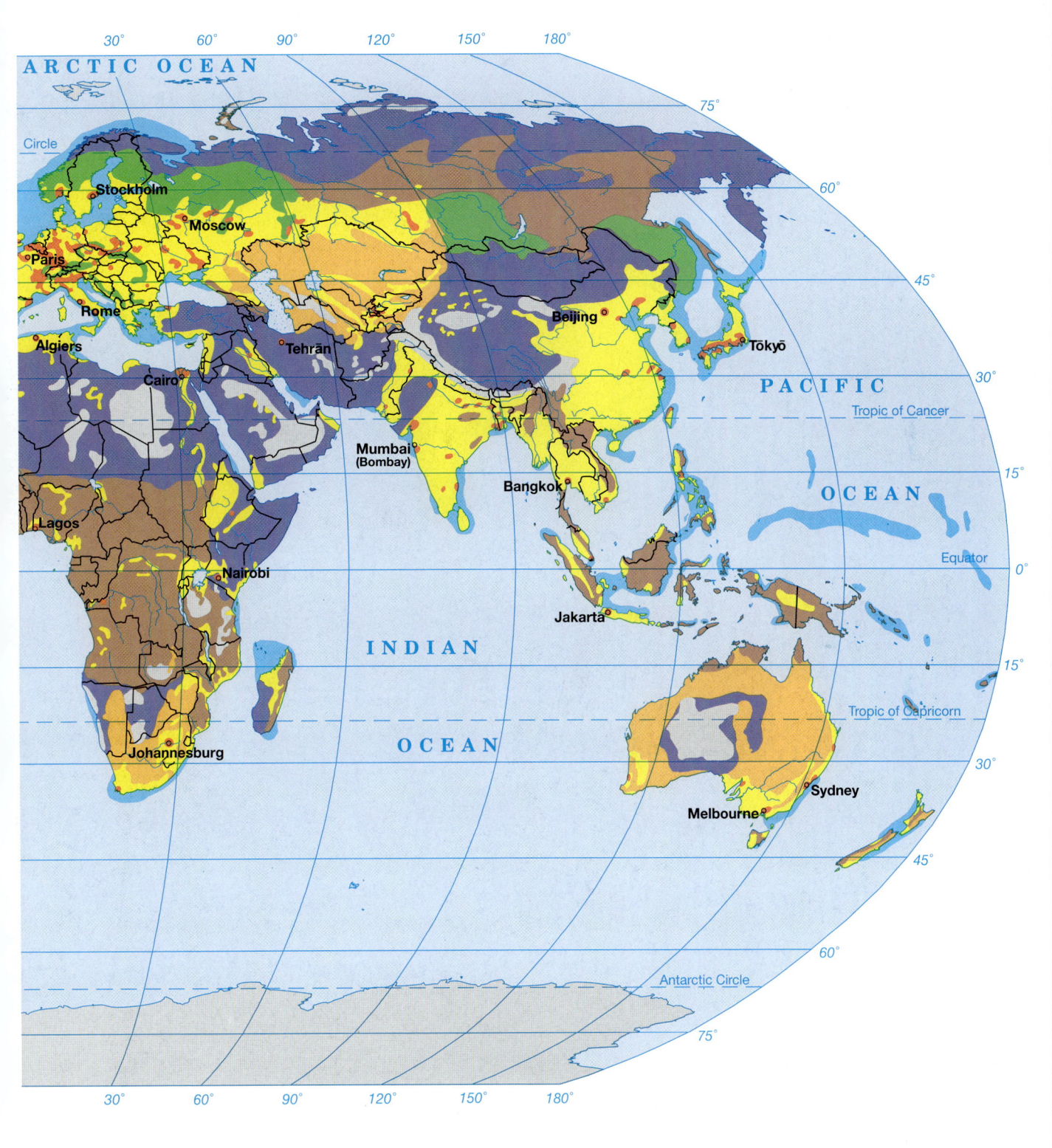

ATLAS

A13

Plate Tectonics

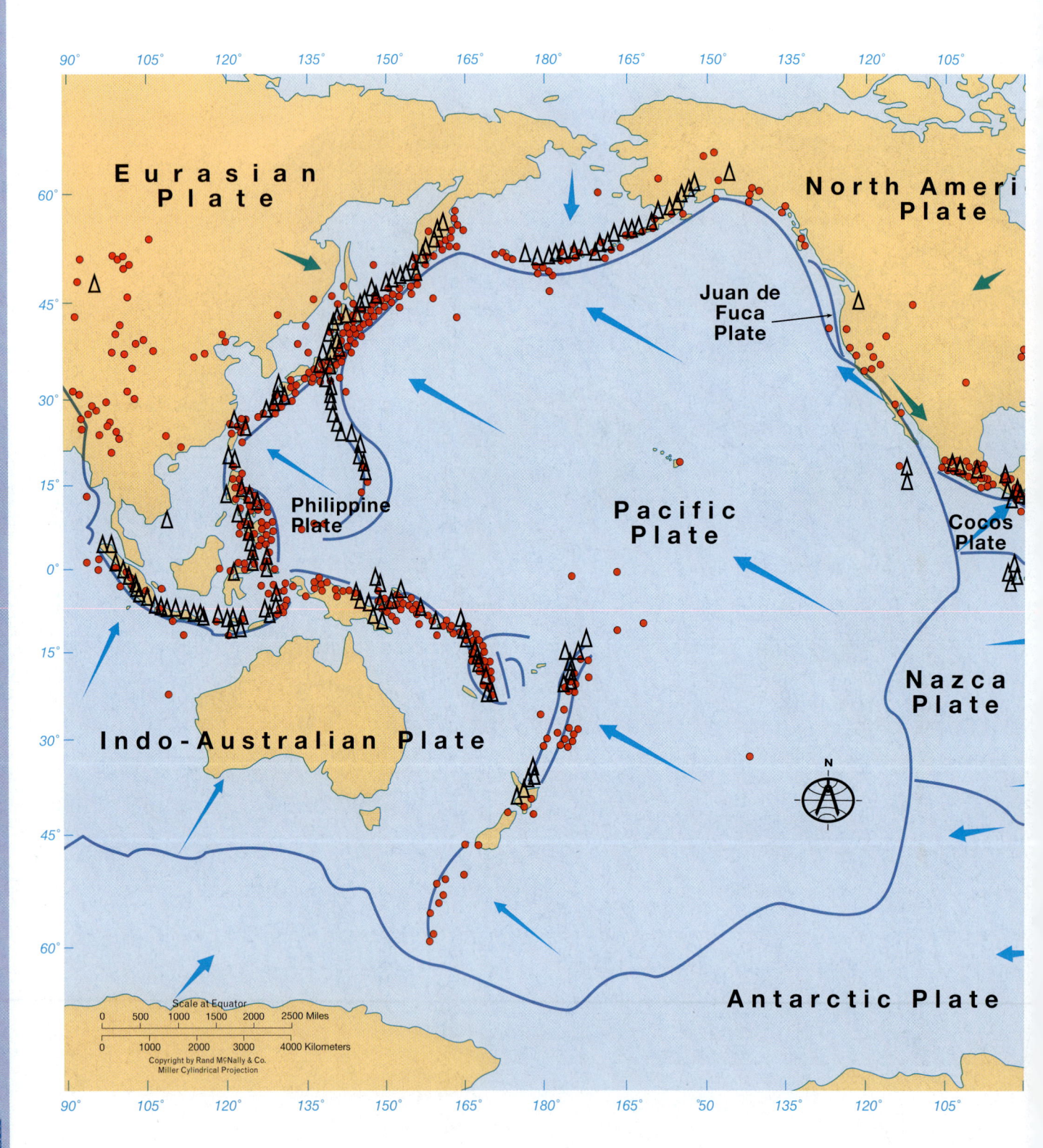

A14

Plate Tectonics

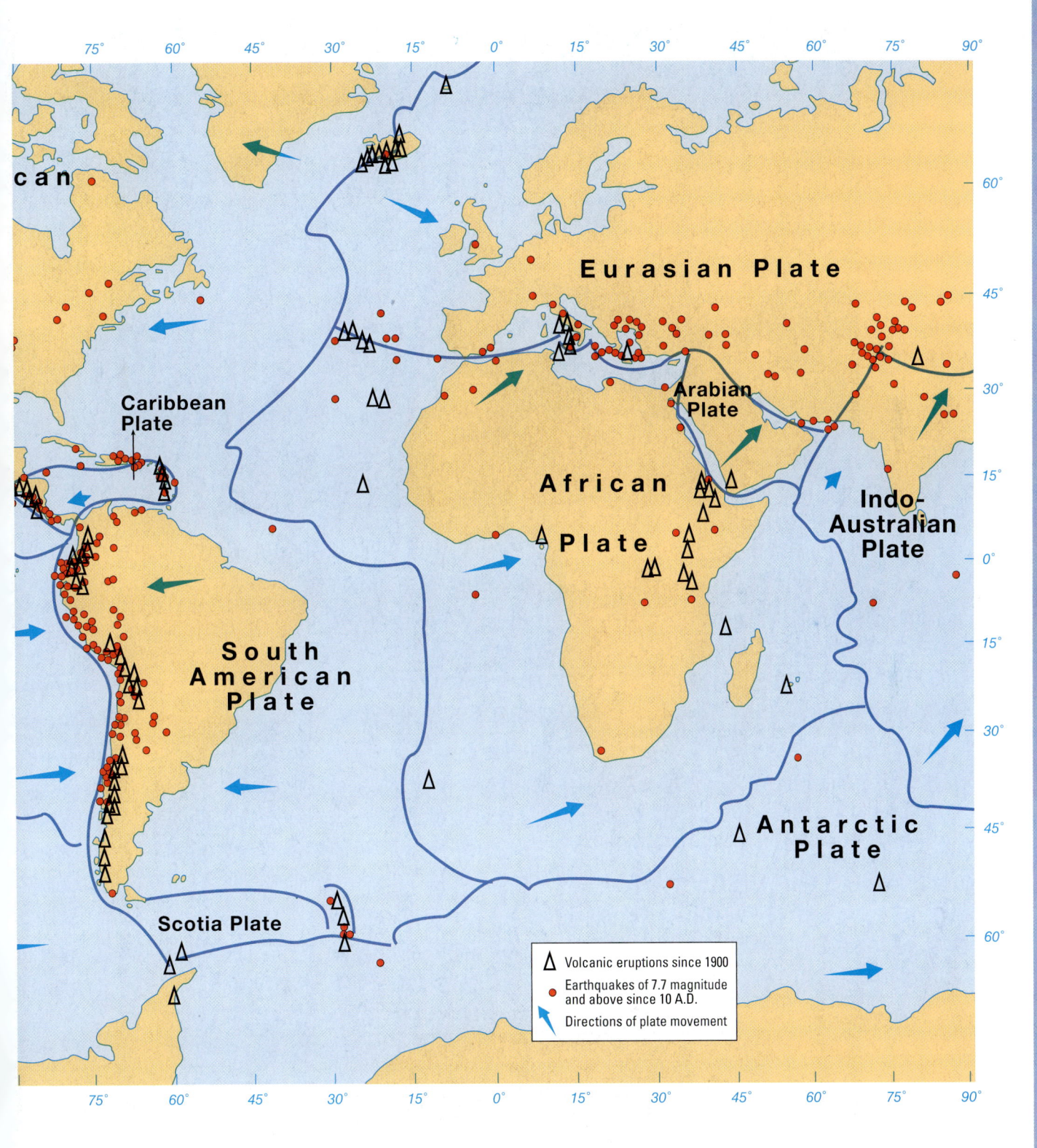

△ Volcanic eruptions since 1900
● Earthquakes of 7.7 magnitude and above since 10 A.D.
→ Directions of plate movement

Eurasian Plate
Caribbean Plate
Arabian Plate
African Plate
Indo-Australian Plate
South American Plate
Antarctic Plate
Scotia Plate

ATLAS

A15

World: Time Zones

11pm | Midnight | 1 am | 2 am | 3 am | 4 am | 5 am | 6 am | 7 am | 8 am | 9 am | 10 am | 11

- Anchorage
- Edmonton
- **NORTH AMERICA**
- Montreal
- Chicago
- New York
- Los Angeles
- INTERNATIONAL DATE LINE
- Mexico City
- Caracas
- Dakar
- Lima
- **SOUTH AMERICA**
- Rio de Janeiro
- Auckland
- Buenos Aires

Nonstandard time zones

11pm | Midnight | 1 am | 2 am | 3 am | 4 am | 5 am | 6 am | 7 am | 8 am | 9 am | 10 am | 11

RAND MCNALLY

A16

World: Time Zones

| 11 am | Noon | 1 pm | 2 pm | 3 pm | 4 pm | 5 pm | 6 pm | 7 pm | 8 pm | 9 pm | 10 pm |

PRIME MERIDIAN

Stockholm
Moscow
Yekaterinburg
Novosibirsk
London
EUROPE
Paris
Madrid
Rome
ASIA
Tehran
Beijing
Tōkyō
Cairo
Mumbai (Bombay)
Bangkok
AFRICA
Lagos
Nairobi
Johannesburg
AUSTRALIA
Sydney

Scale at Equator
0 – 1000 – 2000 – 3000 – 4000 Miles
0 – 1000 – 2000 – 3000 – 4000 – 5000 – 6000 Kilometers
Copyright by Rand McNally & Co.
Mercator Projection

| 11 am | Noon | 1 pm | 2 pm | 3 pm | 4 pm | 5 pm | 6 pm | 7 pm | 8 pm | 9 pm | 10 pm |

ATLAS

RAND McNALLY

A17

United States: Physical

United States: Physical

A19

United States: Political

National Capital
Secondary Capital (State, Province, or Territory)
City over 1,000,000 population
City of 250,000 to 1,000,000 population
City under 250,000 population
0 100 200 300 Miles
0 100 200 300 400 Kilometers
Copyright by Rand McNally & Co.
Alber's Conic Equal Area Projection
ONTARIO
QUÉBEC
NEW BRUNSWICK
Lake Winnipeg
Lake Nipigon
Lake of the Woods
International Falls
Isle Royale
Lake Superior
Duluth
MINNESOTA
St. Cloud
Minneapolis
St. Paul
Mankato
Rochester
Eau Claire
WISCONSIN
Green Bay
Appleton
OshKosh
Sheboygan
Milwaukee
Madison
Racine
Marquette
MICHIGAN
Sault Ste. Marie
Georgian Bay
Lake Huron
Traverse City
Lake Michigan
Saginaw
Flint
Grand Rapids
Lansing
Detroit
Kalamazoo
Ann Arbor
Toronto
Lake Ontario
Lake Erie
Ottawa
Montréal
Lake Champlain
VERMONT
Burlington
Montpelier
Connecticut
NEW HAMPSHIRE
Concord
Manchester
MAINE
Moosehead Lake
Bangor
Augusta
Portland
Gulf of Maine
Watertown
Rochester
NEW YORK
Syracuse
Albany
Buffalo
Binghamton
Hudson
MASSACHUSETTS
Worcester
Boston
Providence
CONNECTICUT
R.I.
Hartford
Bridgeport
Nantucket Island
Long Island
New York
Newark
Trenton
Erie
Oil City
PENNSYLVANIA
Scranton
Allentown
Susquehanna
Harrisburg
Philadelphia
Pittsburgh
Wilmington
NEW JERSEY
Dover
Delaware Bay
DELAWARE
Baltimore
Washington D.C.
Annapolis
MARYLAND
ATLANTIC OCEAN
Sioux City
Waterloo
Dubuque
Cedar Rapids
IOWA
Des Moines
Davenport
Omaha
Rockford
Aurora
Chicago
Moline
Peoria
Bloomington
Illinois
Decatur
Springfield
ILLINOIS
Gary
South Bend
Fort Wayne
INDIANA
Muncie
Indianapolis
Terre Haute
Bloomington
Wabash
Toledo
Cleveland
Akron
Youngstown
Lima
OHIO
Columbus
Springfield
Dayton
Cincinnati
Ohio
WEST VIRGINIA
Charleston
Huntington
VIRGINIA
Richmond
Newport News
Norfolk
Virginia Beach
Roanoke
Albemarle Sound
Pamlico Sound
Missouri
St. Joseph
Kansas City
Topeka
Emporia
Columbia
Jefferson City
St. Louis
MISSOURI
Springfield
Cape Girardeau
Mississippi
Evansville
Owensboro
Louisville
Frankfort
Lexington
KENTUCKY
Clarksville
Cumberland
Nashville
Knoxville
Johnson City
Kentucky Lake
TENNESSEE
Chattanooga
Memphis
Winston-Salem
Greensboro
Durham
Raleigh
NORTH CAROLINA
Asheville
Charlotte
Wilmington
Tulsa
Muskogee
Fayetteville
Jonesboro
Fort Smith
Arkansas
Little Rock
ARKANSAS
Pine Bluff
Ouachita
Texarkana
Greenville
SOUTH CAROLINA
Columbia
Charleston
Huntsville
Birmingham
Tuscaloosa
ALABAMA
Montgomery
Tombigbee
Athens
Atlanta
Augusta
Savannah
GEORGIA
Macon
Columbus
Altamaha
Albany
Chattahoochee
MISSISSIPPI
Jackson
Hattiesburg
Shreveport
Monroe
LOUISIANA
Tyler
Sam Rayburn Res.
Toledo Bend Res.
Red
Trinity
Lake Charles
Baton Rouge
Lafayette
Beaumont
Houston
Galveston
New Orleans
Gulfport
Mobile
Pensacola
Dothan
Tallahassee
Jacksonville
Gainesville
Daytona Beach
Orlando
Tampa
St. Petersburg
Lakeland
FLORIDA
Lake Okeechobee
West Palm Beach
Fort Myers
Fort Lauderdale
Miami
Key West
GULF OF MEXICO
ATLANTIC OCEAN
San Juan
Arecibo
Mayagüez
Caguas
Ponce
PUERTO RICO (U.S.)
0 25 50 Miles
0 25 50 Kilometers
Caribbean Sea
© RMcN.

North America: Physical

North America: Political

South America: Physical

South America: Political

Legend:
- ✪ National Capital
- ★ Secondary Capital (State, Province, or Territory)
- ■ City over 1,000,000 population
- ▣ City of 250,000 to 1,000,000 population
- · City under 250,000 population

Scale: 0 – 1000 Miles / 0 – 1500 Kilometers

Copyright by Rand McNally & Co.
Lambert Azimuthal Equal Area Projection

ATLAS

A25

Europe: Physical

Europe: Physical

Europe: Political

Legend:
- ✪ National Capital
- ★ Secondary Capital (State, Province, or Territory)
- ■ City over 1,000,000 population
- ▫ City of 250,000 to 1,000,000 population
- • City under 250,000 population

Scale: 0–400 Miles / 0–600 Kilometers
Copyright by Rand McNally & Co.
Lambert Conformal Conic Projection

Countries and features labeled on map:

ICELAND (Reykjavík), FAROE ISLANDS (Den.), NORWAY (Oslo, Bergen, Trondheim), SWEDEN (Stockholm, Göteborg, Umeå, Tampere), UNITED KINGDOM (London, Birmingham, Manchester, Liverpool, Glasgow, Edinburgh, Aberdeen, Cardiff, Plymouth), SCOTLAND, NORTHERN IRELAND (Belfast), IRELAND (Dublin, Cork), WALES, ENGLAND, DENMARK (Copenhagen), NETHERLANDS (Amsterdam, The Hague), BELGIUM (Brussels), LUX. (Luxembourg), GERMANY (Berlin, Hamburg, Cologne, Bonn, Frankfurt, Dresden, Stuttgart, Munich), POLAND (Warsaw, Gdańsk, Szczecin, Wrocław, Kraków), LITHUANIA, RUSSIA (Kaliningrad), CZECH REPUBLIC (Prague), SLOVAKIA (Bratislava), AUSTRIA (Vienna), LIECH., SWITZERLAND (Bern, Zürich, Geneva), HUNGARY (Budapest), SLOVENIA (Ljubljana), CROATIA (Zagreb), BOSNIA AND HERZEGOVINA (Sarajevo), YUGOSLAVIA (Belgrade), MACEDONIA (Skopje), ALBANIA (Tiranë), FRANCE (Paris, Nantes, Bordeaux, Toulouse, Lyon, Marseille, Nice, Strasbourg, Le Havre), MONACO, ITALY (Rome, Milan, Turin, Genoa, Venice, Florence, Naples, Bari, Palermo, Catania), VATICAN CITY, SAN MARINO, SPAIN (Madrid, Barcelona, Valencia, Seville, Córdoba, Málaga, Zaragoza, Valladolid, Bilbao, Gijón, A Coruña, Palma), PORTUGAL (Lisbon, Porto), ANDORRA, GIBRALTAR (U.K.), MALTA (Valletta), MOROCCO (Rabat), ALGERIA (Algiers), TUNISIA (Tunis), Corsica (Fr.), Sardinia (It.), Sicily, Cagliari

Seas and waters: ATLANTIC OCEAN, NORWEGIAN SEA, NORTH SEA, BALTIC SEA, Gulf of Bothnia, Irish Sea, St. George's Channel, English Channel, Strait of Dover, Bay of Biscay, MEDITERRANEAN, TYRRHENIAN SEA, ADRIATIC SEA, IONIAN SEA, Skagerrak, Strait of Gibraltar, Arctic Circle

Rivers: Thames, Rhine, Elbe, Oder, Wisła, Seine, Loire, Rhône, Ebro, Tagus, Danube, Po

Rand McNally

A28

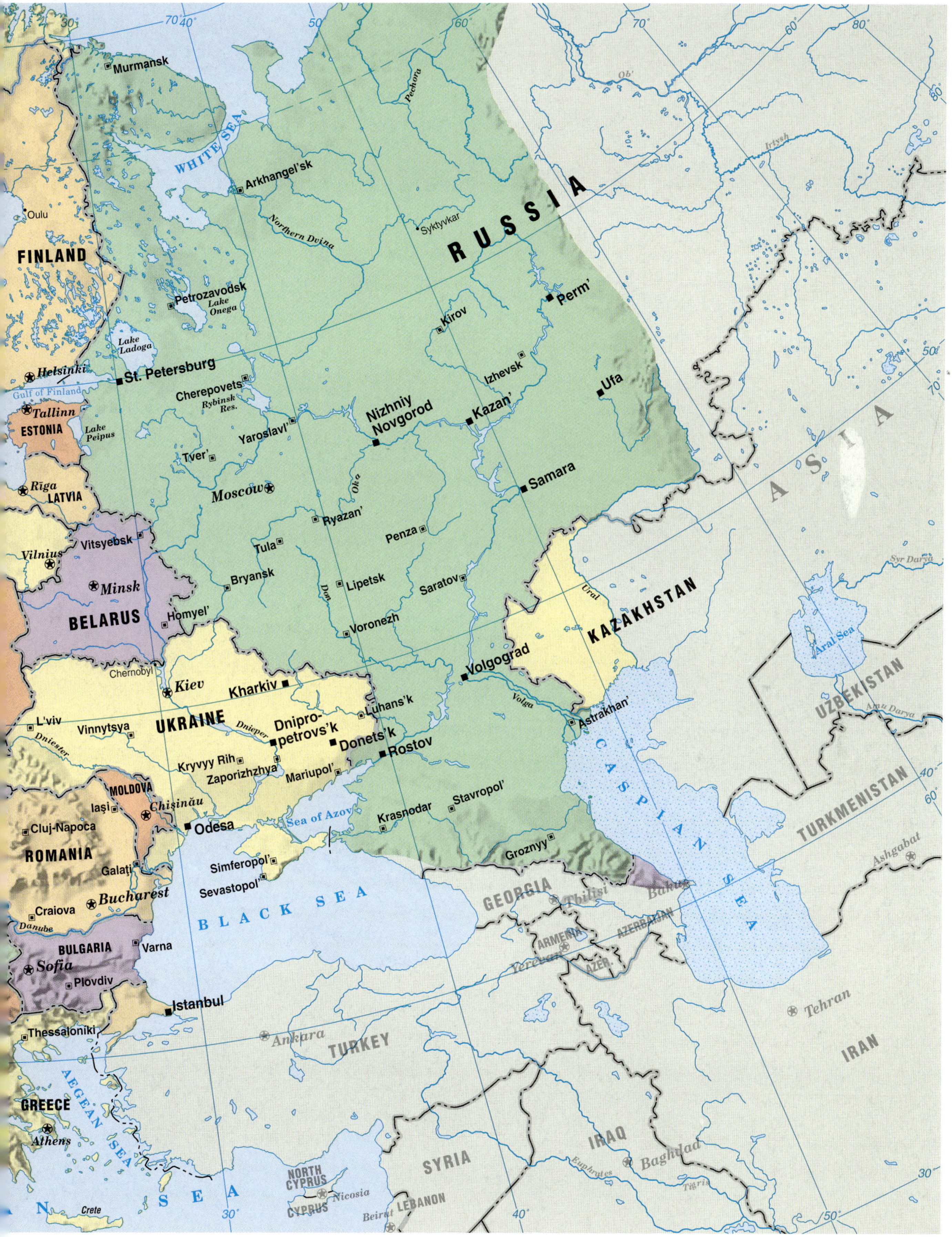

ATLAS

RAND McNALLY

Africa: Physical

Africa: Political

Legend:
- ✪ National Capital
- ★ Secondary Capital (State, Province, or Territory)
- ■ City over 1,000,000 population
- ▪ City of 250,000 to 1,000,000 population
- · City under 250,000 population

Scale: 0–1000 Miles / 0–1500 Kilometers
Copyright by Rand McNally & Co.
Lambert Azimuthal Equal Area Projection

A31

Asia: Physical

Asia: Physical

Asia: Political

Asia: Political

- ★ National Capital
- ★ Secondary Capital (State, Province, or Territory)
- ■ City over 1,000,000 population
- ▣ City of 250,000 to 1,000,000 population
- • City under 250,000 population

ATLAS

A35

Australia and Oceania

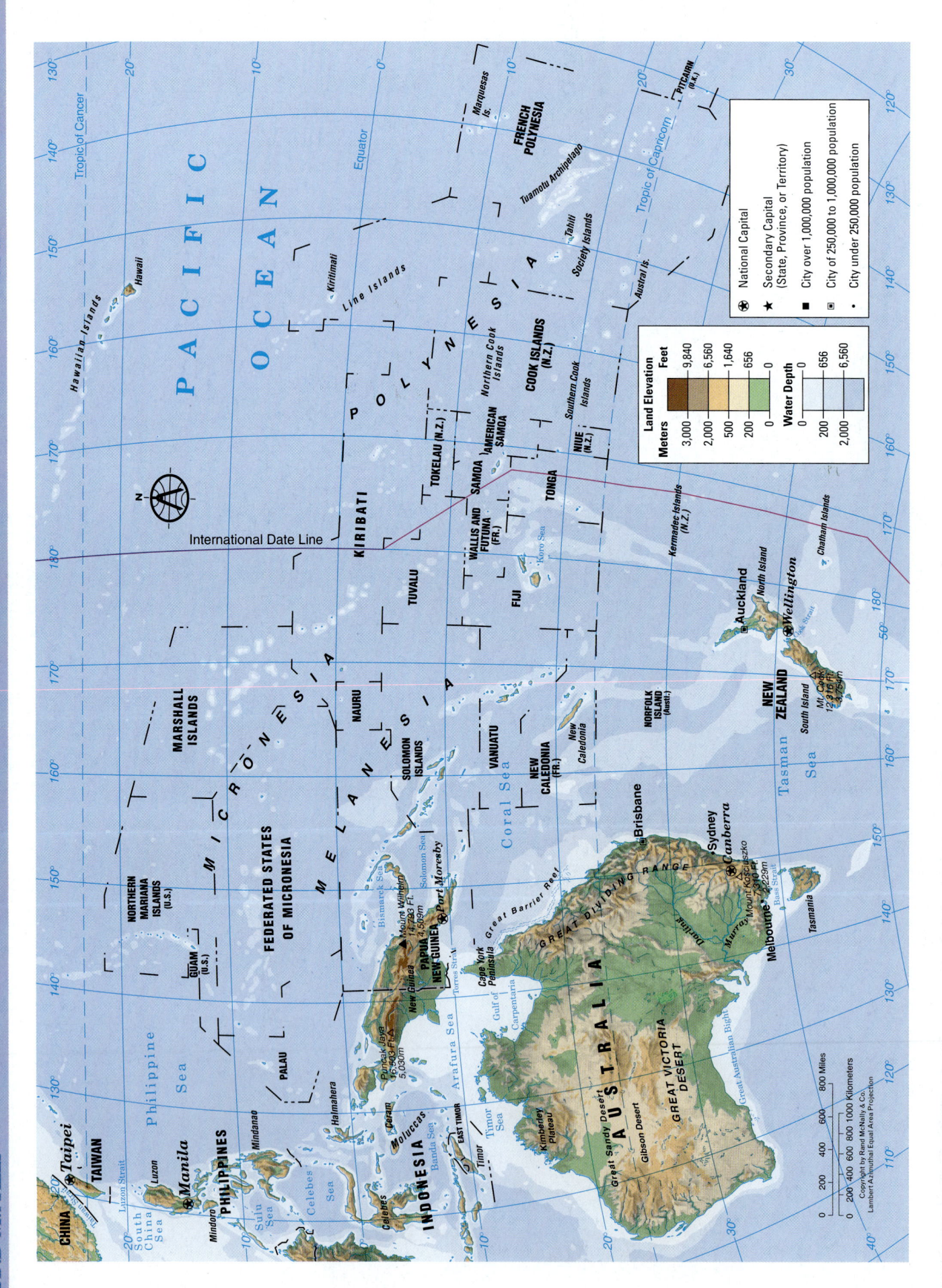

North Pole

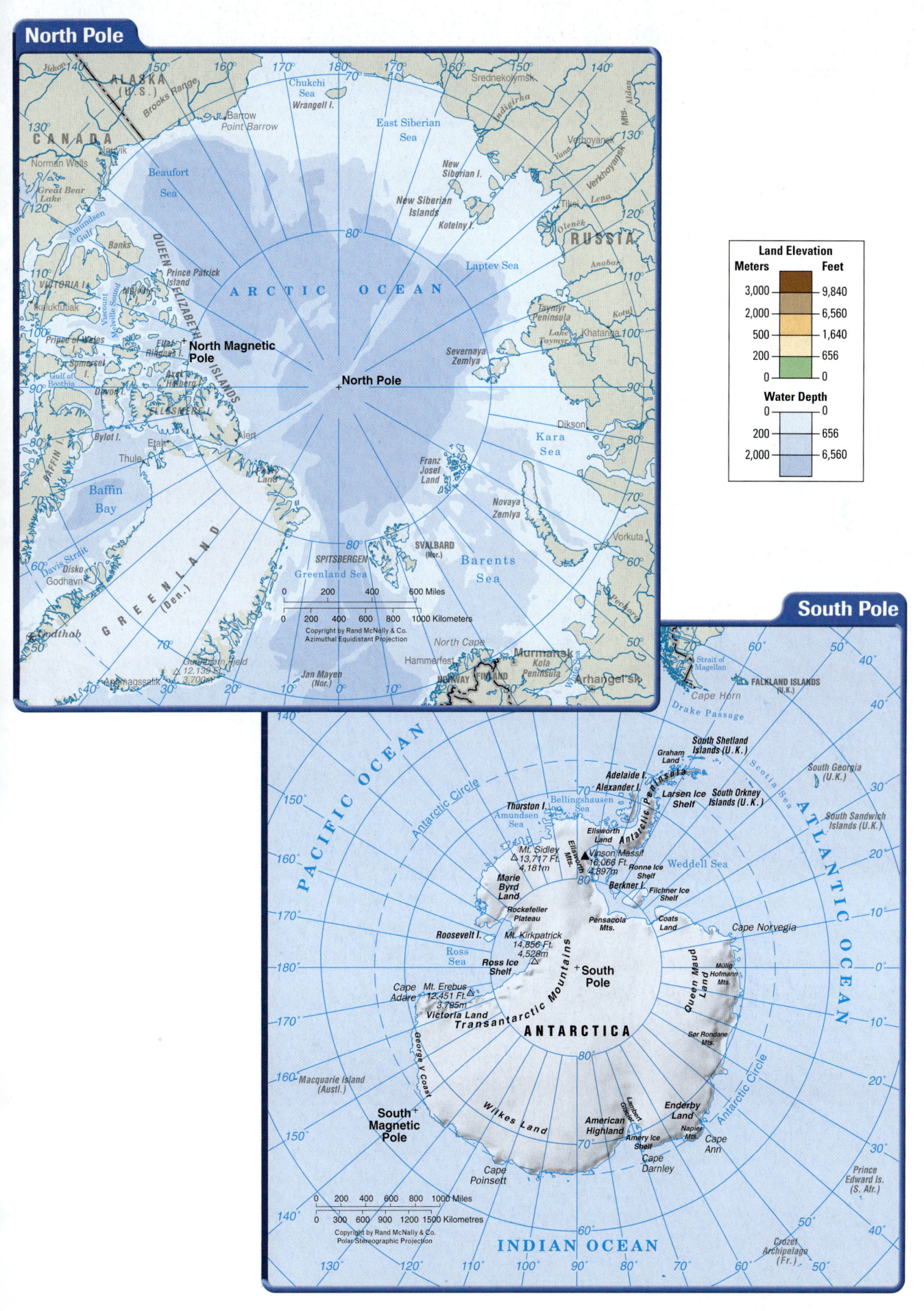

South Pole

Land Elevation

Meters	Feet
3,000	9,840
2,000	6,560
500	1,640
200	656
0	0

Water Depth

0	0
200	656
2,000	6,560

North and South Pole

ATLAS

Rand McNally

A37

FLORIDA
STATE ALMANAC

State Nickname:
THE SUNSHINE STATE

Florida State Flag

State Capitol:
Tallahassee

State Motto:
in god we trust

State Tree:
Sabal Palm

State Insect:
zebra longwing butterfly

State Flower:
Orange Blossom

State Bird:
mockingbird

State Seal

Important Dates in Florida History, 1500–2000

1513 Juan Ponce de Léon claims Florida for Spain.

1565 Pedro Menéndez de Avilés establishes the first permanent European settlement at St. Augustine.

1586 English admiral Sir Francis Drake plunders and burns St. Augustine.

1763 Spain gives Britain Florida in exchange for Havana, Cuba, which Britain captured during the Seven Years' War.

1500 — 1600 — 1700

All photos: Copyright © Photodisc.

Landmass

Florida
58,681 sq mi

Continental United States
3,165,630 sq mi

Population

Florida
16,396,515

United States
284,796,887

Population (in millions): 0, 75, 150, 225, 300

Lakes

World's Largest
Caspian Sea
143,550 sq mi

U.S. Largest
Lake Superior
31,800 sq mi

Florida's Largest
Lake Okeechobee
680 sq mi

GeoFunFacts

FunFact:
The name Florida probably comes from *Pascuar Florida*, the Spanish for Easter. Juan Ponce de Léon named the area *La Florida* shortly after he landed there during Easter of 1513.

1783 Before surrendering to American forces in the Revolutionary War, Britain gives Florida back to Spain to keep it out of American hands.

1819 The United States and Spain negotiate the Adams-Onís Treaty, which gives the United States lawful claim to Florida.

1822 Congress creates the Territory of Florida.

1845 Florida becomes the 27th state in the Union on March 3.

1861 Florida secedes from the United States to join the Confederacy on January 10.

1865 The Confederacy surrenders ending the Civil War. Florida's capital, Tallahassee, is the only Confederate capital east of the Mississippi not occupied by Union forces during the Civil War.

1868 Florida is readmitted to the Union.

1880 Florida's first citrus nursery opens in Tampa.

1937 Florida abolishes the poll tax as a requirement for voting.

1947 Everglades National Park is created.

1969 The first spacecraft to land humans on the moon, Apollo 11, is launched from Cape Canaveral.

1971 Walt Disney World opens near Orlando.

1992 Hurricane Andrew strikes Florida, killing 54 people and causing $22 billion in property damage.

2000 Florida electoral votes are pivotal in the election of Texas Governor George W. Bush as president of the United States.

A39

Florida: Political

GeoFunFact

In terms of land area, Collier County, located in the southwest of the state, is Florida's largest county. It covers more than 2,025 square miles, about 4 percent of Florida's total land area.

Florida: Physical

Florida State Almanac

Map labels:
- Atlantic Ocean
- Gulf of Mexico
- Pensacola
- Britton Hill 345 ft. (105 m.)
- Tallahassee
- Jacksonville
- Apalachicola R.
- Apalachee Bay
- Suwannee R.
- Gainesville
- St. Johns R.
- Lake George
- Lake Apoka
- Orlando
- Lake Tohopekaliga
- Lake Kissimmee
- St. Petersburg
- Tampa
- Tampa Bay
- Lake Istopoga
- Sarasota
- Peace R.
- Caloosahatchee R.
- Lake Okeechobee
- West Palm Beach
- Big Cypress Swamp
- Fort Lauderdale
- Everglades
- Miami
- Biscayne Bay
- Mangrove Swamp
- Florida Bay
- Florida Keys
- Key West

Inset map regions:
- Florida Uplands
- East Gulf Coastal Plain
- Atlantic Coastal Plain

KEY
- ★ State capital
- • Other city
- ▲ Highest elevation
- Wetlands

0 50 100 miles
0 50 100 kilometers
Albers Equal-Area Projection

GeoFunFact

Some 24 percent of Florida's land area consists of wetlands—swamps and marshes.

A41

Florida Precipitation

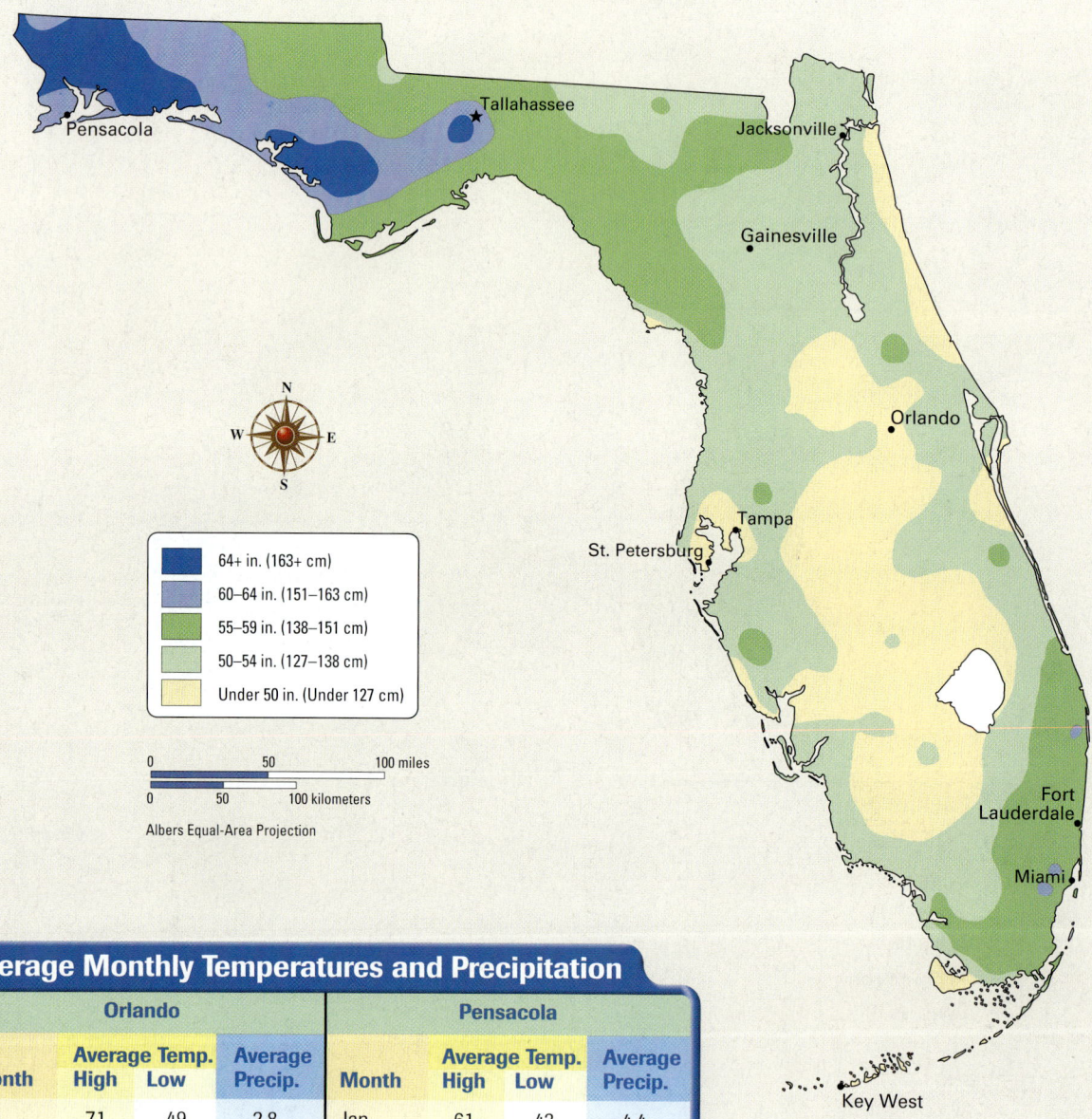

Legend:
- 64+ in. (163+ cm)
- 60–64 in. (151–163 cm)
- 55–59 in. (138–151 cm)
- 50–54 in. (127–138 cm)
- Under 50 in. (Under 127 cm)

Albers Equal-Area Projection

Average Monthly Temperatures and Precipitation

	Orlando				Pensacola		
Month	Average Temp. High	Low	Average Precip.	Month	Average Temp. High	Low	Average Precip.
Jan.	71	49	2.8	Jan.	61	43	4.4
Feb.	73	50	3.1	Feb.	63	46	4.9
Mar.	78	55	2.9	Mar.	68	52	5.5
Apr.	83	59	2.2	Apr.	75	59	4.2
May	88	66	3.5	May	82	66	3.9
June	91	72	6.0	June	87	73	5.1
July	92	73	5.4	July	89	75	6.8
Aug.	92	73	6.2	Aug.	89	75	6.1
Sept.	90	72	6.3	Sept.	86	71	6.5
Oct.	85	69	4.1	Oct.	79	60	4.3
Nov.	79	58	2.8	Nov.	69	51	3.5
Dec.	73	51	2.6	Dec.	63	45	3.9

GeoFunFact

With annual average precipitation of 54 inches, Florida is the nation's second wettest state. Only Louisiana has a higher annual precipitation rate.

Florida: Industry, Agriculture, Resources

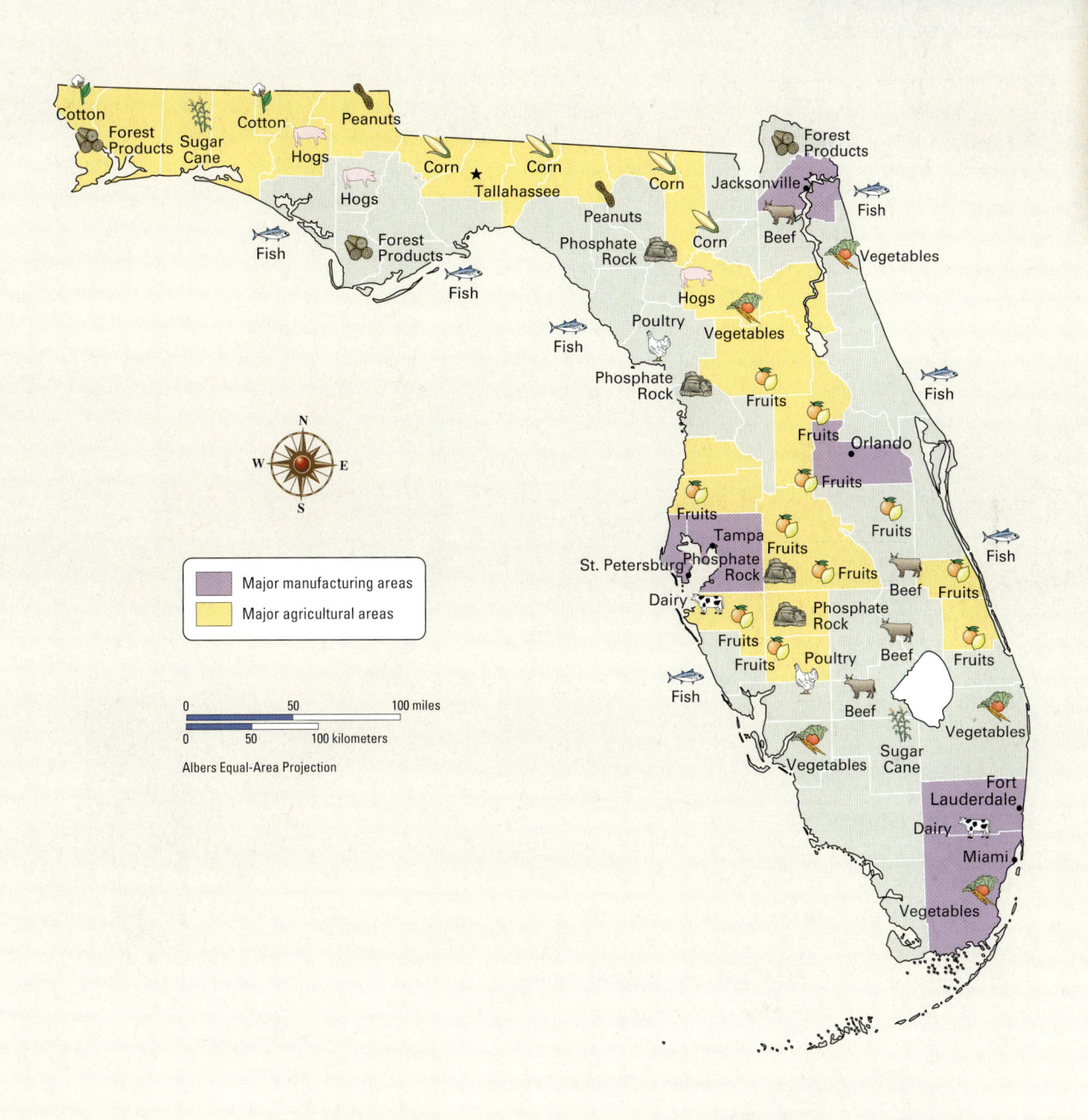

Legend:
- Major manufacturing areas (purple)
- Major agricultural areas (yellow)

Scale: 0–100 miles / 0–100 kilometers
Albers Equal-Area Projection

Labels on map: Cotton, Forest Products, Sugar Cane, Cotton, Hogs, Peanuts, Corn, Corn, Forest Products, Hogs, Tallahassee, Peanuts, Corn, Jacksonville, Fish, Forest Products, Fish, Phosphate Rock, Corn, Beef, Vegetables, Fish, Hogs, Poultry, Vegetables, Fish, Phosphate Rock, Fruits, Fruits, Orlando, Fruits, Fish, Fruits, Tampa, Phosphate Rock, Fruits, St. Petersburg, Fruits, Beef, Fruits, Dairy, Phosphate Rock, Fruits, Poultry, Beef, Fruits, Fish, Beef, Vegetables, Vegetables, Sugar Cane, Fort Lauderdale, Dairy, Miami, Vegetables

GeoFunFact

Florida is responsible for more than 75 percent of citrus production in the United States. The rest of the country's citrus fruit is produced in the states of California, Texas, and Arizona.

Florida State Almanac

A43

Florida Population Density

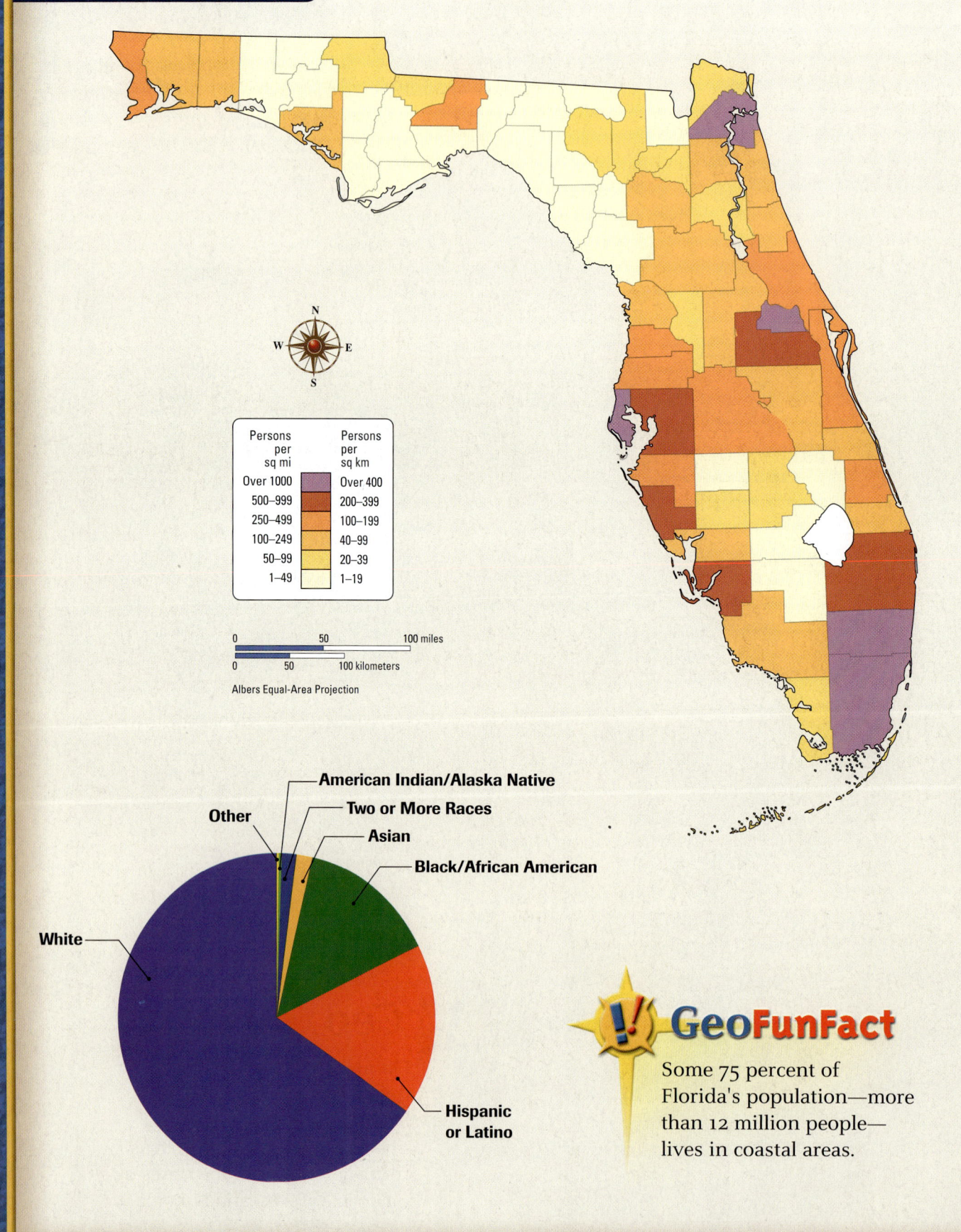

Persons per sq mi
- Over 1000
- 500–999
- 250–499
- 100–249
- 50–99
- 1–49

Persons per sq km
- Over 400
- 200–399
- 100–199
- 40–99
- 20–39
- 1–19

Albers Equal-Area Projection

Pie chart categories:
- White
- Hispanic or Latino
- Black/African American
- Asian
- Other
- American Indian/Alaska Native
- Two or More Races

GeoFunFact

Some 75 percent of Florida's population—more than 12 million people—lives in coastal areas.

Florida State Almanac

Florida National Parks

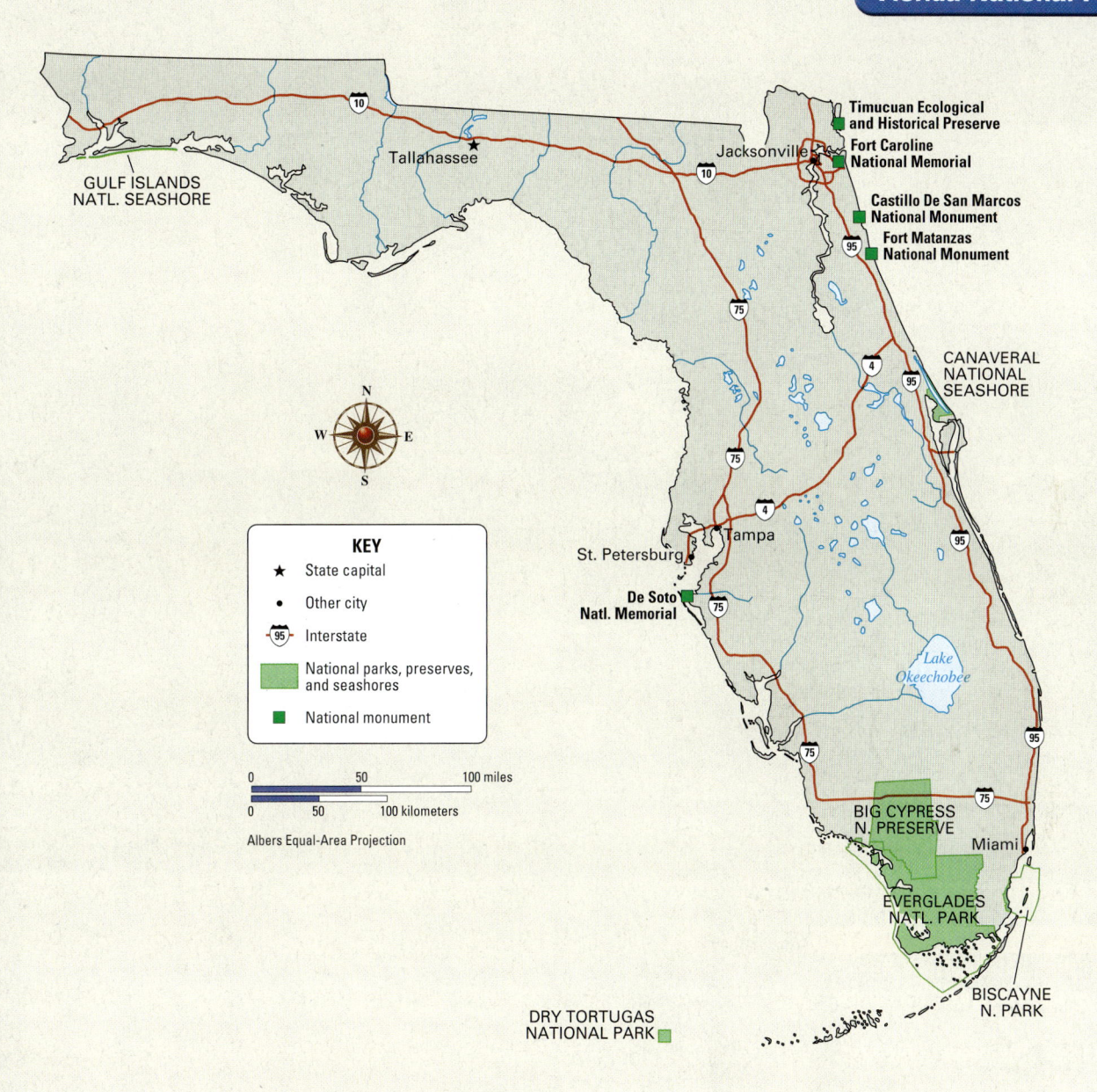

Map labels:
- GULF ISLANDS NATL. SEASHORE
- Tallahassee (state capital)
- Jacksonville
- Timucuan Ecological and Historical Preserve
- Fort Caroline National Memorial
- Castillo De San Marcos National Monument
- Fort Matanzas National Monument
- CANAVERAL NATIONAL SEASHORE
- St. Petersburg
- Tampa
- De Soto Natl. Memorial
- Lake Okeechobee
- BIG CYPRESS N. PRESERVE
- Miami
- EVERGLADES NATL. PARK
- BISCAYNE N. PARK
- DRY TORTUGAS NATIONAL PARK

KEY
- ★ State capital
- • Other city
- Interstate
- National parks, preserves, and seashores
- National monument

0 50 100 miles
0 50 100 kilometers
Albers Equal-Area Projection

GeoFunFact

The Everglades National Park is the only subtropical nature preserve in North America. It also is the only place in the world where alligators and crocodiles live side by side.

UNIT 1

Human-Environment Interaction
An orbiting satellite took these photographs of Earth after dark. They have been combined into one image. The glow of electric lights shows the locations of cities and towns.

INTRODUCTION TO WORLD CULTURES AND GEOGRAPHY

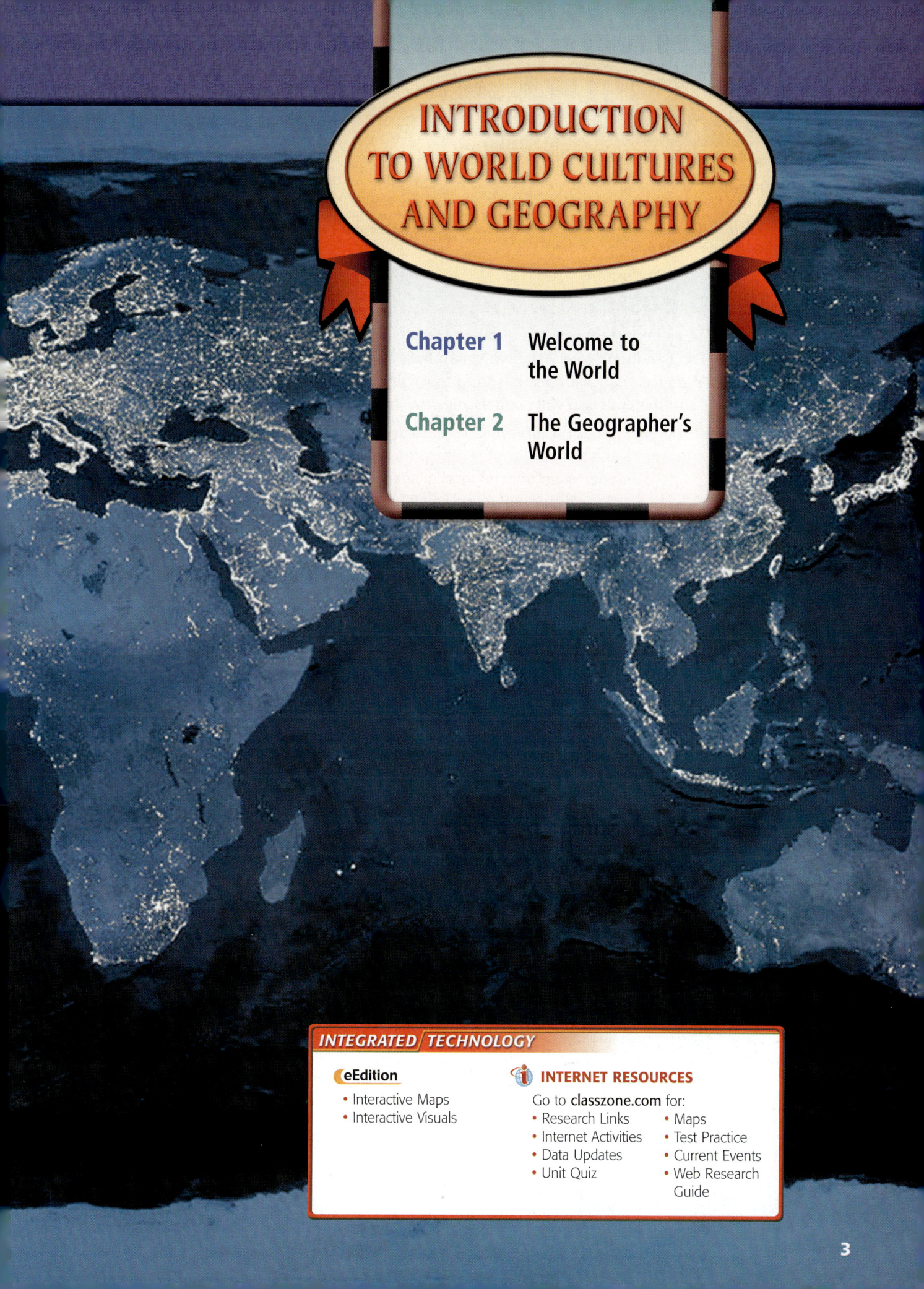

Chapter 1 Welcome to the World

Chapter 2 The Geographer's World

INTEGRATED TECHNOLOGY

eEdition
- Interactive Maps
- Interactive Visuals

INTERNET RESOURCES
Go to **classzone.com** for:
- Research Links
- Internet Activities
- Data Updates
- Unit Quiz
- Maps
- Test Practice
- Current Events
- Web Research Guide

GEOGRAPHY SKILLS HANDBOOK

SUNSHINE STATE STANDARDS
Key Standard SS.B.1.3.1 The student uses various map forms (including thematic maps) and other geographic representations, tools, and technologies to acquire, process, and report geographic information including patterns of land use, connections between places, and patterns and processes of migration and diffusion.
FCAT LA.A.2.3.1 Reading: Identify Main Idea, Facts, and Details

Map Basics

Maps are an important tool for studying the use of space on Earth. This handbook covers the basic map skills and information that geographers rely on as they investigate the world—and the skills you will need as you study geography.

Mapmaking depends on surveying, or measuring and recording the features of Earth's surface. Until recently, this could be undertaken only on land or sea. Today, aerial photography and satellite imaging are the most popular ways to gather data.

Location • Magnetic compasses, introduced by the Chinese in the 1100s, help people accurately determine directions. ▲

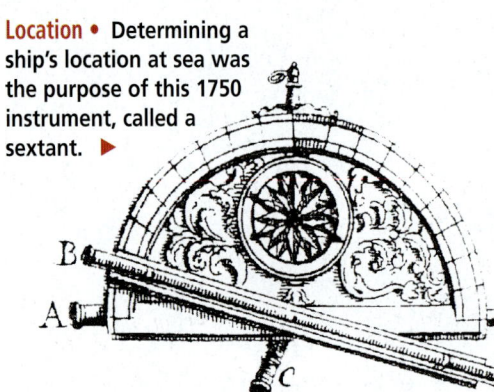

Location • Determining a ship's location at sea was the purpose of this 1750 instrument, called a sextant. ▶

Location • An early example of a three-dimensional geographic grid. ▼

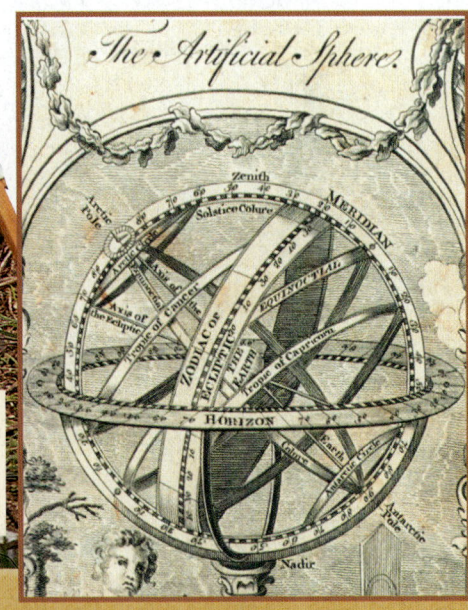

Human-Environment Interaction • Nigerian surveyors use a theodolite, which measures angles and distances on Earth. ▲

4 UNIT 1

South Asia's Economic Activity

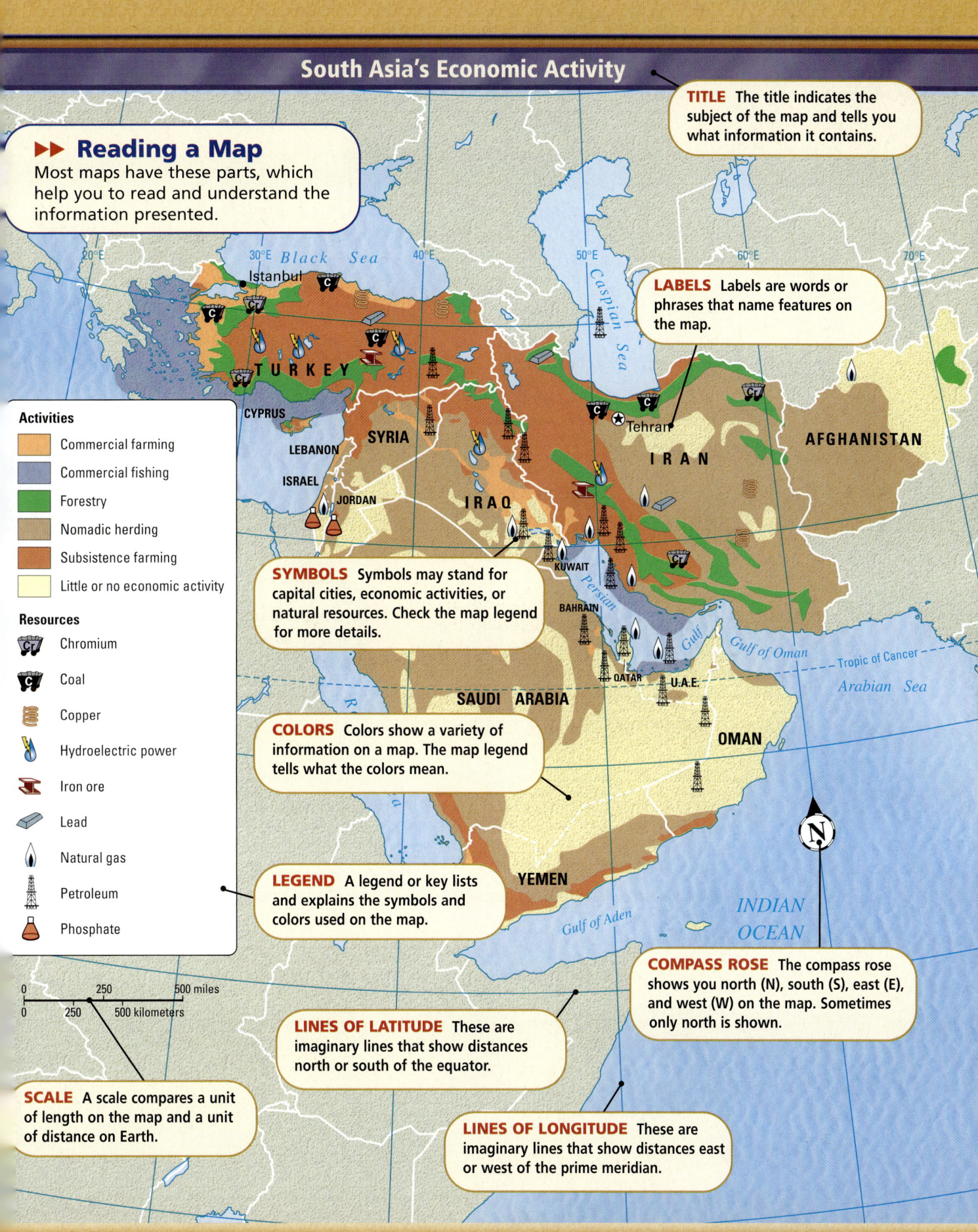

▶▶ Reading a Map
Most maps have these parts, which help you to read and understand the information presented.

TITLE The title indicates the subject of the map and tells you what information it contains.

LABELS Labels are words or phrases that name features on the map.

SYMBOLS Symbols may stand for capital cities, economic activities, or natural resources. Check the map legend for more details.

COLORS Colors show a variety of information on a map. The map legend tells what the colors mean.

LEGEND A legend or key lists and explains the symbols and colors used on the map.

COMPASS ROSE The compass rose shows you north (N), south (S), east (E), and west (W) on the map. Sometimes only north is shown.

LINES OF LATITUDE These are imaginary lines that show distances north or south of the equator.

LINES OF LONGITUDE These are imaginary lines that show distances east or west of the prime meridian.

SCALE A scale compares a unit of length on the map and a unit of distance on Earth.

Activities
- Commercial farming
- Commercial fishing
- Forestry
- Nomadic herding
- Subsistence farming
- Little or no economic activity

Resources
- Chromium
- Coal
- Copper
- Hydroelectric power
- Iron ore
- Lead
- Natural gas
- Petroleum
- Phosphate

Geography Skills Handbook 5

GEOGRAPHY SKILLS HANDBOOK

Map Basics, cont.

▶▶ Longitude and Latitude Lines

Longitude and latitude lines appear together on a map and allow you to pinpoint the absolute locations of cities and other geographic features. You express these locations as coordinates of intersecting lines. These are measured in degrees.

Longitude lines are imaginary lines that run north and south; they are also known as meridians. They show distances in degrees east or west of the prime meridian. The prime meridian is a longitude line that runs from the North Pole to the South Pole through Greenwich, England. It marks 0° longitude.

Latitude lines are imaginary lines that run east to west around the globe; they are also known as parallels. They show distances in degrees north or south of the equator. The equator is a latitude line that circles Earth halfway between the north and south poles. It marks 0° latitude. The tropics of Cancer and Capricorn are parallels that form the boundaries of the tropical zone, a region that stays warm all year.

Longitude Lines (Meridians)

Latitude Lines (Parallels)

▶▶ Hemisphere

Hemisphere is a term for half the globe. The globe can be divided into northern and southern hemispheres (separated by the equator) or into eastern and western hemispheres. The United States is located in the northern and western hemispheres.

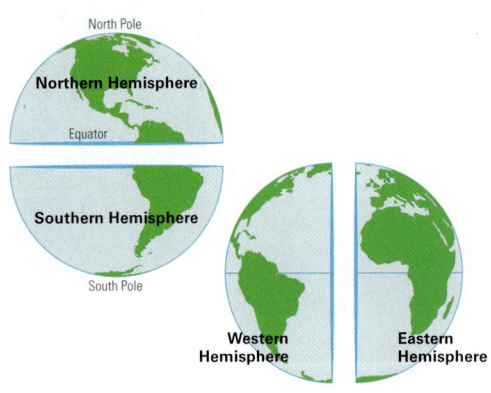

▶▶ Scale

A geographer decides what scale to use by determining how much detail to show. If many details are needed, a large scale is used. If fewer details are needed, a small scale is used.

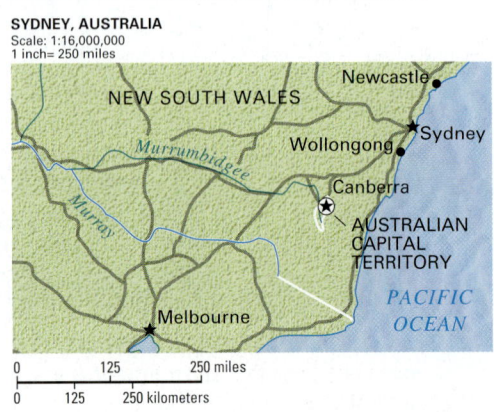

Small scale used, without a lot of detail. ▼

SYDNEY, AUSTRALIA
Scale: 1:16,000,000
1 inch= 250 miles

Larger scale used, with a lot of detail. ▼

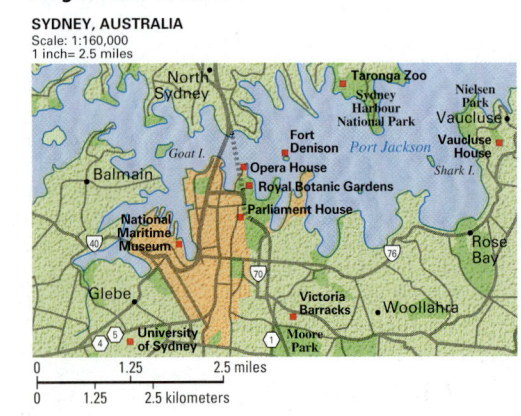

SYDNEY, AUSTRALIA
Scale: 1:160,000
1 inch= 2.5 miles

6   UNIT 1

▶▶ Projections

A projection is a way of showing the curved surface of Earth on a flat map. Flat maps cannot show sizes, shapes, and directions with total accuracy. As a result, all projections distort some aspect of Earth's surface. Below are four projections.

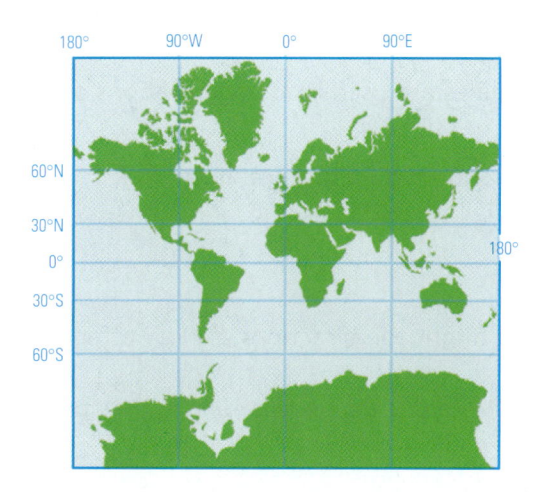

Mercator Projection • The Mercator projection shows most of the continents as they look on a globe. However, the projection stretches out the lands near the north and south poles. The Mercator projection is used for all kinds of navigation. ▲

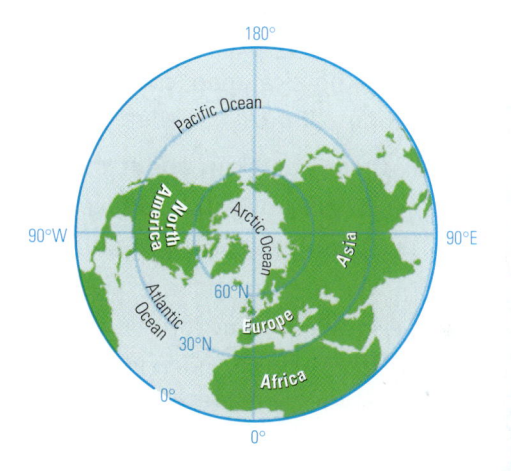

Azimuthal Projection • An azimuthal projection shows Earth so that a straight line from the central point to any other point on the map corresponds to the shortest distance between the two points. Sizes and shapes of the continents are distorted. ▲

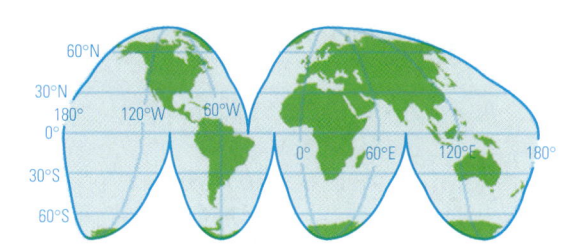

Homolosine Projection • This projection shows landmasses' shapes and sizes accurately, but distances are not correct. ▲

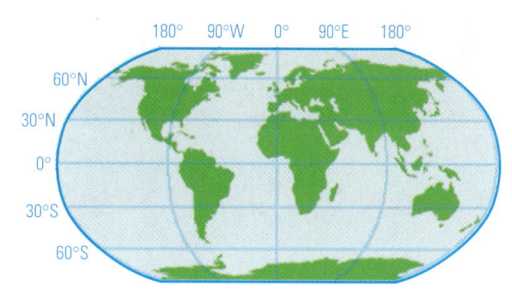

Robinson Projection • For textbook maps, the Robinson projection is commonly used. It shows the entire Earth, with continents and oceans having nearly their true sizes and shapes. However, the landmasses near the poles appear flattened. ▲

MAP PRACTICE

MAIN IDEAS

1. **(a)** What are the longitude and latitude of your city or town?
   (b) What information is provided by the legend in the map on page 5?
   (c) What is a projection? Compare and contrast the depictions of Antarctica in the Mercator and Robinson projections.

CRITICAL THINKING

2. **Making Inferences** Why do you think latitude and longitude are important to sailors?

Think About
- the landmarks you use to find your way around
- the landmarks available to sailors on the ocean

GEOGRAPHY SKILLS HANDBOOK

Different Types of Maps

▶▶ Physical Maps

Physical maps help you see the landforms and bodies of water in specific areas. By studying a physical map, you can learn the relative locations and characteristics of places in a region.

On a physical map, color, shading, or contour lines are used to show elevations or altitudes, also called relief.

Ask these questions about the physical features shown on a physical map:
- Where on Earth's surface is this area located?
- What is its relative location?
- What is the shape of the region?
- In which directions do the rivers flow? How might the directions of flow affect travel and transportation in the region?
- Are there mountains or deserts? How might they affect the people living in the area?

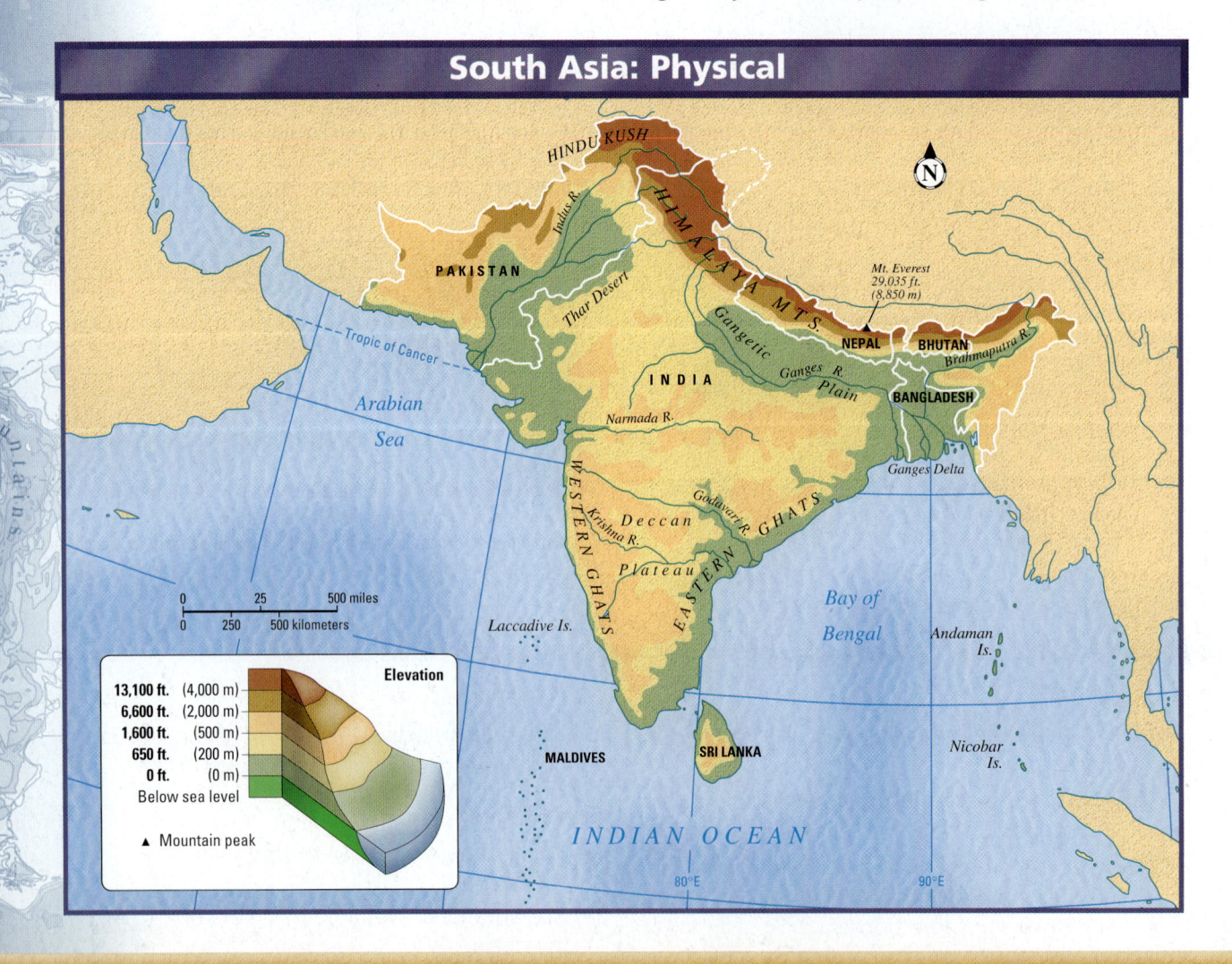

South Asia: Physical

▶▶ Political Maps

Political maps show features that humans have created on Earth's surface. Included on a political map may be cities, states, provinces, territories, and countries.

Ask these questions about the political features shown on a political map:

- Where on Earth's surface is this area located?
- What is its relative location? How might a country's location affect its economy and its relationships with other countries?
- What is the shape and size of the country? How might its shape and size affect the people living in the country?
- Who are the region's, country's, state's, or city's neighbors?
- How populated does the area seem to be? How might that affect activities there?

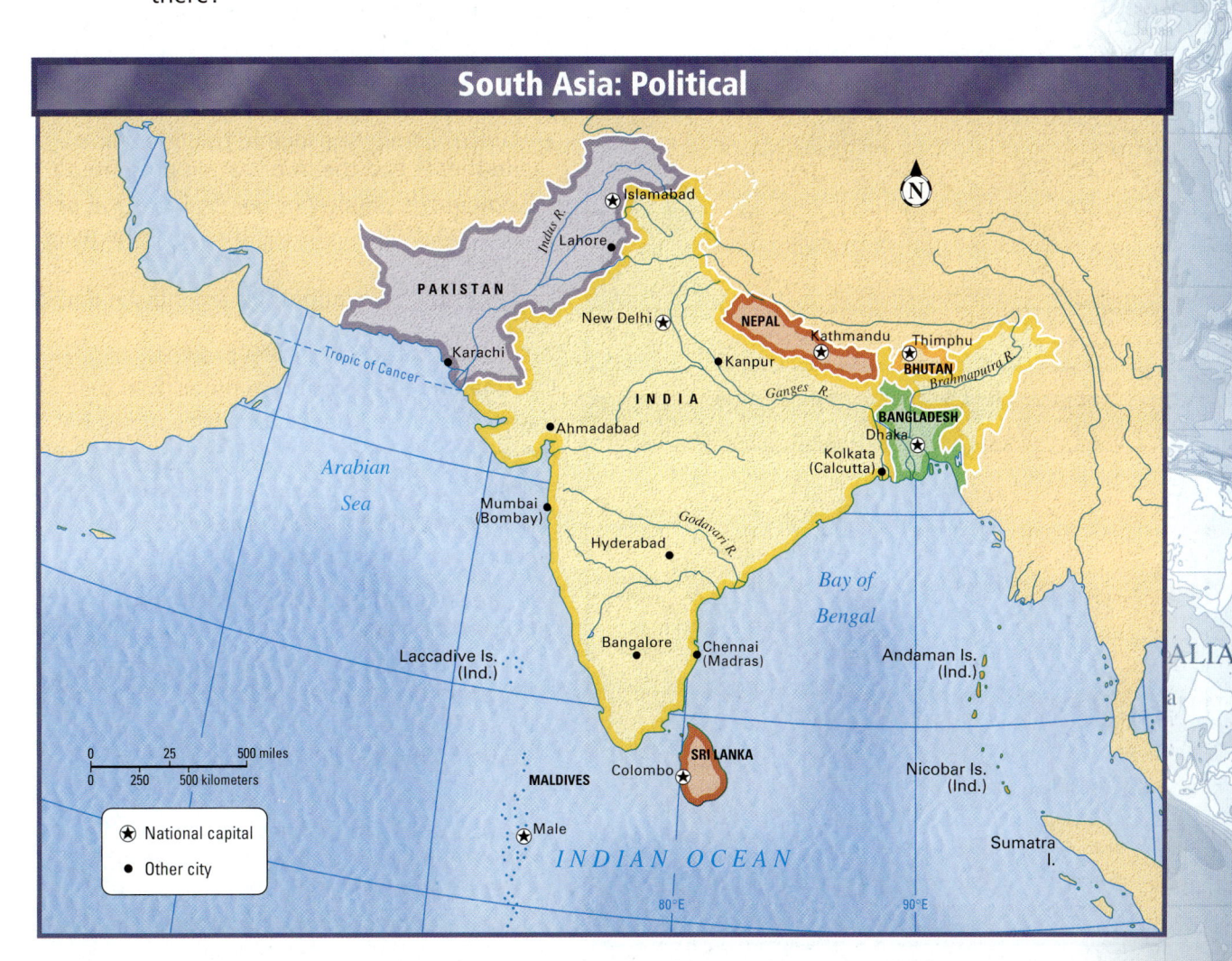

South Asia: Political

Geography Skills Handbook 9

GEOGRAPHY SKILLS HANDBOOK

Different Types of Maps, cont.

▶▶ Thematic Maps

Geographers also rely on thematic maps, which focus on specific ideas. For example, in this textbook you will see thematic maps that show climates, types of vegetation, natural resources, population densities, and economic activities. Some thematic maps show historical trends; others may focus on movements of people or ideas. Thematic maps may be presented in a variety of ways.

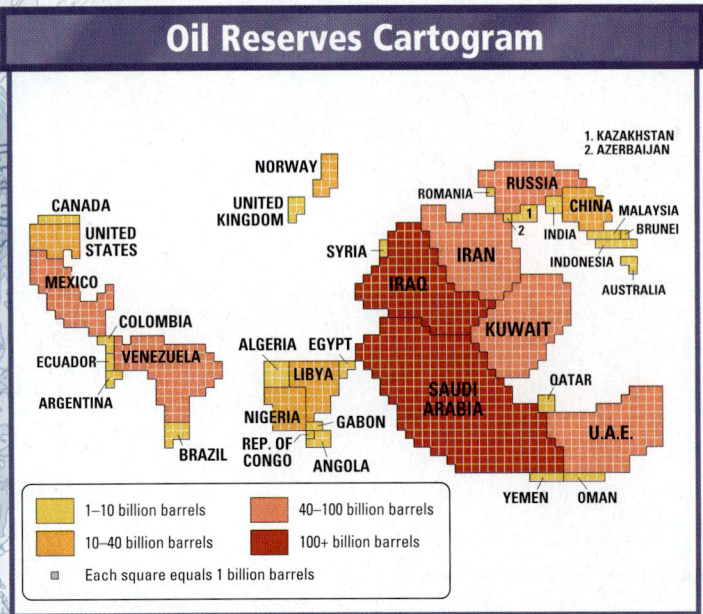

Cultural Legacy of the Roman Empire

Legend:
- Christian areas around A.D. 500
- Romance language spoken, present day
- Boundary of Roman Empire, A.D. 395

Azimuthal Equidistant Projection

Qualitative Maps On a qualitative map, colors, symbols, dots, or lines are used to help you see patterns related to a specific idea. The map shown here depicts the influence of the Roman Empire on Europe, North Africa, and Southwest Asia.

Use the suggestions below to help you interpret the map.

♦ Check the title to identify the theme and the data being presented.

♦ Carefully study the legend to understand the theme and the information presented.

♦ Look at the physical or political features of the area. How might the theme of the map affect them?

♦ What are the relationships among the data?

Oil Reserves Cartogram

Legend:
- 1–10 billion barrels
- 10–40 billion barrels
- 40–100 billion barrels
- 100+ billion barrels
- Each square equals 1 billion barrels

Cartograms A cartogram presents information about countries other than their shapes and sizes. The size of each country is determined by the data being presented, and not by its actual land size. On the cartogram shown here, the countries' sizes show the amounts of their oil reserves.

Use the suggestions below to help you interpret the map.

♦ Check the title and the legend to identify the data being presented.

♦ Look at the relative sizes of the countries shown. Which is the largest?

♦ Which countries are smallest?

♦ How do the sizes of these countries on a physical map differ from their sizes in the cartogram?

♦ What are the relationships among the data?

Flow-Line Maps Flow-line maps illustrate movements of people, goods, or ideas. The movements are usually shown by a series of arrows. Locations, directions, and scopes of movement can be seen. The width of an arrow may show how extensive a flow is. Often the information is related to a period of time. The map shown here portrays the movement of the Bantu peoples in Africa.

Use the suggestions below to help you interpret the map.
- Check the title and the legend to identify the data being presented.
- Over what period of time did the movement occur?
- In what directions did the movement occur?
- How extensive was the movement?

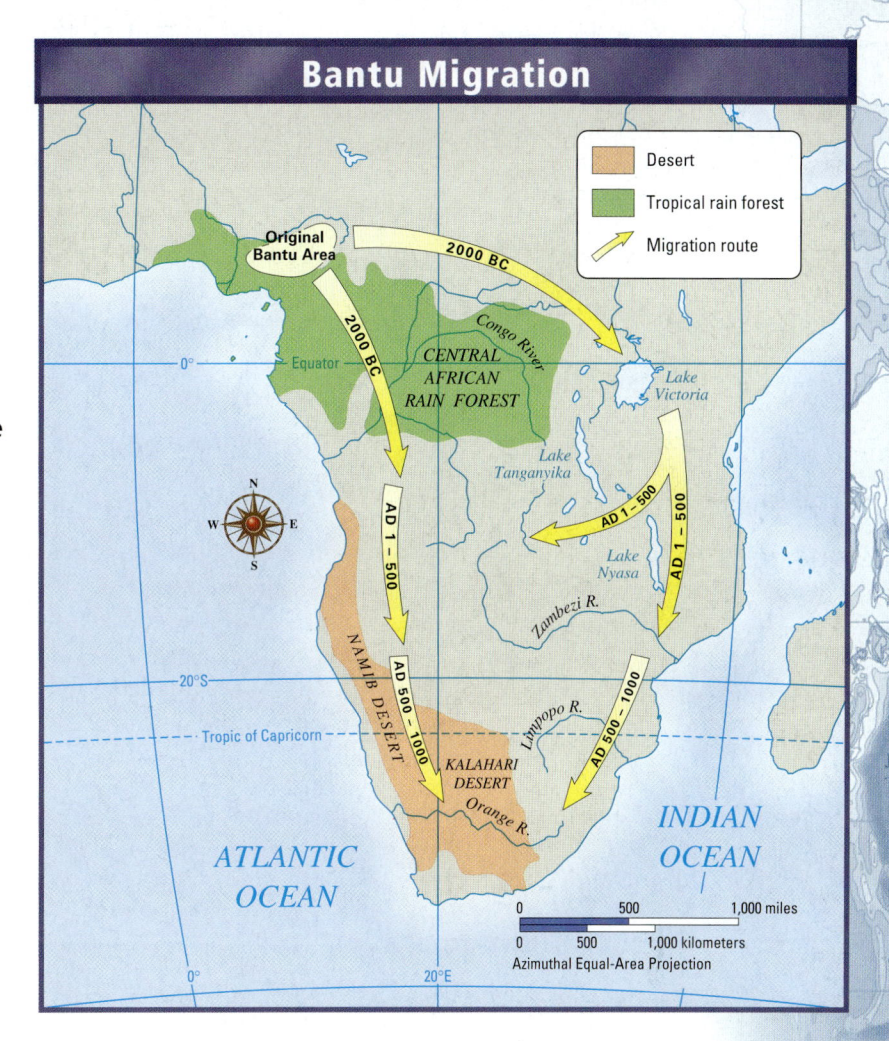

Map Practice

Use pages 8–11 to help you answer these questions. Use the maps on pages 8–9 to answer questions 1–3.

1. In what direction does the Ganges River flow?
2. Kathmandu is the capital of which South Asian nation?
3. Which city is closer to the Thar Desert—Lahore, Pakistan, or New Delhi, India?
4. Why are only a few nations shown in the cartogram?
5. Which kind of thematic map would be best for showing the locations of climate zones?

GeoActivity

Exploring Local Geography Obtain a physical-political map of your state. Use the data on it to create **two separate maps**. One should show physical features only, and the other should show political features only.

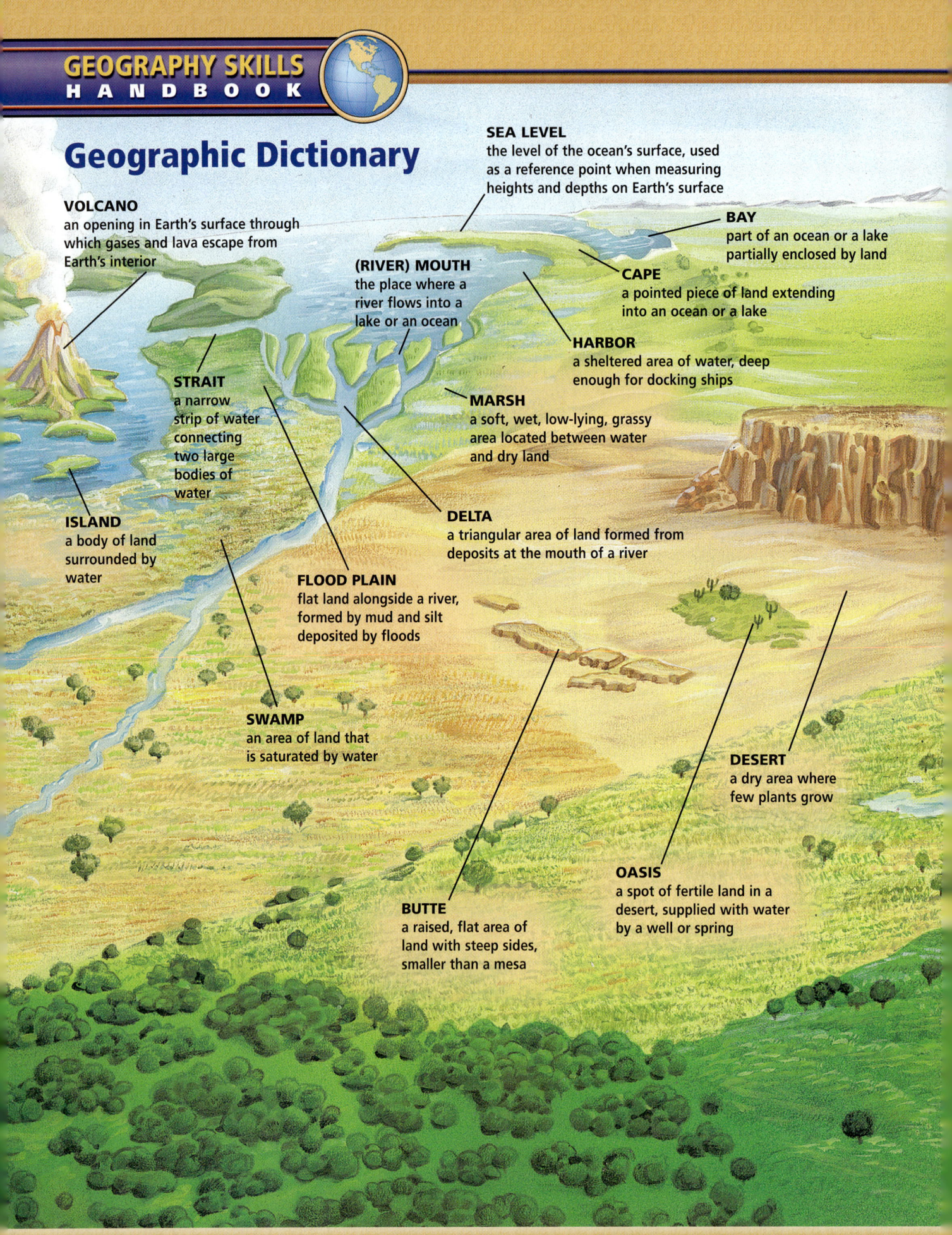

GEOGRAPHY SKILLS HANDBOOK

Geographic Dictionary

SEA LEVEL
the level of the ocean's surface, used as a reference point when measuring heights and depths on Earth's surface

VOLCANO
an opening in Earth's surface through which gases and lava escape from Earth's interior

BAY
part of an ocean or a lake partially enclosed by land

(RIVER) MOUTH
the place where a river flows into a lake or an ocean

CAPE
a pointed piece of land extending into an ocean or a lake

HARBOR
a sheltered area of water, deep enough for docking ships

STRAIT
a narrow strip of water connecting two large bodies of water

MARSH
a soft, wet, low-lying, grassy area located between water and dry land

ISLAND
a body of land surrounded by water

DELTA
a triangular area of land formed from deposits at the mouth of a river

FLOOD PLAIN
flat land alongside a river, formed by mud and silt deposited by floods

SWAMP
an area of land that is saturated by water

DESERT
a dry area where few plants grow

OASIS
a spot of fertile land in a desert, supplied with water by a well or spring

BUTTE
a raised, flat area of land with steep sides, smaller than a mesa

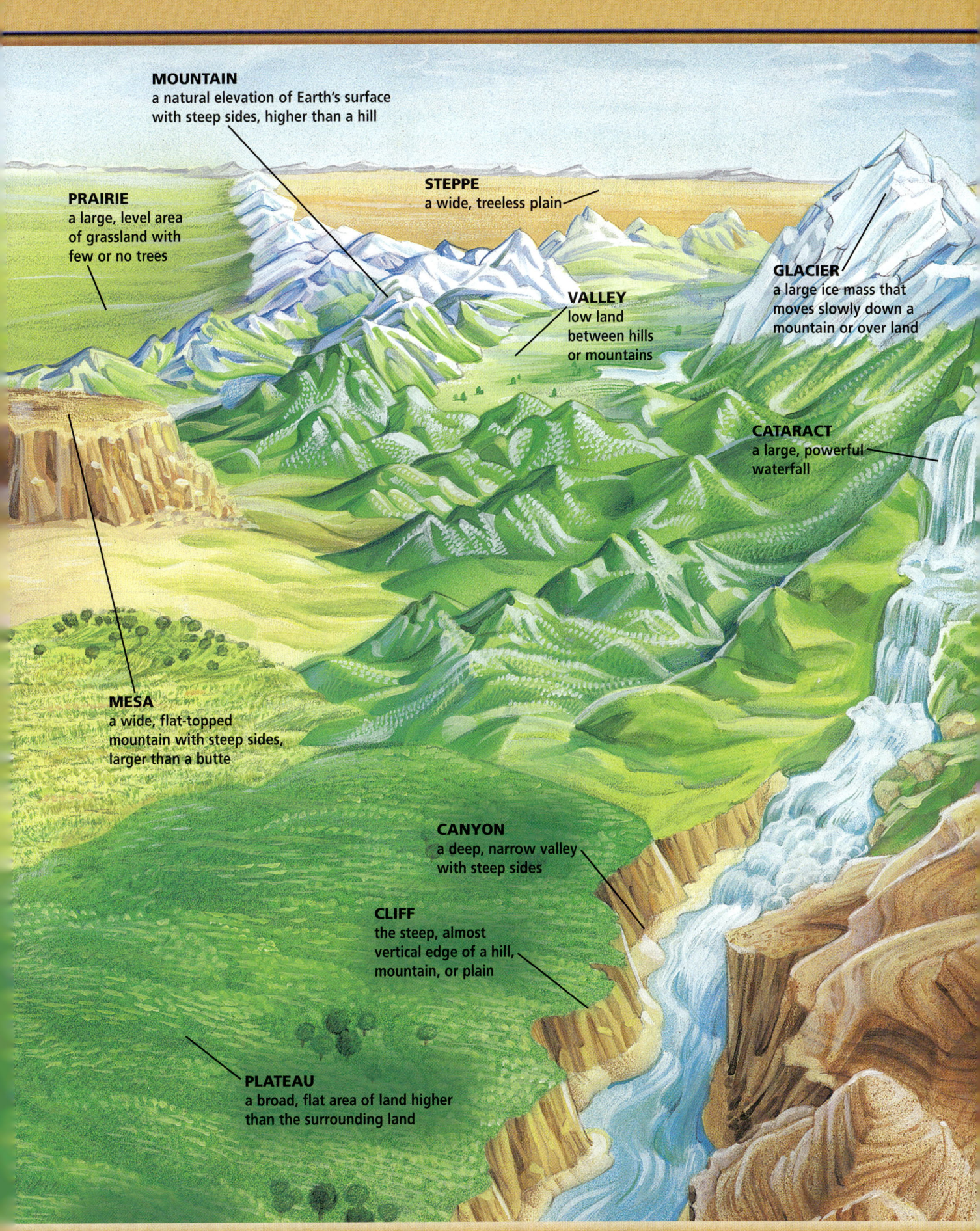

MOUNTAIN
a natural elevation of Earth's surface with steep sides, higher than a hill

PRAIRIE
a large, level area of grassland with few or no trees

STEPPE
a wide, treeless plain

GLACIER
a large ice mass that moves slowly down a mountain or over land

VALLEY
low land between hills or mountains

CATARACT
a large, powerful waterfall

MESA
a wide, flat-topped mountain with steep sides, larger than a butte

CANYON
a deep, narrow valley with steep sides

CLIFF
the steep, almost vertical edge of a hill, mountain, or plain

PLATEAU
a broad, flat area of land higher than the surrounding land

Geography Skills Handbook

CHAPTER 1
Welcome to the World

SECTION 1 The World at Your Fingertips

SECTION 2 Many Regions, Many Cultures

Region The peoples of the world live in an astonishing variety of ways.

FOCUS ON GEOGRAPHY

How have geographic features influenced settlement patterns?

Movement • People settle where they can most easily and comfortably meet their needs for clean water, food, work, communication, trade, and transportation. Before there were good roads, boats were the easiest way to travel or send and receive goods. As a result, people often settled near rivers, lakes, and oceans. They also often settled where the land was suitable for cultivation and the climate was comfortable. You will not find many cities in the frozen wastelands of Siberia.

What do you think?
- Why are there few settlements in the desert?
- Why is there often a city where two rivers meet?

CHAPTER 1 READING SOCIAL STUDIES

BEFORE YOU READ

▶▶ What Do You Know?

You live in the world, but how much do you know about it? The best way to find out is through social studies. *Social studies* is an umbrella term. It covers history, geography, economics, government, and culture. History, as you probably know, is the study of the past. How clearly can you define the other terms? How do you think they can help you to learn about the world?

▶▶ What Do You Want to Know?

Think about what else you need to know before you can come up with clear, complete, and accurate definitions. Record any questions you have in a notebook before you read this chapter.

Region • Citizens have more rights under some governments than others. ▼

READ AND TAKE NOTES

Reading Strategy: Categorizing One way to make sense of information is to organize it in a chart. Writing your notes in a chart with categories can help you remember the most important parts of what you have read.

- Copy the chart below into your notebook.
- As you read the chapter, note the definition of each term listed on the chart.
- Write these definitions next to the appropriate heading.

Region •
Prepared for a flood, this house was built to suit its environment. ▲

Term	Definition
history	
geography	
economics	
government	
culture	

16 CHAPTER 1

SECTION 1
The World at Your Fingertips

TERMS & NAMES
history
geography
government
citizen
economics
scarcity
culture
culture trait

MAIN IDEA
Social studies includes information from five fields of learning to provide a well-rounded picture of the world and its peoples.

WHY IT MATTERS NOW
Understanding your world is essential if you are to be an informed citizen of a global society.

DATELINE

SAN FRANCISCO, USA, JUNE 26, 1945

Fifty nations signed a charter today to establish a new organization called the United Nations. The organization will go into effect October 24.

The United Nations is a successor to the old League of Nations, founded after World War I to prevent another world war, which it failed to do.

The purpose of the new organization is to maintain peace and develop friendly relations among nations.

The member nations hope to cooperate to solve economic, social, cultural, and humanitarian problems and to promote respect for human rights and freedom.

Region • Flags of member countries fly in front of the United Nations headquarters in New York City. ▲

The Peoples of the World

For centuries, people in different parts of the world have been trying to get along with one another, not always with success. Part of the problem is a lack of understanding of other people's ways of life. Certain advances in communication and transportation, such as the Internet and high-speed planes, have brought people closer together. So have increased international trade and immigration. Knowledge of other societies can be a key to understanding them.

TAKING NOTES
Use your chart to take notes about these terms.

Term	Definition
history	
geography	

SUNSHINE STATE STANDARDS
Key Standard SS.B.2.3.2 The student knows the human and physical characteristics of different places in the world and how these characteristics change over time.
Other Standards SS.B.1.3.4, C.1.3.2, D.2.3.1
FCAT LA.A.2.3.1 Reading: Identify Main Idea, Facts, and Details

Welcome to the World 17

Learning About the World

Social studies is a way to learn about the world. It draws on information from five fields of learning—geography, history, economics, government, and culture. Each field looks at the world from a different angle. Consider the approaches you might use if you were starting at a new school. Figuring out how to get around would be learning your school's geography. Asking other students where they come from is learning their history. Making choices about which school supplies you can afford to buy is economics. Learning the school rules is learning about its government. Clubs, teams, styles of clothing, holidays, and even ways of saying things are part of the school's culture.

Place • The five fields of learning in social studies are well represented in daily life. ▲

Connections to Science

Digging into the Past
Archaeologists are scientists who study artifacts to learn about people's culture and history. Artifacts include pots, tools, artworks, and even food remains. Using special techniques and tools, archaeologists carefully remove artifacts from underground or underwater. They use their knowledge about the place and people they are studying to figure out how the artifact was used.

History and Geography

Knowing history and geography helps orient you in time and space. **History** is a record of the past. The people and events of the past shaped the world as it is today. Historians search for primary sources, such as newspapers, letters, journals, and other documents, to find out about past events.

Vocabulary

orient: to become familiar with a situation

A VOICE FROM TODAY

How can we know who we are and where we are going if we don't know anything about where we have come from and what we have been through, the courage shown, the costs paid, to be where we are?

David McCullough, Historian

The Five Themes of Geography **Geography** is the study of people, places, and the environment. Geography deals with the world in spatial terms. The study of geography focuses on five themes: location, region, place, movement, and human-environment interaction.

Region • Israel is part of Southwest Asia. ▲

Location • Israel is on the southeast shore of the Mediterranean. ▲

Human-Environment Interaction • Irrigation systems supply Israel's dry climate with water. ▼

Movement • Immigrants arrive in Israel. ▲

Place • Israel has a dry climate in the south, and a wetter climate in the north, with prosperous farms and thriving cities. ▲

Location tells where a place is. Several countries that have features in common form a region. Place considers an area's distinguishing characteristics. Movement is a study of the migrations of people, animals, and even plants. Human-environment interaction considers how people change and are changed by the natural features of Earth.

Government

Every country has laws and a way to govern itself. Laws are the rules by which people live. **Government** is the people and groups within a society that have the authority to make laws, to make sure they are carried out, and to settle disagreements about them. The kind of government determines who has the authority to make the laws and see that they are carried out.

Limited and Unlimited Governments
In a limited government, everyone, including those in charge, must obey the laws. Some of the laws tell the government what it cannot do. Democracies and republics are two forms of limited government. In a democracy, the people have the authority to make laws directly. In a republic, the people make laws through elected representatives. The governments of the United States, Mexico, and India are examples of republics.

Rulers in an unlimited government can do whatever they want without regard to the law. Totalitarianism is a form of unlimited government. In a totalitarian government the people have no say. Rulers have total control.

BACKGROUND
Local, state, and national governments provide needed services, such as schools, parks, electricity, and roads.

Vocabulary
totalitarian government: a government in which the rulers have total control

Welcome to the World **19**

Citizenship A <u>citizen</u> is a legal member of a country. Citizens have rights, such as the right to vote in elections, and duties, such as paying taxes. Being born in a country can make you a citizen. Another way is to move to a country, complete certain requirements, and take part in a naturalization ceremony.

Vocabulary
naturalization: the process of becoming a citizen

Economics

Looking at the long list of flavors at the ice cream store, you have a decision to make. You have only enough money for one cone. Will it be mint chip or bubble gum flavor? You will have to choose. <u>Economics</u> is the study of how people manage their resources by producing, exchanging, and using goods and services. Economics is about choice.

Movement • One way people become American citizens is by participating in a naturalization ceremony. ▲

Some economists claim that people's desires are unlimited. Resources to satisfy these desires, however, are limited. These economists refer to the conflict between people's desires and their limited resources as <u>scarcity</u>.

Resources Economists identify three types of resources: natural, human, and capital. Natural resources are gifts of nature, such as forests, fertile soil, and water. Human resources are skills people have to produce goods and services. Capital resources are the things people make, such as machines and equipment, to produce goods and services.

Biography

Amartya Sen (b. 1933)
Amartya Sen (ah•MART•yah sen) was born in India. As a professor at Trinity College in Cambridge, England, he taught and studied economics. An important part of his research was to look at catastrophes, such as famine, that happen to the world's poorest people. By showing governments that food shortages are often caused by social and economic conditions, he hoped to prevent famines in the future. In 1998, Sen won the Nobel Prize in Economic Sciences for his research in welfare economics.

Kinds of Economies

Blue jeans are a product. Who decides whether to make them and how many to make and what price to charge? In a command economy, the government decides. In a market economy, individual businesses decide, based on what they think consumers want.

Reading Social Studies
A. Contrasting How does a market economy differ from a command economy?

Levels of Development Different countries and regions have different levels of economic development. In a country with a high level of development, most people are well educated, have good health, and earn decent salaries. Services such as clean running water, electricity, and transportation are plentiful. Technology is advanced, and businesses flourish.

Vocabulary

literacy:
ability to read and write

life expectancy:
average number of years people live

A country with a low level of development is marked by few jobs in industry, poor services, and low literacy rates. Life expectancy is low. These countries are often called developing countries.

Culture

Some people wear saris. Others wear T-shirts. Some people eat cereal and milk for breakfast. Others eat pickled fish. Some people go to church on Sunday morning. Others kneel and pray to Allah five times a day. All these differences are expressions of **culture**. Culture consists of the beliefs, customs, laws, art, and ways of living that a group of people share.

Reading **Social Studies**

B. Recognizing Important Details
What are three characteristics that can define a culture?

Religion is part of most cultures; so is a shared language. The ways people express themselves through music, dance, literature, and the visual arts are important parts of every culture; so are the technology and tools they use to accomplish various tasks. Each kind of food, clothing, or technology, each belief, language, or tool shared by a culture is called a **culture trait**. Taken together, the culture traits of a people shape their way of life.

Citizenship IN ACTION

High Tech for the Developing World Mae Jemison, below, is a former astronaut and the first African-American woman to orbit Earth. In 1993, she left the space program and set up the Jemison Institute for Advancing Technology in Developing Countries. This organization uses space program technology to help developing countries.

One project uses a satellite-based telecommunication system to improve health care in West Africa. Another project is an international science camp for students aged 12 to 16.

SECTION 1 ASSESSMENT

Terms & Names
1. Explain the significance of:
   (a) history
   (b) geography
   (c) government
   (d) citizen
   (e) economics
   (f) scarcity
   (g) culture
   (h) culture trait

Using Graphics
2. Use a chart like this one to list the five themes of geography and their characteristics.

Theme	Characteristics

Main Ideas
3. (a) What five areas of learning does social studies include?
   (b) What are the three main kinds of resources, and how is each one defined?
   (c) What is the difference between limited and unlimited government?

Critical Thinking
4. **Making Inferences**
   Does the United States have a shared, or common, culture?

   Think About
   - what you eat and wear, where you live, how you spend your free time
   - who else shares these activities with you

ACTIVITY -OPTION- Reread the section on citizenship. Make a **poster** showing the rights and responsibilities of a citizen.

Welcome to the World

Interdisciplinary Challenge

Investigate Your World

Suppose that someone has given you a globe as a gift. What a great present! Unlike a flat map, your globe gives you a more accurate view of the world. Best of all, this new globe is programmable. You can input new information about different features and places on Earth. In fact, the manufacturer has set up a contest—the Global Game—giving prizes for the best and most creative approaches to programming the globe. Good luck!

COOPERATIVE LEARNING On these pages are challenges you will meet in trying to win the Global Game. Working with a small group, choose which one you want to solve. Divide the work among group members. Look for helpful information in the Data File. Keep in mind that you will present your solution to the class.

CAPITOL
Tokyo

HISTORY/ECONOMICS CHALLENGE

". . . you want to know more about the world closer to home."

Now that your globe has shown you the worldwide picture, you want to know more about the world closer to home. How has geography influenced the history of your community? What features or resources brought settlers there? Choose one of these options. Look in the Data File for information.

ACTIVITIES

1. Make a time line of major events in the growth of your community. If possible, begin with the Native Americans who originally inhabited the area. Include the arrival of immigrants from various places.
2. Draw or trace an outline of your state. Then make a thematic map of its major products and industries. Use words or symbols (such as a cow, a factory, a computer) and create a map key to identify each product.

SUNSHINE STATE STANDARDS
Key Standard SS.A.6.3.5 The student understands how Florida has allocated and used resources and the consequences of those economic decisions.
FCAT LA.A.2.3.1 Reading: Identify Main Idea, Facts, and Details

22 UNIT 1

LANGUAGE ARTS CHALLENGE

". . . you are taken on an audio journey to new places."

Your new globe has built-in sensors activated by a laser wand. When you point the wand at a spot on the globe, you are taken on an audio journey to new places. The sound clip introduces you to a place's culture—the things that make it unique.

As part of the Global Game, the manufacturer is looking for new ways to present this information. What will you include in your approach? How can you add to the globe's popular appeal? Choose one of these options. Look in the Data File for help.

ACTIVITIES

1. Choose one continent and write a script about it for a seven-minute "audio journey." Remember to include information about geographic features as well as aspects of culture.
2. Design another geography game that the manufacturer can use to market its globe. The game should appeal to students of your age. Write a brief description of the game and its rules.

NICKNAME
Land of the Rising Sun

POPULATION
127,000,000*

*2001 Japanese Government Statistics

Activity Wrap-Up

As a group, review your solution to the challenge you selected. Then present your solution to the class.

DATA FILE

WORLD STATISTICS

- **Circumference** at Equator: 24,902 mi.
- **Earth's speed** of orbit: 18.5 mi./sec.
- **Total area:** 197,000,000 sq. mi.; land area: 57,900,000 sq. mi.
- **Highest point:** 29,035 ft.—Mt. Everest.
- **Lowest point:** 35,800 ft. below sea level—Marianas Trench, Pacific Ocean.
- **Lowest point on land:** 1,312 ft. below sea level, Dead Sea, Israel, and Jordan.

HIGHEST ELEVATIONS BY CONTINENT

- **Asia:** Mt. Everest, Nepal–Tibet, 29,035 ft.
- **South America:** Mt. Aconcagua, Argentina–Chile, 22,834 ft.
- **North America:** Mt. McKinley (Denali), Alaska, 20,320 ft.
- **Africa:** Mt. Kilimanjaro, Tanzania, 19,340 ft.
- **Europe:** Mt. Elbrus, Russia, 18,510 ft.
- **Antarctica:** Vinson Massif, 16,066 ft.
- **Western Europe:** Mont Blanc, France, 15,771 ft.
- **Australia:** Mt. Kosciusko, 7,310 ft.

SOME MAJOR RIVER SYSTEMS

- **Nile,** Africa: 4,160 mi.
- **Amazon,** South America: 4,080 mi.
- **Mississippi**–Missouri, North America (U.S.): 3,740 mi.
- **Chang Jiang** (Yangtze), China: 3,915 mi.
- **Yenisey,** Russia: 2,566 mi.
- **Plata,** South America: 3,030 mi.
- **Huang He** (Yellow), China: 3,010 mi.
- **Congo** (Zaire), Africa: 2,880 mi.

To learn more about Earth's geography, go to

RESEARCH LINKS
CLASSZONE.COM

Introduction to World Cultures and Geography

SECTION 2

Many Regions, Many Cultures

TERMS & NAMES
culture region
interdependence

MAIN IDEA
The world can be divided into regions according to culture.

WHY IT MATTERS NOW
Understanding other cultures can help you understand how people in other regions live and think.

DATELINE

MEERUT, INDIA, MAY 10, 1857— Indian troops serving in the army of the British East India Company rebelled today. Reasons given for the revolt include anger at the way the company has been taking over Indian lands and a lack of respect for Indian customs. The immediate cause was the new Enfield rifles issued to the troops. To load them, soldiers have to bite off the ends of the cartridges.

Word quickly spread that the cartridges were greased with cow and pig fat. This was an insult to both Hindu and Muslim soldiers. Hindus hold cows sacred and never kill them. Muslims believe the meat of pigs is unclean.

Place • The rebellion in Meerut spread to the city of Lucknow and left the Chutter Munzil Palace in ruins. ▲

Different Places, Different Cultures

Indian soldiers and British officials belonged to cultures with different beliefs. The British came from a region of the world where most people ate the meat of pigs and cows. The Indians lived in a region where most people did not. A **culture region** is an area of the world in which many people share similar beliefs, history, and languages. The people in a culture region may have religion, technology, and ways of earning a living in common as well. They may grow and eat similar foods, wear similar kinds of clothes, and build houses in similar styles.

TAKING NOTES
Use your chart to take notes about these terms.

Term	Definition
history	
geography	

SUNSHINE STATE STANDARDS
Key Standard SS.B.1.3.4 The student understands ways factors such as culture and technology influence the perception of places and regions.
FCAT LA.A.2.2.7 Reading: Recognize Compare and Contrast

Culture Regions of the World

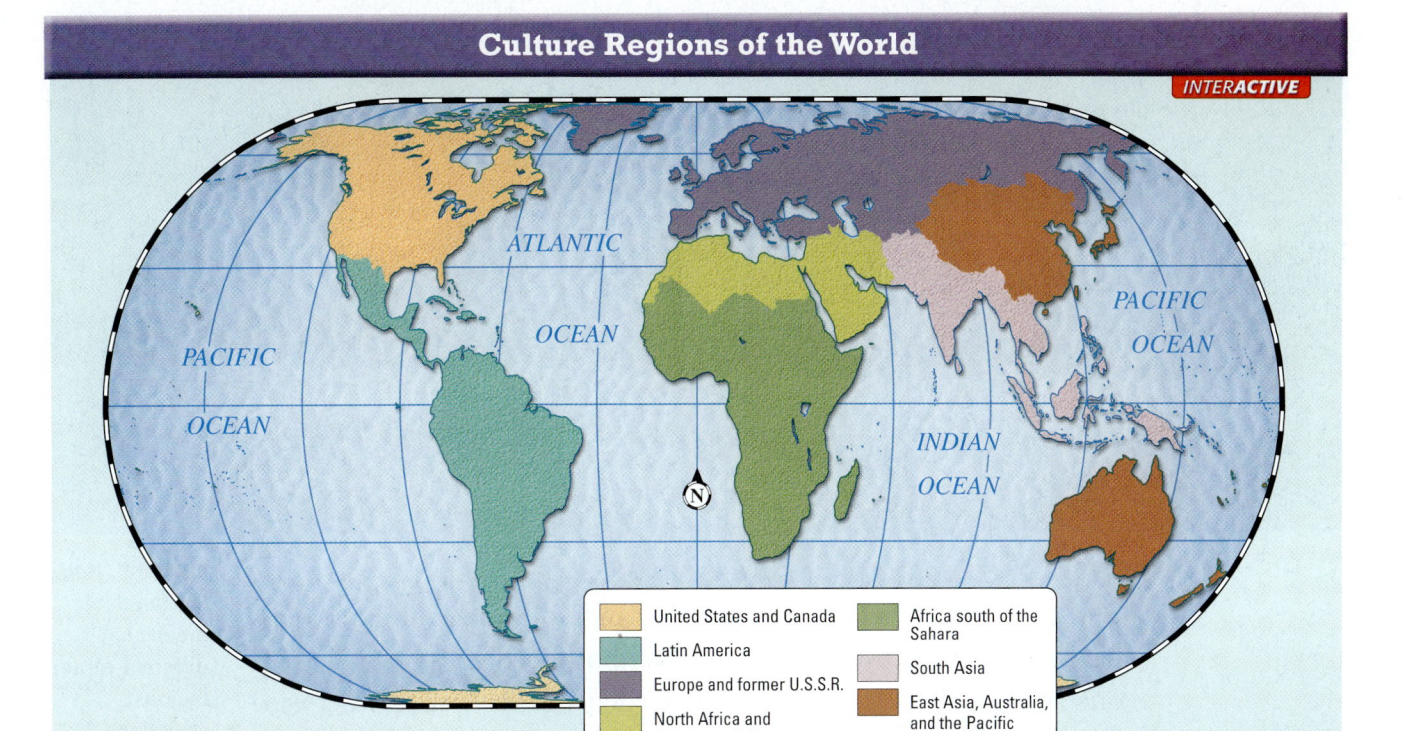

Legend:
- United States and Canada
- Latin America
- Europe and former U.S.S.R.
- North Africa and Southwest Asia
- Africa south of the Sahara
- South Asia
- East Asia, Australia, and the Pacific Islands

GEOGRAPHY SKILLBUILDER:
Interpreting a Map
1. **Region** • How many culture regions are shown on this map?
2. **Location** • Name three culture regions in the Eastern Hemisphere.

The World's Culture Regions

The map above shows the major culture regions of the world. Latin America is one culture region. The Spanish and Portuguese languages help to tie its people together. So does its common history. Southwest Asia and North Africa is another culture region. Most countries in this region share a common desert climate and landscape. People have adapted to the desert in similar ways, thus creating a common culture. Islam, which is the major religion in this region, also helps shape a common culture.

Usually, not every person in a region belongs to the dominant, or mainstream, culture. Some regions are multicultural. For example, the United States and Canada contain other cultures besides the dominant one. Although most people in this region speak English, many people in eastern Canada speak French. Many people in the United States speak Spanish, especially in the Southwest. In both countries, Catholics, Protestants, Jews, Muslims, Buddhists, and members of other religions are free to worship.

Reading **Social Studies**

A. Recognizing Important Details Name two characteristics that make the United States multicultural.

Strange but TRUE

Pictures to Words Did you know that writing began as little more than crude pictures? Writing developed in four stages over many thousands of years. At first, symbols and pictures were used to represent ideas. In the second stage, a sign represented a particular word. The next stage is called syllabic; each sign stood for a word as well as any sound that resembled that word. For example, one sign might be used for both "sea" and "see." Finally came the alphabetic stage, in which each sign represented a sound.

The Greeks perfected the alphabet that we use today. As you can see below, the first two letters of the alphabet evolved from the Egyptian signs for "ox" and "house."

Culture Regions Change For thousands of years, culture regions have changed and evolved as they have borrowed culture traits from one another. They have also come to depend upon each other economically. Decisions and events in one part of the world affect other parts. Advances in transportation and communication have increased this **interdependence**. When oil-producing nations in the Middle East raise the price of oil, for example, the price of gasoline at the neighborhood gas station is likely to rise. If there is an especially abundant banana crop in parts of Latin America, the price of bananas may drop at the local grocery store. More and more, people of different countries are becoming part of one world.

Region • Home life can differ greatly in different culture regions, sometimes depending on a region's climate or natural resources. ▲

SECTION 2 ASSESSMENT

Terms & Names
1. Explain the significance of: (a) culture region   (b) interdependence

Using Graphics

2. Use a chart to list the major culture regions of the world.

Major Culture Regions of the World
1.
2.
3.
4.
5.
6.
7.

Main Ideas

3. (a) List at least three things people in a culture region may have in common.

   (b) Which continents have more than one culture region?

   (c) What is one cause of cultural change?

Critical Thinking

4. **Clarifying**

   Why might Brazilian coffee at your local supermarket suddenly cost more?

   Think About
   • price setting
   • coffee supplies

ACTIVITY -OPTION-   Write a **dialogue** between you and a visitor from another country in which you explain what makes the culture in your region different from others.

SKILLBUILDER

Reading a Time Zone Map

▶▶ Defining the Skill

A time zone map shows the 24 time zones of the world. The prime meridian runs through Greenwich (GREHN•ich), England. Each zone east of Greenwich is one hour later than the zone before. Each zone west of Greenwich is one hour earlier. The International Date Line runs through the Pacific Ocean. It is the location where each day begins. If it is Saturday to the east of the International Date Line, then it is Sunday to the west of it.

SUNSHINE STATE STANDARDS
Key Standard SS.B.1.3.1 The student uses various map forms (including thematic maps) and other geographic representations, tools, and technologies to acquire, process, and report geographic information including patterns of land use, connections between places, and patterns and processes of migration and diffusion.

FCAT LA.A.2.3.1 Reading: Identify Main Ideas, Facts, and Details

▶▶ Applying the Skill

Use the strategies listed below to help you find times and time differences on a time zone map.

How to Read a Time Zone Map

Strategy ❶ Read the title. It tells you what the map is intended to show.

Strategy ❷ Read the labels at the top of the map. They show the hours across the world when it is noon in Greenwich. The labels at the bottom show the number of hours earlier or later than the time in Greenwich.

Strategy ❸ Locate a place whose time you know. Locate the place where you want to know the time. Count the number of time zones between them. Then add or subtract that number of hours.

For example, if it is noon time on the west coast of Africa, you can see that it is 7:00 A.M. on the east coast of the United States. That is a difference of five hours.

▶▶ Practicing the Skill

Practice determining the difference in hours between various time zones. For example, if you select the yellow zone in western Asia and you live in Texas, you will have a time difference of 11 hours. Now select one time zone in Africa, one in Europe, and one in Australia. For each location, determine the number of hours' difference with the time zone in which you live.

Welcome to the World 27

Literature Connections

SUNSHINE STATE STANDARDS
Key Standard SS.A.2.3.1
The student understands how language, ideas, and institutions of one culture can influence other cultures (e.g., through trade, exploration, and immigration).
FCAT LA.E.2.3.1 Literature: Understand Character and Plot Development

The Giant Kuafu Chases the Sun

FROM THE EARLIEST TIMES, people have created myths and legends to explain the natural world. Some stories explain why earthquakes occur or lightning strikes. Others tell how rivers, deserts, canyons, and other landforms came to be. This ancient Chinese myth, dating back at least 2,500 years, comes from the area of northern China where Chinese civilization first began. The myth explains how the province of Shaanxi got its mountains.

Shaanxi, also known as Shensi, is in northern China. The southern part of the province contains the high and rugged Qinling Range, also called the Tsinling Mountains, where the average peak is 8,000 feet high and some are over 12,000 feet high.

Long ago, soon after time began, giants roamed the flat and fertile Earth. One of the largest, bravest, and fastest of them all was named Kuafu—and his strength knew no bounds.

Every day, Kuafu watched the sun rise in the east and set in the west. When night came, he became greatly saddened. He thought, "I do not like the darkness. All life falls into a silent slumber. If I could catch the sun, then I could keep night as bright as day. The plants could grow forever, and it would always be warm. I would never have to sleep again."

The next day, Kuafu stretched his legs and started to race after the sun. He ran like the wind over several thousand miles without rest. Finally, he chased the sun to the Yu Valley where it came to rest every day but Kuafu was thirsty and very, very tired. His thirst grew, and soon it became overwhelming. He had never known a thirst like this, and his body seemed to be drying up like mud bricks in an oven.

Kuafu found the nearest stream and drank it dry. It was not enough. With a giant's stride, he quickly reached the mighty Yellow River. He drank it dry, but again, it was not enough. He continued toward the Great Sea—surely it held water enough to quench his thirst.

On his journey, he drank dry every well and every stream and every lake he came across. His thirst became overpowering, and Kuafu fell to the ground before he reached the Sea. In a fit of anger, with a branch of a peach tree, he made a final swing at the sun. But before the branch reached the sun, Kuafu died of thirst.

The sun set in the Yu Valley, and night came. When the sun rose again, Kuafu's body had been transformed into a mountain range. The peach tree branch extended from his side and formed a peach tree grove. To this day, the peaches in this grove are sweet and moist, always ready to relieve the thirst of those who would choose to chase the sun.

Reading THE LITERATURE

Before you read, examine the title. Why might the title character want to chase the sun? What abilities will he or she need to catch it?

Thinking About THE LITERATURE

Contests involving the sun, as well as efforts to reach the sun, are common in the myths and legends of many societies. Why do you think stories about the sun are told in so many cultures?

Writing About THE LITERATURE

Although Kuafu was not a real person, his myth has survived for thousands of years. Why? What does it teach about human behavior?

Further Reading

Legends of Landforms by Carole G. Vogel explores Native American legends about the origins of many places in the United States.

Why Snails Have Shells by Carolyn Han retells the folk tales of the Han people and other Chinese ethnic groups.

CHAPTER 1 ASSESSMENT

TERMS & NAMES

Explain the significance of each of the following:

1. history
2. geography
3. government
4. citizen
5. economics
6. scarcity
7. culture
8. culture trait
9. culture region
10. interdependence

REVIEW QUESTIONS

The World at Your Fingertips *(pages 17–21)*

1. What are the five themes of geography?
2. What are the main differences between a limited and an unlimited government?
3. How can someone become a citizen of a country?
4. What is the difference between a command economy and a market economy?
5. What are some characteristics of a culture?

Many Regions, Many Cultures *(pages 24–26)*

6. How can decisions made in one part of the world affect people in another part of the world?
7. What aspects of daily life might people in the same culture region share?
8. What makes the United States and Canada a multicultural region?

CRITICAL THINKING

Remembering Definitions

1. Using your completed chart from Reading Social Studies, p. 16, tell how understanding the culture could help you make friends in a new country.

Making Inferences

2. Why might someone's life expectancy be low in a region with a low level of development?

Identifying Problems

3. If countries in the Middle East stopped producing oil, how might that affect the economy of the United States?

Visual Summary

1 The World at Your Fingertips

- History, geography, government, economics, and culture are five ways to understand Earth and its peoples.

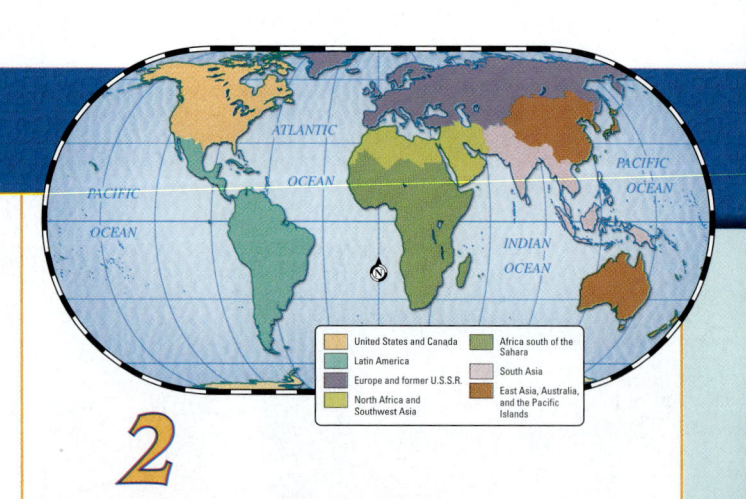

2 Many Regions, Many Cultures

- People live, dress, and think differently in each of the world's culture regions.

> STANDARDS-BASED ASSESSMENT

Use the map and your knowledge of world cultures and geography to answer questions 1 and 2.

Additional Test Practice, pp. S1–S33

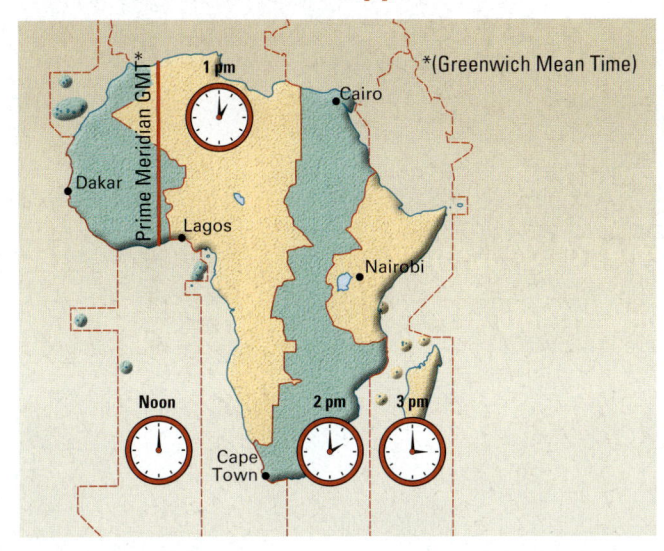

1. Which of these cities is in the same time zone as Cairo?
   A. Cape Town
   B. Dakar
   C. Lagos
   D. Nairobi

2. If it is 6 P.M. in Lagos, what time would it be in Nairobi?
   A. 5 P.M.
   B. 6 P.M.
   C. 7 P.M.
   D. 8 P.M.

In the following quotation, writer Aime Cesair talks about culture. Use the quotation and your knowledge of world cultures and geography to answer question 3.

PRIMARY SOURCE

Culture is everything. Culture is the way we dress, the way we carry our heads, the way we walk, the way we tie our ties—it is not only the fact of writing books or building houses.

AIME CESAIR, speech to the World Congress of Black Writers and Artists in Paris

3. Which of the following statements would Cesair agree with most?
   A. Culture refers to fine art, drama, and classical music.
   B. Culture includes all the things that characterize a group.
   C. Most people in the world do not take part in culture.
   D. Some parts of culture are more important than others.

TEST PRACTICE
CLASSZONE.COM

ALTERNATIVE ASSESSMENT

1. WRITING ABOUT HISTORY

The United States and Canada share a culture region. Think about the elements that contribute to this culture region. Then write a script for a one-act play in which a person from another culture region experiences our culture for the first time. Focus on unique aspects of our language, technology, food, and clothing that a person might find surprising and strange.

2. COOPERATIVE LEARNING

With a group of three to five students, set up a peace conference to help two warring groups make peace. Choose two specific groups and a specific issue that caused the hostility, such as a conflict over the scarcity of water. Do research to understand each side's point of view in the conflict. Group members should take on specific roles, such as conference moderator and spokesperson for each side. Present your peace conference to the class as a skit.

INTEGRATED TECHNOLOGY

Doing Internet Research

Use the Internet to research a culture, such as the people of Lebanon or Hong Kong. Write a report of your findings. List the Web sites you used to prepare your report.

- Specifically find out about the daily life of the people, including what jobs they have, what foods they eat, what clothes they wear, and what their homes are like.
- Also, research what most people in the culture value, what governments they live under, and what common difficulties they face.

For Internet links to support this activity, go to

RESEARCH LINKS
CLASSZONE.COM

CHAPTER 2
The Geographer's World

SECTION 1   The Five Themes of Geography

SECTION 2   The Geographer's Tools

Place "Viewed from the distance of the moon," said scientist and writer Lewis Thomas, "the astonishing thing about the Earth . . . is that it is alive."

FOCUS ON GEOGRAPHY

How has new technology increased our knowledge of Earth?

Human-Environment Interaction • *Terra*, the Earth Observing System (EOS) satellite launched in 1999, helps scientists understand how Earth's lands, oceans, air, ice, and plant and animal life work together as a system. Scientists at the National Aeronautics and Space Administration (NASA) use sensors mounted on satellites to study Earth's air, land, and water.

Terra helps to answer such questions as: Which environmental changes result from natural causes? Which are caused by humans? Satellites like *Terra* also help scientists study natural disasters such as hurricanes, volcanic eruptions, and floods. Today, several countries are working together in the Earth Observing System program to gather information about climate and environmental change on Earth.

What do you think?

- How can *Terra* benefit people?
- Why do countries work together to study climate and environmental change?

CHAPTER 2: READING SOCIAL STUDIES

BEFORE YOU READ

▶▶ What Do You Know?

Do you know how to find important places in your town? Have you visited cities, towns, or rural areas and noticed what made these places special? Do you ever use terms like "up north" or "back east"? Have you ever moved from one neighborhood, town, or country to another? Do you know about the harmful effects of pollution on wildlife habitats? If you answered yes, then you know something about each of geography's five big themes—location, place, region, movement, and human-environment interaction.

▶▶ What Do You Want to Know?

Decide what more you want to learn about geography's five themes. Write your ideas, and any questions you may have, in your notebook before you read this chapter.

READ AND TAKE NOTES

Reading Strategy: Identifying Main Ideas One way to make sense of what you read is to look for main ideas and supporting details. Each paragraph, topic heading, and section in a chapter usually has a main idea. Supporting details help to explain the main idea. Use this spider map to write a main idea and its supporting details from this chapter.

- Copy the spider map in your notebook.
- As you read, look for information about the five themes of geography.
- Write a main idea in the center circle.
- Write details supporting the main idea in the other circles.

Place • Physical and human characteristics reveal patterns in places. ▲

The Five Themes of Geography

34 CHAPTER 2

SECTION 1

The Five Themes of Geography

TERMS & NAMES
continent
absolute location
latitude
longitude
relative location
migrate

MAIN IDEA
The five themes of geography are location, place, region, movement, and human-environment interaction.

WHY IT MATTERS NOW
The five themes enable you to discuss and explain people, places, and environments of the past and present.

DATELINE
EXTRA

FRANKFURT, GERMANY, JANUARY 6, 1912

Scientist Alfred Wegener sent out shock waves today when he proposed a radical new hypothesis. The continents were once joined together as one huge landmass. In time, he suggests, pieces of this landmass broke away and drifted apart.

Wegener calls this supercontinent *Pangaea*. To support his theory, Wegener points out that the continents seem to fit together. He notes, for example, that the east coast of South America fits snugly against the west coast of Africa. Mountain ranges continue across both continents as smoothly as the lines of print across torn pieces of a newspaper.

Other scientists reject Wegener's claim. They say that they know of no force strong enough to cause continents to move.

Movement • Seven continents were once one continent. A <u>continent</u> is a landmass above water on earth. ▲

The Five Themes

Eventually, the scientific community accepted Alfred Wegener's theory. Scientists discovered that giant slabs of Earth's surface, called tectonic plates, move, causing the continents to drift. This creates earthquakes, volcanoes, and mountains. Geographers study the processes that cause changes like these. To help you understand how geographers think about the world, consider geography's five themes—location, place, region, movement, and human-environment interaction.

SUNSHINE STATE STANDARDS
Key Standard SS.B.2.3.2
The student knows the human and physical characteristics of different places in the world and how these characteristics change over time.

Other Standards
SS.B.1.3.2, B.2.3.1

CAT LA.A.2.3.1 **Reading:** Identify Main Ideas, Facts, and Details

TAKING NOTES
Use your web to take notes about the five themes.

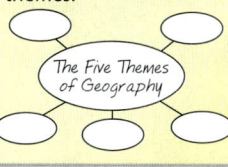

The Geographer's World 35

Australia Today

GEOGRAPHY SKILLBUILDER:
Interpreting a Map
1. **Location** • What is the latitude of Adelaide?
2. **Location** • What island is almost entirely enclosed by the lines 40° and 45° south latitude and 145° and 150° east longitude?

The World's Heritage

Sagarmatha National Park
Sagarmatha National Park is located in mountainous northeastern Nepal. The park includes Mount Everest, the highest peak in the world. Deep gorges and glacial valleys run through the park. Much of the park lies 15,000 feet above sea level. The isolated location of the park helps protect several rare species, such as the Tibetan wolf, the lesser panda, and the snow leopard, shown below.

The park is also famous for its small population of Sherpas. The Sherpa people moved to the region from Tibet more than 500 years ago. They regard Mt. Everest as a holy place. Many Sherpas have acted as guides for people climbing Everest.

Location

Often, the first thing you want to know about a place is where it is located in space. Geography helps you think about things spatially—where they are located and how they got there. Location allows you to discuss places in the world in terms everyone can understand.

Absolute Location If someone asks you where your school is, you might say, "At the corner of Fifth Street and Second Avenue." Ask a geographer where Melbourne, Australia, is located, and you may get the answer "38° south latitude, 145° east longitude." This is the absolute location of the city of Melbourne. **Absolute location** is the exact spot on Earth where a place can be found.

Using a system of imaginary lines drawn on its surface, geographers can locate any place on Earth. Lines that run parallel to the equator are called **latitude** lines. They show distance north and south of the equator. Lines that run between the North and South Poles are called **longitude** lines. They show distance east and west of the prime meridian.

Reading Social Studies

A. Contrasting Contrast absolute location with relative location.

Relative Location Another way to define the location of a place is to describe its relation to other places. You might say your school is "near the fire station" or "two blocks west of the pet store." If someone asks you where Canada is, you might say, "North of the United States." The location of one place in relation to other places is called its **relative location**.

Place • Thousands of years ago, this part of Southwest Asia, then called Mesopotamia, was green and fertile. Today, as you can see, this area is mostly desert. ▲

Place

Another useful theme of geography is place. If you go to a new place, the first thing you want to know is what it is like. Is it crowded or is there a lot of open space? How is the climate? What language do people speak? Every place on Earth has a distinct group of physical features, such as its climate, landforms and bodies of water, and plant and animal life. Places can also have human characteristics, or features that human beings have created, such as cities and towns, governments, and cultural traditions.

Places Change If you could go back to the days when dinosaurs roamed Earth, you would see a world much different from the one you know. Much of Earth had a moist, warm climate, and the continents were not located where they are today. Rivers, forests, wetlands, glaciers, oceans—the physical features of Earth—continue to change. Some changes are dramatic, caused by erupting volcanoes, earthquakes, and hurricanes. Others happen slowly, such as the movement of glaciers or the formation of a delta.

Place • This satellite photo shows the Ganges River delta. It was formed from sediment and mud carried by the river to its mouth. ▼

Region

Geographers group places into regions. A region is a group of places that have physical features or human characteristics, or both, in common. A geographer interested in languages, for example, might divide the world into language regions. All the countries where Spanish is the major language would form one Spanish-speaking language region. Geographers compare regions to understand the differences and similarities among them.

The Geographer's World 37

Natural Regions of the World

Region	Climate	Plant Life
Tropical Rain Forest	Hot and wet all year	Thick trees, broad leaves Trees stay green all year
Tropical Grassland	Hot all year Wet and dry seasons	Tall grasses Some trees
Mediterranean	Hot, dry summers Cool-to-mild winters	Open forests Some clumps of trees Many shrubs, herbs, grasses
Temperate Forest	Warm summers Cold-to-cool winters	Mixed forests; some trees lose leaves in winter, others stay green all year
Cool Forest	Cool-to-mild summers Long, cold winters	Mostly trees with needles; stay green all year; some trees lose leaves in winter
Cool Grassland	Warm summers Cool winters Drier than forest regions	Prairies: Tall, thick grass Higher lands: Shorter grass
Desert	Hot all year Very little rain	Sand or bare soil, few plants May have cactus, some grass and bushes
Tundra	Short, cool summers Long, cold winters Little rain or snow	Rolling plains: No trees Some patches of moss, short grass, flowering plants
Arctic	Very cold Covered in ice all year	None
High Mountain	Varies, depending on altitude	Varies, depending on altitude

SKILLBUILDER: Interpreting a Chart
1. **Region** • How are desert regions and tropical grasslands alike and how are they different?
2. **Region** • In which type of climate are trees most likely to stay green all year?

Natural Regions The world can be divided into ten natural regions. A natural region has its own unique combination of plant and animal life and climate. Tropical rain forest regions are in Central and South America, Africa south of the Sahara, Southeast Asia, Australia, and the Pacific Islands. Where are desert regions located?

Region • The tundra is one of the ten natural regions of the world. ▲

Movement

People, goods, and ideas move from one place to another. So do animals, plants, and other physical features of Earth. Movement is the fourth geographic theme. The Internet is a good tool for the movement of ideas. Sometimes people move within a country. For example, vast numbers of people have migrated from farms to cities. **Migrate** means to move from one area to settle in another. You may have ancestors who immigrated to the United States—perhaps from Africa, Europe, Latin America, or Asia. When people emigrate, they take their ideas and customs with them. They may also adopt new ideas from their new home.

Vocabulary
immigrate: to move to an area

emigrate: to move away from an area

Reasons for Moving Migration is a result of push and pull factors. Problems in one place push people out. Advantages in another place pull people in. Poverty, overcrowding, lack of jobs and schooling, prejudice, war, and political oppression are push factors. Pull factors include a higher standard of living, employment and educational opportunities, rights, freedom, peace, and safety.

Reading Social Studies
B. Synthesizing How do push and pull factors work together?

Human Migration

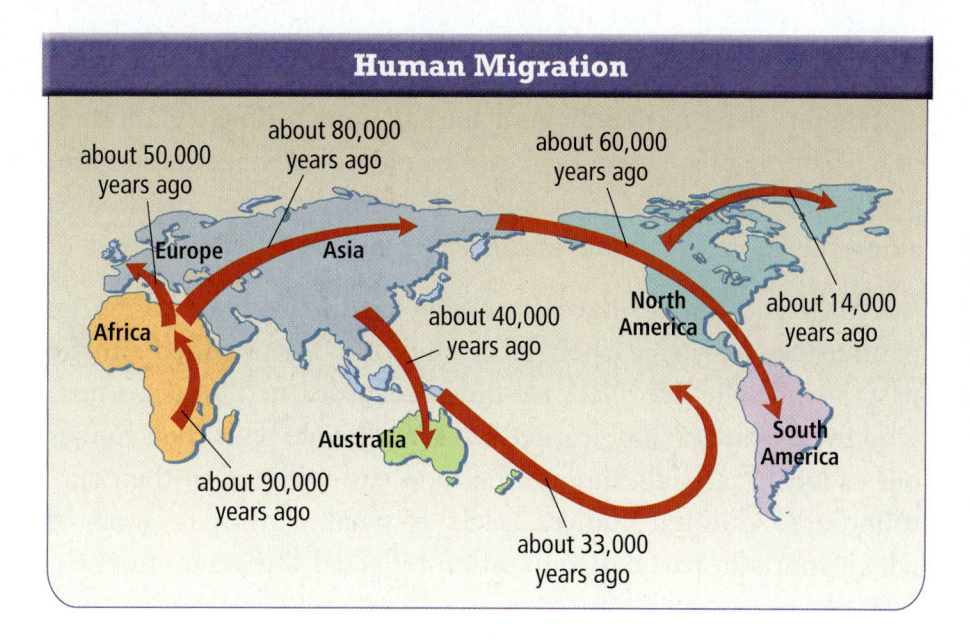

- about 50,000 years ago — Europe
- about 80,000 years ago — Asia
- about 60,000 years ago — (to North America)
- about 40,000 years ago
- about 14,000 years ago — North America / South America
- about 90,000 years ago — Africa / Australia
- about 33,000 years ago

Movement • As you can see, people have been on the move for at least 90,000 years. ◀

Vocabulary
navigable: deep and wide enough for boats to travel on

Barriers to Movement Natural barriers, such as mountain ranges, canyons, and raging rivers, can make migration difficult. Oceans, lakes, navigable rivers, and flat land can make it easier. Modern forms of transportation have made it easier than ever for people to move back and forth between countries.

Human-Environment Interaction

Interaction between human beings and their environment is the fifth theme of geography. Human-environment interaction occurs because humans depend on, adapt to, and modify the world around them. Human society and the environment cannot be separated. Each shapes and is shaped by the other. Earth is a unified system.

Some places are the way they are because people have changed them. For example, if an area has a lot of open meadows, this may be because early settlers cleared the land for farming.

Citizenship IN ACTION

Saving Special Places Many of the most wonderful and special places on Earth may be destroyed or ruined over time unless they are protected. To prevent this, UNESCO (the United Nations Educational, Scientific, and Cultural Organization) set up the World Heritage Committee in 1972. This group identifies human-made and natural wonders all over the world and looks for ways to protect them for the benefit of the world community. So far, the list of World Heritage Sites numbers more than 690. The ancient city of Petra, Jordan (see photograph at right), the Galápagos Islands, the Roman Colosseum, and the Pyramids of Giza are just a few of the places protected for future generations.

The Geographer's World

Human changes may help or hurt the environment. Pollution is an example of a harmful effect. The environment can also harm people. For example, hurricanes wash away beaches and houses along the shore; earthquakes cause fire and destruction.

Adaptation Humans have often adapted their way of life to the natural resources that their local environment provided. In the past, people who lived near teeming oceans learned to fish. Those who lived near rich soil learned to farm. People built their homes out of local materials and ate the food easily grown in their surroundings. Cultural choices, such as what clothes to wear or which sports to participate in, often reflected the environment.

Because of technology, this close adaptation to the environment is not as common as it once was. Airplanes, for example, can quickly fly frozen fish from the coast to towns far inland. Even so, there are many more ice skaters in Canada and surfers in California than the other way around.

Interaction People and the environment continually interact. For example, when thousands of people in a city choose to use public transportation or ride bicycles rather than drive, less gasoline is burned. When less gasoline is burned, there is less air pollution. In other words, when the environment is healthy, the people who live in it are able to lead healthier lives.

SECTION 1 ASSESSMENT

Terms & Names
1. Explain the significance of: (a) continent   (b) absolute location   (c) latitude   (d) longitude
   (e) relative location   (f) migrate

Using Graphics
2. Use a chart like this one to list and explain the five themes of geography.

Theme	Explanation

Main Ideas
3. (a) What physical processes can cause places to change over time?
   (b) How do push and pull factors cause migration?
   (c) What are some ways people have adapted to their environment?

Critical Thinking
4. Making Inferences
   What factors make your part of the United States a region?

Think About
- similar human geography
- similar physical geography

ACTIVITY -OPTION- Write and illustrate a **magazine advertisement** to persuade people to move to a new place. Include several pull factors for the place you are advertising.

SKILLBUILDER

Reading Latitude and Longitude

▶▶ Defining the Skill

To locate places, geographers use a global grid system (see the chart directly below). Imaginary lines of latitude, called parallels, circle the globe. The equator circles the middle of the globe at 0°. Parallels measure distance in degrees north and south of the equator.

Lines of longitude, called meridians, circle the globe from pole to pole. Meridians measure distance in degrees east and west of the prime meridian. The prime meridian is at 0°. It passes through Greenwich, England.

SUNSHINE STATE STANDARDS
Key Standard SS.B.1.3.1 The student uses various map forms (including thematic maps) and other geographic representations, tools, and technologies to acquire, process, and report geographic information including patterns of land use, connections between places, and patterns and processes of migration and diffusion.

FCAT LA.A.2.3.1 Reading: Identify Main Ideas, Facts, and Details

▶▶ Applying the Skill

The world map below shows lines of latitude and longitude. Use the strategies listed directly below to help you locate places on Earth.

How to Read Latitude and Longitude

Strategy ❶ Place a finger on the place you want to locate. With a finger from your other hand, find the nearest parallel. Write down its number. Be sure to include north or south. (You may have to guesstimate the actual number.)

Strategy ❷ Keep your finger on the place you want to locate. Now find the nearest meridian. Write down its number. Be sure to include east or west. (You may have to guesstimate the actual number.)

Strategy ❸ If you know the longitude and latitude of a place and want to find it on a map, put one finger on the line of longitude and another on the line of latitude. Bring your fingers together until they meet.

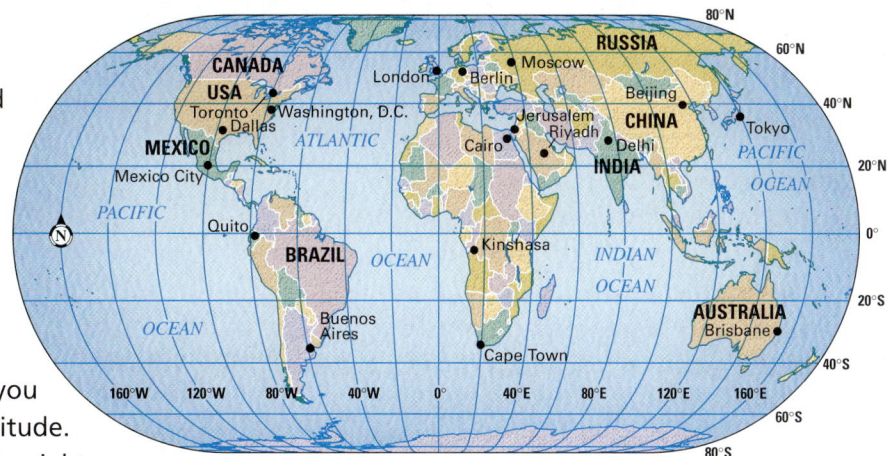

Write a Summary

Writing a summary will help you understand latitude and longitude. The paragraph below and to the right summarizes the information you have learned.

▶▶ Practicing the Skill

Turn to page 36 in Chapter 2, Section 1, "The Five Themes of Geography." Look at the map of Australia and write a paragraph summarizing how you located the city of Adelaide.

> Use latitude and longitude to locate a place on a globe or map. Lines of latitude circle Earth. Lines of longitude run through the poles. The numbers of the lines at the place where two lines cross is the location of that place.

The Geographer's World

Linking Past and Present

The Legacy of World Exploration

Early Pacific Navigation

More than 2,000 years ago, Polynesian sailors were among the first people to sail the Pacific Ocean. Without charts or instruments to help them find their way, these ancient navigators made sea charts from palm sticks tied together with coconut threads, using small shells to represent islands.

Magnetic Compass

In the 1100s, mariners of China and Europe independently discovered the magnetic compass. They discovered that an iron or steel needle touched by a lodestone, or piece of magnetic ore, tends to point roughly in a north-south direction. Today, surveyors and navigators consider the magnetic compass an essential tool for determining direction.

Portolan Charts

Portolan charts were first made in the 1300s in Italy and Spain. *Portolan* comes from an Italian word meaning "navigation instructions." These charts, which were actually rough maps, were based on accounts of medieval Europeans who sailed the Mediterranean and Black seas. Drawn on sheepskin, portolan charts show coastal features and main ports. The straight lines crisscrossing the charts represent the 32 directions of the mariner's compass.

SUNSHINE STATE STANDARDS
Key Standard SS.B.1.3.4 The student understands ways factors such as culture and technology influence the perception of places and regions.
FCAT LA.A.2.3.1 Reading: Identify Main Idea, Facts, and Details

Modern Electronic Navigation

In the 1970s, the U.S. Department of Defense developed the Global Positioning System (GPS). GPS allows people on land, at sea, or in the air to pinpoint their location or to track moving objects in any weather. A network of 24 satellites that orbit Earth beam down data to palm-sized receivers, aiding the military in maneuvers. Civilians use them for hiking or finding shorter travel routes.

Astrolabe

The astrolabe was first used in the 1400s in Europe and the Islamic world. It is a flat, circular piece of either metal or wood. The edge of the circle is marked to show 360 degrees. Sailors used the astrolabe to measure the sun's and stars' angles above the horizon in order to determine their ships' positions at sea.

Chronometer

John Harrison worked for nearly half a century before he perfected, in 1762, a ship's clock that would revolutionize navigation. This tool, called a chronometer, enabled sailors for the first time to determine accurately a ship's longitude, or east-west position. The modern chronometer, which looks like a large, heavy watch, continues to help sailors find their ships' longitude.

Sextant

In the 1730s, the sextant replaced the astrolabe. This device measures the angle between the horizon and the sun, the moon, or a star and is used to calculate latitude, or north-south position. The sextant continues to be a basic navigational tool today.

Find Out More About It!

Study the text and photos on these pages to learn about world exploration. Then choose the item that interests you the most and research it in the library or on the Internet to learn more about it. Use the information you gather to write a short play that you and your classmates can perform.

RESEARCH LINKS
CLASSZONE.COM

Introduction to World Cultures and Geography

Technology: 2004

SUNSHINE STATE STANDARDS
Key Standard SS.B.1.3.1 The student uses various map forms (including thematic maps) and other geographic representations, tools, and technologies to acquire, process, and report geographic information including patterns of land use, connections between places, and patterns and processes of migration and diffusion.
FCAT LA.A.2.3.1 Reading: Identify Main Idea, Facts, and Details

INTERACTIVE

A Map of Earth in 3-D

On February 11, 2000, the space shuttle *Endeavour* was launched into space on an 11-day mission to complete the most in-depth mapping project in history. The Shuttle Radar Topography Mission (SRTM) collected data on 80 percent of Earth's surface. This information was gathered by beaming radar waves at Earth and converting the echoes into images through a process known as interferometry (IHN•tuhr•fuh•RAHM•ih•tree).

With the aid of computers, the resulting information can be used to produce almost limitless numbers of three-dimensional (3-D) maps. These maps show the topography—rivers, forests, mountains, and valleys—of Earth's surface. It took one year to process the data into 3-D maps. These maps, the most accurate topographical maps ever, will help scientists to better study Earth's surface. The data will also be useful to the general public; for example, it can be used to find new locations for cellular-phone towers and to create maps for hikers.

> The data collected on the 11-day SRTM mission can be used by many people—such as the military, the science community, and civic groups—and can be tailored to their needs.

> The 200-foot mast is the longest structure used in space today.

> Radar interferometry uses radar images taken from two different angles to produce a single 3-D image.

THINKING Critically

1. Drawing Conclusions How will new, sophisticated tools such as radar interferometry and computers change the study of Earth and the environment?

2. Making Predictions How will these topographical maps help the world?

UNIT 1 *Introduction to World Cultures and Geography*

SECTION 2
The Geographer's Tools

TERMS & NAMES
cartographer
thematic map
map projection

MAIN IDEA
Geographers use maps, globes, charts, graphs, and new technology to learn about and display the features of Earth.

WHY IT MATTERS NOW
Knowing how to use the tools of geography adds to your ability to understand the world.

DATELINE

BABYLONIA, ABOUT 600 B.C.— Palace officials today released the first map of the world seen in this area. As suspected, Babylon lies at the center of the world. The star-shaped map is drawn on a clay tablet disk about four inches high.

It shows the world surrounded by the Earthly Ocean, which we call the Bitter River. Seven outer regions are also shown as equal triangles rising up out of the oceans. One side of the tablet gives the names of the countries and cities in cuneiform. The other side describes the seven islands. Officials say the map will enable viewers to see the relation of these foreign places to Babylon.

Location • The Babylonian world map was drawn on a clay tablet. ▲

SUNSHINE STATE STANDARDS
Key Standard SS.B.1.3.1
The student uses various map forms (including thematic maps) and other geographic representations, tools, and technologies to acquire, process, and report geographic information including patterns of land use, connections between places, and patterns and processes of migration and diffusion.

FCAT LA.A.2.3.1 Reading: Identify Main Idea, Facts, and Details

Maps and Globes

People have been drawing maps of their world for thousands of years. Geographers today have many tools, such as remote sensing and the Global Positioning System, to help them represent Earth. Increased knowledge and technology allows a **cartographer**, or mapmaker, to construct maps that give a much more detailed and accurate picture of the world. The "Linking Past and Present" and "Technology: 2004" features on pages 42–44 provide more information on modern mapmaking technology.

TAKING NOTES
Use your web to take notes about the five themes.

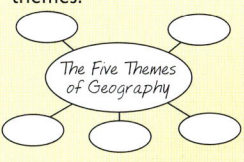

The Five Themes of Geography

The Geographer's World **45**

Location • Draw a picture on the entire surface of an orange and then peel the orange in one continuous piece. After you lay the peel flat, your image will be distorted. ◄

Differences Between Maps and Globes Both maps and globes represent Earth and its features. A globe is an accurate model of the world because it has three dimensions and can show its actual shape. Globes are difficult to carry around, however. Maps are more practical. They can be folded, carried, hung on a wall, or printed in a book or magazine. However, because maps show the world in only two dimensions, they are not perfectly accurate. Look at the pictures above to see why. When the orange peel is flattened out, the picture on the orange is distorted, or twisted out of shape. Cartographers have the same problem with maps.

Reading Social Studies

A. Clarifying Why does a globe represent Earth better than a map?

Three Kinds of Maps General reference maps, which show natural and human-made features, are used to locate a place. **Thematic maps** focus on one specific idea or theme. The population map on page 48 is an example of a thematic map. Pilots and sailors use nautical maps to find their way through air and over water. A nautical map is sometimes called a chart.

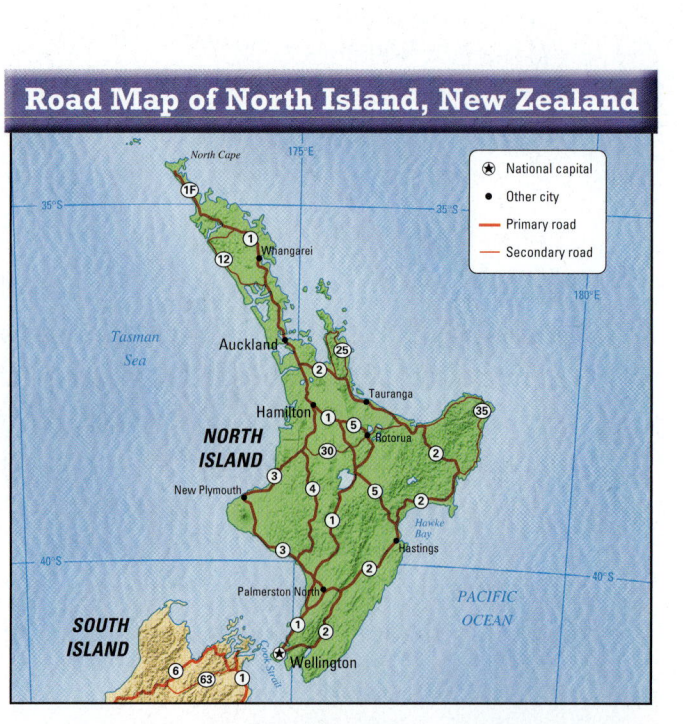

Location • A road map is a reference map that shows how to get from one place to another. ▼

Connections to Math

Measuring Earth In 230 B.C., the Greek scientist Eratosthenes used basic geometry to measure the circumference of Earth. Eratosthenes knew that at noon on June 21, the sun cast no shadow in the Egyptian city of Syene (now Aswan). (See the diagram below.) At the same time, the sun cast a shadow of 7°12′ in Alexandria, about 500 miles from Syene.

The circumference of a circle is 360°; 7°12′ is about 2 percent, or 1/50, of 360°. Therefore, he concluded, 500 miles must be about 2 percent of the distance around Earth, which at the equator would be about 25,000 miles.

7°12′ = 1/50 circumference
N
Syene 512 miles Sun
S

Road Map of North Island, New Zealand

★ National capital
• Other city
— Primary road
— Secondary road

North Cape
Whangarei
Tasman Sea
Auckland
Tauranga
Hamilton
Rotorua
NORTH ISLAND
New Plymouth
Hawke Bay
Hastings
Palmerston North
PACIFIC OCEAN
SOUTH ISLAND
Wellington

46 CHAPTER 2

Mercator Projection

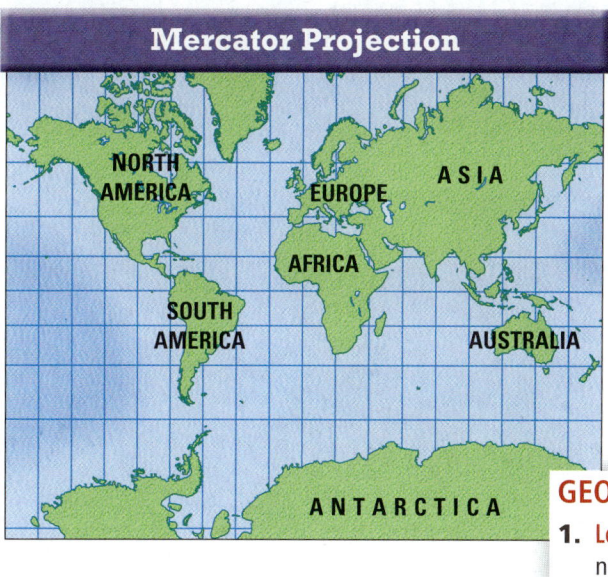

Robinson Projection

GEOGRAPHY SKILLBUILDER: Interpreting a Map
1. **Location** • Compare the size of Africa in relation to other continents on the two projections. How do they differ?
2. **Location** • What other differences do you notice between the Mercator projection and the Robinson projection?

Reading Social Studies

B. Identifying Problems What are the main problems faced by cartographers?

Map Projections The different ways of showing Earth's curved surface on a flat map are called **map projections**. All projections distort Earth, but different projections distort it in different ways. Some make places look bigger or smaller than they really are in relation to other places. Other projections distort shapes. For more than 400 years, the Mercator projection was most often shown on maps of the world. Recently, the Robinson projection has come into common use because it gives a fairer and more accurate picture of the world.

Spotlight on CULTURE

Mercator Map This map of the Arctic was drawn in 1595 by Gerardus Mercator (1512–1594), the famous mapmaker for whom the map projection was named. It is one of many old maps that are rare, beautiful, and important historical artifacts.

THINKING CRITICALLY

1. **Recognizing Important Details** Does Mercator's map show more land or more water?
2. **Identifying Problems** What types of problems might Mercator have faced when he created this map?

For more on Gerardus Mercator, go to

RESEARCH LINKS CLASSZONE.COM

The Geographer's World

World Population and Life Expectancy, 2000

Population

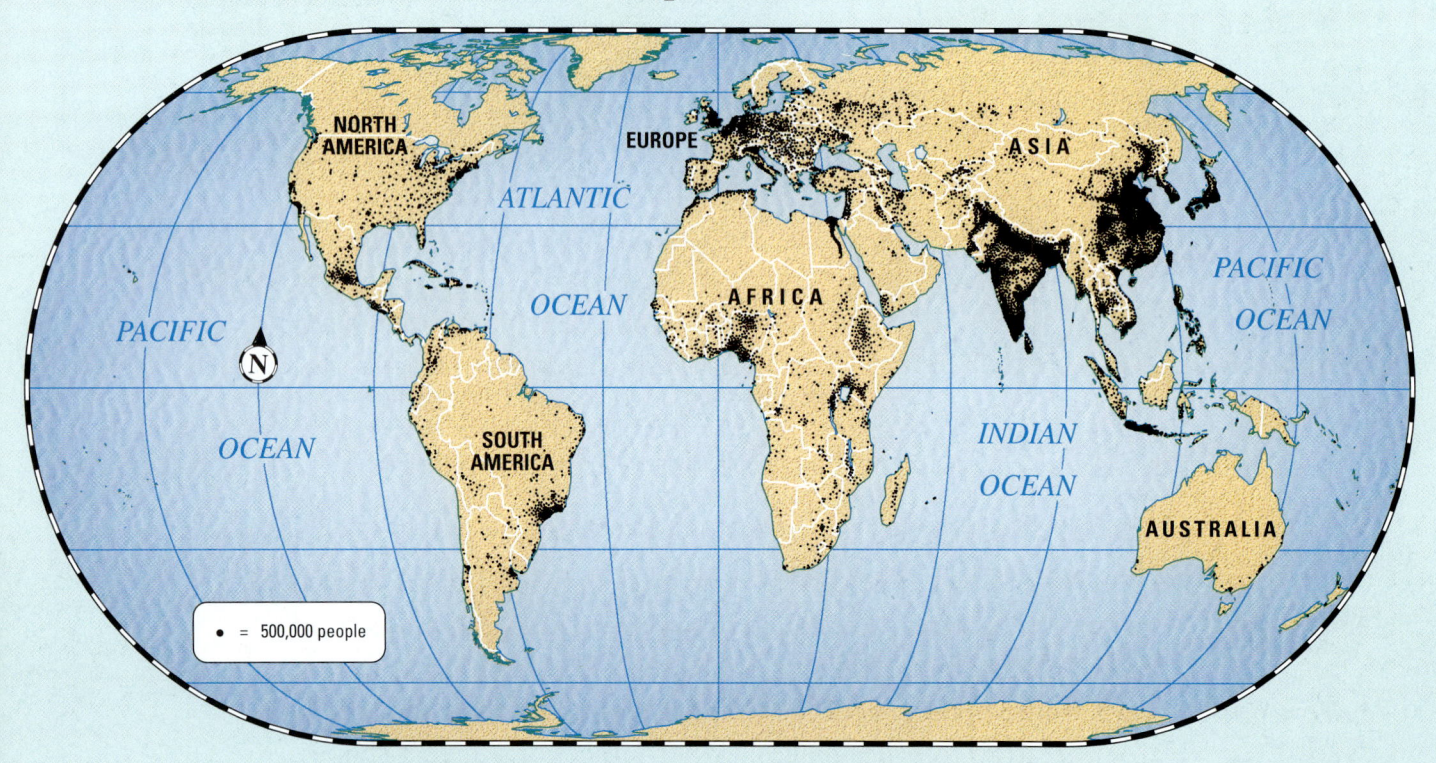

• = 500,000 people

Life Expectancy

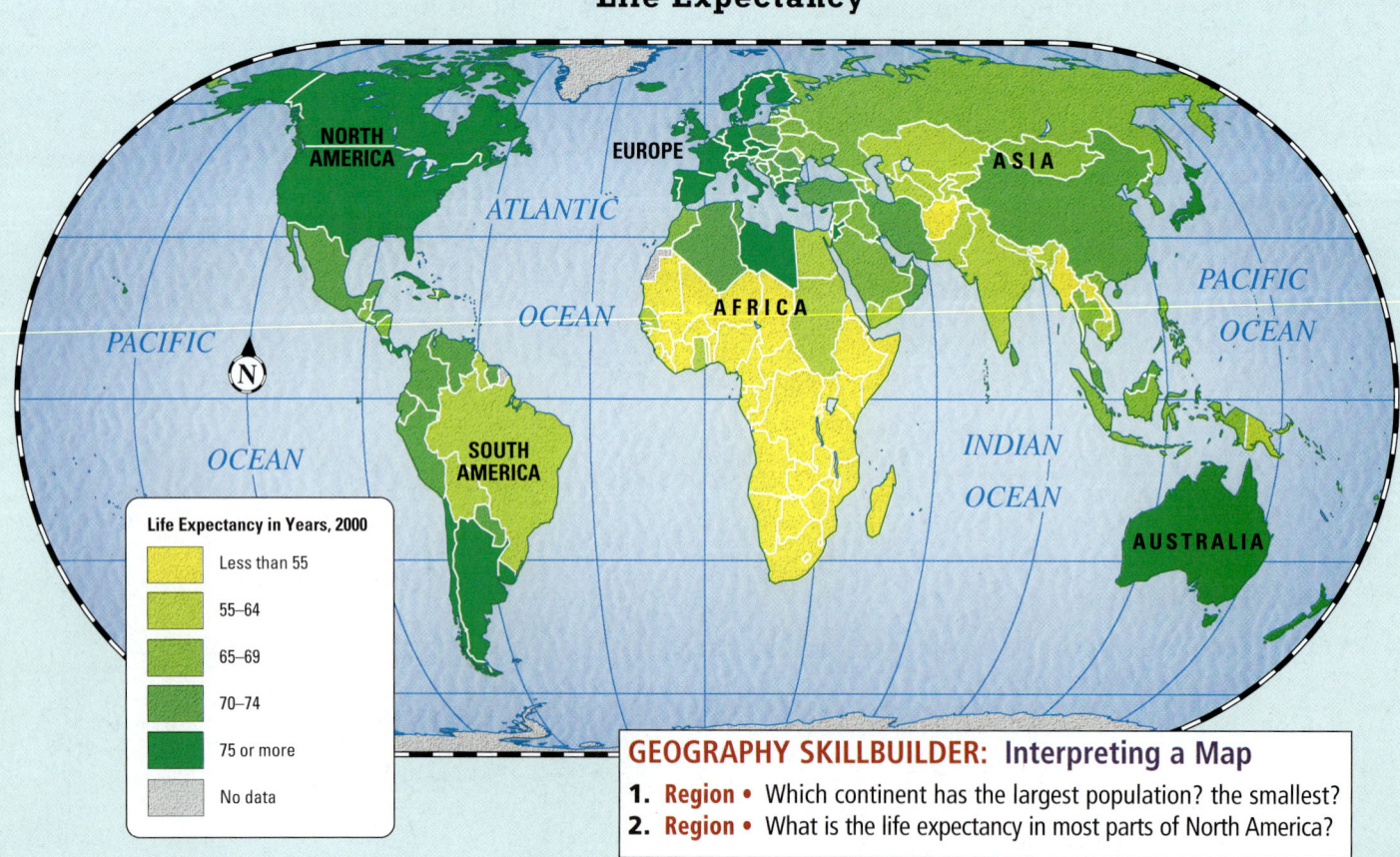

Life Expectancy in Years, 2000
- Less than 55
- 55–64
- 65–69
- 70–74
- 75 or more
- No data

GEOGRAPHY SKILLBUILDER: Interpreting a Map
1. **Region** • Which continent has the largest population? the smallest?
2. **Region** • What is the life expectancy in most parts of North America?

Comparing Maps, Charts, and Graphs

Along with maps, geographers use charts and graphs to display and compare information. The graphs on this page and the maps on page 48 contain related information about the world's population. Notice how each quickly and clearly presents facts that would otherwise take up many paragraphs of text.

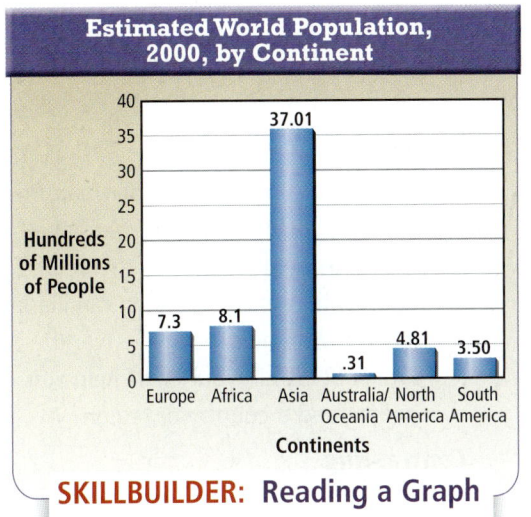

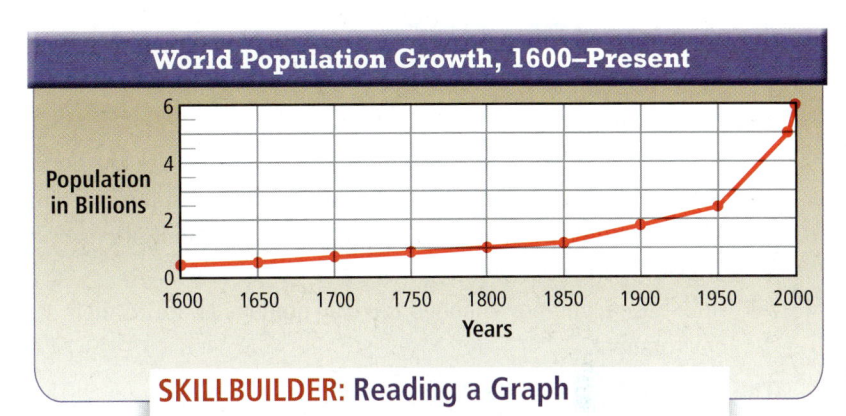

Estimated World Population, 2000, by Continent

(Hundreds of Millions of People)
- Europe: 7.3
- Africa: 8.1
- Asia: 37.01
- Australia/Oceania: .31
- North America: 4.81
- South America: 3.50

SKILLBUILDER: Reading a Graph
1. How many people live in Europe?
2. Which continent has the smallest population?

World Population Growth, 1600–Present

SKILLBUILDER: Reading a Graph
1. How many people lived in the world in 1900?
2. How much did the world's population increase between 1600 and 1900? between 1900 and 2000?

SECTION 2 ASSESSMENT

Terms & Names
1. Explain the significance of: (a) cartographer (b) thematic map (c) map projection

Using Graphics
2. Use a chart like the one below to compare the advantages and disadvantages of maps and globes.

	Maps	Globes
Advantages		
Disadvantages		

Main Ideas
3. (a) What are the differences among the three main kinds of maps?
   (b) How have new tools and knowledge helped cartographers?
   (c) What kinds of information can be displayed in maps and graphs?

Critical Thinking
4. **Using Maps**

   What kind of map would show how many students are in each school in your district?

   Think About
   - the three kinds of maps
   - what information different kinds of population maps show

ACTIVITY -OPTION- Draw a **map** of the route you take to and from school or some other familiar destination. Include the names of streets, landmarks such as shops and other buildings, and any other useful information.

The Geographer's World **49**

CHAPTER 2 ASSESSMENT

TERMS & NAMES

Explain the significance of each of the following:
1. absolute location
2. latitude
3. longitude
4. relative location
5. cartographer
6. thematic map
7. map projection
8. migrate
9. continent

REVIEW QUESTIONS

The Five Themes of Geography *(pages 35–40)*
1. What system do geographers use to determine absolute location?
2. How is relative location different from absolute location?
3. What are some of the natural barriers that made migration difficult in the past?
4. How has technology changed the way humans adapt to their environment?

The Geographer's Tools *(pages 45–49)*
5. Why is a globe an accurate representation of the world?
6. Why would a pilot use a nautical map?
7. How has modern technology helped cartography?
8. Why do most modern cartographers prefer the Robinson projection to the Mercator projection?

CRITICAL THINKING

Drawing Conclusions
1. Using your completed spider map from Reading Social Studies, p. 34, draw a conclusion about which theme of geography is most useful in familiarizing you with an area of the world. Which details in your chart help you understand a country or region?

Contrasting
2. Maps and globes both represent Earth and its features. Contrast the advantages of a map with the advantages of a globe.

Clarifying
3. Why would the leaders of a country find a population density map of their country useful?

Visual Summary

The Five Themes of Geography
- The five themes of geography are location, place, region, movement, and human-environment interaction.
- These themes are the keys to understanding the geography of the world.

The Geographer's Tools
- Maps, globes, charts, graphs, and other tools are available to geographers to help them understand the features of Earth.
- Geographers use these tools to organize and explain Earth's features.

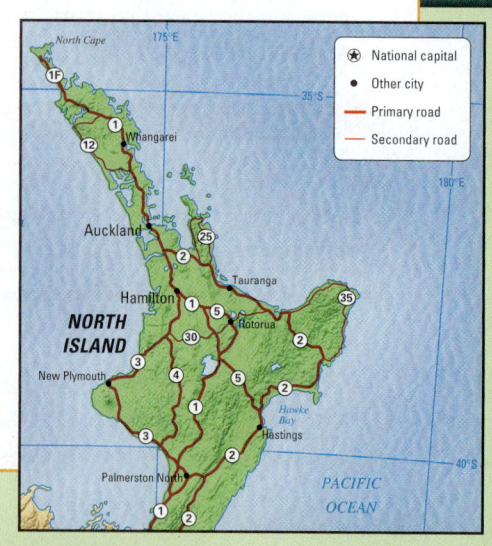

STANDARDS-BASED ASSESSMENT

Use the map and your knowledge of world cultures and geography to answer questions 1 and 2.

Additional Test Practice, pp. S1–S33

In this quotation from a press release, a UNESCO spokesperson describes the archaeological site Mapungubwe. It was the center of the largest kingdom to exist in Africa south of the Sahara before the 14th century. Use the quotation and your knowledge of world cultures and geography to answer question 3.

PRIMARY SOURCE

What survives are the almost untouched remains of the palace sites and also the entire settlement area dependent upon them, as well as two earlier capital sites, the whole presenting an unrivalled picture of the development of social and political structures over some 400 years.

JASMINI SOPOVA, UNESCO spokesperson, *allAfrica.com*

1. The mainland of Australia lies between which lines of latitude?

- **A.** 110°E and 160°E
- **B.** 10°N and 40°S
- **C.** 10°S and 40°S
- **D.** 20°S and 30°S

2. What city is located near 150°E and 35°S?

- **A.** Alice Springs
- **B.** Darwin
- **C.** Perth
- **D.** Sydney

3. Why is it so important that the archaeological remains are untouched?

- **A.** They will be clean, not damaged by dirt and mud.
- **B.** They will accurately show how people once lived.
- **C.** They will make the person who found them famous.
- **D.** They can be rearranged however the archaeologists want.

TEST PRACTICE CLASSZONE.COM

ALTERNATIVE ASSESSMENT

1. WRITING ABOUT HISTORY

The world can be divided into ten natural regions. Find out what these ten regions are. Then choose one region and write a poem about it. In the poem, provide information about where the region is located, what plant life it has, what animal life it has, and what the climate is like in that particular region. Share your poem with the class.

2. COOPERATIVE LEARNING

With a small group of classmates, choose any country in the world and use the five themes of geography to describe it. Divide the tasks of answering these questions: Where is the country located? (location) What are its physical and human characteristics? (place) How can you classify the region? (region) What movement has occurred in the country? (movement) How have the people who live there adapted to the environment? (human-environment interaction) Arrange your findings on a poster board.

INTEGRATED TECHNOLOGY

Doing Internet Research

Use the Internet to research how to technology can be used to study natural events. Write a report of your findings, including a list of the Web sites you used.

- Focus on one natural event, such as tropical rainfall or a hurricane. Look into how technology is helping us understand it.
- Include a prediction about the future uses of technology that involve these kinds of events.

For Internet links to support this activity, go to

RESEARCH LINKS CLASSZONE.COM

The Geographer's World 51

UNIT 2

Place Completed in A.D. 80, the Colosseum in Rome, Italy, held 50,000 spectators. There they watched battles between gladiators, among other contests. The Colosseum is the largest structure that survives from the Roman Empire.

EUROPE, RUSSIA, AND THE INDEPENDENT REPUBLICS

Chapter 3 Western Europe: Its Land and Early History

Chapter 4 The Growth of New Ideas

Chapter 5 Europe: War and Change

Chapter 6 Modern Europe

Chapter 7 Europe Today

THE COLOSSEUM

PACIFIC OCEAN

PACIFIC OCEAN

ATLANTIC OCEAN

EUROPE, RUSSIA, AND THE INDEPENDENT REPUBLICS

INTEGRATED TECHNOLOGY

eEdition
- Interactive Maps
- Interactive Visuals

VIDEO
France: Raphaël in Brittany

INTERNET RESOURCES
Go to **classzone.com** for:
- Research Links
- Internet Activities
- Data Updates
- Unit Quiz
- Maps
- Test Practice
- Current Events
- Web Research Guide

Unit Atlas 2: Physical Geography

Climates of Europe, Russia, and the Independent Republics

Legend:
- Desert
- Semiarid
- Mediterranean
- Marine west coast
- Humid subtropical
- Humid continental
- Subarctic
- Tundra
- Highland

SUNSHINE STATE STANDARDS

Key Standard
SS.B.1.3.1
The student uses various map forms (including thematic maps) and other geographic representations, tools, and technologies to acquire, process, and report geographic information including patterns of land use, connections between places, and patterns and processes of migration and diffusion.

Other Standards
SS.B.1.3.3

FCAT LA.A.2.3.1
Reading: Identify Main Idea, Facts, and Details

Europe, Russia, and the Independent Republics

Europe, Russia, and the Independent Republics: Physical

Fast Facts

✓ **LONG COASTLINE:**
The coastline of Europe alone is 24,000 miles long. Earth measures 24,902 miles around at the Equator.

✓ **BELOW SEA LEVEL:**
Almost a third of the Netherlands and a large portion of the land by the Caspian Sea are below sea level.

✓ **HIGHEST MOUNTAIN:**
Mt. Elbrus in Russia, 18,510 ft.

✓ **DEEPEST LAKE:**
Lake Baikal, 5,714 ft. deep

✓ **LARGEST INLAND SEA:**
Caspian Sea, 149,200 sq. mi.

✓ **LONGEST RIVER:**
Volga River, 2,193 mi.

Elevation
- 13,100 ft. (4,000 m)
- 6,600 ft. (2,000 m)
- 3,275 ft. (1,000 m)
- 650 ft. (200 m)
- 0 ft. (0 m)
- Below sea level
- ▲ Mountain peak

GEOGRAPHY SKILLBUILDER: Interpreting Maps and Visuals

1. **Location** • Which countries have mountains at their borders?
2. **Place** • About how many times larger is the population of Europe, Russia, and the Independent Republics than that of the United States?

Europe, Russia, and the Independent Republics— United States Landmass and Population

LANDMASS
Europe, Russia, and the Independent Republics
10,489,029 square miles

Continental United States
3,165,630 square miles

POPULATION
Europe, Russia, and the Independent Republics
654,628,000

United States
281,421,906

= 50,000,000

Atlas 55

UNIT Atlas 2: Human Geography

Population Density of Europe, Russia, and the Independent Republics

Persons per sq. mi.	Persons per sq. km
Over 520	Over 200
260–520	100–200
130–259	50–99
25–129	10–49
1–24	1–9
0	0

Europe, Russia, and the Independent Republics

Europe, Russia, and the Independent Republics: Political

FAST FACTS

✓ **SMALLEST COUNTRY IN THE WORLD:** Vatican City, less than 0.2 sq. mi.

✓ **LARGEST COUNTRY IN THE WORLD:** Russia, 6,592,800 sq. mi.

✓ **LONGEST ROAD TUNNEL:** Oslo, Norway, 15.3 mi. long

✓ **OLDEST PAINTINGS:** Cave paintings near Verona, Italy, at 32,000 to 37,000 years of age

GEOGRAPHY SKILLBUILDER: Interpreting Maps and Visuals
1. **Location** • Name two countries that do not have seaports.
2. **Movement** • What route would you take to drive from Paris to Bern?

Road Map of Selected European Countries

Atlas 57

Unit 2 Atlas — Data File

For updates on these statistics, go to DATA UPDATE CLASSZONE.COM

Country Flag	Country/Capital	Currency	Population (2001 estimate)	Life Expectancy (years)	Birthrate (per 1,000 pop.) (2000)
	Albania / Tiranë	Lek	3,510,000	71	19
	Andorra / Andorra la Vella	French Franc	68,000	83	11
	Armenia / Yerevan	Dram	3,336,000	75	10
	Austria / Vienna	Euro*	8,151,000	78	10
	Azerbaijan / Baku	Manat	7,771,000	70	15
	Belarus / Minsk	Ruble	10,350,000	68	9
	Belgium / Brussels	Euro*	10,259,000	78	11
	Bosnia-Herzegovina / Sarajevo	Conv. Mark	3,922,000	73	13
	Bulgaria / Sofia	Lev	7,707,000	71	8
	Croatia / Zagreb	Kuna	4,334,000	73	11
	Czech Republic / Prague	Koruna	10,264,000	75	9
	Denmark / Copenhagen	Danish Krone	5,353,000	77	12
	Estonia / Tallinn	Kroon	1,423,000	70	8
	Finland / Helsinki	Euro*	5,176,000	78	11
	France / Paris	Euro*	59,551,000	79	13
	Georgia / Tbilisi	Lavi	4,989,000	73	9
	Germany / Berlin	Euro*	83,029,000	77	9

*On January 1, 2002, the euro became the common currency for 12 of the member nations of the European Union.

Europe, Russia, and the Independent Republics

DATA FILE

Infant Mortality (per 1,000 live births) (2000)	Doctors (per 100,000 pop.) (1990–1998)	Literacy Rate (percentage) (1991–1998)	Passenger Cars (per 1,000 pop.) (1996–1997)	Total Area (square miles)	Map (not to scale)
41.3	129	83	10 (1990)	11,100	
6.4	253	100	552	174	
41.0	316	98	2	11,506	
4.9	302	100	468	32,378	
83.0	360	99	36	33,436	
15.0	443	100	111	80,154	
5.6	395	99	434	11,787	
25.2	143	86	23	19,741	
14.9	345	98	202	42,822	
8.2	229	98	160	21,830	
4.6	303	99	428	30,448	
4.7	290	100	339	16,637	
13.0	297	99	294	17,413	
4.2	299	100	378	130,560	
4.8	303	99	437	212,934	
53.0	436	99	80	26,911	
4.7	350	100	504	137,830	

Atlas 59

Unit 2 Atlas Data File

For updates on these statistics, go to **DATA UPDATE** *CLASSZONE.COM*

Country Flag	Country/Capital	Currency	Population (2001 estimate)	Life Expectancy (years)	Birthrate (per 1,000 pop.) (2000)
	Greece / Athens	Euro*	10,624,000	78	10
	Hungary / Budapest	Forint	10,106,000	71	9
	Iceland / Reykjavik	Krona	278,000	80	15
	Ireland / Dublin	Euro*	3,841,000	76	15
	Italy / Rome	Euro*	57,680,000	78	9
	Kazakhstan / Astana	Tenge	16,731,000	65	14
	Kyrgyzstan / Bishkek	Som	4,753,000	67	22
	Latvia / Riga	Lat	2,385,000	70	8
	Liechtenstein / Vaduz	Swiss Franc	33,000	73	14
	Lithuania / Vilnius	Litas	3,611,000	72	10
	Luxembourg / Luxembourg	Euro*	443,000	77	13
	Macedonia / Skopje	Denar	2,046,000	73	15
	Malta / Valletta	Lira	395,000	77	12
	Moldova / Chisinau	Leu	4,432,000	67	11
	Monaco / Monaco	French Franc	32,000	79	20
	Netherlands / Amsterdam	Euro*	15,981,000	78	13
	Norway / Oslo	Krone	4,503,000	79	13
	Poland / Warsaw	Zloty	38,634,000	74	10

*On January 1, 2002, the euro became the common currency for 12 of the member nations of the European Union.

Europe, Russia, and the Independent Republics

DATA FILE

Infant Mortality (per 1,000 live births) (2000)	Doctors (per 100,000 pop.) (1990–1998)	Literacy Rate (percentage) (1991–1998)	Passenger Cars (per 1,000 pop.) (1996–1997)	Total Area (square miles)	Map (not to scale)
6.7	392	97	223	50,950	
8.9	357	99	222	35,919	
4.0	326	100	489	39,768	
6.2	219	100	292	27,135	
5.5	554	98	540	116,320	
59.0	353	99	61	1,048,300	
77.0	301	97	32	76,641	
16.0	282	100	174	24,595	
5.1	100	100	592 (1993)	62	
15.0	395	100	242	25,174	
5.0	272	100	515	999	
16.3	204	89	132	9,927	
5.3	261	91	321	124	
43.0	400 (1995)	99	46	13,012	
5.9	664	100	548	0.6	
5.0	251	100	372	16,033	
4.0	413	100	399	125,050	
8.9	236	99	195	124,807	

Atlas

Unit 2 Atlas Data File

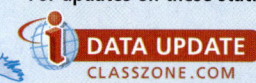

Country Flag	Country/Capital	Currency	Population (2001 estimate)	Life Expectancy (years)	Birthrate (per 1,000 pop.) (2000)
	Portugal Lisbon	Euro*	10,066,000	76	11
	Romania Bucharest	Leu	22,364,000	70	11
	Russia Moscow	Ruble	145,470,000	67	8
	San Marino San Marino	Italian Lira	27,000	80	11
	Slovakia Bratislava	Koruna	5,415,000	73	11
	Slovenia Ljubljana	Tolar	1,930,000	75	9
	Spain Madrid	Euro*	40,038,000	78	9
	Sweden Stockholm	Krona	8,875,000	80	10
	Switzerland Bern	Franc	7,283,000	80	11
	Tajikistan Dushanbe	Ruble	6,579,000	68	21
	Turkmenistan Ashgabat	Manat	4,603,000	66	21
	Ukraine Kiev	Hryvnya	48,760,000	68	8
	United Kingdom London	Pound	59,648,000	77	12
	Uzbekistan Tashkent	Som	25,155,000	69	23
	Vatican City Vatican City	Vatican Lira/Italian Lira	870 (2000)	N/A	N/A
	Yugoslavia Belgrade	New Dinar	10,677,000	73	11
	United States Washington, D.C.	Dollar	281,422,000	77	15

*On January 1, 2002, the euro became the common currency for 12 of the member nations of the European Union.

Europe, Russia, and the Independent Republics

DATA FILE

Infant Mortality (per 1,000 live births) (2000)	Doctors (per 100,000 pop.) (1990–1998)	Literacy Rate (percentage) (1991–1998)	Passenger Cars (per 1,000 pop.) (1996–1997)	Total Area (square miles)	Map (not to scale)
6.0	312	91	295	35,514	
20.5	184	98	106	92,042	
20.0	421	100	120	6,592,812	
8.8	252	99	955	23	
8.8	353	100	185	18,923	
5.2	228	99	343	7,819	
5.7	424	97	384	195,363	
3.5	311	100	417	173,730	
4.8	323	100	460	15,942	
117.0	201	99	31	55,251	
73.0	300 (1997)	98	N/A	188,455	
22.0	299	100	97	233,089	
5.7	164	100	434	94,548	
72.0	309	88	37	173,591	
N/A	N/A	100	N/A	0.17	
10.4	203	98	173	39,448	
7.0	251	97	489	3,787,319	

GEOGRAPHY SKILLBUILDER: Interpreting a Chart
1. **Place** • Which country in the region has the highest life expectancy?
2. **Place** • How many fewer cars per thousand people does Greece have than Germany?

Atlas 63

CHAPTER 3

Western Europe: Its Land and Early History

Section 1 A Land of Varied Riches
Section 2 Ancient Greece
Section 3 Ancient Rome
Section 4 Time of Change: The Middle Ages

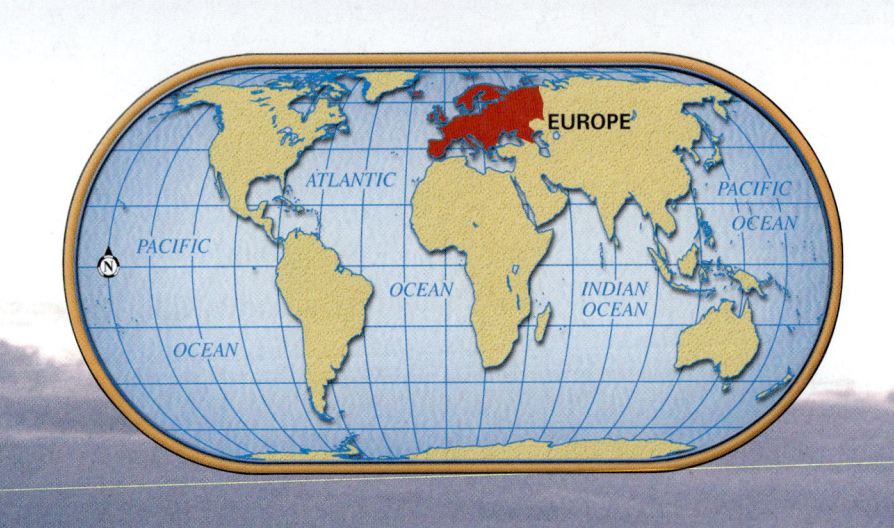

Region Many European cities show their history in their architecture. In Segovia, Spain, an ancient Roman aqueduct lies below the walls of a castle built in the Middle Ages.

FOCUS ON GEOGRAPHY

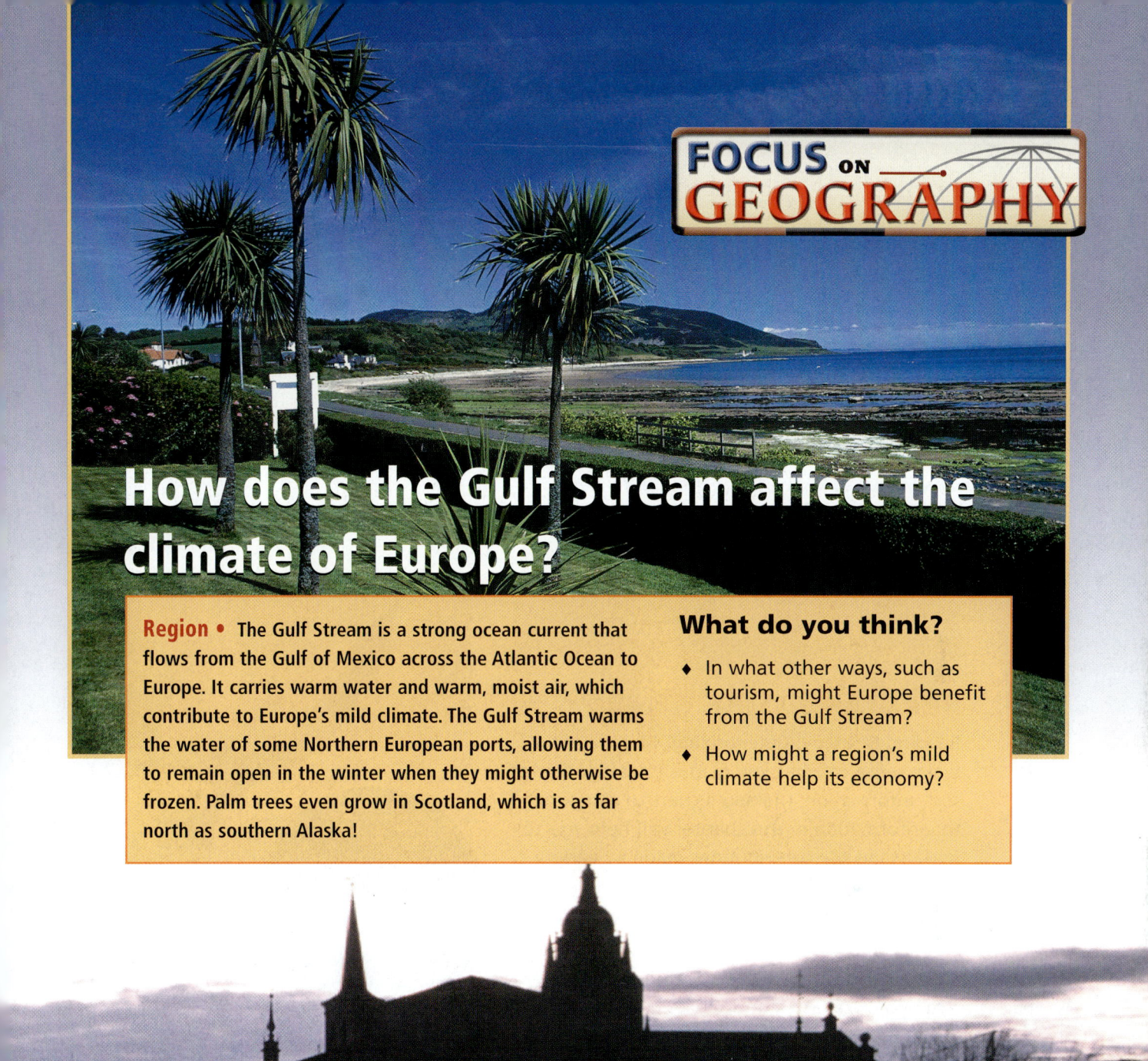

How does the Gulf Stream affect the climate of Europe?

Region • The Gulf Stream is a strong ocean current that flows from the Gulf of Mexico across the Atlantic Ocean to Europe. It carries warm water and warm, moist air, which contribute to Europe's mild climate. The Gulf Stream warms the water of some Northern European ports, allowing them to remain open in the winter when they might otherwise be frozen. Palm trees even grow in Scotland, which is as far north as southern Alaska!

What do you think?

- In what other ways, such as tourism, might Europe benefit from the Gulf Stream?
- How might a region's mild climate help its economy?

CHAPTER 3

READING SOCIAL STUDIES

BEFORE YOU READ

▶▶ *What Do You Know?*

Before you read the chapter, think about what you already know about Europe. What are some of its geographical features? What do you know about its early history? Have you ever read myths from ancient Greece or ancient Rome? Have you ever heard of Julius Caesar or Hercules? What do you know about knights and castles from the Middle Ages?

▶▶ *What Do You Want to Know?*

Decide what you want to know about these early periods of European history. Record your questions in your notebook before you read this chapter.

Region • Ancient Greece made important contributions in literature, philosophy, and architecture. ▼

READ AND TAKE NOTES

Reading Strategy: Categorizing One way to make sense of what you read is to categorize, or sort, information. Making a chart to categorize the information in this chapter will help you to understand the contributions made by early European cultures.

- Copy the chart below into your notebook.
- As you read, look for information relating to the categories of social structure, architecture, religion, and arts and sciences.
- Write your notes under the appropriate headings.

Region • The Middle Ages saw the rise of the Catholic Church and the growth of a middle class. ▲

Region • Ancient Rome made its mark in government, law, and engineering. ▲

Time Period	Social Structure	Architecture	Religion	Arts and Sciences
Ancient Greece				
Ancient Rome				
Middle Ages				

66 CHAPTER 3

SECTION 1

A Land of Varied Riches

TERMS & NAMES
Mediterranean Sea
peninsula
fjord
Ural Mountains
plain

MAIN IDEA
Europe is a continent with varied geographic features, abundant natural resources, and a climate that can support agriculture.

WHY IT MATTERS NOW
The development of Europe's diverse cultures has been shaped by the continent's diverse geography.

DATELINE *EXTRA*

LONDON, ENGLAND, MAY 6, 1994

Rough waters have always made the English Channel, which separates England and France, difficult to cross. Now, however, you can travel under the water! Today, a tunnel nicknamed "the Chunnel" opens, allowing high-speed trains to travel between London and Paris in about three hours. The Chunnel—short for Channel Tunnel—was carved through chalky earth under the sea floor and took seven years to build. It is the largest European construction project of the 20th century.

Movement • Eurostar trains make the 31-mile trip under the English Channel in only 20 minutes. ▲

ation • The Channel nel connects England France. ▲

The Geography of Europe

Today, cars, airplanes, and trains are common forms of high-speed transportation across Europe. Before the 19th century, however, the fastest form of transportation was to travel by water—on top of it, rather than under it.

TAKING NOTES
Use your chart to take notes about Western Europe.

Time Period	Social Structure	Architecture
Ancient Greece		
Ancient Rome		

SUNSHINE STATE STANDARDS
Key Standard SS.B.2.3.2 The student knows the human and physical characteristics of different places in the world and how these characteristics change over time.
Other Standards SS.B.2.3.8
FCAT LA.A.2.3.1 Reading: Identify Main Idea, Facts, and Details

Western Europe: Its Land and Early History

Waterways Look at the map of Europe on page 71. Water surrounds the continent to the north, south, and west. The southern coast of Europe borders the warm waters of the **Mediterranean Sea**. Europe also has many rivers. The highly traveled Rhine and Danube rivers are two of the most important. The Volga, which flows nearly 2,200 miles through western Russia, is the continent's longest. For hundreds of years, these and other waterways have been home to boats and barges carrying people and goods inland across great distances.

Landforms Several large **peninsulas,** or bodies of land surrounded by water on three sides, form the European continent. In Northern Europe, the Scandinavian Peninsula is home to Norway and Sweden. Along the jagged shoreline of this peninsula are beautiful fjords (fyawrdz). A **fjord** is a long, narrow, deep inlet of the sea located between steep cliffs. In Western Europe, the Iberian Peninsula includes Portugal and Spain. The Iberian Peninsula is separated from the rest of the continent by a mountain range called the Pyrenees (PEER·uh·NEEZ). The entire continent of Europe, itself surrounded by water on three sides, is a giant peninsula.

Reading Social Studies
A. Clarifying Why were waterways important for the movement of people and goods?

BACKGROUND
Europe can be divided into four areas: Western Europe, Northern Europe, Eastern Europe, and Russia and its neighboring countries.

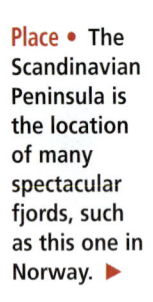

Place • The Scandinavian Peninsula is the location of many spectacular fjords, such as this one in Norway. ▶

Place • The Alps remain snowcapped year-round. ▶

Reading Social Studies

B. Clarifying What natural landform separates Europe from Asia?

Mountain ranges, including the towering Alps, also stretch across much of the continent. Along Europe's eastern border, the **Ural Mountains** (YUR•uhl) divide the continent from Asia. The many mountain ranges of Europe separated groups of people from one another as they settled the land thousands of years ago. This is one of the reasons why different cultures developed across the continent.

The Great European Plain Not all of Europe is mountainous. A vast region called the Great European Plain stretches from the coast of France to the Ural Mountains. A **plain** is a large, flat area of land, usually without many trees. The Great European Plain is the location of some of the world's richest farmland. Ancient trading centers attracted many people to this area, which today includes some of the largest cities in Europe—Paris, Berlin, Warsaw, and Moscow.

Vocabulary

Gulf Stream: a warm ocean current that flows northeast from the Gulf of Mexico through the Atlantic Ocean.

Climate

Although the Gulf Stream brings warm air and water to Europe, the winters are still severe in the mountains and in the far north. In some of these areas, cold winds blow southward from the Arctic Circle and make the average temperature fall below 0°F in January. The Alps and the Pyrenees, however, protect the European countries along the Mediterranean Sea from these chilling winds. In these warmer parts of southern Europe, the average temperature in January stays above 50°F.

Western Europe: Its Land and Early History **69**

The summers in the south are usually hot and dry, with an average July temperature around 80°F. This makes the Mediterranean coast a popular vacation spot. Elsewhere in Europe, in all but the coldest areas of the mountains and the far north, the average July temperature ranges from 50°F to 70°F.

Natural Resources

Europe has a large variety of natural resources, including minerals. The rich coal deposits of Germany's Ruhr (rur) Valley region have helped to make that area one of the world's major industrial centers. Russia and Ukraine have large deposits of iron ore, which is used to make iron for automobiles and countless other products.

Region • Western Europe benefits from a varied landscape rich in natural resources. ▼

Land Use in Europe Today

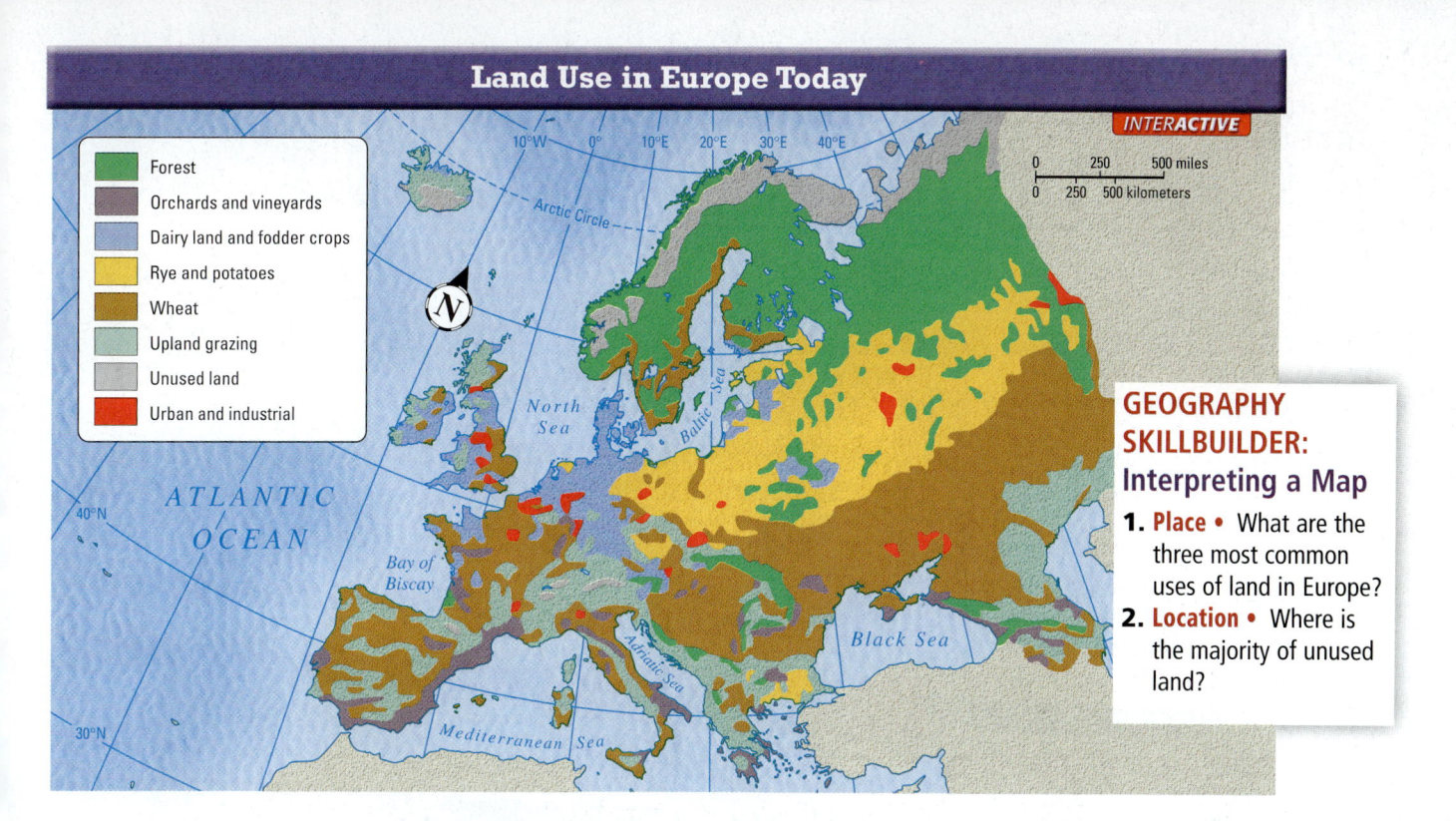

Legend:
- Forest
- Orchards and vineyards
- Dairy land and fodder crops
- Rye and potatoes
- Wheat
- Upland grazing
- Unused land
- Urban and industrial

GEOGRAPHY SKILLBUILDER: Interpreting a Map

1. **Place** • What are the three most common uses of land in Europe?
2. **Location** • Where is the majority of unused land?

Vocabulary

precipitation: moisture, including rain, snow, and hail, that falls to the ground

Europe also has rich soil and plentiful rainfall. The average precipitation for the Great European Plain, for example, is between 20 and 40 inches per year. The map above shows the agricultural uses of the land, highlighting the major crops. Notice that few parts of the continent are too cold or too hot and dry to support some form of agriculture. These characteristics have made Europe a world leader in crop production.

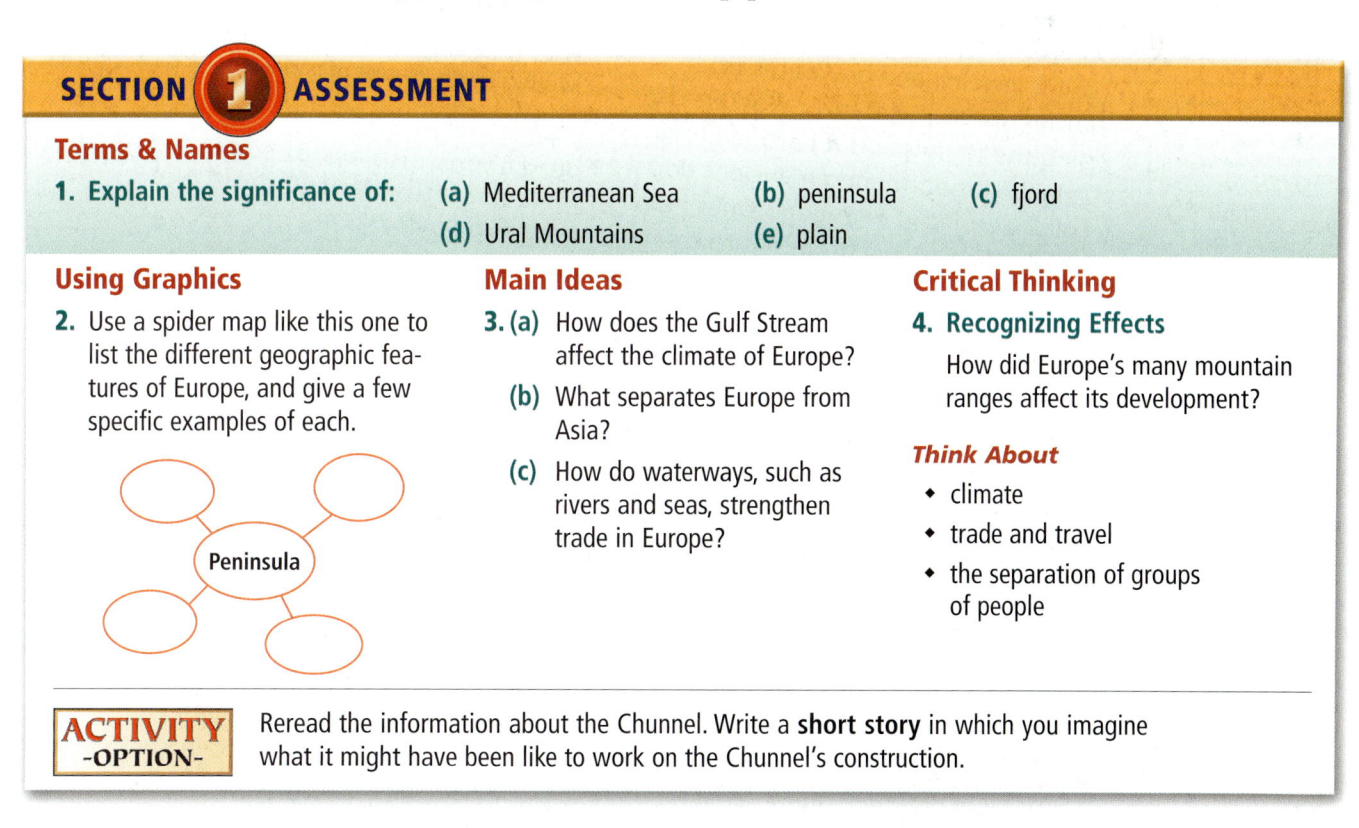

SECTION 1 ASSESSMENT

Terms & Names
1. Explain the significance of:
   - (a) Mediterranean Sea
   - (b) peninsula
   - (c) fjord
   - (d) Ural Mountains
   - (e) plain

Using Graphics
2. Use a spider map like this one to list the different geographic features of Europe, and give a few specific examples of each.

(Peninsula spider map)

Main Ideas
3. (a) How does the Gulf Stream affect the climate of Europe?
   (b) What separates Europe from Asia?
   (c) How do waterways, such as rivers and seas, strengthen trade in Europe?

Critical Thinking
4. **Recognizing Effects**
   How did Europe's many mountain ranges affect its development?

   Think About
   - climate
   - trade and travel
   - the separation of groups of people

ACTIVITY -OPTION- Reread the information about the Chunnel. Write a **short story** in which you imagine what it might have been like to work on the Chunnel's construction.

Western Europe: Its Land and Early History

SECTION 2

Ancient Greece

TERMS & NAMES
city-state
polis
Aegean Sea
oligarchy
Athens
philosopher
Aristotle
Alexander the Great

MAIN IDEA
The ancient Greeks developed a complex society, with remarkable achievements in the arts, sciences, and government.

WHY IT MATTERS NOW
The achievements of the ancient Greeks continue to influence culture, science, and politics in the world today.

DATELINE

ATHENS, GREECE, FEBRUARY 2, 1997—Five years after construction workers began building the new Athens subway, artifacts from ancient Greek civilization are still being discovered. When completed, the new subway will reduce traffic and air pollution in the capital. Historians and archaeologists, however, have been the first to benefit from this massive public works project.

Workers have discovered statues, coins, jewelry, and gravesites from ancient Greece. Recently, workers digging the foundation for a downtown Athens station found an ancient dog collar decorated with gemstones. Local officials have promised to create permanent displays of some artifacts in stations throughout the new subway system.

Place • Building the subway in Athens led to spectacular discoveries of ancient artifacts. ▲

The Land and Early History of Greece

The Greek Peninsula is mountainous, which made travel by land difficult for early settlers. Most of the rocky land also contains poor soil and few large trees, but settlers were able to cultivate the soil to grow olives and grapes. The greatest natural resource of the peninsula is the water that surrounds it. The ancient Greeks depended on these seas for fishing and trade, and they became excellent sailors.

TAKING NOTES
Use your chart to take notes about Western Europe.

Time Period	Social Structure	Architecture
Ancient Greece		
Ancient Rome		

SUNSHINE STATE STANDARDS
Key Standard SS.A.2.3.1 The student understands how language, ideas, and institutions of one culture can influence other cultures (e.g., through trade, exploration, and immigration).
Other Standards SS.A.2.3.4
FCAT LA.A.2.3.1 Reading: Identify Main Idea, Facts, and Details

The Formation of City-States As the ancient Greek population grew, people created city-states. A **city-state** included a central city, called a **polis**, and surrounding villages. Each ancient Greek city-state had its own laws and form of government. The city-states were united by a common language, shared religious beliefs, and a similar way of life.

The Growth of Colonies By the mid-eighth century B.C., the Greeks were leaving the peninsula in search of better land and greater opportunities for trade. During the next 200 years, they built dozens of communities on the islands and coastline of the **Aegean Sea** (ih·JEE·uhn). Some Greeks settled as far away as modern-day Spain and North Africa.

Once established, these distant Greek communities traded with each other and with those communities on the Greek Peninsula. This made a great variety of goods available to the ancient Greeks, including wheat for bread, timber for building boats, and iron ore for making strong tools and weapons.

Connections to Language

Metropolis When ancient Greeks moved away from a large polis to a distant community, they referred to their former city-state as their metropolis. In Greek, this means "mother-city." Today, we use the word *metropolis* to mean any large urban area, such as Los Angeles, London, Tokyo, or Athens (shown below).

Greek Colonization, 800 B.C.

GEOGRAPHY SKILLBUILDER: Interpreting a Map

1. **Place** • What was the value to the Greeks of controlling Byzantium?
2. **Location** • What was the southernmost Greek territory at this time?

Western Europe: Its Land and Early History

Strange but TRUE

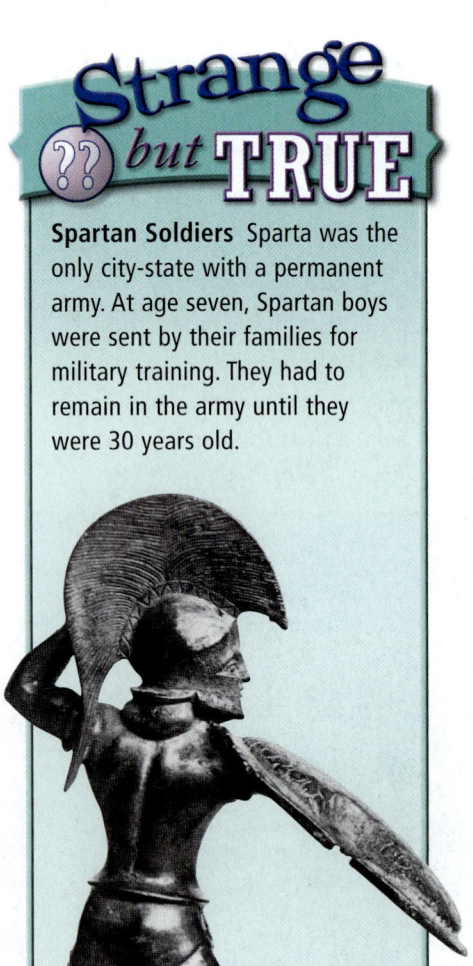

Spartan Soldiers Sparta was the only city-state with a permanent army. At age seven, Spartan boys were sent by their families for military training. They had to remain in the army until they were 30 years old.

Individual Forms of Government Some ancient Greek city-states were oligarchies (AHL·ih·GAHR·kees). An <u>oligarchy</u> is a system in which a few powerful, wealthy individuals rule. The word *oligarchy* comes from an ancient Greek word meaning "rule by the few." Other city-states were ruled by a tyrant, a single person who took control of the government against the wishes of the community. Still other ancient Greek city-states developed an early form of democracy. The word *democracy* comes from an ancient Greek word meaning "rule by the people." In a democracy, citizens take part in the government.

Reading Social Studies

A. Comparing Compare the three forms of government most common in ancient Greek city-states.

Athens and Sparta

<u>Athens,</u> centrally located on the Greek Peninsula, was one of the largest and most important ancient Greek city-states. By the end of the sixth century B.C., Athens had developed a democratic form of government. Athenian citizens took part in political debates and voted on laws, but not everyone who lived in Athens enjoyed these rights. Participation in government was limited to free, adult males whose fathers had been citizens of Athens. Women, slaves, and foreign residents could not take part in government.

Athens's chief rival among the other Greek city-states was Sparta. Located in the southernmost part of the Greek Peninsula, Sparta was an oligarchy. It was ruled by two kings, who were supported by other officials. Sparta, like Athens, had a powerful army. Each city-state's army helped protect it from slave rebellions, guard against attack by rival city-states, and defend it from possible foreign invaders.

Learning and the Arts

In 480 B.C., the Persians, who controlled a large empire to the east, tried to conquer the Greek Peninsula. Several Greek city-states, including Athens and Sparta, joined forces to defeat the Persians. In the years following this victory, the ancient Greeks made remarkable achievements in literature, learning, and architecture.

BACKGROUND

After the defeat of Persia, Athens became the most powerful Greek city-state. The most important Athenian leader of the time was Pericles (PEHR·ih·KLEEZ), who lived from c. 495 to 429 B.C.

Literature To honor their gods and goddesses, the ancient Greeks created myths and wrote poems and plays. Some of the greatest Greek plays were written during the fifth century B.C. During that time, the playwrights Aeschylus (EHS·kuh·luhs), Sophocles (SAHF·uh·KLEEZ), and Euripides (yu·RIHP·ih·DEEZ) wrote tragedies, which are serious plays that end unhappily. Many of these stories have been the basis for modern films and operas.

In addition to using the gods as characters, ancient Greek playwrights sometimes poked fun at important citizens, including generals and politicians. Aristophanes (ar·ih·STAHF·uh·NEEZ) was a popular writer of comedies of this type.

Philosophy Ancient Greece was the birthplace of some of the finest thinkers of the ancient world. Socrates (SAHK·ruh·TEEZ) was an important philosopher of the fifth century B.C. A **philosopher** studies and thinks about why the world is the way it is. Socrates studied and taught about friendship, knowledge, and justice. Another great philosopher, Plato (PLAY·toh), was a student of Socrates who studied and taught about human behavior, government, mathematics, and astronomy.

The ancient Greek philosopher Heraclitus (HEHR·uh·KLY·tuhs) wrote the following lines.

Reading Social Studies
B. Making Inferences Why do you think philosophers felt the need to teach?

> **A VOICE FROM ANCIENT GREECE**
>
> One cannot step twice into the same river, for the water into which you first stepped has flowed on.
>
> — Heraclitus

Many people continue to study and write about the same philosophical questions that these, and other, ancient Greek philosophers explored.

The World's Heritage

Ancient Greek Architecture
Ancient Greek builders created some of the world's most impressive works of architecture. They built several beautiful temples atop the Acropolis (uh·KRAHP·uh·lihs) in Athens, shown at right. The most famous of the temples is the Parthenon (PAHR·thuh·nahn).

In the United States and elsewhere, government buildings, such as courthouses and post offices, have been built similar in style to the Parthenon. This use of ancient architecture echoes the democratic ideals of ancient Greece.

Biography

Aristotle At the age of 17, Aristotle (384–322 B.C.) began studying philosophy with Plato. After Plato died, Aristotle received his most important assignment—to teach Alexander, the teenage son of King Philip II of Macedonia.

After teaching Alexander, Aristotle returned to Athens. There he taught and wrote about poetry, government, and astronomy. He started a famous school called the Lyceum (ly•SEE•uhm). Aristotle also collected and studied plants and animals. The work of this brilliant philosopher continues to greatly influence scientists and philosophers today.

The Spread of Greek Culture The city-states of ancient Greece were constantly at war with one another. By the fourth century B.C., this fighting had weakened their ability to defend themselves against foreign invaders. In 338 B.C., King Philip II of Macedonia conquered the land. After Philip died, his son, Alexander—who had been taught by **Aristotle**—took control.

Alexander the Great was an excellent military leader, and his armies conquered vast new territories. As Alexander's empire expanded, Greek culture, language, and ideas were spread throughout the Mediterranean region and as far east as modern-day India. Upon Alexander's death, however, his leading generals fought for control of his territory and divided it among themselves. This marked the end of one of the great empires of the ancient world.

Region • In this mosaic Alexander the Great is shown riding into battle on his beloved horse, Bucephalus (byoo•SEHF•ah•luhs). ▲

SECTION 2 ASSESSMENT

Terms & Names

1. Explain the significance of:
   - (a) city-state
   - (b) polis
   - (c) Aegean Sea
   - (d) oligarchy
   - (e) Athens
   - (f) philosopher
   - (g) Aristotle
   - (h) Alexander the Great

Using Graphics

2. Use a chart like this one to list and describe the ancient Greek achievements in government, literature, and architecture.

Government	Literature	Architecture

Main Ideas

3. (a) Why were the surrounding areas of water an important natural resource of the Greek Peninsula?

   (b) Which people were allowed to participate in the government of ancient Athens?

   (c) How did Alexander the Great help to spread Greek culture?

Critical Thinking

4. Summarizing

   Why was the fifth century B.C. a remarkable time in ancient Greek history?

   Think About
   - warfare
   - leaders
   - literature and philosophy

ACTIVITY -OPTION- Reread the information about the individual forms of government common in ancient Greece. Present an **oral report** to the class that compares and contrasts two of the forms.

SKILLBUILDER

Making a Generalization

SUNSHINE STATE STANDARDS
Key Standard SS.A.2.3.8 The student knows the political, social, and economic institutions that characterized the significant aspects of Eastern and Western civilizations.
FCAT LA.A.2.3.1 Reading: Identify Main Idea, Facts and Details

▶▶ Defining the Skill

To make generalizations means to make broad judgments based on information. When you make generalizations, you should gather information from several sources.

▶▶ Applying the Skill

The following three passages contain different information on the government of ancient Athens. Use the strategies listed below to make a generalization about Athenian government based on the passages.

How to Make a Generalization

Strategy ❶ Look for all the information that the sources have in common. These three sources all explain about Athenian government.

Strategy ❷ Form a generalization that describes ancient Athenian government in a way that all three sources would support. State your generalization in a sentence.

Make a Chart

Using a chart can help you make generalizations. The chart below shows how the information you just read can be used to generalize about the government of ancient Athens.

❶ Athenian citizens took part in political debates and voted on laws, but not everyone who lived in Athens enjoyed these rights. Participation in government was limited to free, adult males whose fathers had been citizens in Athens.
—*World Cultures and Geography*

In return for playing their parts as soldiers or sailors, ❶ ordinary Athenians insisted on controlling the government.
—*Encyclopaedia Britannica*

Unlike representative democracies or republics, in which one man is elected to speak for many, Athens was a true ❶ democracy: every citizen spoke for himself.
—*Classical Greece*

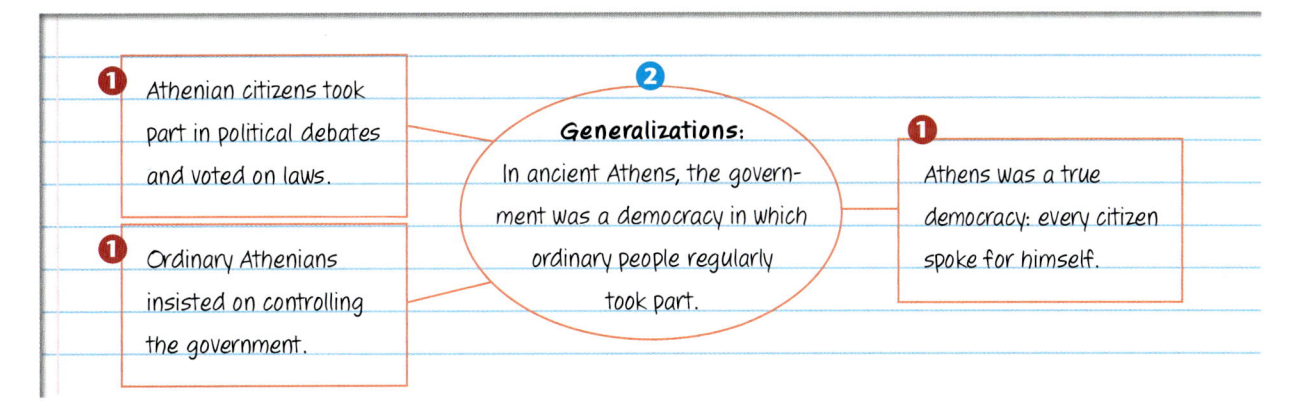

❶ Athenian citizens took part in political debates and voted on laws.

❶ Ordinary Athenians insisted on controlling the government.

❷ **Generalizations:** In ancient Athens, the government was a democracy in which ordinary people regularly took part.

❶ Athens was a true democracy: every citizen spoke for himself.

▶▶ Practicing the Skill

Turn to Chapter 3, Section 2, "Ancient Greece." Read the sections on literature and philosophy. Also read about ancient Greek writings in an encyclopedia, a library book, or on the Internet. Then make a chart like the one above to form a generalization about the importance of knowledge and learning to the ancient Greeks.

Section 3: Ancient Rome

TERMS & NAMES
- republic
- Senate
- patrician
- plebeian
- Julius Caesar
- empire
- Augustus
- Constantine

MAIN IDEA
The ancient Romans made important contributions to government, law, and engineering.

WHY IT MATTERS NOW
The cultural achievements of the Romans continue to influence the art, architecture, and literature of today.

DATELINE

ROME, 295 B.C.

Yet another Roman road was completed today! Rome is famous for its vast network of roadways. Repairing old roads and adding new ones keeps Roman engineers busy. Construction is time-consuming because the lengthy roads, which are paved with large stones, must be carefully planned. However, the benefits are worth the effort.

The roads connect the great city to distant lands under Roman rule. These roadways also enable the army to move quickly. These days, it seems that almost all roads lead to Rome. In fact, when this massive undertaking is finished, Roman roads will stretch for tens of thousands of miles across the land.

Location • All roads lead to Rome—including the Via Appia (VEE•uh APP•ee•uh) shown here. ▲

The Beginnings of Ancient Rome

Ancient Rome began as a group of villages located along the banks of the Tiber River in what is now Italy. There, early settlers herded sheep and grew wheat, olives, and grapes. Around 750 B.C., these villages united to form the city of Rome.

TAKING NOTES
Use your chart to take notes about Western Europe.

Time Period	Social Structure	Architecture
Ancient Greece		
Ancient Rome		

SUNSHINE STATE STANDARDS
Key Standard SS.A.2.3.6 The student knows the major events that shaped the development of various cultures (e.g., the spread of agrarian societies, population movements, technological and cultural innovation, and the emergence of new population centers).
Other Standards SS.A.2.3.1, A.2.3.5
FCAT LA.A.2.3.1 Reading: Identify Main Idea, Facts, and Details

The Formation of the Roman Republic For more than 200 years, kings ruled Rome. Then, in 509 B.C., Rome became a republic. A **republic** is a nation in which power belongs to the citizens, who govern themselves through elected representatives.

BACKGROUND
In ancient Rome, a senator held his position for life.

The Senate The Roman **Senate** was an assembly of elected representatives. It was the single most powerful ruling body of the Roman Republic. Each year, the Senate selected two leaders, called consuls, to head the government and the military.

Patricians At first, most of the people elected to the Senate were patricians (puh·TRIHSH·uhns). In ancient Rome, a **patrician** was a member of a wealthy, landowning family who claimed to be able to trace its roots back to the founding of Rome. The patricians also controlled the law, since they were the only citizens who were allowed to be judges.

Plebeians An ordinary, working male citizen of ancient Rome—such as a farmer or craftsperson—was called a **plebeian** (plih·BEE·uhn). Plebeians had the right to vote, but they could not hold public office until 287 B.C., when they gained equality with patricians.

The Expansion of the Roman World

Over hundreds of years, Rome grew into a mighty city. By the third century B.C., Rome ruled most of the Italian Peninsula. This gave Rome control of the central Mediterranean.

The city-state of Carthage, which ruled North Africa and southern Spain, controlled the western Mediterranean. To take control over this area as well, Rome fought Carthage and eventually won.

As Rome's population grew, its army also expanded in size and strength. Under the leadership of ambitious generals, Rome's highly trained soldiers set out to conquer new territories one by one.

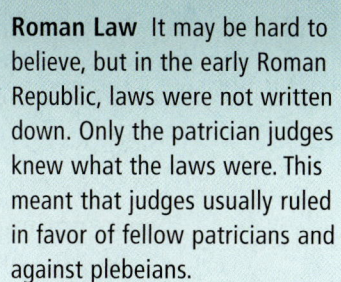

Strange but TRUE

Roman Law It may be hard to believe, but in the early Roman Republic, laws were not written down. Only the patrician judges knew what the laws were. This meant that judges usually ruled in favor of fellow patricians and against plebeians.

The plebeians grew tired of unfair treatment and demanded that the judges create a written code of laws that applied to all Roman citizens. This code, called the Law of the Twelve Tables, was written around 450 B.C. It formed the foundation of Roman law.

Western Europe: Its Land and Early History

Extent of Roman Control, 509 B.C. to 146 B.C.

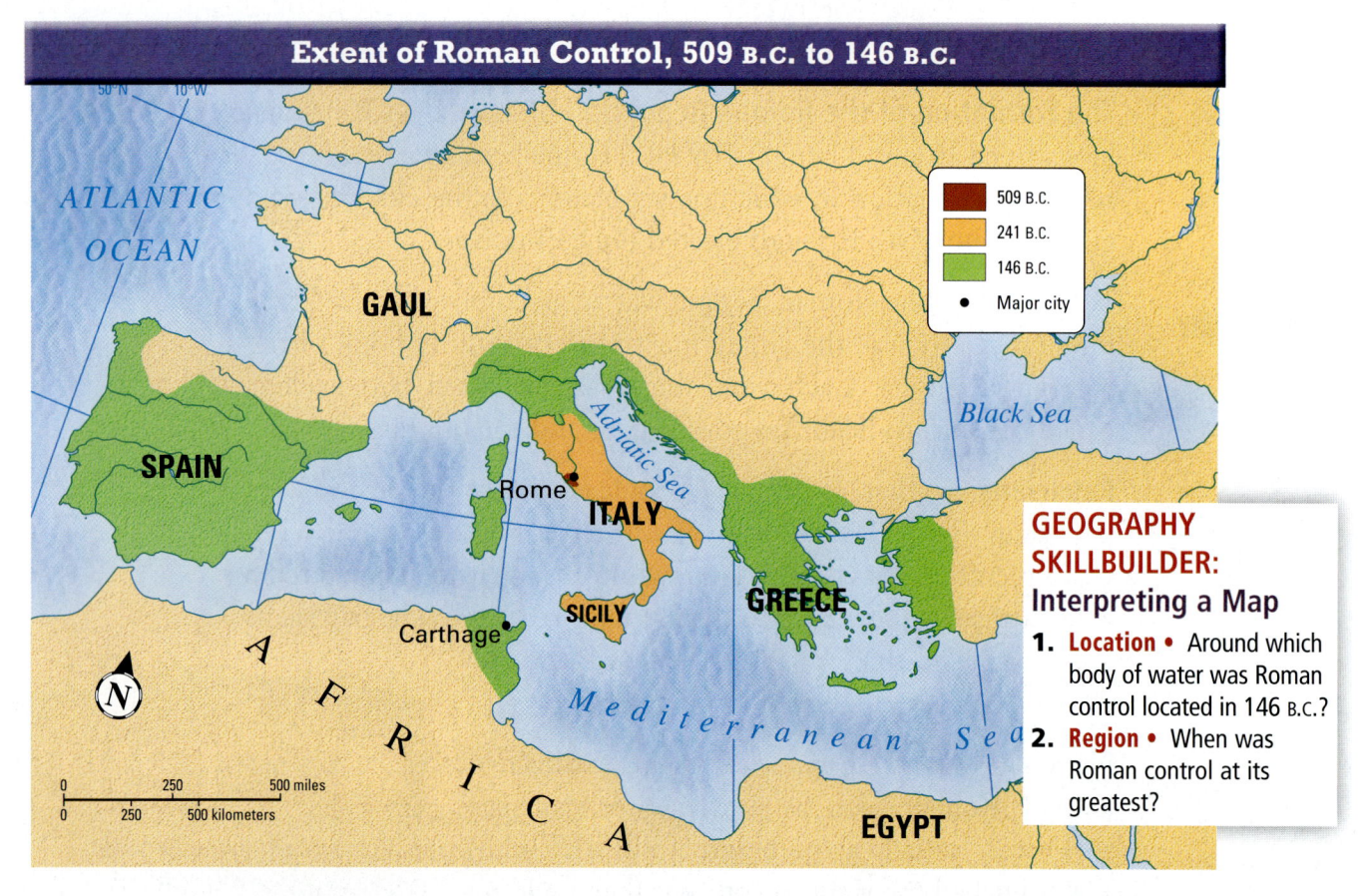

- 509 B.C.
- 241 B.C.
- 146 B.C.
- Major city

GEOGRAPHY SKILLBUILDER: Interpreting a Map
1. **Location** • Around which body of water was Roman control located in 146 B.C.?
2. **Region** • When was Roman control at its greatest?

As Rome's control over its neighbors expanded, its culture and language continued to spread into Spain and Greece. By the end of the second century B.C., the Romans ruled most of the land surrounding the Mediterranean Sea. The ancient Romans even called the Mediterranean *mare nostrum* (MAH•ray NOH•struhm), which means "our sea."

Region • Once in power, Julius Caesar had his likeness stamped on coins such as this one. ▼

From Republic to Empire

As the Roman Republic grew, its citizens became a more and more diverse group of people. Many Romans practiced different religions and followed different customs, but they were united by a common system of government and law. In the middle of the first century B.C., however, Rome's form of government changed.

The End of the Roman Republic
Julius Caesar, a successful Roman general and famous speaker, was the governor of the territory called Gaul. By conquering nearby territories to expand the land under his control, he increased both his power and his reputation. The Roman Senate feared that Caesar might become too powerful, and they ordered him to resign. Caesar, however, had other ideas.

BACKGROUND

Ancient Gaul included the lands that are modern-day France, Belgium, and parts of northern Italy.

Rather than resign, Caesar fought a long, fierce battle for control of the Roman Republic. In 45 B.C., he finally triumphed and returned to Rome. Caesar eventually became dictator of the Roman world. A dictator is a person who holds total control over a government. Caesar's rule marked the end of the Roman Republic.

The Beginning of the Roman Empire Julius Caesar had great plans to reorganize the way ancient Rome was governed, but his rule was cut short. On March 15, 44 B.C., a group of senators, angered by Caesar's plans and power, stabbed him to death on the floor of the Roman Senate. A civil war then erupted that lasted for several years.

In 27 B.C., Caesar's adopted son, Octavian, was named the first emperor of Rome. This marks the official beginning of the Roman Empire. An **empire** is a nation or group of territories ruled by a single, powerful leader, or emperor. As emperor, Octavian took the name **Augustus**.

The Augustan Age Augustus ruled the Roman Empire for more than 40 years. During this time, called the Augustan Age, the empire continued to expand. To help protect the enormous amount of land under his control, Augustus sent military forces along its borders, which now extended northward to the Rhine and Danube rivers.

Reading Social Studies
A. Recognizing Important Details How many years separated the rules of Julius Caesar and Augustus?

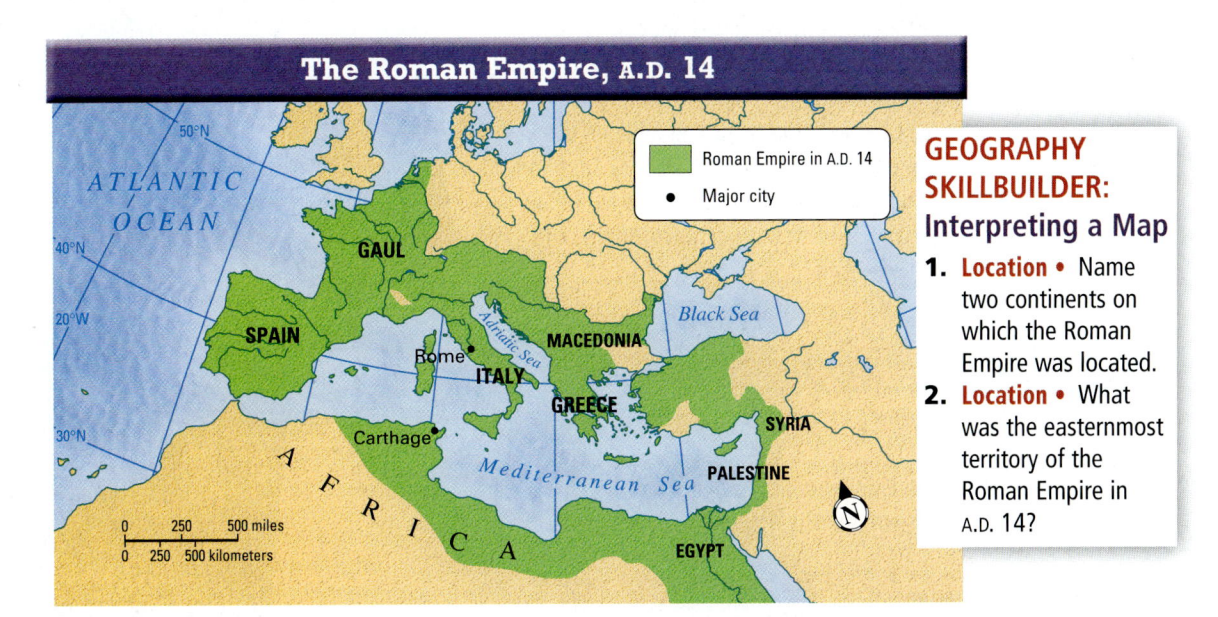

Region • Sculptures of Augustus were sent all over the Roman Empire to let people know what their leader looked like. ▲

The Roman Empire, A.D. 14

GEOGRAPHY SKILLBUILDER: Interpreting a Map

1. **Location •** Name two continents on which the Roman Empire was located.
2. **Location •** What was the easternmost territory of the Roman Empire in A.D. 14?

Western Europe: Its Land and Early History

While the Roman army kept peace, architects and engineers built many new public buildings. Trade increased, with olive oil, wine, pottery, marble, and grain being shipped all across the Mediterranean. Lighthouses were constructed, too, to help ships find their way into port.

The Augustan Age was also a time of great Roman literature. One of the most famous works of the age is the *Aeneid* (ih·NEE·ud). This long poem tells the story of Rome's founding. Augustus himself asked the famous poet Virgil to write it. This period of peace and cultural growth that Augustus created in the Roman Empire was called the "Pax Romana" (pahks roh·MAH·nah). The Pax Romana, or Roman Peace, lasted for 200 years.

Vocabulary

marble: a hard, smooth stone, often white in color

Region • A diver holds an artifact from an ancient Roman shipwreck in the Mediterranean Sea. ▲

Spotlight on CULTURE

Architecture Various inventions helped the Roman Empire grow and prosper. In addition to buildings and roads, Roman architects and engineers constructed water systems called aqueducts. Ancient aqueducts were raised tunnels that carried fresh water over long distances.

Built throughout the empire, aqueducts poured millions of gallons of water into Rome and other cities every day. They supplied clean water to private homes, fountains, and public baths. Today, some ancient Roman aqueducts still stand in France, Spain, and even on the outskirts of Rome itself.

THINKING CRITICALLY

1. **Analyzing Motives**
   Why did Romans want a way to transport water?
2. **Hypothesizing**
   Do you think the Roman Empire would have grown so large and prosperous without the aqueducts?

For more on Roman architecture, go to **RESEARCH LINKS** CLASSZONE.COM

82 CHAPTER 3

The Rise of Christianity

Reading Social Studies

B. Making Inferences How do you think the Roman Empire indirectly helped the spread of Christianity?

Region • Constantine (died A.D. 337) was the first Christian emperor of Rome. ▼

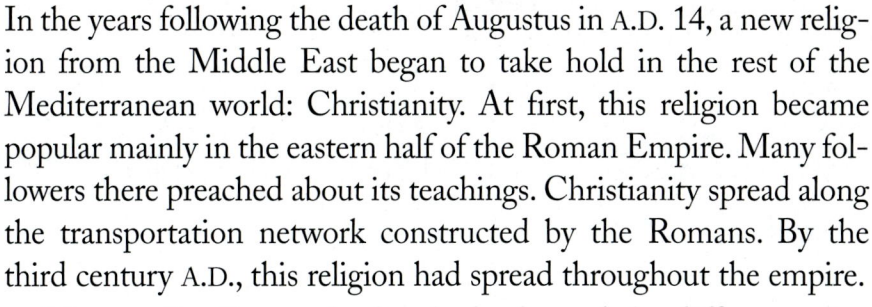

In the years following the death of Augustus in A.D. 14, a new religion from the Middle East began to take hold in the rest of the Mediterranean world: Christianity. At first, this religion became popular mainly in the eastern half of the Roman Empire. Many followers there preached about its teachings. Christianity spread along the transportation network constructed by the Romans. By the third century A.D., this religion had spread throughout the empire.

Most earlier Roman leaders had tolerated the different religions practiced throughout the empire. Christians, however, were viewed with suspicion and suffered persecution as early as A.D. 64. Roman leaders and people of other religions even blamed the Christians for natural disasters. Many Christians during this time were punished or killed for their beliefs.

The First Christian Emperor

Things changed when **Constantine** became emperor of Rome in A.D. 306. In A.D. 312, before a battle, Constantine claimed to have had a vision of a cross in the sky. The emperor promised that if he won the battle, he would become a Christian. Constantine was victorious, and the next year he fulfilled his promise. Christianity became the official religion of the Roman Empire. Today, Christianity has nearly two billion followers worldwide.

SECTION 3 ASSESSMENT

Terms & Names

1. Explain the significance of:
   - (a) republic
   - (b) Senate
   - (c) patrician
   - (d) plebeian
   - (e) Julius Caesar
   - (f) empire
   - (g) Augustus
   - (h) Constantine

Using Graphics

2. Use a chart like this one to outline the achievements of ancient Rome's Augustan Age.

Achievement	Effects

Main Ideas

3. (a) On what waterway is the city of Rome located?
   (b) What helped to unite the many different citizens of the Roman Republic?
   (c) How did Christianity spread throughout the Roman Empire?

Critical Thinking

4. **Drawing Conclusions**

   Why was ancient Rome able to control most of the land surrounding the Mediterranean Sea?

   Think About
   - the location of the Italian Peninsula
   - Rome's army
   - Rome's wars with Carthage

ACTIVITY -OPTION- Review the information about the beginnings of ancient Rome. Create a **chart** that compares the two important classes of Roman society: patricians and plebeians.

Section 4
Time of Change: The Middle Ages

TERMS & NAMES
medieval
Charlemagne
feudalism
manorialism
guild
Magna Carta

MAIN IDEA
The Middle Ages was a time of great change in Western Europe.

WHY IT MATTERS NOW
Some developments that occurred during the Middle Ages continue to affect life in Europe today.

DATELINE

ROME, A.D. 476—A Germanic tribe called the Visigoths has attacked our city of Rome and overthrown the emperor, Romulus Augustulus. The Roman army—no longer as large or as well organized as it was during the height of the empire—was unable to fight off the invaders.

After looting the great city, fierce bands of warriors and bandits have continued raiding towns and villages throughout Western Europe. They are stealing jewels and money, killing both people and animals, and even seizing control of entire territories. The Roman Empire seems to have breathed its last breath.

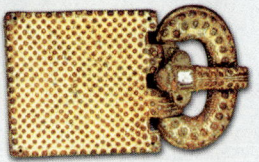

Region • Visigoth artifacts, like these saddle buckles, were found near Rome. ▲

Western Europe in Collapse

As the Roman Empire collapsed in the fifth century, more and more people fled to the countryside to escape invaders from the north and east. Eventually, there was no central government to maintain roads, public buildings, or water systems. Most towns and cities in Western Europe shrank or were totally abandoned. Long-distance travel became unsafe, and trade less common.

TAKING NOTES
Use your chart to take notes about Western Europe.

Time Period	Social Structure	Architecture
Ancient Greece		
Ancient Rome		

SUNSHINE STATE STANDARDS
Key Standard SS.A.2.3.8 The student knows the political, social, and economic institutions that characterized the significant aspects of Eastern and Western civilizations.
Other Standards SS.B.1.3.5, C.2.3.4, D.2.3.1
FCAT LA.A.2.3.1 Reading: Identify Main Idea, Facts, and Details

Reading Social Studies

A. Clarifying Who provided leadership during the Middle Ages?

The Beginning of the Medieval Era The period of history between the fall of the Roman Empire and the beginning of the modern world is called the Middle Ages, or **medieval** (MEE·dee·EE·vuhl) era. During this time, many of the advances and inventions of the ancient world were lost. Without a strong central government, many Europeans turned to military leaders and the Roman Catholic Church for leadership and support.

Charlemagne and the Christian Church

Among the most famous military leaders was the Germanic King Charlemagne (SHAHR·luh·mayn). In the late 700s, **Charlemagne,** or Charles the Great, worked to bring political order to the northwestern fringes of what had been the Roman Empire. This great warrior not only fought to increase the size of his kingdom, he also worked to improve life for those who lived there.

A New Roman Emperor Eventually, news of Charlemagne's accomplishments spread to Rome. Although the old empire was gone, Rome was now the center of the Catholic Church. The Pope recognized that joining forces with Charlemagne might bring greater power to the Church.

In 800, the Pope crowned Charlemagne as the new Holy Roman Emperor. During Charlemagne's rule, education improved, the government became stronger, and Catholicism spread. But after Charlemagne's death, Western Europe was once again without a strong political leader.

Region • Charlemagne established order and supported education and culture for a brief period in the early Middle Ages. ▲

The Role of the Church

Throughout Western Europe in medieval times, each community was centered around a church. The church offered religious services, established orphanages, and helped care for the poor, sick, and elderly. They also hosted feasts, festivals, and other celebrations. As communities grew, their members often donated money and labor to build new and larger churches.

Monks and Nuns Some people chose to dedicate their lives to serving God and the Church. These religious people were called monks and nuns. Monks were men who devoted their time to praying, studying, and copying and decorating holy books by hand. Monks lived in communities called monasteries. Many monasteries became important centers of learning in medieval society.

Western Europe: Its Land and Early History

Women who served the Church were called nuns. In the Middle Ages, it was common for a woman to become a nun after her husband died. Nuns prayed, sewed, taught young girls, cared for the poor, and also copied and decorated books. They lived in secluded communities called convents.

Vocabulary
secluded: to be separate or hidden away

Location •
Convents and monasteries often were located in hard-to-reach areas. ▲

Two Medieval Systems

During the Middle Ages, almost all the land was owned by powerful nobles—lords, kings, and high church officials. The central government was not very strong. The nobles sometimes even controlled the king and constantly fought among themselves. To protect their lands and position, nobles developed a system known as feudalism.

The Feudal System
Feudalism was a system of political ties in which the nobles, such as kings, gave out land to less powerful nobles, such as knights. In return for the land, the noble, called a vassal, made a vow to provide various services to the lord. The most important was to furnish his lord with knights, foot soldiers, and arms for battle.

The parcel of land granted to a vassal by his lord was called a fief (feef). The center of the lord's fief was the manor, which consisted of a large house or castle, surrounding farmland, villages, and a church. A fief might also include several other manors or castles belonging to the fief-owner's vassals.

Connections to History

The Bayeux Tapestry This famous work of art depicts the invasion of England by William the Conqueror in 1066. The Bayeux (by•YOO) Tapestry is a series of scenes from the point of view of the invaders, who came from Normandy. Normandy is a part of what is now France. The work is an important source of information about not only the conquest of England, but also medieval armor, clothing, and other aspects of culture.

Although called a tapestry, the work is really an embroidered strip of linen about 230 feet long. It includes captions in Latin. The Bayeux Tapestry was probably made by nuns in England about 1092.

Manorialism On the manor, peasants lived and farmed, but they usually did not own the land they lived on. In exchange for their lord's protection, the peasants contributed their labor and a certain amount of the food they raised. Some peasants, known as serfs, actually belonged to the fief on which they lived. They were not slaves, but they were not free to leave the land without the permission of the lord. This system, in which the lord received food and work in exchange for his protection, is known as **manorialism**.

Place • Although castles were large, they were built for defense. Castles were usually located on high ground with a series of walls and towers. ▲

Medieval Ways of Life

Medieval nobles had more power than the peasants. However, the difference in the standard of living between the very rich and the very poor was not as great as the difference today.

Castle Life The manor houses or castles may have been large, but they were built more for defense than for comfort. Thick stone walls and few windows made the rooms cold, damp, and dark. Fires added warmth but made the air smoky. Medieval noble families may have slept on feather mattresses, but lice and other pests were a constant annoyance. Most castles did not have indoor plumbing.

Western Europe: Its Land and Early History

Peasant Life Peasants lived outside the castle walls in small dwellings, often with dirt floors and straw roofs. They owned little furniture and slept on straw mattresses. It was common for peasant families to keep their farm animals inside their homes.

Peasants often worked two or three days a week for their lord, harvesting crops and repairing roads and bridges. The rest of the week they farmed their own small plots. Many days were religious festivals during which no one worked.

Connections to Economics

The Middle Class In the early Middle Ages, only a small percentage of people in Western Europe were wealthy landowners. Most people worked on manor lands or at some sort of craft. However, those workers who found jobs in towns often were able to save money and build businesses. Eventually, their improved status led to the rise of a middle class.

Unlike nobles, the members of this new middle class did not live off the land they owned. They had to continuously earn money, as most people do today.

The Growth of Medieval Towns

By the middle of the 11th century, life was improving for many people in Western Europe. New farming methods increased the supply of food and shortened the time it took to harvest crops. Fewer farmers were needed, and workers began to leave the countryside in search of other opportunities. People moved back into towns or formed new ones that grew into booming centers of trade. The population increased, and more and more people owned property or started businesses.

Guilds As competition among local businesspeople grew, tradespeople and craftspeople created their own guilds, or business associations. Similar to modern trade unions, a **guild** protected workers' rights, set wages and prices, and settled disputes. Membership in a guild was also a common requirement for citizens who sought one of the few elective public offices.

Reading Social Studies

B. Analyzing Motives Why did people create guilds?

The Late Middle Ages

Over time, the towns of the late Middle Ages grew in size, power, and wealth. The citizens of these towns began to establish local governments and to elect leaders.

Governments Challenge the Church The Pope insisted that he had supreme authority over all the Christian lands. Kings and other government leaders, however, did not agree that the Pope was more powerful than they were. This is an issue that continues to be discussed today.

The Magna Carta The rulers of Western Europe also struggled for power with members of the nobility. In England, nobles rebelled against King John. In 1215, the nobles forced the English king to sign a document called the **Magna Carta** (MAG·nuh KAHR·tuh), or Great Charter. This document limited the king's power and gave the nobles a larger role in the government.

Region • High taxes and failures on the battlefield made King John one of the most hated kings of England. ▼

Region • The Magna Carta influenced the creators of the U.S. Constitution. ▲

SECTION 4 ASSESSMENT

Terms & Names
1. Explain the significance of:
   (a) medieval
   (b) Charlemagne
   (c) feudalism
   (d) manorialism
   (e) guild
   (f) Magna Carta

Using Graphics
2. Use a flow chart like this one to show how Europe changed over four time periods: A.D. 476, the 800s, the mid-1000s, and the 1200s.

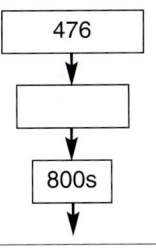

   476
   ↓
   [ ]
   ↓
   800s
   ↓

Main Ideas
3. (a) Why is this era of European history called the Middle Ages?
   (b) Describe the role of the Church in medieval society.
   (c) How did manorialism help both nobles and peasants?

Critical Thinking
4. **Contrasting**
   How did life differ for nobles and peasants under feudalism?

   Think About
   • where they lived
   • what they ate
   • how they did their work

ACTIVITY -OPTION- Review the information about serfs. Write a series of short **journal entries** describing what a week in the life of a serf might have been like during the Middle Ages.

Western Europe: Its Land and Early History 89

CHAPTER 3 ASSESSMENT

TERMS & NAMES

Explain the significance of each of the following:

1. peninsula
2. plain
3. city-state
4. Aegean Sea
5. Athens
6. republic
7. empire
8. Constantine
9. feudalism
10. Magna Carta

REVIEW QUESTIONS

A Land of Varied Riches (pages 67–71)
1. What is special about Europe's physical environment?
2. Why is the Great European Plain an important region?

Ancient Greece (pages 72–76)
3. What helped to unite the separate city-states of ancient Greece?
4. What caused the people of Athens to join forces with their rival city-state, Sparta, in 480 B.C.?

Ancient Rome (pages 78–83)
5. Why did the ancient Romans call the Mediterranean Sea "our sea"?
6. Why did the Roman Senate ask Julius Caesar to resign?

Time of Change: The Middle Ages (pages 84–89)
7. Why did the people turn to the Roman Catholic Church for leadership and support during the Middle Ages?
8. What contributed to the growth of towns during the Middle Ages?

CRITICAL THINKING

Recognizing Effects
1. Using your completed chart from Reading Social Studies, p. 66, identify changes in art, culture, religion, and social structure from the time of ancient Rome to the Middle Ages.

Hypothesizing
2. Many myths and plays of ancient Greece have been the basis for modern films and dramas. What does this indicate about these ancient stories and characters?

Analyzing Causes
3. How did the long, peaceful reign of Augustus help to promote architecture, literature, and art in the Roman Empire?

Visual Summary

1 A Land of Varied Riches
- The rich natural resources and varied geography of Europe helped to shape its development.

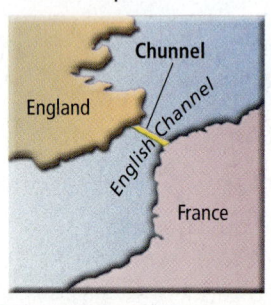

2 Ancient Greece
- The ancient Greeks developed a complex society and system of government.
- The achievements of the ancient Greeks in architecture, literature, and philosophy had a lasting impact on the world.

3 Ancient Rome
- Under strong leadership, ancient Rome experienced a time of great growth.
- Ancient Rome's contributions to government, engineering, and literature influenced Western culture.

4 Time of Change: The Middle Ages
- The social order and government of the Middle Ages transformed Europe into a modern society.

STANDARDS-BASED ASSESSMENT

Use the map and your knowledge of world cultures and geography to answer questions 1 and 2.

Additional Test Practice, pp. S1–S33

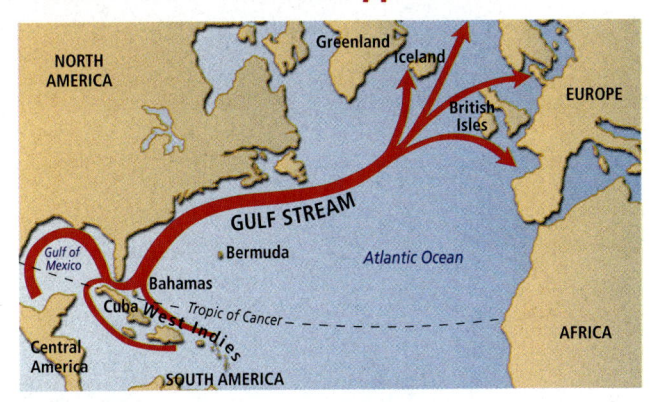

The following passage is from a biography of Julius Caesar. Use the quotation and your knowledge of world cultures and geography to answer question 3.

PRIMARY SOURCE

The conspirators who murdered Julius Caesar . . . failed miserably to destroy him. Though they killed his body, they could not extinguish his spirit, his vision for Rome's future. . . . Many plebes [common people] . . . and soldiers saw him as their champion. And his bloody death unleashed the pent-up distrust and anger they felt for the . . . ruling class.

DON NARDO, *Julius Caesar*

1. What bodies of water does the Gulf Stream flow through on the way to Europe?
   - **A.** Atlantic Ocean and Gulf of Mexico
   - **B.** Atlantic Ocean and Tropic of Cancer
   - **C.** Atlantic Ocean and West Indies
   - **D.** Gulf of Mexico and Tropic of Cancer

2. Which of the following regions do you think is most directly affected by the Gulf Stream?
   - **A.** Africa
   - **B.** Central America
   - **C.** Europe
   - **D.** South America

3. The passage supports which of the following observations?
   - **A.** Caesar's assassination was celebrated by the masses in Rome.
   - **B.** Caesar's energy and his hopes for Rome lived on in spite of his death.
   - **C.** The soldiers joined with the conspirators to remove Caesar from power.
   - **D.** The death of Caesar signaled the end to his vision for Rome.

TEST PRACTICE CLASSZONE.COM

ALTERNATIVE ASSESSMENT

1. **WRITING ABOUT HISTORY**

   TThe Pope crowned Charlemagne as the Holy Roman Emperor in 800. Research this event and write a biography of Charlemagne in which you focus on his reign as emperor.
   - Use the Internet or library resources to research Charlemagne and his impact on political, economic, and religious life in Europe.
   - As a biographer, focus on the facts and important details you found in your research. Also, include your impressions of his reign.

2. **COOPERATIVE LEARNING**

   Work with a small group of classmates to design and create a playbill for a Greek tragedy. Your playbill, or program for the audience, should include a cover illustration, a list of the characters, a summary of the story, and information about the playwright. Group members can share the responsibilities of researching, writing, and illustrating the playbill.

INTEGRATED TECHNOLOGY

Doing Internet Research

Different regions of Europe contain different natural resources. Focus on one European region, such as the Ruhr Valley, the Mediterranean Sea, or the independent republics of Eastern Europe. Use the Internet to research the region and its natural resources.
- Use the Internet, as well print encyclopedias, atlases, and other reference books to learn about the region.
- Focus your research on the natural resources found there, how they contributed to the region's development, and how the region has developed in modern times.
- Organize your findings into a report. Include a map that shows the region and its resources.

For Internet links to support this activity, go to

RESEARCH LINKS CLASSZONE.COM

CHAPTER 4
The Growth of New Ideas

Section 1   Renaissance Connections

Section 2   Traders, Explorers, and Colonists

Section 3   The Age of Revolution

Section 4   The Russian Empire

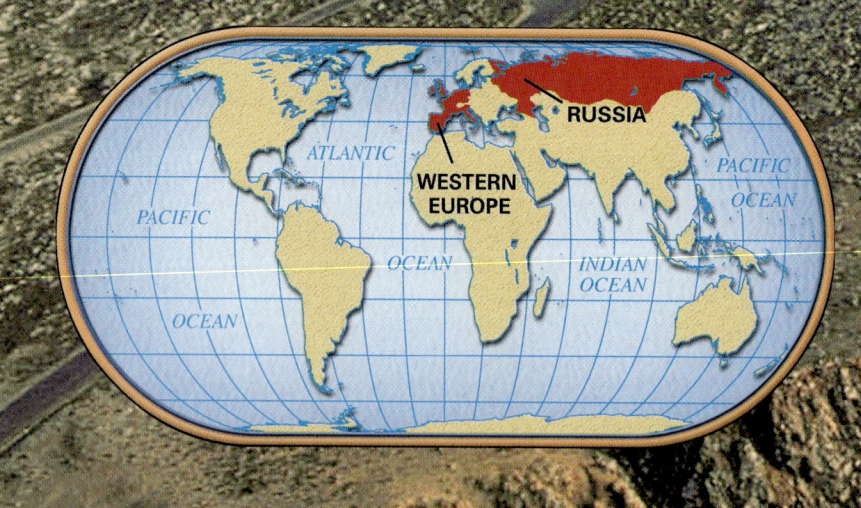

How can trade spread disease?

FOCUS ON GEOGRAPHY

Movement • In 1347, an epidemic of bubonic plague (boo·BAHN·ihk playg) hit Europe. This plague, also called the Black Death, started in Asia. Caravans and trading ships carried it to port cities on the Mediterranean Sea. The plague spread from Sicily to the Italian Peninsula and then to France, Spain, and England.

The Black Death was carried by fleas that infected both rats and humans. Rats did not die from the plague. Instead, they served as hosts, or carriers, for the disease. By 1349, the horrors of the epidemic reached Switzerland, Austria, and Hungary. Later, it even reached as far north and east as Scandinavia and Russia. Historians estimate that this plague killed one out of every three persons in Europe.

What do you think?

- Why might the plague have reached Italy before it spread to England?
- How do you think the Black Death might have affected the economy of Europe?

Place The Cape of Saint Vincent is at the southwest tip of Portugal, jutting into the Atlantic Ocean. This was the location of Prince Henry's School of Navigation, where Portuguese sailors learned ways to explore the oceans of the world.

CHAPTER 4

READING SOCIAL STUDIES

BEFORE YOU READ

▶▶ What Do You Know?

Do you know who first sailed around the world? Do you know that Leonardo da Vinci drew plans for a helicopter 400 years before it was actually built? Think of other discoveries, inventions, events, and famous people. What do you think life was like for common people during this time? Think about movies you have seen, books you have read, and what you have learned in other classes about the Renaissance, the Industrial Revolution, and political revolutions in France, Russia, and the United States.

▶▶ What Do You Want to Know?

Decide what you know about changes in the West from the Renaissance into the 1800s. In your notebook, record what you hope to learn from this chapter.

READ AND TAKE NOTES

Reading Strategy: Categorizing One way to make sense of what you read is to categorize ideas. Categorizing means sorting information by certain traits, ideas, or characteristics. Use the chart below to categorize details about the topics covered in this chapter.

- Copy the chart into your notebook.
- As you read each section, look for information about ideas, people, and events.
- Record key details in each category.

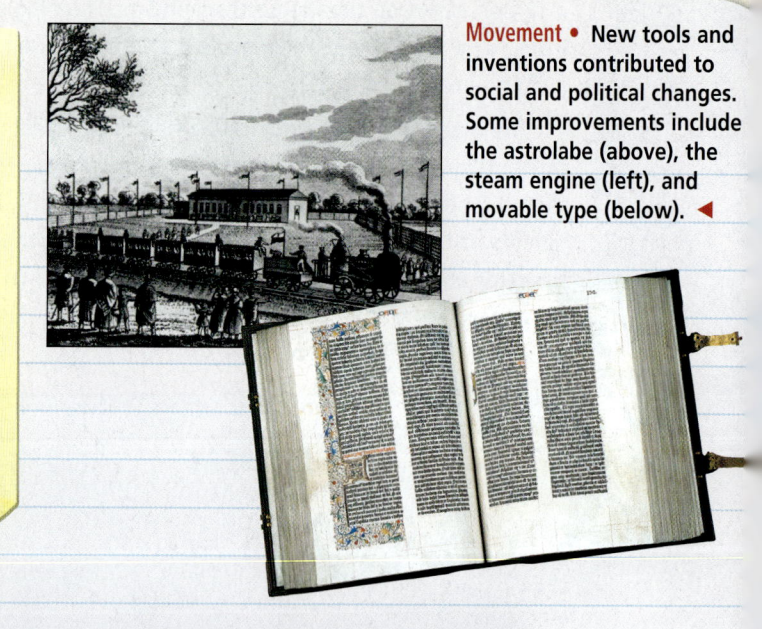

Movement • New tools and inventions contributed to social and political changes. Some improvements include the astrolabe (above), the steam engine (left), and movable type (below). ◀

Influences	New Ideas	People/Achievements	Events/Effects
The Renaissance			
European Exploration and Conquest			
Scientific and Industrial Revolutions			
Political Revolutions			
The Russian Empire			

94 CHAPTER 4

Section 1: Renaissance Connections

TERMS & NAMES
- Crusades
- Renaissance
- Florence
- Leonardo da Vinci
- William Shakespeare
- Reformation
- Martin Luther
- Protestant

MAIN IDEA
The rebirth of art, literature, and ideas during the Renaissance changed European society.

WHY IT MATTERS NOW
Many accomplishments of the Renaissance are high points of Western culture and continue to inspire artists, writers, and thinkers of today.

DATELINE — EXTRA

PARIS, FRANCE, 1269

Paris is buzzing with activity as thousands of European soldiers assemble here. This is the starting-off point for the eighth Crusade, which has nearly a thousand miles to travel. King Louis IX of France, who is in command, is confident that his armies can restore European power over the Holy Land.

Since the Crusades began in 1096, the Christians have fought against the Muslims and founded four states in the eastern Mediterranean. European power has weakened since then. However, King Louis's army looks ready to recapture the lost territory for Christianity.

Movement • Crusaders will make their way toward the Holy Land. ▲

Europeans Encounter New Cultures

The **Crusades**—a series of expeditions from the 11th to the 13th centuries by Western European Christians to capture the Holy Lands from Muslims—greatly changed life in Western Europe. The Crusades opened up trade routes, linking Western Europe with southwestern Asia and North Africa. They also helped Europeans rediscover the ideas of ancient Greece and Rome.

TAKING NOTES
Use your chart to take notes about people and ideas.

	Influences	New Ideas	People/Achievements
The Renaissance			
European Exploration			

SUNSHINE STATE STANDARDS
Key Standard SS.A.2.3.6 The student knows the major events that shaped the development of various cultures (e.g., the spread of agrarian societies, population movements, technological and cultural innovation, and the emergence of new population centers).
Other Standards SS.A.2.3.1, A.2.3.5, A.2.3.7
FCAT LA.A.2.3.1 Reading: Identify Main Idea, Facts, and Details

The Growth of New Ideas

Italian City-States, c. 1350

GEOGRAPHY SKILLBUILDER:
Interpreting a Map
1. **Location** • Which city-state does not have access to water?
2. **Location** • Which city-state was in the best position to trade by land and sea with Asia?

Over time, this interest in the ancient world sparked a new era of creativity and learning in Western Europe. This cultural era, which lasted from the 14th to the 16th century, is called the **Renaissance**.

The Rebirth of Europe

The Renaissance began on the Italian Peninsula in the mid-14th century. During this time, many artists, architects, writers, and scholars created works of great importance. These included beautiful paintings, large sculptures, impressive buildings, and thought-provoking literature. As new ideas and achievements spread across the continent of Europe, they changed the way people viewed themselves and the world.

The Italian City-States In the 14th century, the Italian Peninsula was divided into many independent city-states. Some of these city-states, such as **Florence**, were bustling centers of banking, trade, and manufacturing.

BACKGROUND
After Rome fell, many achievements of ancient times were lost. Many books and manuscripts, however, were preserved by Muslim and Christian scholars.

Region •
Florence, once a wealthy city-state, remains an important economic and cultural center. The Duomo, shown here, is a symbol of the city's Renaissance past. ▼

Region • The wealthy merchants in Italy built large palaces, called palazzos, such as Florence's Palazzo Medici shown here. ▶

The wealthy businesspeople who lived in these city-states were members of a new class of aristocrats. Unlike the nobles of the feudal system, these aristocrats lived in cities, and their wealth came from money and goods rather than from the lands they owned.

A Changing View of the World Religion was important to people's daily life during the Renaissance, but many wealthy Europeans began to turn increased attention to the material comforts of life.

New wealth allowed aristocratic families to build large homes for themselves in the city centers, decorating them with luxurious objects. They ate expensive food and dressed in fine clothes and jewels, often acquired as a result of the expanded trade routes. Aristocrats also placed increased emphasis on education and the arts.

Learning and the Arts Flourish

BACKGROUND
Some Renaissance architects, such as Filippo Brunelleschi (BROO•nuh•LEHS•kee), studied the ruins of Roman buildings and modeled their new buildings after ancient designs.

Wealthy citizens were proud of their city-states and often became generous patrons. A patron gave artists and scholars money and, sometimes, a place to live and work. They hired architects and designers to improve local churches, to design grand new buildings, and to create public sculptures and fountains. As one Italian city-state made additions and improvements, others competed to outdo it.

Biography

The Medici Family Among the most famous patrons of the Renaissance were the Medici (MEHD•uh•chee). They were a wealthy family of bankers and merchants. In fact, they were the most powerful leaders of Florence from the early 1400s until the 18th century.

Along with Lorenzo, pictured below, the Medici family included famous princes and dukes, two queens, and four popes. Throughout the 15th and 16th centuries, the Medici supported many artists, including Botticelli, Michelangelo, and Raphael. Today, Florence is still filled with important works of art made possible by the Medici.

The Growth of New Ideas

Culture •
Leonardo da Vinci completed the painting *La Belle Ferronnière* in 1495. ▲

As part of the competition to improve the appearance and status of their individual city-states, patrons wanted to attract the brightest and best-known scholars and poets of the time. Patrons believed that the contributions of these individuals would, in turn, add to the greatness of their city-states and attract more wealth.

The Visual Arts: New Subjects and Methods Most medieval art was based on religious subjects. Painters and sculptors of the early Renaissance created religious art too, but they also began to depict other subjects. Some made portraits for wealthy patrons. Others created works showing historical scenes or mythological stories.

Leonardo da Vinci One of the most famous artists and scientists of the Renaissance was **Leonardo da Vinci** (lee·uh·NAHR·doh duh VIHN·chee) (1452–1519). Among his best-known paintings are the *Mona Lisa*, a portrait of a young woman with a mysterious smile, and *The Last Supper*. Da Vinci was more than just a talented painter, however.

Throughout his life, da Vinci observed the world around him. He studied the flow of water, the flight of birds, and the workings of the human body. Da Vinci, who became a skilled engineer, scientist, and inventor, filled notebooks with thousands of sketches of his discoveries and inventions. He even drew ideas for flying machines, parachutes, and submarines—hundreds of years before they were built.

Reading Social Studies

A. Contrasting How did the subject matter of Renaissance art differ from medieval art?

Connections to Math

Perspective During the Renaissance, artists began to use a technique called linear perspective. Linear perspective is a system of using lines to create the illusion of depth and distance. In the drawing below, notice how the perspective lines move toward a single point in the distance, giving the picture depth.

The Northern Renaissance

As the new Renaissance ideas about religion and art spread to Northern Europe, they inspired artists and writers working there. The Dutch scholar and philosopher Desiderius Erasmus (ih·RAS·muhs) (1466–1536), for example, criticized the church for its wealth and poked fun at its officials. During the late 16th and early 17th centuries, another writer—the Englishman **William Shakespeare**—wrote a series of popular stage plays. Many of his works, including *Romeo and Juliet* and *Macbeth*, are still read and performed around the world.

The Reformation

BACKGROUND
In 1516, the English writer Thomas More published a famous book called *Utopia*. It describes the author's idea of a perfect society. Today, the word "utopia" is used to describe any ideal place.

Roman Catholicism was still the most powerful religion in Western Europe. Some of the views of the northern Renaissance writers and scholars, however, were in conflict with the Roman Catholic Church. These new ideas would eventually lead to the **Reformation,** a 16th-century movement to change church practices.

Martin Luther The German monk **Martin Luther** (1483–1546) was one of the most important critics of the church. The wealth and corruption of many church officials disturbed him. Luther also spoke out against the church's policy of selling indulgences—the practice of forgiving sins in exchange for money.

In 1517, Luther wrote 95 theses, or statements of belief, attacking the sale of indulgences and other church practices. Copies were printed and handed out throughout Western Europe. After this, Luther was excommunicated, or cast out and no longer recognized as a member of a church, and went into hiding. While in hiding, he translated the Bible from Latin into German so that all literate, German-speaking people could read it. Under Luther's leadership, many Europeans began to challenge the practices of the Roman Catholic Church.

Spotlight on CULTURE

The Printing Press Until the Renaissance, each copy of a book had to be written by hand—usually by monks or nuns. A Renaissance invention, however, changed that forever. Around 1450, a German printer named Johann Gutenberg (Yoh·HAHN GOO·tuhn·BERG) began to use a method of printing with movable type. This meant that multiple copies of books, such as this Bible, could be printed quickly and less expensively.

Although many Renaissance books dealt with religious subjects, printers also published plays, poetry, works of philosophy and science, and tales of travel and adventure. As greater numbers of books were published, more and more Europeans learned to read.

For more on the printing press, go to
RESEARCH LINKS CLASSZONE.COM

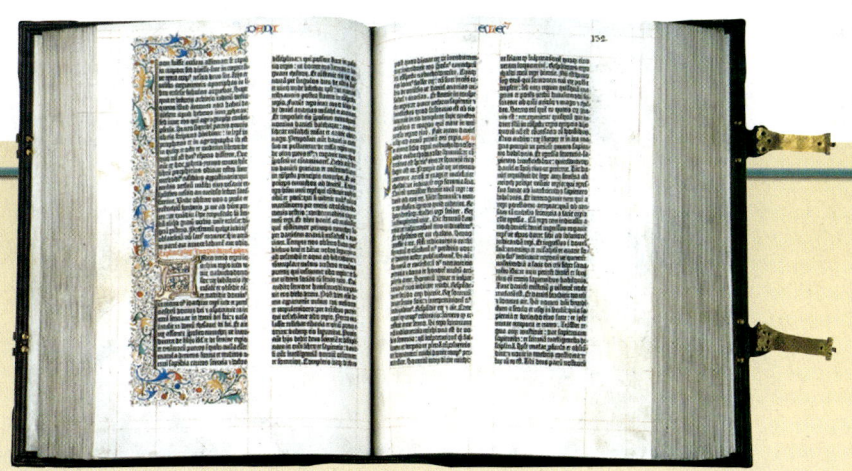

THINKING CRITICALLY
1. **Recognizing Effects**
What were three effects of the invention of Gutenberg's printing press?

2. **Synthesizing**
Before the printing press, who produced the books?

The Growth of New Ideas

A Conflict over Religious Beliefs

Reading Social Studies

B. Clarifying How did Protestants get their name?

Luther's followers were called **Protestants** because they protested events at an assembly that ended the church's tolerance of their beliefs. Many people in Western Europe still supported the church, however. This conflict led to religious wars that ended in 1555. At that time, the Peace of Augsburg declared that German rulers could decide the official religion of their own state.

The Spread of Protestant Ideas
By 1600, Protestantism had spread to England and the Scandinavian Peninsula. Protestants pushed to expand education for more Europeans. They did this because being able to read meant being able to study the Bible. They also encouraged translation of the Bible into the native language of each country.

The Counter Reformation
The Roman Catholic Church responded to Protestantism by launching its own movement in the mid-16th century. As part of this movement, called the Counter Reformation, the church stopped selling indulgences. It also created a new religious order called the Society of Jesus, or the Jesuits. Jesuit missionaries and scholars worked to spread Catholic ideas across Europe, to Asia, and to the lands of the "new world" across the Atlantic Ocean.

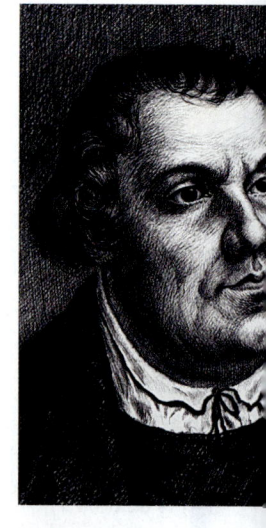

Region • Martin Luther's writings and actions changed Christianity forever. ▲

SECTION 1 ASSESSMENT

Terms & Names

1. Explain the significance of:
   - (a) Crusades
   - (b) Renaissance
   - (c) Florence
   - (d) Leonardo da Vinci
   - (e) William Shakespeare
   - (f) Reformation
   - (g) Martin Luther
   - (h) Protestant

Using Graphics

2. Use a spider map like this one to chart the characteristics and accomplishments of the Renaissance.

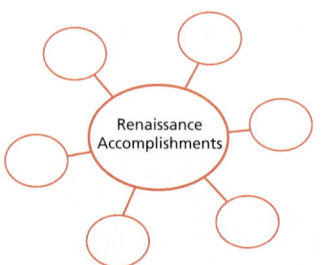

   (Renaissance Accomplishments)

Main Ideas

3. (a) Where and when did the Renaissance begin?
   (b) In what ways were the wealthy Europeans of the Renaissance different from the wealthy Europeans of feudal times?
   (c) What was the Counter Reformation?

Critical Thinking

4. **Hypothesizing**

   Why do you think Protestantism spread so quickly in Northern Europe?

   Think About
   - new methods of printing
   - the ideas of the northern Renaissance
   - the work of Martin Luther

ACTIVITY -OPTION-

Write a **letter** to an imagined patron asking for support to create a project—such as a public sculpture, park, fountain, or building—to beautify your community.

Section 2: Traders, Explorers, and Colonists

TERMS & NAMES
Prince Henry the Navigator
Christopher Columbus
Ferdinand Magellan
circumnavigate
imperialism

MAIN IDEA
European trade and exploration changed the lives of many people on both sides of the Atlantic.

WHY IT MATTERS NOW
Today, citizens of the Americas continue to feel the effects of European exploration and colonization.

DATELINE

SAGRES, PORTUGAL, 1421— Portugal's Prince Henry may not have journeyed to sea, but he has earned a well-deserved nickname: "The Navigator." He has organized expeditions of sailors to explore the west coast of Africa. Five years ago, Henry also founded a School of Navigation. It is here in Sagres, at Portugal's southwestern tip, which juts into the Atlantic Ocean.

Astronomers, geographers, and mathematicians gather here to study and teach new methods of traveling across the seas. They plan expeditions using the latest maps, tools, and information about the winds and currents of the Atlantic Ocean. Sometimes the scholars add to their knowledge by talking with sea captains about their voyages.

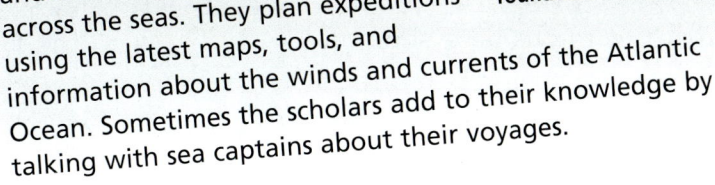

Movement • Prince Henry of Portugal founded the School of Navigation. ▲

Trade Between Europe and Asia

For centuries before the Renaissance, European traders traveled back and forth across the Mediterranean. Merchants commonly journeyed from southern Europe to North Africa and to the eastern Mediterranean. Spices were one of the most important items traded at this time.

TAKING NOTES
Use your chart to take notes about people and ideas.

Influences	New Ideas	People/Achievements
The Renaissance		
European Exploration		

SUNSHINE STATE STANDARDS
Key Standard SS.A.2.3.2 The student knows how major historical developments have had an impact on the development of civilizations.
Other Standards SS.A.2.3.5, A.2.3.6
FCAT LA.A.2.3.1 Reading: Identify Main Idea, Facts, and Details

The Growth of New Ideas **101**

The Spice Trade Spices were in great demand by Europeans. Before refrigeration, meat and fish spoiled quickly. To help preserve food and to improve its flavor, people used spices such as pepper, cinnamon, nutmeg, and cloves. These spices came from Asia.

For centuries, Italian merchants from Genoa and Venice controlled the spice trade. They sailed to ports in the eastern Mediterranean, where they would purchase spices and other goods from traders who had traveled across Asia. The Italian merchants would then bring these goods back to Europe.

The Possibility of Great Wealth Transporting goods across these great distances was costly. Everyone along the way had to be paid and wanted to earn a profit. By the time the spices reached Europe, they had to be sold at extremely high prices.

European merchants knew that if they could trade directly with people in Asia, they could make enormous profits. In the 15th century, Europeans began to search for a new route to Asia.

BACKGROUND
In addition to spices, European countries traded for precious metals, which they used to make coins. Metals such as gold and silver were scarce in Europe.

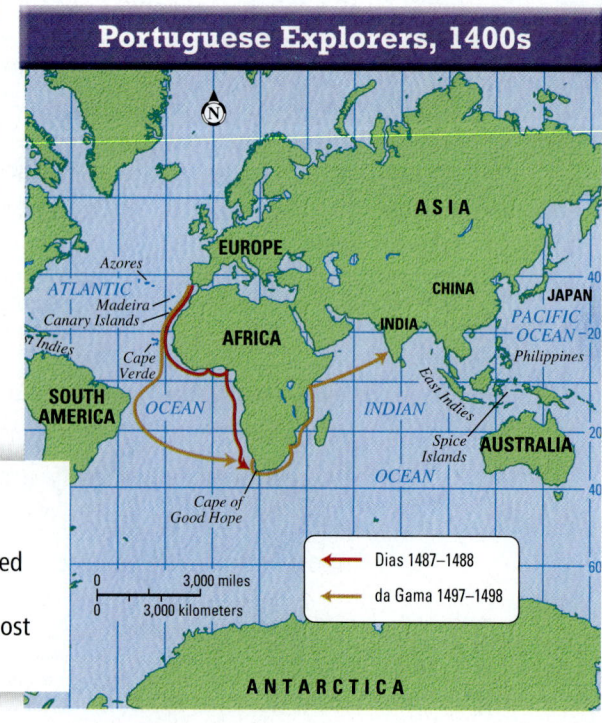

Leaders in Exploration

The small country of Portugal is at the westernmost part of the European continent. Portuguese sailors had navigated the waters of the Atlantic Ocean for centuries. As shown on the map below, they traveled down the west coast of Africa and as far west into the Atlantic as Madeira, the Azores, and the Canary Islands.

Exploring the African Coast In the early 1400s, Portugal's **Prince Henry the Navigator** decided to send explorers farther down the coast of Africa. He believed that if explorers could find a way around Africa, it might be a shortcut to Asia. Portuguese explorers returned home from these expeditions with gold dust, ivory, and more knowledge of navigation. By the time Henry died in 1460, the Portuguese had ventured around the great bulge of western Africa to present-day Sierra Leone.

Portuguese Explorers, 1400s

GEOGRAPHY SKILLBUILDER:
Interpreting a Map
1. **Movement** • Which explorer reached Asia?
2. **Location** • Which continent was most explored by the Portuguese?

102 CHAPTER 4

The Race Around Africa Bold Portuguese explorers continued to push farther down the African coast. Finally, in 1488, Bartolomeu Dias (BAHR·too·loo·MAY·oo DEE·uhsh) rounded the southern tip of Africa. The Portuguese named the tip the Cape of Good Hope.

Less than ten years later, Vasco da Gama (vas·KOH deh GAH·muh) led a sea expedition all the way to Asia. Da Gama and his crew traveled for 317 days and 13,500 miles before reaching the coast of India. They were the first Europeans to discover a sea route to Asia. Now, the riches of Asia could be brought directly to Europe. After setting up trading posts along the coast of the Indian Ocean, Portugal ruled these waterways.

Europe Enters a New Age

Portugal was not the only European country to understand that whoever controlled trade with Asia would have great power and wealth. Spain and England quickly entered the race to find a direct sea route of their own.

Christopher Columbus Some explorers believed that the shortest way to Asia was to sail west across the Atlantic Ocean. Queen Isabella of Spain agreed to fund an expedition across the Atlantic.

In August 1492, an Italian named **Christopher Columbus** and 90 crew members left Spain aboard three ships—the *Santa Maria*, the *Pinta*, and the *Niña*. The Atlantic Ocean proved to be wider than maps of the time suggested. On October 12, after weeks at sea, the crew spotted land. Although Columbus thought he had found Asia, they were off the coast of an island in the Caribbean. This was still a great distance from their spice-rich destination.

Ferdinand Magellan In 1519, Spain funded an expedition for the Portuguese explorer **Ferdinand Magellan** (muh·JEHL·uhn). Magellan left Spain with five ships and more than 200 sailors. As they traveled west, the crew battled violent storms and rough seas. Food was in short supply, and starving sailors ate rats and sawdust. Some died of disease.

Connections to Science

New Ships In the early 15th century, Portuguese shipbuilders designed a sturdy ship called a caravel, pictured below. Built for exploration and trade, the caravel was small and had a narrow body. This helped the ship to cut through waves and to travel in shallow water.

The caravel also used a combination of square and triangular sails. These made sailing easier against strong, shifting winds.

Reading Social Studies

A. Recognizing Important Details What continent did Columbus reach, and where did he think he was?

The Growth of New Ideas

Movement • Sailors figured their ship's position with the astrolabe. It measured the position of the sun and stars in relation to the horizon. ▼

By the time Magellan and his ships reached the Philippines in Asia, the sailors had spent 18 long months at sea. Then, during a battle there, Magellan and several crew members were killed. The expedition returned to Spain after a three-year journey. Only one boat and 18 crew members succeeded. They had to **circumnavigate,** or sail completely around, the world.

Reading Social Studies

B. Identifying Problems What were the main problems faced by Magellan and his crew?

John Cabot King Henry VII of England did not want Portugal and Spain to claim all the riches of Asia. He funded a voyage by Italian-born Giovanni Caboto, called John Cabot by the English, who believed that a northern route across the Atlantic Ocean might be a shortcut to Asia.

Aboard one small ship, Cabot and 18 crew members sailed west from England in May 1497. When they reached land the following month, Cabot thought they had found Asia. Most likely, they landed in present-day Newfoundland in Canada.

The Outcomes of Exploration

The kings and queens of Europe sent explorers in search of a direct trade route to Asia. These expeditions, however, turned out to have unexpected results.

A Clash of Cultures European countries founded many new colonies along the coastal areas of Africa and North and South America. This practice of one country controlling the government and economy of another country or territory is called **imperialism.** These conquered lands were already home to large, self-ruling populations. They had their own cultural traditions. After the arrival of the Europeans, the lives of these indigenous peoples would never be the same.

Vocabulary
indigenous: born and living in a place, rather than having come from somewhere else

Religious Conversion The European monarchs were Christians. They had strong religious beliefs, and they sent missionaries and other religious officials to help convert conquered peoples to Christianity. The European rulers also hoped that these new converts would help Christianity overcome other powerful religions, especially Islam.

The Spread of Diseases Without knowing it, the European explorers and colonists carried diseases with them, including smallpox, malaria, and measles. These diseases were unknown in the Americas, and killed tens of thousands of people there.

Columbus, Cabot, and Magellan, 1492–1522

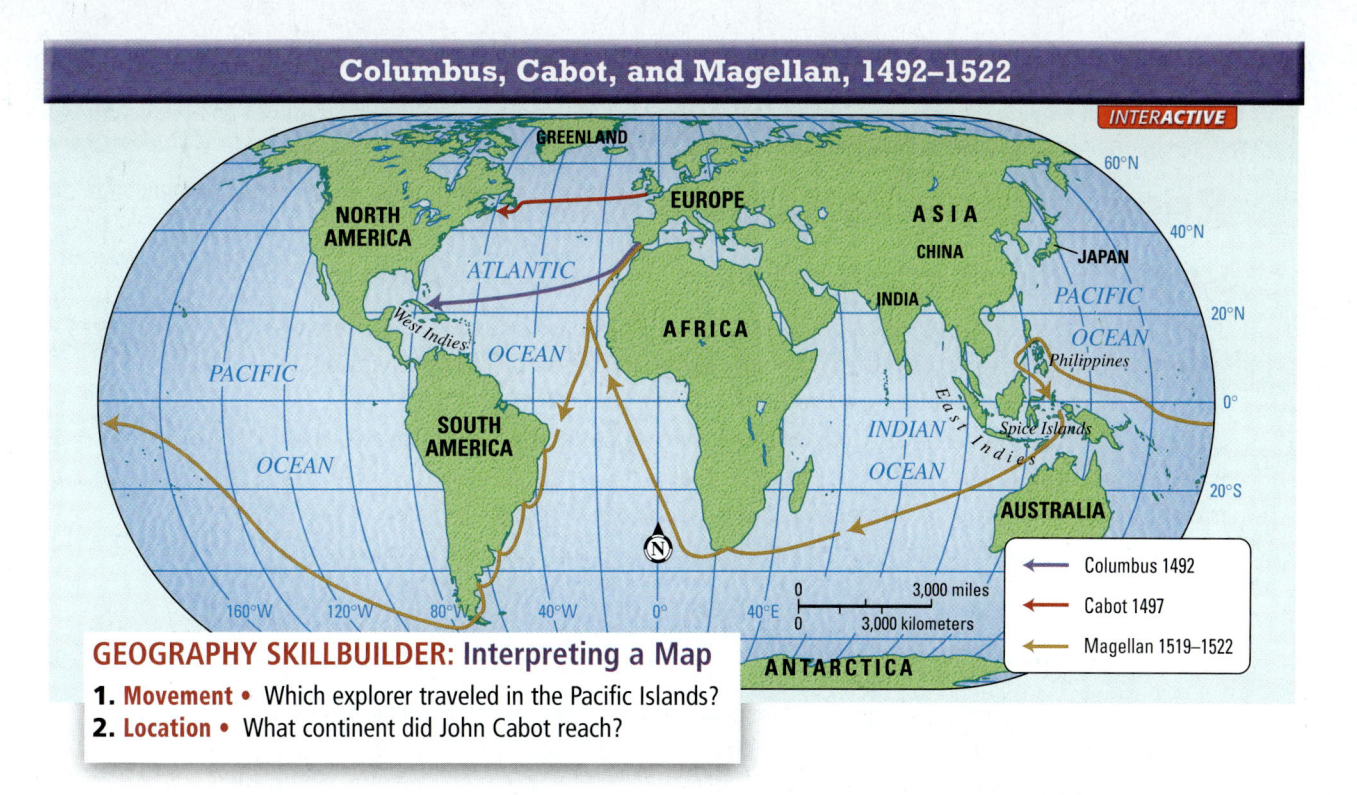

GEOGRAPHY SKILLBUILDER: Interpreting a Map
1. **Movement** • Which explorer traveled in the Pacific Islands?
2. **Location** • What continent did John Cabot reach?

Slavery European explorations also led to an expanding slave trade. The Portuguese purchased West Coast African people to work as slaves back in Portugal, where the work force had been reduced by plague. In other colonized areas, such as Mexico and parts of South America, Europeans forced conquered peoples to work the land where they lived. For hundreds of years, Africans and conquered peoples of the Americas would be forced to work under horrible conditions.

SECTION 2 ASSESSMENT

Terms & Names
1. Explain the significance of:
   (a) Prince Henry the Navigator
   (b) Christopher Columbus
   (c) Ferdinand Magellan
   (d) circumnavigate
   (e) imperialism

Using Graphics
2. Use a chart like this one to compare characteristics of the voyages of Christopher Columbus and Vasco da Gama.

Columbus's Voyage	Da Gama's Voyage

Main Ideas
3. (a) Why were spices so important to Europeans?
   (b) Why did Europeans want to find a new route to Asia?
   (c) Name three ways in which European exploration affected the indigenous peoples of North and South America.

Critical Thinking
4. **Making Inferences**
   Why do you think the Portuguese became leaders of European exploration?

   Think About
   - the location of Portugal
   - early Portuguese voyages
   - Prince Henry and his School of Navigation

ACTIVITY -OPTION- Reread the information about Magellan's voyage around the world. Write a **journal entry** describing the events of the voyage from the point of view of a crew member.

The Growth of New Ideas **105**

SKILLBUILDER

Researching Topics on the Internet

SUNSHINE STATE STANDARDS
Key Standard SS.A.1.3.2
The student knows the relative value of primary and secondary sources and uses this information to draw conclusions from historical sources such as data in charts, tables, graphs.
FCAT LA.A.2.3.6 Reading: Use Variety of Reference Materials

▶▶ Defining the Skill

The Internet is a computer network that connects libraries, museums, universities, government agencies, businesses, news organizations, and private individuals all over the world. Each location on the Internet has a home page with its own address, or URL (universal resource locator). With a computer connected to the Internet, you can reach the home pages of many organizations and services. The international collection of home pages, known as the World Wide Web, is an excellent source of up-to-date information about the regions and countries of the world.

▶▶ Applying the Skill

The Web page shown below is the European Reading Room at the Library of Congress Web site. Use the strategies listed below to help you understand how to research topics on the Internet.

How to Research Topics on the Internet

Strategy ❶ Once on the Internet, go directly to the Web page. For example, type http://www.loc.gov/rr/european/extlinks.html in the box at the top of the Web browser and press ENTER. The Web page will appear on your screen.

Strategy ❷ Explore the European Reading Room links. Click any of the links to find more information about a subject. These links take you to other Web sites.

Strategy ❸ Always confirm information you have found on the Internet. The Web sites of universities, government agencies, museums, and trustworthy news organizations are more reliable than others. You can often find information about a site's creator by looking for copyright information or reviewing the home page.

▶▶ Practicing the Skill

Turn to Chapter 4, Section 1, "Renaissance Connections." Reread the section and make a list of topics you would like to research.

For Internet links to support this activity, go to

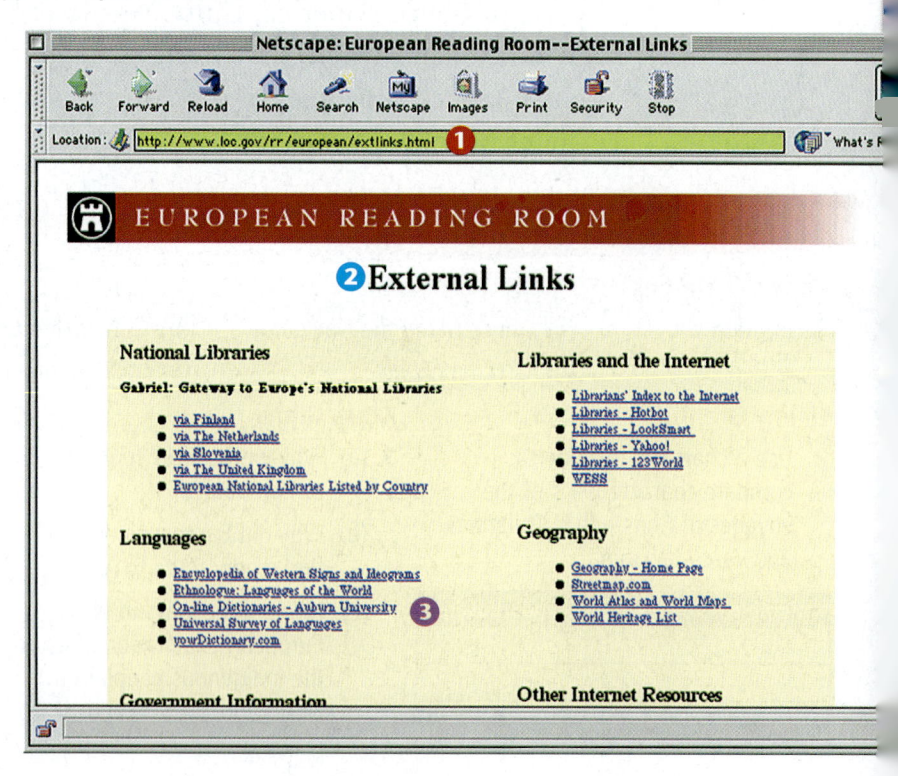

RESEARCH LINKS
CLASSZONE.COM

SECTION 3
The Age of Revolution

TERMS & NAMES
Scientific Revolution
Industrial Revolution
labor force
capitalism
French Revolution
Reign of Terror
Napoleon Bonaparte

MAIN IDEA
Scientific, industrial, and political revolutions transformed European society.

WHY IT MATTERS NOW
European revolutions in science, technology, and politics helped to create modern societies throughout the world.

DATELINE EXTRA

LEIPZIG, GERMANY, APRIL 1839

A new era in German history has begun. The Leipzig-Dresden railway is open for business. Although short rail lines have been in service for a few years, this is the first long-distance railway in this part of Europe.

The steam locomotive that powers the German train was made in England. It is the latest improvement to George Stephenson's "Rocket" train, which set a speed record of 30 mph in 1829. Already, this new form of transportation is changing Europe. The railroads are attracting many passengers and are also ideal for hauling goods. It seems that wherever new train stations are built, growth and prosperity soon follow.

Region • Leipzig's railway will now take passengers all the way to Dresden. ▲

Changes in Science and Industry

The steam-powered locomotive was only one in a long line of technological improvements made in Europe since the 1600s. In fact, scientists and inventors made so many discoveries during these years that Europe experienced both a scientific and an industrial revolution. These periods of great change would help to create modern societies.

TAKING NOTES
Use your chart to take notes about people and ideas.

Influences	New Ideas	People/Achievements
The Renaissance		
European Exploration		

SUNSHINE STATE STANDARDS
Key Standard SS.A.3.3.2 The student understands the historical events that have shaped the development of cultures throughout the world.
Other Standards SS.A.3.3.5, B.1.3.4
FCAT LA.A.2.3.1 Reading: Identify Main Idea, Facts, and Details

The Growth of New Ideas **107**

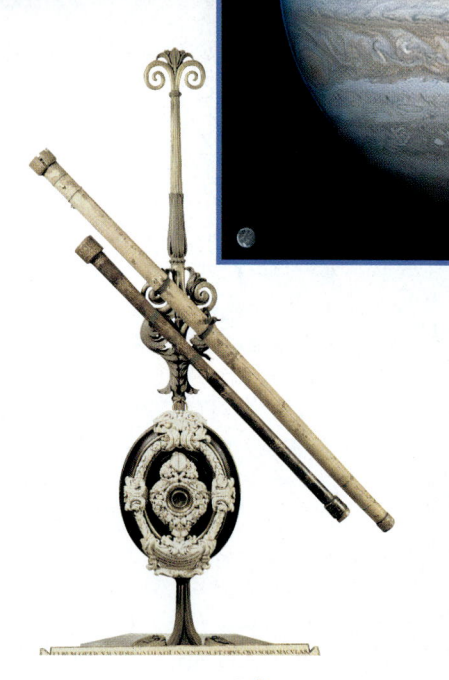

The Scientific Revolution In the 16th and 17th centuries, scientific discoveries changed the way Europeans looked at the world. This led to the **Scientific Revolution**.

In Italy, Galileo Galilei (GAL·uh·LEE·oh GAL·uh·LAY) (1564–1642) studied the stars and planets using a new invention called the telescope. Later in Holland, Antoni van Leeuwenhoek (LAY·vuhn·huk) (1632–1723) used a microscope to explore an unknown world found in a drop of water. The Swedish botanist Carolus Linnaeus (lih·NEE·uhs) (1707–1778) even developed a system to name and classify all living things on Earth.

Culture •
In 1610, Galileo used his telescope to observe that Jupiter had moons. ▲

The World's Heritage

The Scientific Method During the Scientific Revolution, scientists began doing research in a new way, called the scientific method. This scientific method is still used by scientists today.

First, scientists identify a problem. Next, they collect data about the problem. Using this data, they develop an explanation for the problem and test the explanation by performing experiments. Finally, they reach a conclusion.

The Industrial Revolution Many inventions of the Scientific Revolution began to change the way people worked all across Europe. Machines performed jobs that once had been done by humans and animals. This brought about such great change that it led to a revolution in the way goods were produced: the **Industrial Revolution**.

Machines were grouped together to make products in large factories. Early factories were built in the countryside near streams and rivers so that they could be powered by water. By the late 1700s, however, new steam engines were used to power the machinery. More and more factories could now be built in cities. People, in turn, moved from the countryside to the cities in search of work.

Reading Social Studies

A. Finding Causes How did the Scientific Revolution lead to the Industrial Revolution?

The Workshop of the World

The Industrial Revolution began in England in the late 1700s. The first English factories made textiles, or cloth. The steam-powered machines of the textile industry produced large amounts of goods quickly and cheaply. So many factories were built in England that the country earned the nickname "The Workshop of the World."

108 CHAPTER 4

BACKGROUND

In the 1850s, laws were finally passed to help protect women and children from long hours and harsh working conditions.

Hard Work for Low Pay The Industrial Revolution created a need for workers, or a **labor force**, in cities. The workers who ran the textile machines made up part of this labor force. Most workers could earn more income in cities than on farms, but life could be hard. Factory laborers worked long hours and received low pay. In fact, many families often sent their children to work to help create more income.

In 1838, women and children made up more than 75 percent of all textile factory workers. Children as young as seven were forced to work 12 hours a day, six days a week.

Population Growth in European Cities

SKILLBUILDER: Interpreting a Chart
1. Which city had the largest growth in population?
2. What was the population of Paris in 1890?

The Spread of Industrialization
The textile industry in 18th-century England was one step in the development of an economic system called **capitalism**. In this system, factories and other businesses that make and sell goods are privately owned. Private business owners make decisions about what goods to produce. They sell these goods at a price that will earn a profit.

Industrialization spread from England to other countries, including Germany, France, Belgium, and the United States. Cities in these countries grew rapidly and became more crowded and dirtier. Diseases, such as cholera (KAHL·uhr·uh) and typhoid (TY·foyd) fever, spread. Smoke from factories blackened city skies, and pollution fouled the rivers.

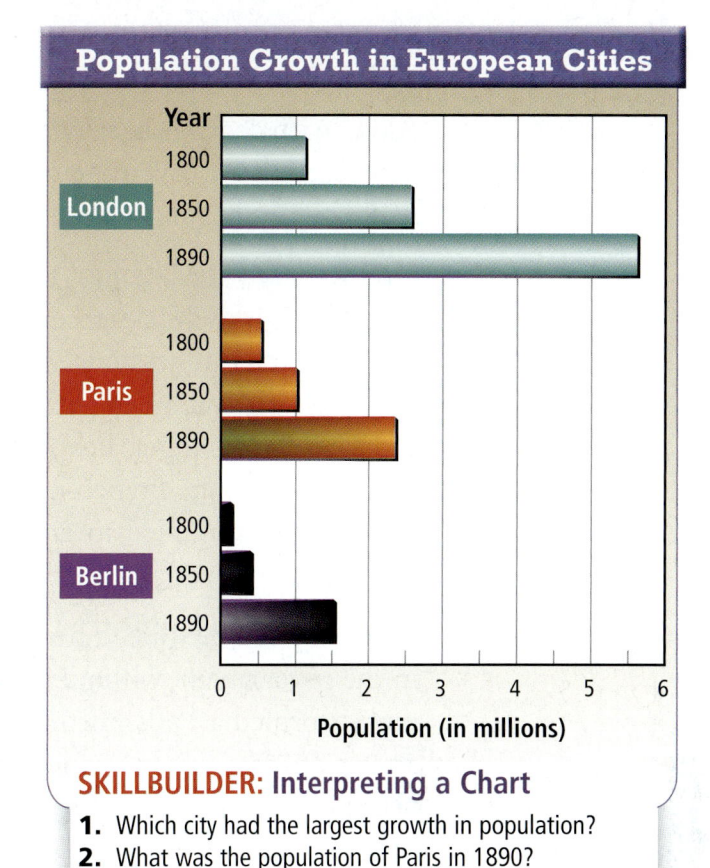

Place •
Factories, like this one in Sheffield, England, were found throughout Western Europe by the mid-19th century. ▶

The Growth of New Ideas **109**

The French Revolution

Along with changes in science, technology, and the economy came new ideas about government. In the late 18th century, many ordinary citizens began to fight for more political rights.

Ripe for Political Change By the 1780s, the French government was deeply in debt because of bad investments and the costs of waging wars. Life was miserable for the common working people. Poor harvests combined with increased population had led to food shortages and hunger. People were forced to pay heavy taxes. At the same time, the French king, Louis XVI, and his queen, Marie Antoinette, continued to enjoy an expensive life at court, entertaining themselves and the French nobility.

Storming the Bastille The citizens of France demanded changes in the government, without success. Then, on July 14, 1789, angry mobs stormed a Paris prison called the Bastille (ba·STEEL). The attack on this prison, which reflected the royal family's power, became symbolic of the **French Revolution**.

Revolts spread from Paris to the countryside, and poor and angry workers burned the homes of the nobility. By 1791, France had a new constitution that made all French citizens equal under the law.

Reading Social Studies
B. Analyzing Motives Why did the French citizens demand a new government?

Region • The storming of the Bastille remains a symbol of the French Revolution. ▼

BACKGROUND

Until the French Revolution, the guillotine was only used to execute nobles. It was considered the most humane type of execution.

The French Republic In 1792, France became a republic. King Louis XVI was found guilty of treason, or betraying one's country. In 1793, he and Marie Antoinette were sentenced to death. They were beheaded on the guillotine (GIHL·uh·teen).

Still, France was not at peace. The new revolutionary leaders refused to tolerate any disagreement. Between 1793 and 1794, these new leaders executed 17,000 people. This period of bloodshed became known as the **Reign of Terror**.

Napoleon French leaders continued to struggle for power until 1799, when General **Napoleon Bonaparte** (nuh·POH·lee·uhn BOH·nuh·PAHRT) took control. The French Revolution and the disorder that followed were finally over.

However, the new sense of equality brought about by the Revolution stirred feelings of nationalism among the French. Nationalism is pride in and loyalty to one's nation. Soon, the citizens of other European nations began to fight for more political power. Slowly, they, too, won more rights.

Region • Napoleon Bonaparte crowned himself emperor of France in 1804. He led France to victory in what became known as the Napoleonic Wars. ▲

SECTION 3 ASSESSMENT

Terms & Names
1. Explain the significance of:
   (a) Scientific Revolution (b) Industrial Revolution (c) labor force (d) capitalism
   (e) French Revolution (f) Reign of Terror (g) Napoleon Bonaparte

Using Graphics

2. Use a chart like this one to list some of the scientific, industrial, and political changes that occurred during the Age of Revolution.

Scientific Changes	Industrial Changes	Political Changes

Main Ideas

3. (a) Describe at least three inventions or discoveries of the Scientific Revolution.
   (b) How did the Industrial Revolution change the way people in Europe worked?
   (c) What changes occurred in France after the French Revolution?

Critical Thinking

4. **Recognizing Effects**
   How did industrialization change the cities to which it spread?

   Think About
   • population
   • diseases
   • the environment

ACTIVITY -OPTION- Reread the section about the French Revolution. Write a **poem** or **lyrics** for a folk song that describe the events from the point of view of a common citizen or a member of the royal family.

The Growth of New Ideas

SECTION 4: The Russian Empire

TERMS & NAMES
czar
Ivan the Terrible
Peter the Great
Catherine the Great
Russian Revolution

MAIN IDEA
Strong leaders built Russia into a large empire, but the country's citizens had few rights and struggled with poverty.

WHY IT MATTERS NOW
Russia has had a great influence on world politics and is experiencing a period of great change.

DATELINE

MOSCOW, RUSSIA, 1560—Today, the most magnificent church in Moscow opened with a grand celebration. The Cathedral of St. Basil has ten domes—each one unique. The massive structure, built of bricks and white stone, is decorated with brilliant colors.

Ivan IV built this cathedral to celebrate his victory eight years ago over the Tatars (TAH•tuhrz). These Turkish people who live in Central Asia have long threatened Russia's security.

The victory also added the lands of the Tatars, including their capital at Kazan, to our growing empire. Russians everywhere should be proud of Moscow's new church and of the victory it symbolizes.

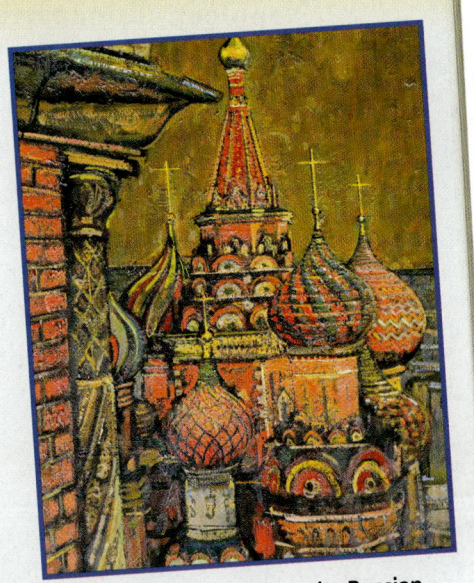

Place • Ivan IV has honored a Russian victory over the Tatars with the construction of St. Basil's Cathedral. ▲

Russia Rules Itself

Russia, geographically the world's largest nation, is located in both Europe and Asia. It takes up large parts of both continents, and both continents have helped shape its history.

Mongols from eastern Asia conquered Russia in the 13th century and ruled it for about 200 years. During the 15th century, Russia broke free of Mongol rule. At this time, the most important Russian city was Moscow, located in the west.

TAKING NOTES
Use your chart to take notes about people and ideas.

Influences	New Ideas	People/Achievements
The Renaissance		
European Exploration		

SUNSHINE STATE STANDARDS
Key Standard SS.A.3.3.2 The student understands the historical events that have shaped the development of cultures throughout the world.
Other Standards SS.A.2.3.5, A.3.3.4
FCAT LA.A.2.3.1 Reading: Identify Main Idea, Facts, and Details

112 CHAPTER 4

Reading Social Studies

A. Clarifying Why did the Russian people give Ivan IV the nickname Ivan the Terrible?

The First Czars of Russia In 1547, a 16-year-old leader in Moscow was crowned the first **czar** (zahr), or emperor, of modern Russia. His official title was Ivan IV, but the people nicknamed him **Ivan the Terrible.** Ivan was known for his cruelty, especially toward those he viewed as Russia's enemies. During his rule of 37 years, the country was constantly at war.

During the reigns of Ivan the Terrible and the czars who followed him, Russia had an unlimited government. This is a form of government in which a single ruler holds all the power. The people have no say in how the country is run.

Conflicts at Home The first Russian czars were often in conflict with the Russian nobles, who possessed much land and wealth. The czars viewed the nobles as a threat to their control over the people. Ivan the Terrible ordered his soldiers to murder Russian nobles and church leaders who opposed him.

The poor farmers, or peasants, of Russia also suffered under the first czars. New laws forced the peasants to become serfs, who had to remain on the farms where they worked.

Region • Ivan the Terrible is said to have worn this fur-trimmed crown at his coronation in 1547. ▲

The Expansion of Russia

In addition to strengthening their control over the Russian people, the czars wanted to gain new territory. Throughout the 17th and 18th centuries, rulers such as Peter the Great and Catherine the Great conquered neighboring lands.

A Window on the West An intelligent man with big ideas for his country, **Peter the Great** ruled Russia from 1682 to 1725. After defeating Sweden in war and winning land along the Baltic Sea, Peter built a port city called St. Petersburg. This city, which Peter saw as Russia's "window on the west," became the new capital.

BACKGROUND
In 1721, Peter the Great changed his title from *czar* to *emperor*, a title that he thought sounded more European.

One of Peter's goals was to have closer ties with Western Europe. He hoped to use the ideas and inventions of the Scientific Revolution to modernize and strengthen Russia. During his rule, Peter reformed the army and the government and built new schools. He even ordered Russians to dress like Europeans and to shave off their beards. Peter's reforms made Russia stronger, but they did not improve life for Russian peasants.

Movement • Peter the Great brought to Russia many of the improvements of the Scientific and Industrial Revolutions. ▲

The Growth of New Ideas

The Expansion of Russia, 1584–1796

GEOGRAPHY SKILLBUILDER: Interpreting a Map
1. **Location** • What body of water did Russia gain access to in 1796?
2. **Place** • When did Russia gain the most land?

A Great Empress <u>Catherine the Great</u> took control of Russia in 1762 and ruled until her death in 1796. Catherine added vast new lands to the empire, including the present-day countries of Ukraine (yoo·KRAYN) and Belarus (behl·uh·ROOS). Like Peter the Great, Catherine borrowed many ideas from Western Europe. She started new schools and encouraged art, science, and literature. Catherine also built new towns and expanded trade.

During Catherine's reign, Russia became one of Europe's most powerful nations. The lives of the peasants, however, remained miserable. Catherine thought about freeing them, but she knew the nobles would oppose her. When the peasants rebelled in the 1770s, Catherine crushed their uprising.

Movement • Catherine the Great continued Peter the Great's practice of bringing the ideas of Western Europe to Russia. ▼

A Divided Russia

In the 19th century, Russia remained a divided nation. Most people were poor peasants, and most of the wealth belonged to the nobles. This division would lead to conflict and eventually to a political revolution.

The Nobles Many Russian nobles sent their children to be educated in Germany and France. In fact, many noble families spoke French at home, speaking Russian only to their servants. The Western Europeans introduced many new ideas to the Russian nobles, among them the idea that a nation's government should reflect the wishes of its citizens.

BACKGROUND
Catherine the Great was born in Germany. She came to Russia at 15 to marry the heir to the throne, Peter III. He was a weak ruler, however, and Catherine, supported by the army and the people, overthrew him.

Many Russian nobles were army officers or government officials. Most supported the czar and were proud of Russia's growing power. In 1825, one group of nobles tried to replace the government. Their attempt to gain more power failed.

The Serfs In the 19th century, the Russian serfs still had no land or money of their own. They worked on farms owned by others and received little help from the Russian government.

In 1861, Alexander II decided to end serfdom in Russia. He hoped that freeing the serfs would help his country compete with Western Europe. The serfs had to pay a heavy tax, though, and the land they were given was often not good for farming. Most former serfs felt that they had gained very little.

Bloody Sunday The serfs were not the only unhappy Russians. Many university students, artists, and writers believed that the government's treatment of the serfs was unfair. Some joined groups that tried to overthrow the government. In addition, workers in Russia's cities complained about low pay and poor working conditions.

In 1905, a group of workers marched to the royal palace in St. Petersburg with a list of demands. Government troops shot many of them. News of the events of this "Bloody Sunday" spread across Russia, making people even angrier with the government and czar.

BACKGROUND
In the 1850s, Russia fought the Crimean War against Turkey. Two of Turkey's allies were Britain and France. When Russia lost, Alexander II thought this proved that his country was still far less advanced than Western European nations.

Spotlight on CULTURE

The Hermitage Museum One of the world's largest art museums is the Hermitage in St. Petersburg. It contains many works of art, including French, Spanish, and British paintings. Part of the collection is in the Winter Palace, a former royal residence.

Both Peter the Great and Catherine the Great collected European art. On a trip to Amsterdam in 1716, Peter bought paintings by the famous Dutch artist Rembrandt. About 50 years later, Catherine bought more than 200 works of art when she visited Germany. These royal collections became part of the Hermitage when it opened as a public museum in 1852.

THINKING CRITICALLY

1. **Analyzing Motives**
Why did Peter the Great and Catherine the Great collect art from Western Europe?

2. **Making Inferences**
Why do you think the works of art were displayed in a museum?

For more on the Hermitage Museum, go to
RESEARCH LINKS CLASSZONE.COM

The End of the Russian Empire

In 1914, World War I began. Nicholas II—a quiet, shy man who did not want war—ruled Russia, but he failed to keep his country out of the battle. Russia, whose allies included the United Kingdom and France, suffered terrible losses fighting Germany and its allies.

During World War I, there were food shortages in the cities and workers went on strike. Russian revolutionaries organized the workers against the czar. Even the Russian army turned against their ruler, and in 1917, Nicholas was forced to give up power. This overturning of the Russian monarchy is known as the **Russian Revolution**.

Nicholas II and the royal family (the Romanovs) were imprisoned by the revolutionaries. On July 17, 1918, they were all shot to death. This execution ended more than 300 years of rule by the Romanov family and nearly 400 years of czarist rule.

Reading Social Studies

B. Analyzing Motives Why did Russian workers strike?

Strange but TRUE

Rasputin One of the most influential people at the court of Czar Nicholas II was Rasputin. He came from Siberia in eastern Russia and was a self-styled holy man. Crown prince Alexis suffered from the disease hemophilia, and no doctor in Russia could cure him. Rasputin seemed to mysteriously heal the boy, gaining favor with Nicholas's wife, Czarina Alexandra. However, in 1916, Russian nobles killed Rasputin out of fear of the considerable power and influence the monk had.

SECTION 4 ASSESSMENT

Terms & Names
1. Explain the significance of:
   (a) czar
   (b) Ivan the Terrible
   (c) Peter the Great
   (d) Catherine the Great
   (e) Russian Revolution

Using Graphics
2. Use a chart like this one to describe three characteristics of czars of Russia.

Ivan the Terrible	Peter the Great	Catherine the Great	Nicholas II

Main Ideas
3. (a) What effects did an unlimited government have on Russian peasants?
   (b) How did Peter the Great help reform Russia?
   (c) Alexander II ended serfdom in 1861, but this did little to help the serfs. Why?

Critical Thinking
4. **Finding Causes**
   What events led to the Russian Revolution?

Think About
- the life of the serfs
- Bloody Sunday
- the events of World War I

ACTIVITY -OPTION- Look at the map on page 114 that shows the expansion of Russia. Write a brief **summary** to describe how the Russian nation grew from the 1500s to 1800.

Technology: 1781

SUNSHINE STATE STANDARDS
Key Standard SS.A.3.3.2 The student understands the historical events that have shaped the development of cultures throughout the world.
FCAT LA.A.2.3.1 Reading: Identify Main Idea, Facts, and Details

INTERACTIVE

James Watt's Double-Action Steam Engine

Amid the excitement of the Industrial Revolution, James Watt (1736–1819), a Scottish inventor, patented a new steam engine. Steam power had been used for many years, but Watt's invention was an improved, double-action steam engine. This system, in which the steam pushes from both sides of the piston rather than from just one, enhanced efficiency and increased power. Watt's invention helped to advance manufacturing and transportation and influenced later inventions. Watt's double-action steam engine was one of the most important inventions of the Industrial Revolution.

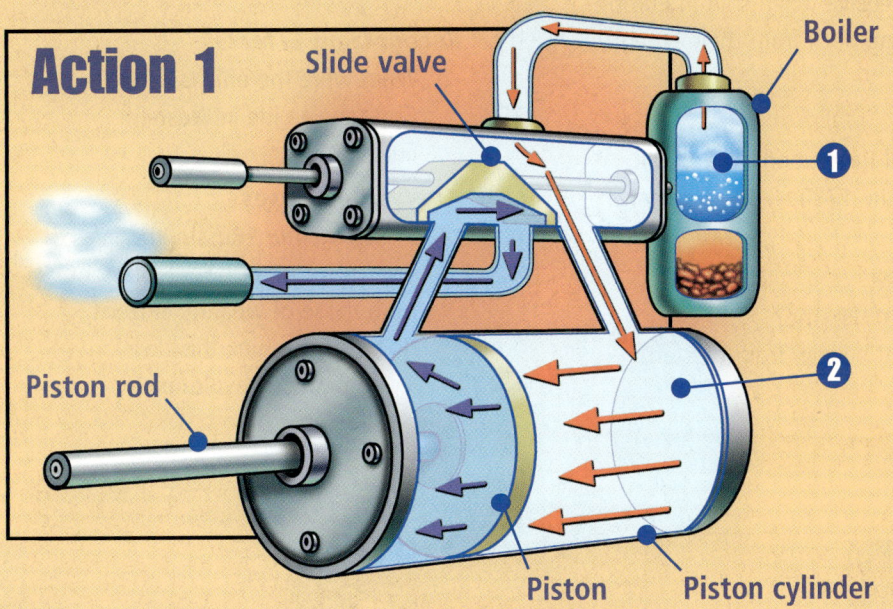

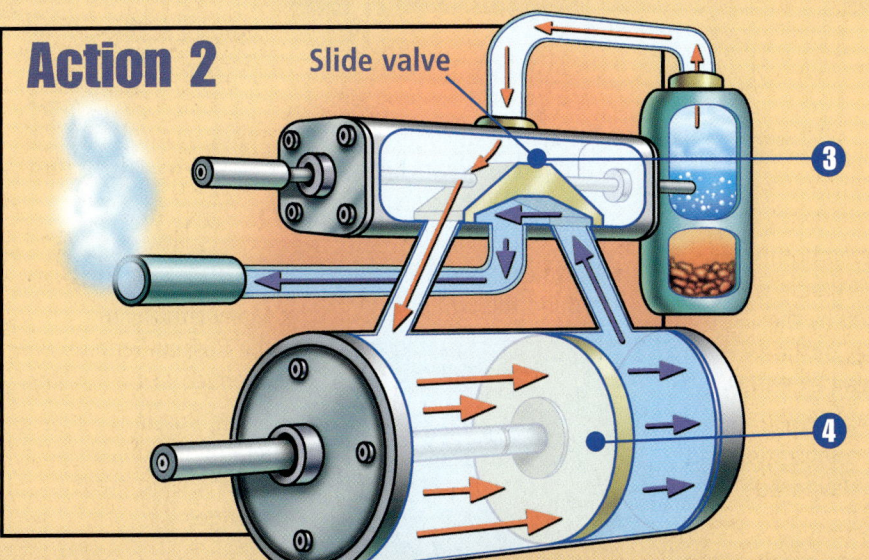

How the Engine Works

Steam from the **boiler** enters the **piston cylinder**. The pressure of the steam pushes the **piston** to one side, moving the **piston rod**. When the piston reaches the end of the stroke, the **slide valve** shifts the steam to the other side of the piston, forcing it back and releasing the steam it compresses as exhaust.

① As water is converted to steam, its volume increases 1,600 percent.

② When the steam enters the piston cylinder, it forces the piston rod to one side.

③ As the piston reaches the end of its stroke, the slide valve channels steam to the other side of the piston.

④ The piston rod is pushed back, forcing the "old" steam out as exhaust.

Action 1 — Slide valve, Boiler, Piston rod, Piston, Piston cylinder

Action 2 — Slide valve

Key: Steam | Exhaust

THINKING Critically

1. Drawing Conclusions
How did the steam engine help power the Industrial Revolution?

2. Recognizing Effects
How did Watt's steam engine change the lives of working people?

UNIT 2 *Europe, Russia, and the Independent Republics*

CHAPTER 4 ASSESSMENT

TERMS & NAMES

Explain the significance of each of the following:
1. Renaissance
2. Leonardo da Vinci
3. Reformation
4. Ferdinand Magellan
5. circumnavigate
6. imperialism
7. Industrial Revolution
8. Napoleon Bonaparte
9. Peter the Great
10. Russian Revolution

REVIEW QUESTIONS

Renaissance Connections (pages 95–100)
1. How did the subjects chosen by artists change during the Renaissance?
2. Why were the followers of Martin Luther called Protestants?

Traders, Explorers, and Colonists (pages 101–105)
3. Why were spices from Asia so expensive when sold in Europe?
4. What did Portuguese explorers bring back from their expeditions to western Africa?

The Age of Revolutions (pages 107–111)
5. When and where did the Industrial Revolution begin?
6. What conditions in France during the 1780s led to the French Revolution?

The Russian Empire (pages 112–116)
7. How did Ivan the Terrible earn his nickname?
8. What ideas did Catherine the Great borrow from Western Europe?

CRITICAL THINKING

Finding Causes
1. Using your completed chart from Reading Social Studies, p. 94, list the events that led to the growth of cities during the Industrial Revolution.

Recognizing Effects
2. What were the effects of the Crusades on life in Western Europe?

Analyzing Causes
3. In 19th-century Russia, the lives of poor citizens were very different from those of wealthy citizens. How do you think this division led to political revolution?

Visual Summary

1 Renaissance Connections
- European society was transformed by the art, literature, and ideas of the Renaissance.
- The accomplishments of this period are an important part of Western culture.

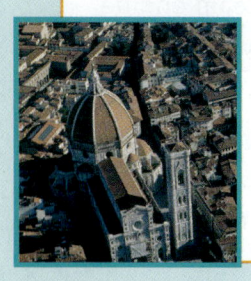

2 Traders, Explorers, and Colonists
- People on both sides of the Atlantic were changed by the voyages of the European explorers.
- European exploration led to colonization and to the slave trade.

3 The Age of Revolution
- The Age of Revolution resulted in great changes in European society, industry, and politics.
- These changes were felt around the world.

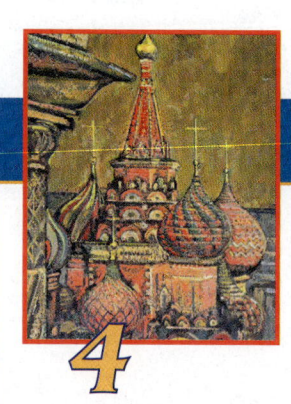

4 The Russian Empire
- Many citizens of the Russian Empire were deprived of their rights.
- Today, Russia is a large nation experiencing great change.

STANDARDS-BASED ASSESSMENT

Use the map and your knowledge of geography to answer questions 1 and 2.

Additional Test Practice, pp. S1–S33

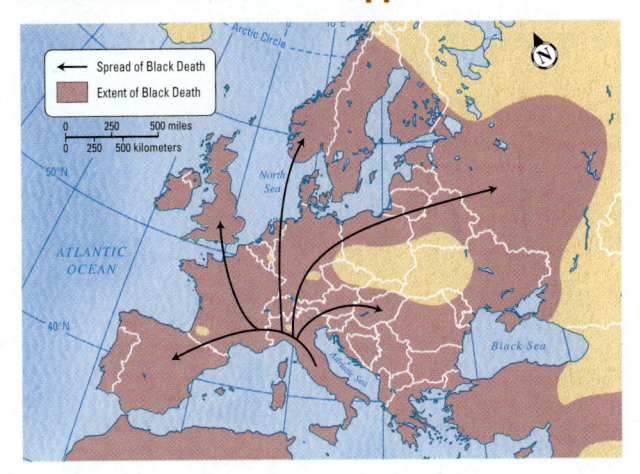

The following passage is from a biography of Leonardo da Vinci. Use the quotation and your knowledge of world cultures and geography to answer question 3.

PRIMARY SOURCE

Although we have called Leonardo a scientist, it is not a title he would have understood. The word "scientist" was not used before 1840. Leonardo did, however, use the word "science." To him it meant knowledge proved true by experience. He contrasted it with "speculation," by which he meant guesswork not proved by experience.

STEWART ROSS, *Leonardo da Vinci*

1. Judging from the arrows on the map, how might the plague have spread?
   A. mostly from north to south
   B. through the center of Eastern Europe
   C. along trade routes out of Italy
   D. in a circular pattern

2. According to the map, which body of water did the plague cross as it spread through Europe?
   A. Adriatic Sea
   B. Atlantic Ocean
   C. Black Sea
   D. North Sea

3. What did Leonardo da Vinci consider the basis of science?
   A. guesses
   B. experience
   C. dedication
   D. speculations

TEST PRACTICE CLASSZONE.COM

ALTERNATIVE ASSESSMENT

1. WRITING ABOUT HISTORY

Imagine that you are a film maker. Write a proposal for a documentary film about Leonardo da Vinci and one of his inventions. In your proposal, describe the invention, tell how it works, and explain how da Vinci came up with the idea. Remember that the purpose of your documentary is to inform and entertain the viewer.

- Research the Internet or library books about Leonardo da Vinci to find an interesting invention.
- If possible, include a copy of da Vinci's sketch or a photograph of the invention.

2. COOPERATIVE LEARNING

With a group of three or four classmates, research the voyage of Ferdinand Magellan, the first explorer to lead an expedition that sailed around the world. Then prepare a presentation for your class. Group members can share the responsibilities of finding out who funded the trip, what hardships the sailors faced, and what eventually happened to Magellan. One member can create a map of Magellan's route.

INTEGRATED TECHNOLOGY

Doing Internet Research

The Scientific Revolution changed the way people viewed the world. Use the Internet to research one discovery or invention of a great scientist of the time, such as Galileo Galilei.

- Using the Internet, as well as other library resources, find out about the discovery or invention. You might find information in a biography of the scientist.
- Another source of information might be a science museum.
- Create a poster to explain your findings. Include a diagram or other illustration of the scientific discovery. Explain how the discovery or invention has affected life in modern times.

For Internet links to support this activity, go to

RESEARCH LINKS CLASSZONE.COM

The Growth of New Ideas

CHAPTER 5
Europe: War and Change

SECTION 1 European Empires

SECTION 2 Europe at War

SECTION 3 The Soviet Union

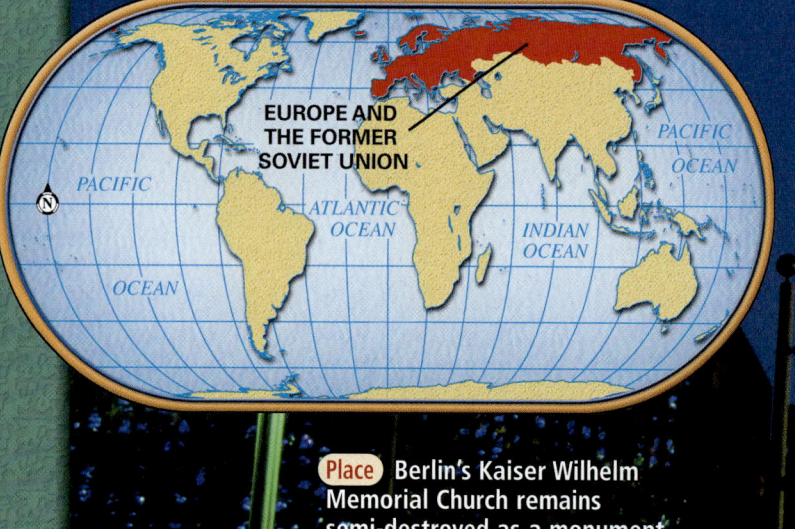

EUROPE AND THE FORMER SOVIET UNION

Place Berlin's Kaiser Wilhelm Memorial Church remains semi-destroyed as a monument to World War II. Germany has since rebuilt its cities. It is once again an important part of Europe's economy, politics, and culture.

FOCUS ON GEOGRAPHY

How has Europe's small landmass affected its history?

Place • The continent of Europe is home to more than 40 countries. Yet, it is approximately the same size as the United States. Since many European nations share borders with several other countries, Europeans often speak three or more languages. Across Europe, approximately 50 languages are spoken.

Europe is densely populated. In fact, the continent has almost three times as many people as the United States. So many people, living so close together, has sometimes led to competition and warfare over land and resources.

What do you think?

- How might the differences among Europeans cause conflict?
- How might the closeness of so many countries help to unite Europe?

CHAPTER 5

READING SOCIAL STUDIES

BEFORE YOU READ

▶▶ *What Do You Know?*

Do you know that during World War I, armies trained dogs to guard supplies and assist soldiers? What do you know about World War I and World War II? Have you ever seen a movie or read a book about either conflict? What do you hear in the news about current events in Europe? Think about how events in Europe in the past century might have contributed to life there today.

▶▶ *What Do You Want to Know?*

Decide what you know about Europe's history in the 1900s and what it is like there today. In your notebook, record what you hope to learn from this chapter.

Region • The image of the hammer and sickle became the symbol of the Soviet Union. ▲

READ AND TAKE NOTES

Reading Strategy: Analyzing Causes and Effects

Analyzing causes and effects is an essential skill for understanding what you read in social studies, because events are caused by other events or situations. This sequence is called a chain of events. Understanding which causes lead to which events is essential in understanding history and other areas of social studies. Use the chart below to show causes and effects discussed in Chapter 5.

- Copy the chart into your notebook.
- As you read, record causes and effects for each event.

Region • During World War I, armies trained dogs to assist them. ▲

Causes	Event	Effects
	World War I	
	World War II	
	Growth of Soviet Union	

122 CHAPTER 5

SECTION 1

European Empires

TERMS & NAMES
nationalism
colonialism
Austria-Hungary
dual monarchy

MAIN IDEA
The beginning of the 20th century was a time of change in Europe, as feelings of nationalism began to take hold.

WHY IT MATTERS NOW
Feelings of nationalism continue to lead to conflicts that change the map of Europe.

DATELINE

NORWAY, SEPTEMBER 1905—It could have been war in the Scandinavian Peninsula. The armies of Norway and Sweden had begun preparations.

Instead, Sweden ended the crisis peacefully by granting Norway independence. Norway had been under Swedish control since 1814. Although Norway ran its own affairs within the country, Sweden set foreign policy and controlled Norway's international shipping and trade.

Prince Charles of Denmark has been invited to become king of Norway. The Norwegians will vote to approve their new leader. If chosen, he will become King Haakon VII.

The king's role will be largely ceremonial. His chief task will be to help unite the newly independent people of Norway.

Region • Prince Charles of Denmark, pictured here with his family, hopes to become King Haakon VII of Norway.

The Spread of Nationalism

Norway's independence from Sweden was a sign of new ideas that were sweeping across Europe at the time. During the late 19th and early 20th centuries, **nationalism,** or strong pride in one's nation or ethnic group, influenced the feelings of many Europeans. An ethnic group includes people with similar languages and traditions, but who are not necessarily ruled by a common government.

TAKING NOTES
Use your chart to take notes about war and change in Europe.

Causes	Event	Effects
	World War I	
	World War II	

SUNSHINE STATE STANDARDS
Key Standard SS.B.1.3.3 The student knows the social, political, and economic divisions on Earth's surface.
FCAT LA.A.2.3.1 Reading: Identify Main Idea, Facts and Details

Europe: War and Change 123

Constitutional Monarchies In part, the spread of nationalism was fueled by the fact that more Europeans than ever before could vote. For centuries, many monarchs had unlimited power. In country after country, however, citizens demanded the right to elect lawmakers who would limit their monarch's authority. This kind of government is called a constitutional monarchy. A constitutional monarchy not only has a king or queen, but also a ruling body of elected officials. The United Kingdom is one example of a constitutional monarchy.

By 1900, many countries in Western Europe had become constitutional monarchies. Citizens of these countries strongly supported the governments that they helped to elect. When one country threatened another, most citizens were willing to go to war to defend their homeland.

Reading Social Studies

A. Contrasting How does a constitutional monarchy differ from a democracy?

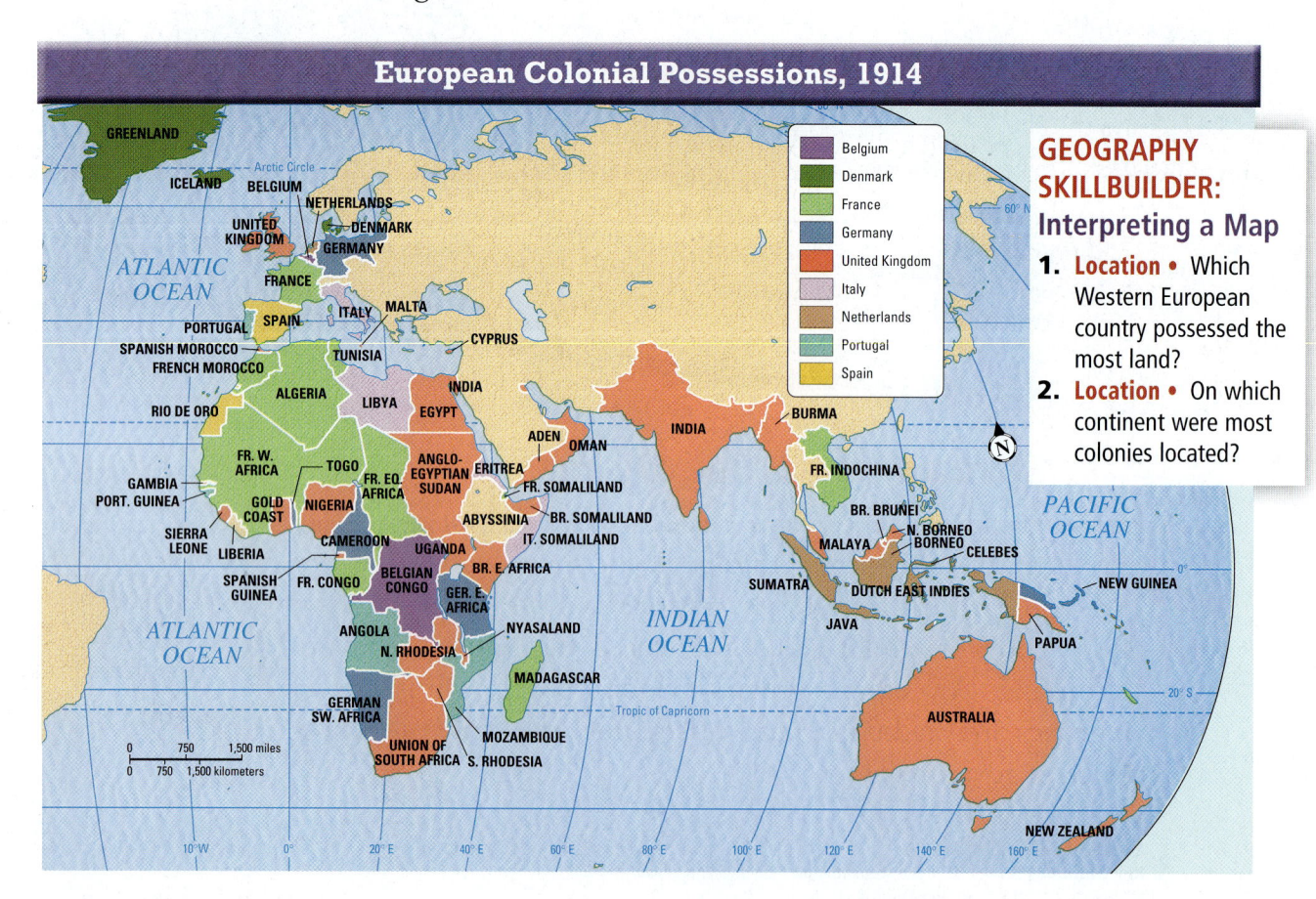

The Defense of Colonial Empires At the beginning of the 20th century, many Western European countries—including France, Italy, the United Kingdom, Germany, and even tiny Belgium—had colonies in Asia and Africa. Colonies supplied the raw materials that the ruling countries needed to produce goods in their factories back home. Asian and African colonies, sometimes larger than the ruling country, were also important markets for manufactured goods.

European Colonial Possessions, 1914

GEOGRAPHY SKILLBUILDER: Interpreting a Map

1. **Location** • Which Western European country possessed the most land?
2. **Location** • On which continent were most colonies located?

Location • In 1914, the United Kingdom could truthfully state that the sun never set on the British Empire. ◀

During this period of **colonialism,** Western European nations spent much of their wealth on building strong armies and navies. Their military forces helped to defend borders at home as well as colonies in other parts of the world. Colonies were so important that the ruling countries sometimes fought one another for control of them. They also struggled to extend their territories.

Spotlight on CULTURE

The Ballets Russes Begun in Paris, France, in 1909, the Ballets Russes (ba•LAY ROOS) was a dance company under the direction of the Russian producer Sergey Diaghilev (dee•AH•guh•LEHF). It was a critical and commercial success, and it spread artistic ideas.

Talented dancers and choreographers, such as Nijinsky, worked for Diaghilev. Famous composers—including Claude Debussy (duh•BYOO•see) and Igor Stravinsky—wrote music for performances. Pablo Picasso, Marc Chagall, and other great artists designed the sets. The Ballets Russes continued until Diaghilev's death in 1929.

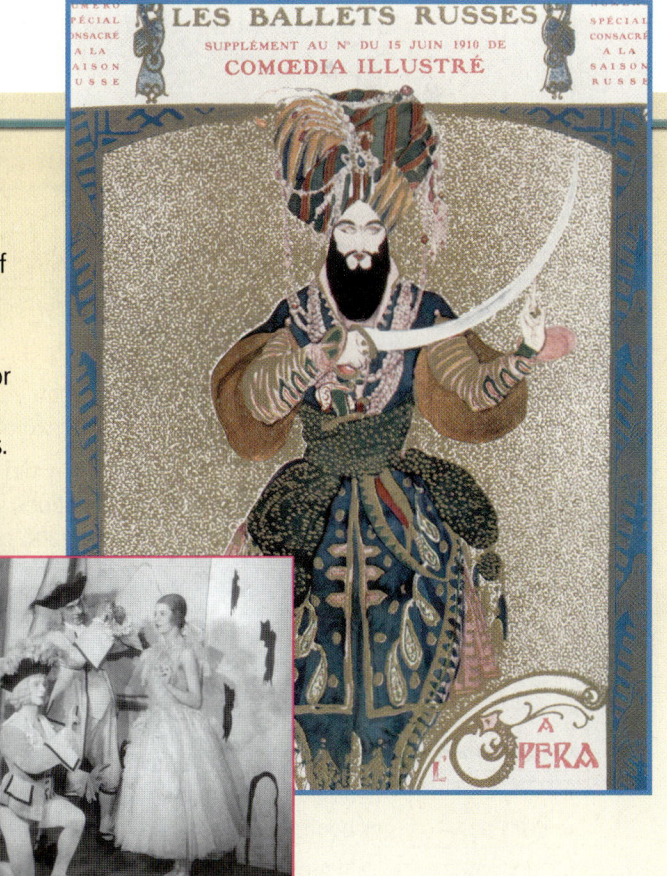

THINKING CRITICALLY

1. **Synthesizing**
   How did the Ballets Russes benefit the European art and theater communities?
2. **Clarifying**
   How was the Ballets Russes more than a collection of dancers, musicians, and artists?

For more on the Ballets Russes, go to
RESEARCH LINKS CLASSZONE.COM

Austria-Hungary, 1900

GEOGRAPHY SKILLBUILDER: Interpreting a Map

1. **Location** • Name three countries that bordered Austria-Hungary.
2. **Region** • What was the capital of Austria-Hungary?

Austria-Hungary By the end of the 19th century, most nations of Western and Northern Europe had become industrialized. The majority of Eastern Europe, including Russia, remained agricultural. These Eastern European countries imported most of their manufactured goods from Western and Northern Europe.

The largest empire in Eastern Europe in 1900 was **Austria-Hungary**. The empire was a **dual monarchy**, in which one ruler governs two nations. As you can see in the map above, Austria-Hungary also included parts of many other present-day countries, including Romania, the Czech Republic, and portions of Poland.

Reading Social Studies

B. Making Inferences Why do you think governing a dual monarchy was difficult?

SECTION 1 ASSESSMENT

Terms & Names
1. Explain the significance of:
   (a) nationalism
   (b) colonialism
   (c) Austria-Hungary
   (d) dual monarchy

Using Graphics

2. Look at the map on page 124 that shows European colonial territories. Use a chart like the one below to list the major colonial powers and their colonies.

Nation	Locations of Colonies

Main Ideas

3. (a) Identify one reason for the spread of nationalism in Europe.
   (b) Why did Western European nations spend much of their wealth on armies and navies?
   (c) How did the nations of Eastern Europe differ from those of Western and Northern Europe at the end of the 19th century?

Critical Thinking

4. **Drawing Conclusions**
   Why were their colonies so important to European nations?

   Think About
   - land and people
   - competition among nations
   - the production and sale of goods

ACTIVITY -OPTION- Reread the information about the Ballets Russes. Write an **outline** of a story or book that might be a good choice for a ballet. Explain your choice.

SECTION 2

Europe at War

TERMS & NAMES
World War I
alliance
Adolf Hitler
fascism
Holocaust
World War II
NATO

MAIN IDEA
During the first half of the 20th century, European countries fought each other over land, wealth, and ideals.

WHY IT MATTERS NOW
The changes brought about by the two world wars continue to affect Europe today.

DATELINE

SARAJEVO, BOSNIA-HERZEGOVINA, JUNE 28, 1914—Today, Archduke of Austria-Hungary Franz Ferdinand and his wife, Duchess Sophie, were murdered as they drove through Sarajevo. A nineteen-year-old Serb, Gavrilo Princip, jumped on the Archduke's automobile and fired two shots. The first killed the Duchess. The second killed the Archduke, who was next in line to be emperor of Austria-Hungary.

The Serbians have protested against Austria-Hungary since 1908, when the empire took over Bosnia and Herzegovina (BAHZ•nee•uh HEHRT•suh•GOH•VEE•nuh). Princip has been arrested.

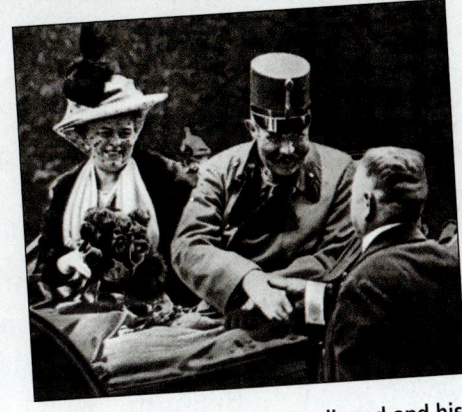

Region • Archduke Franz Ferdinand and his wife, Duchess Sophie, were fatally shot in Sarajevo. ▲

The World at War

Because of the murder of Archduke Franz Ferdinand in 1914, the emperor of Austria-Hungary declared war on Serbia. When Russia sent troops to defend Serbia, Germany declared war on Russia. Russia supported Serbia because both Russians and Serbians share a similar ethnic background—they are both Slavic peoples. This was the beginning of **World War I**.

SUNSHINE STATE STANDARDS
Key Standard
SS.A.3.3.2 The student understands the historical events that have shaped the development of cultures throughout the world.
FCAT LA.A.2.3.1
Reading: Identify Main Idea, Facts, and Details

TAKING NOTES
Use your chart to take notes about war and change in Europe.

Causes	Event	Effects
	World War I	
	World War II	

Europe: War and Change **127**

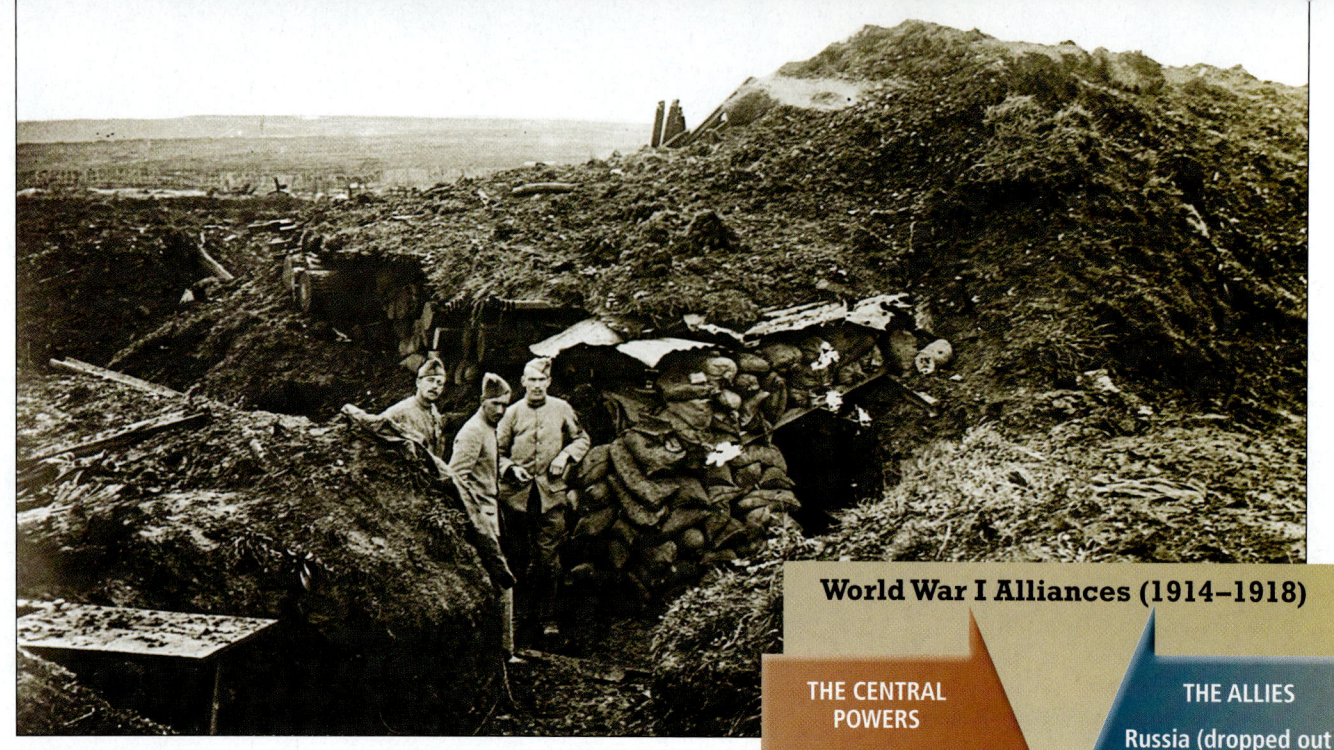

Place • World War I was primarily fought in trenches, which were dug by the armies for better defense. ▲

World War I Alliances (1914–1918)

THE CENTRAL POWERS
- Austria-Hungary
- Germany
- Turkey (Ottoman Empire)
- Bulgaria

THE ALLIES
- Russia (dropped out in 1917)
- France
- United Kingdom
- Italy (joined 1915)
- United States (joined 1917)

World War I Alliances European rulers wanted other leaders to think twice before declaring war on their countries. To help defend themselves, several countries joined alliances (uh·LY·uhn·sez). An **alliance** is an agreement among people or nations to unite for a common cause. Each member of an alliance agrees to help the other members in case one of them is attacked.

When Germany joined the war to support Austria-Hungary, France came in on the side of Russia. Germany then invaded Belgium, which was neutral, to attack France. Because Great Britain had promised to protect Belgium, it, too, declared war on Germany. After German submarines sank four American merchant ships, the United States joined the side of Russia, France, and Great Britain.

The chart above shows the major powers on both sides of World War I. Italy had originally been allied with Germany and Austria-Hungary but joined the Allies after the war began. Russia dropped out of the war completely after the revolution in that country in 1917.

Reading Social Studies

A. Recognizing Important Details Why did Great Britain enter World War I?

SKILLBUILDER: Interpreting a Political Cartoon
1. What does the artist mean by naming the figure "Progress"?
2. Why is the man wearing a gas mask?

World War I was costly in terms of human life. When it was over, nearly 22 million civilians and soldiers on both sides were dead. The Allies had won, and Europe had been devastated.

Europe After World War I

More people were killed during World War I than during all the wars of the 19th century combined. Afterward, people in many countries on both sides of the costly war—and even those not directly involved—were poor, homeless, and without work.

The Allies blamed Germany for much of the killing and damage during the war. In 1919, Germany and the Allies signed the Treaty of Versailles (vuhr•SY).

Strange but TRUE

War Dogs During World War I, dogs were trained to guard ammunition, to detect mines, and to carry messages. Dogs even helped to search for the wounded.

War dogs saved many lives. They were especially helpful in forested areas and at night. These dogs are wearing protective masks to keep them safe from poison gas attacks.

GEOGRAPHY SKILLBUILDER: Interpreting a Map

1. **Location** • What body of water does the coast of Yugoslavia reach?
2. **Location** • Name three countries that border Czechoslovakia.

Europe: War and Change **129**

The Treaty of Versailles demanded that Germany be punished by being forced to pay for the damage done to the Allied countries. Germany was also made to give up valuable territory.

A New Map of Europe Additional treaties during the following year also altered the political boundaries of many European countries. As the map on page 129 shows, Austria-Hungary was divided as a result of the war, becoming two separate countries. This allowed several Eastern European ethnic groups that had been part of Austria-Hungary to gain their independence.

World War II

By the 1930s, Germany was still paying for the damage done to the Allied countries during World War I. The German economy was in ruins, and the Germans greatly wished to rebuild their own country. In 1933, citizens elected **Adolf Hitler** and the National Socialist, or Nazi, Party. The Nazi Party believed in fascism. **Fascism** (FASH·IHZ·uhm) is a philosophy that supports a strong, central government controlled by the military and led by a powerful dictator. People believed that this new leader would help Germany recover.

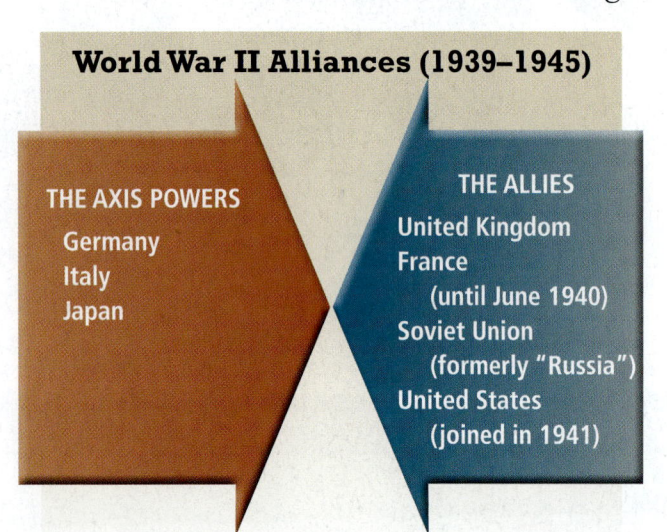

World War II Alliances (1939–1945)

THE AXIS POWERS
Germany
Italy
Japan

THE ALLIES
United Kingdom
France
(until June 1940)
Soviet Union
(formerly "Russia")
United States
(joined in 1941)

Reading Social Studies

B. Finding Causes What conditions led Germans to find hope in Adolf Hitler?

BACKGROUND

Like Germany, Italy was also ruled by a fascist dictator after World War I: Benito Mussolini (1883–1945).

Hitler and the Nazi Party Fascists practiced an extreme form of patriotism and nationalism. Fascists also had racist beliefs.

In the 1930s, Hitler unjustly blamed the Jewish citizens of Germany, among other specific groups, for the country's problems. His Nazi followers seized Jewish property and began to send Jews, along with disabled people, political opponents, and others, to concentration camps. During this **Holocaust,** millions of people were deliberately killed, and others starved or died from disease.

In 1934, Hitler took command of the armed forces. Then, in 1939, Hitler's army invaded Poland. **World War II** had begun. By June 1940, Hitler's army had swept through Western Europe, conquering Belgium, the Netherlands, Luxembourg, France, Denmark, and Norway. A year later, Germany invaded the Soviet Union.

WWII Alliances The chart on page 130 shows the major powers on both sides of World War II. As in World War I, the United States at first tried to stay out of the conflict but entered the war after Japan bombed U.S. military bases at Pearl Harbor in Hawaii on December 7, 1941.

Europe After World War II

World War II turned much of Europe into a battleground. By the end of the war, the United States, France, and the United Kingdom occupied Western Europe. The Soviet Union occupied Eastern Europe, including the eastern part of Germany.

Once peace was established, the western allies helped to set up free governments in Western Europe. In 1949, the countries of Western Europe joined Canada and the United States to form a defense alliance called **NATO** (NAY·toh). The members of this alliance, whose name stands for North Atlantic Treaty Organization, agreed to defend one another if they were attacked by the Soviet Union or any other country. Without a common enemy, political differences quickly separated the Soviet Union from Western Europe and the United States.

Place • The Kaiser Wilhelm Memorial Church in Berlin was nearly destroyed by Allied bombs. The ruins still stand today as a World War II monument. See pages 120–121. ▲

Biography

Anne Frank In July 1942, during World War II, Anne Frank and her family went into hiding in Amsterdam—a city in the Netherlands. The Frank family were Jewish and were afraid they would be sent to a concentration camp. Anne was only thirteen.

For two years, Anne, her father, mother, sister, and four other people lived in rooms in an attic. Their rooms were sealed off from the rest of the building. While in hiding, Anne kept a diary. Although the family was discovered and Anne died in a concentration camp, her diary was eventually published. Today, this famous book—translated into many languages and the basis for a play and a film—lives on.

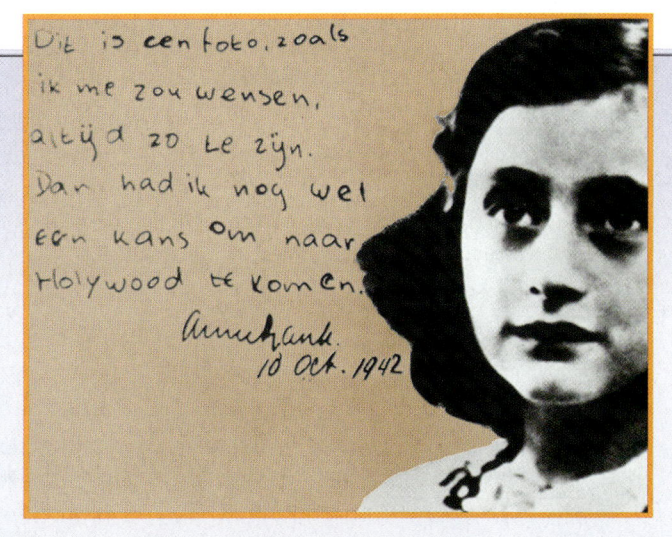

Europe: War and Change

Europe After World War II

GEOGRAPHY SKILLBUILDER: Interpreting a Map

1. **Location** • In what country is Berlin located?
2. **Location** • Name three countries that border the Soviet Union.

The Marshall Plan United States Secretary of State George C. Marshall created the Economic Cooperation Act of 1948, also known as the Marshall Plan. This plan provided U.S. aid—agricultural, industrial, and financial—to countries of Western Europe. The Marshall Plan greatly benefited war-torn Europe. It may also have prevented economic depression or political instability.

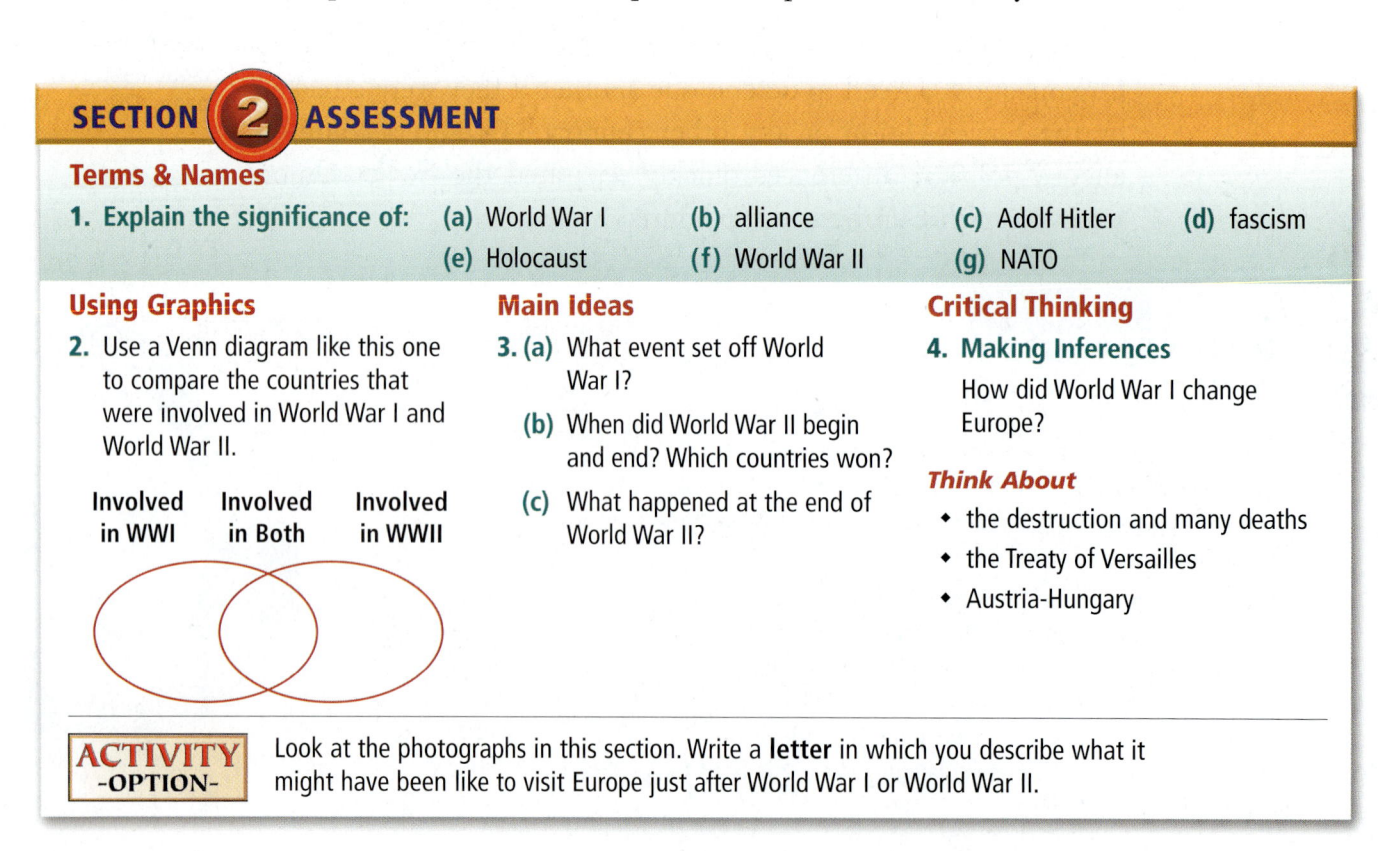

SECTION 2 ASSESSMENT

Terms & Names

1. Explain the significance of:
   (a) World War I
   (b) alliance
   (c) Adolf Hitler
   (d) fascism
   (e) Holocaust
   (f) World War II
   (g) NATO

Using Graphics

2. Use a Venn diagram like this one to compare the countries that were involved in World War I and World War II.

   Involved in WWI | Involved in Both | Involved in WWII

Main Ideas

3. (a) What event set off World War I?
   (b) When did World War II begin and end? Which countries won?
   (c) What happened at the end of World War II?

Critical Thinking

4. **Making Inferences**
   How did World War I change Europe?

   Think About
   • the destruction and many deaths
   • the Treaty of Versailles
   • Austria-Hungary

ACTIVITY -OPTION- Look at the photographs in this section. Write a **letter** in which you describe what it might have been like to visit Europe just after World War I or World War II.

SKILLBUILDER

Reading a Political Cartoon

▶▶ **Defining the Skill**

Political cartoons—also known as editorial cartoons—express an opinion about a serious subject. A political cartoonist uses symbols, familiar objects, and people to make his or her point quickly and visually. Sometimes the caption and words in the cartoon help to clarify the meaning. Although a cartoonist may use humor to make a point, political cartoons are not always funny.

SUNSHINE STATE STANDARDS
Key Standard SS.A.3.3.1 The student understands ways in which cultural characteristics have been transmitted from one society to another (e.g., through art, architecture, language, other artifacts, traditions, beliefs, values, and behaviors).

FCAT LA.A.2.3.2 Reading: Identify Purpose and Point of View

▶▶ **Applying the Skill**

This political cartoon was created in the period between World War I and World War II. However, Europeans were already concerned about developments in Germany.

How to Read a Political Cartoon

Strategy ❶ Read the cartoon's title and any other words. For example, some cartoons have labels, captions, and thought balloons. Then study the cartoon as a whole.

Strategy ❷ If the cartoon has people in it, are they famous? Sometimes the cartoonist wants to comment on a famous person, such as a world leader. Look for symbols or details in the cartoon. For example, in this cartoon a German soldier is climbing out of the Versailles Treaty. Think about the relationships between the words and the images.

Strategy ❸ Summarize the cartoonist's message. What is the cartoonist's point of view about the subject? What does this cartoonist think was the cause of Hitler's rise to power?

Make a Chart

A chart can help you to analyze the information in a political cartoon. Once you understand the cartoon's elements, you can summarize its meaning. Use a chart such as this one to help you organize the information.

Important Words	Hitler Party; Versailles Treaty
Important Symbols/Images	German soldier with "Hitler Party" on his helmet crawling out of the Versailles Treaty that officially ended World War I.
Summary ❸	The terms of the Versailles Treaty led to the rise of Hitler's party in Germany; Hitler's party, symbolized by a soldier, is war-like and threatens Europe.

▶▶ **Practicing the Skill**

Study the political cartoon in Chapter 5, Section 2, on page 128. Make a chart similar to the one above in which you list the important parts of the cartoon and write a summary of the cartoon's message.

Europe: War and Change

Literature Connections

Fionn Mac Cumhail and the Giant's Causeway [1]

SUNSHINE STATE STANDARDS
Key Standard SS.A.3.3.1
The student understands ways in which cultural characteristics have been transmitted from one society to another (e.g., through art, architecture, language, other artifacts, traditions, beliefs, values, and behaviors).

FCAT LA.E.2.3.1 Literature: Understand Character and Plot Development

FIONN MAC CUMHAIL, more commonly known as Finn MacCool, is a familiar figure in Irish folk tales. He first appears in the ancient Celtic tales known as the Fenian cycle. In the following story, retold by Una Leavy, Fionn is portrayed as a clever giant, hard at work with the Fianna, his band of Irish warriors. They begin to build a bridge from Ireland to Scotland, because, as the boastful Fionn says, "There are giants over there that I'm longing to conquer." Plans suddenly change, however, and Fionn must go home.

1. The Giant's Causeway, which takes its name from this legend, is a striking natural rock formation on the coast of Ireland.

2. The region of Ireland where Fionn and the Fianna are building their bridge to Scotland. It is the location of the actual Giant's Causeway.

Fionn Mac Cumhail and the Fianna worked quickly on the bridge, splitting stones into splendid pillars and columns. Further and further they stretched out into the ocean. From time to time, there came a distant rumble. "Is it thunder?" asked the Fianna, but they went on working. Then one of their spies came ashore. "I've just been to Scotland!" he said. "There's a huge giant there called Fathach Mór. He's doing long jumps—you can hear the thumping. He has a magic little finger with the strength of ten men! He's in training for the long jump to Antrim." [2]

Fionn's face paled. "The strength of ten men!" he thought. "I'll never fight him. He'll squash me into a pancake." But he could not admit that he was nervous, so he said to the Fianna, "I've just had a message from Bláithín, my wife. I must go home at once—you can all take a holiday."

He set off by himself and never did a man travel faster. Bláithín was surprised to see him. "And is the great causeway finished already?" she asked.

"No indeed," replied Fionn.

"What's the matter?" Bláithín asked. So Fionn told her.

"What will I do, Bláithín?" he asked. "There's the strength of ten men in his magic little finger. He'll squish me into a jelly!"

Bláithín laughed. "Just leave him to me. Stoke up the fire and fetch me the sack of flour. Then go outside and find nine flat stones." Fionn did as he was told. Bláithín worked all night making ten oatcakes. In each she put a large flat stone, all except the last. This one she marked with her thumbprint. "Go and cut down some wood," she said. "You must make an enormous cradle."

Fionn worked all morning. The cradle was just finished when there was a mighty rumble and the dishes shook.

"It's him," squealed Fionn.

"Don't worry!" said Bláithín. "Put on this bonnet. Now into the cradle and leave me to do the talking."

"Does Fionn Mac Cumhail live here?" boomed a great voice above her.

"He does," said Bláithín, "though he's away at the moment. He's gone to capture the giant, Fathach Mór."

"I'm Fathach Mór!" bellowed the giant. "I've been searching for Fionn everywhere."

"Did you ever see Fionn?" she asked. "Sure you're only a baby compared with him. He'll be home shortly and you can see for yourself. But now that you're here, would you do me a favor? The well has run dry and Fionn was supposed to lift up the mountain this morning. There's spring water underneath it. Do you think you could get me some?"

"Of course," shouted the giant as he scooped out a hole in the mountain, the size of a crater.

Fionn shook with fear in the cradle and even Bláithín turned pale. But she thanked the giant and invited him in. "Though you and Fionn are enemies, you are still a guest," she said. "Have some fresh bread." And she put the oatcakes before him. Fathach Mór began to eat. Almost at once he gave a piercing yell and spat out two teeth.

"What kind of bread is this?" he screeched. "I've broken my teeth on it."

"How can you say such a thing?" asked Bláithín. "Even the child in the cradle eats them!" And she gave Fionn the cake with the thumbprint. Fathach looked at the cradle. "Whose child is that?" he asked in wonder.

"That's Fionn's son," said Bláithín.

"And how old is he?" he asked then.

"Just ten months," replied Bláithín.

"Can he talk?" asked the giant.

"Not yet, but you should hear him roar!" At once, Fionn began to yell.

"Quick, quick," cried Bláithín. "Let him suck your little finger. If Fionn comes home and hears him, he'll be in such a temper. With an anxious glance at the door, the giant gave Fionn his finger. Fionn bit off the giant's magic little finger. Screeching, the giant bolted from the house. Fionn leaped from the cradle in bib and bonnet and danced his Bláithín round the kitchen.

Reading THE LITERATURE

Before reading this story, how did you expect Fionn Mac Cumhail to act? Did you expect him to be the hero of the story? Who is? How does the character solve the problem in the story? What skills are used to solve it?

Thinking About THE LITERATURE

In many European myths and legends, the heroes are powerful and fearless. How does Fionn act in this story? What words does the author use to make clear Fionn's attitude toward the danger he faces? How does he differ from other legendary figures that you have read about?

Writing About THE LITERATURE

Often, myths are created in order to answer questions about or explain mysteries in the world. This legend explains why the causeway was never finished. How might the story about Fionn be different if the causeway had been finished?

About the Author

Una Leavy, the author of *Irish Fairy Tales & Legends,* is an Irish writer who lives with her husband and children in County Mayo, Ireland.

Further Reading *The Names upon the Harp* by Marie Heaney recounts myths and legends of early Irish literature, including the stories about Fionn Mac Cumhail that make up the Fenian cycle.

SECTION 3

The Soviet Union

TERMS & NAMES
Iron Curtain
puppet government
one-party system
Joseph Stalin
collective farm
Warsaw Pact
Cold War

MAIN IDEA
After World War II, the Soviet Union was the most powerful country in Europe, but life for most Soviet citizens was difficult.

WHY IT MATTERS NOW
Russia, the former Soviet Union, remains powerful and is currently experiencing great change.

DATELINE

WARSAW, POLAND, MAY 14, 1955—Today, the Soviet Union and most Eastern European countries announced that they have signed the Warsaw Treaty of Friendship, Cooperation, and Mutual Assistance. The members of this alliance agree to offer military defense to one another for a period of 20 years.

Yugoslavia is the only country in Eastern Europe that did not sign the agreement.

The new treaty, also called the Warsaw Pact, allows the Soviet Union to keep troops in the countries that are located between the Soviet Union and Western Europe. The Warsaw Pact is a response to the formation of NATO, an alliance that Western European countries joined six years ago.

Region • Warsaw hosted Eastern European officials who signed a military alliance here in the Palace of Culture. ▲

East Against West

After World War II, political differences divided the Soviet-controlled countries of Eastern Europe from those of Western Europe. These differences gave rise to an invisible wall known as the **Iron Curtain**. While there was no actual curtain, people of the East were restricted from traveling outside of their countries. Westerners who wished to visit the East also faced restrictions.

TAKING NOTES
Use your chart to take notes about war and change in Europe.

Causes	Event	Effects
	World War I	
	World War II	

SUNSHINE STATE STANDARDS
Key Standard SS.A.3.3.5 The student understands the differences between institutions of Eastern and Western civilizations (e.g., differences in governments, social traditions and customs, economic systems and religious institutions).
Other Standards SS.A.3.3.4, B.1.3.3
FCAT LA.A.2.3.1 Reading: Identify Main Idea, Facts, and Details

The Strongest Nation in Europe
The Union of Soviet Socialist Republics, or USSR, was the official name of the Soviet Union. It included 15 republics, of which Russia was the largest. The Soviet Union entered World War II in 1941, when Germany invaded its borders. German troops destroyed much of the western Soviet Union and killed millions of people. This invasion brought the Soviet Union close to collapse. However, with the defeat of Germany, the Soviet Union rose to become the strongest nation in Europe.

Communism
After World War II, the Soviet Union established Communist governments in Eastern Europe. The Soviets made sure—either by politics or by force—that these new Eastern European governments were loyal to the Soviet Union.

Soviet Control of Eastern Europe
The Soviet Union controlled the countries of Eastern Europe through puppet governments. A **puppet government** is one that does what it is told by an outside force. In this case, the Eastern European governments followed orders from Soviet leaders in Moscow.

Most Eastern Europeans did have the chance to vote, but they had only one political party to choose from: the Communist Party. All other parties were outlawed. This meant that there was only one candidate to choose from for each government position. This is an example of a **one-party system.** Soviet citizens could not complain about the government. In fact, they could be jailed for expressing any view that the Soviet leaders did not like.

Vocabulary
establish: set up; create

Reading Social Studies
A. Making Inferences
How do you think the Soviet Union enforced a one-party system in Eastern Europe?

Region • The hammer and sickle became the symbol of Soviet Communism. The tools represent the unity of the peasants (sickle) with the workers (hammer). ▲

Movement • The government-controlled factories in the Soviet Union did not produce enough of certain items. When goods that were often in short supply—such as bread and shoes—finally became available, people had to wait in long lines to buy them. ◀

Europe: War and Change

Joseph Stalin

Joseph Stalin (STAH•lihn) (1879–1953) ruled the Soviet Union during World War II. Stalin took power after the death of Vladimir Lenin. Lenin was a Communist leader who had helped overthrow the czar and ruled the Soviet Union from 1917 until his death in 1924. The name Stalin is related to the Russian word for "steel." Stalin was greatly feared, and his rule was indeed as tough as steel. He controlled the government until his death.

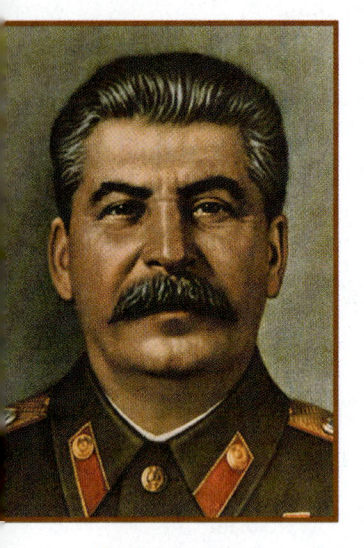

Region • Joseph Stalin ruled the Soviet Union from 1928 to 1953. ▲

The Five-Year Plans Under Stalin, the government controlled every aspect of Soviet life. Stalin hoped to strengthen the country with his five-year plans, which were sets of economic goals. For example, Stalin ordered many new factories to be built. The Soviet government decided where and what types of factories to build, how many goods to produce, and how to distribute them. These decisions were based on the Communist theory that this would benefit the most people.

GEOGRAPHY SKILLBUILDER: Interpreting a Map

1. **Region** • Which countries were behind the Iron Curtain but not in the Soviet Union?
2. **Location** • What was the westernmost country in the Warsaw Pact?

Region • The Soviet government managed the factories while citizens provided the actual labor. ◀

138   CHAPTER 5

The Iron Curtain and the Warsaw Pact Nations, 1955

Legend:
- Soviet Union
- Warsaw Pact members
- Western European Nations
- Iron Curtain

Soviet Agriculture Stalin also hoped to strengthen the Soviet Union by controlling the country's agriculture. During the 1930s, peasants were forced to move to collective farms. A **collective farm** was government-owned and employed large numbers of workers. All the crops produced by the collective farms were distributed by the government. Sometimes farm workers did not receive enough food to feed themselves and their families.

Region • Similar to urban factory workers, Russian peasants labored on government-controlled collective farms. ▼

The Secret Police Stalin used his secret police to get rid of citizens he did not trust. The secret police arrested those who did not support the Soviet government. Suspects were transported to slave-labor camps in Siberia. Millions of men and women were sent to this remote and bitterly cold region of northeastern Russia. Many never returned home.

The Cold War

From 1941 to 1945, the United Kingdom, the United States, and the Soviet Union shared a goal: to defeat the Axis Powers. They became allies to make that happen. Once the war ended, however, these countries no longer had a common enemy—and had little reason to work together. Most Western European countries were constitutional monarchies or democracies, and most Eastern European countries had Communist, largely Soviet-controlled, governments.

Spotlight on CULTURE

Soviet Film The Russian director Sergey Eisenstein (EYE•zen•stine) (1898–1948), bottom right, made only six movies, but they are among the most important works in film history. The silent film *Battleship Potemkin* (1925), whose poster is to the right, is one of Eisenstein's most famous. It is about a mutiny at sea. The director's use of close-ups and his method of combining short scenes changed the way films were made all over the world.

Just before the start of World War II, Eisenstein made the film *Alexander Nevsky* (1938). It tells the story of a historic battle that the Russians won against German-speaking invaders in the 1200s. This film became very popular during World War II, which it seemed to foreshadow.

THINKING CRITICALLY

1. **Clarifying**
   What influenced Eisenstein to direct war films?
2. **Synthesizing**
   What did Eisenstein want to show about the relationship between Russians and Germans?

For more on Sergey Eisenstein, go to RESEARCH LINKS CLASSZONE.COM

Region • The Brandenburg Gate was a part of the Berlin Wall that separated East Berlin from West Berlin. ◄

The members of NATO and the nations in the **Warsaw Pact**—the alliance of Eastern European countries behind the Iron Curtain—refused to trade or cooperate with each other. The countries never actually fought, so this period of political noncooperation is called the **Cold War**. Both sides in the Cold War were hesitant to start a war that would involve the use of newly developed nuclear weapons, which could cause destruction on a global scale.

The United States and Western Europe feared that the Soviet Union would influence other countries to become Communist. At the same time, the Soviet Union wanted to protect itself against invasion. This led the countries on either side of the Iron Curtain to view and treat each other as possible threats. The tense international situation caused by the Cold War would continue for almost 40 years.

Reading **Social Studies**

B. Comparing Compare the Soviet Union's fears in the Cold War with those of the United States and Western Europe.

SECTION 3 ASSESSMENT

Terms & Names

1. Explain the significance of:
   - (a) Iron Curtain
   - (b) puppet government
   - (c) one-party system
   - (d) Joseph Stalin
   - (e) collective farm
   - (f) Warsaw Pact
   - (g) Cold War

Using Graphics

2. Use a chart like this one to describe three elements of Joseph Stalin's rule of the Soviet Union.

Five-Year Plans	Agriculture	Secret Police

Main Ideas

3. (a) What happened to the Soviet Union during World War II?

   (b) How did the governments of most Western and Eastern European countries differ?

   (c) How did Joseph Stalin rule the Soviet Union?

Critical Thinking

4. **Analyzing Motives**

   Why do you think the Soviet Union wanted to control the countries of Eastern Europe?

   Think About
   - the events of World War II
   - the location of the Eastern European countries
   - the governments of the Soviet Union and Western Europe

ACTIVITY -OPTION- Reread the information about the secret police. Write a dramatic **scene** in which the main character is sent to a labor camp in Siberia.

Europe: War and Change

CHAPTER 5 ASSESSMENT

TERMS & NAMES

Explain the significance of each of the following:
1. nationalism
2. colonialism
3. World War I
4. alliance
5. World War II
6. NATO
7. Adolf Hitler
8. Warsaw Pact
9. Iron Curtain
10. Cold War

REVIEW QUESTIONS

European Empires (pages 123–126)
1. What was the largest empire in Eastern Europe in 1900?
2. What is one reason why European nations built up their military?

Europe at War (pages 127–132)
3. Why did European countries join alliances?
4. What did the Treaty of Versailles require Germany to do?
5. What country did Germany invade to begin World War II?

The Soviet Union (pages 136–141)
6. Why did most Eastern European voters have only one political party to choose from?
7. How did the Iron Curtain affect the lives of Eastern Europeans?
8. Why were both sides in the Cold War hesitant to start a war?

CRITICAL THINKING

Identifying Problems
1. Using your completed chart from Reading Social Studies, p. 122, list some of the causes and effects of World Wars I and II.

Making Inferences
2. Why might a citizen who has helped elect a government be more willing to fight to defend it?

Hypothesizing
3. How do you think Soviet peasants felt about collective farms? Why?

Visual Summary

1 European Empires
- In early-20th-century Europe, feelings of nationalism arose.
- Western European nations ruled colonial empires.

2 Europe at War
- Due to a complex set of alliances, most of Europe was drawn into World War I.
- The Treaty of Versailles set the stage for an even more widespread conflict—World War II.

3 The Soviet Union
- After World War II, the Soviet Union was very powerful.
- However, life was difficult for many Soviet citizens.

STANDARDS-BASED ASSESSMENT

Use the map and your knowledge of geography to answer questions 1 and 2.

Additional Test Practice, pp. S1–S33

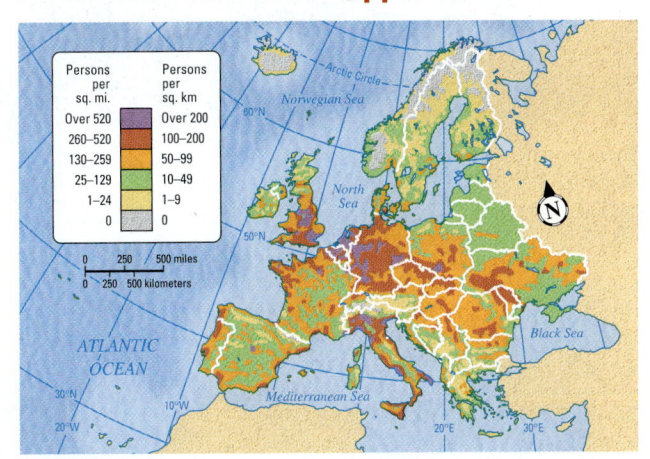

The excerpt is from a famous speech that Winston Churchill gave during the Cold War. Use the quotation and your knowledge of world cultures and geography to answer question 3.

PRIMARY SOURCE

From Stettin in the Baltic to Trieste in the Adriatic, an iron curtain has descended across the Continent. Behind that line lie all the capitals of the ancient states of Central and Eastern Europe. . . . All these famous cities and the populations around them lie in what I might call the Soviet sphere, and all are subject, in one form or another, not only to Soviet influence but to a very high and in some cases increasing measure of control from Moscow.

WINSTON CHURCHILL,
"Iron Curtain" speech, Fulton, Missouri

1. Which areas of Europe are the least densely populated?
  A. The area just south of the North Sea
  B. Areas on the Atlantic Coast
  C. Areas along the Mediterranean Sea
  D. Areas near the Arctic Circle

2. Judging from this map, why do you think some areas are more densely populated than others?
  A. Many people tend to move to mountainous regions.
  B. Many people tend to settle in cities near coasts or rivers.
  C. Many people tend to avoid living on peninsulas.
  D. Many people like to live on islands because of the fishing.

3. According to the passage, what threat did the iron curtain provide?
  A. The Communist Soviet Union controlled the region behind the iron curtain.
  B. Famine and disease threatened countries in Central and Eastern Europe.
  C. Hitler and his forces wanted to reconquer the region behind the iron curtain.
  D. A barrier prevented people from visiting the cities of Central and Eastern Europe

TEST PRACTICE
CLASSZONE.COM

ALTERNATIVE ASSESSMENT

1. WRITING ABOUT HISTORY

Imagine that you are a government official from a European nation living in one of the nation's colonies in Asia or Africa. Write a letter to your family telling them what life in the colony is like in the year 1900.
  • Use the Internet or the library to research one of the European colonies in Asia or Africa.
  • In your letter, identify the colony and describe its location. Include information about the colony's climate, geography, culture, and people. Describe your country's plans for the colony.

2. COOPERATIVE LEARNING

With a small group, design a monument to commemorate an event in 20th-century Europe, such as a particular battle from World War I, the Holocaust, or World War II. Share the responsibilities of researching the event, designing the monument, and presenting it to your class. In your presentation, provide some background information and suggest a permanent location for your monument.

INTEGRATED TECHNOLOGY

Doing Internet Research

Countries such as Switzerland and Sweden were not directly involved in World War I or World War II. Use the Internet to research one of the neutral countries and include your findings in a report.
  • Use the Internet and other library resources to identify a country that wasn't directly involved in the wars.
  • Another source of information might be a historical museum or archive.
  • Look for information about the country's government and economy in the first half of the 20th century, how the country was affected by the wars, and what life was like for its citizens.

For Internet links to support this activity, go to

RESEARCH LINKS
CLASSZONE.COM

Europe: War and Change

Chapter 6
Modern Europe

Section 1 Eastern Europe Under Communism

Section 2 Eastern Europe and Russia

Section 3 The European Union

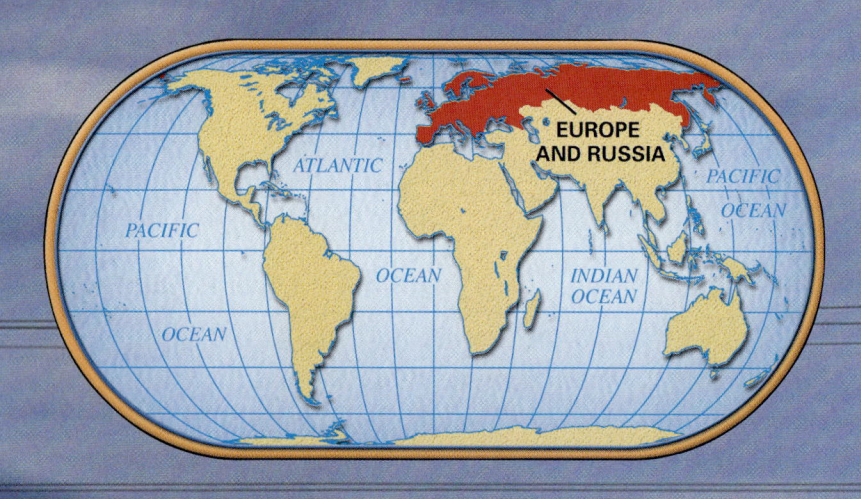

Movement High-speed trains, like this one in France, make travel in Europe very convenient.

FOCUS ON GEOGRAPHY

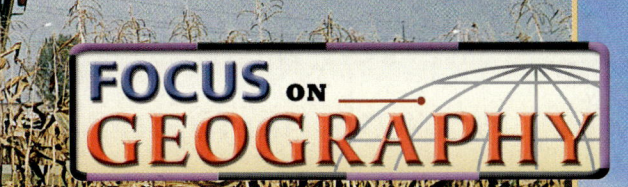

How are the new republics of Eastern Europe using natural resources to build their economies?

Human-Environment Interaction • Natural resources are often an important part of a nation's economy. When the Soviet Union broke up in 1991, the newly independent nations of Eastern Europe chose to develop market economies.

In Ukraine, which is rich in coal and iron, mining and manufacturing are major industries. (Ukraine once had vast petroleum and natural gas resources, but heavy production used up much of them.) Estonia, Latvia, and Lithuania have large forests and good farmland. Estonia is also rich in oil shale, which it uses to make electricity.

What do you think?

- How do natural resources affect the types of goods a country produces?
- Why is it important for countries to use natural resources carefully?

CHAPTER 6

READING SOCIAL STUDIES

BEFORE YOU READ

▶▶ What Do You Know?

Before you read the chapter, think about what you already know about Europe. Do you have family, friends, or neighbors who were born in Europe? Have you read books, such as the Harry Potter series, that take place in Europe? Think about what you have seen or heard about Italy, England, France, or Germany in the news, during sporting events, and in your other classes.

▶▶ What Do You Want to Know?

Decide what you know about Europe today. Then, in your notebook, record what you hope to learn from this chapter.

Region • Euros are the most visible symbol of economic unity in Europe. ▲

READ AND TAKE NOTES

Reading Strategy: Comparing Comparing is a useful strategy for understanding how events change societies. As you read this chapter, compare Eastern Europe under Communism with Eastern Europe after Communism. Use the chart below to take notes.

- Copy the chart into your notebook.
- As you read, notice how government, economics, and culture differ under the old and new systems.
- After you read each section, record key ideas on your chart.

Place • Some Christians in Ukraine dye Easter eggs brilliant colors. ▲

Aspect	Under Communism	After Communism
Government		
Economy		
Culture		

SECTION 1
Eastern Europe Under Communism

TERMS & NAMES
propaganda
private property rights
Nikita Khrushchev
deposed
détente

MAIN IDEA
The Communist government of the Soviet Union controlled the lives of its citizens.

WHY IT MATTERS NOW
Today, many republics of the former Soviet Union have become independent nations.

DATELINE
EXTRA

THE KREMLIN, MOSCOW, APRIL 12, 1961 — A 27-year-old Soviet pilot has become the first person to travel into space. Soviet officials proudly announced today that cosmonaut Yuri Gagarin had orbited Earth in 1 hour and 29 minutes.

His 4.75-ton spacecraft, *Vostok I*, flew at a maximum altitude of 187 miles above the planet. Its top speed was 18,000 miles per hour.

Gagarin graduated from the Soviet Air Force cadet school just four years ago. He is the son of a carpenter and began to study flying while in college. Gagarin's space flight puts the Soviet Union a giant step ahead of the United States in the space race.

Movement • Yuri Gagarin becomes the first human in space. ▶

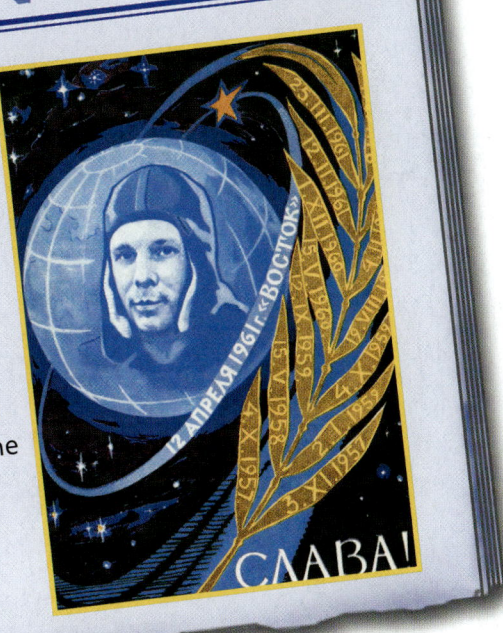

Soviet Culture

The Soviet space program of the 1950s and 1960s brought international attention to that country. Daily life for citizens of the Soviet Union and of the Eastern European countries under its control, however, was difficult. Most people were poor and had little, if any, say in their government.

TAKING NOTES
Use your chart to take notes about modern Europe.

Aspect	Under Communism	After Communism
Government		
Economy		

SUNSHINE STATE STANDARDS
Key Standard SS.D.2.3.1 The student understands ways production and distribution decisions are determined in the United States economy and how these decisions compare to those made in market, tradition-based, command, and mixed economic systems.
Other Standards SS.A.3.3.1, B.1.3.3
FCAT LA.A.2.3.1 Reading: Identify Main Idea, Facts, and Details

Modern Europe **147**

Strange but TRUE

Space Dogs Four years before Yuri Gagarin blasted into space, a Russian dog orbited the planet. Her name was Laika (LY•kuh), which means "Barker." Laika, pictured below, was launched into space on *Sputnik 2* in November 1957. The Soviets did not then have the ability to bring a spacecraft down safely, and Laika lived in space for only a few days.

In August 1960, however, the Russians sent two other dogs into space. Named Belka and Strelka, they were the first living creatures to go into space and return safely to Earth.

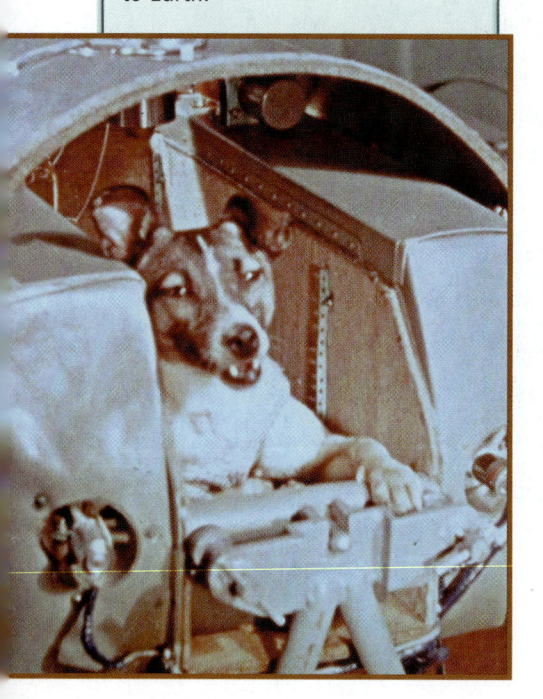

Creating a National Identity The Soviet government was fearful that some ethnic groups might want to break away from the Soviet Union. To keep this from happening, Soviet leaders tried to create a strong national identity. They wanted people in the republic of Latvia, for example, to think of themselves as Soviets, not as Latvians.

To help achieve its goals, the Soviet government created and distributed **propaganda** (PRAHP•uh•GAN•duh), or material designed to spread certain beliefs. Soviet propaganda included pamphlets, posters, artwork, statues, songs, and films. It praised the Soviet Union, its leaders, and Communism.

Soviet Control of Daily Life To prevent different ethnic groups from identifying with their individual cultures rather than with the Soviet Union, the Soviet government outlawed many cultural celebrations. It destroyed churches and other religious buildings and killed thousands of religious leaders. The members of many ethnic groups were not allowed to speak their native languages or celebrate certain holidays.

The Soviet government also controlled communications media, such as newspapers, books, and radio. This meant that most Soviet citizens could not learn much about other nations around the world.

Region • This statue, a form of propaganda, displays the Soviet belief in the unity of the worker (hammer) and the farmer (sickle). ▼

Literature and the Arts The works of many writers, poets, and other artists who lived during the Soviet era often were banned or censored. Soviet artists were forced to join government-run unions. These unions told artists what kinds of works they could create. Artists who disobeyed were punished. Some were imprisoned or even killed.

Ethnic and Cultural Groups of the Soviet Union, c. 1950

GEOGRAPHY SKILLBUILDER:
Interpreting a Map
1. **Place** • Where in the Soviet Union do most Uralic and Altaic people live?
2. **Region** • What is the most common ethnicity of the Soviet Union?

Legend:
- Caucasian peoples
- Indo-European peoples
- Uralic and Altaic peoples
- Sparsely populated

Sports The leaders of the Soviet Union wanted their country to be seen as equal to, if not better than, other powerful nations. One way to achieve this goal was to become a strong competitor in the Olympics and in other international sports competitions.

The Soviet government supported its top athletes and provided for all their basic needs. It even hired and paid for the coaches and paid for all training. The hockey teams and gymnasts of the Soviet Union were among the best in the world.

Region • Romanian gymnasts, like Nadia Comaneci, won medals at the Olympics. ▼

The Soviet Economy

In addition to controlling the governments of the Soviet Union and of those Eastern European countries under its influence, Soviet leaders also ran the economy. When the Soviets installed Communist governments in Eastern Europe after World War II, they promised to improve industry and to bring new wealth to be shared among all citizens. This did not happen.

Government Control Communism in the Soviet Union did not support **private property rights,** or the right of individuals to own land or an industry. The Soviets wanted all major industries to be owned by the government rather than by private citizens. So the government took over factories, railroads, and businesses.

Modern Europe

The Soviet government decided what would be produced, how it would be produced, and who would get what was produced. These choices were made based on Soviet interests, not on the interests of the republics or of individuals. Communist countries of Eastern Europe were often unable to meet the needs—including bread, meat, and clothing—of their citizens.

Reading Social Studies

A. Clarifying Who benefited most from Soviet industry?

Attempts at Change

Starting in the 1950s, Eastern Europeans began to demand more goods of better quality. They also wanted changes in the government. In 1956, Hungary and Poland tried to free their governments and economies from Soviet control. But the Communist army put an end to these attempts at change.

Khrushchev From 1958 until 1964, **Nikita Khrushchev** (KRUSH•chehf) ruled the Soviet Union. During this period, called "The Thaw," writers and other citizens began to have greater freedoms. Khrushchev even visited the United States in 1959, but the thaw in the Cold War did not last. In 1964, with the Soviet economy growing weaker, Khrushchev was **deposed,** or removed from power.

Spotlight on CULTURE

Solzhenitsyn In 1945, army officer Aleksandr Solzhenitsyn (SOHL•zhuh•NEET•sihn), far right, called the Soviet leader Joseph Stalin "the boss." For this, he was sentenced to eight years in slave-labor camps. Later, Solzhenitsyn wrote books about his experiences in those camps. He also wrote a letter against censorship. The government called him a traitor, and in 1969 it forced Solzhenitsyn to leave the writers' union. Five years later, Solzhenitsyn left the country.

Although Solzhenitsyn's works were banned, many Soviet citizens read them in secret. Copies of his and other banned books were passed from person to person across the nation. Through such writings, Soviet citizens learned many things that the government had tried to hide from them.

THINKING CRITICALLY

1. **Analyzing Motives** Why would the Soviet government stop people from reading Solzhenitsyn's books?
2. **Comparing** Compare the censorship of literature in the Soviet Union with censorship in the United States.

For more on Aleksandar Solzhenitsyn, go to

RESEARCH LINKS
CLASSZONE.COM

Reading Social Studies

B. Recognizing Important Details How did the Soviet Union maintain control over other Eastern European nations?

The Prague Spring In January 1968 in Czechoslovakia, Alexander Dubček (DOOB•chek) became the First Secretary of the Czechoslovak Communist Party. His attempts to lessen the Soviet Union's control over Czechoslovakia led to a period of improvement called the "Prague Spring." Czech citizens enjoyed greater freedoms, including more contact with Western Europe. In August of that year, however, the Soviet Union sent troops to force a return to strict Communist control. Dubček was later replaced, and Soviet controls were back in place.

Détente The member nations of NATO, which were concerned about starting an all-out war with the Soviet Union, were unable to stop the Soviet control of Eastern Europe. In the 1970s, however, leaders of the Soviet Union and the United States began to have more contact with each other. This led to a period of **détente** (day•TAHNT), or lessening tension, between the members of NATO and the Warsaw Pact nations.

Place • Nikita Khrushchev, the son of a miner and grandson of a peasant, lessened government control of Soviet citizens. ▲

Region • Citizens of Czechoslovakia protested Soviet control in 1968. ◀

151

Place • The old city of Dubrovnik is in Croatia, a part of the former Yugoslavia, which was a Communist country in Eastern Europe. ▶

Economic Crisis By the 1980s, economic conditions in the Soviet Union and in those countries under its control had still not improved. Even after détente, the Soviet government continued to spend most of its money on the armed forces and nuclear weapons. In addition, people who lived in the non-Russian republics of the Soviet Union now wanted more control over their own affairs. Many citizens began to reject the Soviet economic system, but the Soviet leaders refused to give up any of their power or control.

SECTION 1 ASSESSMENT

Terms & Names
1. Explain the significance of:
   (a) propaganda
   (b) private property rights
   (c) Nikita Khrushchev
   (d) deposed
   (e) détente

Using Graphics
2. Use a chart like this one to list and describe major aspects of Soviet culture.

Aspects of Soviet Culture

Main Ideas
3. (a) Why did Soviet leaders try to create a strong national identity?
   (b) What began to happen in Eastern Europe in the 1950s?
   (c) Describe the significance of the "Prague Spring."

Critical Thinking
4. **Analyzing Motives**
   Why do you think the works of many writers, poets, and artists were banned or censored during the Soviet era?

   Think About
   • what Soviet citizens learned from Solzhenitsyn's works
   • the government's use of propaganda
   • what life was like for most Soviet citizens

ACTIVITY -OPTION- Reread the information under "Literature and the Arts" and the Spotlight on Culture feature. Write a **speech** for or against censorship in the arts.

SKILLBUILDER

Using an Electronic Card Catalog

▶▶ Defining the Skill

To find books, magazines, or other sources of information in a library, you may use an electronic card catalog. This catalog is a computerized search program on the Internet that lists every book, periodical, or other resource found in the library. You can search for resources in the catalog in four ways: by title, by author, by subject, and by keyword. Once you have typed in your search information, the catalog will give you a list of every resource that matches it. This is called bibliographic information. You can use an electronic card catalog to build a bibliography, or a list of books, on the topic you are researching.

SUNSHINE STATE STANDARDS
Key Standard SS.A.1.3.2
The student knows the relative value of primary and secondary sources and uses this information to draw conclusions from historical sources such as data in charts, tables, graphs.
FCAT LA.A.2.3.6 Reading: Use Variety of Reference Materials

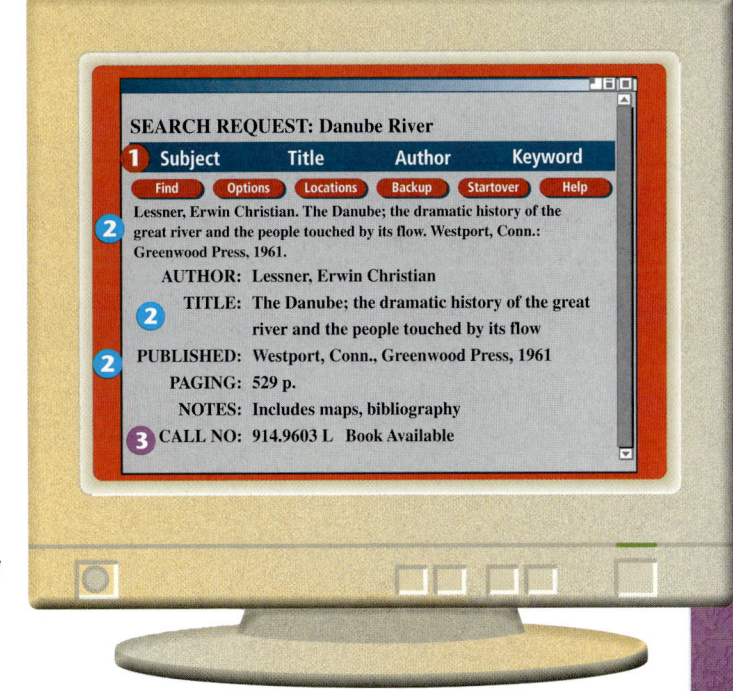

▶▶ Applying the Skill

The screen below shows the results of an electronic search for information about the Danube River. To use the information on the screen, follow the strategies listed below.

How to Use an Electronic Card Catalog

Strategy ❶ To begin your search, choose Subject, Title, Author, or Keyword. The student doing this search chose "Subject" and then typed in "Danube River."

Strategy ❷ Based on your search, the catalog will give you a list of records that match that subject. You must then select one of the records to view the details about the resource. The catalog will then give you a screen like the one to the right. This detailed record lists the author, title, and information about where and when the resource was published, and by whom.

Strategy ❸ Locate the call number for the book. The call number indicates the section in the library where you will find the book. You can also find out if the book is available in the library you are using. If not, it may be available in another library in the network.

```
SEARCH REQUEST: Danube River
❶ Subject    Title    Author    Keyword
  Find  Options  Locations  Backup  Startover  Help

❷ Lessner, Erwin Christian. The Danube; the dramatic history of the
  great river and the people touched by its flow. Westport, Conn.:
  Greenwood Press, 1961.
       AUTHOR: Lessner, Erwin Christian
❷       TITLE: The Danube; the dramatic history of the great
               river and the people touched by its flow
❷   PUBLISHED: Westport, Conn., Greenwood Press, 1961
        PAGING: 529 p.
         NOTES: Includes maps, bibliography
❸     CALL NO: 914.9603 L   Book Available
```

▶▶ Practicing the Skill

Review the text in Chapter 6, Section 1 to find a topic that interests you, such as Yuri Gagarin. Use the Subject search on an electronic card catalog to find information about your topic. Make a bibliography about the subject. Organize your bibliography alphabetically by author. For each book you list, also include the title, city, publisher, and date of publication.

Modern Europe

Eastern Europe and Russia

SECTION 2

TERMS & NAMES
Mikhail Gorbachev
parliamentary republic
coalition government
ethnic cleansing
Duma

MAIN IDEA
After the breakup of the Soviet Union, many former Soviet republics and countries of Eastern Europe became independent.

WHY IT MATTERS NOW
Nations once under Soviet rule are taking steps toward new economies and democratic governments.

DATELINE

THE KREMLIN, MOSCOW, 1988—To reduce military spending, the Soviet Union has begun removing large numbers of troops and arms from Eastern Europe. This latest news is just one of many changes in the Soviet government since Mikhail Gorbachev (GAWR•buh•chawf) came to power three years ago.

Although Gorbachev believes in the ideals of the Soviet system, he thinks that change is necessary to help solve the country's economic and political problems. Since 1985 Gorbachev has reduced Cold War tensions with the United States. At home in the Soviet Union, he has allowed more political and economic freedom.

Region • Mikhail Gorbachev leads the Soviet Union toward a freer society. ▲

The Breakup of the Soviet Union

<u>Mikhail Gorbachev</u>'s reforms did not solve the problems of the Soviet Union. The economy continued to get worse. When Gorbachev did not force the countries of Eastern Europe to remain Communist, this further displeased many Communists.

SUNSHINE STATE STANDARDS
Key Standard SS.A.3.3.5 The student understands the differences between institutions of Eastern and Western civilizations (e.g., differences in governments, social traditions and customs, economic systems and religious institutions).
Other Standards SS.A.3.3.4
FCAT LA.A.2.2.7 Reading: Recognize Compare and Contrast

TAKING NOTES
Use your chart to take notes about modern Europe.

Aspect	Under Communism	After Communism
Government		
Economy		

154 CHAPTER 6

Vocabulary

coup d'état: the overthrow of a government, usually by a small group in a position of power; often shortened to "coup"

In 1991, a group of more traditional Soviet leaders tried to take over the Soviet government. Thousands of people opposed this coup d'état (KOO•day•TAH), and the coup failed. Then, one by one, the Soviet republics declared independence. The Warsaw Pact was dissolved. By the end of 1991, the Soviet Union no longer existed. The huge country had become 15 different nations.

Modern Eastern Europe

Each former Soviet republic set up its own non-Communist government. The countries of Eastern Europe that had been under Soviet control held democratic elections, and many wrote or revised their constitutions.

In some countries, such as the Czech Republic, former Communists were banned from important government posts. In other countries, such as Bulgaria, the former Communists reorganized themselves into a new political party and have won elections. Many different ethnic groups also tried to create new states within a nation or to reestablish old states that had not existed in many years.

BACKGROUND

The Central Asian Soviet republics were mostly Muslim. These republics are now the countries of Kazakhstan, Turkmenistan, Uzbekistan, Kyrgyzstan, and Tajikistan.

Parliamentary Republics Today, most of the countries of Eastern Europe are parliamentary republics. A **parliamentary republic** is a form of government led by the head of the political party with the most members in parliament. The head of government, usually a prime minister, proposes the programs that the government will undertake. Most of these countries also have a president who has ceremonial, rather than political, duties.

Former Soviet Republics and Warsaw Pact Members, 2001

GEOGRAPHY SKILLBUILDER: Interpreting a Map
1. **Location** • Which former Soviet republics and Warsaw Pact members border Russia?
2. **Region** • On which continent are most of these countries located?

Modern Europe **155**

In some countries, small political parties have joined forces to work together to form a government. This is called a **coalition government.**

New Economies Under Soviet rule, Eastern Europe struggled economically and its people's freedoms were severely restricted. Although Eastern Europeans gained their freedom, they also faced problems such as inflation and unemployment.

Eastern Europe's countries are changing from command economies to free-market economies. Some countries, such as Slovakia, made this change slowly. Others, such as Poland, reformed their economic system and achieved economic success.

Many former Soviet republics, which did not quickly reform their economic systems, are in bad economic shape. Some of these nations are terribly poor. Struggles for power have led to violence and sometimes civil war. Pollution from the Soviet era threatens people's health. Still, some republics, including Ukraine, Latvia, Lithuania, and Estonia, are making progress as independent nations.

Defense After the breakup of the Soviet Union, Eastern European nations no longer looked to the Soviet government to defend them. Many wanted to become members of NATO. Belonging to NATO would help assure them of protection in case of invasion.

Reading Social Studies

A. Comparing Compare a command economy with a free-market economy.

Spotlight on CULTURE

Easter in Ukraine In Ukraine, most Christians belong to the Orthodox Church. These Ukrainians are known for the special way in which they celebrate the Easter holiday. They create beautiful Easter eggs, which are dyed bright colors and covered with intricate designs. These eggs are so beautiful that people around the world collect them.

Ukrainians also bake a special bread for Easter. They decorate it with designs made from pieces of dough. Families bring the bread and other foods to church to be blessed on Easter. Then they eat the foods for the holiday feast.

THINKING CRITICALLY

1. **Analyzing Issues**
Why were Ukrainian Easter eggs not common during the Soviet era?
2. **Comparing**
How do your family's holiday customs compare with Ukrainian customs?

For more on Easter in Ukraine, go to RESEARCH LINKS CLASSZONE.COM

In 1999 three new members joined NATO: Poland, Hungary, and the Czech Republic. In 2001 Bulgaria, Romania, Slovakia, Slovenia, and the Baltic states were also working to become NATO members.

War in the Balkan Peninsula

Since the late 1980s, much of Eastern Europe has been a place of turmoil and struggle. Yugoslavia, one of the countries located on Europe's Balkan Peninsula, has experienced terrible wars, extreme hardships, and great change.

Under Tito After World War II, Yugoslavia came under Marshal Tito's (TEE·toh) dictatorship. Tito controlled all the country's many different ethnic groups, which included Serbs, Croats, and Muslims. His rule continued until his death in 1980. Slobodan Milošević (sloh·boh·DON muh·LAW·shuh·vich) became Yugoslavia's president in 1989, after years of political turmoil.

Milosevic Slobodan Milošević, a Serb, wanted the Serbs to rule Yugoslavia. The Serbs in Bosnia began fighting the Croats and Muslims living there. The Bosnian Serbs murdered many Muslims so that Serbs would be in the majority. The Serbs called these killings of members of minority ethnic groups **ethnic cleansing**. Finally, NATO attacked the Bosnian Serbs and ended the war.

Vocabulary
Baltic states: Estonia, Latvia, and Lithuania—former Soviet republics that are on the Baltic Sea

BACKGROUND
By 1991 Croatia, Slovenia, Macedonia, and Bosnia-Herzegovina had gained independence from Yugoslavia. Only Serbia and Montenegro were still part of the Yugoslavian federation.

Connections to Science

Pollution Soviet leaders thought that industry would improve life for everyone. Developing industry was so important that the Soviet government did not worry about pollution. Few laws were passed to protect the environment.

In the 1970s and 1980s there was not enough money to modernize industry or to reduce pollution. Some areas also could not afford proper sewage systems or recycling plants. Today, Eastern Europe has some of the worst pollution problems on the continent.

The Balkan States, 1991 and 2001

GEOGRAPHY SKILLBUILDER: Interpreting a Map
1. **Location** • Which Balkan state borders Greece?
2. **Region** • How many countries developed from Yugoslavia?

In 1995 the Serbs, Croats, and Muslims of Bosnia signed a peace treaty. In 1999 Milošević began using ethnic cleansing against the Albanians in Kosovo, a region of Serbia. NATO launched an air war against Yugoslavia that ended with the defeat of the Serbs. In 2000, public protests led to Milošević's removal. He was subsequently arrested and tried for war crimes by the United Nations.

Modern Russia

Life in Russia has improved since the breakup of the Soviet Union. Russian citizens can elect their own leaders. They enjoy more freedom of speech. New businesses have sprung up, and some Russians have become wealthy.

Unfortunately, Russia still faces serious problems. Many leaders are dishonest. The nation has been slow to reform its economic system. Most of the nation's new wealth has gone to a small number of people, so that many Russians remain poor. The crime rate has grown tremendously. The government has also fought a war against Chechnya (CHECH•nee•yah), a region of Russia that wants to become independent.

Reading Social Studies
B. Identifying Problems What are the main problems that face Russia today?

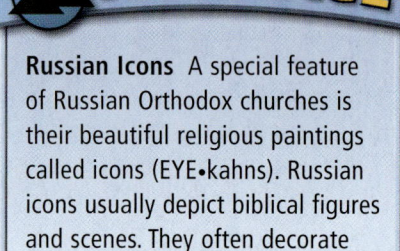

The World's Heritage

Russian Icons A special feature of Russian Orthodox churches is their beautiful religious paintings called icons (EYE•kahns). Russian icons usually depict biblical figures and scenes. They often decorate every corner of a church.

The greatest Russian icon painter was Andrei Rublev (AHN•dray ruhb•LYAWF). He worked in the late 1300s and early 1400s. Rublev's paintings, one of which is shown below, are brightly colored and highlighted in gold. His work influenced many later painters, and today he is considered one of the world's great religious artists.

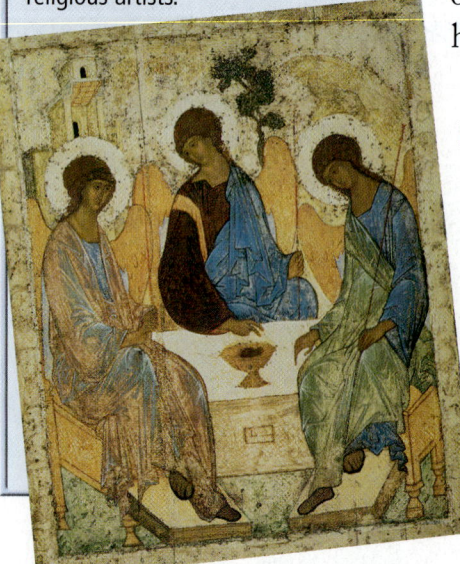

Russian Culture The fall of communism helped most Russians to follow their cultural practices more freely. Russians gained the freedom to practice the religion of their choice. They can also buy and read the great works of Russian literature that once were banned. At the beginning of the 21st century, writers and other artists also have far more freedom to express themselves.

New magazines and newspapers are being published. Even new history books are being written. For the first time in decades, these publications are telling more of the truth about the Soviet Union.

Russia's Government Russia has a democratic form of government. The president is elected by the people. The people also elect members of the **Duma** (DOO•muh), which is part of the legislature.

BACKGROUND
One of the most popular pastimes in Russia is the game of chess. In fact, many of the world's greatest chess players, such as Boris Spassky, have been Russian.

158 CHAPTER 6

Russia's Natural Resources Today

Legend: Forest, Grassland, Desert, Tundra, Farmland, Fishing, Natural gas, Coal, Oil, Iron, Gold, Lead

GEOGRAPHY SKILLBUILDER: Interpreting a Map

1. **Human-Environment Interaction** • Name three of Russia's more common natural resources.
2. **Place** • What is the most common type of land in Russia?

BACKGROUND

Russian highways are in poor condition. Also, many rivers and major ports are closed by ice in the winter. As a result, most Russian goods are transported by railroad.

Democracy is still new to the Russian people. Some citizens are working to improve the system to reduce corruption and to ensure that everyone receives fair treatment. Even the thought of changing the government is new to most Russians. Under the Soviets, people had to accept things the way they were.

Resources and Industry The map above shows Russia's major natural resources. The country is one of the world's largest producers of oil. Russia also contains the world's largest forests. Its trees are made into lumber, paper, and other wood products.

Russian factories produce steel from iron ore. Other factories use that steel to make tractors and other large machines. Since Russian ships can reach both the Pacific and Atlantic oceans, Russia also has a large fishing industry.

Economics Following the lead of Eastern European countries, Russia has been moving toward a free-market economy. Citizens can own land, and foreign companies are encouraged to do business in Russia. These changes have given many Russians more opportunities, but they have also brought difficulties.

Connections to Language

The Russian Language More than 150 million people speak Russian. It is related to other Slavic languages of Eastern Europe, including Polish, Serbian, and Bulgarian.

Russian is written using the Cyrillic (suh•RIHL•ihk) alphabet, which has 33 characters.

Many of the newly independent republics are now returning to the Latin alphabet, used to write English and most other languages of the Western world. The major powers in the world economy base their languages on the Latin alphabet, making communication easier with other countries.

Hello
Привет

Modern Europe 159

Place • Forestry is a major industry in Russia. These harvested logs are being floated downriver to be processed. ▶

Prices are no longer controlled by the government. This means that companies can charge a price that is high enough for them to make a profit. At the beginning of the 21st century, however, people's wages have not risen as fast as prices. Many people cannot afford to buy new products.

Some Russians have done well in the new economy. On the other hand, people with less education and less access to power have not done as well. Also, today most new businesses and jobs are in the cities, which means that people in small towns have fewer job opportunities.

BACKGROUND
The Russian government is unable to enforce tax laws. Many people don't pay their taxes. Without that money, the government cannot provide basic services, such as health care.

SECTION 2 ASSESSMENT

Terms & Names
1. Explain the significance of:
   (a) Mikhail Gorbachev
   (b) parliamentary republic
   (c) coalition government
   (d) ethnic cleansing
   (e) Duma

Using Graphics
2. Use a flow chart like this one to outline the changes in Eastern Europe and Russia from 1988 through 2000.

   1988:
   ↓
   [ ]
   ↓
   [ ]

Main Ideas
3. (a) What happened to the governments of the former Soviet republics after independence?
   (b) How have the economies of Eastern European countries changed now that those countries are free?
   (c) In what ways has life in Russia improved since the breakup of the Soviet Union?

Critical Thinking
4. **Making Inferences**
   Why do you think many Eastern European countries would like to join NATO?

   Think About
   • what happened to the Warsaw Pact
   • the economies of Eastern Europe
   • the relationship between Eastern Europe and Russia

ACTIVITY -OPTION- Reread the information in the Spotlight on Culture feature. Write a short, personal **essay** that describes a special family, school, neighborhood, or holiday celebration in which you participated.

160 CHAPTER 6

SECTION 3

The European Union

TERMS & NAMES
European Union
currency
euro
tariff
standard of living
Court of Human Rights

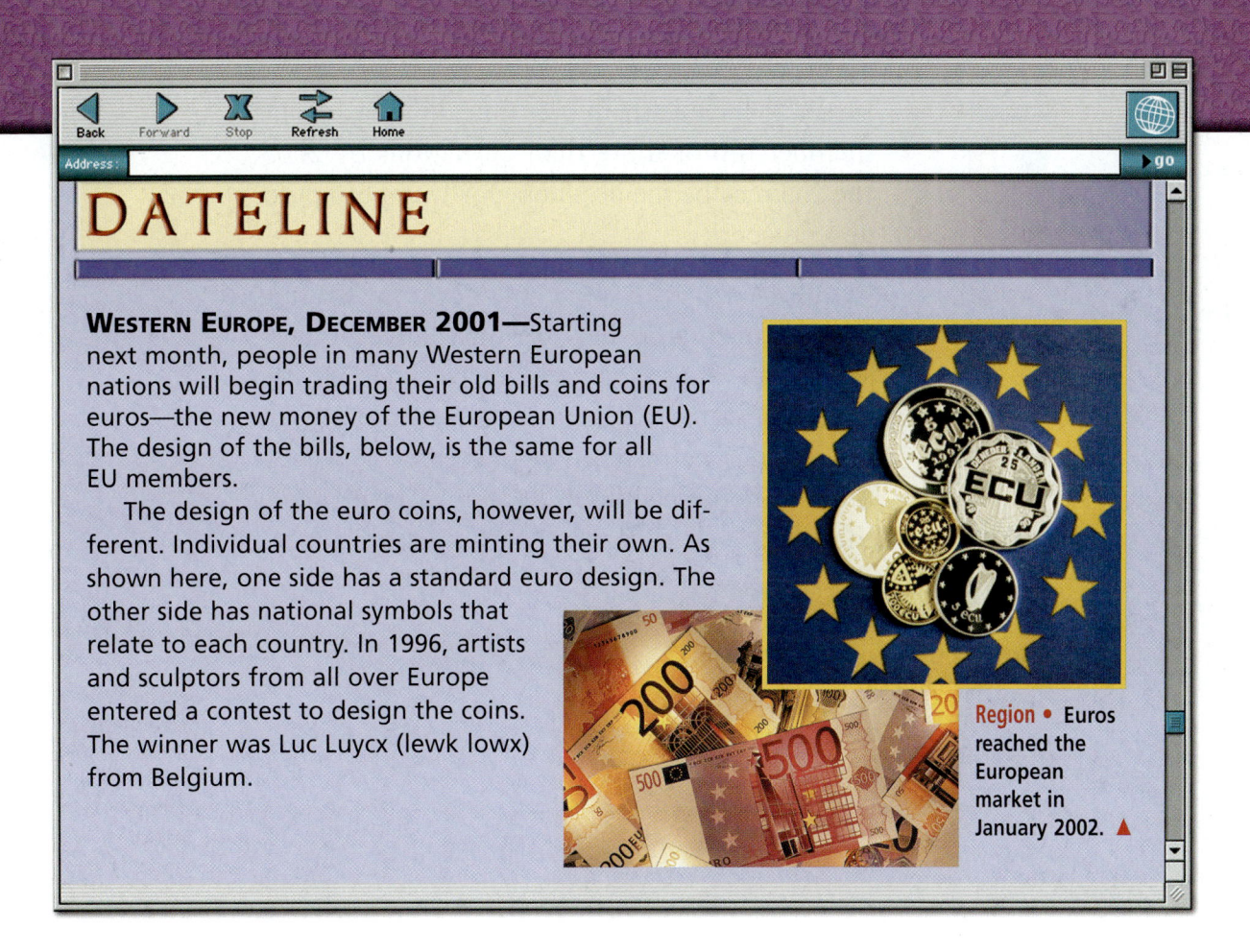

MAIN IDEA
Europeans want to maintain a high quality of life for all citizens while preserving their unique cultures.

WHY IT MATTERS NOW
A prosperous and culturally diverse Europe provides goods and markets for the rest of the world.

DATELINE

WESTERN EUROPE, DECEMBER 2001—Starting next month, people in many Western European nations will begin trading their old bills and coins for euros—the new money of the European Union (EU). The design of the bills, below, is the same for all EU members.

The design of the euro coins, however, will be different. Individual countries are minting their own. As shown here, one side has a standard euro design. The other side has national symbols that relate to each country. In 1996, artists and sculptors from all over Europe entered a contest to design the coins. The winner was Luc Luycx (lewk lowx) from Belgium.

Region • Euros reached the European market in January 2002. ▲

Western Europe Today

Today, in Western Europe, all national leaders share their power with elected lawmakers. Citizens take part in government by voting and through membership in a variety of political parties. The Unit Atlas on pages 54–63 shows modern Europe.

TAKING NOTES
Use your chart to take notes about modern Europe.

Aspect	Under Communism	After Communism
Government		
Economy		

SUNSHINE STATE STANDARDS
Key Standard SS.D.2.3.1 The student understands ways production and distribution decisions are determined in the United States economy and how these decisions compare to those made in market, tradition-based, command, and mixed economic systems.
Other Standards SS.B.1.3.3, B.2.3.2
FCAT LA.A.2.3.1 Reading: Identify Main Idea, Facts, and Details

Modern Europe 161

Members of the European Union, 2001

Austria	
Belgium	
Denmark	
Finland	
France	
Germany	
Greece	
Ireland	
Italy	
Luxembourg	
Netherlands	
Portugal	
Spain	
Sweden	
United Kingdom	

The European Union Many countries of Western Europe belong to a group called the **European Union** (EU). At first, countries joined the EU to encourage trade. This economic group, however, is becoming a loose political union.

Many former Communist countries of Eastern Europe want to join the Union too. They know that membership will help them economically and politically. Eastern European countries, however, cannot automatically join the EU. Many must first make legal, economic, and environmental improvements. The EU has agreed to include them over time. With a possible membership of more than 20 nations by 2003, the EU may be the best hope for European peace and prosperity.

Regional Governments In Western Europe, each nation also has regional governments, similar to those of individual states in the United States. Regional governments are demanding—and receiving—greater power. As a result, many people in Western Europe enjoy increased self-rule and participation in the political process.

BACKGROUND

In 2001, the EU gave initial approval to the Czech Republic, Estonia, Hungary, Poland, and Slovenia to join in the near future.

Region • The headquarters of the European Central Bank is located in Frankfurt, Germany. ◀

EU Economies

BACKGROUND
Some EU nations, including the United Kingdom and Denmark, have not agreed to give up their existing currency.

Traditionally, each European nation has had its own **currency,** or system of money. The EU is meant to make international trade much simpler. With more Europeans using the **euro,** the currency of the EU, currency no longer has to be exchanged every time a payment crosses a border.

Improved Trade To encourage trade, members have also done away with tariffs on the goods they trade with one another. A **tariff** is a duty or fee that must be paid on imported or exported goods, making them more expensive. EU members have lifted border controls as well. This means that goods, services, and people flow freely among these member nations.

Another goal of the EU is to achieve economic equality among its members. To reach this goal, EU members are sharing their wealth. Poorer countries such as Ireland receive money to help them build businesses.

Reading Social Studies
A. Clarifying How would improved trade raise the standard of living?

A Higher Standard of Living Member nations hope that increased trade and shared wealth will help give all citizens of the EU a high standard of living. A person's **standard of living,** or quality of life, is based on the availability of goods and services.

People who have a high standard of living have enough food and housing, good transportation and communications, and access to schools and health care. They also have a high rate of literacy, meaning that most adults are able to read.

Additional Benefits The members of the EU are helping the countries of Eastern Europe to raise their environmental standards. They are willing to pay up to 75 percent of the cost for a new waste treatment system in Romania, for example. The program includes recycling centers for paper, glass, and plastics. It will clean up and close old dumping grounds, which were leaking pollution into the ground water.

Connections to Economics

Tourism For many European nations, tourism is an important part of the economy. In fact, the continent represents about 60 percent of the world's tourist market. Visitors come to enjoy Europe's climate, historic sites, museums, and food.

Popular destinations include Spain, Italy, Austria, and the United Kingdom. France, below, is the most visited country in the world. In 1999 it hosted more than 73 million tourists.

Modern Europe 163

The EU also runs programs that train people for jobs. As citizens of a member nation, people are not limited to a job in their own country. They may work in any part of the EU. They can even vote in local elections wherever they live. In addition, the EU's **Court of Justice** protects the rights of all its citizens in whichever member country they live.

Cultural Diversity

Although many European nations are part of the EU, they still have their own distinct cultural traditions. These traditions may include different languages, unique foods, certain ways of doing business, and even special games and celebrations. Many of these traditions developed over hundreds of years.

Some nations are a mix of several cultures. In Belgium, for example, Flemings live in the north and speak Dutch. Another major group, the Walloons, lives in the south. They speak French. A third group of German-speaking Belgians lives in the eastern part of the country. Many Belgian cities include people from all three groups.

City Life Many of the world's famous and exciting cities are located in Western Europe. London, Madrid, Paris, Amsterdam, and Rome are just a few of the major centers for the arts, business, and learning. These cities are centuries old, and Europeans work hard to preserve them.

Europeans also take pride in the conveniences that their cities offer. Most major urban areas have excellent public transportation, including subways, buses, and trains. Sidewalk cafés are also popular, where people come to meet friends, eat, and relax.

Reading Social Studies

B. Identifying Problems What are the main problems facing the European Union?

Region • Many Europeans center their social lives around urban sidewalk cafés, such as this one in Italy. ▼

Region • Quaint small European villages are popular tourist attractions. ▶

BACKGROUND

Many European families cannot make a living on a small farm. The government may offer support to such families, to help preserve the nation's rural culture.

Country Life European cities have much to offer, but the countryside is also popular—especially for vacationers. The Italian region of Tuscany (TUHS·kuh·nee) and the French region of Provence (pruh·VAHNS) are two of the best-known examples of the many beautiful rural areas.

Small European villages may have only a café, a grocery store, a post office, a town square, and a collection of houses. Many families who live in such areas have been farming or raising animals on the same land for generations. Some even live in houses that their families have owned for hundreds of years.

SECTION 3 ASSESSMENT

Terms & Names

1. Explain the significance of:
   (a) European Union (EU)
   (b) currency
   (c) euro
   (d) tariff
   (e) standard of living
   (f) Court of Human Rights

Using Graphics

2. Use a chart like this one to compare aspects of city life and country life in Europe.

City Life	Country Life

Main Ideas

3. (a) Describe the importance of the new shared currency that is based on the euro.

   (b) Can any European country automatically join the EU? Why or why not?

   (c) List at least two benefits, other than a shared currency, for countries that are members of the EU.

Critical Thinking

4. **Synthesizing**

   Why may the EU be the best hope for European peace and prosperity?

   Think About
   - the number of member countries
   - the goals of the EU
   - modern European conflicts

ACTIVITY -OPTION-

Choose one photograph from this section that shows a place in Europe. Write a **postcard** or **e-mail** to a friend or family member as if you were there. What sights and sounds will you describe?

Modern Europe 165

Linking Past and Present

The Legacy of Europe

Movable Type

Before Johann Gutenberg (1400–1468) invented the printing press in Germany, European monks copied books by hand. Movable type made it possible to print multiple copies of books quickly, allowing people access to them. The printing process advanced greatly in the 1930s. By the mid-1940s, printed works included complex illustrations and color. Today, people create text and images and print them directly from their computers.

Early printing press ▲

Nitroglycerin

For almost 20 years, Alfred Nobel (1833–1896), shown at left, worked on developing a way to safely contain and ignite nitroglycerin, a powerful explosive. Eventually, chemists and doctors realized that nitroglycerin widens blood vessels and can be used to treat patients with heart conditions. Given in tablet, patch, or oral-spray form, nitroglycerin has saved countless lives.

Architecture

The White House in Washington, D.C., is one of many buildings in the United States that has been influenced by Roman architecture. Roman buildings often featured vaulted domes, columns, and large interior spaces. This type of architecture has influenced other buildings in the United States, including many banks and courthouses.

Democracy

Around 500 B.C., several Greek city-states established democracies, replacing their single-ruler governments. The word *democracy* derives from two Greek words: *demos,* meaning "people," and *kratos,* meaning "power." Today, the idea of rule by the people is found around the world, from the United States to France to India.

The agora, or marketplace, of ancient Athens was often the scene of political activities. ▲

Find Out More About It!

Study the text and photos on these pages to learn about inventions, creations, and contributions that have come from Europe. Then choose the item that interests you the most and use the library or the Internet to learn more about it. Use the information you gather to create a poster celebrating the contribution.

RESEARCH LINKS
CLASSZONE.COM

SUNSHINE STATE STANDARDS
Key Standard SS.A.3.3.1 The student understands ways in which cultural characteristics have been transmitted from one society to another (e.g., through art, architecture, language, other artifacts, traditions, beliefs, values, and behaviors).

FCAT LA.A.2.3.2 Reading: Identify Purpose and Point of View

Yacht ▼

Robot ▶

Flamingo ▶

European Languages

Many words of different European languages have made their way into English. For example, the word *dinner* is actually French in origin. As English people traveled and settled around the world, they borrowed words from such European languages as German, Spanish, and Norwegian to use in their everyday communication. Examples of some of these words we use today are *kindergarten* (German), *dinner* (French), *yacht* (Dutch), *corridor* (Italian), *vanilla* (Spanish), *flamingo* (Portuguese), *robot* (Czech), and *ski* (Norwegian).

Europe, Russia, and the Independent Republics

CHAPTER 6 ASSESSMENT

TERMS & NAMES

Explain the significance of each of the following:

1. propaganda
2. Nikita Khrushchev
3. détente
4. Mikhail Gorbachev
5. ethnic cleansing
6. Duma
7. currency
8. euro
9. tariff
10. standard of living

REVIEW QUESTIONS

Eastern Europe Under Communism (pages 147–152)
1. Why did the Soviet government outlaw many cultural celebrations?
2. Explain why most Soviet citizens learned little about other nations around the world.
3. How did the Soviet Union maintain control over Eastern European countries?

Eastern Europe and Russia (pages 154–160)
4. How did the Soviet Union change during 1991?
5. List at least three of Russia's major natural resources.

The European Union (pages 161–165)
6. What is the importance of the European Union (EU)?
7. Name one benefit of being a member of the EU.
8. Identify at least three of Europe's major centers of the arts, business, and learning.

CRITICAL THINKING

Comparing
1. Using your completed chart from Reading Social Studies, p. 146, compare Eastern Europe under Communism with Eastern Europe after Communism.

Summarizing
2. Outline the changes to the Russian economy since the breakup of the Soviet Union.

Recognizing Important Details
3. What types of changes must Eastern European countries make in order to join the EU?

Visual Summary

1. Eastern Europe Under Communism
- The Soviet Union's communist government controlled the lives of its citizens.
- Under Nikita Khrushchev, citizens began to have greater freedom.

2. Eastern Europe and Russia
- Today, independent nations once under Soviet rule are taking steps toward new economies and greater freedom.

3. The European Union
- Many European countries are members of an economic and political alliance called the European Union (EU).

STANDARDS-BASED ASSESSMENT

Use the map and your knowledge of geography to answer questions 1 and 2.

Additional Test Practice, pp. S1–S33

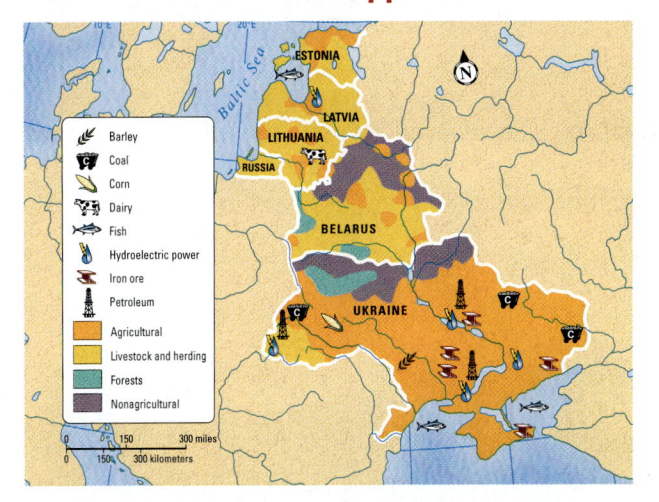

1. Which of the following countries has the greatest variety of power resources?
   A. Estonia
   B. Latvia
   C. Lithuania
   D. Ukraine

2. If you were a dairy farmer, in which country would you probably live?
   A. Belarus
   B. Lithuania
   C. Russia
   D. Ukraine

In the following passage, Mikhail Gorbachev explains his reasons for reforming the Soviet economy. Use the quotation and your knowledge of world cultures and geography to answer question 3.

PRIMARY SOURCE

The country began to lose momentum. Economic failures became more frequent. Difficulties began to accumulate and deteriorate, and unresolved problems to multiply. . . . Analyzing the situation, we first discovered a slowing economic growth. In the last fifteen years the national income growth rates had declined by more than a half.

MIKHAIL GORBACHEV, *Perestroika*

3. According to Gorbachev, what difficulty did the Soviet economy face?
   A. Jobs were being eliminated.
   B. Prices were rapidly rising.
   C. Growth rates were declining.
   D. Factories were being closed.

TEST PRACTICE
CLASSZONE.COM

ALTERNATIVE ASSESSMENT

1. **WRITING ABOUT HISTORY**
   During "The Thaw" in the Soviet Union (1958–1964), people gained many freedoms. Research these freedoms and find out how these changes affected the lives of average citizens in the Soviet Union. Then write a journal entry that might have been written by a citizen after he or she experienced one of these freedoms for the first time. Share your entry with the class.

2. **COOPERATIVE LEARNING**
   When the Soviet Union broke apart into 15 nations, each country had to set up a new government. In a group of three to five classmates, create a government and constitution. Assign each group member a role in the new government, such as a representative or president. Outline the responsibilities of each member. Work together to write a brief constitution for your government including sections that outline basic rights, freedoms, and responsibilities of citizens.

INTEGRATED TECHNOLOGY

Doing Internet Research
Use the Internet and library resources to research the economy of any one of the Balkan states. Write a short report of your findings. List the Web sites that you used to prepare your report.
- Specifically look for information about the types of industry that exist in that state as well as any economic problems the state might face.
- Include graphs or charts that show the state's major imports and exports.

For Internet links to support this activity, go to

RESEARCH LINKS
CLASSZONE.COM

Modern Europe

Chapter 7

Europe Today

- **Section 1** The United Kingdom
- **Section 2** Sweden
- **Section 3** France
- **Section 4** Germany
- **Section 5** Poland

Place London's Piccadilly Circus is an intersection of major roads, with an Underground, or subway, stop at the center. Piccadilly Circus is a popular tourist attraction and shopping district.

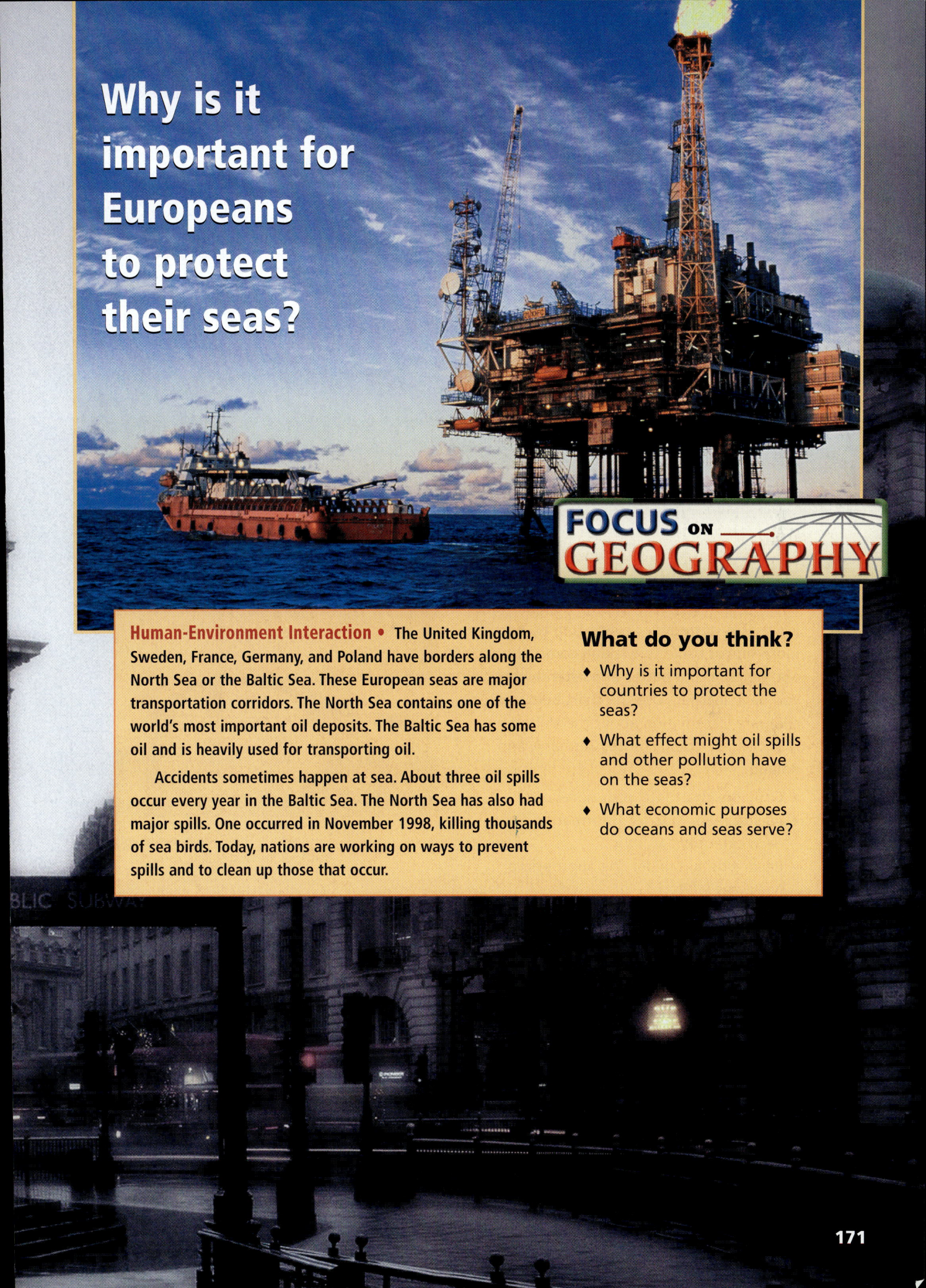

Why is it important for Europeans to protect their seas?

FOCUS ON GEOGRAPHY

Human-Environment Interaction • The United Kingdom, Sweden, France, Germany, and Poland have borders along the North Sea or the Baltic Sea. These European seas are major transportation corridors. The North Sea contains one of the world's most important oil deposits. The Baltic Sea has some oil and is heavily used for transporting oil.

Accidents sometimes happen at sea. About three oil spills occur every year in the Baltic Sea. The North Sea has also had major spills. One occurred in November 1998, killing thousands of sea birds. Today, nations are working on ways to prevent spills and to clean up those that occur.

What do you think?

- Why is it important for countries to protect the seas?
- What effect might oil spills and other pollution have on the seas?
- What economic purposes do oceans and seas serve?

CHAPTER 7 READING SOCIAL STUDIES

BEFORE YOU READ

What Do You Know?

Did you know that from the end of WW II until 1990, Germany was two separate countries and Poland was controlled by the Soviet Union? Do you have relatives or friends who come from the United Kingdom, Sweden, France, Germany, or Poland? Have you ever seen the Queen of England or the Pope, who is from Poland, on television? Have you heard of the Nobel Prize, which is awarded in Sweden? Think about what you have learned in other classes, what you have read, and what you have heard or seen in the news about these countries.

Region • Sweden's Nobel Prize honors great achievements worldwide. ▲

What Do You Want to Know?

Consider what you know about the countries covered in Chapter 7. In your notebook, record what you hope to learn from this chapter.

READ AND TAKE NOTES

Reading Strategy: Comparing Comparing is a useful strategy for evaluating two or more similar subjects. Making comparisons also helps you to better understand what you have learned. Use the chart below to compare information about the United Kingdom, Sweden, France, Germany, and Poland.

- Copy the chart into your notebook.
- As you read, look for information for each category.
- Record details under the appropriate headings.

Movement • The German-made Volkswagen Beetle is the best-selling car ever. ▲

Country	Physical Geography	Government	Economy	Culture	Interesting Facts
United Kingdom					
Sweden					
France					
Germany					
Poland					

172 CHAPTER 7

SECTION 1
The United Kingdom

TERMS & NAMES
London
secede
Good Friday Accord
Charles Dickens

MAIN IDEA
The United Kingdom is a small nation in Western Europe with a history of colonization.

WHY IT MATTERS NOW
British economic, political, and cultural traditions have influenced nations around the world.

DATELINE

BARCELONA, SPAIN, MAY 30, 1999—They did it! Manchester United won the triple crown of soccer. The British fans here are going wild, and their excitement is easy to understand. Manchester United is only the third soccer team to win its league championship, cup titles, and the Champions League final.

Football, or "soccer" as Americans call it, is the world's most popular sport. The British invented a form of the game, called "mob football," in the 1300s. Back then, the playing field was the size of a small town, and there might have been as many as 500 players. A set of rules for the game was developed in 1863. Today, football is the national pastime in the United Kingdom.

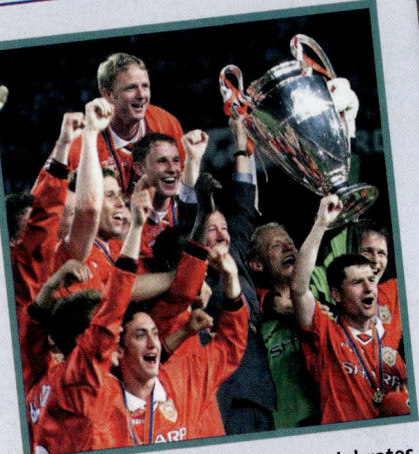

Region • Manchester United celebrates after winning soccer's triple crown. ▲

A Kingdom of Four Political Regions

The United Kingdom is a small island nation of Western Europe. Its culture has had an enormous impact on the world. The nation's official name is the United Kingdom of Great Britain and Northern Ireland. **London**, located in southeastern England, is the capital.

TAKING NOTES
Use your chart to take notes about Europe today.

Country	Physical Geography	Government
United Kingdom		
Sweden		

SUNSHINE STATE STANDARDS
Key Standard SS.A.3.3.5 The student understands the differences between institutions of Eastern and Western civilizations (e.g., differences in governments, social traditions and customs, economic systems and religious institutions).
Other Standards SS.B.1.3.3, D.2.3.2
FCAT LA.A.2.3.1 Reading: Identify Main Idea, Facts, and Details

Europe Today 173

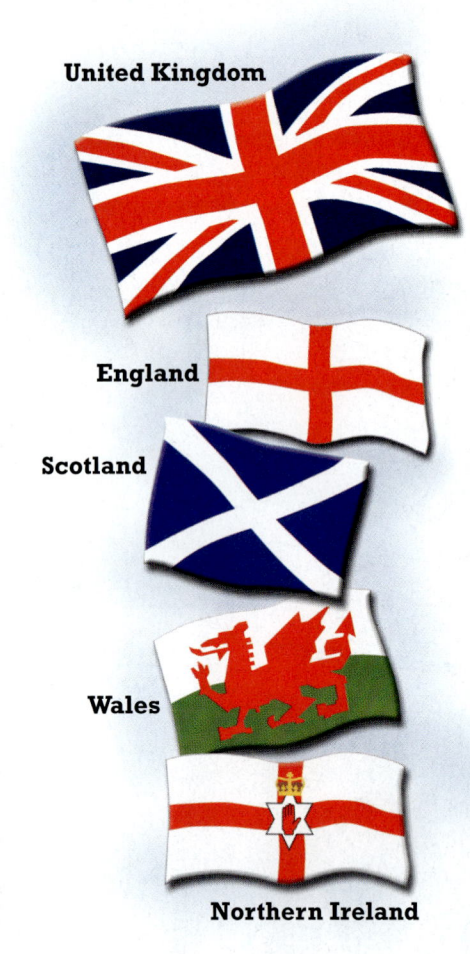

Four different political regions make up the United Kingdom: Scotland, England, Wales, and Northern Ireland (see the map below). The British monarchy has ruled over the four regions for hundreds of years.

Vocabulary
monarchy: government by king or queen

National Government
Today, the government of the United Kingdom is a constitutional monarchy. The British monarch is a symbol of power rather than an actual ruler. The power to govern belongs to Parliament, which is the national lawmaking body.

The British Parliament has two parts. The House of Lords is made up of nobles. Elected representatives make up the House of Commons. The House of Commons is the more powerful of the two houses.

The prime minister leads the government. He or she is usually the leader of the political party that wins the most seats in the House of Commons. The other political parties go into "opposition," which means their role is to question government policies.

Reading Social Studies
A. Clarifying Who is the head of government in the United Kingdom?

Regional Government in Great Britain
Recently, the national government of the United Kingdom has returned some self-rule to some regions of Great Britain. In the late 1990s, voters in Wales approved plans for their own assembly, or body of lawmakers. Also at this time, the Scots voted to create their own parliament. Both Wales's assembly and Scotland's parliament met for the first time in 1999.

GEOGRAPHY SKILLBUILDER: Interpreting a Map
1. **Location** • Which region of the United Kingdom is on a different island?
2. **Location** • Which body of water separates the United Kingdom from France?

174 CHAPTER 7

BACKGROUND

The roots of division in Northern Ireland go back to at least the 1600s, when English and Scottish colonists settled there. These Protestant settlers took over the lands of Irish Catholics.

Governing Northern Ireland Throughout the 20th century, there were conflicts in Northern Ireland between Irish Catholic nationalists and Irish Protestants who supported the government of the United Kingdom. In fact, during the 1960s, many Irish Catholics wanted Northern Ireland to **secede,** or withdraw from, the United Kingdom. They hoped to unite Northern Ireland with the Republic of Ireland. Irish Protestants—a majority in the region—generally wanted to remain part of the United Kingdom.

In 1969, riots broke out, and the British government sent in troops to stop them. Violence between groups of Protestants and Catholics continued for almost 30 years. In 1998, representatives from both sides signed the **Good Friday Accord**. This agreement set up the Northern Ireland Assembly, which represents both Catholic and Protestant voters. For this government to succeed in Northern Ireland, however, the former enemies will need to work together.

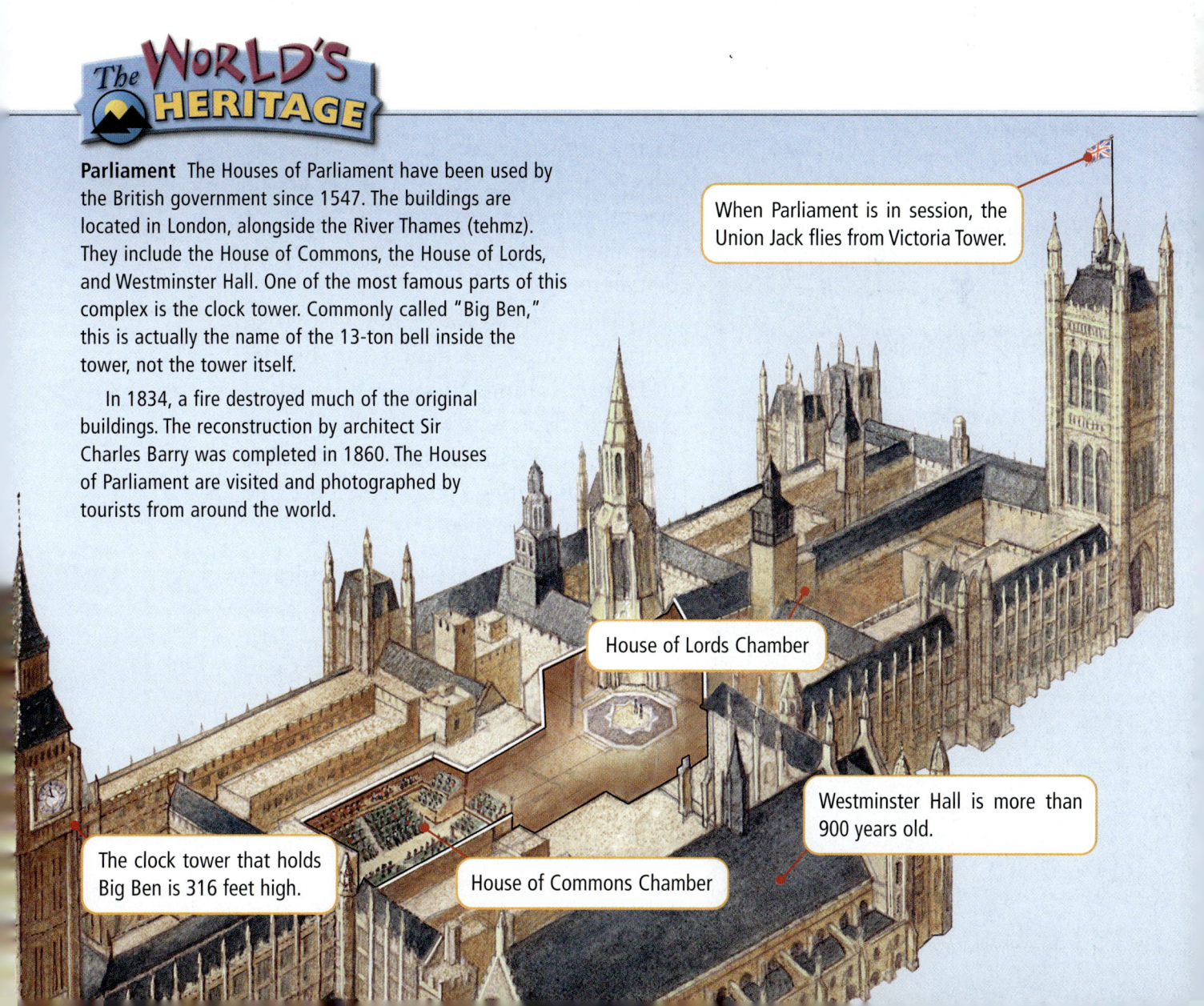

The World's Heritage

Parliament The Houses of Parliament have been used by the British government since 1547. The buildings are located in London, alongside the River Thames (tehmz). They include the House of Commons, the House of Lords, and Westminster Hall. One of the most famous parts of this complex is the clock tower. Commonly called "Big Ben," this is actually the name of the 13-ton bell inside the tower, not the tower itself.

In 1834, a fire destroyed much of the original buildings. The reconstruction by architect Sir Charles Barry was completed in 1860. The Houses of Parliament are visited and photographed by tourists from around the world.

When Parliament is in session, the Union Jack flies from Victoria Tower.

House of Lords Chamber

Westminster Hall is more than 900 years old.

The clock tower that holds Big Ben is 316 feet high.

House of Commons Chamber

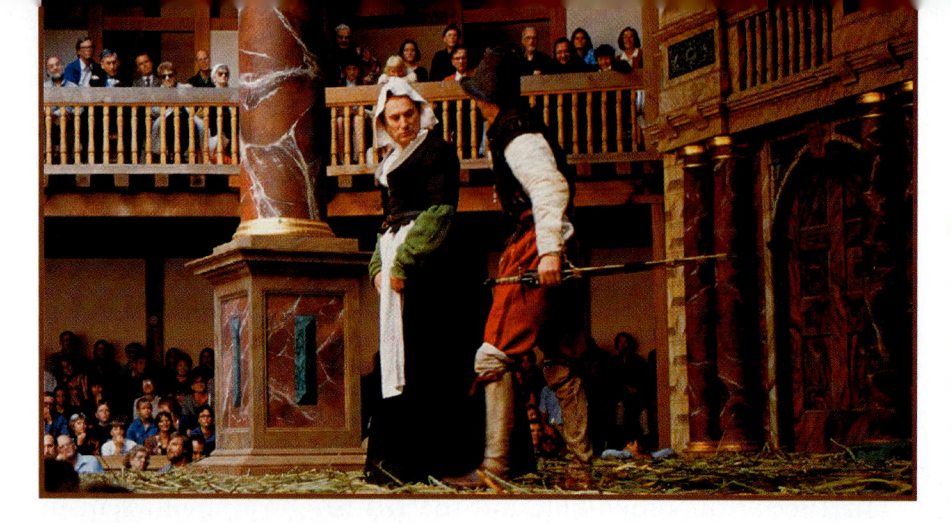

Region • London's New Globe Theater is a replica of the 17th-century playhouse that originally hosted William Shakespeare's works. ◄

Cultural Heritage

The United Kingdom has a rich cultural heritage that includes the great Renaissance playwright William Shakespeare. With a long history as an imperial power, the nation has been exporting its culture around the world for hundreds of years. For example, India, Canada, and other former British colonies modeled their governments on the British parliamentary system. British culture has also set trends in sports, music, and literature.

Music British music influenced the early music of Canada and the United States, both former British colonies. One British tune long familiar to people in the United States is "God Save the Queen." You probably know it as "My Country, 'Tis of Thee." Several countries have put the words of their national anthems to this traditional British melody.

Region • In the early 1960s, the Beatles became wildly popular, not only in the United Kingdom, but also around the world. ▼

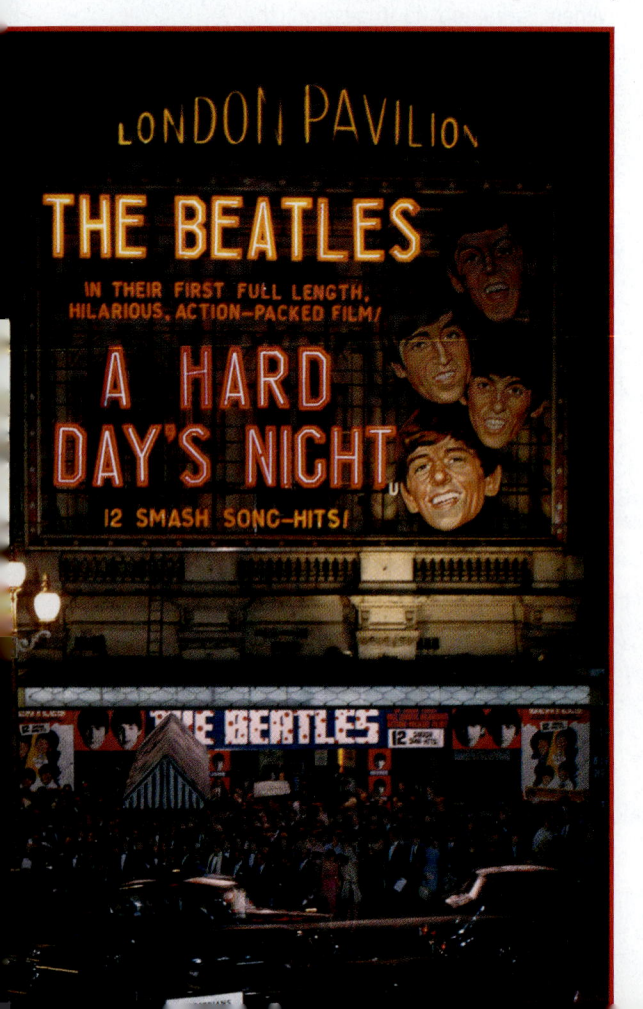

During the 1960s, many British musical groups—including the Beatles and the Rolling Stones—dominated music charts around the world. In later decades, other British singers, including Elton John, Sting, and Dido, became popular favorites.

Literature The best-known cultural export of the United Kingdom, aside from the English language itself, may be literature. In the 19th century, Mary Shelley dreamed up Frankenstein's monster, and Sir Arthur Conan Doyle first wrote about Sherlock Holmes. Another popular author of the time was **Charles Dickens** (1812–1870), who wrote *Oliver Twist* and *A Christmas Carol*.

Reading Social Studies

B. Recognizing Important Details Why was the United Kingdom able to spread British culture across the world?

Two gifted British writers of the 20th century are Virginia Woolf and George Orwell. Modern British authors have also given the world many popular stories for young people. They include C. S. Lewis, who wrote *The Chronicles of Narnia,* and J. K. Rowling, who created the Harry Potter books.

The British Economy

The United Kingdom is an important trading and financial center. Many British citizens also make their living in mining and manufacturing. Factories in the United Kingdom turn out a variety of products ranging from china to sports cars. The nation has plenty of coal, natural gas, and oil to fuel its factories, but it has few other natural resources.

The need for imported goods makes trade another major industry of the United Kingdom. The nation imports many raw materials used in manufacturing. It also imports food, because the farms of this nation produce only enough to feed about two-thirds of its large population.

Region • J. K. Rowling's Harry Potter books have captured the imaginations of children worldwide. ▲

SECTION 1 ASSESSMENT

Terms & Names
1. Explain the significance of:
   (a) London
   (b) secede
   (c) Good Friday Accord
   (d) Charles Dickens

Using Graphics
2. Use a chart like this one to describe the major aspects of the United Kingdom's modern government, economy, and culture.

Modern United Kingdom	
Government	
Economy	
Culture	

Main Ideas
3. (a) Identify the four regions that make up the United Kingdom.
   (b) What role does the British monarch play in the government of the modern United Kingdom?
   (c) What impact has the culture of the United Kingdom had on its colonies and on other parts of the world?

Critical Thinking
4. **Analyzing Issues**
   Why do you think the conflict in Northern Ireland is so difficult to resolve?

   Think About
   ◆ differences in religious beliefs
   ◆ recent changes in British regional governments
   ◆ the long period of continued violence

ACTIVITY -OPTION- Reread the information about British football from the "Dateline" feature that opens the section. Write a **description** of a sport that interests you.

Europe Today **177**

SECTION 2

Sweden

TERMS & NAMES
Riksdag
ombudsman
armed neutrality
hydroelectricity
acid rain
skerry

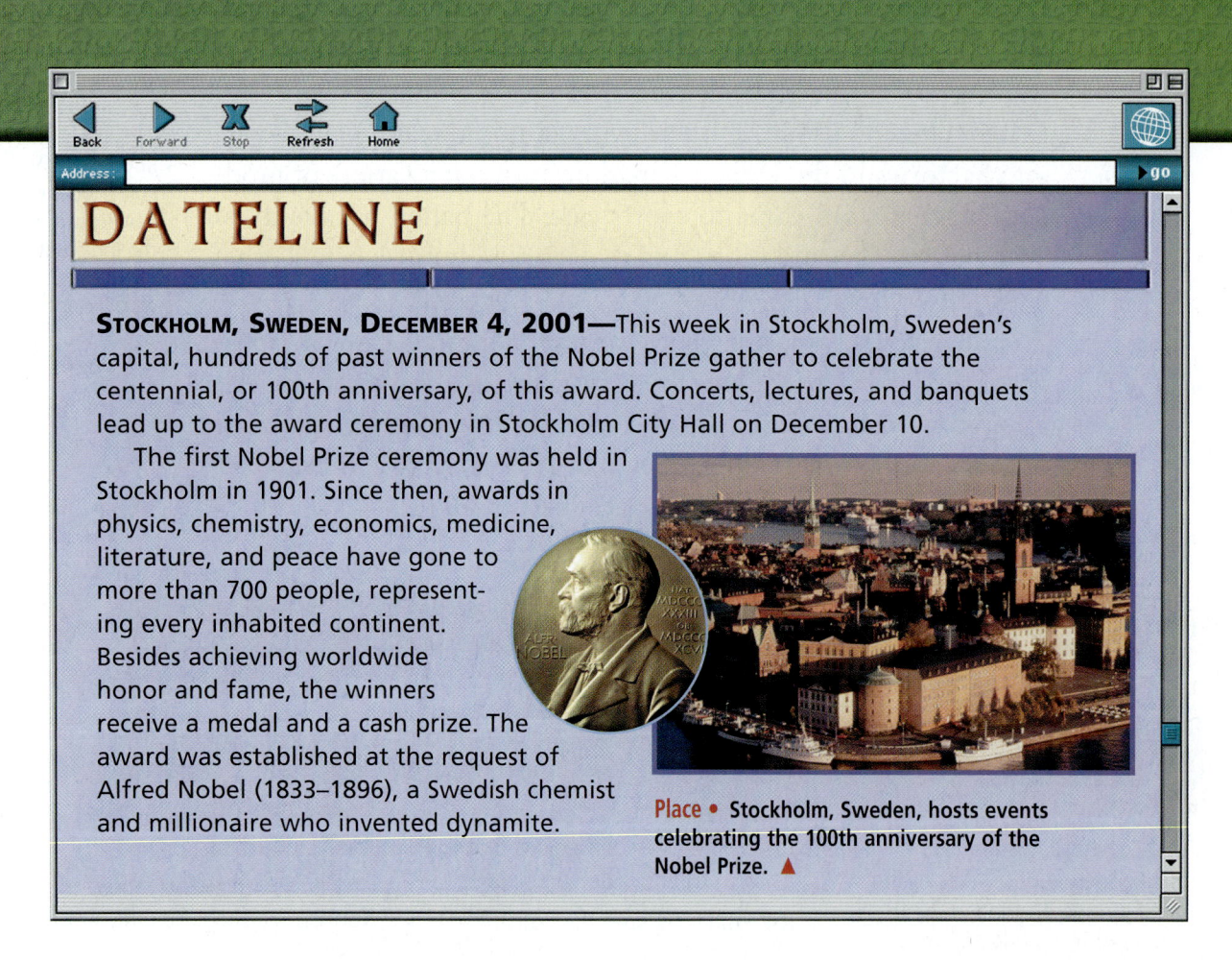

MAIN IDEA
Sweden offers its people a high standard of living, although it also faces environmental problems.

WHY IT MATTERS NOW
Modern Sweden is dealing with environmental issues that affect many countries around the world.

DATELINE

STOCKHOLM, SWEDEN, DECEMBER 4, 2001—This week in Stockholm, Sweden's capital, hundreds of past winners of the Nobel Prize gather to celebrate the centennial, or 100th anniversary, of this award. Concerts, lectures, and banquets lead up to the award ceremony in Stockholm City Hall on December 10.

The first Nobel Prize ceremony was held in Stockholm in 1901. Since then, awards in physics, chemistry, economics, medicine, literature, and peace have gone to more than 700 people, representing every inhabited continent. Besides achieving worldwide honor and fame, the winners receive a medal and a cash prize. The award was established at the request of Alfred Nobel (1833–1896), a Swedish chemist and millionaire who invented dynamite.

Place • Stockholm, Sweden, hosts events celebrating the 100th anniversary of the Nobel Prize. ▲

Sweden's Government

Home of the Nobel Prize, Sweden shares the Scandinavian Peninsula with Norway in Northern Europe (see the map on page 179). The country is a constitutional monarchy; the Swedish monarch has only ceremonial powers and cannot make laws. Instead, the people elect representatives to four-year terms in the Swedish parliament, called the **Riksdag** (REEKS·DAHG).

TAKING NOTES
Use your chart to take notes about Europe today.

Country	Physical Geography	Government
United Kingdom		
Sweden		

SUNSHINE STATE STANDARDS
Key Standard SS.B.2.3.6 The student understands the environmental consequences of people changing the physical environment in various world locations.
Other Standards SS.A.3.3.5
FCAT LA.A.2.3.1 **Reading:** Identify Main Idea, Facts, and Details

The Riksdag The 349 members of the Riksdag nominate Sweden's prime minister. They also appoint ombudsmen. **Ombudsmen** are officials who protect citizens' rights and make sure that the Swedish courts and civil service follow the law.

Swedish citizens vote to determine how many members of each political party serve in the Riksdag. Before 1976, the Social Democratic Labour Party had been in power for nearly 44 years. Today, the Swedish government includes four other parties.

Region •
Women are active in Swedish government. ▶

Foreign Policy Since World War I, Sweden's foreign policy has been one of **armed neutrality**. This means that in times of war, the country has its own military forces but does not take sides in other nations' conflicts.

Even during peacetime, the Swedish government tries not to form military alliances. Unless Sweden is directly attacked, it will not become involved in war. The country is a strong supporter of the United Nations.

Reading Social Studies
A. Synthesizing How does Sweden's neutrality affect its foreign relations?

The Economy and the Environment

Privately owned businesses and international trade are important to Sweden's economy. It exports many goods, including metals, minerals, and wood. Engineering and communications are major industries. The automobile industry also provides many jobs.

Sweden Today

- National boundary
- ★ National capital
- • Other city

GEOGRAPHY SKILLBUILDER: Interpreting a Map
1. **Location •** Which country shares the Scandinavian Peninsula with Sweden?
2. **Region •** What is the national capital of Sweden?

Europe Today **179**

The Swedish Labor Force After World War II, many Swedes left their towns and villages to find work in the large cities in the south. Today, more than 80 percent of the population lives in these urban areas. Much of Sweden's labor force is highly educated and enjoys a high standard of living.

Power Sources <u>Hydroelectricity</u>, or power generated by water, is the main source of electrical power in Sweden. Nuclear power is also widely used. The Swedish government is looking into other, safer sources of energy, which include solar- and wind-powered energy.

Place • Many in Sweden's highly educated labor force work in the high-tech and engineering industries. ▲

Acid Rain Sweden and its neighboring countries share similar environmental problems. One of the most severe problems is <u>acid rain</u>. Acid rain occurs when air pollutants come back to Earth in the form of precipitation. These pollutants may soon poison many trees throughout the region. Sweden and neighboring countries are working to clean up the environment by trying to control air pollutants produced by cars and factories.

Region • December 13 is St. Lucia's Day, one of Sweden's most important Christian holidays. ▼

Reading Social Studies

B. Clarifying What causes acid rain?

Daily Life and Culture

Culturally and ethnically, Sweden is primarily a homogeneous country. Ninety percent of the population are native to Sweden and are members of the Lutheran Church of Sweden. The majority of people speak Swedish.

Since World War II, immigrants from Turkey, Greece, and other countries have brought some cultural diversity to Sweden's population. Today, about one in nine people living in Sweden is an immigrant or the child of an immigrant.

Vocabulary

homogeneous: the same throughout

Recreation Workers in Sweden have many benefits, including long vacations. The Swedes love taking time to enjoy both winter and summer sports. Sweden, with its cold weather and many hills and mountains, is a great place for cross-country and downhill skiing. Skating, hockey, and ice fishing are also popular.

180 CHAPTER 7

Place • Sweden's cold winters have made downhill and cross-country skiing popular. ▶

Many small islands, called **skerries**, dot the Swedish coast. In the summer, many people visit these islands to hike, camp, and fish. Tennis, soccer, and outdoor performances such as concerts are popular as well.

Contributions to World Culture Sweden is well-known for its contributions to drama, literature, and film. The late 19th-century and early 20th-century plays of August Strindberg are produced all over the world. Astrid Lindgren's children's books, including *Pippi Longstocking* (1945), still delight readers everywhere. Ingmar Bergman is famous for the many great films he directed.

SECTION 2 ASSESSMENT

Terms & Names
1. Explain the significance of:
   (a) Riksdag
   (b) ombudsman
   (c) armed neutrality
   (d) hydroelectricity
   (e) acid rain
   (f) skerry

Using Graphics
2. Use a spider map like this one to outline the major aspects of Sweden's government, economy, and culture.

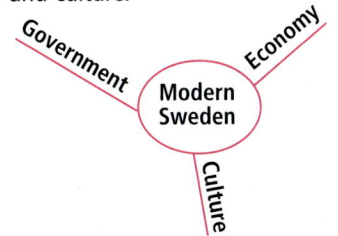

(Spider map with "Modern Sweden" in center, branches to Government, Economy, Culture)

Main Ideas
3. (a) On which European peninsula is Sweden located? What other country shares this peninsula?
   (b) What happened to the Swedish labor force after World War II?
   (c) How has immigration since World War II changed the population of Sweden?

Critical Thinking
4. **Evaluating Decisions**
   What do you think might be the advantages and disadvantages of armed neutrality for Sweden?

   Think About
   ◆ Sweden's location
   ◆ the damage and expense of war
   ◆ the benefits of alliances

ACTIVITY -OPTION- Reread the "Dateline" feature at the beginning of this section. Write a short **description** of which category you would like to earn a Nobel Prize in and why.

Europe Today 181

Interdisciplinary Challenge

Spend a Day in Renaissance Florence

You are a traveler visiting Florence, Italy, in the year 1505. It is exciting to be here now. All over Europe, people have heard about the Renaissance, or cultural rebirth, that is taking place in this beautiful city. Artists, architects, writers, and scientists are turning out brilliant work. In the day you spend here, you want to learn about this new cultural movement. You want to be able to tell people at home about Renaissance Florence.

COOPERATIVE LEARNING On these pages are challenges you will encounter as you tour Renaissance Florence. Working with a small group, choose one of these challenges to solve. Divide the work among group members. Look for helpful information in the Data File. Keep in mind that you will present your solution to the class.

LANGUAGE ARTS CHALLENGE

"Florence is home to brilliant artists and writers."

Why did the Renaissance start here? Florence is home to brilliant artists and writers. Successful merchants and craftworkers, along with several powerful families, have made the city rich. Many wealthy people are patrons, or sponsors, of artists' work. You are curious about the people of Florence. Who are the leading figures? What is life like here? Choose one of these options to discover the answers. Use the Data File for help.

ACTIVITIES

1. Choose one major figure who lived in Florence during the Renaissance and research his or her life. Then write a short first-person monologue in which, speaking as that person, you describe your life and work.
2. Imagine you are an ordinary young Florentine living in 1505—for example, a goldsmith's apprentice. Write journal entries for a week in your life.

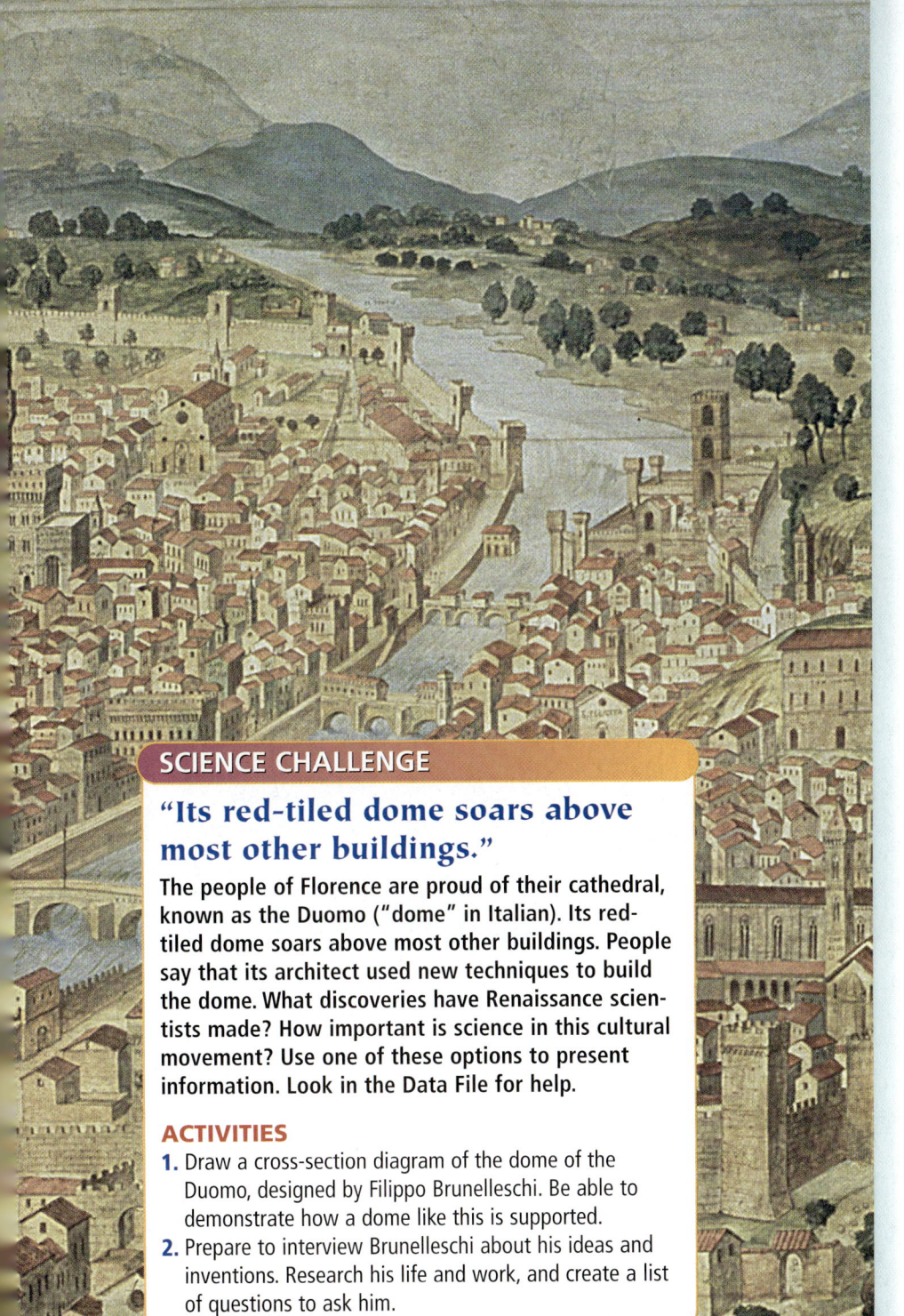

SUNSHINE STATE STANDARDS
Key Standard SS.A.2.3.1 The student understands how language, ideas, and institutions of one culture can influence other cultures (e.g., through trade, exploration, and immigration).
FCAT LA.B.1.3.1 Writing: Organize for Type and Purpose

SCIENCE CHALLENGE

"Its red-tiled dome soars above most other buildings."

The people of Florence are proud of their cathedral, known as the Duomo ("dome" in Italian). Its red-tiled dome soars above most other buildings. People say that its architect used new techniques to build the dome. What discoveries have Renaissance scientists made? How important is science in this cultural movement? Use one of these options to present information. Look in the Data File for help.

ACTIVITIES

1. Draw a cross-section diagram of the dome of the Duomo, designed by Filippo Brunelleschi. Be able to demonstrate how a dome like this is supported.
2. Prepare to interview Brunelleschi about his ideas and inventions. Research his life and work, and create a list of questions to ask him.

Activity Wrap-Up

As a group, review your solution to the challenge you selected. Then present your solution to the class.

DATA FILE

LANDMARKS OF RENAISSANCE FLORENCE

- Florence is built on both sides of the **Arno River**. Its population during the Renaissance was about 100,000. Most of the famous buildings are on the right bank. Besides its artists, Renaissance Florence was known for its craftworkers, such as goldsmiths and leatherworkers.

- The **Duomo** stands on the Piazza del Duomo, an open square. In 1418, Filippo Brunelleschi won a contest to build a dome over the unfinished church. He invented new methods and machines to build it. As in earlier domes, vaults or pointed arches support the dome. Brunelleschi added a circular support wall, called a drum, to build it higher.

- The **Ponte Vecchio** ("Old Bridge"), built in 1345, is one of several bridges across the Arno River. Shops, especially those of goldsmiths, line both sides of the bridge.

- The **Pitti Palace**, built in 1458, is on the left bank of the river.

MAJOR FIGURES OF THE RENAISSANCE

- **Filippo Brunelleschi** (1377–1446), architect of the Duomo and the Pitti Palace.
- **Dante** (1265–1321), poet, author of *Divine Comedy*. Dante pioneered the usage of everyday language, instead of Latin, in literature.
- **Isabella d'Este** (1474–1539), noblewoman and patron of many artists.
- **Leonardo da Vinci** (1452–1519), painter, sculptor, engineer, scientist.
- **Michelangelo** (1475–1564), sculptor, painter, architect; sculptor of *David* (1504).
- **Raphael** (1483–1520), painter and architect.

To learn more about Renaissance Florence, go to

RESEARCH LINKS
CLASSZONE.COM

Europe, Russia, and the Independent Republics

SECTION 3
France

TERMS & NAMES
Charles de Gaulle
French Resistance
Jean Monnet
socialism
European Community
impressionism

MAIN IDEA
France was ruined politically and economically by World War II but has since made a full recovery.

WHY IT MATTERS NOW
France is an important member of the European Union and continues to influence the world's economy and cultures.

DATELINE EXTRA

PARIS, FRANCE, AUGUST 26, 1944

Paris is free! The church bells are still ringing from yesterday's celebrations. After four long years of German control, Paris finally has been liberated. General Charles de Gaulle returned from the United Kingdom yesterday and celebrated the liberation by leading a parade from the Arc de Triomphe to Notre Dame Cathedral.

The liberation of Paris is the result of a two-and-a-half-month advance of Allied forces from the beaches of Normandy in northern France. The French Resistance in Paris began disrupting the German occupiers on August 19, and yesterday, the French army entered Paris.

Region • The liberation of Paris is a significant symbolic victory for the Allies. ▲

The Fifth Republic

During World War II, **Charles de Gaulle** (1890–1970) was a general in the French army. After Germany conquered France in 1940, de Gaulle fled to the United Kingdom. There, he became the leader of the French in exile and stayed in contact with the French Resistance. The **French Resistance** established communications for the Allied war effort, spied on German activity, and sometimes assassinated high-ranking German officers.

TAKING NOTES
Use your chart to take notes about Europe today.

Country	Physical Geography	Government
United Kingdom		
Sweden		

SUNSHINE STATE STANDARDS
Key Standard SS.D.2.3.2 The student understands that relative prices and how they affect people's decisions are the means by which a market system provides answers to the three basic economic questions: What goods and services will be produced? How will they be produced? Who will buy them?
Other Standards SS.A.3.3.1, A.3.3.5
FCAT LA.A.2.3.1 Reading: Identify Main Idea, Facts, and Details

France Today

GEOGRAPHY SKILLBUILDER:
Interpreting a Map

1. **Location** • Name three countries that border France.
2. **Location** • Which bodies of water does France have access to?

On December 21, 1958, Charles de Gaulle was elected president of France. He reorganized the French constitution and instituted the Fifth Republic of France.

The Government of the Fifth Republic
France is a parliamentary republic. Governmental power is split between the president and parliament. The president is elected by the public to a seven-year term; beginning in 2002, the president will serve a five-year term. The president's primary responsibilities are to act as guardian of the constitution and to ensure proper functioning of other authorities.

Parliament has two parts: the Senate and the National Assembly. The president chooses a prime minister, who heads parliament and is largely responsible for the internal workings of the government. The French government is very active in the country's economy.

A Centralized Economy

World War II left France poor and in need of rebuilding. The National Planning Board, established by **Jean Monnet** (moh•NAY) in 1946, launched a series of five-year plans to modernize France and set economic goals for the country.

Reading Social Studies

A. Comparing Compare the term and role of the president of France with the president of the United States.

Connections to History

Lascaux Cave Paintings On September 12, 1940, while hiking in the hills of Lascaux (lah•SKOH) near the town of Montignac in southern France, four teenage boys discovered ancient cave paintings. They found the caves after their dog fell in a hole in the ground.

Henri Breuil (broy), one of the first archaeologists on the scene, counted more than 600 images of horses (shown here), deer, and bison. The cave paintings are about 17,000 years old, making them some of the oldest works of art yet discovered.

Europe Today 185

The result of these plans was a mixed economy, with both public and private sectors. The French government nationalized, or took over, major banks; insurance companies; the electric, coal, and steel industries; schools; universities; hospitals; railroads; airlines; and even an automobile company.

This nationalization of industry is a form of socialism. **Socialism** is an economic system in which some businesses and industries are controlled by the government. The government also provides many health and welfare benefits, such as health care, housing, and unemployment insurance. However, today the French government is slowly placing more of the economy under the control of private companies.

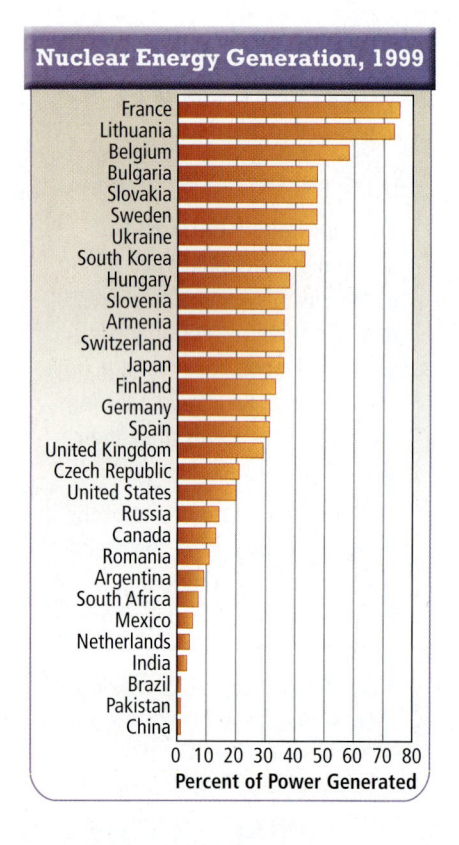

Nuclear Energy Generation, 1999

France, Lithuania, Belgium, Bulgaria, Slovakia, Sweden, Ukraine, South Korea, Hungary, Slovenia, Armenia, Switzerland, Japan, Finland, Germany, Spain, United Kingdom, Czech Republic, United States, Russia, Canada, Romania, Argentina, South Africa, Mexico, Netherlands, India, Brazil, Pakistan, China

0 10 20 30 40 50 60 70 80
Percent of Power Generated

Region • Nuclear power plants are a common sight in the French countryside. ▼

Energy The French economy grew rapidly after 1946, and the country's industry was powered mainly by coal, oil, and gas. When worldwide oil prices rose in the 1970s, the French economy suffered. In the 1980s, France turned to nuclear power so that its economy would be less dependent on oil. Today France draws 75 percent of its power from nuclear energy, a higher percentage than any other nation in the world.

Most famous for its wines, France also exports grains, automobiles, electrical machinery, and chemicals. Although only about 7 percent of the labor force works on farms, France exports more agricultural products than any other nation in the European Community.

The **European Community** is an association developed after World War II to promote economic unity among the countries of Western Europe. Its success gave rise to greater unity, both politically and economically, in the European Union.

Reading Social Studies

B. Analyzing Motives Why does France produce a large amount of nuclear energy?

BACKGROUND

Tourism is a major industry in France. The country hosts more than 70 million visitors annually, making it the most visited country in the world.

The Culture of Paris

Paris, the capital city of France, is famous for its contributions to world culture, most especially in the arts. Nicknamed "City of Light," Paris has long been an intellectual and artistic center.

Edouard Manet (muh·NAY) (1832–1883) helped influence one of the most important art movements of modern times, impressionism. **Impressionism** is an art style that uses light to create an impression of a scene rather than a strictly realistic picture. Manet inspired such artists as Claude Monet (moh·NAY), Pierre Renoir (ruhn·WAHR), and Paul Cézanne (say·ZAHN). This group of artists worked together in Paris and shared their thoughts and opinions of art.

Paris's Musée d'Orsay and the Louvre (loove) house two of the greatest collections of fine art in the world. The School of Fine Arts leads a tradition of education and art instruction that has produced artists such as Pierre Bonnard (baw·NAHR) (1867–1947) and Balthus (1908–2001).

Region • Monet and his family often modeled for Manet, as in this 1874 painting, *Monet Working on His Boat in Argenteuil.* ▲

Literature France has a rich tradition of literature as well. Marcel Proust, who wrote *Remembrance of Things Past*, was an influential writer in the early 20th century. Other significant writers include Albert Camus (kah·MOO), who wrote *The Stranger*, and Simone de Beauvoir (boh·VWAHR), author of *The Mandarins*.

SECTION 3 ASSESSMENT

Terms & Names
1. Explain the significance of:
   (a) Charles de Gaulle
   (b) French Resistance
   (c) Jean Monnet
   (d) socialism
   (e) European Community
   (f) impressionism

Using Graphics
2. Use a chart like this one to list the major aspects of French government, economy, and culture.

	Major Aspects
Government	
Economy	
Culture	

Main Ideas
3. (a) What role does the French government play in the country's economy?
   (b) What is France's primary source of power?
   (c) Name three contributions of French culture to the world.

Critical Thinking
4. **Clarifying**
   How was the liberation of Paris a symbolic victory?

   Think About
   • the actions of the French Resistance
   • the cultural life of Paris

ACTIVITY -OPTION- Reread the text on Manet. Draw an impressionist **portrait** of a classmate, friend, or family member.

Europe Today

SECTION 4

Germany

TERMS & NAMES
Berlin Wall
reunification
Ludwig van Beethoven
Rainer Maria Rilke

MAIN IDEA
Germany has overcome many obstacles to become both a unified and a modern nation.

WHY IT MATTERS NOW
Germany has helped to shape recent European history and contemporary Western culture.

DATELINE

BERLIN, GERMANY, OCTOBER 3, 1990— It is just past midnight. Church bells are ringing, fireworks are exploding, bands are playing, and the streets are filled with celebrating Germans. At midnight, the treaty to reunite East and West Germany became official. Germany is whole once more!

Just a year ago, the Berlin Wall—a 103-mile-long barrier of concrete and barbed wire—still separated East and West Berlin. Constructed in 1961, the Wall kept East Germans from escaping from their Communist government to democratic West Germany. Then, in 1989, as the Communist government weakened, the Wall came down.

Location • Germans celebrate unification in front of the Reichstag, the seat of the federal government. ▲

A Divided Germany

Today, the reunified nation of Germany is one of the largest countries in Europe. When World War II ended in 1945, however, Germany was divided. United States, French, and British soldiers occupied the new West German nation, and Soviet soldiers occupied the new East Germany.

TAKING NOTES
Use your chart to take notes about Europe today.

Country	Physical Geography	Government
United Kingdom		
Sweden		

SUNSHINE STATE STANDARDS
Key Standard SS.B.1.3.3 The student knows the social, political, and economic divisions on Earth's surface.
Other Standards SS.A.3.3.1
FCAT LA.A.2.3.1 Reading: Identify Main Idea, Facts, and Details

188 CHAPTER 7

West Germany The United States helped West Germany set up a democratic government. In part, the United States supported the new nation because it was located between the Communist countries of Eastern Europe and the rest of Western Europe.

With the help of U.S. loans, West Germany experienced a so-called economic miracle. In 20 years, it rebuilt its factories and became one of the world's richest nations. Its economy later became the driving force behind the European Union.

East Germany In contrast to West Germany, East Germany remained poor. Most East Germans saw West Germany, and Western Europe in general, as a place where people had better lives. East Germany's Communist government, however, discouraged contact between east and west.

By 1989, the Soviet Union's control of Eastern Europe was weakening. Hungary, a Soviet ally, relaxed control over its borders with Western Europe. East Germans began crossing the Hungarian border into Austria and eventually made their way into West Germany. After the **Berlin Wall** came down in 1989, more East Germans fled to West Germany.

BACKGROUND
Although Berlin was inside East Germany, it had a large free zone defended by the Allies. The Berlin Wall separated the two parts of the city: East Berlin and West Berlin.

Germany Today

GEOGRAPHY SKILLBUILDER: Interpreting a Map

1. **Location** • Which country is nearest to Germany's national capital?
2. **Place** • Which was larger, East or West Germany?

Reunified Germany

Since the 1990 **reunification**, or the reuniting of East and West Germany, the German government has spent billions of dollars rebuilding the eastern part of the country. The effort has included roads, factories, housing, and hospitals. The city of Berlin, once again the nation's capital, was also rebuilt. The newly reunified nation also restored the Reichstag (RYK·shtahg), where the Federal Assembly meets.

However, reunification has also caused tensions between "Ossies" (OSS·eez) and "Wessies" (VEHSS·eez). Many Ossies complain about the lack of jobs and the cost of housing. Many Wessies complain about paying taxes to rebuild the nation and to help support the former East Germans.

Region • The new Volkswagen Beetle is typical of German car design, known for its simplicity and style. The first Volkswagen was designed by Ferdinand Porsche (POOR·sheh) in 1934. ▲

Reading Social Studies

Clarifying Why did East Germany need to be rebuilt and not West Germany?

Vocabulary

Ossies: former East Germans

Wessies: former West Germans

German Culture

Germany's rich cultural traditions may help to unite its people, who are especially proud of their music and literature. Germans are also famous for designing high-quality products, such as cars, electronic appliances, and other complex machinery.

Music Three of Germany's best-known composers are Johann Sebastian Bach (bahck) (1685–1750), George Frederick Handel (HAHN·duhl) (1685–1759), and **Ludwig van Beethoven** (LOOD·vig vahn BAY·TOH·vuhn) (1770–1827). Their music is still performed and recorded all over the world. German composer Richard Wagner (VAHG·nuhr) (1813–1883) wrote many operas, including a series based on German myths and legends known as the Ring Cycle.

Biography

Beethoven Perhaps the best-loved German composer is Ludwig van Beethoven. Beethoven began to lose his hearing when he was in his 20s. By the time he was 50, he was almost deaf.

Beethoven refused to let his deafness stop him from creating music, however. "I will grapple with Fate, it shall not overcome me," he wrote. In 1824, he finished his Ninth Symphony, which ends with a section containing the well-known "Ode to Joy." An orchestra played this same symphony at an open-air concert during the destruction of the Berlin Wall.

Place • Half-timber architecture, shown here, is common throughout Germany. ▲

BACKGROUND
More than 100 million people around the world speak German.

Literature One of the greatest writers in the German language was **Rainer Maria Rilke** (RIHL·kuh) (1875–1926). His poems, which are still admired and studied today, were a way for Rilke to communicate his feelings and experiences.

Other important 20th-century German authors include Günter Grass (grahs) (b. 1927) and Thomas Mann (man) (1875–1955). Grass has written about the horrors of World War II, the setting for his novel *The Tin Drum*. Both writers were awarded the Nobel Prize in Literature—Mann in 1929 and Grass in 1999.

SECTION 4 ASSESSMENT

Terms & Names
1. Explain the significance of: (a) Berlin Wall   (b) reunification   (c) Ludwig van Beethoven   (d) Rainer Maria Rilke

Using Graphics
2. Use a chart like this one to compare aspects of Germany before and after reunification.

Before Reunification	After Reunification

Main Ideas
3. (a) Describe the economic miracle that occurred in West Germany.
   (b) Why has there been tension between the Ossies and the Wessies?
   (c) On what projects has Germany spent billions of dollars since 1990?

Critical Thinking
4. **Synthesizing**
   What makes Germany an important European country?

   Think About
   - its location
   - its size
   - its role in modern history

ACTIVITY -OPTION- Reread the "Dateline" feature at the beginning of the section. Write a **short story** describing what it might have been like to celebrate the reunification of Germany in 1990.

Europe Today 191

SKILLBUILDER

Making an Outline

▶▶ Defining the Skill

Before writing a research report, you must decide on your topic and then gather information about it. When you have all of the information you need, then you begin to organize it. One way of organizing your information before writing the report is to make an outline. An outline lists the main ideas in the order in which they will appear in the report. It also organizes the main ideas and supporting details according to their importance. The form of every outline is the same. Main ideas are listed on the left and labeled with capital Roman numerals. Supporting ideas are indented and labeled with capital letters. Supporting details are indented farther and labeled with numerals.

SUNSHINE STATE STANDARDS
Key Standard SS.A.3.3.4
The student knows significant historical leaders who have influenced the course of events in Eastern and Western civilizations since the Renaissance.

FCAT LA.B.1.3.1 Writing: Organize for Type and Purpose

▶▶ Applying the Skill

The outline to the right is for a biography of Marie Curie, one of the great physicists of all time. Use the strategies listed below to help you learn how to make an outline.

How to Make an Outline

Strategy ❶ Read the main ideas of this report. They are labeled with capital Roman numerals. Each main idea will need at least one paragraph.

Strategy ❷ Read the supporting ideas for each main idea. These are labeled with capital letters. Notice that some of the main ideas require more supporting ideas than others.

Strategy ❸ Read the supporting details that are included in this outline. These are labeled with numerals. The writer of this outline did not include the supporting details for some of the supporting ideas. It is not necessary to include every piece of information that you have. An outline is intended merely as a guide for you to follow as you write the report.

Strategy ❹ A report can be organized in different ways. This biography is organized chronologically, that is, according to time. It starts with Curie's birth and ends with her legacy after death. The outline follows the order of events in her life. A report can be organized in other ways, such as comparing and contrasting or according to advantages and disadvantages. The outline should clearly reflect the way the report is organized.

❶ I. Who Was She?
    A. Polish-born physicist
❷ B. Birth and early life
    C. Schooling
       1. In secret in Poland (women were not allowed to enter
❸   higher education)
       2. In France at the Sorbonne
❹   a. license of physical sciences, 1893
          b. license of mathematical sciences, 1894
II. The Physicist
    A. Life and work with husband, Pierre Curie
       1. Discoveries
         a. polonium, summer 1898
         b. radium, fall 1898
       2. Nobel Prize in Physics, 1903
         a. shared with Henri Becquerel
         b. Marie was the first woman to ever be awarded a Nobel Prize
    B. Her own accomplishments
       1. Became the first female professor at the Sorbonne
         a. took over Pierre's position after his death, 1906
       2. Her research on radioactivity was published, 1910
       3. Nobel Prize in Chemistry, 1911

▶▶ Practicing the Skill

Look through Chapter 7 and find a topic that interests you. Gather information about that topic, and then write an outline for a report about that topic. Be sure to use the correct outline form.

SECTION 5 Poland

TERMS & NAMES
Solidarity
Lech Walesa
Czeslaw Milosz
censorship
dissident

MAIN IDEA
Poland has gone through the difficulties of establishing a new democratic government and a new economic system.

WHY IT MATTERS NOW
Poland is an excellent example of the success that has been achieved by the newly independent Eastern European nations.

DATELINE

GDAŃSK, POLAND, 1980

In response to recent increases in food prices, many strikes have broken out across Poland. Today's strikes are much larger than the strikes that occurred in 1976. The shipyards in Gdańsk have 17,000 striking workers. One of the strikers' demands is the right to form labor unions. The recent strikes are yet another sign of the country's weakening economy, which has continued to decline over the past decade. Poland's attempts to improve its economic health by borrowing money from other nations have not helped, as the government is unable to repay those loans.

Place • Polish workers protest poor conditions under the Communist government. ▲

Political and Economic Struggles

The strikes and riots of the 1970s and 1980s were not the first actions Polish citizens took against their government. In 1956, Polish workers had rioted to protest their low wages.

In fact, there have been political and economic struggles in Poland since World War II ended in 1945. At that time, Communists took over the government and set strict wage and price controls.

TAKING NOTES
Use your chart to take notes about Europe today.

Country	Physical Geography	Government
United Kingdom		
Sweden		

SUNSHINE STATE STANDARDS
Key Standard SS.A.3.3.4 The student knows significant historical leaders who have influenced the course of events in Eastern and Western civilizations since the Renaissance.
Other Standards SS.A.3.3.1, D.2.3.1
FCAT LA.A.2.3.1 Reading: Identify Main Idea, Facts, and Details

Europe Today 193

Poland Today

GEOGRAPHY SKILLBUILDER:
Interpreting a Map

1. **Location** • Name a port city in Poland.
2. **Location** • How many different countries border Poland?

Solidarity In 1980, labor unions throughout Poland joined an organization called **Solidarity**. This trade union was led by **Lech Walesa** (LEK wah·LEHN·suh), an electrical worker from the shipyards of Gdańsk (guh·DAHNSK).

In the beginning, Solidarity's goals were to increase pay and improve working conditions. Before long, however, the organization set its sights on bigger goals. In late 1981, members of Solidarity were calling for free elections and an end to Communist rule. Even though Solidarity had about 10 million members, the government fought back. It suspended the organization, cracked down on protesters, and arrested thousands of members, including Walesa.

BACKGROUND
Poland's capital and largest city is Warsaw. The nation's citizens are called Poles.

Region • In 1980, Solidarity leader Lech Walesa gained the support of labor unions. Ten years later, he became Poland's president. ◄

Region • Poland's senate helps ensure that all the country's citizens have representation. ◄

A Free Poland

In the late 1980s, economic conditions continued to worsen in Poland. The government asked Solidarity leaders to help them solve the country's economic difficulties. Finally, the Communists agreed to Solidarity's demand for free elections.

When the elections were held in 1989, many Solidarity candidates were elected, and the Communists lost power. In 1990, Lech Walesa became the president of a free Poland.

A New Constitution Today, Poland is a parliamentary republic. The country approved a new constitution in 1997. This constitution guarantees civil rights such as free speech. It also helps to balance the powers held by the president, the prime minister, and parliament.

Parliament Poland's parliament is made up of two houses. The upper house, or senate, has 100 members. The lower house, which has 460 members, chooses the prime minister. Usually, as in the United Kingdom, the prime minister is a member of the largest party or alliance of parties within parliament.

A number of seats in parliament are reserved for representatives of the small German and Ukrainian ethnic groups in Poland. In this way, all Polish citizens are ensured a voice in their government.

A Changing Economy

Besides a new government, the Poles have also had to deal with a changing economy. In 1990, Poland's new democratic government quickly switched from a command economy to a free market economy. Prices were no longer controlled by the government, and trade suddenly faced international competition.

Reading Social Studies
A. Recognizing Important Details What led to free elections in Poland?

BACKGROUND
The Polish president, who is elected every five years, is the head of state.

Europe Today

Inflation Although Polish shops were able to sell goods that had not been available before, prices rose quickly—by almost 80 percent. With this inflation, or a continual rise in prices, people's wages could not keep up with the cost of goods.

Many Polish companies, which could not compete with high-quality foreign goods, went out of business. This, in turn, resulted in high unemployment. As more and more people lost their jobs, Poland's overall standard of living fell.

An Improving Economy In time, new Polish businesses found success, giving more people work. Inflation started to drop. By 1999, inflation was down to around 7 percent. By 2000, Poland no longer needed the economic aid it had been receiving from the United States.

One way to measure the strength of a country's economy is to look at consumer spending. Between 1995 and 2000, Poles bought new cars at a high rate of half a million each year. Today, Poland has 2 million small and medium-sized businesses. The success of these small businesses is another sign of Poland's healthy economy.

Region • With Poland's economy on the rise, unemployment has decreased. ▲

Poland's Culture

The history of Poland has been one of ups and downs. In the 1500s and 1600s, Poland was a large and powerful kingdom. By 1795, Russia, Prussia, and Austria had taken control of its land, and Poland ceased to exist as an independent country. Poland did not become a republic until 1918, after World War I. Throughout the centuries, however, Poland has had a rich culture.

Literature Polish literature is full of accounts of struggles for national independence and stories about glorious kingdoms won and lost by heroic patriots.

One of Poland's best-known writers of recent times is **Czeslaw Milosz** (CHEH·slawv MEE·LAWSH) (b. 1911). Milosz published his first book of poems in the 1930s. After World War II, he worked as a diplomat in the United States and then France.

BACKGROUND

A famous Polish general and patriot, Thaddeus Kosciusko (KAHS·ee·UHS·koh), fought on the side of the colonists during the American Revolution.

Milosz, who became a professor at the University of California at Berkeley, won the Nobel Prize in Literature in 1980.

Censorship Under Communist rule, the Polish media were controlled by the government. The government decided what the media could and could not say. It outlawed any information that did not support and praise the accomplishments of Communism. As a result of this **censorship**, many writers could not publish their works. Some of them became dissidents. A **dissident** is a person who openly disagrees with a government's policies.

Supporting the Arts In order to help Polish writers, the government now allows publications printed in Poland to be sold tax-free. To help Polish actors, screenwriters, and directors, movie theaters are repaid their costs for showing Polish movies. Public-sponsored television stations are supported not only by free-market advertising but also by fees the public pays to own television sets.

Reading Social Studies
B. Analyzing Motives Why did the Communist government control the media?

Place • In 1978, Poland's pride was greatly boosted when Polish-born John Paul II was elected pope. He was the first non-Italian to be elected pope in 456 years. ▲

SECTION 5 ASSESSMENT

Terms & Names
1. Explain the significance of:
   (a) Solidarity
   (b) Lech Walesa
   (c) Czeslaw Milosz
   (d) censorship
   (e) dissident

Using Graphics
2. Use a chart like this one to compare and contrast one aspect of Poland with the same aspect of the United Kingdom, Sweden, France, or Germany.

Poland	Other Country

Main Ideas
3. (a) How did the Polish government respond to Solidarity's goals?
   (b) What was the outcome of Poland's free election in the late 1980s?
   (c) Describe the recent changes in the economy of Poland.

Critical Thinking
4. **Summarizing**
   How would you describe what life was like in Poland before the changes of 1990?

   Think About
   • strikes and riots
   • the Communist government
   • censorship

ACTIVITY -OPTION- Reread the information about Solidarity. Write a short **speech** that might have been given to gain support for the organization in the 1980s.

Europe Today

CHAPTER 7 ASSESSMENT

TERMS & NAMES

Explain the significance of each of the following:

1. London
2. Good Friday Accord
3. armed neutrality
4. hydroelectricity
5. Charles de Gaulle
6. socialism
7. Berlin Wall
8. reunification
9. censorship
10. dissident

REVIEW QUESTIONS

The United Kingdom (pages 173–177)
1. What are the two houses that form the British Parliament? Which is more powerful?
2. Why is it necessary for the United Kingdom to import foods and other goods?

Sweden (pages 178–181)
3. What role do ombudsmen play in the Swedish government?
4. Why is Sweden an excellent place for skiing?

France (pages 184–187)
5. What is France's main source of energy?
6. Identify at least three Impressionist painters.

Germany (pages 188–191)
7. What role did the United States government play in West Germany after World War II?
8. Identify at least three famous German composers.

Poland (pages 193–197)
9. Why is Lech Walesa important to modern Poland?
10. Describe the new constitution that Poland approved in 1997.

CRITICAL THINKING

Comparing
1. Using your completed chart from Reading Social Studies, p. 172, compare the governments and economies of the United Kingdom, Sweden, France, Germany, and Poland.

Hypothesizing
2. One of Sweden's severe environmental problems is acid rain. Why might it be difficult for a country to solve this problem?

Making Inferences
3. Why do you think it was important to the United States that West Germany have a democratic government?

Visual Summary

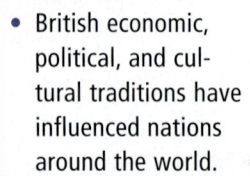

1 The United Kingdom
- British economic, political, and cultural traditions have influenced nations around the world.

2 Sweden
- Sweden offers its people a high standard of living.
- Sweden is dealing with environmental issues such as nuclear power and acid rain.

3 France
- France has made a speedy recovery from World War II.

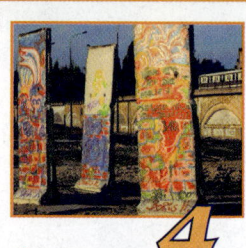

4 Germany
- Germany has overcome many obstacles to become a unified and modern nation.

5 Poland
- Poland is an example of the success made possible by the recent independence of Eastern European nations.

STANDARDS-BASED ASSESSMENT

Use the map and your knowledge of geography to answer questions 1 and 2.

Additional Test Practice, pp. S1–S33

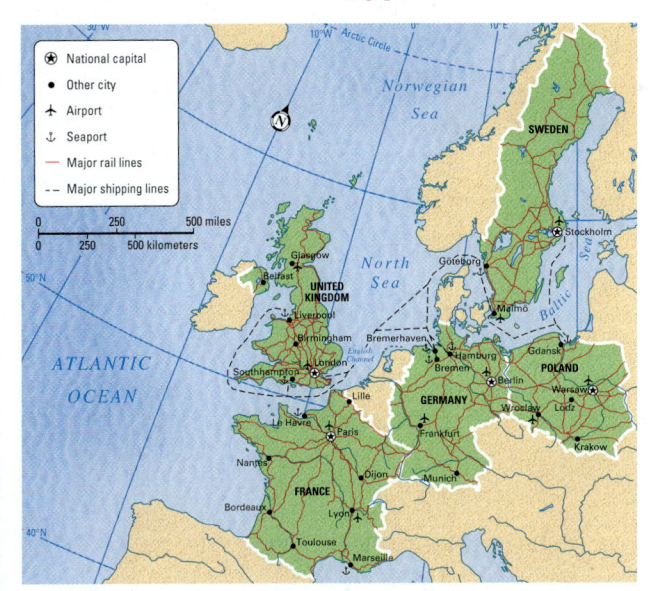

The following excerpt is from a speech about Lech Walesa when he won the Nobel Peace Prize in 1983. Use the quotation and your knowledge of world cultures and geography to answer question 3.

PRIMARY SOURCE

He was faced with overwhelming difficulties; the choice of strategy was not easy. The goal was clear enough; the workers' right to organize and the right to negotiate with the country's officials on the workers' social and economic situation. But which of the many available paths would lead him to this goal? . . . Walesa's chosen strategy was that of peace and negotiation.

EGIL AARVIK, excerpt of presentation speech

1. Which of these cities has an airport but is not a capital?

- **A.** Birmingham
- **B.** Paris
- **C.** Stockholm
- **D.** Wroclaw

2. If a ship is traveling along a major shipping line between Liverpool and Göteborg, what seaport would it pass?

- **A.** Gdansk
- **B.** Lille
- **C.** Southhampton
- **D.** Stockholm

3. What peaceful strategy did Walesa use to achieve his goal?

- **A.** opposing Communists
- **B.** negotiating with officials
- **C.** facing overwhelming difficulties
- **D.** choosing a clear path

TEST PRACTICE
CLASSZONE.COM

ALTERNATIVE ASSESSMENT

1. WRITING ABOUT HISTORY

On November 9, 1989, the Berlin Wall was torn down, and East and West Germany were reunited. Write a headline and a feature article that might have appeared in a newspaper the next day. Include historic information about the wall. Conduct research to find quotes from people who were present at the event and include several of them in your article. Share your article with the class.

2. COOPERATIVE LEARNING

Many festivals and holidays are celebrated in the United Kingdom, Sweden, France, Germany, and Poland. Working in a small group, create a presentation about one of these. Work together to research the meaning of the holiday or festival you choose, when it is celebrated, and the foods and activities associated with it. Decide what form your presentation will take and divide the tasks needed to complete the project.

INTEGRATED TECHNOLOGY

Doing Internet Research

Use the Internet or other library resources to research the life and work of a well-known artist, author, or poet from the United Kingdom, Sweden, France, Germany, or Poland. Prepare a presentation of your findings.

- You might research biographies of the person and collections of his or her work.
- In your research, find out what was historically or socially significant about your subject's writing or artwork.
- Include a copy of the person's artwork or an excerpt from his or her writing.

For Internet links to support this activity, go to

RESEARCH LINKS
CLASSZONE.COM

Europe Today

UNIT 3

Place The Blue Mosque was built in the 17th century in Constantinople (now Istanbul, Turkey). On the land around the mosque, there is a religious school, a public bath, souvenir shops, and a kitchen to feed the poor.

NORTH AFRICA AND SOUTHWEST ASIA

Chapter 8 North Africa and Southwest Asia: Place and Times

Chapter 9 North Africa and Southwest Asia Today

THE BLUE MOSQUE

NORTH AFRICA AND SOUTHWEST ASIA

INTEGRATED TECHNOLOGY

eEdition
- Interactive Maps
- Interactive Visuals

VIDEO
Israel: Muhammad in Judea

INTERNET RESOURCES
Go to **classzone.com** for:
- Research Links
- Internet Activities
- Data Updates
- Unit Quiz
- Maps
- Test Practice
- Current Events
- Web Research Guide

Unit Atlas 3: Physical Geography

SUNSHINE STATE STANDARDS

Key Standard SS.B.1.3.1 The student uses various map forms (including thematic maps) and other geographic representations, tools, and technologies to acquire, process, and report geographic information including patterns of land use, connections between places, and patterns and processes of migration and diffusion.

Other Standards SS.B.1.3.3

FCAT LA.A.2.3.1 Reading: Identify Main Idea, Facts, and Details

North Africa and Southwest Asia: Physical

Elevation
- 13,100 ft. (4,000 m)
- 6,600 ft. (2,000 m)
- 3,275 ft. (1,000 m)
- 650 ft. (200 m)
- 0 ft. (0 m)
- Below sea level
- ▲ Mountain peak

North Africa and Southwest Asia

North Africa and Southwest Asia: Precipitation

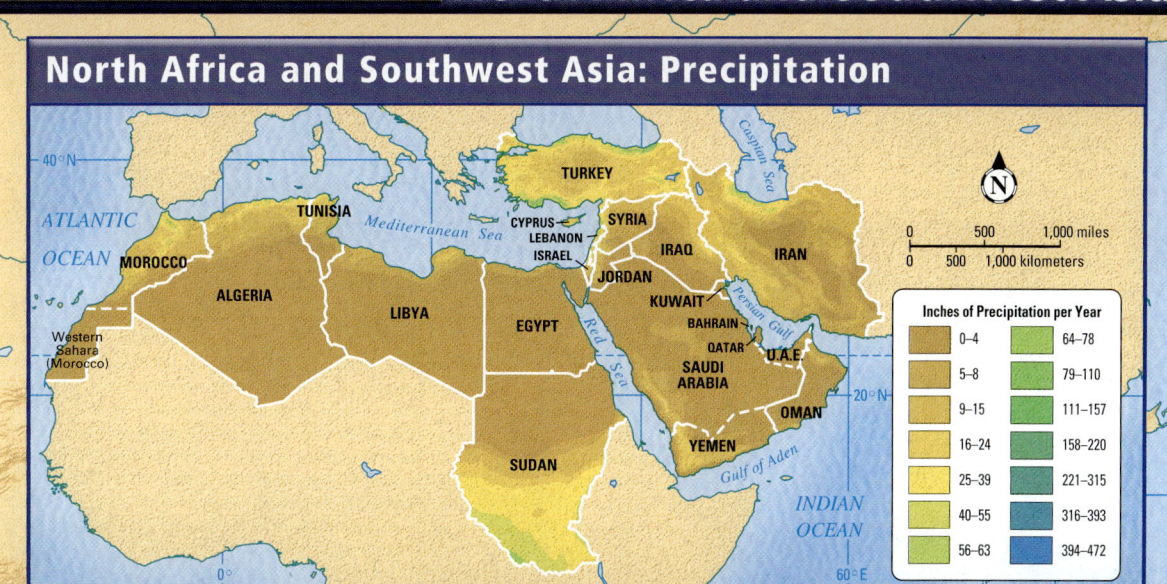

Inches of Precipitation per Year
0–4 / 64–78
5–8 / 79–110
9–15 / 111–157
16–24 / 158–220
25–39 / 221–315
40–55 / 316–393
56–63 / 394–472

Comparisons of Landmass and Population of the United States, North Africa, and Southwest Asia

LANDMASS
- North Africa and Southwest Asia: 5,600,859 square miles
- Continental United States: 3,165,630 square miles

POPULATION
- North Africa and Southwest Asia: 412,667,364
- United States: 281,421,906
- 👤 = 50,000,000

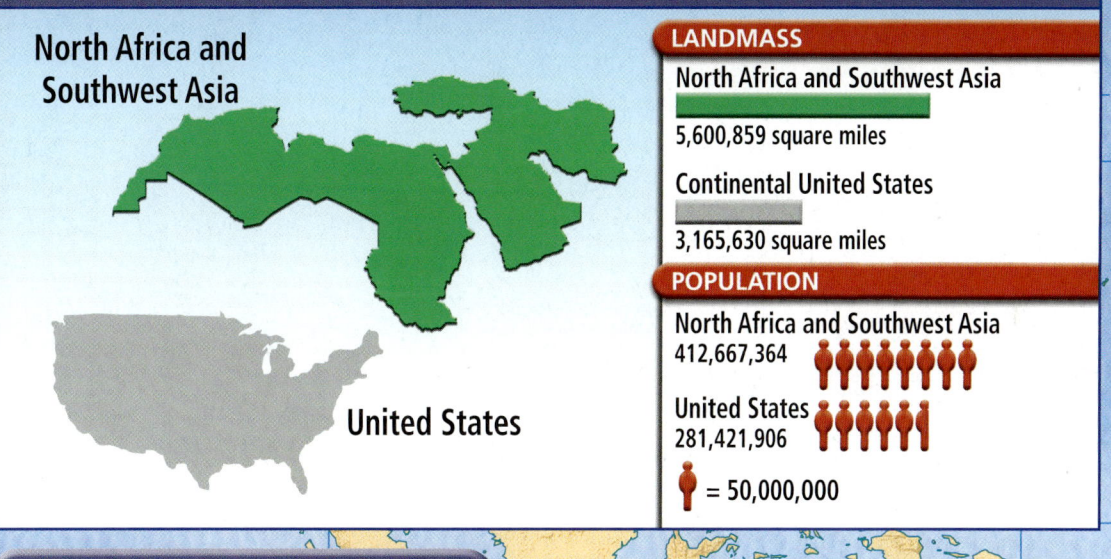

Fast Facts

✓ **WORLD'S LONGEST RIVER:** Nile, 4,132 mi.

✓ **WORLD'S LARGEST DESERT:** Sahara, 3,350,000 sq. mi.

✓ **WORLD'S HIGHEST RECORDED TEMPERATURE:** 136°F at El Azizia, Libya, on September 13, 1922

✓ **WORLD'S LARGEST SUPPLY OF OIL:** 259 billion barrels of proven oil reserves in Saudi Arabia

✓ **DRIEST AREA IN THE WORLD:** Nearly two-thirds of this region is desert.

GEOGRAPHY SKILLBUILDER: Interpreting Maps and Visuals

1. **Region** • Name three countries that get less than 10 inches of rain per year.
2. **Region** • Name the countries that border the Red Sea.

Unit Atlas 3: Human Geography

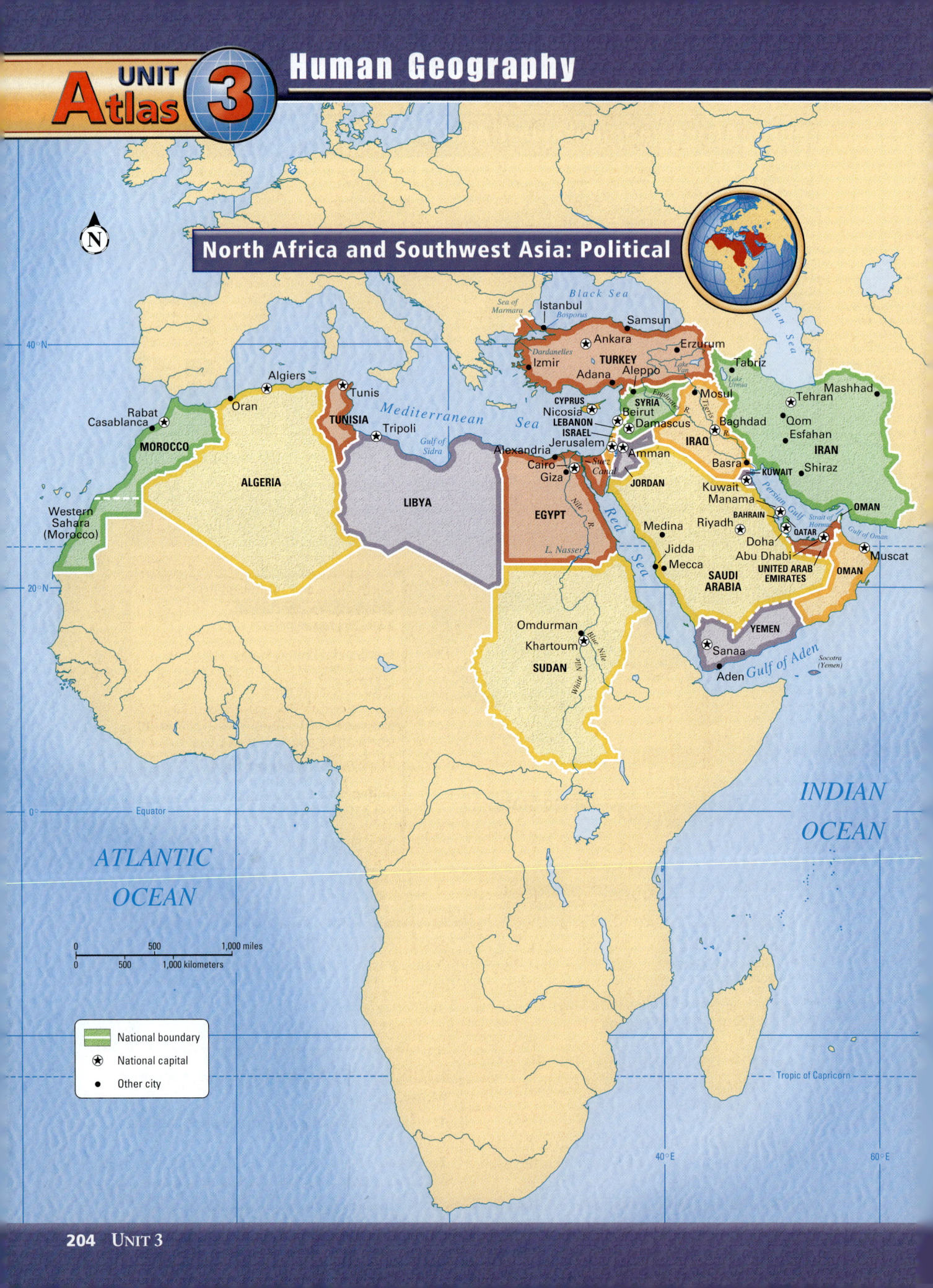

North Africa and Southwest Asia: Political

Legend:
- National boundary
- ★ National capital
- • Other city

Scale: 0–1,000 miles / 0–1,000 kilometers

North Africa and Southwest Asia

Religions of North Africa and Southwest Asia

Religious group:
- Christian
- Druze
- Jewish
- Sunni Muslim
- Shi'ite Muslim

Ethnic Groups of North Africa and Southwest Asia

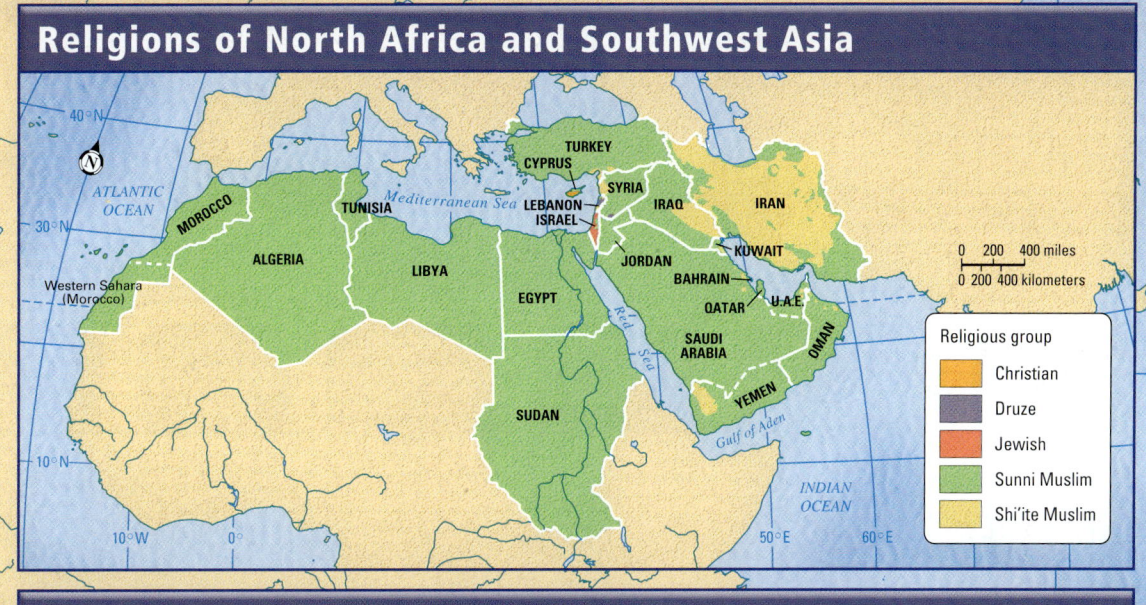

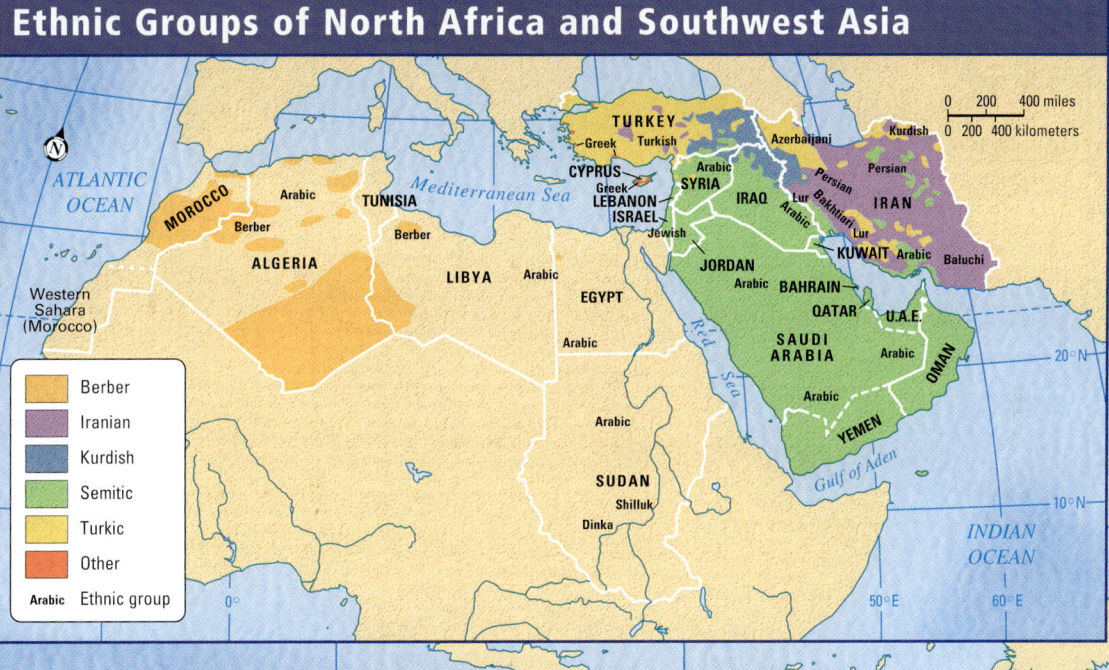

- Berber
- Iranian
- Kurdish
- Semitic
- Turkic
- Other

Arabic Ethnic group

FAST FACTS

✓ **LARGEST COUNTRY (in land area):** Sudan, with 966,757 sq. mi.

✓ **LARGEST ETHNIC GROUP WITHOUT A COUNTRY:** The Kurds, with 20 million living in Iran, Iraq, Syria, and Turkey

✓ **ORIGIN OF MAJOR RELIGIONS:** Islam, Judaism, and Christianity all originated in this area.

✓ **LOWEST POPULATION DENSITY:** Libya, with 7.5 people per sq. mi.

GEOGRAPHY SKILLBUILDER: Interpreting Maps and Visuals

1. **Movement** • What is the largest ethnic group in this region?
2. **Region** • What is the most common religion in this region?

Atlas 205

UNIT 3 Atlas Data File

For updates on these statistics, go to
DATA UPDATE CLASSZONE.COM

Country Flag	Country/Capital	Currency	Population (2001 estimate)	Life Expectancy (years)	Birthrate (per 1,000 pop.) (2000 estimate)
	Algeria Algiers	Dinar	31,736,000	70	23
	Bahrain Manama	Dinar	645,000	73	21
	Cyprus Nicosia	Pound	763,000	77	13
	Egypt Cairo	Pound	69,537,000	63	25
	Iran Tehran	Rial	66,129,000	70	18
	Iraq Baghdad	Dinar	23,332,000	67	35
	Israel Jerusalem	New Shekel	5,938,000	79	19
	Jordan Amman	Dinar	5,453,000	77	26
	Kuwait Kuwait	Dinar	2,042,000	76	22
	Lebanon Beirut	Pound	3,628,000	71	20
	Libya Tripoli	Dinar	5,241,000	75	28
	Morocco Rabat	Dirham	30,645,000	69	23
	Oman Muscat	Rial Omani	2,622,000	72	38
	Qatar Doha	Riyal	769,000	72	16
	Saudi Arabia Riyadh	Riyal	22,757,000	68	38
	Sudan Khartoum	Pound	36,080,000	57	39

206 UNIT 3

North Africa and Southwest Asia

DATA FILE

Infant Mortality (per 1,000 live births) (2000)	Doctors (per 100,000 pop.) (1992–1998)	Literacy Rate (percentage) (1995–2000)	Passenger Cars (per 1,000 pop.) (1996–1997)	Total Area (square miles)	Map (not to scale)
42.2	85	62	17	919,595	
14.0	100	85	242	268	
7.4	255	97	316	3,572	
65.7	202	51	20	385,230	
28.1	85	79	26	636,300	
62.4	55	58	32	167,975	
7.6	385	96	224	7,992	
32.1	166	87	40	34,342	
9.8	189	79	318	6,880	
29.4	210	92	325	3,950	
26.4	128	76	126	678,400	
37.0	46	44	39	274,461	
23.9	133	59	108	82,009	
16.4	126	79	151	4,416	
36.3	166	63	89	865,000	
69.2	9	46	1	966,757	

Unit Atlas 3: Data File

For updates on these statistics, go to **DATA UPDATE** CLASSZONE.COM

Country Flag	Country/Capital	Currency	Population (2001 estimate)	Life Expectancy (years)	Birthrate (per 1,000 pop.) (2000)
	Syria Damascus	Pound	16,729,000	68	31
	Tunisia Tunis	Dinar	9,705,000	74	17
	Turkey Ankara	Lira	66,494,000	71	19
	United Arab Emirates Abu Dhabi	Dirham	2,407,000	74	18
	Yemen Sanaa	Rial	18,078,000	60	43
	United States Washington, D.C.	Dollar	281,422,000	77	15

The Blue Mosque in Istanbul ◄

Queen Hatshepsut ▲

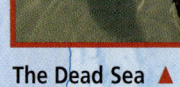

The Dead Sea ▲

North Africa and Southwest Asia

DATA FILE

Infant Mortality (per 1,000 live births) (2000)	Doctors (per 100,000 pop.) (1992–1998)	Literacy Rate (percentage) (1996–1998)	Passenger Cars (per 1,000 pop.) (1991–1998)	Total Area (square miles)	Map (not to scale)
35.2	144	79	9	71,498	
30.1	70	67	28	63,378	
33.3	121	82	53	300,948	
13.4	181	79	144	32,278	
67.4	23	43	15	203,796	
7.0	251	97	489	3,787,319	

GEOGRAPHY SKILLBUILDER: Interpreting a Chart

1. **Region** • How much higher is Lebanon's literacy rate than Iran's?
2. **Region** • In general, how can a country's literacy rate be a predictor of its infant mortality rate in this region?

A shadoof in Egypt ▼

An oil well in Saudi Arabia ▲

Palestinians in Israel ▲

Atlas 209

CHAPTER 8
North Africa and Southwest Asia: Place and Times

SECTION 1 Physical Geography

SECTION 2 Ancient Mesopotamia and the Fertile Crescent

SECTION 3 Ancient Egypt

SECTION 4 Birthplace of Three Religions

SECTION 5 Muslim Empires

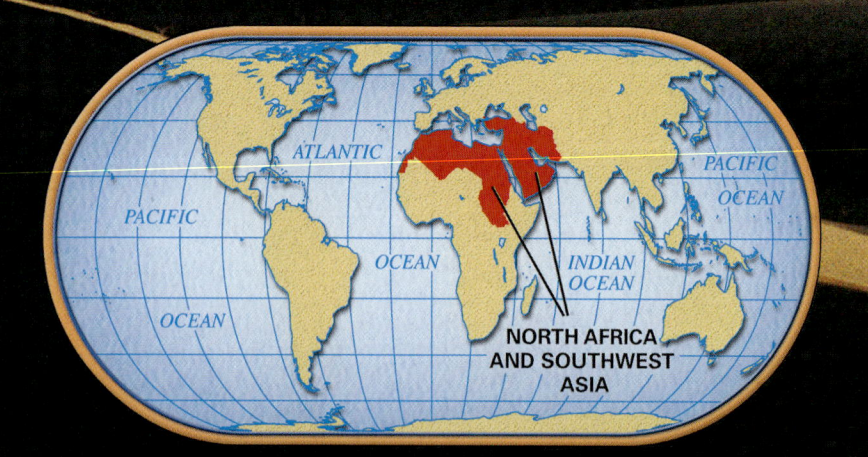

Region The Sahara stretches across much of North Africa.

FOCUS ON GEOGRAPHY

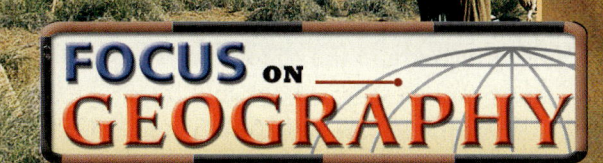

How have sheep contributed to the spread of deserts in North Africa?

Human-Environment Interaction • Overgrazing, or allowing livestock such as sheep and goats to eat too much vegetation, has contributed to the spread of deserts in North Africa. Desertification from overgrazing is particularly bad in northwestern countries such as Morocco.

As population increases, more strain is put on fragile areas. When people plant too many crops, graze too many animals, or cut down trees in the dry lands—especially during periods of drought—the land becomes unusable. People have difficulty growing food, and famine may follow. Countries in North Africa are working to change political, economic, and social problems that contribute to desertification.

What do you think?

- What might cause people to plant or graze their animals on dry lands?
- What can countries do to prevent desertification?

CHAPTER 8 READING SOCIAL STUDIES

BEFORE YOU READ

▶▶ What Do You Know?

Before you read the chapter, consider what you already know about North Africa and Southwest Asia. Look at a physical map of the region, and think about features, such as the Sahara. How might living in a desert affect the lives of people who live there? What do you know about the pyramids of ancient Egypt? Are you familiar with any of these sacred books—the Hebrew Scriptures, the Christian Bible, or the Qur'an of Islam? Many of the events in these books took place in this region. Try to imagine the changes that have occurred here in 5,000 years of human history.

▶▶ What Do You Want to Know?

Decide what you know about the physical features of the region and about ancient Mesopotamia, Egypt, and the Muslim Empires. In your notebook, record what you hope to learn from this chapter.

Place • Ziggurats were stepped towers on which temples were built in ancient Mesopotamia. ▲

READ AND TAKE NOTES

Reading Strategy: Making Generalizations Making generalizations is a useful strategy for understanding universal themes in social studies. A generalization is a statement expressed in general terms but supported by detailed evidence. As you read this chapter, think about how the civilizations that arose in North Africa and Southwest Asia influenced world history. Use the chart below to record details that support each generalization.

- Copy the chart into your notebook.
- As you read, notice how civilization has developed in this region.
- Beside each generalization, record some key details that support it.

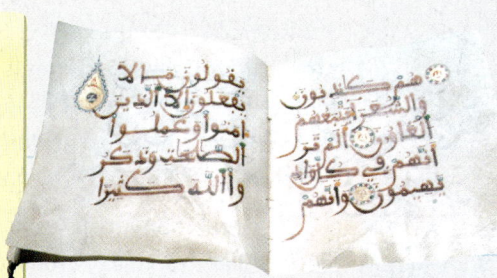

Culture • The Qur'an is the sacred book of Islam. ▲

Generalizations	Supporting Details
1. Bodies of water provide resources for people in North Africa and Southwest Asia.	
2. Complex civilizations developed religions and laws in ancient Mesopotamia.	
3. An ancient Egyptian culture based on shared beliefs and goals left a monumental legacy.	
4. Three of the world's major religions began in Southwest Asia.	
5. Islamic beliefs and achievements spread throughout the world.	

SECTION 1

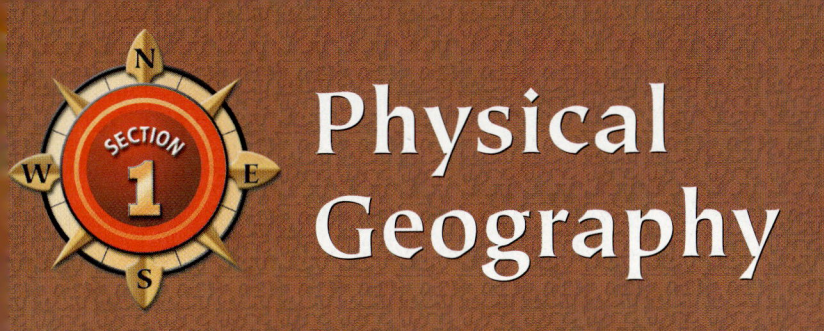

Physical Geography

TERMS & NAMES
fertile
hunter-gatherer
irrigation

MAIN IDEA
Water and the lack of it has shaped this region of flooding rivers, little rainfall, and surrounding seas.

WHY IT MATTERS NOW
Today the region enjoys the benefits of rich oil resources, but its people continue to struggle with problems of both dry land and flooding rivers.

DATELINE EXTRA

MESOPOTAMIA, 3000 B.C.

Yesterday, the yearly spring flooding of the Euphrates River began. The river is high this year because of heavy rains. Farmers from nearby villages are afraid their homes will be lost. But they need the rich soil the swollen river brings. As soon as the river settles back in its bed, they can begin to plant.

It's like this every year. The gods tell the river to bring good soil, and the river obeys. To Mesopotamians, it means that life will go on.

Human-Environment Interaction • The Euphrates River brings rich soil to the land. ▲

Rivers and Deserts

Water and the lack of it has shaped North Africa and Southwest Asia, a region where little rain falls. Seas of sand cover the deserts, which are dry all year. In these deserts, water is found only in oasis areas. Other areas have depended on the annual flooding of the rivers to make the soil **fertile**, or productive. Fertile soil provides the nutrients that plants need to grow.

TAKING NOTES
Use your chart to take notes about North Africa and Southwest Asia.

Generalizations	Details
1. Bodies of water provide resources for people in North Africa and ...	
2. Complex civilizations developed religions and ...	

SUNSHINE STATE STANDARDS
Key Standard SS.B.2.3.7 The student knows how various human systems throughout the world have developed in response to conditions in the physical environment.
FCAT LA.A.2.3.1 Reading: Identify Main Idea, Facts, and Details

North Africa and Southwest Asia: Place and Times 213

Three Rivers

Some of the ancient peoples who lived in North Africa and Southwest Asia benefited from three major rivers in the region—the Nile, the Tigris (TY·grihs), and the Euphrates (yoo·FRAY·teez). The 4,000-mile-long Nile, the longest river in the world, flows from its source in east central Africa to the Mediterranean in northeast Egypt. The Tigris and Euphrates flow to the southeast from Turkey into the northern end of the Persian Gulf. (See the Unit Atlas map on page 202).

From Hunter-Gatherers to Farmers Thousands of years ago, <u>hunter-gatherers</u> roamed the east coast of the Mediterranean and the valleys formed from the rivers. These people found food by hunting, fishing, and gathering wild grains, fruits, and nuts. For 99 percent of the time human beings have been on Earth, they have been hunter-gatherers. Eventually, hunter-gatherers settled permanently in places where they could raise animals and grow crops. Some places where hunter-gatherers may have first become farmers are the valleys of the Nile, Tigris, and Euphrates rivers about 8,000 years ago.

How Rivers Enrich the Soil Most of the soil in the desert regions of North Africa and Southwest Asia is not good for farming. It contains a lot of salt or sand. Only the rivers make farming possible. In summer, when melted snow flowing from the Ethiopian mountains raises the level of the Nile, the river floods. Heavy spring and summer rains also cause the Nile to flood. When these flooding waters flow over the riverbanks, they leave behind fertile soil that has been carried from one area to another.

Snows also melt in the Turkish highlands, where the Tigris and Euphrates rivers begin. As a result, these rivers also flood yearly, bringing fertile soil into the river valleys.

The World's Heritage

The Plow No one knows who invented the plow, the farmer's most essential tool. The earliest plows were only sharpened sticks used to dig holes for planting.

Plows like the one shown below are still used in some parts of the world. Modern plows have more parts and are mechanized, but their function is the same.

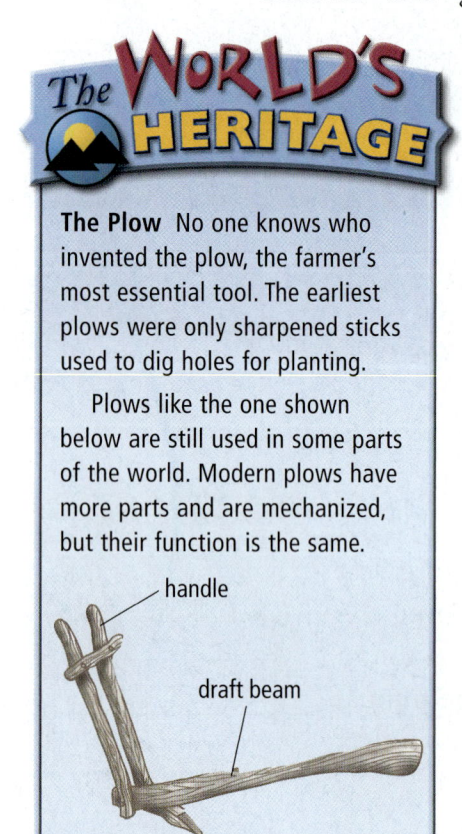

handle

draft beam

Human-Environment Interaction • Hunter-gatherers lived off the food they found in the natural world. ▲

Reading Social Studies

Finding Causes Why might farming have begun in the valleys of the Nile, Tigris, and Euphrates rivers?

Human-Environment Interaction • This modern irrigation system is in the Draa Valley in Morocco. ▼

Human-Environment Interaction • For thousands of years farmers in the region have used simple irrigation tools, such as this shadoof, to water the land. ▲

Irrigation Few places in the region are close enough to the three major rivers to depend on them for deposits of fertile soil. Farmers in other areas have had to develop **irrigation** methods, or ways of bringing water to dry land.

Surrounding Waters

The Mediterranean Sea, the Red Sea, and the Persian Gulf have shaped the climate, resources, and societies of the region. The Mediterranean is the largest body of water in the region. The mild climate of the lands around the Mediterranean attracted settlers. Early civilizations formed on its eastern shores.

Trade Routes Since ancient times, the Red Sea has been an important trade route. Goods and ideas that have traveled through the Red Sea have shaped the cultures that lie on either side of it. The Persian Gulf has also been an important trade route. Today, it draws the interest of the world because of its key position in the middle of oil-rich Southwest Asia.

Energy from an Ancient Sea Millions of years ago, a huge sea covered North Africa and Southwest Asia. When sea creatures died, their remains sank to the bottom.

Strange but TRUE

The Dead Sea It's not actually a sea—it's a lake—and it's not completely dead—some bacteria can survive in its salty depths. The Dead Sea has an area of about 394 square miles. At 1,312 feet below sea level, it is the lowest point on Earth, and it is about ten times saltier than any ocean. Salt and minerals make the water so dense, you can easily float on it.

North Africa and Southwest Asia: Place and Times

Turkey: Vegetation Map

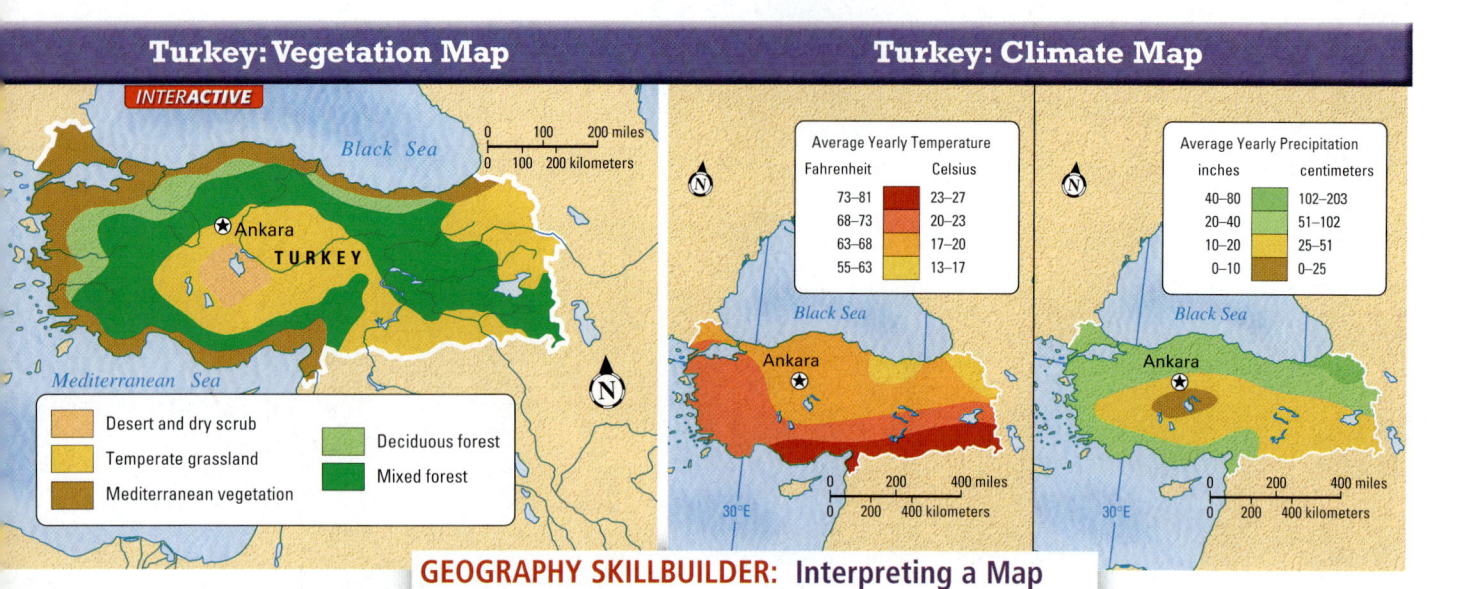

Legend:
- Desert and dry scrub
- Temperate grassland
- Mediterranean vegetation
- Deciduous forest
- Mixed forest

Turkey: Climate Map

Average Yearly Temperature
Fahrenheit	Celsius
73–81	23–27
68–73	20–23
63–68	17–20
55–63	13–17

Average Yearly Precipitation
inches	centimeters
40–80	102–203
20–40	51–102
10–20	25–51
0–10	0–25

GEOGRAPHY SKILLBUILDER: Interpreting a Map
1. **Place** • How does the amount of yearly precipitation affect the type of vegetation that grows?
2. **Location** • What is the average yearly temperature in Ankara?

Over long periods of time, mud and sand and other materials were deposited on top of them. Heat and pressure from these materials changed the dead matter into petroleum, or oil.

Turkey Not all of North Africa and Southwest Asia is hot and dry. Turkey is cooler than the rest of the region and gets more rain. As a result, instead of deserts, Turkey has grasslands and even forest areas.

SECTION 1 ASSESSMENT

Terms & Names
1. Explain the significance of: (a) fertile   (b) hunter-gatherer   (c) irrigation

Using Graphics
2. Use a spider map like this one to map the importance of water in North Africa and Southwest Asia.

(spider map with center "bodies of water" and four empty circles)

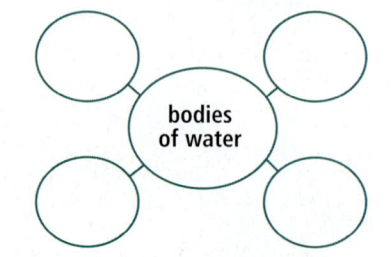

Main Ideas
3. (a) How did the area around the Persian Gulf come to be a rich source of petroleum?
   (b) How did hunter-gatherers in North Africa and Southwest Asia become farmers?
   (c) How did rivers in Southwest Asia enrich the soil?

Critical Thinking
4. **Analyzing Causes**
   Why might the earliest farming communities have developed along the Nile, Tigris, and Euphrates rivers?

   Think About
   - needs of farmers
   - annual flooding

ACTIVITY -OPTION- Make a **chart** of the major rivers and bodies of water discussed in this section and list the effects each has had on the region.

216 CHAPTER 8

SECTION 2

Ancient Mesopotamia and the Fertile Crescent

TERMS & NAMES
Hammurabi
Fertile Crescent
Sumerian
ziggurat
class system
cuneiform
scribe

MAIN IDEA
Ancient Mesopotamia's complex civilization, based on city-states, developed a code of laws and a written language.

WHY IT MATTERS NOW
Mesopotamia's achievements led the way to the law codes and written languages in use today.

DATELINE

BABYLON, HAMMURABI'S EMPIRE, 1750 B.C.— Emperor Hammurabi has unveiled a huge black stone containing 282 laws given to him by the god Shamash. For one of the first times ever, a code of laws has been presented to the people of the empire.

According to the Code of Hammurabi, punishment for breaking the law will depend upon the status of the offender and the victim. Most serious crimes, such as murder, will be punished by death. If a house falls down on its owner, the builder of the house will be killed. If the owner's son is killed, then the builder's son will be killed as well. The idea is that a crime should be repaid with a similar punishment. Many of the laws can be boiled down to this statement: "An eye for an eye, a tooth for a tooth."

Culture • Emperor Hammurabi receives a code of laws from the god Shamash, patron of justice. ▲

The Mesopotamian City-State

Hammurabi (HAM•uh•RAH•bee), a famous emperor of ancient Mesopotamia, ruled from 1792 to 1750 B.C. (See the map on page 424.) Mesopotamia, which means "land between the rivers" in Greek, covers about the same area as modern Iraq, northeast Syria, and part of southeast Turkey. The region is sometimes called the **Fertile Crescent** because of its shape and fertile soil.

TAKING NOTES
Use your chart to take notes about North Africa and Southwest Asia.

Generalizations	Details
1. Bodies of water provide resources for people in North Africa and ...	
2. Complex civilizations developed religions and ...	

SUNSHINE STATE STANDARDS
Key Standard SS.A.2.3.2 The student knows how major historical developments have had an impact on the development of civilizations.
Other Standards SS.A.2.3.8
FCAT LA.A.2.3.1 Reading: Identify Main Idea, Facts, and Details

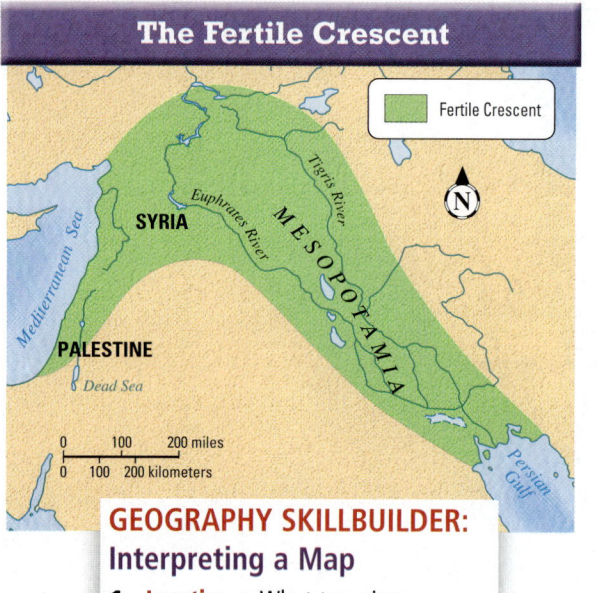

The Fertile Crescent

GEOGRAPHY SKILLBUILDER:
Interpreting a Map
1. **Location** • What two rivers formed Mesopotamia?
2. **Place** • What does the map tell you about the importance of water in forming the Fertile Crescent?

City-States Around 3000 B.C., the **Sumerians**, the first inhabitants of the area, organized the first city-states. A city-state is made up of a city and the areas it controls. Three major challenges influenced the development of city-states. One was the threat of hostile invaders. To protect themselves, the Sumerians surrounded their cities with strong, high walls. The second challenge was lack of water. There was very little rainfall in the region. City-states built and maintained irrigation canals for local use.

The third challenge involved trade. The Sumerians lacked stones, metals, and timber for building and had to import these materials. The Sumerians wanted to export grain, dates, and cloth, but trade was risky. Traders often had to cope with bandits, pirates, and wild animals. Well-protected city-states would have helped traders feel more confident about doing business.

Reading Social Studies
A. Recognizing Effects What were three effects of the founding of city-states?

Government by Priests and Kings Mesopotamian city-states were centers of religious worship. The Sumerians believed in many gods. The most important gods, Enlil and Utu, controlled the rain and sun. Other gods, such as Inanna, Goddess of Love and War, cured diseases and helped kings fight wars. Each city-state built a temple to a specific god. The people believed this god was the city's special guardian. The temple was built on a pyramid-shaped tower called a **ziggurat**. From the winding terraces wrapped around the ziggurat, people could watch celebrations honoring their god.

Place • This is the gateway to a ziggurat built around 1250 B.C. ▼

Temple priests were the first governors of Mesopotamian city-states. When the city-states began to argue about land and water rights, leaders were elected to defend their interests. Later these rulers became kings. Each king chose who would rule after his death. From then on, the city-states were governed by two groups. The priests controlled religious and economic life, and the king controlled political and military life.

From Kings to Emperors Occasionally, kings conquered other city-states. Sometimes these kings allowed the conquered cities to keep worshiping their own special gods. They let the ruling families and temple priests keep local control. Other kings built empires from the lands they had conquered. An empire is a group of countries under one ruler's control. These emperors demanded that the conquered people honor them as gods. Local rulers could no longer turn to their own gods for advice. Now they had to take orders directly from the emperor.

Reading Social Studies

B. Analyzing Causes How did some kings become emperors?

The Class System

Mesopotamia had a **class system**. This meant society was divided into different social groups. Each social group, or class, possessed certain rights and was protected by law. The most favored classes enjoyed more rights than anyone else.

The Three Classes Kings, priests, and wealthy property owners were at the top of the class system. The middle class included skilled workers, merchants, and farmers. Skilled workers specialized in one craft, such as making pottery or spinning thread. Merchants often sold goods brought from other Mesopotamian cities or from other countries. Farmers worked fields that belonged to the temple or the palace.

Many workers in Mesopotamia were enslaved. These people were at the bottom of the class system. Some had been captured in war. Others sold themselves and their families into slavery to pay off a debt. Once they paid the debt, their masters had to set them free. Even former slaves had some rights in Mesopotamian society.

Culture •
These necklaces, earrings, and headress were worn by a Sumerian queen. ▲

Place •
People in Mesopotamia raised animals, caught fish, raised crops, and traded goods. ▶

North Africa and Southwest Asia: Place and Times   219

A Culture Based on Writing

The Sumerians developed one of the first systems of writing, called **cuneiform** (KYOO•nee•uh•FAWRM). With this wedge-shaped writing, they kept lists and records. They sent business letters. They recorded their history, their religious beliefs, and their knowledge of medicine, mathematics, and astronomy. Few Sumerians actually learned to read and write. Schools trained **scribes** to be society's record keepers and meet the different needs of the temple, the royal government, and the business world.

Educating Scribes Only the wealthy could afford to send their children to school. Most of these children were boys, but a few girls also studied at the schools—called tablet houses. Most scribes were children of government officials, priests, and wealthy merchants. Some were orphans who had been adopted by rich people and sent to school. The school day lasted from sunrise to sunset. There were about 600 different characters which students had to memorize. Students who misbehaved were punished by "the man in charge of the whip." Here is how one student scribe described his monthly school schedule:

Spotlight on CULTURE

The Development of Cuneiform The Sumerians created one of the world's first written languages more than 5,000 years ago. Cuneiform—which means "wedge-shaped"—developed from pictographs. Early pictographs looked like the object they represented, such as a fish or a bird. Sumerians used a pen made from a sharpened reed to draw pictographs in vertical rows on soft clay tablets. Over time, the pictograph forms became more simplified and people began to write in horizontal rows. Eventually the forms became wedge-shaped. Scribes began using a pen that created the wedge-shaped signs when it was pushed into the clay.

THINKING CRITICALLY

1. **Analyzing Information** Why do you think Sumerians wrote on clay tablets?
2. **Contrasting** What were the differences between early pictographs and cuneiform writing?

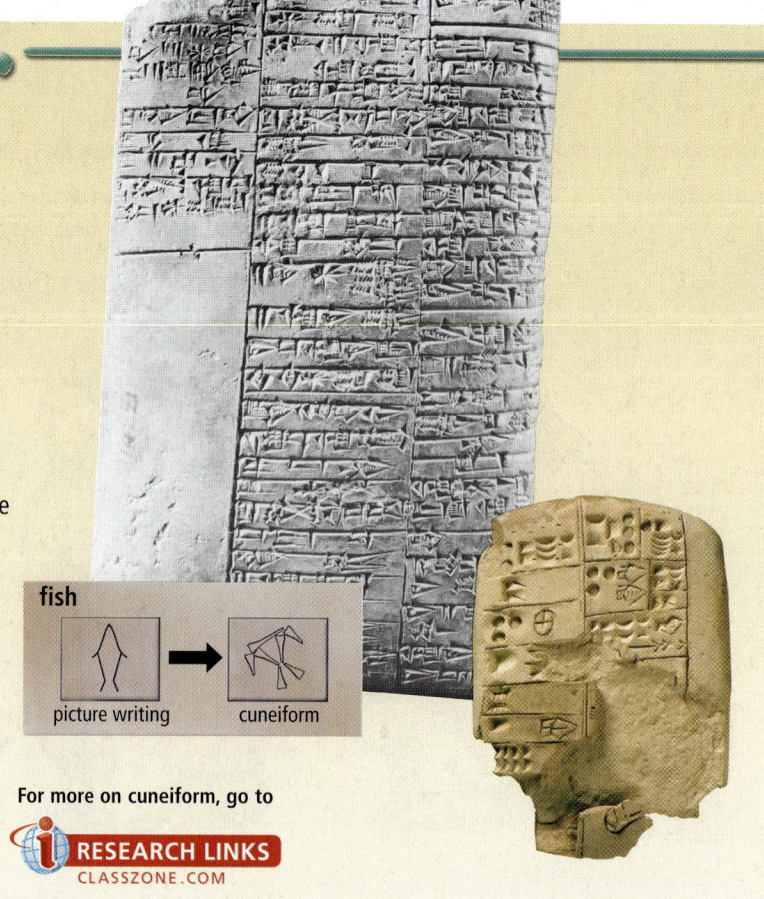

fish
picture writing → cuneiform

For more on cuneiform, go to
RESEARCH LINKS
CLASSZONE.COM

A VOICE FROM SUMERIA

The reckoning of my monthly stay in the tablet house is (as follows):

My days of freedom are three per month.
Its festivals are three days per month.
Within it, twenty-four days per month
(is the time of) my living in the tablet house.
They are long days.

a student scribe

Scribes Played Many Roles Scribes did more than make lists, keep records, and write letters for their employers. Some wrote literary and scientific works of their own. Certain lullabies and love songs were written by women scribes. Traveling scribes from Mesopotamia shared their writings with people from neighboring countries.

Since few people in Mesopotamia could read, scribes read out loud to audiences. One favorite tale was about a flood that covered the earth. It is one of a collection of tales in a book called *The Epic of Gilgamesh*, which relates the adventures of a semi-divine hero.

Culture • The hero Gilgamesh was both a king and a god. ▲

SECTION 2 ASSESSMENT

Terms & Names
1. Explain the significance of:
   (a) Hammurabi
   (b) Fertile Crescent
   (c) Sumerian
   (d) ziggurat
   (e) class system
   (f) cuneiform
   (g) scribe

Using Graphics
2. Use a chart like this one to show how building city-states solved challenges faced by the Mesopotamians.

Challenge	Solution

Main Ideas
3. (a) Why do geographers refer to Mesopotamia as the Fertile Crescent?
   (b) How did some Mesopotamian kings become emperors?
   (c) How did scribes contribute to Mesopotamian civilization?

Critical Thinking
4. **Forming and Supporting Opinions**

   Are the laws set forth in Hammurabi's Code too harsh?

   Think About
   ◆ the meaning of justice
   ◆ the reasons for punishment
   ◆ the role mercy plays in justice

ACTIVITY -OPTION- Design a **mural** of ancient Mesopotamia showing the roles and activities of typical citizens.

North Africa and Southwest Asia: Place and Times

SKILLBUILDER

Comparing Climate and Vegetation Maps

SUNSHINE STATE STANDARDS
Key Standard SS.B.1.3.1 The student uses various map forms (including thematic maps) and other geographic representations, tools, and technologies to acquire, process, and report geographic information including patterns of land use, connections between places, and patterns and processes of migration and diffusion.
FCAT LA.A.2.2.7 Reading: Recognize Compare and Contrast

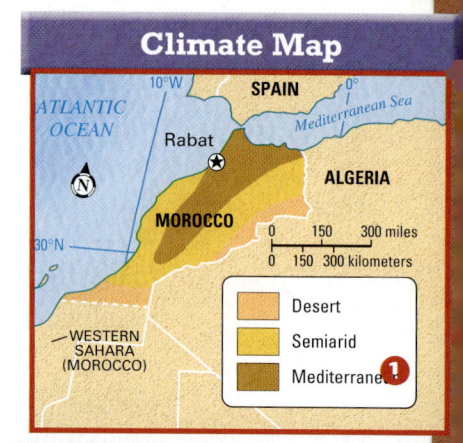

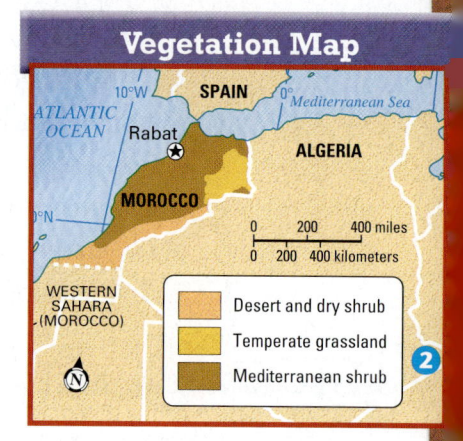

▶▶ Defining the Skill

A climate map shows the climate of a country or region. Climate has two important factors—average temperature and precipitation. A vegetation map shows what grows in the region. It shows, for example, whether the region has forests or deserts. The climate of a region influences its vegetation. The key shows what each map color means.

▶▶ Applying the Skill

The maps shown here are of the country of Morocco in northwestern Africa. The top map shows Morocco's climate and the bottom map shows its vegetation.

How to Compare Climate and Vegetation Maps

Strategy ❶ Look at the climate map. Read the key to see what types of climates are represented on the map. Then study the map to see where each of those climate types can be found in the country of Morocco.

Strategy ❷ Look at the vegetation map. Read the key, and then look at the map. What kind of vegetation is found in Morocco, and where?

Strategy ❸ Compare the maps. Look at the different climates and at the vegetation in those areas. What kind of vegetation grows where there is little rain? What kind grows where it rains some of the year?

Make a Chart

A chart can help you organize the information that you gain from comparing the two maps. The chart below lists the types of vegetation found in Morocco and the kind of climate that vegetation is located in.

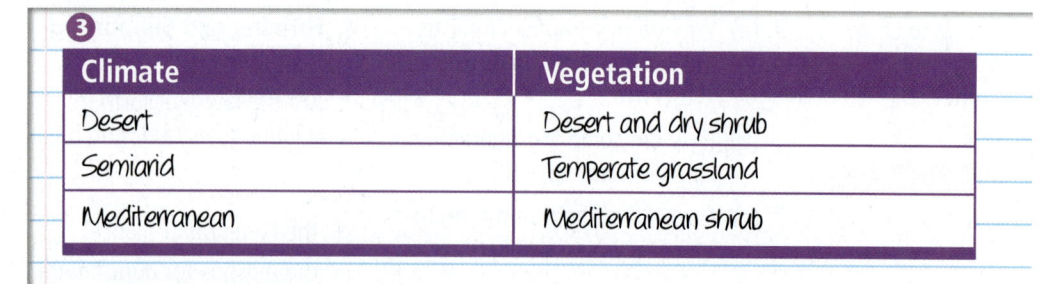

❸

Climate	Vegetation
Desert	Desert and dry shrub
Semiarid	Temperate grassland
Mediterranean	Mediterranean shrub

▶▶ Practicing the Skill

Turn to page 216 in Chapter 8, Section 1. Look at the climate map and the vegetation map found there. Create a chart to organize and analyze the information found in those two maps.

SECTION 3
Ancient Egypt

TERMS & NAMES
papyrus
pyramid
pharaoh
hieroglyphics
Re
Horus

MAIN IDEA
The civilization of the ancient Egyptians developed in response to both its desert environment and the flooding waters of the Nile River.

WHY IT MATTERS NOW
The ancient Egyptian civilization is a model of a well-organized society with limited natural resources.

DATELINE EXTRA

CAIRO, EGYPT, 1458 B.C.—A new building project got under way this week. Our new ruler, Thutmose III, has decided to build a temple near the Nile River. Thousands of workers are needed to work on it.

The foreman of the project told this reporter, "We will need stone cutters, water carriers, painters, and cooks. We can find work for almost anyone who wants a job." They hope the temple will be finished in a few years.

Thutmose III ▲

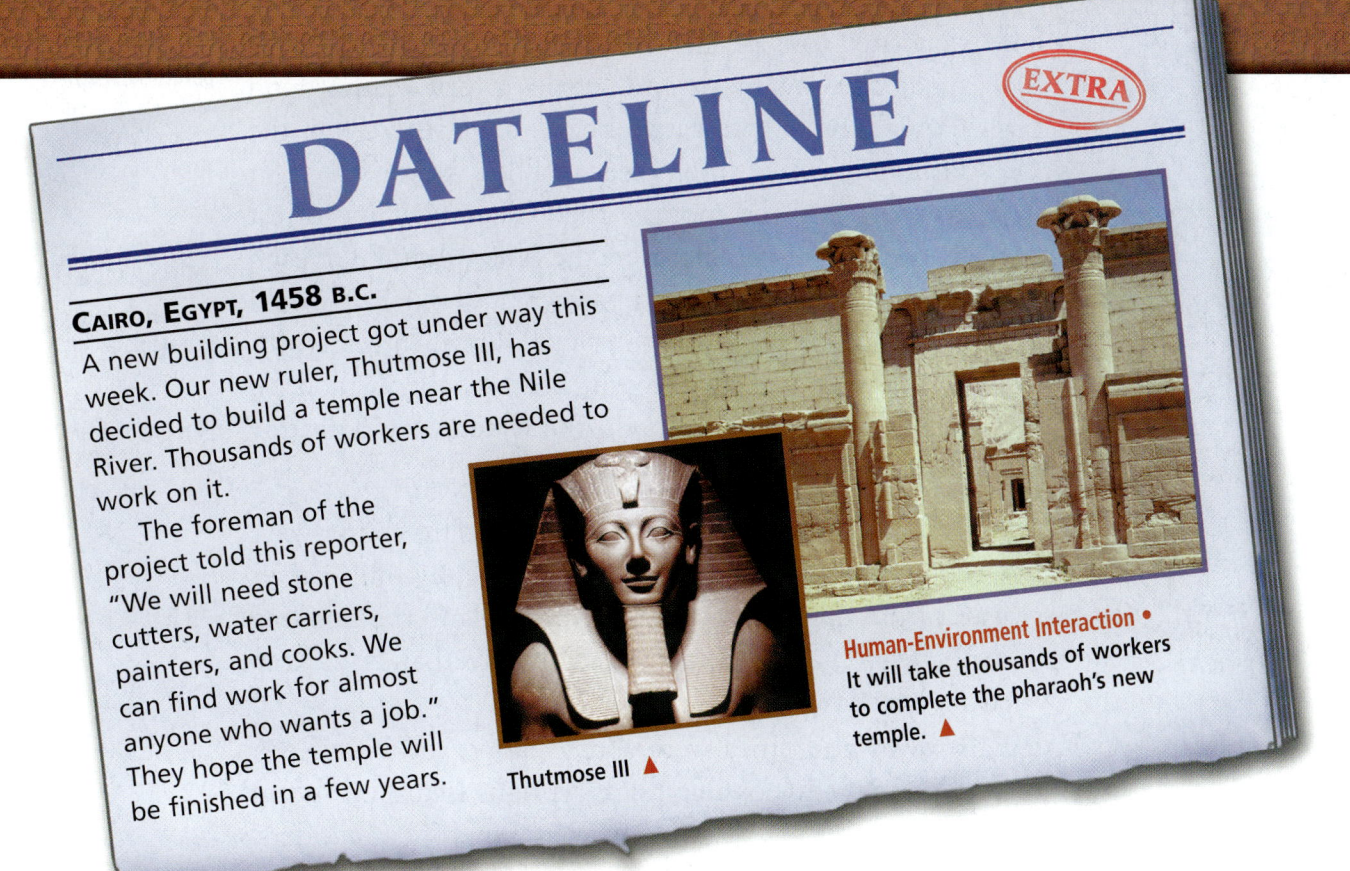

Human-Environment Interaction •
It will take thousands of workers to complete the pharaoh's new temple. ▲

Ancient Egypt and the Nile

Many of the temples and other monumental structures of ancient Egypt still stand. Without the Nile River, however, they probably would never have been built. As the Greek historian Herodotus (hih·RAHD·uh·tuhs) said approximately 2,500 years ago, Egyptian civilization was "the gift of the Nile."

TAKING NOTES
Use your chart to take notes about North Africa and Southwest Asia.

Generalizations	Details
1. Bodies of water provide resources for people in North Africa and ...	
2. Complex civilizations developed religions and ...	

SUNSHINE STATE STANDARDS
Key Standard SS.A.2.3.4 The student understands the impact of geographical factors on the historical development of civilizations.
Other Standards SS.A.2.3.7, A.2.3.8
FCAT LA.A.2.3.1 Reading: Identify Main Idea, Facts, and Details

North Africa and Southwest Asia: Place and Times **223**

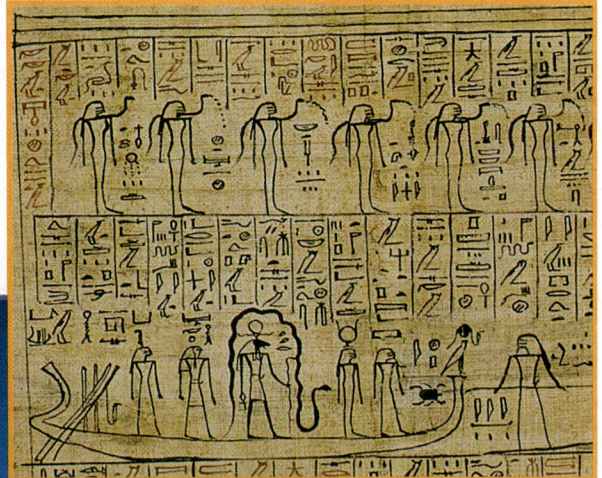

Human-Environment Interaction • This page from the Book of the Dead was drawn on papyrus. ◄

The River in the Sand Desert covers most of Egypt. The sands spread for hundreds of miles to the west and the south, discouraging outsiders from invading. The Nile River, which runs through the desert, is sometimes called "the river in the sand."

The Nile's yearly floods deposited tons of silt in the river valley. The deposits made the soil black and fertile. Every year, around October, the floodwaters began to retreat. Then the farmers planted their seeds. They harvested their crops during the months the Nile was at its lowest levels. The Egyptians knew the Nile would flood each year. But they could not predict how much it would flood or how high the water would rise. In years with very low floods, there might not be enough food. In years with very high floods, the waters would destroy fields and homes.

Taming the Nile The ancient Egyptians found ways to manage the unpredictable river. They built canals to carry water from the Nile to the parts of the land the flooding water did not reach. They strengthened the riverbanks to keep the river from overflowing.

Egyptian towns and cities were spread along the Nile River valley. The Nile made it possible for Egyptians living in distant places to come together. The Egyptians were expert boat builders. They built harbors and ports for large cargo boats. The Nile provided such good transportation that there were few roads in ancient Egypt. Because goods moved easily along the Nile, trade was very profitable.

The Nile's Gifts The ancient Egyptians used Nile mud to make pottery and bricks. They made a paperlike material called **papyrus** (puh·PY·ruhs) from the papyrus plant. This tall plant grew in marshes and swamps around the Nile. In fact, the English word *paper* comes from "papyrus." It was easier to write on papyrus than on the bulky clay tablets the Mesopotamians used.

Place • Papyrus reeds grow along the Nile River. ▲

Vocabulary
silt: particles of earth and rock that build up in rivers or streams

Reading Social Studies
A. Identifying Problems What problems did the Nile River cause Egyptian farmers?

Tutankhamen's Tomb

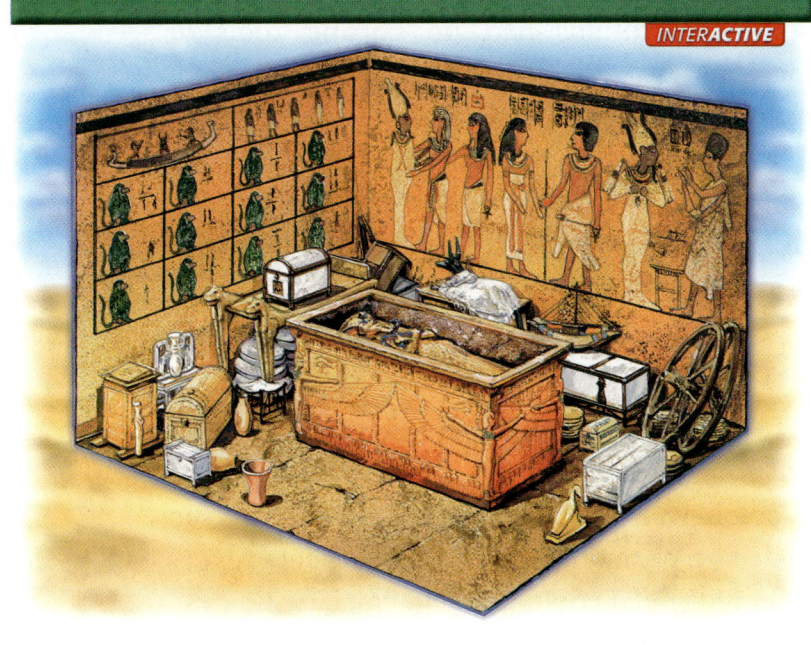

INTERACTIVE

Place • In 1922, the tomb of Egyptian king Tutankhamen (TOOT·ahng·KAH·muhn) was found almost exactly as it had been left thousands of years before. Although his tomb may be the most famous, Tutankhamen was not buried in a pyramid. He was buried in an area now known as the Valley of the Tombs of the Kings. ◀

The Great Builders

The Egyptians noticed that bodies buried in the sand on the edge of the desert resisted decay. It may have affected their beliefs in an afterlife. The concept of an afterlife played a central role in ancient Egyptian life and culture. It led the Egyptians to build huge **pyramids,** as well as many other temples and monuments.

Vocabulary
afterlife: a life believed to follow death

The Pyramids Pyramids are easily recognized by their shape. Four triangular sides on a rectangular base meet at a single point. The Egyptians built the pyramids for their kings, or **pharaohs** (FAIR·ohz). Each pyramid is a palace where an Egyptian king planned to spend the afterlife.

BACKGROUND
Nubia (NOO·bee·uh), a country to the south of Egypt, was a source of the gold the Egyptians used in their pyramids.

Materials and Labor To build the pyramids, the Egyptians used large blocks of stone. A single pyramid might contain 92 million cubic feet of stone, enough to fill a large sports stadium. The tips of pyramids were often capped with gold.

Building a pyramid was complicated. The pharaoh appointed a leader to organize the project. The leader and his staff used **hieroglyphics**—a writing system that uses pictographs to stand for words or sounds—to make lists of the workers and supplies they needed for the project.

Citizenship IN ACTION

Recording the Past The great statues and monuments of ancient Egypt have lasted thousands of years, but they will not last forever. They are threatened by pollution and other changes in the environment. Now a nonprofit group called INSIGHT (Institute for the Study and Implementation of Graphic Heritage Techniques) is using the latest technology, such as digital photography and laser scanning, to record Egypt's cultural heritage.

Working with archaeologists, INSIGHT volunteers record ancient tombs, temples, and statues before they fall apart or are destroyed. The results will be used for research and educational purposes.

North Africa and Southwest Asia: Place and Times   225

Biography

Hatshepsut (hat•SHEHP•soot) was the first woman to rule Egypt. Like male pharaohs, she wore a tightly braided false beard.

Hatshepsut came to the throne around 1500 B.C., when her husband, the pharaoh Thutmose II, died. The throne passed to Thutmose III, Hatshepsut's son. Because he was a child, Hatshepsut acted as ruler. Even when he grew up, she refused to give him the throne. Instead, she had herself proclaimed pharaoh and ruled for 20 years.

She encouraged foreign trade and building projects, including a number of magnificent temples.

The Egyptians had no cutting tools or machines to get the stone they needed. Removing the stone and shaping it into blocks was very difficult work. The work was also dangerous. Every Egyptian family had to help with the project. They either worked as laborers or provided food for the workers.

The Pharaoh and the Gods

Egyptians believed that the ruling pharaoh was the living son of the sun god, **Re** (RAY). The pharaoh was also linked with **Horus,** the sun god. The pharaoh was not only ancient Egypt's chief judge and commander in chief, he was also the chief religious figure. His religious example guided the common people in their daily lives and in their preparations for the afterlife.

Religion in Daily Life Temples were everywhere in ancient Egypt. Some were dedicated to major gods, like Re. Others were dedicated to local gods. Pharaohs had temples built in their honor so that people could worship them.

Ordinary citizens did not gather for prayer in the temples. Only priests carried out the temple rituals. Smaller buildings stood outside the temple grounds where common people could pray or leave offerings to the gods. Many private homes also contained small shrines where family members worshiped their gods and honored the spirits of dead family members.

Reading Social Studies

B. Making Inferences How important was their religion to Egyptians?

Culture • Egyptian artists' drawings followed rules. Eyes and shoulders were drawn as if from the front, the rest of the body sideways. Important people were drawn larger than others. ▶

Preparing for the Afterlife Average Egyptians were not buried in pyramids. They made careful preparations for the afterlife, however. Family members were responsible for burying their dead relatives and tending their spirits. Egyptians believed they could help the dead person live comfortably in the afterlife. They prevented bodies from decaying by treating them with preservatives, or mummifying them. The Egyptians filled tombs with items for the dead to use in the afterlife and they decorated the tombs with art. They also made regular offerings to honor the dead.

Culture • Osiris and Isis were the Egyptian god and goddess of the dead. ◀

Culture • A mask covers this mummy's face. ▲

SECTION 3 ASSESSMENT

Terms & Names
1. Explain the significance of:
   (a) papyrus   (b) pyramid   (c) pharaoh
   (d) hieroglyphics (e) Re   (f) Horus

Using Graphics
2. Use a spider map like this one to record all the ways the Nile River benefited the ancient Egyptians.

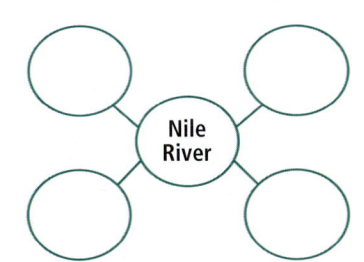

Main Ideas
3. (a) Why did the Egyptians build pyramids?
   (b) How did the use of hieroglyphics help Egyptian builders?
   (c) Why was the pharaoh so important to the Egyptians?

Critical Thinking
4. Summarizing

   How did belief in an afterlife affect the culture of the ancient Egyptians?

   Think About
   ◆ burial practices
   ◆ buildings

ACTIVITY -OPTION-
Suppose that you are an ancient Egyptian. Write a **journal entry** about the daily work of an inhabitant of ancient Egypt.

North Africa and Southwest Asia: Place and Times

Technology: 3500 B.C.

The Potter's Wheel

Archaeologists can trace the origin of the wheel back to flat stones used to make pottery about 8,500 years ago. An ancient potter's wheel consisted of a stone, wood, or baked-clay disk resting on a short stone or clay stand. A potter's helper would spin the disk while the potter shaped clay. The spinning motion allowed potters to make symmetrical containers. Some ancient potters had artists decorate their finished pots. By 3500 B.C., the Sumerians of Mesopotamia had developed the first true potter's wheel, which rotated at a much greater speed. This enabled potters to produce larger quantities of containers, helping to turn pottery into an industry.

INTERACTIVE

SUNSHINE STATE STANDARDS
Key Standard SS.A.2.3.3 The student understands important technological developments and how they influenced human society.
FCAT LA.E.2.3.1 Literature: Understand Character and Plot Development

The wheel has provided not only a surplus of goods to be traded far and wide but also a means of transporting them.

The potter's wheel makes possible the mass production of a wide variety of inexpensive goods.

Archaeologists study broken pieces of pottery, called potsherds, to learn about lifestyles and practices of past civilizations.

The centrifugal force of the spinning wheel causes the clay to move outward, allowing the potter to form stronger, lighter vessels and to fashion such useful features as spouts.

THINKING Critically

1. Drawing Conclusions
As production of pottery increased, the amount of decoration decreased. Why?

2. Making Inferences
Which mechanical devices used today were adapted from the wheel?

SECTION 4

Birthplace of Three Religions

TERMS & NAMES
Abraham
Judaism
Jesus
Christianity
Muhammad
Islam
Muslim
Qur'an

MAIN IDEA
Southwest Asia was the birthplace of Judaism, Christianity, and Islam.

WHY IT MATTERS NOW
Today, these three religions continue to attract believers and influence world events.

DATELINE

JERUSALEM, JUNE 10, 1967—The third war between Arab States and Israel ended today—after just six days of fighting. Israeli forces have gained control of Jerusalem's Old City. In 1948, Jerusalem was divided between Arabs and Israelis. Now the entire city is in Israeli hands.

The Old City includes sites sacred to three religions. Muslims revere the Dome of the Rock, built over the rock from which Muhammad made a night journey to heaven. The Wailing Wall, all that remains of the ancient Temple of Solomon, is sacred to the Jews. The Christian Church of the Holy Sepulcher marks the spot where Jesus Christ is believed to have been buried after his crucifixion.

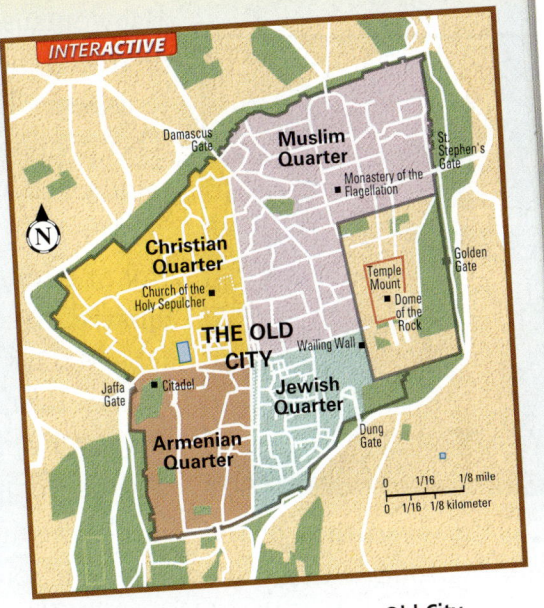

Location • This map of Jerusalem's Old City section shows the location of many sacred sites. ▲

Three Religions

Jerusalem is a city in which Jews, Christians, and Muslims have lived for centuries. These religions all share common traits. They all got their start in Southwest Asia.

The members of each group believe that there is only one god, a belief called monotheism. The Sumerians and Egyptians believed in many gods, a belief called polytheism. In addition, each religion was first led by a single person and has a set of sacred writings.

TAKING NOTES
Use your chart to take notes about North Africa and Southwest Asia.

Generalizations	Details
1. Bodies of water provide resources for people in North Africa and...	
2. Complex civilizations developed religions and...	

North Africa and Southwest Asia: Place and Times 229

Abraham and the Origin of Judaism

The Hebrew people were the first monotheists. They believed in a god they called Yahweh. According to the Hebrew scripture, Yahweh spoke to a man named **Abraham**. Abraham was from the city of Ur, in southeastern Mesopotamia. Yahweh told Abraham to leave his native land. Abraham obeyed and settled in Canaan, which is now in the land of Israel. Abraham's descendants are known as Jews, and their religious belief is called **Judaism**.

> **Vocabulary**
> scripture: sacred writing

Movement • Abraham led his household into the land of Canaan. ▲

How Judaism Adapted over Time The story of Judaism is the story of exile. In 586 B.C., the Babylonians from southern Mesopotamia destroyed the First Temple built by the Jews in Jerusalem. The Jews were exiled to Babylon. They continued to worship by praying and reading their holy texts.

> **Vocabulary**
> exile: forced removal from one's native country

About 50 years later, the Persians took control of Mesopotamia. The Persian ruler Cyrus allowed the Jews to return to Jerusalem and rebuild their Temple. Much later, the Jews came under Roman control. The Jews revolted against Rome in A.D. 66. Jerusalem and the Second Temple were destroyed in the struggle.

Place • The Wailing Wall is all that remains of Solomon's Temple. ▲

Although the Temple was never rebuilt, Judaism did not die out. Jewish teachers and religious leaders encouraged their people to replace worship in the Temple with prayer, study, and good deeds. For the next 1,800 years, most Jews lived outside Jerusalem. They hoped that Jerusalem might once again become the home of Judaism.

Jesus and the Birth of Christianity

Sometime during the years 8 to 4 B.C., a Jewish boy named **Jesus** was born in Bethlehem, a small town in ancient Palestine. (See the map on page 233.) The story of his life is told in the four Gospels, part of the Christian scripture collected in the Bible. The first of the Gospels was written about 30 years after Jesus died.

Early Life According to the Gospels, Jesus grew up in Galilee, a region in northern Palestine. His father trained him to be a carpenter.

Culture • This famous painting, *The Last Supper* by Leonardo da Vinci, shows Jesus with his disciples shortly before his death. ◄

Vocabulary

baptize: to purify and admit into a new way of life

disciple: a follower of the teachings of another

When he was about 30, his cousin John the Baptist baptized him. For the next three years, he traveled around the countryside, preaching a religion of love and forgiveness and performing miracles. People flocked to hear his words. Disciples gathered around him.

The Jewish people believed that someday a Messiah, or savior, would come to lead them out of exile. Some people believed Jesus was the Messiah. He came to be called Christ, the Greek word for *messiah*. Those who believed in him and his teachings were called Christians.

Final Days Some government and religious leaders considered Jesus' teachings and his large following a threat to their own power. When Jesus came to Jerusalem to celebrate the Jewish feast of Passover, the authorities decided to get rid of him. Judas Iscariot, one of the 12 disciples who were closest to Jesus, betrayed him to the authorities. Jesus was arrested. After a brief trial, he was crucified and died. He was put into a tomb. After three days, according to his disciples, he was resurrected and later went up into heaven.

Vocabulary

crucify: to put to death by fastening the hands and feet to a cross

resurrect: to bring back to life

Place • Many Christians believe Jesus was buried at the site of the Church of the Holy Sepulcher in Jerusalem. ▼

Beginnings of Christianity Jesus' disciples spread his teachings and their belief that he was the Messiah promised in Jewish scripture. From its roots in Judaism, a new religion developed called **Christianity**. It is based on the life and teachings of Jesus. Eventually, the new religion spread to other parts of the world. Today, only a small number of Christians live in Southwest Asia, the region where Christianity began. (See the Unit Atlas map on page 205.)

Muhammad, the Prophet of Islam

Less than 600 years after Christ's death, a third monotheistic religion arose in Southwest Asia. A man named **Muhammad** (mu·HAM·ihd) was born in Mecca (MEHK·uh) about A.D. 570.

North Africa and Southwest Asia: Place and Times   231

He is the founder of **Islam,** a religion whose followers believe there is one god and that Muhammad is his prophet. A believer in Islam is called a **Muslim.**

One day about A.D. 610, according to Muslim beliefs, when Muhammad was alone, he heard a voice commanding him: "Recite in the name of your Lord who created! He created man from that which clings. Recite; and thy Lord is Most Bountiful, He who has taught by the pen, taught man what he knew not."

Vocabulary
prophet: a person who speaks through divine inspiration

Place • The Sultan of Morocco donated this copy of the Qur'an to the city of Jerusalem. ▼

Muhammad's Teachings Muhammad believed that the command came from the angel Gabriel, who was revealing to him the will of God. For the next 22 years, Gabriel continued to send revelations to Muhammad. Later, the revelations were collected into the **Qur'an** (kuh·RAN), the sacred text of Islam. Muhammad told other people about the divine messages he received. He criticized the wealthy people of Mecca for turning their backs on the poor and needy. He encouraged them to reject their wicked ways and to worship the one true God.

Reading **Social Studies**
Comparing What did the founders of Judaism, Christianity, and Islam have in common?

The leaders of Mecca thought Muhammad's teachings threatened their traditions and businesses. Some plotted to kill him. In 622, Muhammad and a group of followers escaped to the nearby city of Medina (mih·DEE·nuh), where they were welcomed. Muslims date the beginning of their calendar from this important year in their history.

SECTION 4 ASSESSMENT

Terms & Names
1. Explain the significance of:
   (a) Abraham (b) Judaism (c) Jesus (d) Christianity
   (e) Muhammad (f) Islam (g) Muslim (h) Qur'an

Using Graphics
2. Use a time line like this one to write important dates in the early history of Judaism, Christianity, and Islam.

586 B.C. ├──┼──┼──┼──┤ A.D. 622

Main Ideas
3. (a) What do Judaism, Christianity, and Islam have in common?
   (b) What role did Jesus' disciples play in establishing Christianity?
   (c) What does the Qur'an contain?

Critical Thinking
4. **Making Inferences**
   Why do you think Judaism was able to flourish in exile for so many centuries?

   Think About
   • religious beliefs
   • the role of religious leaders and teachers

ACTIVITY -OPTION- Suppose that you have just seen and heard one of the religious leaders mentioned in this section. Write a **letter** to a friend describing your experience.

Holy Places of Three Religions

Holy city or site
- 🟢 Christian
- ⚫ Jewish
- 🔴 Muslim
- -- Intermittent Stream

GEOGRAPHY SKILLBUILDER: Interpreting a Map

1. **Location** • Which religions have holy sites on the Sea of Galilee?
2. **Region** • What does this map indicate about the importance of this region to Christians, Jews, and Muslims?

233

SECTION 5: Muslim Empires

TERMS & NAMES
Five Pillars of Islam
caliph
theocracy
Ottoman Empire
Constantinople
Suleiman I
Janissary
Sultan Mehmed V

MAIN IDEA
Islamic beliefs and culture spread throughout Southwest Asia and much of the world.

WHY IT MATTERS NOW
Islam, the world's second largest religion, influences society and governments in most Southwest Asian countries today.

DATELINE

MECCA, ARABIA, 9TH DAY OF DHUL HIJJAH, A.D. 622 — The Prophet Muhammad today preached a sermon to 140,000 followers who have come to Mecca from all over Arabia on a pilgrimage. In his sermon, Muhammad reviewed all his teachings over the years. Many say it was the most important sermon he has ever preached. Some fear it may be his last.

He began by saying, "O People, lend me an attentive ear, for I know not whether after this year I shall ever be among you again." It is well-known that for the past few years the Prophet has been anxious to spread word of his religion wherever he can.

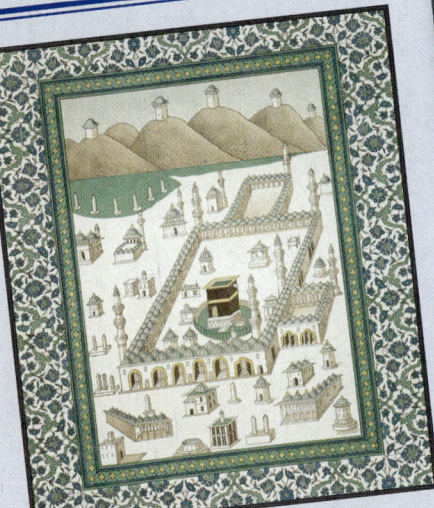

Place • Mecca is the holiest city in Islam. ▲

The Five Pillars of Islam

The most important teachings of Muhammad are summed up in the **Five Pillars of Islam**. All members of the Muslim community believe in the central importance of these five religious duties. The Five Pillars of Islam unite Muslims around the world.

TAKING NOTES
Use your chart to take notes about North Africa and Southwest Asia.

Generalizations	Details
1. Bodies of water provide resources for people in North Africa and ...	
2. Complex civilizations developed religions and ...	

SUNSHINE STATE STANDARDS
Key Standard SS.A.2.3.8 The student knows the political, social, and economic institutions that characterized the significant aspects of Eastern and Western civilizations.
FCAT LA.A.2.3.1 Reading: Identify Main Idea, Facts, and Details

234 CHAPTER 8

The Five Pillars of Islam

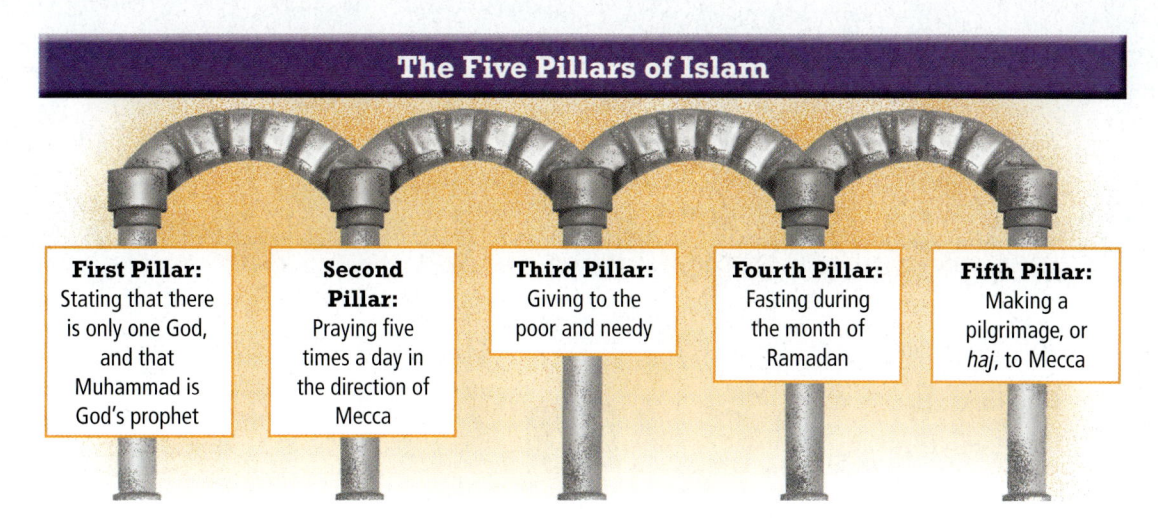

First Pillar: Stating that there is only one God, and that Muhammad is God's prophet

Second Pillar: Praying five times a day in the direction of Mecca

Third Pillar: Giving to the poor and needy

Fourth Pillar: Fasting during the month of Ramadan

Fifth Pillar: Making a pilgrimage, or *haj*, to Mecca

Muslim Empires

Muhammad died without choosing someone to continue his work. His close associates soon selected a **caliph** (KAY·lihf) to succeed him. The title of caliph was used by rulers of the Muslim community from 632 until 1924. The caliph's duty was to spread God's rule. In carrying out this task, the caliphs founded a new empire, the caliphate. The caliphate was a **theocracy** (thee·AHK·ruh·see), a government ruled by a religious leader.

Reading Social Studies

A. Analyzing Causes How did the caliphs' trading system lead to the spread of culture?

Conquest, Trade, and Learning The caliphs created a vast trading system throughout their empires. Islamic ideas spread as books were exchanged along trade routes. Metalwork, pottery, and fabrics exposed other people to new and unique Muslim artwork.

In the early Middle Ages, Muslims collected and translated important books and papers in order to preserve knowledge. During the 1100s and 1200s, these texts were translated from Arabic into Hebrew and Latin. These translations helped European scholars study the knowledge of the ancient world. They could see how Islamic thinkers had further developed this knowledge.

Islam in Europe The caliphs conquered Christian Spain and introduced Islamic culture there. They had hoped to spread their influence elsewhere in Europe. In 732, however, that hope was dashed. Muslim armies trying to capture Tours, in what is now west-central France, were defeated by Charles Martel (sharl mahr·TEHL), Charlemagne's grandfather. By 1400, however, the Muslims had succeeded in conquering parts of Europe.

Culture • The influence of Islamic art left its mark in southern Spain, where Muslims built such works of art as the Alhambra, a magnificent palace. ▲

The Ottoman Empire

The Muslim **Ottoman Empire** controlled what is now Turkey and parts of North Africa, Southwest Asia, and Southeast Europe. The Ottomans made **Constantinople,** called Istanbul in present-day Turkey, their capital city. The rulers of the Ottoman Empire were called sultans. The vast Ottoman Empire included people of different backgrounds. The sultans were tolerant of other religions. Christians and Jews could pay a tax that allowed them to worship as they pleased. Some achieved prominent positions in banking and business.

Region • Suleiman I was a 16th-century sultan of the Ottoman Empire. ▼

Suleiman, "The Magnificent" From 1520 to 1566, **Suleiman I** (SOO•lay•MAHN) ruled the Ottoman Empire. Christians called Suleiman "The Magnificent." Muslims called him "The Lawgiver." Suleiman published a code of laws that established a system of justice throughout his empire. Suleiman's chief architect, Sinan (suh•NAHN), transformed Christian Constantinople into an Islamic capital. Sinan designed famous mosques in Istanbul and elsewhere in the Ottoman Empire. As long as Suleiman ruled the Ottoman Empire, it was the richest and most powerful empire in Europe and Southwest Asia.

Reading **Social Studies**

B. Forming and Supporting Opinions Do you think Suleiman I deserved to be called "The Magnificent"?

Slaves and Soldiers

Not everyone shared in the empire's wealth and glory. Many people were slaves, often prisoners from conquered nations. They served at court or in the homes of wealthy people. Many of the male slaves became soldiers.

The Janissaries A special group of soldiers loyal to the sultan, called **Janissaries**, developed in the late 1300s out of a small force of slaves. By the 1600s, they had become so powerful that even the sultans feared them. They refused to learn modern ways of fighting, however, and grew weak. In 1826, a group of Janissaries attacked the sultan. Forces loyal to the sultan fired on the attacking Janissaries, killing 6,000. The sultan then disbanded the force.

The Decline of the Ottoman Empire

Over the centuries, the Ottoman Empire grew weak. It fought wars constantly to hold on to its empire. By the 1800s, the empire came close to bankruptcy several times. It also had trouble competing in trade with industrialized Europe. **Sultan Mehmed V** fought on the losing side of World War I. After the war ended, the empire lost control of Arab lands. By 1924, the Ottoman Empire no longer existed. The modern country of Turkey had taken its place.

Culture • Three Janissaries (on the right) stand in front of their sultan. ▲

SECTION 5 ASSESSMENT

Terms & Names

1. Explain the significance of:
   - (a) Five Pillars of Islam
   - (b) caliph
   - (c) theocracy
   - (d) Ottoman Empire
   - (e) Constantinople
   - (f) Suleiman I
   - (g) Janissary
   - (h) Sultan Mehmed V

Using Graphics

2. Use a time line like this one to record major events in the spread of Islamic empires.

   632 —————— 1924

Main Ideas

3. (a) How did the caliphs contribute to the growth of Islamic empires?
   (b) What regions of the world did the Ottoman Empire include?
   (c) What was Constantinople?

Critical Thinking

4. **Hypothesizing** How might the modern world be different if Muslim armies had won the battle of Tours?

   Think About
   - cultural change
   - religious differences

ACTIVITY -OPTION- Create an illustrated **report** on the religious buildings of Judaism, Christianity, or Islam.

CHAPTER 8 ASSESSMENT

TERMS & NAMES

Explain the significance of each of the following:
1. fertile
2. irrigation
3. Hammurabi
4. Fertile Crescent
5. pyramid
6. hieroglyphics
7. Re
8. Muhammad
9. caliph
10. theocracy

REVIEW QUESTIONS

Physical Geography (pages 213–216)
1. What makes it possible to farm the desert near the Nile?
2. Name the three important bodies of water that helped to shape the region of North Africa and Southwest Asia.

Ancient Mesopotamia and the Fertile Crescent (pages 217–221)
3. What three problems faced the city-states of Mesopotamia?
4. List the three classes of people in Mesopotamia.

Ancient Egypt (pages 223–227)
5. Why did the ancient Egyptians build canals on the Nile?
6. Why did the ancient Egyptians fill their tombs with everyday items?

Birthplace of Three Religions (pages 229–233)
7. What do Judaism, Christianity, and Islam have in common?
8. Why is Jerusalem an important city for Jews, Christians, and Muslims?

Muslim Empires (pages 234–237)
9. Why did the Muslims call Suleiman I "The Lawgiver"?
10. What caused the Ottoman Empire to grow weak?

CRITICAL THINKING

Comparing
1. Use the details in your completed chart from Reading Social Studies, p. 212, to compare the religion of ancient Egypt with the religion of Mesopotamia.

Evaluating Decisions
2. The nonprofit group INSIGHT is using technology to record Egypt's culture. (See page 225.) Based on the amount of work involved, do you think the work of INSIGHT is a good idea? Why or why not?

Making Inferences
3. The Greek historian Herodotus called Egypt "the gift of the Nile." What do you think he meant?

Visual Summary

1 Physical Geography
- The climate, resources, and soil conditions of North Africa and Southwest Asia are determined by the water and rainfall of the region.
- Dry land and flooding rivers still affect the region today.

2 Ancient Mesopotamia and the Fertile Crescent
- A complex civilization arose as Mesopotamia struggled with challenges.
- Early achievements in Mesopotamia led the way for later societies.

3 Ancient Egypt
- Environment influenced the development of civilization in ancient Egypt.
- The ancient Egyptians created a well organized and complex civilization.

4 Birthplace of Three Religions
- Three major world religions began in Southwest Asia.
- Judaism, Christianity, and Islam have a great deal in common.

5 Muslim Empires
- Islamic beliefs have spread through Southwest Asia and other parts of the world.
- These beliefs influence both society and government.

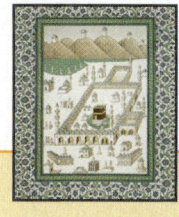

> STANDARDS-BASED ASSESSMENT

Use the map and your knowledge of geography to answer questions 1 and 2.

Additional Test Practice, pp. S1–S33

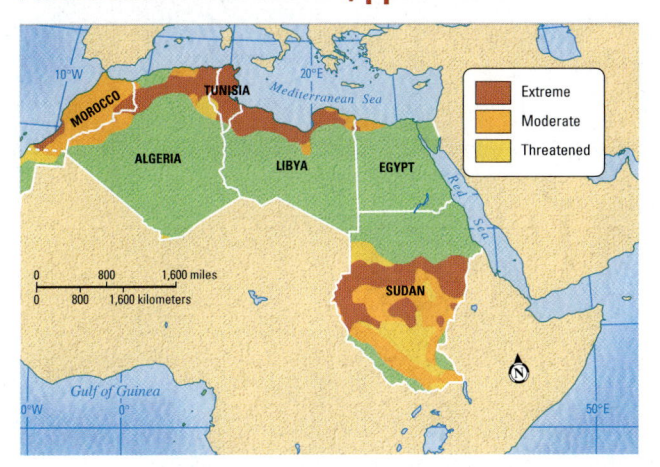

The following passage describes the reasons for a food shortage in Sudan. Use the quotation and your knowledge of world cultures and geography to answer question 3.

PRIMARY SOURCE

Following two consecutive years of serious drought, extensive floods in northern Sudan have displaced tens of thousands of people, destroyed crops and aggravated the already precarious food supply situation in the affected areas. Heavy rains in the . . . Ethiopian highlands caused an overflow of the Nile river and submerged many villages and settlements. Water levels in the Nile are reported to be higher than those of 1988, when the river burst its banks causing massive destruction.

FOOD AND AGRICULTURE ORGANIZATION
SPECIAL ALERT, Aug. 22, 2001

1. Which of the following countries has lost the greatest amount of land to the desert?
   A. Algeria
   B. Egypt
   C. Libya
   D. Sudan

2. Which of the following statements best describes Tunisia?
   A. It is almost entirely desert.
   B. Almost half of it is desert.
   C. Desertification has just begun.
   D. It has no desertification.

3. What two natural events caused a food shortage in Sudan?
   A. flood and overflow
   B. drought and flood
   C. drought and displacement
   D. flood and displacement

TEST PRACTICE
CLASSZONE.COM

ALTERNATIVE ASSESSMENT

1. WRITING ABOUT HISTORY

Scribes worked long hours and had many roles. Imagine you are learning to be a scribe in Mesopotamia. Research the lives of students learning to be scribes. Then write a letter home to your family describing what you are learning, your daily routine at school, and the responsibilities you will be taking on.

2. COOPERATIVE LEARNING

Two women, Hatshepsut and Cleopatra, won fame as rulers of ancient Egypt. In a group of three to five classmates, plan a documentary about one of these rulers. Conduct research to find out when she ruled, how she came to power, and what she accomplished during her rule. To complete the documentary, share the responsibilities of writing a script, locating or creating illustrations, and presenting the documentary to the class.

INTEGRATED TECHNOLOGY

Doing Internet Research

Use the Internet to research hieroglyphic symbols. Then create a poster that presents your findings. List the Web sites you used to prepare your poster.

- Find out how many types of picture symbols were used and how they were organized to communicate written information.
- Include a chart that shows the sounds, words, actions, and ideas the symbols represented.
- Show some words or simple sentences translated into hieroglyphics

For Internet links to support this activity, go to

RESEARCH LINKS
CLASSZONE.COM

North Africa and Southwest Asia: Place and Times

CHAPTER 9

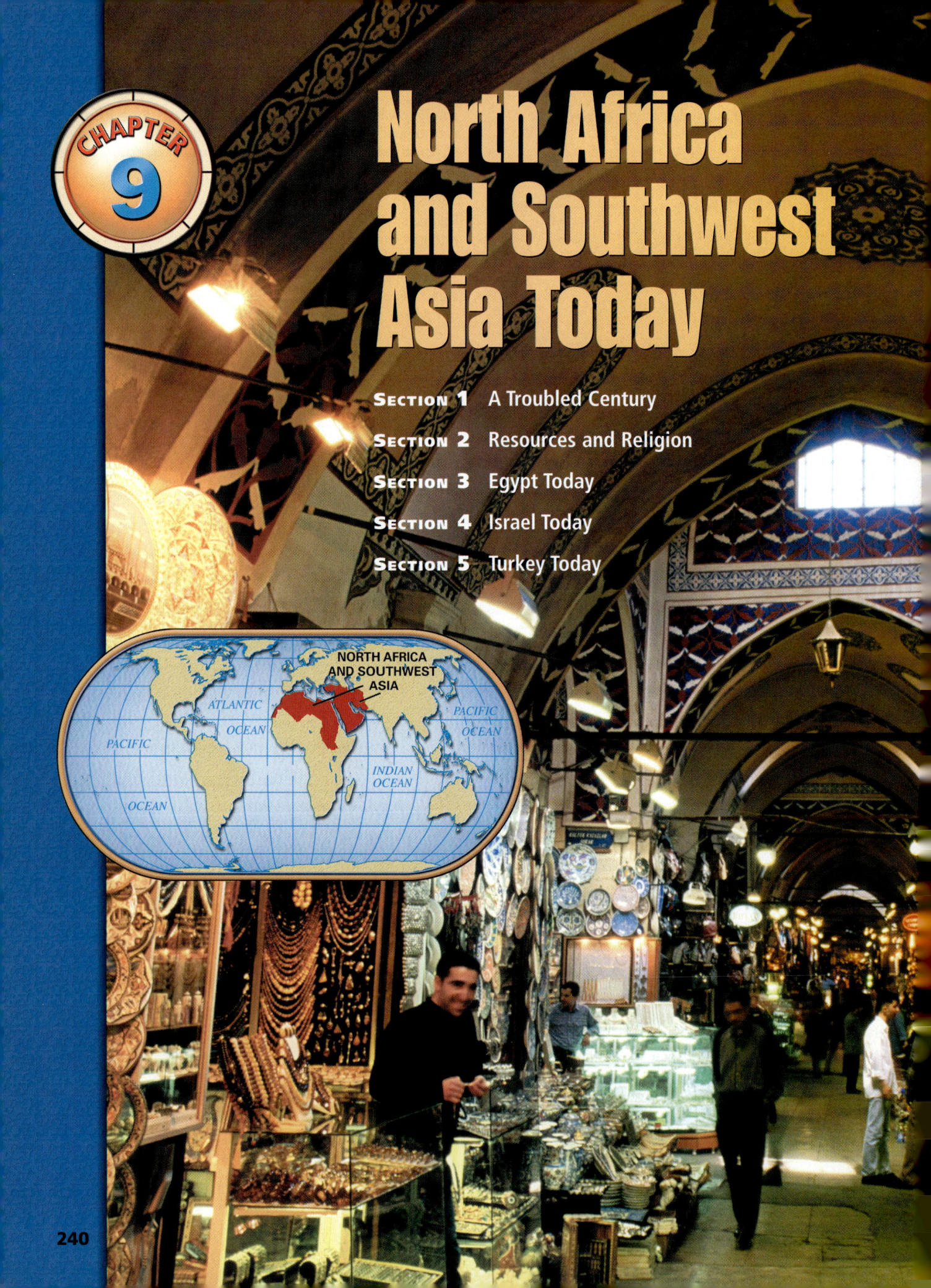

North Africa and Southwest Asia Today

SECTION 1 A Troubled Century
SECTION 2 Resources and Religion
SECTION 3 Egypt Today
SECTION 4 Israel Today
SECTION 5 Turkey Today

How have rich oil deposits affected Southwest Asia and the world?

FOCUS ON GEOGRAPHY

Human-Environment Interaction • Enormous amounts of petroleum, or oil, lie beneath the land surrounding the southern and eastern shores of the Mediterranean Sea, a region often called the Middle East. Experts believe the Middle East supplies about 40 percent of the world's oil. Other countries have come to depend on the oil produced here. The importance of providing energy resources for the planet has given the region great political and economic power. The governments of Middle Eastern nations try to control the price and amount of oil that is produced in their region.

What do you think?

- How are politics and economics related in the Middle East?
- How might the importance of this region change as nations develop alternative sources of energy?

Place A wealth of goods is sold in this vast indoor bazaar in Istanbul, Turkey.

CHAPTER 9
READING SOCIAL STUDIES

BEFORE YOU READ

▶▶ What Do You Know?

Before you read the chapter, consider what you know about North Africa and Southwest Asia today. You may know something about countries like Israel, Saudi Arabia, Iran, Egypt, Turkey, and Iraq from televised news reports about conflicts in this area. Think about the region's role as a major producer of oil. You, or people you know, may have been born in the region or may have lived or visited there. Review what you have learned about recent history and current events in this part of the world.

▶▶ What Do You Want to Know?

Decide what you want to know about contemporary North Africa and Southwest Asia. In your notebook, record what you hope to learn from this chapter.

Region • These girls live in Cairo, Egypt, the largest city in the region. ▼

READ AND TAKE NOTES

Reading Strategy: Identifying Problems and Solutions Recognizing problems and how they are solved will help you understand complicated issues you read about in social studies. Use the chart below to identify problems, solutions, and new problems discussed in Chapter 9.

- Copy the chart into your notebook.
- As you read, look for information related to each problem listed on the chart. Some issues are discussed more than once.
- Take notes on solutions that have been tried and problems that resulted.

Region • This sign is in three languages—Hebrew, Arabic, and English. ▲

Problems	Solutions	Resulting Problems
History of foreign influence		
Changes in world markets		
Severe water shortage		
Poverty in villages in Egypt		
Lack of a homeland for Jews		
Forced modernization in Turkey		

SECTION 1
A Troubled Century

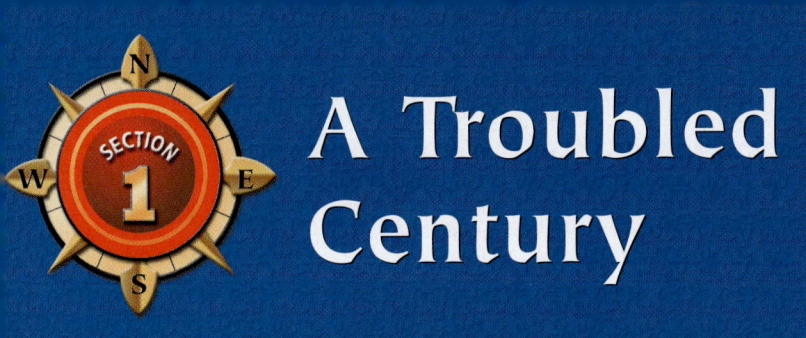

TERMS & NAMES
mandate
Palestine
Arab-Israeli Wars
Kurd
Persian Gulf War

MAIN IDEA
Today's conflicts in North Africa and Southwest Asia have roots in the history of the region.

WHY IT MATTERS NOW
Regional conflicts affect the security and well-being of people around the world.

DATELINE

SÈVRES, FRANCE, AUGUST 10, 1920

Turkey's Ottoman Empire, the "sick man of Europe" is dead at last. Today, Turkey agreed to surrender most of its territory to Great Britain and France. Revolts by Arab nationalists in recent years had weakened the once-great empire. Being on the losing side in the recent World War marked its end. Mesopotamia and Palestine will now be under British control. Syria, which includes Lebanon, goes to the French.

Region • European nations divided up the Ottoman Empire at the Sèvres conference. ▲

European Nations Take Over

When World War I ended, the history of modern Southwest Asia and North Africa began. During the war, the Turkish Ottoman Empire had sided with Germany against Great Britain, France, and Russia. After the Ottoman Empire's defeat, most of its former territory was divided between Great Britain and France. The stage was set for major conflicts that still trouble the region today. (See the map on page 248.)

TAKING NOTES
Use your chart to take notes about North Africa and Southwest Asia.

Problems	Solutions	Resulting Problems
History of foreign influence		
Changes in world markets		

SUNSHINE STATE STANDARDS
Key Standard SS.B.2.3.2 The student knows the human and physical characteristics of different places in the world and how these characteristics change over time.
Other Standards SS.A.3.3.3, A.3.3.5
FCAT LA.A.2.3.1 Reading: Identify Main Idea, Facts, and Details

North Africa and Southwest Asia Today **243**

Independence Days in Southwest Asia and North Africa

Country	Controlling Power	Taken Over	Achieved Independence
Algeria	France	1847	July 5, 1962
Bahrain	Great Britain	1880	August 15, 1971
Egypt	Great Britain	1882	February 28, 1922
Iraq	Great Britain	1920	October 3, 1932
Jordan	Great Britain	1921	May 25, 1946
Kuwait	Great Britain	1899	June 19, 1961
Lebanon	France	1920	November 22, 1943
Libya	Italy	1932	December 24, 1951
Morocco	France (1/3 under Spain)	1912	March 2, 1956 (April 1956 from Spain)
Oman	Portugal	late 1500s	1650
Qatar	Great Britain	1916	September 3, 1971
Sudan	Egypt/Great Britain	1898	January 1, 1956
Syria	France	1920	April 17, 1946
Tunisia	France	1881	March 20, 1956
United Arab Emirates	Great Britain	1952	December 2, 1971
Yemen	Great Britain	1882	1967 (South Yemen) May 22, 1990 (union of North and South Yemen)

SKILLBUILDER: Interpreting a Chart

1. Which European nation controlled the most countries in the region?
2. In which century did most countries on the chart achieve independence?

A History of Foreign Control Europeans had been taking control of the region since before the 19th century. After World War I, this control often took the form of mandates. A **mandate** is a country placed under the control of another power by international agreement. The European powers promised to give their mandates independence by a certain date. Countries that were not mandates often had to fight for independence.

Conflict Over Palestine

After World War I, Great Britain controlled **Palestine,** an Arab region that was also the land the Jews had lived in 2,000 years earlier. Starting in the late 1800s, Jews fleeing persecution in Eastern Europe had begun migrating there again. After World War II and the Holocaust, many Jews were left homeless and the number who wanted to migrate to Palestine increased.

Palestine, however, was already home to Arabs who had no desire to see their homeland become a Jewish state. Arabs in other countries backed them up. In 1947, Great Britain asked the United Nations to solve the problem. The United Nations divided Palestine—one part for Jews and another for Arabs. The Jews accepted the plan, but the Arabs did not. In May 1948, Jewish leaders declared Israel an independent state. Iraq, Syria, Egypt, Jordan, and Lebanon immediately declared war on Israel. The Israelis won the first of the **Arab-Israeli Wars.** (See the map on page 245.)

Reading Social Studies

A. Summarizing What was the main source of conflict between the Jews and Arabs in Palestine?

Changing Boundaries in Palestine, 1947–49

The Arab-Israeli Wars, 1967 and 1973

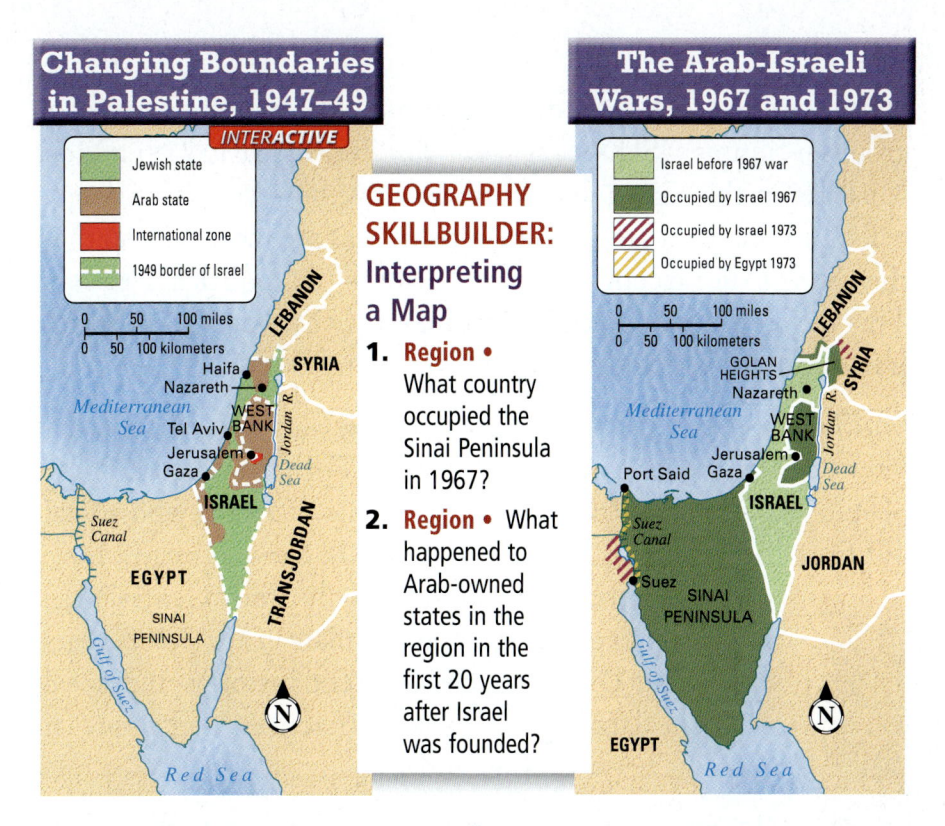

GEOGRAPHY SKILLBUILDER: Interpreting a Map

1. **Region** • What country occupied the Sinai Peninsula in 1967?
2. **Region** • What happened to Arab-owned states in the region in the first 20 years after Israel was founded?

Palestinian Refugees About 700,000 Palestinian Arabs had to leave their homes. They fled to other Arab countries or settled in camps set up by the UN. In 1964, some Palestinian people formed the Palestine Liberation Organization (PLO). The PLO refused to recognize Israel's right to exist.

Continuing Conflict In 1967 and 1973, Israel won the third and fourth of the Arab-Israeli Wars. Conflict continued even in peacetime. Over the years, territory passed back and forth between Israel and Arab countries. (See the map above.)

Attempts at Peace In 1979, Egypt became the first Arab country in the region to make peace with Israel. Leaders of Egypt and Israel discussed the Palestinians' wish for their own state. Ten years later, Palestinian Arabs rebelled in the territories controlled by Israel. Finally, in 1993, Israel and the PLO signed an agreement. The PLO recognized Israel's right to exist. Israel returned land to the Palestinians. The next year, Israel and Jordan signed a peace treaty. In 2000, however, another Palestinian uprising broke out.

Sources of Conflict

Among all the peoples of the Middle East, religious differences contribute to conflict. Jews and Arabs claim holy sites in Jerusalem. Religious conflicts between Christians and Muslims have erupted in Egypt, Lebanon, and Sudan. Conflicts also occur within religions.

North Africa and Southwest Asia Today

Sunnis and Shi'ites Islam, for example, has two main sects, or groups—Sunnis (SUN·eez) and Shi'ites (SHEE·yts). Most Muslims in the region are Sunni. In Iran, however, most people belong to the Shi'a branch of Islam. Shi'ites are more willing than the Sunni to accept religious leaders as political leaders. This difference has contributed to conflict between neighboring Iran and Iraq. The most powerful Iraqis are Sunni.

Conflict Between Ethnic Groups Trouble also occurs when different ethnic groups come into conflict. For example, like most people in the region, Iraqis are descendants of Arabs who spread out from the Arabian Peninsula in the 600s. Most Iranians, however, are Persian, people originally from Central Asia who have lived on the Iranian plateau for 3,000 years. Arabs and Persians have different histories and speak different languages. These differences contribute to conflicts between Iran and Iraq.

Nationalism Some ethnic groups want their own countries. At least 20 million **Kurds**, for example, live in mountainous areas of Iran, Iraq, Syria, Turkey, and other countries of the region. Most Kurds are Sunni Muslims and speak a language related to Persian. Many Kurds have died in their fight to gain their own state.

Fundamentalism Muslim fundamentalists believe Islam should be strictly observed. In 1979, Shi'ite leader Ayatollah Khomeini (EYE·yuh·TOH·luh koh·MAY·nee) took over the government of Iran. Khomeini objected to the way the former ruler had been westernizing the country. Khomeini's government passed laws forbidding the sale of alcohol and limiting the freedom of women. Fundamentalist movements have also arisen in other countries in the region, often coming into conflict with people who have less strict beliefs.

Wars in the Region

The neighboring countries of Iran and Iraq had long disputed who owned the oil-rich territory between them. In 1980, Iraq, led by its absolute ruler Saddam Hussein, invaded Iran.

The Iran-Iraq War The war lasted eight years. As many as one million people died, including soldiers as young as 11 and 12. Neither side could gain a clear victory. In 1988, both countries finally signed a cease-fire agreement developed by the United Nations.

Region •
Hebrew (top line) is the official language of Israel. Arabic (second line) is the language of many other countries in the region. ▼

Reading Social Studies

B. Contrasting What is an important difference between Sunnis and Shi'ites?

Vocabulary
ethnic group: people who share a common and distinctive culture, heritage, and language

Vocabulary
ayatollah: respected religious leader

The Persian Gulf War In 1990, Iraq invaded the small oil-rich country of Kuwait. The United Nations imposed a trade embargo to prevent Iraq from importing goods or exporting oil. The embargo took away most of Iraq's income, but Hussein continued to fight. On January 16, 1991, the **Persian Gulf War** began when an international armed force began missile attacks on Iraq, followed by a ground attack on February 24. One hundred hours later, Iraq surrendered. Iraq was out of Kuwait, but Saddam Hussein stayed in power. The UN-imposed embargo remained in effect.

Vocabulary
embargo: a government order forbidding trade with other countries

Culture • In Baghdad, a statue of Saddam Hussein is toppled to show the end of his rule. ▼

War with Iraq By the early 2000s, President George W. Bush had come to believe that Iraqi leader Saddam Hussein was hiding dangerous illegal weapons. The Bush administration was afraid that terrorist groups might use these weapons to attack the United States. The United States was unable to persuade the UN Security Council to support an invasion of Iraq. On March 20, 2003, however, the United States, joined by Britain, Australia, and other allies, invaded Iraq.

Rebuilding Iraq On April 9, 2003, U.S. forces gained control of Baghdad and toppled Hussein's regime. By early May 2003, President Bush announced that combat operations in Iraq had ended. (See the Special Report on page 544.)

SECTION 1 ASSESSMENT

Terms & Names
1. Explain the significance of: (a) mandate (b) Palestine (c) Arab-Israeli Wars (d) Kurd (e) Persian Gulf War

Using Graphics
2. Use a time line like this one to write the dates of major wars in Southwest Asia and North Africa.

1948 ├───┼───┼───┼───┤ 2003

Main Ideas
3. (a) How have European nations contributed to turmoil in Southwest Asia and North Africa?
   (b) In what ways has religion been a source of conflict in this region?
   (c) What are some of the different ethnic groups in this region and how have they come into conflict?

Critical Thinking
4. **Forming and Supporting Opinions**
   Do you think the United Nations should be more involved in settling conflicts in Southwest Asia and North Africa?

   Think About
   • the system of mandates
   • conflict in the region
   • the UN in the Persian Gulf War

ACTIVITY -OPTION- Trace a **map** of the countries of Southwest Asia and North Africa. Write each country's name and the year it achieved independence on the map.

North Africa and Southwest Asia Today **247**

SKILLBUILDER

Reading a Historical Map

▶▶ Defining the Skill

Historical maps show an area of the world as it was in the past. Different historical maps contain different kinds of information. Some show trade routes or routes of exploration. Some show how an empire or nation has increased or decreased in size. Some show how political boundaries have changed over time. The map key tells what the symbols, lines, and colors on a historical map represent.

SUNSHINE STATE STANDARDS
Key Standard SS.B.1.3.1
The student uses various map forms (including thematic maps) and other geographic representations, tools, and technologies to acquire, process, and report geographic information including patterns of land use, connections between places, and patterns and processes of migration and diffusion.

FCAT LA.A.2.3.5 Reading: Locate, Organize, Interpret Information

▶▶ Applying the Skill

The historical map below shows how the Ottoman Empire gradually collapsed. During the 15th and 16th centuries, the Ottoman Empire was one of the most powerful empires in the world. It lasted for more than 600 years, but by 1922 the empire was gone.

How to Read a Historical Map

Strategy ❶ Read the title to learn the time period that is shown on the map.

Strategy ❷ Read the key. Shown first on this key is a dotted line, which represents the boundary of the Ottoman Empire in 1807. Look at the map and find that boundary. As you follow the boundary, notice which bodies of water it touches and which continents it covers.

Strategy ❸ Look at each color on the key and the time period represented by that color. Then look for each color on the map. Some of the color regions are scattered. Be sure to locate all of them.

Strategy ❹ Read the map. Notice when different regions were lost to the Ottoman Empire. Some of these regions became independent; others fell under the rule of other nations.

Write a Summary

Writing a summary will help you gain a clearer understanding of the map. The paragraph to the right summarizes the information from this historical map.

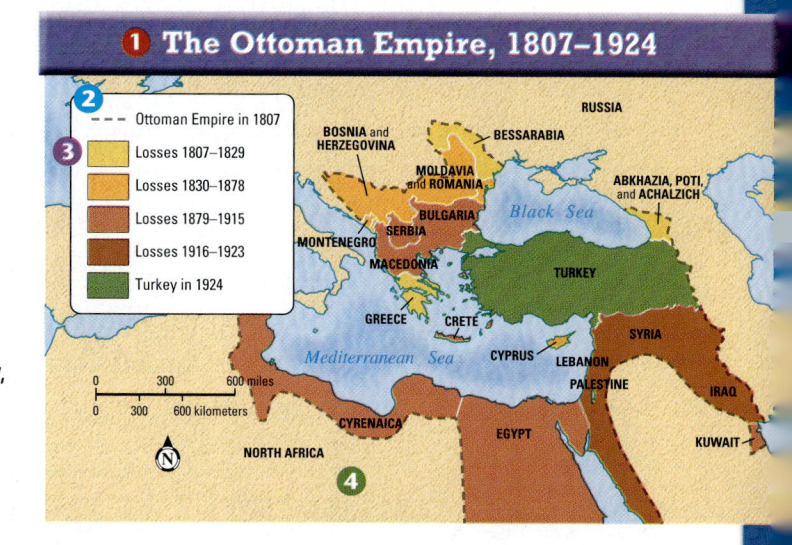

❶ The Ottoman Empire, 1807–1924

❷
- - - Ottoman Empire in 1807
❸
Losses 1807–1829
Losses 1830–1878
Losses 1879–1915
Losses 1916–1923
Turkey in 1924

SUMMARY In 1807 the Ottoman Empire stretched from Bosnia and North Africa in the west to Kuwait in the east, and from Russia in the north to Egypt in the south. Beginning in 1807, the area claimed by the Ottomans was gradually taken over by Greece, Austria-Hungary, Italy, and Great Britain.

▶▶ Practicing the Skill

Turn to page 245 in Chapter 9, Section 1. Look at the historical map entitled *Changing Boundaries in Palestine, 1947–49,* and then write a paragraph summarizing what you learned from it.

SECTION 2
Resources and Religion

TERMS & NAMES
OPEC
primary product
secondary product
petrochemical
haj
Ramadan

MAIN IDEA
Oil resources are a powerful influence on the region's economies, and religion, especially Islam, is a powerful influence on its culture.

WHY IT MATTERS NOW
Peace in Southwest Asia and North Africa depends on prosperity and the ability of different religions to coexist.

DATELINE

KHUZISTAN PROVINCE, PERSIA (IRAN), 1908—A British company has just discovered oil here in Khuzistan. Both the British and the Persians expect it to bring their countries great wealth. The Shah of Iran (Persia) has given British businessman William Knox D'Arcy the rights to drill for oil here. D'Arcy plans to create the Anglo-Persian Oil Company and to begin exporting oil by 1912. The world's increasing dependence on oil for energy has led experts to predict that the value of oil will increase dramatically. The Middle East, they say, has the potential to become the greatest oil-producing area in the world.

Human-Environment Interaction • Workers lay an oil pipeline in the Khuzistan plain. ▶

The Importance of Oil

Oil was soon discovered in other countries of Southwest Asia and North Africa. Great Britain, France, the United States, and other western countries made agreements with the oil-rich nations to build and run companies to develop the oil fields. Today, nearly half the world's oil is found here, mainly in Saudi Arabia, Iran, Kuwait, and Iraq. Saudi Arabia, the world's largest oil-producing country, is also one of the largest oil exporters to the United States.

TAKING NOTES
Use your chart to take notes about North Africa and Southwest Asia.

Problems	Solutions	Resulting Problems
History of foreign influence		
Changes in world markets		

North Africa and Southwest Asia Today

Human-Environment Interaction • OPEC's oil embargo in 1973 led to long lines at gas stations. ◄

Gaining Control After World War II, many nations in the region chose to nationalize, or have their governments take over the running of, their oil industries. In 1960, four of these countries—Iran, Iraq, Saudi Arabia, and Kuwait—joined with Venezuela, an oil-rich country in South America, to form the Organization of Petroleum Exporting Countries, or **OPEC**. OPEC would decide the price and amount of oil produced in each country each year. In a world dependent on oil as its major energy source, OPEC had a great deal of power. In 1973, OPEC placed an embargo on the export of oil to countries that supported Israel. As a result, the price of gasoline shot way up as its supply went down, leading to shortages.

Developing New Products Since the early 1900s, oil has been the most important **primary product**, or raw material, in Southwest Asia and North Africa. The countries of the region export mostly primary products. (See the map below.) Many countries have also developed **secondary products**, or goods manufactured from primary products. In Iraq, for example, date palms are an important primary product. From them, industries in Iraq manufacture date syrup, paper from palm leaves, and other secondary products.

Reading Social Studies

Analyzing Causes How did OPEC's oil embargo lead to a rise in the price of gasoline?

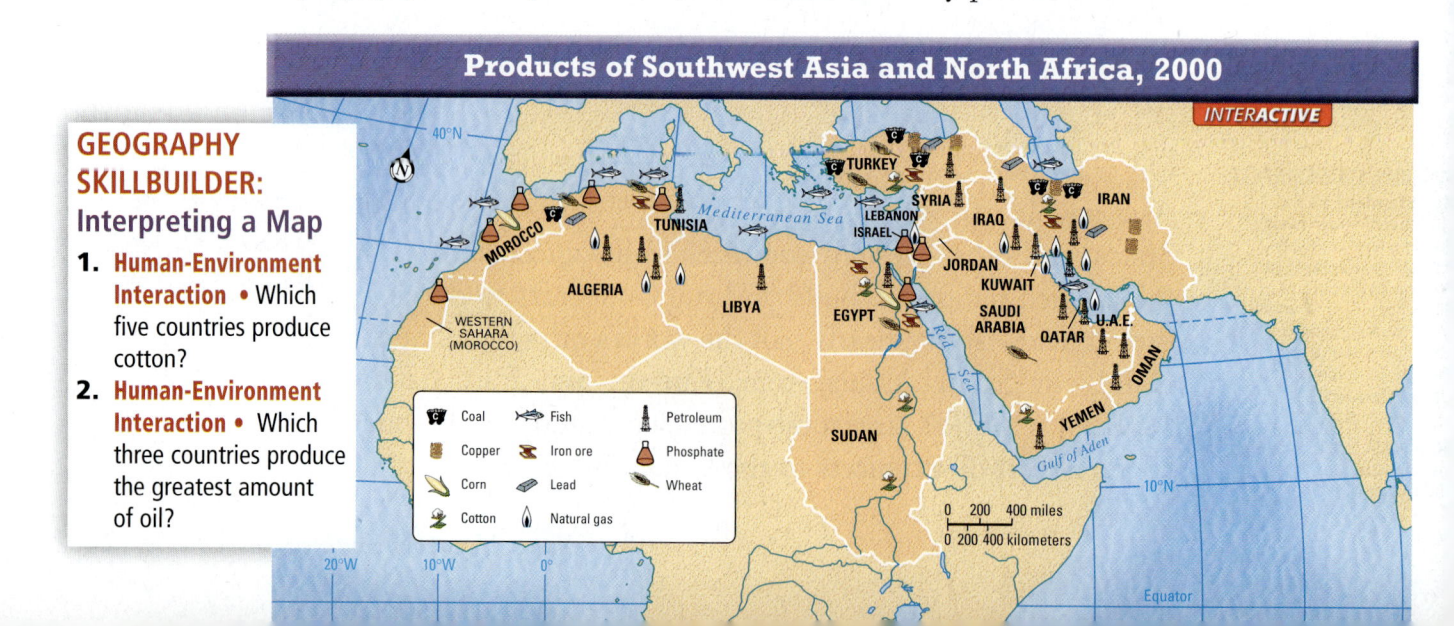

Products of Southwest Asia and North Africa, 2000

GEOGRAPHY SKILLBUILDER: Interpreting a Map

1. **Human-Environment Interaction** • Which five countries produce cotton?
2. **Human-Environment Interaction** • Which three countries produce the greatest amount of oil?

Oil Industries The oil-rich countries also use the oil to make secondary products. For over 30 years, Saudi Arabia and other Persian Gulf countries have been refining crude oil in modern refineries. They also make **petrochemicals** from crude oil and natural gas. Petrochemicals are used in the manufacture of cosmetics, plastics, synthetic materials, detergents, fertilizers, and many other products.

Religion in the Region

BACKGROUND
The Israeli city of Haifa is the world center of the Bahai religion, which split off from Islam. Bahais believe in the equality of men and women and a universal God.

Islam is the dominant religion in the region, but not the only one. Jews and Christians have lived there for thousands of years. Most Jews in the region moved to Israel once it was created, but small communities of Jews remain in Turkey, Egypt, and Iran. Many Christians left after the breakup of the Ottoman Empire. Today the Copts of Egypt and the Maronites of Lebanon are the region's two largest Christian communities.

The Influence of Islam on Culture
Every country in the region shows the influence of Islam. The Five Pillars of Islam (see page 235) are woven into the fabric of daily life. People stop to pray five times a day, no matter what they are doing—at home, in the streets, at school, at work. Radio and television stations air programs devoted to readings from the Qur'an many times a day. All Muslims try to go on a **haj**, or pilgrimage to Mecca, once in a lifetime.

Place • During a *haj*, the holy city of Mecca is packed with pilgrims. ▲

Ramadan During the ninth month of the Islamic year, called **Ramadan** (RAM•uh•DAHN), Muslims fast from sunrise to sunset. Only the very young or sick or those on a journey are allowed to eat or drink during this time. During Ramadan, believers eat a light breakfast before dawn. Then they do not eat or drink again until dusk. The joyous *'Id al-Fitr* (ihd uhl•FIHT•uhr), the Feast of the Breaking of the Fast, ends Ramadan and lasts for several days.

The Muslim Calendar
For Muslims, the calendar begins the year Muhammad fled to Medina, A.D. 622 according to the Western calendar. Each Islamic year has 12 months of about 29 days each, which makes the Islamic year about 11 days shorter than the Western year. Each day starts at sunset.

North Africa and Southwest Asia Today

Westernization vs. Traditional Culture

Many people in Southwest Asia and North Africa think western nations exert too much influence over their culture. Others are more open to westernization, adopting aspects of the way of life common in Europe and the United States. Fast-food restaurants, T-shirts, television, and rap music are examples of westernization. So are many technological advances in business, science, medicine, and agriculture. Some people in the region believe westernization will give them a higher standard of living and an easier, more exciting, more enjoyable way of life. For others, the loss of their traditional culture is too great a price to pay.

The Roles of Women

Women in the region have different roles in society. In countries like Israel, Jordan, and Egypt, many women are well educated and hold important positions in business, politics, and the military. In some countries, however, religious beliefs limit the roles women can play. For example, Saudi Arabian women have fewer rights than do Saudi men. Women are not allowed to attend gatherings with men, and they are forbidden to drive cars. A Saudi woman may have only one husband, but a Saudi man is allowed by Islamic law to have up to four wives. Very few Saudi women work outside the home. Those that do usually teach in all-girl schools or treat patients at maternity clinics.

Spotlight on CULTURE

Persian Carpets Persians—now called Iranians—have been making carpets for more than 2,500 years. Brightly colored intricate designs made the carpets valued for their beauty. Craftspeople spent months and even years carefully weaving dyed sheep's wool into artistic patterns. Today Persian carpets decorate palaces, important buildings, and museums.

THINKING CRITICALLY

1. **Drawing Conclusions**
   What do you think makes Persian carpets valuable?
2. **Summarizing**
   What role have Persian carpets played in Iranian culture?

For more on Persian carpets, go to
RESEARCH LINKS
CLASSZONE.COM

Clothing and Culture

Clothing reveals much about the region's cultures. In Israel, for instance, some women and men dress in fashionable Western clothing. Orthodox Jewish women, however, wear more modest dress as their religious beliefs dictate. Orthodox men often wear black suits and hats and grow long ringlets of hair in front of their ears. In some Islamic countries, women wear *chadors*, floor-length cloaks that cover everything but the women's eyes. In Iran and Saudi Arabia, such clothing is not a choice; it's the law. Men, too, dress and grow facial hair as Islamic law demands.

Culture • This woman is wearing a *chador.* ▲

Vocabulary
nomads: people with no fixed home who move about in search of food, water, and grazing land

A Disappearing Nomadic Culture

Once nomads lived in the desert places of the region. Most nomads herded sheep from place to place in search of grazing lands. Other nomads escorted camel caravans of traders across the desert. Today, only one percent of the population is nomadic. Now trucks, not camels, cross the desert on paved roads. Droughts have decreased grazing lands. Governments encourage nomads to settle down. They have also made it more difficult for nomads from other countries to cross their borders.

SECTION 2 ASSESSMENT

Terms & Names
1. Explain the significance of: (a) OPEC (b) primary product (c) secondary product (d) petrochemical (e) *haj* (f) Ramadan

Using Graphics
2. Use a chart like this one to list major products in Southwest Asia and North Africa.

Primary Products	Secondary Products

Main Ideas
3. (a) How are oil resources important to Southwest Asia and North Africa?
   (b) How does Islam affect the culture of the region?
   (c) What is the status of women in most Islamic countries?

Critical Thinking
4. **Making Inferences**
   Why do you think some people in Southwest Asia and North Africa welcome westernization while others resist it?

   Think About
   ◆ modern technology
   ◆ role of religion
   ◆ standard of living

ACTIVITY -OPTION- Make a **poster** showing crude oil and the products made from it. Label them as primary or secondary products.

North Africa and Southwest Asia Today

Interdisciplinary Challenge

Explain the Pyramids of Ancient Egypt

SUNSHINE STATE STANDARDS
Key Standard SS.A.2.3.7 The student knows significant achievements in art and architecture in various urban areas and communities to the time of the Renaissance (e.g., the Hanging Gardens of Babylon, pyramids in Egypt, temples in ancient Greece, bridges and aqueducts in ancient Rome, changes in European art and architecture between the Middle Ages and the High Renaissance).
FCAT LA.A.2.3.1 Reading: Identify Main Idea, Facts, and Details

You are a tour guide and Egyptologist—an expert on ancient Egypt. Your specialty is the age of pyramid building, about 4,700 to 4,200 years ago (c. 2686–2160 B.C.). Pyramids, large and small, were built as tombs for the pharaohs of the Old Kingdom and members of their families. The most famous are the three pyramids at Giza, near Cairo, where you work. In the course of your work, tourists come to you with questions about the pyramids. You want to find interesting ways to share your knowledge with them.

COOPERATIVE LEARNING On these pages are challenges you will meet while dealing with visitors to the pyramids. Working with a small group, choose one challenge to solve. Divide the work among group members. Look for helpful information in the Data File. Keep in mind that you will present your solution to the class.

MATH CHALLENGE

"... the Great Pyramid of Khufu was the world's tallest structure."

The three pyramids at Giza were built for Khufu, his son Khafre, and his grandson Menkure. For more than 4,300 years, the Great Pyramid of Khufu was the world's tallest structure. Khafre's pyramid is almost as big. How can you explain these huge structures to your visitors? Choose one of these options. Look in the Data File for information.

ACTIVITIES
1. Make an accurate drawing of the Great Pyramid of Khufu on graph paper, using the measurements given. Use blocks or clay to build a scale model.
2. How does the present height of the Great Pyramid compare with its original height? How does its height compare with the heights of the pyramids of Khafre and Menkure? Express your answers as percentages.

ARTS CHALLENGE

". . . what [is it] like to explore the interior of a pyramid?"

Most of what we know about ancient Egypt comes from hieroglyphics and artifacts found in tombs—jewelry, statues, cosmetics, mummies. Today, most pyramids are closed to outsiders. How can you give visitors an idea of what it is like to explore the interior of a pyramid? How can they have the same experience that an archaeologist has?

ACTIVITIES

1. Draw the interior of a tomb, including objects such as statues, jewelry, and mummies.
2. Sketch a series of scenes you would use in making a video about an archaeologist exploring the interior of a pyramid.

Activity Wrap-Up

As a group, review your solution to the challenge you selected. Then present your solution to the class.

DATA FILE

THE PYRAMIDS OF EGYPT

- The pyramids at Giza were one of the **Seven Wonders of the Ancient World.** The oldest of all the wonders, they are the only ones that still stand today.
- Builders used mainly **limestone** and **granite blocks.** Originally, the pyramids were faced with smooth, white limestone. Vandals have stripped off most of this surface stone.
- Building the **Great Pyramid** took about 20 years. Ancient historians said that it took 100,000 workers. Archaeologists today, however, think that there were **20,000 to 30,000 workers.** The workers were probably not slaves, but farmers and villagers who worked in exchange for food and the chance to serve their god-king.

GREAT PYRAMID OF KHUFU

- Oldest and largest of pyramids at Giza, built about **4,500 years ago.**
- Square base: length of each side about **756 feet.**
- Original height: **481 feet;** now about 451 feet.
- Covers about **13 acres**—about seven city blocks.
- Contains about **2.3 million blocks** of stone, each weighing about 2.5 tons.

PYRAMID OF KHAFRE

- Square base: length of each side about **708 feet.**
- Original height: **471 feet.**
- Covers about **11.5 acres.**

PYRAMID OF MENKURE

- Square base: length of each side about **356.5 feet.**
- Original height: **218 feet.**
- Covers about **2.9 acres.**

To learn more about the pyramids, go to

RESEARCH LINKS
CLASSZONE.COM

SECTION 3
Egypt Today

TERMS & NAMES
King Farouk
Gamal Abdel Nasser
Aswan High Dam
tradeoff
Anwar Sadat
Muslim Brotherhood
fellahin

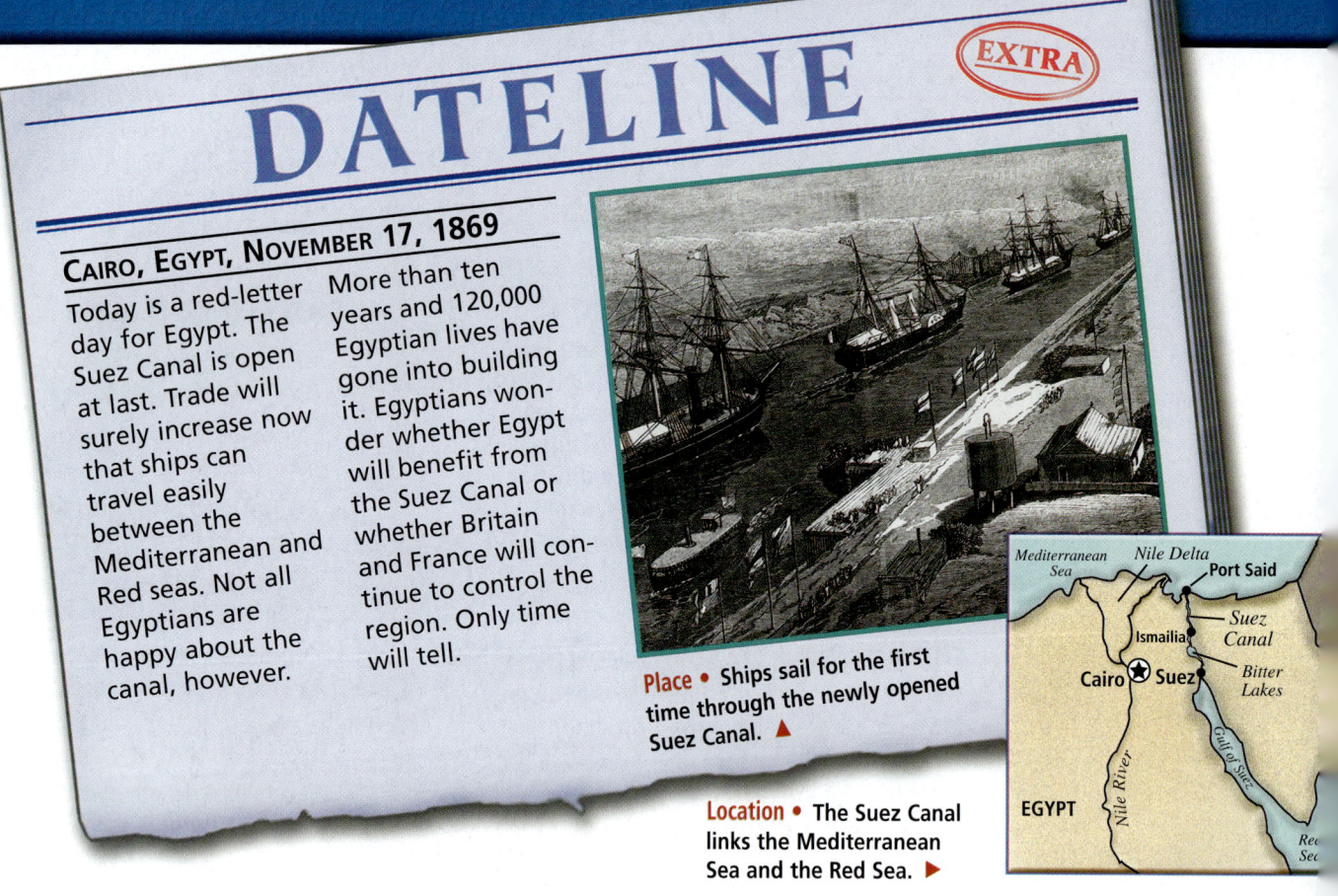

MAIN IDEA
Egypt's modernization has brought progress and problems.

WHY IT MATTERS NOW
Egypt often sets the pace in the region for social and political change.

DATELINE EXTRA

CAIRO, EGYPT, NOVEMBER 17, 1869

Today is a red-letter day for Egypt. The Suez Canal is open at last. Trade will surely increase now that ships can travel easily between the Mediterranean and Red seas. Not all Egyptians are happy about the canal, however. More than ten years and 120,000 Egyptian lives have gone into building it. Egyptians wonder whether Egypt will benefit from the Suez Canal or whether Britain and France will continue to control the region. Only time will tell.

Place • Ships sail for the first time through the newly opened Suez Canal. ▲

Location • The Suez Canal links the Mediterranean Sea and the Red Sea. ▶

SUNSHINE STATE STANDARDS
Key Standard SS.B.2.3.2 The student knows the human and physical characteristics of different places in the world and how these characteristics change over time.
Other Standards SS.B.2.3.4, B.2.3.7
FCAT LA.A.2.3.1
Reading: Identify Main Idea, Facts, and Details

The Suez Canal

The Suez Canal was the grand project of Egyptian ruler Ismail Pasha (ihs·MAH·eel PAH·shuh). He wanted it built to make Egypt the equal of Western nations. But the cost of the canal and other expensive projects drove Egypt into bankruptcy. Ismail had to sell Egypt's shares in the Suez Canal Company to the British government. From then until 1956, Great Britain had some control over Egypt.

TAKING NOTES
Use your chart to take notes about North Africa and Southwest Asia.

Problems	Solutions	Resulting Problems
History of foreign influence		
Changes in world markets		

256 CHAPTER 9

From Ancient to Modern Times

Great Britain was not the first foreign power to rule Egypt after the time of the pharaohs. For 2,500 years, Egypt was under foreign influence. It was conquered in turn by Persians, Macedonians, and Romans. Arab Muslims from the Arabian peninsula invaded in A.D. 639–642. A military group called the Mamelukes (MAM·uh·LOOKS) seized control in about 1250 and ruled until Ottoman troops invaded in 1517. From the late 1700s to the early 1900s, France and then Great Britain controlled much of Egypt. Britain gave up absolute control in 1922, and Egypt became a monarchy, a country ruled at first by King Fuad (FOO·ahd), and after 1936 by his son, **King Farouk** (fuh·ROOK). Foreign policy, defense, and communications, however, remained under British control.

Place • Gamal Abdel Nasser was President of Egypt for 16 years. ▼

Nasser Takes Over An Egyptian army officer, **Gamal Abdel Nasser,** resented the weakness of his government and the strong British influence on his country. In 1952, he and other officers overthrew King Farouk. The next year Egypt became a republic. Nasser was Egypt's leader from 1954 to 1970.

Controlling the Nile Nasser's most significant accomplishment was the construction of the **Aswan High Dam,** begun in 1956, to control the flooding of the Nile River. The dam gives Egyptian farmers a more dependable source of water for their crops and allows them to grow crops year round. It also gives Egypt electrical power and has made fishing an important industry.

Human-Environment Interaction • The Aswan High Dam, opened in 1971, cost about $1 billion to build. ▼

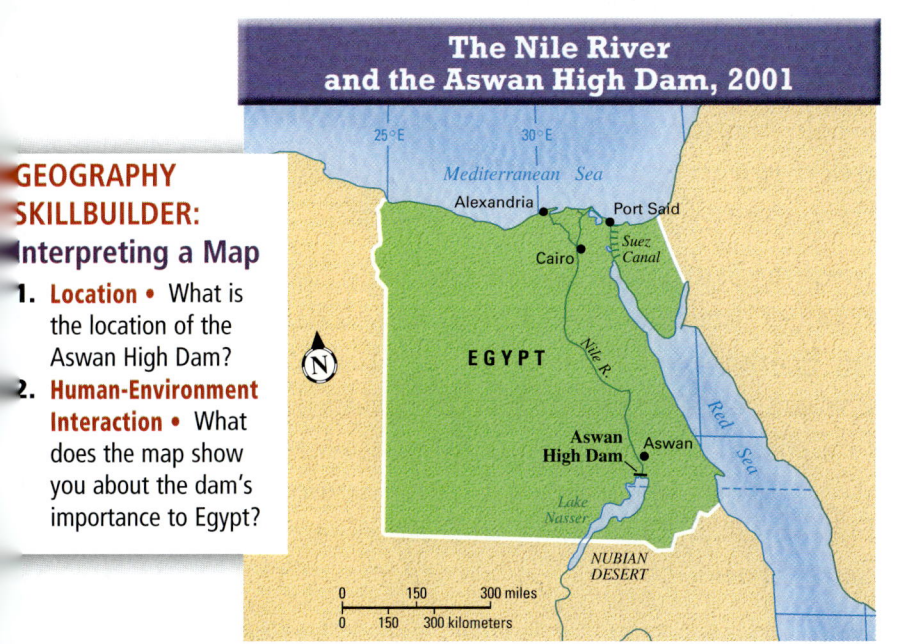

The Nile River and the Aswan High Dam, 2001

GEOGRAPHY SKILLBUILDER: Interpreting a Map
1. **Location** • What is the location of the Aswan High Dam?
2. **Human-Environment Interaction** • What does the map show you about the dam's importance to Egypt?

North Africa and Southwest Asia Today

Place • Egyptian women campaigned for the vote in Cairo in the 1920s. ▲

Biography

Anwar Sadat, 1918–1981
Anwar Sadat (below, left) took part in the 1952 seizure of the government of King Farouk. When President Nasser died in 1970, Vice President Sadat was elected President.

Sadat led Egypt to war with Israel in 1973. A few years later, however, he became the first Arab leader to seek peace between the two countries. He shared the 1978 Nobel Peace Prize with Israeli Prime Minister Menachem Begin (right, below). In 1979, Israel and Egypt signed a peace treaty. Muslim extremists objected to Sadat's peace treaty with Israel and his close ties with the United States. On October 6, 1981, extremists assassinated him.

Because of the dam, however, the river no longer deposits the rich soil from the south as it did during yearly flooding. Instead, over 100 million tons of earth settle behind the dam each year. Farmers now have to use artificial fertilizers which pollute the water. The Aswan High Dam is an example of a tradeoff. A **tradeoff** is an exchange of one benefit for another.

Rights for Women Women were active in the movement for Egyptian independence in the years from 1919 to 1922, yet were denied the vote. Although they gradually acquired the right to higher education, women were still subject to the Muslim Personal Status Law, which gave men far more rights in marriage. Women continued to demand their rights. In 1956, in Nasser's new government, they gained the right to vote and to run for office. A revised Muslim Personal Status Law in 1979 somewhat improved women's rights within the family. In 2000, Egypt passed a law making it easier for women to get a divorce.

A Search for Peace Egypt actively opposed Israel for many years. However, in 1979, led by President **Anwar Sadat**, Egypt became the first Arab state to sign a peace treaty with Israel. Egypt also led the region in opposing Iraq's 1990 invasion of Kuwait. Egypt has tried to settle arguments between Iraq and the United Nations. In the fall of 2000, President Hosni Mubarak met with other regional leaders to talk about how to end Israeli-Palestinian violence.

The Muslim Brotherhood Not everyone in Egypt values freedom and compromise. The **Muslim Brotherhood** is an extremist Muslim group which insists that Egypt be governed solely by Islamic law. The Brotherhood claims the Egyptian government is being untrue to the principles of Islam by working with Israel and the United States.

Population Distribution in Egypt, 1998

Persons per sq. mi.	Persons per sq. km
260–520	100–200
130–259	50–99
25–129	10–49
1–24	1–9
0	0

Vegetation in Egypt, 1998

- Desert
- Tropical desert shrub
- Swamp grass
- Salt flats

GEOGRAPHY SKILLBUILDER: Interpreting a Map

1. **Place** • What do you notice about the Nile River on each map?
2. **Human-Environment Interaction** • What relationship do you notice between population and vegetation?

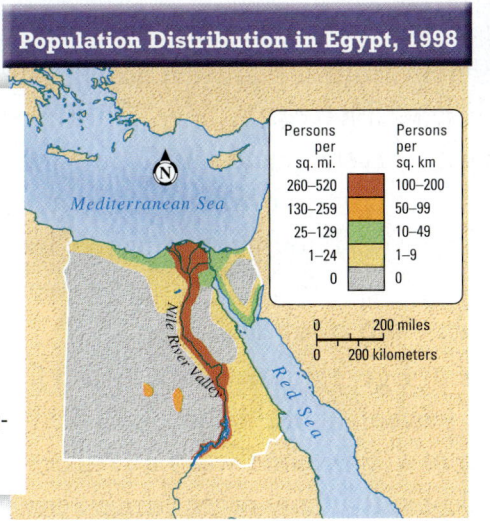

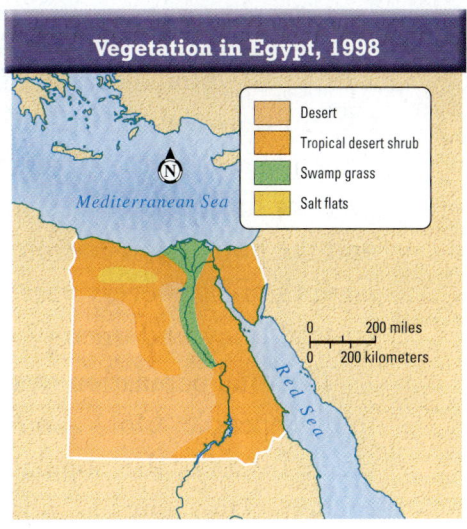

The Land and the People

Most of Egypt consists of desert lands where no one can live. Just about all of Egypt's 70 million people live in a narrow strip of land along either side of the Nile or in a few desert oases. Some live in big cities. Others farm the fields made fertile by the Nile.

Egyptian Cotton Cotton is a major primary product and agricultural export. Cotton-growing developed in Egypt during the 1860s when the Civil War in the United States disrupted cotton exports from southern states. Egypt produces some of the finest cotton in the world. It has also developed a textile industry that manufactures cotton yarns and cotton fabrics as secondary products.

Village Life More than half the population of Egypt lives in villages. Most villagers are **fellahin** (FEHL·uh·HEEN), or peasant farmers. The fellahin are some of the poorest Egyptians. Most rent land or work in their own fields. Many do not know how to read or write. Many fellahin children do not go to school.

Fellahin wear traditional Arab clothing. Men wear pants and loose-fitting, hooded gowns. Women wear long, flowing gowns. Like poor people in the cities, they eat a simple diet of bread and beans, which leads to malnutrition. Infectious diseases, such as tuberculosis, also afflict the fellahin. Only a lucky few are ever treated by doctors.

Reading Social Studies

A. **Identifying Problems** What are the main problems the fellahin face?

Human-Environment Interaction • These fellahin raise sheep. ▼

Africa's Largest City

Life in Egyptian cities is different from life in rural areas. Cairo (KY·roh) is the capital of Egypt. The city's older inhabitants remember when the city had gardens, trees, and birds. Now those gardens have been paved over. The city is crowded and polluted, and the population continues to grow. Thousands of people leave Egypt's villages every year and come to Cairo looking for work. Instead, they find unemployment and overcrowding.

The total population of ancient Egypt was never more than four million people. Only about 5 percent of the population lived in cities. In 2000, the population of Cairo alone was more than 12 million. Cairo now has more people than any other African city.

Life in Cairo Cairo has both historic and modern sections. Many poor people live in the older sections. Some poor Cairenes live in cemeteries or on roofs. Others live in poorly built apartment buildings. Many have no steady work. Some are unskilled workers in factories. Others work in the city's small shops that sell jewelry and tourist souvenirs. Cairo's newer areas are along the west bank of the Nile. Most well-educated Cairenes live near the government buildings, foreign embassies, hotels, museums, and universities located there. They are doctors, lawyers, teachers, factory managers, and government officials.

Reading Social Studies

B. Analyzing Causes What is the main reason for Cairo's increase in population?

The WORLD'S HERITAGE

The Pyramids and the Great Sphinx
The current residents of Cairo, Egypt, live in the shadows of some of the ancient world's most magnificent architecture—the pyramids and the Great Sphinx.

Egyptians built the pyramids as tombs for their kings more than 4,000 years ago. Near the pyramids, they also carved an enormous sphinx—a mythological creature with a lion's body and human head—out of natural rock. The head of the Great Sphinx is fashioned to look like King Khafre (c. 2575–c. 2465 B.C.).

Place • Cairo is a huge city crowded with buildings, cars, and millions of people. ▶

Place • These girls live in Cairo within sight of the Sphinx and pyramids of ancient Egypt. ▼

The Region's Cultural Leader

Egypt has been the Arab world's cultural leader for over a century. It has led the region in education. In 1829, it opened the first modern school for girls in the Arab world. In the 1950s, it became the first Arab country to require that all children attend elementary school. It has also had a strong feminist movement for many years. Arabs throughout the region get much of their information and entertainment from Egyptian television, radio, movies, newspapers, and magazines.

SECTION 3 ASSESSMENT

Terms & Names

1. Explain the significance of:
   - (a) King Farouk
   - (b) Gamal Abdel Nasser
   - (c) Aswan High Dam
   - (d) tradeoff
   - (e) Anwar Sadat
   - (f) Muslim Brotherhood
   - (g) fellahin

Using Graphics

2. Use a time line like this one to write the dates when control of Egypt changed hands.

   639–642 ——————————— 1952

Main Ideas

3. (a) What were Nasser's major achievements?
   (b) How have Egyptian women's rights improved over the last century?
   (c) What has Egypt done to improve the search for peace in the region?

Critical Thinking

4. **Evaluating Decisions**

   Do you think the building of the Aswan Dam was a worthwhile tradeoff?

   Think About
   - its value to farmers
   - the consequences of pollution

ACTIVITY -OPTION-

Write a **letter** telling about daily life as a young person in Cairo or in a farming village along the Nile.

Literature Connections

Thread by Thread

OVER THE PAST 60 YEARS, wars in Southwest Asia have left a bitter legacy of anger, frustration, and despair. Despite continuing conflicts, however, many people in the region share a hope for peace. The author of this poem, Bracha Serri, believes that one day peace will be achieved.

> Thread by thread
> knot by knot
> like colonies of ants
> we weave a bridge
>
> Thread by thread
> piece by piece
> knitting embroidering
> sewing decorating
> thread by thread
> we weave
> the map of conciliation.[1]

1. Friendship.

Rachel's is white
Yemima's purple
Amal's is green
Salima's rose-colored
thread by thread
we stitch together
torn hearts
bind the map of conciliation.

I pray for the life of Ami and Nitsi
you pray for Ilan, Shoshi and Itsik
and she prays
for Jehan, Asheraf and Fahed
with the same tear.
Word and another word
prayer and another prayer
and our heart is one
we embroider in hope
with the sisterhood of workers
a map of love
to tear down the borders . . .

Reading THE LITERATURE

What technique does the poet use to let the reader know that the "weavers" are people from different countries or ethnic backgrounds? Why is that important?

Thinking About THE LITERATURE

Why do you think this poem is called "Thread by Thread"? What do the threads represent? Who are the weavers and what are they making?

Writing About THE LITERATURE

Describe how you think the finished cloth would look. What size and shape would it be? What colors would it have in it? Where would it be placed or displayed?

About the Author

Bracha Serri, born in Yemen, grew up speaking Arabic. Later, her family moved to Israel. Serri has written, "I want my childhood spoken language, Arabic, to come together with my university education in linguistics. . . . I feel I have written my poems for women who do not have a voice, who can't speak up for themselves."

Further Reading *The Space Between Our Footsteps,* edited by Naomi Shihab Nye, contains poems by more than 100 poets and artists from 19 Southwest Asian countries.

SUNSHINE STATE STANDARDS
Key Standard SS.A.3.3.1
The student understands ways in which cultural characteristics have been transmitted from one society to another (e.g., through art, architecture, language, other artifacts, traditions, beliefs, values, and behaviors).
FCAT LA.E.2.3.1 Literature: Understand Character and Plot Development

Section 4: Israel Today

TERMS & NAMES
Zionism
kibbutz
Law of Return
Orthodox Jews
Rosh Hashanah
Yom Kippur
secular

MAIN IDEA
Israel's current problems are rooted in a long and complicated history.

WHY IT MATTERS NOW
Peace in the region depends on peace between Israelis and Palestinians.

DATELINE

TEL AVIV, PALESTINE, JULY 14, 1921— Newcomers from America arrived here today after a long and difficult trip. All have been active in the movement to establish a Jewish homeland in Palestine. Goldie Mabovitch and her husband, Morris Myerson, born in Russia, hope to join a kibbutz. Riots in the port city of Jaffa delayed their arrival. Palestinian Arabs are protesting the immigration of Jews from America, Russia, and other countries who plan to settle in the land the Arabs consider their own.

Movement • Jewish immigrants from Europe arrive in Palestine. Some took Hebrew names; for example, Goldie Mabovitch became Golda Meir. ▲

From Zionism to a Modern State

After A.D. 70, when the Romans destroyed the Temple in Jerusalem, Jews no longer had a country of their own. They lived scattered around the world, but still considered Palestine their homeland. **Zionism** was a Jewish movement that encouraged Jews to return to that homeland, which many called Zion. In the late 1800s, Jews began immigrating there and establishing colonies.

TAKING NOTES
Use your chart to take notes about North Africa and Southwest Asia.

Problems	Solutions	Resulting Problems
History of foreign influence		
Changes in world markets		

SUNSHINE STATE STANDARDS
Key Standard SS.A.3.3.3 The student knows how physical and human geographic factors have influenced major historical events and movements.
Other Standards SS.A.3.3.5, B.1.3.4, B.2.3.1
FCAT LA.A.2.3.1 Reading: Identify Main Idea, Facts, and Details

Reading Social Studies

A. Analyzing Motives What were the Jewish immigrants' main reasons for forming kibbutzim?

Life on a Kibbutz Many new arrivals came from Eastern Europe, where Jews were often denied the right to be landowners. Seizing the chance to own land, even in the desert, the newcomers formed communities called kibbutzim. A **kibbutz** (kih·BUTS; *kibbutzim* is the plural) is a farming village whose members own everything in common. Members share labor, income, and expenses. The people of the kibbutzim saw themselves as brave, hard-working pioneers.

> **A VOICE FROM ISRAEL**
>
> The kibbutz would break new ground, literally; it would make the parched earth bloom and beat back the attacks of marauders who sought to destroy our pioneering lives.
>
> *David Ben Gurion*

Kibbutzim Today About 270 kibbutzim still exist in Israel today. Some manufacture and sell products or welcome tourists. Others are still farming communities. Israel produces nearly all of its food. To improve the dry soil, Israelis practice drip irrigation. Tubes in the ground deliver the exact amount of water each plant needs.

The People of Israel

Israel was established in 1948 as a Jewish state. Judaism is the state religion. Hebrew is the official language. The second official language is Arabic. In Jewish and Arab schools in Israel, English is a required language. Of its six million inhabitants, over 80 percent are Jews. The Declaration of the Establishment promised that Israel would treat all its inhabitants equally. Some Israelis feel their country has not always lived up to that promise.

Place • A modern kibbutz sprawls over a desert landscape. ▲

Palestinian Arabs About 20 percent of the people in Israel are Palestinian Arabs. Arab Israelis carry Israeli passports and vote, but they do not have to serve in the Israel Defense Forces (IDF). More than 90 percent of Arab Israelis are Sunni Muslim. In 2003, Arab Israelis were elected to 8 of the 120 seats in the Knesset, the Israeli parliament. This was down from 11 seats in 1996. Most Arab Israelis do not have as high a standard of living as other groups in Israel. In 2000, the government announced a billion-dollar program to improve schools, housing, and job opportunities for Arab Israelis.

Some Palestinians are refugees from Israel who fled to the Gaza Strip and the West Bank after the 1948 Arab-Israeli War. (See the map on page 245.) Israel occupies these territories. Constant tension between Arabs and Israelis often leads to violence.

Women in Israel Even before Israel was a state, its women were encouraged to work outside the home. To free mothers from child-care duties, children on kibbutzim lived and slept in separate children's houses and visited their parents during evenings and weekends. An American-educated woman, Golda Meir (MY•uhr), was the prime minister of Israel from 1969 to 1974.

Culture • Israeli women must serve in the military for two years; men must serve for three. ▲

Reading Social Studies
B. Making Inferences Why might Jews in other countries want to emigrate to Israel?

The Law of Return

Since 1948, Israel has taken in nearly 3 million Jewish immigrants. The 1950 **Law of Return** states that Jews anywhere in the world can immigrate to Israel and become citizens.

Recent Immigrants In 1987, the Soviet Union allowed Jews within its borders to leave. In May 2000, Israel welcomed its millionth immigrant from the former Soviet Union. Many Soviet immigrants are highly skilled.

Israeli society is increasingly diverse. Since the 1980s, about 20,000 Ethiopians of Jewish origin have settled in Israel. Another 20,000 Ethiopian Jews were expected to move to Israel in 2003. Immigrants from Eastern Europe and North Africa have also arrived in the country. Many immigrant groups

Connections to Citizenship

Neve Shalom/Wahat al-Salem The cooperative community of Neve Shalom/Wahat al-Salem was established in 1972 by Jews and Palestinian Arabs of Israeli citizenship. The village occupies 100 acres of land halfway between Jerusalem and Tel Aviv. Described as an "oasis of peace," Neve Shalom/Wahat al-Salem is not connected with any political party. It is democratically governed and owned by its members. Through its School for Peace, the Neve Shalom/Wahat al-Salem community sponsors dialogue between Arabs and Jews in high schools and universities. It also conducts training courses in conflict management.

publish newspapers in their native languages. New arrivals from North Africa and other countries in the Middle East have brought skills such as pottery making and weaving to enrich Israeli society.

Religion in Israel Today

Only about one in four of Israel's Jews strictly follows Jewish law. They are called **Orthodox Jews.** These Jews believe that Jewish law should help form government policy. Orthodox rabbis have official control over marriage, divorce, and burial. They also limit what Israeli Jews can do on the Sabbath and holidays. **Rosh Hashanah** (RAWSH huh•SHAW•nuh) is the Jewish New Year. **Yom Kippur** (YAWM KIHP•uhr) is the Day of Atonement, a day for fasting and reflecting on one's sins. It is the holiest day in the Jewish year. No government employee can work on these Jewish High Holy Days. No newspapers appear on either holiday. Most of Israel's Jews are **secular,** meaning that religious practices play a less important role in their lives. They are more interested in living a modern way of life. Many resent Orthodox control of daily life.

Movement • Jewish children from Ethiopia make a new home in Israel. ▲

SECTION 4 ASSESSMENT

Terms & Names
1. Explain the significance of:
   (a) Zionism   (b) kibbutz   (c) Law of Return   (d) Orthodox Jews
   (e) Rosh Hashanah   (f) Yom Kippur   (g) secular

Using Graphics

2. Use a cause-and-effect chart like this one to write the reasons for Jewish immigration to Palestine.

   Causes → Effect: Jewish immigration to Palestine

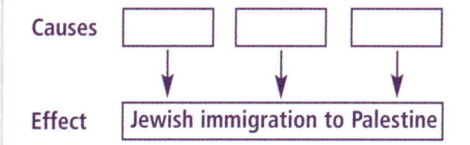

Main Ideas

3. (a) Why did early Jewish settlers in Israel establish kibbutzim?
   (b) What have immigrants contributed to Israeli society?
   (c) What are the major differences between Orthodox and secular Jews?

Critical Thinking

4. **Forming and Supporting Opinions**

   In what ways is Israeli society diverse?

   Think About
   - recent immigrants
   - non-Jewish citizens
   - variety of languages

ACTIVITY -OPTION- Write an **interview** you might have with a new immigrant to Israel. Include information on where the immigrant comes from, the date and method of arrival, reasons for coming, and reactions to a new land.

Linking Past and Present

The Legacy of North Africa and Southwest Asia

SUNSHINE STATE STANDARDS
Key Standard SS.A.2.3.2 The student knows how major historical developments have had an impact on the development of civilizations.
FCAT LA.A.2.3.1 Reading: Identify Main Idea, Facts, and Details

Religion

Three major religions—Judaism, Christianity, and Islam—began in Southwest Asia. Judaism is based on the laws Moses received from God, which are written in the Torah. Christianity is based on the teachings of Jesus, which appear in the New Testament. Islam is based on the teachings of the prophet Muhammad and the sacred text called the Qur'an. The teachings and beliefs of Judaism, Christianity, and Islam spread east and south through Asia, north and west to Europe, south through Africa, and west to the Americas. All three religions share a belief in one God and encourage people to live a life of tolerance and peace.

Writing

About 5,500 years ago, Mesopotamians began to use what is considered the first developed system of writing. They made marks that represented words on wet clay tablets, some of which survive today. Two thousand years later, the Egyptians developed a sophisticated writing system, known as hieroglyphics, in which pictures were used to represent sounds and words. Today, people continue to communicate, not only by writing with pen and paper but also by using electronic mail.

Cosmetics

Archaeologists believe that cosmetics were used as early as 4000 B.C. Ancient Egyptians used plants and powdered minerals to make cosmetics. During and after the Renaissance, the use of cosmetics flourished in Europe, as both men and women made up their faces. Italy and France became cosmetic-manufacturing centers. By the 1900s, people of all social classes were using cosmetics. Since the 1930s, the cosmetic industry has developed into a big business.

268 UNIT 3

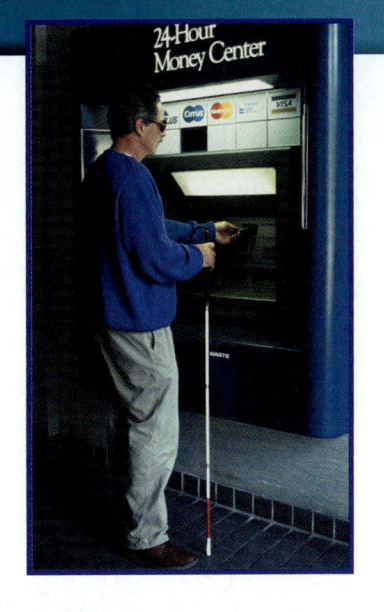

Banking

Almost 5,500 years ago, before the invention of coins or paper money, a form of banking existed in ancient Mesopotamia. In Italy in the 1200s, banking took place on benches in the street. In fact, the word *bank* comes from the Italian word *banco,* which means "bench." By the 1600s, customers of banks in England were using written drafts, or checks, to make payments. Modern banking is electronic. Though some people use written checks, many take advantage of automated teller machines and telephone-banking systems to meet their banking needs.

Find Out More About It!
Study the text and photos on these pages to learn about inventions, creations, and contributions that have come from North Africa and Southwest Asia. Then choose the item that interests you the most and, in a short essay, describe how your life would be different if it did not exist.

RESEARCH LINKS
CLASSZONE.COM

Lever

A lever is a rod or bar that pivots on a fulcrum, acting like a seesaw to help people perform work. Early people used levers to move and lift heavy rocks. In 1500 B.C., Egyptians used the shadoof—a lever with weights on one end and a bucket on the other—to lift water from rivers and canals into their fields. They also developed a balance scale based on the lever. Balance scales and wheelbarrows are examples of levers we use today.

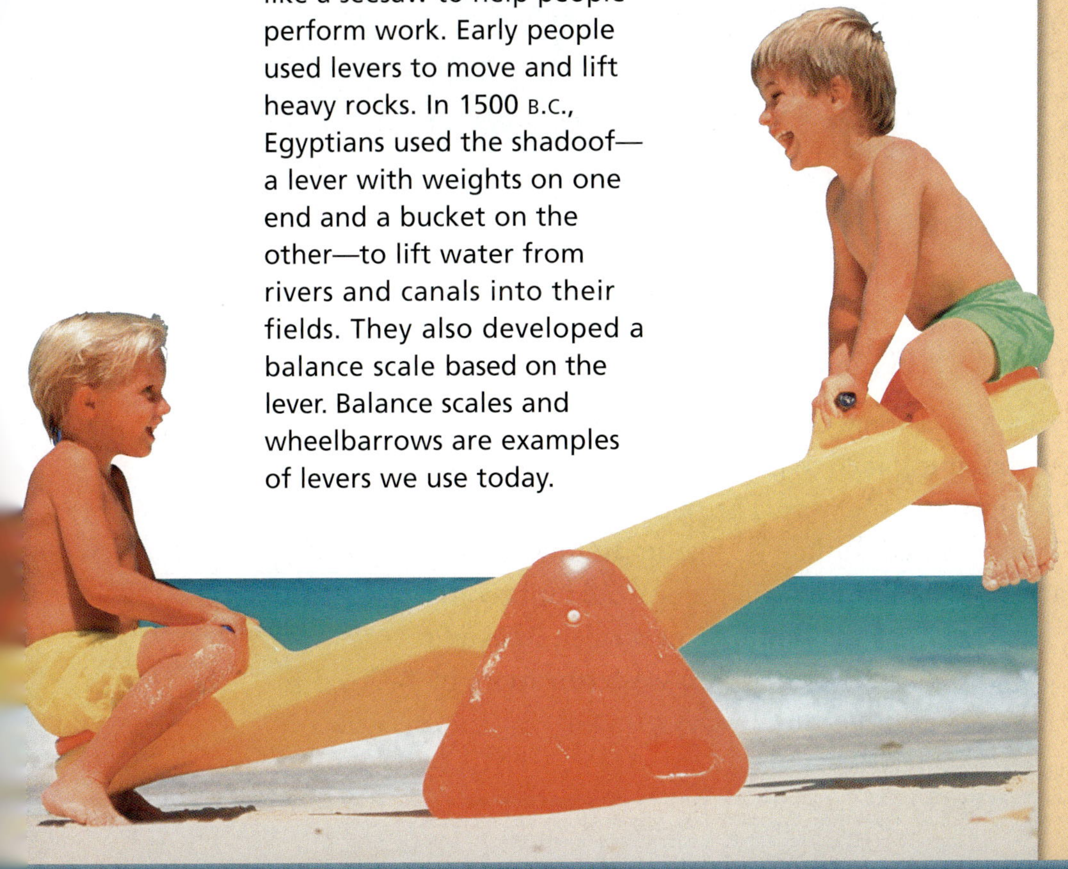

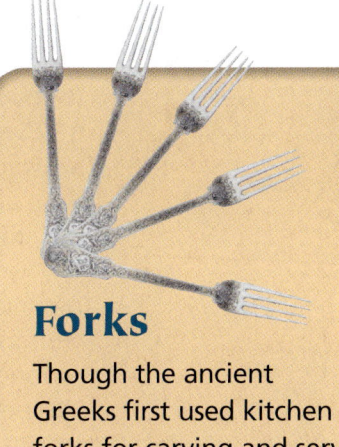

Forks

Though the ancient Greeks first used kitchen forks for carving and serving meat, it was not until the 800s that nobles in Southwest Asia used forks for dining. For the next 900 years, wealthy people continued to use forks for eating. Because the common people believed forks were unnecessary and even odd, they continued to use their hands, knives, and spoons for eating. Forks were not commonly used in the West until the 1800s.

North Africa and Southwest Asia

SECTION 5
Turkey Today

TERMS & NAMES
Mustafa Kemal
Grand National Assembly
Atatürk
Tansu Ciller

MAIN IDEA
Turkey's culture blends modern European and traditional Islamic ways.

WHY IT MATTERS NOW
Turkey is an important military ally and trade partner of the United States and Europe.

DATELINE

ANKARA, TURKEY, NOVEMBER 25, 1925—No more fez. Turkish leader Mustafa Kemal has declared that Turkish men are no longer allowed to wear the fez, their traditional head covering.

According to the new Hat Law, hats are now the acceptable head covering for men. Muslim women are being strongly encouraged to give up the veil. These changes are in keeping with Kemal's drive to westernize Turkey. Many Turks are happy to see Turkey become more like Europe. Others are unhappy with this move away from the traditional Islamic way of life.

Culture • Turkish men are getting used to wearing hats. ▲

Between Two Worlds

If you look at Turkey on the map on page 273, you will see that it is joined to Southwest Asia on the east and to Europe on the west. The question after World War I was: Would Turkey be like its Islamic neighbors and hold on to its traditions, or would it become more like the West? Its powerful new ruler, **Mustafa Kemal** (kuh·MAHL), believed in westernization, by force if necessary.

TAKING NOTES
Use your chart to take notes about North Africa and Southwest Asia.

Problems	Solutions	Resulting Problems
History of foreign influence		
Changes in world markets		

SUNSHINE STATE STANDARDS
Key Standard SS.A.3.3.5 The student understands the differences between institutions of Eastern and Western civilizations (e.g., differences in governments, social traditions and customs, economic systems and religious institutions).
Other Standards SS.A.3.3.4, B.1.3.3
FCAT LA.A.2.3.1 Reading: Identify Main Idea, Facts, and Details

Place • Mustafa Kemal Atatürk was the founder and first president of the Republic of Turkey (1923–38). ▲

Reading Social Studies

Forming and Supporting Opinions Which of Mustafa Kemal's changes do you think had the greatest effect on Turkish life?

A Powerful Ruler

Mustafa Kemal was the founder of modern Turkey. He had been a Turkish officer and war hero for the Ottoman forces during World War I. The Ottomans had continued to rule Turkey even after the empire became weak. Turkey fought on the losing side during the war, which weakened it even more. In 1920, Great Britain occupied Turkey.

Mustafa Kemal Becomes Atatürk Kemal opposed Britain's action. He organized Turkey's first **Grand National Assembly,** or legislature. The assembly elected Kemal president. At his suggestion, the assembly officially adopted the name Turkey, the land of the Turkish people. In 1923, Kemal declared Turkey a republic and got rid of the old Islamic government the following year.

While Kemal was in the Ottoman army, he spent time in European cities. He admired the way of life he saw there. He believed adopting modern, "Western" ways and ideas would benefit Turkey. Over the next nine years, Kemal introduced his changes. The Western alphabet replaced the Arabic alphabet. The Western calendar replaced the Islamic calendar.

Before 1934, many Turks used only first names. In 1934, a new law required the use of last names. The National Assembly gave Kemal the name **Atatürk,** which means "Father of Turks."

Changes Brought by Modernization

For nearly 1,000 years, Islamic law had shaped Turkish life. Atatürk, however, believed in secular government. He closed all institutions that had been founded on Islamic law. He replaced religious schools with secular schools. Since people were used to having Islam play a major role in all aspects of their lives, many protested Atatürk's reforms.

Women in Turkey Turkish women benefited from Atatürk's reforms. He made it easier for women to divorce their husbands. Marriages could no longer be arranged by a woman's parents unless she agreed. Men were no longer able to have more than one wife at the same time.

Women could now also vote and run for office. In the mid-1930s, women were elected to the national parliament. The world's first woman supreme court justice was a Turk. For several years during the 1990s, a woman named **Tansu Ciller** was Turkey's prime minister.

Movement • In 1993, Prime Minister Tansu Ciller traveled from Turkey to the United States where she met with President Bill Clinton. ▼

Rights and Freedoms Today

Turkey adopted its most recent constitution in 1982. The Turkish Constitution promises freedom of religion, freedom of speech, freedom of the press, and other rights. The government, however, does not always live up to these promises. It sometimes limits freedoms. Turkish journalists can be arrested for writing articles against the government. The government also bans some publications.

The Kurds The Kurds are a group of people who live in the mountainous regions of southeastern Turkey, Iraq, Iran, and Syria. They have been fighting for their own state since 1984. The Turkish government has made suspected Kurd fighters leave their homes. It limits the right to teach Kurdish in schools. It also limits the use of Kurdish in television and radio programs.

International Alliances

Turkey and the United States are both members of the North Atlantic Treaty Organization (NATO). This alliance was formed in 1949 to keep the Soviet Union and its allies from attacking non-Communist countries in Western Europe. Turkey joined the alliance in 1952. When the Soviet Union fell apart in 1991, some NATO members felt the alliance was no longer necessary. Turkey disagreed because NATO membership helps protect its borders. Membership also gives Turkey a say in major decisions other members make.

Connections to Literature

Looking for Troy Two of the world's best-known epic poems tell about a long-ago war in the eastern Mediterranean. In the *Iliad*, Greeks besiege the city of Troy. Greek soldiers hide inside a giant wooden horse to trick the Trojans into opening the gates of the city. The photo at right shows a model of the Trojan Horse. In the *Odyssey*, the hero, Odysseus, has many adventures on his way home from the same war. Both poems may have been composed by the Greek poet Homer sometime around 800 B.C.

While many people thought the Trojan War was just a legend, Heinrich Schliemann, a German archaeologist, dreamed of finding the real Troy. In the 1870s, he began to dig at a site in northwestern Turkey. He found ruins of palaces and golden artifacts. In fact, Schliemann had found Troy—but not the city of the poems. Over centuries, people had built new cities on the ruins of older ones. Archaeologists think that the seventh city down on the site is the Troy of the *Iliad*. It was destroyed about 1250 B.C.

Joining the European Union Most of Turkey's trade is with Western Europe. In 1987, Turkey applied to join the European Union (EU). The EU was reluctant to accept Turkey, partly because of the size of its population. There are not enough jobs in Turkey for all the people who want them. Two million Turks have gone to Germany to work. Millions more work in other European countries. Workers from EU countries are allowed to move freely within the region. European countries worried that membership in the EU would let more Turkish workers into their countries than they could handle.

Region •
The city of Istanbul is partly in Europe and partly in Asia. ▲

SECTION 5 ASSESSMENT

Terms & Names
1. Explain the significance of:
   (a) Mustafa Kemal
   (b) Grand National Assembly
   (c) Atatürk
   (d) Tansu Ciller

Using Graphics
2. Use a chart like this one to list changes made by Mustafa Kemal.

Old Ways	New Ways
1.	
2.	
3.	
4.	
5.	

Main Ideas
3. (a) How does Turkey limit the rights of the Kurds?
   (b) How did Atatürk's reforms benefit women?
   (c) Why does Turkey value its membership in NATO?

Critical Thinking
4. **Analyzing Issues**
   How does the issue of unemployment affect Turkey's chances of joining the European Union?

   Think About
   ◆ Turkey's population
   ◆ jobs in Europe

ACTIVITY -OPTION-
Write a **dialogue** between two Turks, one who welcomes Mustafa Kemal's changes and one who opposes them.

CHAPTER 9 ASSESSMENT

TERMS & NAMES

Explain the significance of each of the following:
1. Arab-Israeli Wars
2. OPEC
3. primary product
4. Aswan High Dam
5. Anwar Sadat
6. Zionism
7. kibbutz
8. Yom Kippur
9. Mustafa Kemal
10. Tansu Ciller

REVIEW QUESTIONS

A Troubled Century *(pages 243–247)*
1. What was the United Nations solution to the conflicting claims of Arabs and Zionists to Palestine?

Resources and Religion *(pages 249–253)*
2. Why is oil the most important resource in the region?
3. How does Islam influence the culture of the region?

Egypt Today *(pages 256–261)*
4. Why did France and Britain build the Suez Canal?
5. What are the main benefits and drawbacks of the Aswan Dam?
6. How is life in Egypt's rural areas different from life in Cairo?

Israel Today *(pages 264–267)*
7. Why do Jews and Arabs come into conflict in Israel?
8. From what countries and regions have recent immigrants come to Israel?

Turkey Today *(pages 270–273)*
9. What changes did Mustafa Kemal make in Turkey?
10. Why has Turkey had difficulty joining the European Union?

CRITICAL THINKING

Identifying Problems
1. Using your completed chart from Reading Social Studies, p. 242, list times when the solution to a problem in the region caused a new problem.

Analyzing Motives
2. Why have Muslim fundamentalists and others objected to westernization?

Comparing
3. Compare the progress of women's rights in modern-day Turkey to those of women in modern-day Saudi Arabia.

Visual Summary

1 A Troubled Century
- The conflicts of the past have contributed to problems today in North Africa and Southwest Asia.

2 Resources and Religion
- Oil and Islam are major factors in the region's economy and culture.

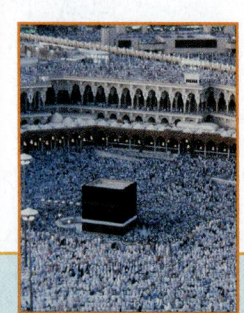

3 Egypt Today
- Modernization has brought both benefits and problems to Egypt.

4 Israel Today
- Conflict continues because both Jews and Arabs claim the land of Israel.

5 Turkey Today
- Modern Turkey is the result of Mustafa Kemal's forcible westernization of a traditional Islamic culture.

STANDARDS-BASED ASSESSMENT

Use the map and your knowledge of world cultures and geography to answer questions 1 and 2.

Additional Test Practice, pp. S1–S33

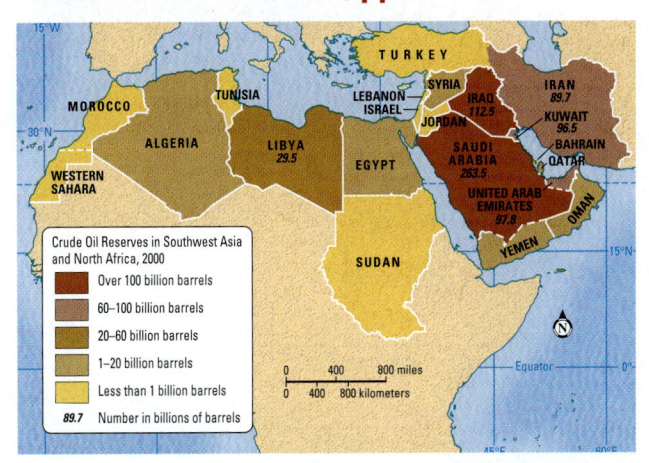

Crude Oil Reserves in Southwest Asia and North Africa, 2000

1. Which country has less crude oil reserves than Algeria?
   - A. Iraq
   - B. Libya
   - C. Saudi Arabia
   - D. Sudan

2. Which country has more than 98 billion barrels of crude oil reserves?
   - A. Iraq
   - B. Kuwait
   - C. Morocco
   - D. United Arab Emirates

In 1977, Egyptian President Anwar Sadat took the courageous step of visiting Israel, the enemy of his country. The following passage is from a speech he gave there about his desire for peace. Use the quotation and your knowledge of world cultures and geography to answer question 3.

PRIMARY SOURCE

Any life lost in war is a human life, irrespective of its being that of an Israeli or an Arab. A wife who becomes a widow is a human entitled to a happy family life, whether she be an Arab or an Israeli. Innocent children who are deprived of the care and compassion of their parents are ours, be they living on Arab or Israeli land. They command our top responsibility to afford them a comfortable life today and tomorrow.

ANWAR SADAT, *speech to the Israeli Knesset, November 20, 1977*

3. Why did Sadat want to prevent future Arab-Israeli wars?
   - A. He did not want his country to lose more land to Israel.
   - B. He believed that his country had been wrong in the past.
   - C. He did not want any more Arabs or Israelis to die in war.
   - D. He wanted to make life more comfortable for children.

TEST PRACTICE CLASSZONE.COM

ALTERNATIVE ASSESSMENT

1. WRITING ABOUT HISTORY

Although the Persian Gulf War lasted only 100 hours, many lives were lost and much of Kuwait was devastated. Imagine you are a war correspondent during that war. File a report at the end of the war that describes the reasons for the war, the missile and ground attacks, the fires in the oil fields, and the numbers of lives lost by all the countries involved. Share your report with your class.

2. COOPERATIVE LEARNING

In pairs, present information to the class about religious observances that involve fasting. Research one observance, such as Ramadan, Lent, or Yom Kippur. Write a paragraph that explains the observance. Include information about how long the observance and fasting lasts and what activities are associated with it. Try to find photographs to accompany your report.

INTEGRATED TECHNOLOGY

Doing Internet Research
Use the Internet to research any of the major cities discussed in this chapter, such as Cairo, Istanbul, or Tel Aviv. Then create a tourist brochure of your findings. Keep a list of the Web sites you used to prepare your brochure.

- Find information that would be helpful to a tourist visiting that city for the first time, such as what language is spoken there, what the climate is like, and what historic sites and cultural events there are to experience.
- Include a map or an illustration of a major tourist attraction.

For Internet links to support this activity, go to

RESEARCH LINKS CLASSZONE.COM

UNIT 4

Place Elephants are one of many kinds of animals that inhabit the 5,700-square-mile Serengeti National Park in Tanzania, Africa. The Serengeti Plain is the last place in Africa where vast land-animal migrations take place.

AFRICA SOUTH OF THE SAHARA

Chapter 10 Africa South of the Sahara: Geography and History

Chapter 11 Western and Central Africa

Chapter 12 Eastern and Southern Africa

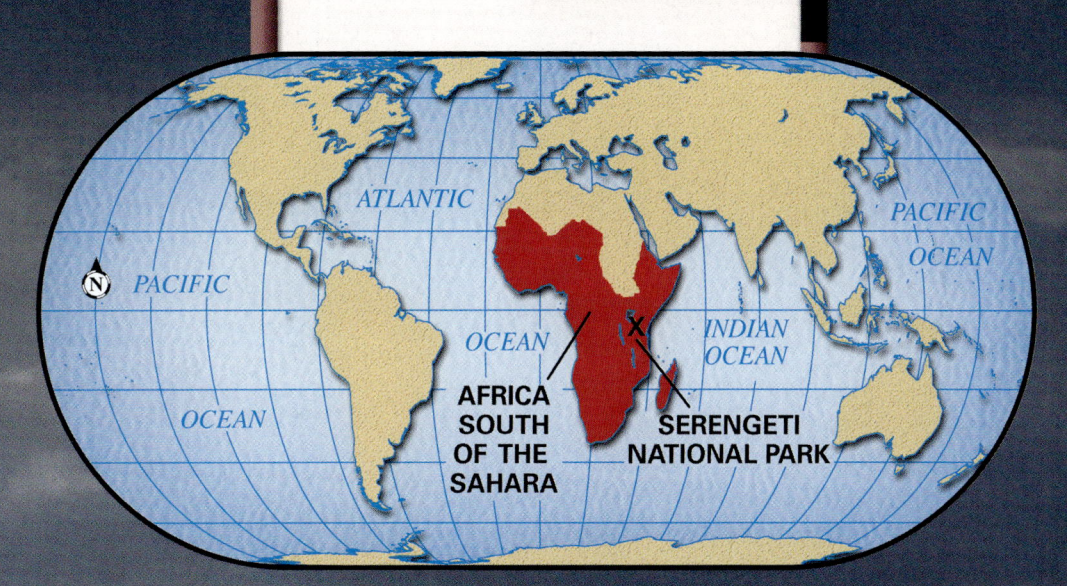

AFRICA SOUTH OF THE SAHARA

SERENGETI NATIONAL PARK

INTEGRATED TECHNOLOGY

eEdition
- Interactive Maps
- Interactive Visuals

VIDEO
Senegal: Cheik in Senegal

INTERNET RESOURCES
Go to **classzone.com** for:
- Research Links
- Internet Activities
- Data Updates
- Unit Quiz
- Maps
- Test Practice
- Current Events
- Web Research Guide

UNIT 4 Atlas — Physical Geography

Africa South of the Sahara: Physical

SUNSHINE STATE STANDARDS

Key Standard SS.B.1.3.1 The student uses various map forms (including thematic maps) and other geographic representations, tools, and technologies to acquire, process, and report geographic information including patterns of land use, connections between places, and patterns and processes of migration and diffusion.

Other Standards SS.B.1.3.3

FCAT LA.A.2.3.1 Reading: Identify Main Idea, Facts, and Details

278 UNIT 4

Africa South of the Sahara

Resources of Africa South of the Sahara

Legend:
- Aluminum
- Coal
- Copper
- Diamonds
- Gold
- Iron ore
- Petroleum
- Phosphate
- Tin
- Uranium

Africa South of the Sahara–U.S. Landmass and Population

LANDMASS
Africa South of the Sahara
8,389,419 square miles

Continental United States
3,165,630 square miles

POPULATION
Africa South of the Sahara
625,535,088

United States
281,421,906

= 50,000,000

Fast Facts

COUNTRY WITH LEAST RAINFALL: Namibia, with 10.63 in. per yr.

MOST DIAMONDS: Africa produces about 50 percent of the world's diamonds.

GOLD RESERVES: South Africa produces 495 tons of gold per year—about 30 percent of the world's total—and accounts for more than half of the world's known reserves.

GEOGRAPHY SKILLBUILDER: Interpreting Maps and Visuals

1. **Place** • Which country has the greatest number of mineral resources?
2. **Region** • Find Lesotho on the map on page 484. What are some issues that might arise due to its location?

Atlas 279

UNIT 4 Atlas — Human Geography

Africa South of the Sahara: Political

Legend:
- National boundary
- ★ National capital
- • Other city

Scale: 0–1,000 miles / 0–1,000 kilometers

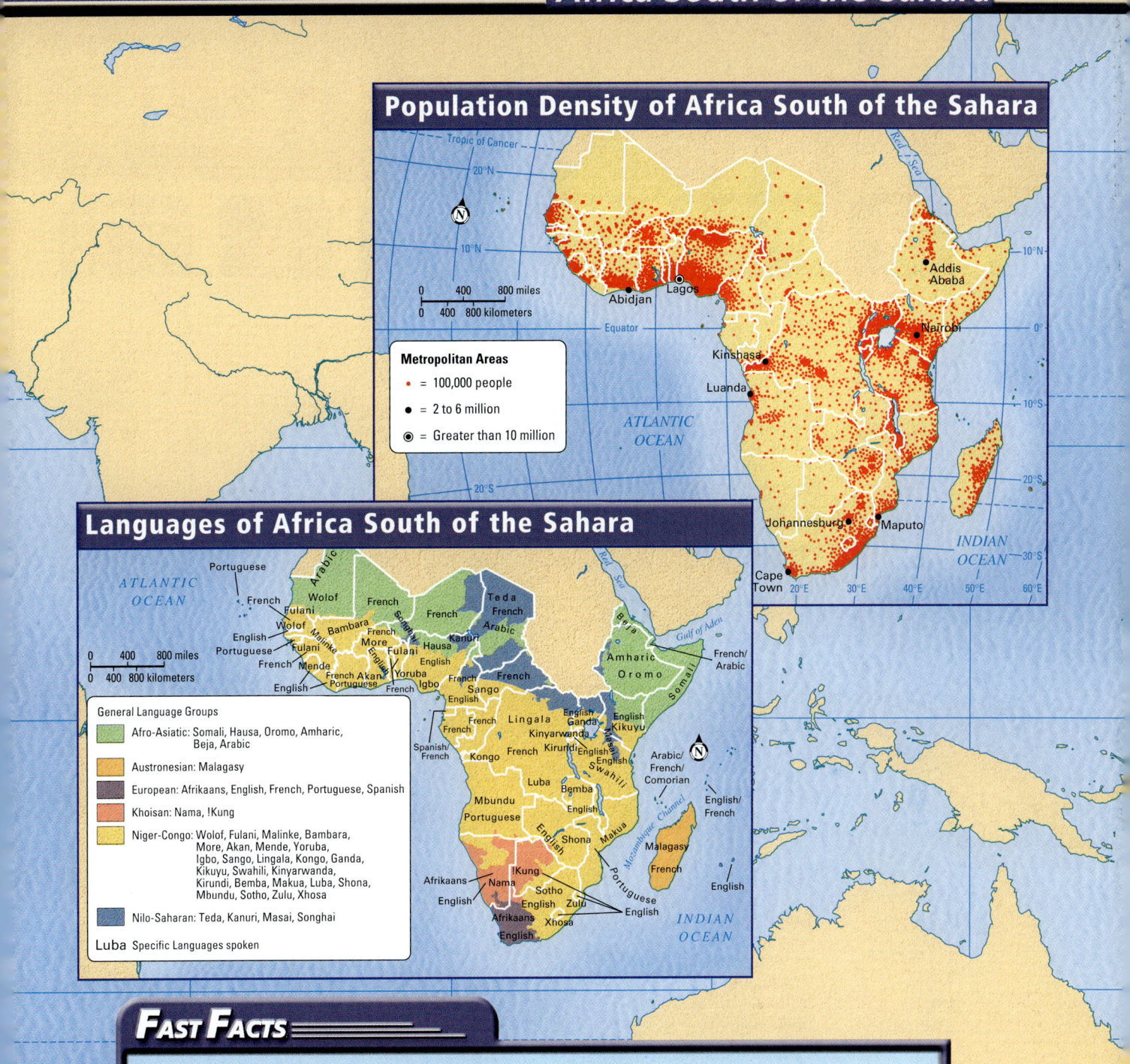

Africa South of the Sahara

Population Density of Africa South of the Sahara

Metropolitan Areas
- • = 100,000 people
- ● = 2 to 6 million
- ⊙ = Greater than 10 million

Languages of Africa South of the Sahara

General Language Groups
- Afro-Asiatic: Somali, Hausa, Oromo, Amharic, Beja, Arabic
- Austronesian: Malagasy
- European: Afrikaans, English, French, Portuguese, Spanish
- Khoisan: Nama, !Kung
- Niger-Congo: Wolof, Fulani, Malinke, Bambara, More, Akan, Mende, Yoruba, Igbo, Sango, Lingala, Kongo, Ganda, Kikuyu, Swahili, Kinyarwanda, Kirundi, Bemba, Makua, Luba, Shona, Mbundu, Sotho, Zulu, Xhosa
- Nilo-Saharan: Teda, Kanuri, Masai, Songhai

Luba Specific Languages spoken

Fast Facts

✓ **LARGEST FAMILY OF LANGUAGES:**
Niger-Congo language family, with 890 known member languages

✓ **FEWEST PHONES:**
Africa has less than 2 percent of the world's telephone lines. Most Africans have to travel two hours to find a phone. Eighty percent of Africa's population has never placed a phone call. More people use the Internet in London than in all of Africa.

✓ **MOST SPARSELY POPULATED:**
After Mongolia, Namibia is the most sparsely populated country in the world, with 5.7 people per square mile.

GEOGRAPHY SKILLBUILDER: Interpreting Maps and Visuals
1. **Movement** • In which two countries is Afrikaans spoken?
2. **Place** • Name two countries that have low population densities.

Atlas 281

UNIT Atlas 4 — Data File

For updates on these statistics, go to
DATA UPDATE CLASSZONE.COM

Country Flag	Country/Capital	Currency	Population (2001 estimate)	Life Expectancy (years)	Birthrate (per 1,000 pop.) (2000)
	Angola Luanda	Readjusted Kwanza	10,366,000	47	48
	Benin Porto-Novo	CFA Franc	6,591,000	50	45
	Botswana Gaborone	Pula	1,586,000	44	32
	Burkina Faso Ouagadougou	CFA Franc	12,272,000	47	47
	Burundi Bujumbura	Franc	6,224,000	47	42
	Cameroon Yaoundé	CFA Franc	15,803,000	55	37
	Cape Verde Praia	Escudo	405,000	68	37
	Central African Republic Bangui	CFA Franc	3,577,000	45	38
	Chad N'Djamena	CFA Franc	8,707,000	48	50
	Comoros Moroni	Franc	596,000	59	38
	Congo, Democratic Republic of the Kinshasa	Congolese Franc	53,625,000	49	48
	Congo, Republic of the Brazzaville	CFA Franc	2,894,000	48	40
	Côte d'Ivoire Yamoussoukro	CFA Franc	16,393,000	47	38
	Djibouti Djibouti	Djibouti Franc	461,000	48	39
	Equatorial Guinea Malabo	CFA Franc	486,000	50	41
	Eritrea Asmara	Birr	4,298,000	55	43
	Ethiopia Addis Ababa	Birr	65,892,000	46	45

Africa South of the Sahara

DATA FILE

Infant Mortality (per 1,000 live births) (2000)	Doctors (per 100,000 pop.) (1997–1998)	Literacy Rate (percentage) (1996–1998)	Passenger Cars (per 1,000 pop.) (1991–1998)	Total Area (square miles)	Map (not to scale)
125.0	8	42	21	481,351	
93.9	6	38	6	43,483	
57.2	24	76	53	231,804	
105.3	3	22	3	105,869	
74.8	6	46	2	10,759	
77.0	7	74	7	183,591	
76.9	17	73	29	1,557	
96.7	4	44	3	240,534	
109.8	3	39	1	459,752	
77.3	7	59	18	719	
108.6	7	59	7	905,365	
108.6	25	78	10	132,047	
112.2	9	45	11	124,503	
115.0	14	62	31	8,958	
108.0	25	81	9	10,830	
81.8	3	52	2	10,830	
116.0	4	36	0.8	471,776	

Atlas 283

Unit 4 Atlas Data File

Country Flag	Country/Capital	Currency	Population (2001 estimate)	Life Expectancy (years)	Birthrate (per 1,000 pop.) (2000)
	Gabon Libreville	CFA Franc	1,221,000	52	38
	Gambia, The Banjul	Dalasi	1,411,000	45	43
	Ghana Accra	Cedi	19,894,000	58	34
	Guinea Conakry	Franc	7,614,000	45	42
	Guinea-Bissau Bissau	CFA Franc	1,316,000	45	42
	Kenya Nairobi	Shilling	30,766,000	49	35
	Lesotho Maseru	Maloti	2,177,000	53	33
	Liberia Monrovia	Dollar	3,226,000	50	50
	Madagascar Antananarivo	Malagasy Franc	15,983,000	52	44
	Malawi Lilongwe	Kwacha	10,548,000	39	41
	Mali Bamako	CFA Franc	11,009,000	53	47
	Mauritania Nouakchott	Ouguiya	2,747,000	54	41
	Mauritius Port Louis	Rupee	1,190,000	70	17
	Mozambique Maputo	Metical	19,371,000	40	41
	Namibia Windhoek	Rand	1,798,000	46	36
	Niger Niamey	CFA Franc	10,355,000	41	54
	Nigeria Abuja	Naira	126,636,000	52	42

Africa South of the Sahara

DATA FILE

Infant Mortality (per 1,000 live births) (2000)	Doctors (per 100,000 pop.) (1997–1998)	Literacy Rate (percentage) (1996–1998)	Passenger Cars (per 1,000 pop.) (1991–1998)	Total Area (square miles)	Map (not to scale)
87.0	19	63	21	103,346	
130.0	4	35	7	4,127	
56.2	6	69	5	92,100	
98.0	13	36	2	94,925	
130.0	17	37	3	13,948	
73.7	13	81	10	224,960	
84.5	5	82	3	11,720	
139.1	2	38	9	43,000	
96.3	11	65	4	226,658	
126.8	2	58	3	47,747	
122.5	5	38	3	478,764	
92.0	14	41	7	397,955	
19.4	85	84	61	790	
133.9	4	42	4	302,328	
68.3	30	81	38	318,000	
123.1	4	15	4	489,189	
77.2	19	61	5	356,669	

Atlas **285**

UNIT 4 Atlas Data File

For updates on these statistics, go to DATA UPDATE CLASSZONE.COM

Country Flag	Country/Capital	Currency	Population (2001 estimate)	Life Expectancy (years)	Birthrate (per 1,000 pop.) (2000)
	Rwanda Kigali	Franc	7,313,000	39	43
	São Tomé and Príncipe São Tomé	Dobra	165,000	64	43
	Senegal Dakar	CFA Franc	10,285,000	52	41
	Seychelles Victoria	Rupee	80,000	71	18
	Sierra Leone Freetown	Leone	5,427,000	45	47
	Somalia Mogadishu	Shilling	7,489,000	46	47
	South Africa, Pretoria/Cape Town/Bloemfontein	Rand	43,586,000	55	25
	Swaziland Mbabane	Lilangeni	1,104,000	38	41
	Tanzania Dar es Salaam	Shilling	36,232,000	53	42
	Togo Lomé	CFA Franc	5,153,000	49	42
	Uganda Kampala	Shilling	23,986,000	42	48
	Zambia Lusaka	Kwacha	9,770,000	37	42
	Zimbabwe Harare	Dollar	11,365,000	40	30
	United States Washington, D.C.	Dollar	281,422,000	77	15

Africa South of the Sahara

DATA FILE

Infant Mortality (per 1,000 live births) (2000)	Doctors (per 100,000 pop.) (1997–1998)	Literacy Rate (percentage) (1996–1998)	Passenger Cars (per 1,000 pop.) (1991–1998)	Total Area (square miles)	Map (not to scale)
120.9	4	64	2	10,169	
50.8	47	73	30	372	
67.7	8	36	12	76,124	
8.5	132	84	85	178	
157.1	7	31	4	27,699	
125.8	4	24	2	246,200	
45.4	56	85	102	471,445	
107.7	15	78	29	6,705	
98.8	5	74	2	364,898	
79.7	8	55	17	21,853	
81.3	4	65	1	91,134	
109.0	7	76	16	290,585	
80.0	14	87	3	150,820	
7.0	251	97	489	3,787,319	

GEOGRAPHY SKILLBUILDER: Interpreting a Chart
1. **Place** • How many more doctors per 100,000 people does Cape Verde have than Burkina Faso?
2. **Place** • How much higher is Lesotho's literacy rate than Guinea's?

Atlas 287

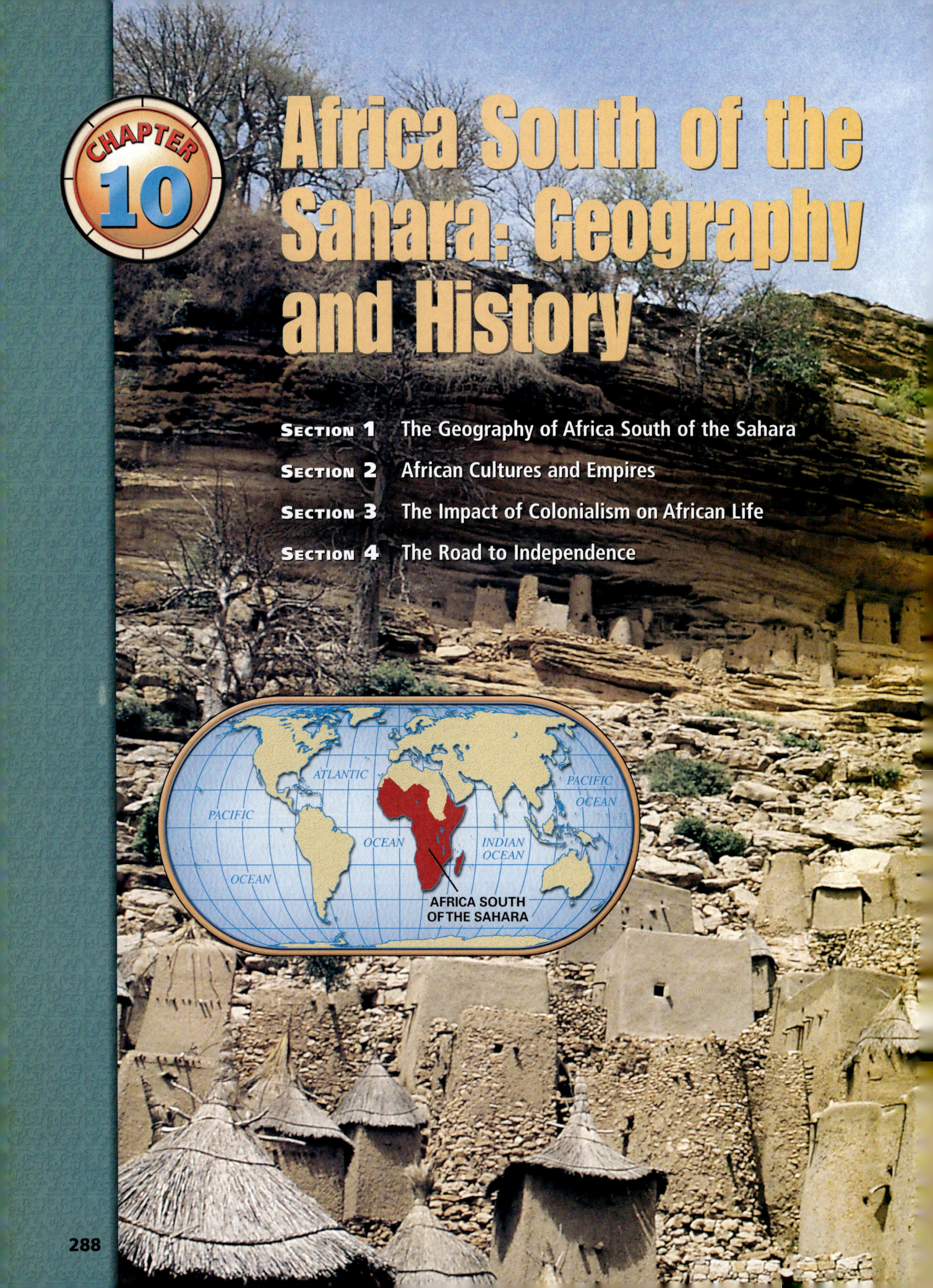

CHAPTER 10
Africa South of the Sahara: Geography and History

Section 1 The Geography of Africa South of the Sahara

Section 2 African Cultures and Empires

Section 3 The Impact of Colonialism on African Life

Section 4 The Road to Independence

AFRICA SOUTH OF THE SAHARA

Who owns a country?

FOCUS ON GEOGRAPHY

Place • This 1892 drawing of a British imperialist illustrates the United Kingdom's claim on Africa. In the late 1800s, many European nations wanted to control a piece of the continent. By the early 1900s, all but two African nations were colonized by European powers. What did Africans think about this? Who owned Africa: the Africans or the European colonizers?

What do you think?

- Why do you think the artist drew the British man with his feet planted on Egypt and South Africa?
- What are the benefits and disadvantages of being a colony?

Place Most Africans live in villages, not in cities. The cliffside dwellings of the Tellem tribe are built above a Banani village in Mali.

CHAPTER 10 READING SOCIAL STUDIES

BEFORE YOU READ

▶▶ What Do You Know?

Africa south of the Sahara is a land rich in natural resources. Despite this, many countries in this part of Africa do not have strong economies. What do you know of Africa's early history? How did Europeans affect the development of this region? Reflect on what you have learned in other classes, what you have read, and what you have seen in movies or on television about the countries in Africa south of the Sahara.

▶▶ What Do You Want to Know?

Decide what you know about Africa south of the Sahara. In your notebook, record what you hope to learn from this chapter.

Place • Baule gold masks sometimes represent the face of an enemy killed in battle. ▲

READ AND TAKE NOTES

Reading Strategy: Analyzing Causes and Effects
As you read about history, it is important to understand not only historical events, but also why the events happened (causes) and what resulted from the events (effects). Use the chart below to record the causes and effects of processes that shaped the history of Africa south of the Sahara.

- Copy the chart into your notebook.
- As you read, look for information about the geographic and human processes listed on the chart.
- Record the causes and effects of each process.

Culture • Traditional dances in Zambia are used for tribal ceremonies and entertainment. ▲

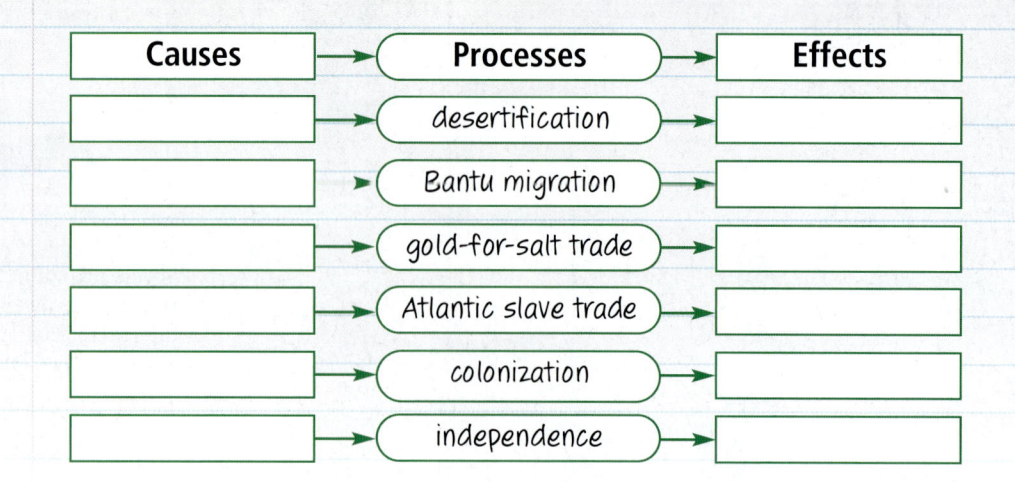

Causes	→	Processes	→	Effects
	→	desertification	→	
	→	Bantu migration	→	
	→	gold-for-salt trade	→	
	→	Atlantic slave trade	→	
	→	colonization	→	
	→	independence	→	

290 CHAPTER 10

SECTION 1

The Geography of Africa South of the Sahara

TERMS & NAMES
plateau
Great Rift Valley
Sahel
desertification
drought
savanna
nonrenewable resource
renewable resource

MAIN IDEA

Africa south of the Sahara is a region with dramatically different landforms and climates. This provides for a variety of natural resources.

WHY IT MATTERS NOW

Tourists come from all over the world to explore this region's natural landscapes.

DATELINE EXTRA

BAMAKO, MALI, MARCH 8, 2000

Families in Mali are watching in despair as their farmland turns to sand. This problem—called desertification—is affecting many families in Africa. Experts have come to Mali for a United Nations–sponsored meeting to decide what can be done. In the past, efforts have focused on grand plans, such as planting thousands of trees to stop the advancing desert. When there was no money to water the trees, they died. Soon, the desert marched on.

Today's plans are more modest. One idea is to convince villagers to collect firewood from far away, leaving trees near the sand in place. Another idea is to change how people farm so that soil doesn't blow away. In these small ways, experts hope they can stop desertification.

Human-Environment Interaction • This brushwood fence is an attempt to stabilize sand dunes and fight against the advance of the desert. ▲

SUNSHINE STATE STANDARDS
Key Standard SS.B.2.3.2 The student knows the human and physical characteristics of different places in the world and how these characteristics change over time.
Other Standards SS.B.2.3.6, B.2.3.8
FCAT LA.A.2.3.1 Reading: Identify Main Idea, Facts, and Details

The African Continent

Natural changes in Africa's lands, such as desertification, affect its people. Africa is roughly three times the size of the United States. About 225 million years ago, Africa was the center of Earth's only continent, called Pangaea (pan•JEE•uh). Pangaea broke up into separate continents that drifted apart over many millions of years. The piece that became Africa stayed where it was.

TAKING NOTES
Use your chart to take notes about Africa South of the Sahara.

Causes → Processes → Effects
→ colonization →
→ independence →

Africa South of the Sahara: Geography and History **291**

Landforms of Africa South of the Sahara

Africa has two major land types: lowlands and highlands. Locate the two regions on the Unit Atlas map on page 278. The lowlands are in the north and west, and the highlands are in the south and east. Several peaks rise out of the highlands of Kenya and Tanzania. The highest is Mount Kilimanjaro. The name *Kilimanjaro* comes from the Swahili (swah·HEE·lee) phrase *kilima njaro*, which means "shining mountain." From the sweltering rain forest below, Kilimanjaro looks as though it is shining in the sun. That's because its peak is snowcapped all year even though Kilimanjaro sits almost on the Equator.

Plateaus Look again at the Unit Atlas map on page 278. Most of Africa south of the Sahara—both highlands and lowlands—lies on a high plateau. A **plateau** is a raised area of relatively level land. The African plateau rises from coastal plains along much of the north and west coastlines. Steep cliffs line much of the southern and eastern coasts, rising sharply from the Atlantic and Indian oceans. The east side of the plateau is higher than the west, at about 5,000 feet above sea level. The western plateau averages about 1,500 feet above sea level.

BACKGROUND
Mount Kilimanjaro is a volcanic massif, or large, independent mountain mass. It is made up of three distinct parts: Kibo, Mawensi, and Shira. Kibo is still actively volcanic and, as the highest peak, has a permanent ice cap.

Region • The Congo Basin is drained by the 2,900-mile-long Congo River (also called the Zaire River). ▼

Place • Mount Kenya, at 17,058 feet, is the second highest mountain in Africa. It is an extinct volcano. ▼

Region • The Great Rift Valley is nearly 4,000 miles long. It is 9,850 feet below sea level at its deepest point. ▶

Vocabulary

rift: a deep crack formed when plates of Earth separate

Rifts The tectonic plates on which Africa sits have been slowly pulling apart for 50 million years. The separation of the plates has been forming a series of broad, steep-walled valleys called rifts. The rifts make up the **Great Rift Valley,** which stretches from the Red Sea to Mozambique. Locate the valley on the Unit Atlas map on page 278. The Great Rift Valley will become larger and larger as East Africa pulls away from the rest of the continent. Eventually, East Africa may become an island. The island of Madagascar was formed in this way. Look again at the map on page 278 to find where Madagascar fit before it broke away.

Waterways of Africa South of the Sahara

Parts of the Great Rift Valley have filled with water to form huge lakes, such as Lake Tanganyika. Africa's largest lake, Lake Victoria, is pictured at the bottom of this page. It lies in a shallow basin between two rift valleys on the borders of Uganda, Kenya, and Tanzania. Lakes and rivers provide fresh water and fish. However, waterfalls and rapids make boat travel difficult.

Reading Social Studies

A. Summarizing What are some benefits provided by Africa's lakes and rivers?

Rivers Many of Africa's rivers have exceptional features. The Nile River, flowing northward out of the mountains of central Africa, is the world's longest river. The Okavango River crosses Angola, Namibia, and Botswana before emptying into marshes north of the Kalahari Desert. The Zambezi River features many powerful waterfalls, including Victoria Falls. The mist from these falls can be seen 25 miles away.

Place • Lake Victoria is the second largest freshwater lake in the world. It is the major source of the Nile River. ▼

Africa's Deserts

Desert	Area (sq. mi)	High Temp.	Annual Rainfall
Sahara	3,320,000	136°F	1" to 5"
Kalahari	360,000	115°F	<5" south; more northeast
Namib	52,000	over 100°F	0.5" to 2"

SKILLBUILDER: Reading a Chart
1. **Place** • Which desert is the largest?
2. **Place** • Which desert is the hottest?

Many Climates

Four major climatic regions of Africa south of the Sahara are desert (arid), semiarid, tropical, and equatorial. The different temperatures and amounts of rainfall affect which plants and animals live in each region.

Desert and Semiarid Regions
Desert climates are found in the Sahara to the north and the Namib (NAH•mihb) and Kalahari to the south. These areas have little rain, high temperatures, and few plants and animals. Around the desert areas are semiarid regions that also have high temperatures but have more rainfall than the deserts.

The **Sahel** (suh•HAYL) is a semiarid region south of the Sahara. This area is experiencing **desertification**—a process by which a desert spreads. **Drought,** or the lack of rain, is one cause of desertification. The lack of rain causes fewer plants to grow. Without plants, soil blows away, leaving a dry, barren landscape. Other causes are overgrazing and overuse of the land for farming. People in Africa and around the world are trying to stop this process because a lack of enough arable land contributes to the widespread hunger in many African countries.

Tropical and Equatorial Regions
The tropical climate extends from the semiarid areas toward the Equator. There is a rainy season of up to six months, and the rest of the year is dry.

Savannas, found in both semiarid and tropical areas, are flat grasslands with scattered trees and shrubs. More than 4.5 million square miles of Africa are savannas. Many African animals, including lions, elephants, giraffes, and zebras, live on these grasslands.

The equatorial region has two rainy seasons and two brief dry seasons each year. Located at the Equator, this climate has high temperatures year-round and annual rainfall of 50 to 60 inches.

Citizenship IN ACTION

Helping the Hungry Since 1977, a global volunteer organization called the Hunger Project has been working to end hunger in developing nations. In Africa, where poverty and hunger are widespread, the Hunger Project is sponsoring the African Woman Food Farmer Initiative.

So far, the program has loaned money to more than 14,000 women farmers like this one, in eight countries. The initiative has also provided health, nutrition, and literacy training for 9,000 more women in agriculture.

Reading Social Studies

B. Analyzing Issues How does the great area of desert and semiarid land impact the lives of many Africans?

Rain forests with trees as tall as 195 feet grow here. Many animals, including the chimpanzee, gorilla, hippopotamus, and African gray parrot, live in the rain forest.

Resources of Africa South of the Sahara

Africa is rich in mineral resources, such as gold and diamonds, that form over hundreds of millions of years. Other plentiful minerals are copper, tin, chrome, nickel, and iron ore. **Nonrenewable resources,** such as copper and diamonds, cannot be replaced or can be replaced only over millions of years.

Renewable resources can be used and replaced over a relatively short time period. The renewable resources of this region include trees used to make wood products, cocoa beans, cashew nuts, peanuts, vanilla beans, coffee, bananas, rubber, sugar, and tea. Africa's natural wildlife and historic sites are important resources that draw tourists from all over the world.

Region • In 1866, a child found a pebble on the banks of a river in South Africa. The pebble turned out to be a 21-carat diamond! ▼

Strange but TRUE

The Fish That Did Not Die In 1938, off the coast of South Africa, some fishermen caught something surprising. The blue fish in their net was 5 feet long, weighed about 127 pounds, and had several rows of small, pointed teeth. The fishermen had never seen anything like it. Nor, according to scientists, should they have.

The fish, a coelacanth (SEE•luh•KANTH), was thought to have been extinct for 70 million years. Now here was proof that it wasn't. However, they aren't plentiful. It wasn't until 1952 that a second live coelacanth was found. Only a few hundred exist today.

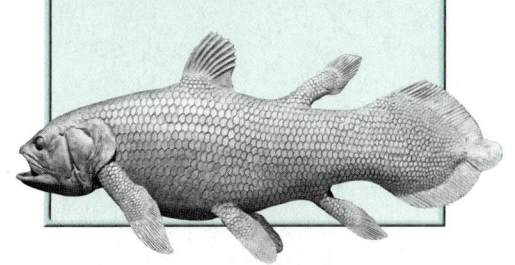

SECTION 1 ASSESSMENT

Terms & Names
1. **Explain the significance of:**
   - (a) plateau
   - (b) Great Rift Valley
   - (c) Sahel
   - (d) desertification
   - (e) drought
   - (f) savanna
   - (g) nonrenewable resource
   - (h) renewable resource

Using Graphics
2. Use a chart like this one to list some of this region's renewable and non-renewable resources.

Renewable Resources	Nonrenewable Resources

Main Ideas
3. (a) Describe the landforms and waterways of Africa.

   (b) Describe four climatic regions of Africa south of the Sahara.

   (c) Explain the differences between renewable and nonrenewable resources. Give examples of each.

Critical Thinking
4. **Using Maps**

   Look at the map of Africa on page 486. Has the Great Rift Valley affected modern political boundaries in Africa? Explain your answer.

   Think About
   - the location of the Great Rift Valley
   - current national borders in Africa

ACTIVITY -OPTION- Draw a **commemorative stamp** honoring a climatic region or landform in Africa south of the Sahara.

SECTION 2
African Cultures and Empires

TERMS & NAMES
paleontologist
Bantu migration
Mansa Musa

MAIN IDEA
Africa south of the Sahara has a rich and significant history.

WHY IT MATTERS NOW
Many scientists think Africa south of the Sahara is the cradle of the human race. The oldest fossil remains of humans have come from this region.

DATELINE

SOUTHERN AFRICA, A.D. 500—There is a group of newcomers in the area. They come from the north and speak languages unlike ours. Instead of hunting in the forests as we do, they raise animals for food. They plant grain in fields near their settlement.

The newcomers, who call themselves "Bantu," have sharp spears and blades made of a cold, dark metal. They use a short, sharp metal tool for digging—much better than our stone and wood tools. Many of our people have begun to trade goods for the newcomers' fine tools and pottery.

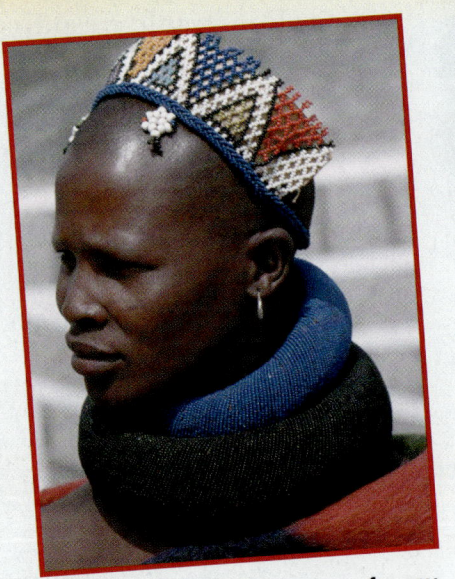

Movement • This woman is one of many Bantu who have settled in southern Africa. ▲

The First Humans

The roots of the Bantus can be traced back thousands of years. Fossil evidence shows that the first known humans lived in Africa several million years ago. **Paleontologists**, or scientists who study fossils, have discovered human remains in Kenya, South Africa, and other African nations. Fossilized human footprints 3.6 million years old have been found in Tanzania. It is now known that humans in Africa were the first to develop language, tools, and culture. Then, over tens of thousands of years, they migrated to other continents.

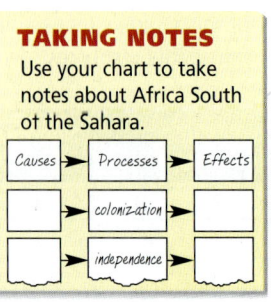

SUNSHINE STATE STANDARDS
Key Standard
SS.A.2.3.4 The student understands the impact of geographical factors on the historical development of civilizations.
Other Standards
SS.A.2.3.2, B.2.3.1
FCAT LA.A.2.3.1
Reading: Identify Main Idea, Facts, and Details

TAKING NOTES
Use your chart to take notes about Africa South of the Sahara.

Early African Farmers

The first humans lived in small groups. For food, they collected berries, plants, and nuts and hunted wild animals. As plants and animals became scarce in one place, the people moved on. During this time, a group known as Bantu lived in what is now Cameroon. Around 5,000 years ago, the Bantu became farmers instead of hunter-gatherers. They learned to grow grain and herd cattle, sheep, and other animals. Later, they learned how to work with iron to make tools and weapons.

On the Move The Bantu began to move to other parts of Africa around 1000 B.C. Perhaps the desert was spreading, or they needed more land for a growing population. For about 2,000 years, the Bantu gradually spread across the continent. Their great movement is called the **Bantu migration**. In their new homes, they learned to grow and use different plants. In some places, the native hunter-gatherers lived in separate villages or moved away, as did the Sans, or Bushmen. In other places, the Bantu and the local people, such as the Pygmies, intermarried. Over time, the Bantu culture became widespread throughout Africa. Today, many Africans speak Swahili, Zulu, and other Bantu languages.

Culture • These headdresses represent Tyi Wara—an antelope spirit who, according to Bantu mythology, taught the first people how to grow crops. ▲

Reading Social Studies

A. Recognizing Effects How did the Bantu migration influence the character of Africa south of the Sahara?

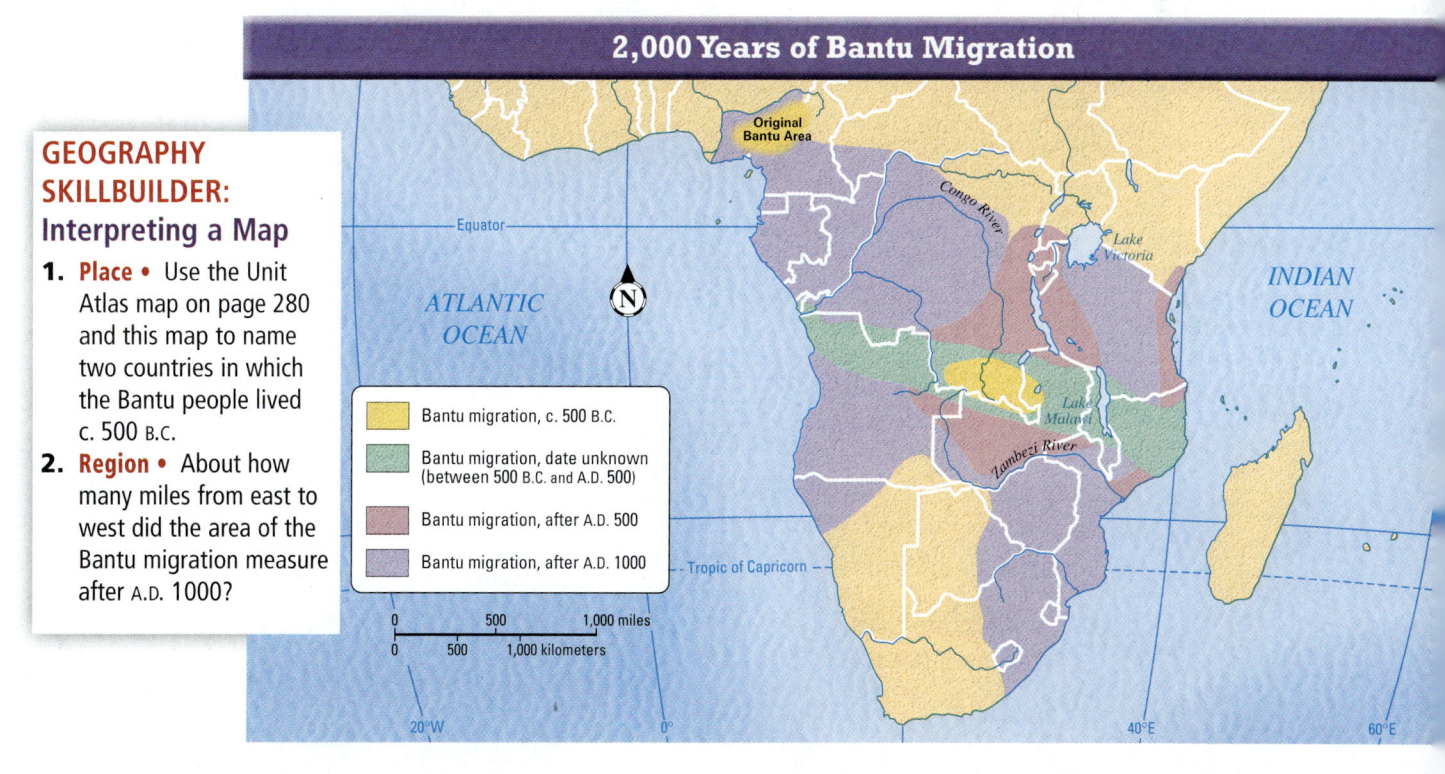

2,000 Years of Bantu Migration

GEOGRAPHY SKILLBUILDER: Interpreting a Map

1. **Place •** Use the Unit Atlas map on page 280 and this map to name two countries in which the Bantu people lived c. 500 B.C.
2. **Region •** About how many miles from east to west did the area of the Bantu migration measure after A.D. 1000?

Map legend:
- Bantu migration, c. 500 B.C.
- Bantu migration, date unknown (between 500 B.C. and A.D. 500)
- Bantu migration, after A.D. 500
- Bantu migration, after A.D. 1000

Africa South of the Sahara: Geography and History

Trade Networks

Eventually, the Bantu built permanent villages. Trade routes began to develop between these communities across Africa.

The Salt Trade Salt was as precious to ancient Africans as gold and diamonds. People needed salt each day to stay alive. They also used it to preserve food. However, most of Africa south of the Sahara had no salt deposits. The closest source was in the Sahara, where giant salt slabs, some as heavy as 200 pounds, were mined. A vast trade network developed between the salt mines and the area south of the Sahara. To get salt, people in southern Africa traded gold, slaves, ivory, and cola nuts.

Camels and Caravans African trade expanded even further when the Arabian camel was introduced to Africa in the A.D. 600s. Camels are well adapted for long treks across the desert. Using camels, salt traders could carry goods from the savannas and forests across the desert to Northern Africa. There they traded for goods from Europe and Asia, such as glass from Italy or cotton and spices from India. The desert trade was profitable but risky. Robbers lived in the desert. For protection, traders traveled together in caravans.

BACKGROUND
Salt cakes were used as currency in ancient Ethiopia.

Place •
Adapted to their desert environment, camels can drink up to 20 gallons of water in 10 minutes and store it in their bloodstream. ▼

Why Camels Are Well Adapted to Desert Travel

A double row of **long, curly eyelashes** keeps sand out of eyes, and **bushy eyebrows** shield eyes from the sun.

Fur-lined ears filter out sand.

The fat-filled hump provides many days' worth of energy.

A large mouth, 34 **sharp teeth,** and a **tough mouth lining** enable the camel to eat thorn bushes.

Long, thin legs have powerful muscles; a camel can walk 25 miles in a day and carry 330 pounds of cargo.

Broad, flat feet don't sink into the sand.

An Empire Built by Trade

In the fourth century A.D., a kingdom called Ghana arose in the Niger River Valley. Ancient Ghana's location allowed it to control trade between northern and southern Africa. Traders had to pay a tax in gold nuggets to pass through the kingdom on their way to Europe and Southwest Asia. In addition, ancient Ghana had many gold mines. Ghana had so much gold from these two sources that the kingdom was called the Land of Gold.

People eagerly traded gold for other precious items, such as salt. The merchants of Ghana also traded gold and slaves for cooking utensils, cloth, jewelry, copper, and weapons.

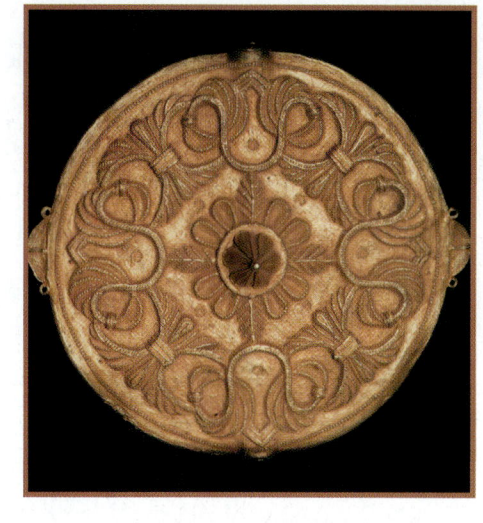

Reading Social Studies
B. Synthesizing Why was Ghana called the Land of Gold?

Human-Environment Interaction • This 18th- or 19th-century gold jewelry from Ghana was probably worn by members of an Ashanti king's court. ▲

The Mali Empire

Muslim armies began a war with Ghana in 1054. The fighting continued for many years and interfered with the trade upon which Ghana depended. This weakened the empire. By the 1200s, the people under Ghana's rule began to break away.

Mali Absorbs Ghana Around 1235, a Muslim leader named Sundiata united warring tribes. He then brought neighboring states under his rule to create the Mali Empire. In the year 1240, he took control of what was left of the Ghana Empire. The Mali Empire included most of the area that Ghana had ruled, along with lands to the east.

Culture • This daughter of a Fanti chief continues a long tradition of Ghanian royalty by wearing gold jewelry and ornaments. ▶

Africa South of the Sahara: Geography and History

It controlled trade routes across the Sahara and from the south, as well as along the Niger River. Many rulers and people of Mali became Muslims but still continued to practice their traditional religions, too.

Mali's Golden Age **Mansa Musa** ruled Mali from about 1312 to 1332. Under his rule, Mali expanded and flourished. In 1324, he made a religious pilgrimage to Mecca in Arabia. During his journey, he persuaded Muslim scholars and artisans to return to Mali with him. Timbuktu, Mali's major city, became a cultural center. Architects built beautiful mosques in and around the city. Scholars brought their knowledge of Islamic law, astronomy, medicine, and mathematics. Universities in several West African cities became centers of Islamic education.

Culture • Mansa (emperor) Musa spread interest in Mali as he traveled to Arabia. Tales of his wealth reached as far away as Europe. ▲

The Songhai Empire

Mali's power declined after Mansa Musa's death in 1337. Eventually, Mali was conquered by nearby Songhai. Like Mali and Ghana had in the past, Songhai controlled trade across the Sahara. It ruled neighboring states, and by the early 1500s was larger than Mali had been. Timbuktu again became a center of Muslim culture. In the early 1590s, a Moroccan army defeated

---

SECTION 2 ASSESSMENT

Terms & Names
1. Explain the significance of: (a) paleontologist (b) Bantu migration (c) Mansa Musa

Using Graphics
2. Use a time line like this one to list important events in this region's history.

   1000 B.C.
   ↓
   ↓
   A.D. 1600

Main Ideas
3. (a) How did the introduction of the camel influence trade in ancient Africa?
   (b) What were the two most valuable minerals in ancient Ghana? Why?
   (c) How did a location in the Niger River valley help empires flourish?

Critical Thinking
4. **Recognizing Effects**
   What were the effects of Mansa Musa's pilgrimage on Mali?

   Think About
   • who came to Mali after the pilgrimage
   • what changes occurred in the culture of Mali

ACTIVITY -OPTION- Make a **diorama** showing a camel caravan traveling through the Sahara, carrying salt to people in southern Africa.

SECTION 3: The Impact of Colonialism on African Life

TERMS & NAMES
missionary
Hutu
Tutsi

MAIN IDEA
The slave trade and colonialism destroyed traditional cultures and social systems in Africa south of the Sahara.

WHY IT MATTERS NOW
Africa is still recovering from the effects of the slave trade and colonialism.

DATELINE

THE ROYAL PALACE, KONGO, JULY 6, 1526 — King Affonso of Kongo has sent a letter to the king of Portugal, protesting the criminal behavior of Portuguese merchants and sailors in Kongo. Traders are kidnapping the young men of his kingdom to sell into slavery. They use European goods to bribe Kongolese to capture their own people. Even noblemen and the king's own relatives have been taken.

Affonso says that European ways are corrupting the Kongolese. Some of the king's courtiers believe the slave trade can bring Kongo a great deal of wealth. But the king's position remains firm.

Movement • Elmina is a slave-trading fortress through which the Portuguese move enslaved Africans. ▲

Africa Before the Europeans

Before Europeans came, Africans had varied ways of life under different kinds of governments. Kings ruled great empires like Mali. Some states had aspects of democratic rule. Some groups had no central government. Some Africans lived in great cities like Timbuktu, while others lived in small forest villages. Some were nomadic hunters, and some were skilled artists who sculpted masks and statues.

TAKING NOTES
Use your chart to take notes about Africa South of the Sahara.

Causes	Processes	Effects
	colonization	
	independence	

SUNSHINE STATE STANDARDS
Key Standard SS.A.2.3.1 The student understands how language, ideas, and institutions of one culture can influence other (e.g., through trade, exploration, and immigration).
Other Standards SS.A.2.3.8
FCAT LA.A.2.3.1 Reading: Identify Main Idea, Facts, and Details

The Slave Trade

Slavery existed in Africa long before Europeans arrived. Rulers in Mali and Songhai had thousands of slaves who worked as servants, soldiers, and farm workers. Villages raided one another to take captives and sell them. Often, a slave could work to earn his or her freedom. In the 1400s, however, Europeans introduced a form of slavery that devastated African life and society.

From Africa to the Americas In the early 15th century, European traders began to sell slaves. They raided towns to capture unwilling Africans. Some Africans captured in wars were sold to European traders by other Africans. One estimate is that 10 to 12 million Africans were forced into slavery and sent to European colonies in North and South America from 1520 to 1860. Many more were captured but died of disease or starvation before arriving. About 1750, movements to stop the slave trade had begun. By 1808, the United States, the United Kingdom, and Denmark had made it illegal to bring in slaves from Africa. However, it would take longer for countries to make owning a slave illegal.

Impact on Africa In addition to the Africans captured and sold, many were killed during raids. About two-thirds of those taken were men between the ages of 18 and 30. Slave traders chose young, strong, healthy people, leaving few behind to lead families and villages. African cities and towns did not have enough workers. Family structures were destroyed.

BACKGROUND
Conditions on slave ships were so bad that about 16 percent of slaves died during transport.

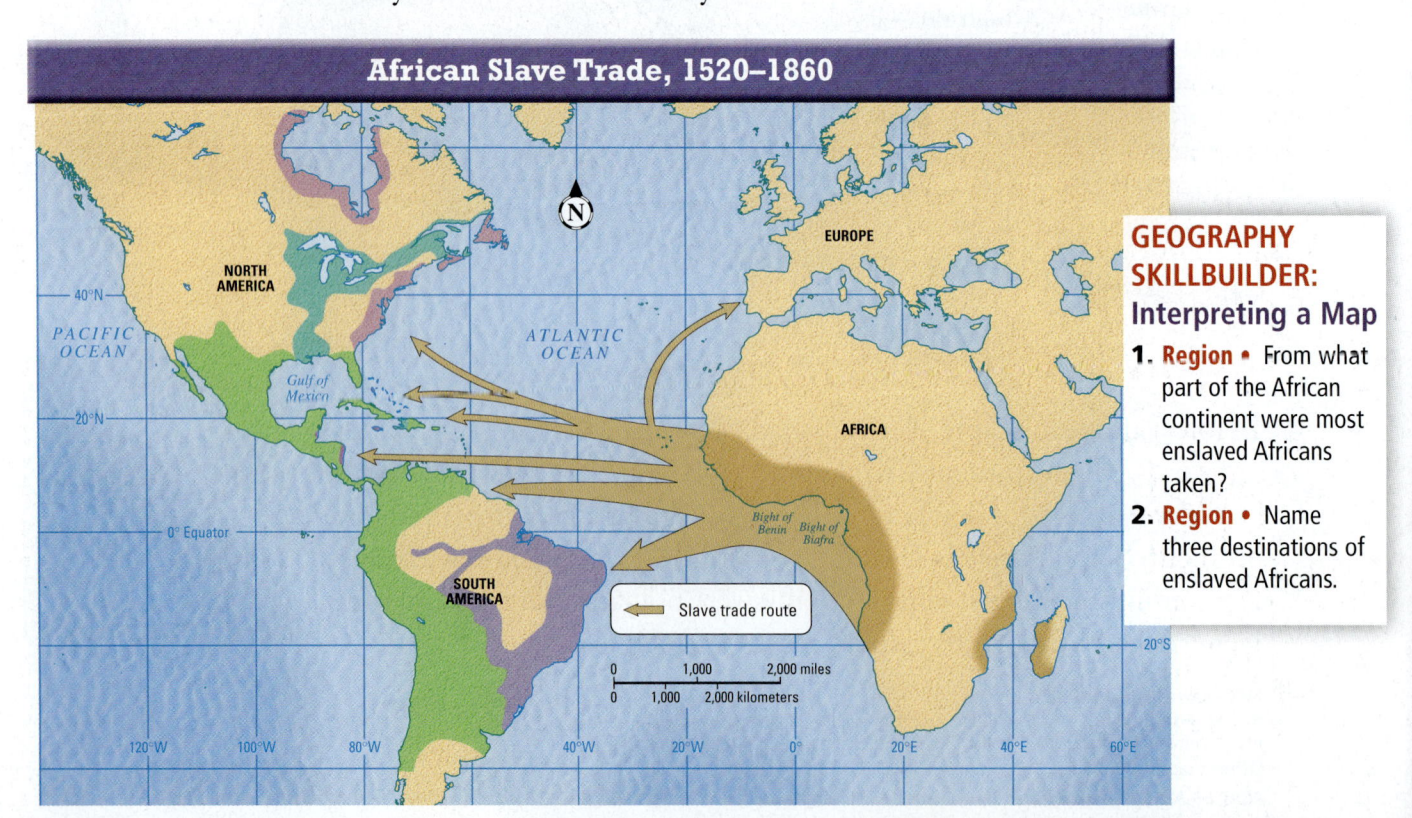

African Slave Trade, 1520–1860

GEOGRAPHY SKILLBUILDER: Interpreting a Map
1. **Region** • From what part of the African continent were most enslaved Africans taken?
2. **Region** • Name three destinations of enslaved Africans.

BACKGROUND
During the Industrial Revolution, inventions increased the speed of making goods. This created a need for more raw materials and markets.

European Colonialism

When Europeans ended the slave trade, they did not lose interest in Africa. The Industrial Revolution had changed economies in Europe and the United States. Africa could supply both raw materials, such as minerals, and new markets for goods.

Explorers and Missionaries Europeans knew little about the interior of Africa, but many were curious. Scientists and explorers were interested in African wildlife and natural resources. European missionaries also traveled to Africa. A **missionary** is a person who goes to another country to do religious and social work. Missionaries wanted to convert Africans to Christianity and bring education and health care to Africa. Many also taught European ways of thinking, which often conflicted with, and destroyed, African traditions.

Competition for Africa In the 19th century, European nations began to compete for control of Africa. Each wanted the biggest or richest colonies and control of trade. To avoid wars over territory, European and U.S. leaders met in Berlin in 1884. There, and in later meetings, they discussed how to divide Africa. No Africans were consulted. Over the next 20 years, Belgium, France, the United Kingdom, Germany, Italy, Spain, Portugal, and the Ottoman Empire all established colonies in Africa. By 1912, only Ethiopia and Liberia remained independent.

The World's Heritage

A Wealth of Animals When European explorers came to Africa, they saw impressive sights—lions and cheetahs stalking zebras, elephants trumpeting messages to their young, giraffes delicately nibbling the tops of trees. Today, Tanzania's Serengeti National Park is where modern explorers watch animals in the wild—animals that most non-Africans have seen only in zoos.

The Serengeti is home to an astonishing variety of life. It is also the last place in Africa where huge migrations of animals take place. The sight of a million gnus, zebras, and gazelles moving majestically through the park is one of the wonders of the world.

Africa South of the Sahara: Geography and History

European Colonies in Africa, 1912

GEOGRAPHY SKILLBUILDER: Interpreting a Map

1. **Region** • Which country had the greatest number of colonies in Africa in 1912?
2. **Region** • Which countries remained independent?

Legend:
- Belgian
- British
- French
- German
- Italian
- Portuguese
- Spanish
- Independent state

Territories and labels shown on map:

Madeira Is. (Port.), Spanish Morocco, Morocco, Tunisia, Canary Is. (Sp.), Ifni, Spanish Sahara, Algeria, Libya, Egypt, Rio de Oro, Cape Verde Is. (Port.), French West Africa, Anglo-Egyptian Sudan, Eritrea, French Somaliland, The Gambia, Portuguese Guinea, Sierra Leone, Liberia, Gold Coast, Togo, Nigeria, Cameroon, British Somaliland, Ethiopia, Fernando Póo, Rio Muni, Príncipe (Port.), São Tomé (Port.), French Equatorial Africa, Uganda, British East Africa, Italian Somaliland, Belgian Congo, Cabinda (Port.), German East Africa, Zanzibar I. (Br.), Comoros Is. (Fr.), Angola, Northern Rhodesia, Nyasaland, Mozambique, Madagascar, German Southwest Africa, Southern Rhodesia, Walvis Bay, Bechuanaland, Swaziland, Union of South Africa, Basutoland

Mediterranean Sea, Red Sea, Atlantic Ocean, Indian Ocean, Mozambique Channel, Tropic of Cancer, Equator, Tropic of Capricorn

Impact of Colonial Rule

When Europeans divided Africa, most colonizers cared mainly about gold, diamonds, and other resources. The Europeans knew little about Africa's political and social systems. Many Europeans looked down on Africa's rich cultures and tried to make Africans more like Europeans.

Europeans also worsened conflicts among ethnic groups. For example, the Belgian rulers of Rwanda-Burundi insisted that everyone carry identity cards saying whether they were **Hutu,** the ethnic majority, or **Tutsi,** the minority that had ruled the Hutu. Many people did not know which of these they were. The Belgians decided that anyone who owned more than ten cows was Tutsi. The Tutsi got the best education and jobs. Soon the Hutu were resentful, and a violent conflict began. In 1994, the conflict between the Hutu and the Tutsi escalated into a brutal civil war. The Tutsi were victorious and formed a new government in Rwanda.

Movement • During and after the civil war, thousands of Tutsi were massacred, and thousands of Hutu refugees, such as these, were driven from their homeland. ▼

SECTION 3 ASSESSMENT

Terms & Names
1. Explain the significance of: (a) missionary (b) Hutu (c) Tutsi

Using Graphics

2. Use a chart like this one to list the ways in which Europeans changed Africa, and the effects of the changes on African life.

Change	Effect

Main Ideas

3. (a) How did Europeans change the institution of slavery in Africa?

   (b) Why did European interest in Africa turn from the slave trade to colonization?

   (c) How is the modern conflict between the Hutu and Tutsi a result of the actions of European rulers?

Critical Thinking

4. **Comparing**

   How was the way of life of many Africans different after the arrival of Europeans?

   Think About
   - goals of missionaries and European countries
   - history and traditions of ethnic peoples

ACTIVITY -OPTION- Write an **opinion paper** explaining the negative effects of colonization.

Africa South of the Sahara: Geography and History **305**

SKILLBUILDER

Interpreting a Chart

SUNSHINE STATE STANDARDS
Key Standard SS.A.1.3.2
The student knows the relative value of primary and secondary sources and uses this information to draw conclusions from historical sources such as data in charts, tables, graphs.
FCAT LA.A.2.3.1 Reading: Identify Main Idea, Facts, and Details

▶▶ Defining the Skill

A chart organizes information in a visual form. The information is simplified or summarized and then arranged so that it is easy to read and understand.

▶▶ Applying the Skill

The chart below lists the population, number of radios, and number of televisions in several West African nations and the United States. Use the strategies listed below to help you interpret the chart.

How to Interpret a Chart

Strategy ❶ Read the title to learn the main idea of the chart.

Strategy ❷ Read the labels across the top and down the first column of the chart. The labels in the column list the countries represented in the chart. The labels across the top tell what information is provided for each country.

Strategy ❸ Study the information in the chart. Read down the columns to compare one country with another. Read across the rows to see the communications available in each country.

Strategy ❹ Summarize the information in the chart. The title helps you clarify the main idea of the chart.

❶ **Communication in Western Africa and the United States, 2000**

❷ Country	Population	Radios	Televisions
Benin	❸ 6.6 million	620,000	60,000
Ghana	❸ 19.9 million	4,400,000	1,730,000
Liberia	❸ 3.2 million	❸ 790,000	❸ 70,000
Mali	11 million	570,000	45,000
Niger	10.4 million	680,000	125,000
Nigeria	126.6 million	23,500,000	6,900,000
United States	284.5 million	575,000,000	219,000,000

❹ This chart compares the population, the number of radios, and the number of televisions in several West African nations and the United States. In the countries of Benin and Mali, there are very few radios and televisions compared with the number of people. For example, in Mali there is one television for every 244 people. In the United States, there is more than one radio per person. In Nigeria, there is one television for every 18 people.

Write a Summary

To gain a clear understanding of the information in this chart, write a summary. It is possible to produce other data from the information in this chart. To find out how many people there are for one television or radio in each nation, divide the population by the number of televisions or radios. The paragraph above summarizes the chart.

▶▶ Practicing the Skill

Turn to page 294 in Chapter 10. Study the chart titled "Africa's Deserts," and write a paragraph that summarizes the information in that chart.

SECTION 4

The Road to Independence

TERMS & NAMES
racism
diversity
apartheid

MAIN IDEA
During the 20th century, African nations gained independence from their colonial rulers.

WHY IT MATTERS NOW
Many independent nations in Africa are now struggling to form democratic governments.

DATELINE

NAIROBI, KENYA, DECEMBER 12, 1963—Thousands of Kenyans watched today as the British flag was lowered for the last time over the former colony. The new national flag of independent Kenya was raised in its place.

The new flag's stripes of black, red, and green stand for the country's people, their struggle for independence, and the country's rich resources. The center symbol is a Masai shield and spears.

To mark the change from British rule, Prince Philip of England attended the ceremony. All over Kenya, people cheered their new country, shouting "Uhuru!" the Swahili word for freedom.

Place • Prince Philip and Kenya's President Jomo Kenyatta attend the ceremony marking Kenya's independence. ▲

Moving Toward Independence

Colonial rule in Africa disrupted social systems and governments, and robbed Africa of resources. Many Africans objected, but they did not have enough power to act. During the 1920s and 1930s, colonial rulers sent a few Africans to attend universities in Europe and the United States. These educated young people started to dream of independence. Nationalism grew strong.

TAKING NOTES
Use your chart to take notes about Africa South of the Sahara.

SUNSHINE STATE STANDARDS
Key Standard SS.A.3.3.2 The student understands the historical events that have shaped the development of cultures throughout the world.
Other Standards SS.B.1.3.3
FCAT LA.A.2.3.1 Reading: Identify Main Idea, Facts, and Details

Africa South of the Sahara: Geography and History 307

African Political Systems, 2001

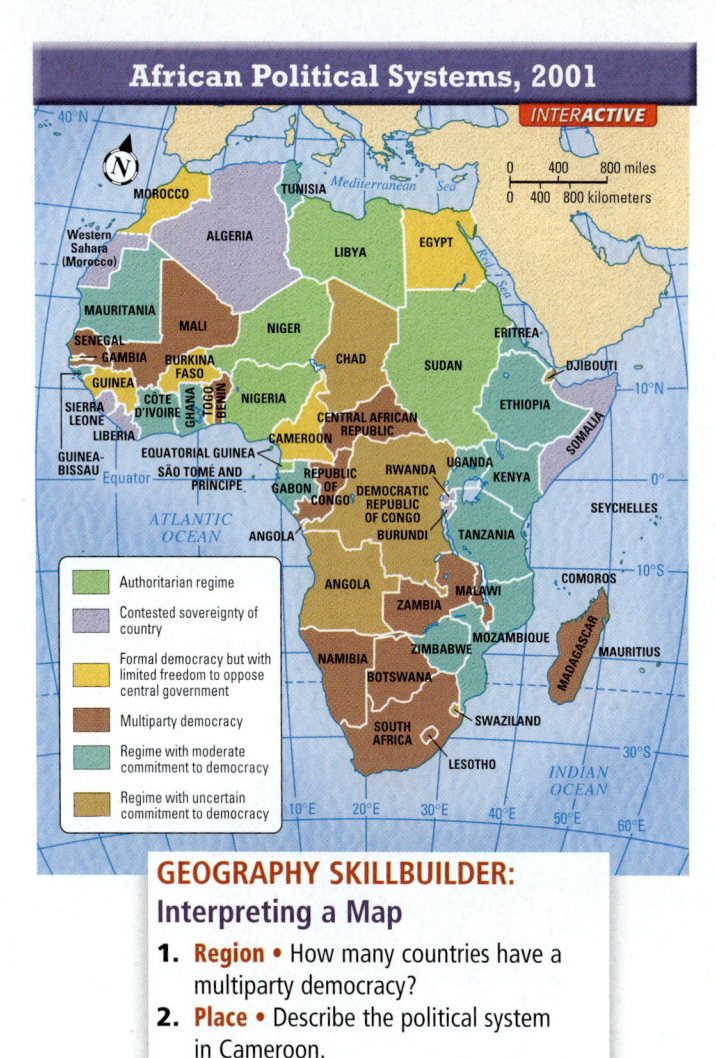

GEOGRAPHY SKILLBUILDER:
Interpreting a Map
1. **Region** • How many countries have a multiparty democracy?
2. **Place** • Describe the political system in Cameroon.

Map legend:
- Authoritarian regime
- Contested sovereignty of country
- Formal democracy but with limited freedom to oppose central government
- Multiparty democracy
- Regime with moderate commitment to democracy
- Regime with uncertain commitment to democracy

Journey to Freedom

European nations wanted to keep their colonies for their valuable resources although they were expensive to maintain. Many Europeans believed that Africans were unable to govern themselves. This attitude is an example of **racism,** the unfounded belief that one race is inferior to another race.

Pan-African Congresses Educated Africans believed they could govern themselves. African men had fought for the European Allies during World War I, and thousands had died. Ex-soldiers wanted self-rule. Pan-Africanism, an idea that people of African descent around the world should work together for their freedom, attracted more supporters. In 1919, the first Pan-African Congress was organized. Africans again fought in World War II. After this war, many felt that they now deserved independence.

> **A VOICE FROM AFRICA**
>
> …We are determined to be free. We want education. We want the right to earn a decent living; the right to express our thoughts and emotions, to adopt and create forms of beauty. We demand for Black Africa autonomy and independence….
>
> *The Pan-African Congress, 1945*

Reading Social Studies
A. Analyzing Causes How did the two world wars and the Pan-African congresses affect the struggle for African independence?

At the fifth Pan-African Congress in 1945, there were 90 delegates; 26 were from all over Africa. Several were men who would become the political leaders of their countries, including Kwame Nkrumah of Ghana and Jomo Kenyatta of Kenya.

New African Countries

Between 1951 and 1980, most of the colonies in Africa south of the Sahara gained independence. For some countries, the path to nationhood was smooth. For others, it was not. Nigeria and South Africa had different experiences in achieving independence.

Nigeria: Diversity Brings Division

Before Nigeria gained independence from the United Kingdom in 1960, it had experienced a well-organized government, rich resources, and a strong economy under British rule. It was hoped that Nigeria's **diversity**—its many different cultures and viewpoints—would be a source of strength. Many Nigerians are Muslim, while others are Christian or follow traditional African religions. Nigerians speak more than 400 languages. However, instead of being a source of strength, this diversity caused problems.

Reading Social Studies

B. Finding Causes What led to the 1966 rioting in Nigeria?

Riots and War The slave trade and colonial rule had worsened hostility between the ethnic groups in Nigeria. Many Nigerian politicians focused on their ethnic group and not the whole country. Some leaders stole money and gave or took bribes.

Spotlight on CULTURE

Yam Festivals People celebrate what is precious to them. In Ghana, Nigeria, and Côte d'Ivoire, the yam is traditionally the most important crop. Among the Igbo people of Nigeria, a man's first prayer to God is for children. His second is for many yams.

Every year, people in these countries celebrate the harvest of the new yams with special dances and ceremonies. Côte d'Ivoire's King Kofti is shown at right accepting offerings at the Yam Festival. Yam paste is prepared in a large bowl.

Among the Akan people of Aburi in Ghana, a priest begins the festival by slicing and dropping three pieces from a yam. If the pieces fall skin-side down, the village will have good luck. If the slices fall cut-side down, trouble is ahead.

THINKING CRITICALLY

1. **Comparing** How is the American holiday Thanksgiving similar to the Yam Festival?
2. **Making Inferences** Why do you think a priest is involved with the Yam Festival in Ghana?

For more on the yam festivals, go to

RESEARCH LINKS
CLASSZONE.COM

Africa South of the Sahara: Geography and History

In 1966, deadly riots broke out, and many people were killed. The next year, people in the eastern part of Nigeria announced the formation of a separate country, Biafra. After three years of civil war between Biafran Nigerians and the Nigerian army, Biafra was defeated and rejoined Nigeria. Since then, military leaders have primarily ruled Nigeria.

Independence of South Africa

The United Kingdom gave South Africa independence in 1910. This action did not bring freedom to most South Africans. Only white South Africans could vote, and many laws were passed to restrict nonwhites.

In 1948, an official policy of racial segregation known as **apartheid** (uh·PAHRT·HYT) was adopted. Apartheid strictly separated people by color. Many people resisted apartheid. Protesters held marches, went on strike, and sometimes became violent. Although many protesters were jailed or killed, they did make progress. In 1991, apartheid ended. In 1994, for the first time, all South African adults could vote.

Place • Signs such as these were common in South Africa during apartheid. Everything from businesses to bathrooms was segregated. ▲

BACKGROUND
The word *apartheid* is from the Afrikaans language. It means "apartness."

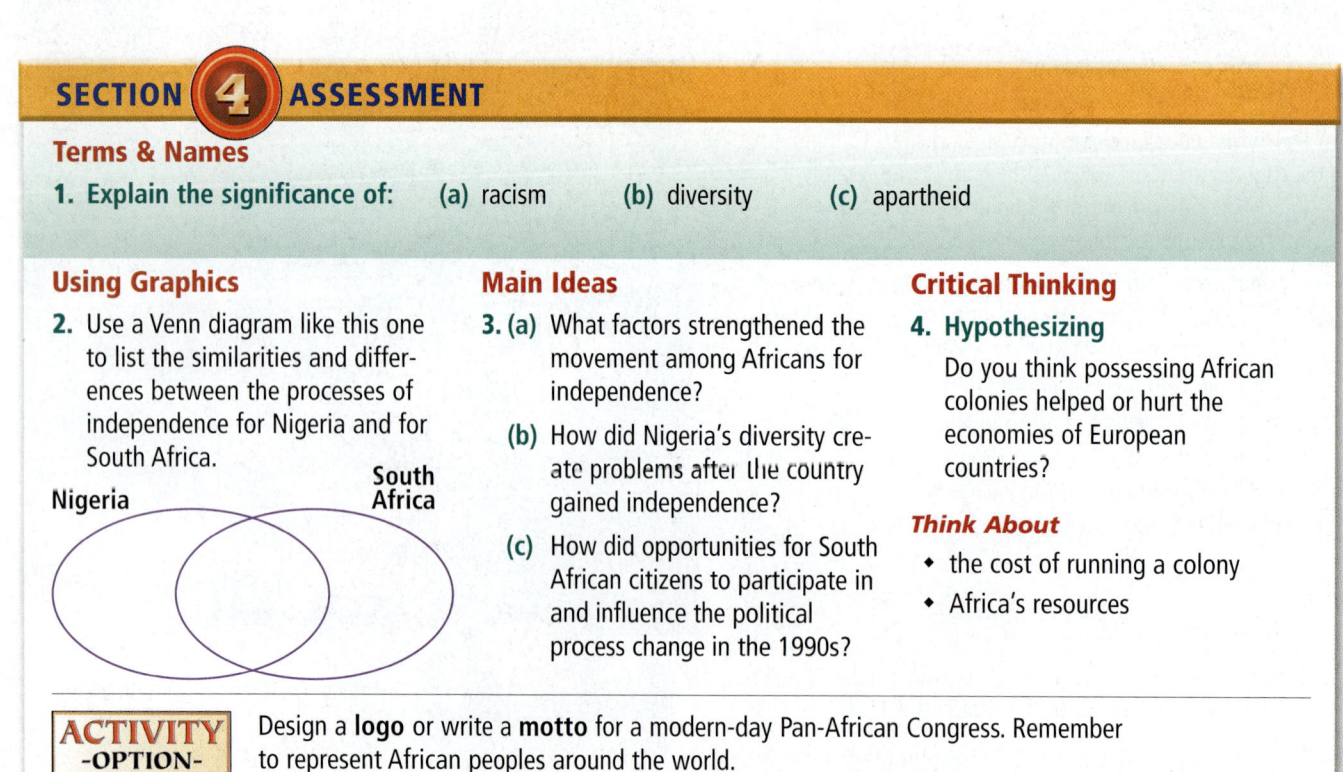

SECTION 4 ASSESSMENT

Terms & Names
1. Explain the significance of: (a) racism (b) diversity (c) apartheid

Using Graphics
2. Use a Venn diagram like this one to list the similarities and differences between the processes of independence for Nigeria and for South Africa.

Nigeria   South Africa

Main Ideas
3. (a) What factors strengthened the movement among Africans for independence?
  (b) How did Nigeria's diversity create problems after the country gained independence?
  (c) How did opportunities for South African citizens to participate in and influence the political process change in the 1990s?

Critical Thinking
4. **Hypothesizing**
  Do you think possessing African colonies helped or hurt the economies of European countries?

Think About
- the cost of running a colony
- Africa's resources

ACTIVITY -OPTION- Design a **logo** or write a **motto** for a modern-day Pan-African Congress. Remember to represent African peoples around the world.

Technology: 1100

House of Stone

Scattered across southeastern Africa are hundreds of stone ruins built between A.D. 1100 and 1500. The most spectacular, Great Zimbabwe, covers almost 1,800 acres. The word *zimbabwe* means "house of stone."

In the early 1900s, archaeologists proved that the city's builders were ancestors of the present-day Shona people. Artifacts from India, China, and Asia have been found at the site. The area was a trade center for gold, ivory, cloth, beads, and ceramics.

SUNSHINE STATE STANDARDS
Key Standard SS.A.2.3.7 The student knows significant achievements in art and architecture in various urban areas and communities to the time of the Renaissance (e.g., the Hanging Gardens of Babylon, pyramids in Egypt, temples in ancient Greece, bridges and aqueducts in ancient Rome, changes in European art and architecture between the Middle Ages and the High Renaissance).
FCAT LA.A.2.3.1 Reading: Identify Main Idea, Facts, and Details

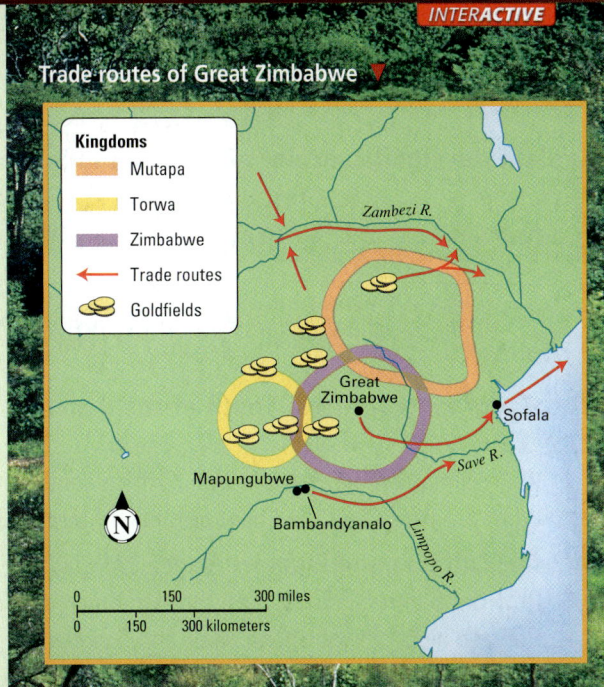

INTERACTIVE
Trade routes of Great Zimbabwe

Kingdoms
- Mutapa
- Torwa
- Zimbabwe
- Trade routes
- Goldfields

Builders used 900,000 granite slabs to create stone walls. The slabs were laid together without any type of mortar.

Natural weathering causes slabs of granite to break off hills in this area. Builders of Great Zimbabwe cut these slabs into smaller pieces and used them to create the stone walls.

Even though Great Zimbabwe has high walls and towers, archaeologists do not believe it was used as a fortress. Some archaeologists believe it was a religious center for the ancestors of the Shona.

THINKING Critically

1. Drawing Conclusions
The stone walls and towers of Great Zimbabwe were not built to protect the city. Why did its builders construct the walls and towers?

2. Making Inferences
How do trading networks of today differ from those of Great Zimbabwe?

UNIT 4 *Africa South of the Sahara*

CHAPTER 10 ASSESSMENT

TERMS & NAMES

Explain the significance of each of the following:
1. plateau
2. Great Rift Valley
3. Sahel
4. desertification
5. drought
6. savanna
7. Bantu migration
8. Mansa Musa
9. racism
10. diversity

REVIEW QUESTIONS

The Geography of Africa South of the Sahara (pages 291–295)
1. What climatic regions are found in Africa south of the Sahara?
2. What are rift valleys, and how are they formed?

African Cultures and Empires (pages 296-300)
3. How did Bantu culture spread through much of Africa?
4. How did kingdoms of Ghana, Mali, and Songhai become powerful?

The Impact of Colonialism on African Life (pages 301–305)
5. How did the European slave trade affect life in this region?
6. What factors did European countries consider while dividing up Africa?

The Road to Independence (pages 307–310)
7. What events increased the determination of Africans to gain independence from European rule?
8. What were some of the problems that accompanied independence in some African countries?

CRITICAL THINKING

Finding Causes
1. Using your completed chart from Reading Social Studies, p. 290, explain the causes and effects of desertification.

Analyzing Motives
2. Why were European nations so interested in establishing colonies in Africa?

Recognizing Effects
3. How did slave trade and colonialism in the past make it difficult for African leaders to build new, independent nations?

Visual Summary

1 The Geography of Africa South of the Sahara
- Africa south of the Sahara is a region of highlands and lowlands, with a variety of landforms and rich resources.

2 African Cultures and Empires
- Africa is the cradle of humankind.
- For over a thousand years (A.D. 400–1600), Africans built great empires based on trade.

3 The Impact of Colonialism on African Life
- Slave trade weakened African social systems by removing many healthy, young people from Africa.
- In the late 1800s, European nations divided Africa and established colonies, destroying existing governmental and social systems.

4 The Road to Independence
- In the late 20th century, most European colonies in Africa became independent nations.

> STANDARDS-BASED ASSESSMENT

Use the map and your knowledge of world cultures and geography to answer questions 1 and 2.

Additional Test Practice, pp. S1–S33

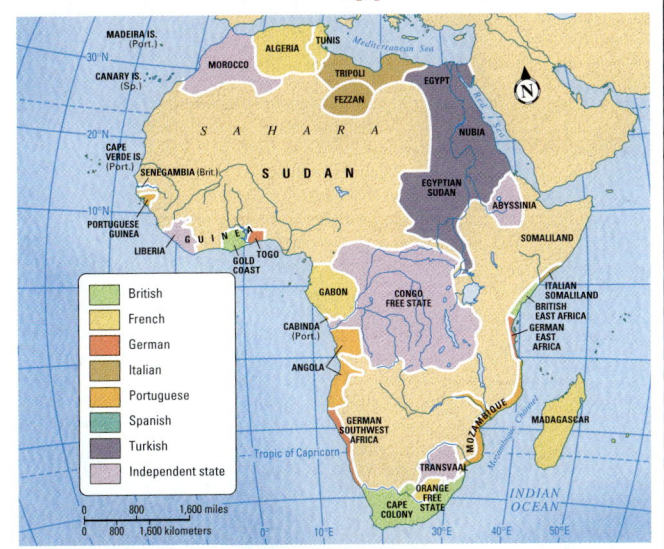

The explorer David Livingstone described his first sight of Victoria Falls in the following passage from his diary. Use the quotation and your knowledge of world cultures and geography to answer question 3.

PRIMARY SOURCE

After twenty minutes' sail from Kalai we came in sight, for the first time, of the columns of vapor appropriately called 'smoke,' rising at a distance of five or six miles. . . . Five columns now arose, and, bending in the direction of the wind, they seemed placed against a low ridge covered with trees; the tops of the columns at this distance appeared to mingle with the clouds. They were white below, and higher up became dark, so as to simulate smoke very closely. The whole scene was extremely beautiful.

DAVID LIVINGTONE, excerpt from his diary

1. Which of the following was a Turkish colony in 1886?
   A. Abyssinia
   B. Fezzan
   C. Nubia
   D. Togo

2. Which of the following countries probably controlled a port on the Mediterranean Sea?
   A. France
   B. Germany
   C. Portugal
   D. Spain

3. What do you think is the most likely explanation for the columns of "smoke" that Livingstone described?
   A. a forest fire on the shore
   B. mist from the water falls
   C. cooking fires in nearby villages
   D. tall storm clouds on the horizon

TEST PRACTICE
CLASSZONE.COM

ALTERNATIVE ASSESSMENT

1. WRITING ABOUT HISTORY

At the Berlin Conference of 1884–1885, European leaders came up with a plan to divide Africa. Research the conference. What countries were represented? How was the land divided? How did countries attain specific pieces of land to colonize? Write a report on your findings. Share your report with your class.

2. COOPERATIVE LEARNING

In a group of three to five classmates, gather photocopies, museum postcards, or magazine clippings showing art from countries in Africa south of the Sahara. Each group member can choose a different country. Organize the art around a map of Africa on the bulletin board or on a poster. Use string to connect each work of art to its country. Add a label telling when and where the artwork was created.

INTEGRATED TECHNOLOGY

Doing Internet Research

Use the Internet to research wildlife parks and refuges in Africa south of the Sahara. Then write a report of your findings. List the Web sites you used to prepare your report.

- Locate information about where these sites are located, what animals live there, what the goals of these parks and refuges are, and what problems they face.
- Include information about opportunities for visitors.

For Internet links to support this activity, go to

RESEARCH LINKS
CLASSZONE.COM

Africa South of the Sahara: Geography and History

CHAPTER 11
Western and Central Africa

SECTION 1 History and Political Change
SECTION 2 Economies and Cultures
SECTION 3 Nigeria Today

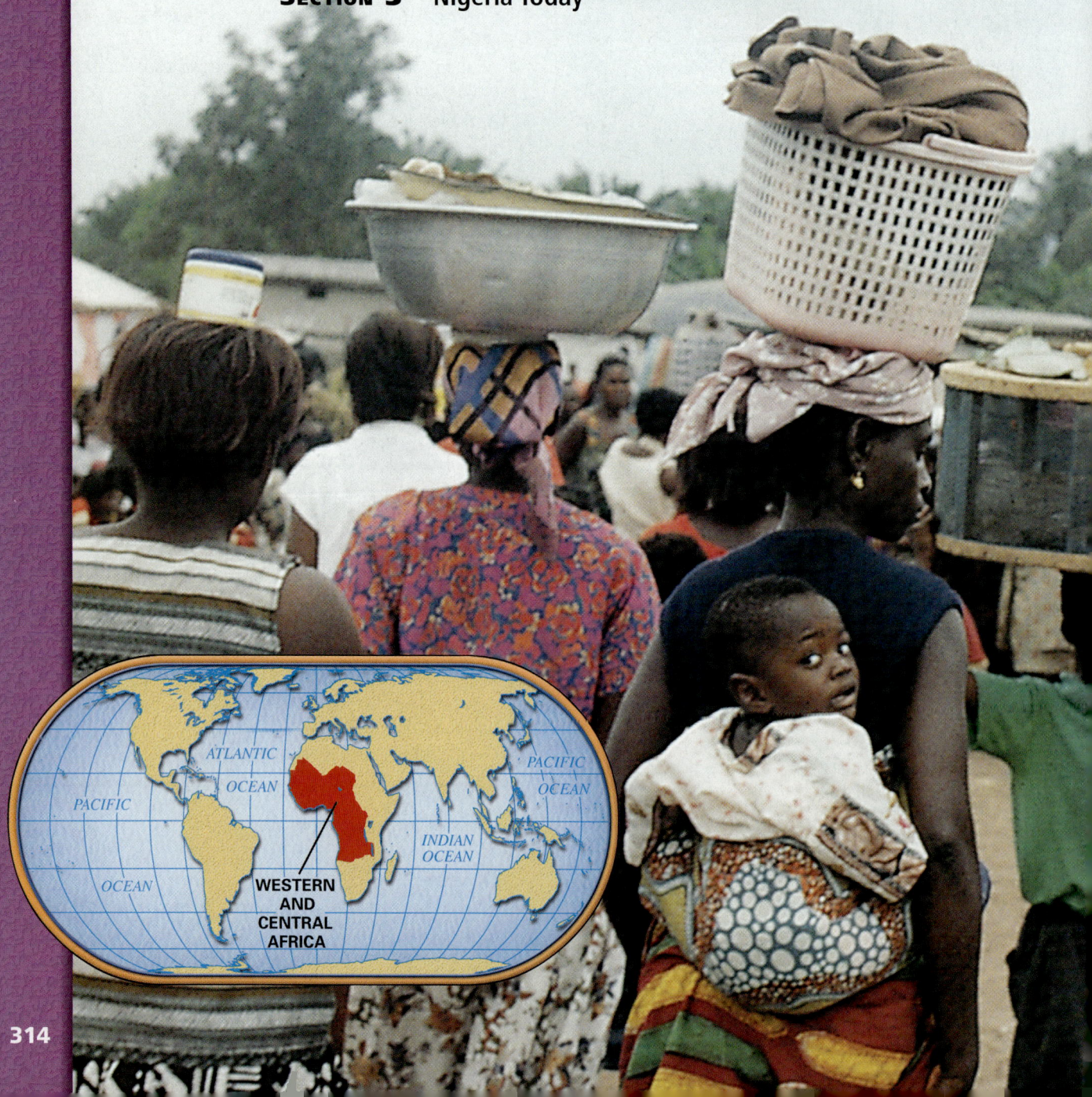

How can an entire town move across a country?

FOCUS ON GEOGRAPHY

Movement • Many African villages are far away from pharmacies, stores, airports, and other modern services.

In the Democratic Republic of the Congo, dense forests separate many villages from cities and towns.

Instead of building roads, the Congolese use their rivers as highways. Great barges run up and down the Congo River, carrying thousands of people on each trip. These barges are moving towns, with clinics, churches, markets, restaurants, and more.

What do you think?

- In what other ways do you think Africans use their waterways?
- What benefits do you think the barge offers over airplane travel in the Democratic Republic of the Congo?

Place Most African towns and villages host daily or weekly outdoor markets. Many of the vendors live in the countryside and travel into town to sell their goods.

CHAPTER 11 READING SOCIAL STUDIES

BEFORE YOU READ

▶▶ What Do You Know?
Western and Central African countries export many products to the United States, including gold and the cacao beans used to make chocolate. What else do you know about this region? Did you know that Liberia was founded by Americans? How did European colonialism affect the region? Reflect on what you have learned in other classes, what you read in Chapter 10, and what you have seen in the news about recent events in this area.

▶▶ What Do You Want to Know?
Decide what else you want to know about Western and Central Africa. In your notebook, record what you hope to learn from this chapter.

Culture • Cameroon's soccer team celebrated after winning the gold medal at the Olympic Games in 2000. ▼

READ AND TAKE NOTES

Reading Strategy: Making Inferences Making inferences is an important skill in reading social studies. Making inferences involves thinking beyond the text and interpreting the information you read. To make inferences, read carefully and use common sense and previous knowledge to make connections between ideas. Use the chart below to record inferences you can build on as you read.

- Copy the chart into your notebook.
- Read each statement. Use what you know to make inferences. Record your interpretations, connections, and ideas.
- As you read, record key evidence that confirms, changes, or builds on your inferences.

Culture • At one time only royalty in Ghana could wear this colorful Kente cloth. Today, it is popular among all Ghanaians. ▲

Statements	My Inferences	Key Evidence
European colonial powers divided Africa. Territories created by colonial powers became separate countries.		
In most African countries, governments are either too strong or too weak.		
Most countries of Western and Central Africa have a mix of different types of economies.		
Africa is culturally diverse. Before colonial rule, Africa had many different types of societies. There are some things that most of the peoples of Western and Central Africa have in common.		
Nigeria has more than 250 ethnic groups. Conflicts among these groups have sometimes led to civil war. This diversity has also led to a rich artistic and literary heritage.		

SECTION 1
History and Political Change

TERMS & NAMES
coup d'état
OAU
mediate
ECOWAS

MAIN IDEA
Since gaining independence, some of the countries of Western and Central Africa have had trouble establishing stable governments.

WHY IT MATTERS NOW
Unstable governments are the basis for many conflicts in Western and Central Africa.

DATELINE EXTRA

BERLIN, GERMANY, FEBRUARY 26, 1885
The competition for the riches of Africa has caused growing conflict. But today, the countries of Europe finally agreed on the rules for dividing up the African continent. The rules will enable the countries to claim land in Africa without going to war with one another.

When the powers of Europe take land in Africa, they must make sure that no other country has already claimed that land. Also, the agreement will allow open trade among the colonies. All countries will be able to freely move goods on the Congo River. At last, the takeover of Africa will be orderly.

Region • This political cartoon makes clear that European nations have been fighting for control of African lands and resources.

Dividing Western and Central Africa

European nations divided the African continent in the late 1800s. They were not thinking about creating new nations. Their goal was to control Africa's rich resources. To avoid war with one another, the European powers made trades. They traded one advantage—such as coastal land—for another.

TAKING NOTES
Use your chart to take notes about Western and Central Africa.

Statements	My Inferences	Key Evidence
European colonial powers divided Africa...		
In most African countries, governments are...		

SUNSHINE STATE STANDARDS
Key Standard SS.A.3.3.5 The student understands the differences between institutions of Eastern and Western civilizations (e.g., differences in governments, social traditions and customs, economic systems and religious institutions).
Other Standards SS.B.2.3.5
FCAT LA.A.2.2.7 Reading: Recognize Compare and Contrast

Western and Central Africa 317

New Maps of West Africa

When Europeans divided Africa, they ignored traditional borders between Africa's ethnic groups. They used other factors to draw new maps, such as the location of rivers or lakes.

Let's Make a Deal Look at The Gambia on the political map of Africa on page 280. The country is only 30 miles across at its widest point. How was a country with such strange borders formed? In 1816, the British bought an island at the mouth of the Gambia River. They used the island as a base to extend their control over the banks of the river. However, France claimed all the land around the river. When the Europeans drew borders in the late 1880s, the British kept The Gambia, with access to the river. In return, the French got more land for Senegal.

Dividing the Congo Basin European interest in a river affected borders in Central Africa too. The Congo River is the second-longest river in Africa. Belgium, France, and Portugal all wanted to claim the river and the lands around it. That rivalry was the main reason for the conference in Berlin that you read about on page 523. At the conference, the three nations agreed to divide the huge Congo Basin. King Leopold of Belgium took the land that is now the Democratic Republic of the Congo as his personal property. France possessed what is now the Republic of the Congo. Portugal controlled what is present-day Angola.

Human-Environment Interaction • The Gambia's width was in large part determined by the firing range of the British gunboats that patrolled the Gambia River. ▲

Reading Social Studies

A. Analyzing Motives Why was controlling a river so important to the Europeans?

Governments in Western and Central Africa

When African nations became independent, many of their colonial borders stayed the same. These borders split ethnic groups and regions that historically had been united, making it difficult

The Congo Basin, 2001

GEOGRAPHY SKILLBUILDER: Interpreting a Map

1. **Region** • What physical feature forms the border between the Republic of the Congo and the Democratic Republic of the Congo?
2. **Place** • What is the capital of the Republic of the Congo?

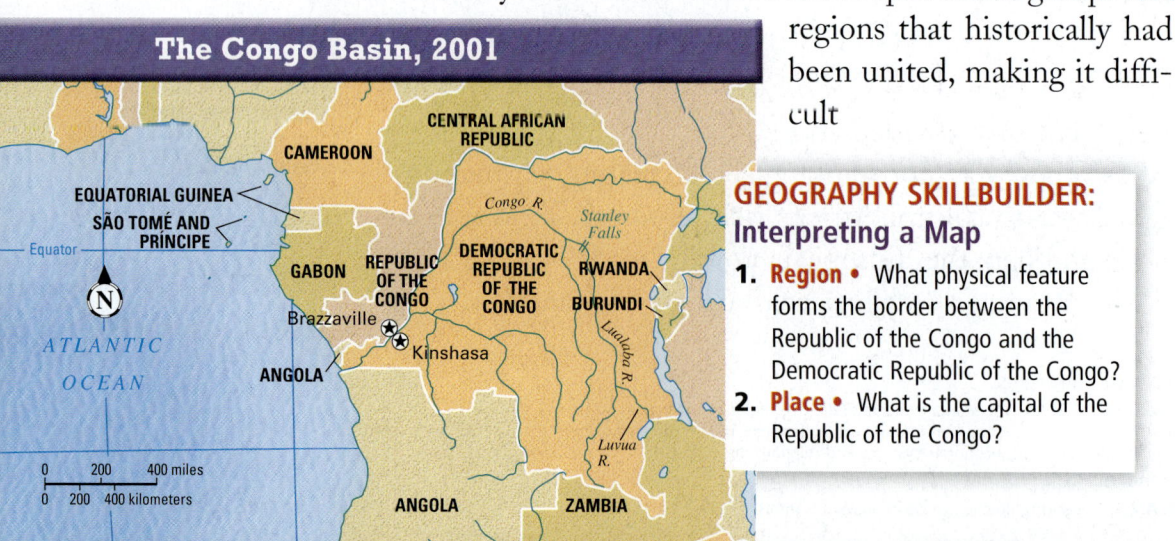

Since 1963, about 200 African governments have been ousted by coups d'état (KOO day·TAH). A **coup d'état** is an overthrow of a government by force. Two of the many countries that have struggled to create stable democratic governments are the Democratic Republic of the Congo and Ghana.

Government in the Democratic Republic of the Congo

In 1960, the former Belgian Congo gained independence, but a series of coups d'état toppled each established government. Five years later, an army general, Joseph Désiré Mobutu, took power. Mobutu tried to wipe out all traces of colonialism. He changed the name of the country to Zaire (ZY·eer) and his own name to Mobutu Sese Seko (SAY·say SAY·koh). He made people wear African-style clothing and take names that were African instead of Belgian.

Mobutu ruled as a dictator, calling the people of Zaire his "children." He allowed no criticism of his rule. At the same time, he built up a personal fortune by stealing government money intended for roads, schools, and hospitals.

Place • This banknote was printed in 1993, four years before Zaire became the Democratic Republic of the Congo. ▼

BACKGROUND
Joseph Kabila was not elected president. He was chosen by his father's handpicked parliament.

Civil War A brutal civil war began in Zaire in 1994. It resulted in Laurent-Désiré Kabila overthrowing Mobutu's government. Kabila changed the country's name to the Democratic Republic of the Congo. However, the country was not a true democracy, and civil war started again. Kabila was assassinated in 2001. His son, Joseph Kabila, replaced him as president.

Place • Kwame Nkrumah is shown here, at left, shortly after Ghana gained independence. ▼

Government in Ghana

In 1957, the British colony of Gold Coast became the first independent country in Africa south of the Sahara. The new nation took its name, Ghana, from a great ancient empire. The country's first leader was Kwame Nkrumah (uhn·KROO·muh). Nkrumah wanted to make Ghana modern. He built a new seaport, roads, and railroads to make shipping natural resources to factories and sending manufactured goods to stores easier and cheaper. Foreign trade improved. Ghana also became the first country in Africa south of the Sahara to have compulsory primary education.

Reading Social Studies
B. Drawing Conclusions Why do you think some African leaders have decided to change their nations' names?

Place • This billboard in Accra, Ghana, showed Jerry John Rawlings (center) with the two candidates for the presidency in 2000. ▲

Military Rulers Although Nkrumah helped the new nation, he ruled as a dictator. He sent his opponents to prison. Some were tortured and killed. In 1966, the police and the army organized a coup d'état against Nkrumah. The coup d'état leaders freed political prisoners. They tried to help small businesses. Still, conditions in Ghana grew worse. People lost their jobs and did not have money for food. They went on strike to protest. When military leaders tried to take control, fighting began, and more coups d'état followed. In 1979, Jerry John Rawlings, a soldier, took power.

The Coming of Democracy In 1992, Rawlings allowed an election to take place. Ghana then became more democratic. A new constitution and parliament put limits on his power. In 2000, Rawlings became the first modern African military ruler to give up power peacefully. Elections brought in a new president. Today, Ghana is one of the most stable nations in Africa. In 1998, UN Secretary General Kofi Annan commented on Ghana's success.

Reading Social Studies

C. Forming and Supporting Opinions What do you think of Rawlings's decision to give up power peacefully? Why might he have decided to do so?

Vocabulary

status quo: existing state of affairs

> **A VOICE FROM GHANA**
>
> I grew up in Ghana at the time when we were fighting for independence, and so I saw lots of changes in my youth. I saw that it was possible to challenge the status quo and do something about it. And change did occur.
>
> *Kofi Annan, 1998*

Citizenship IN ACTION

Aid for Children In cities all over Africa, growing numbers of children can be found living on the streets. In Accra, Ghana, which has thousands of street children (shown at right), two local organizations are working to help them: Street Girls Aid (S.Aid) and Catholic Action for Street Children (CAS).

CAS provides places where children can wash, eat, rest, take classes, or simply play. For teenage mothers with children, S.Aid offers daycare so the mothers can work. Both groups provide health care and counseling to help children cope with the harshness of life on the streets.

Region • In 2001, the OAU was being transformed into the African Union, whose new Secretary General, Amara Essy, is shown here on the right. ▶

Nations Helping Nations

Like Ghana, many African nations have had to struggle for peace and democracy. Some nations are working together to help one another. In 1963, the **OAU**, or the Organization of African Unity, was formed. The organization tries to promote unity among all Africans. For example, the OAU would like to establish a single currency for Africa. The OAU also mediates disputes between countries. To **mediate** means to help find a peaceful solution.

ECOWAS The nations of Western Africa also cooperate economically. **ECOWAS**, or the Economic Community of West African States, was formed in 1975. It works to improve trade within Western Africa and with countries outside the region. ECOWAS also has mediated disputes between countries in Western Africa and tried to end government corruption.

SECTION 1 ASSESSMENT

Terms & Names
1. Explain the significance of: (a) coup d'état (b) OAU (c) mediate (d) ECOWAS

Using Graphics
2. Use a chart like this one to compare the governments of the Democratic Republic of the Congo and Ghana.

Democratic Republic of the Congo	Ghana

Main Ideas
3. (a) What was the impact of European colonization on the governments of modern Africa?
   (b) What example was given in this section of a government with unlimited power? What example was given in this section of a government with limited power?
   (c) How did Kwame Nkrumah influence Ghana?

Critical Thinking
4. **Making Inferences**

   Why do you think it was important for the power of Jerry John Rawlings, the former president of Ghana, to be limited?

   Think About
   - other dictatorships around the world
   - the progression of human rights

ACTIVITY -OPTION- Pretend you have been commissioned by the OAU to design a common currency for all of Africa. Draw a **model** or write a **description** of your design.

Western and Central Africa

Linking Past and Present

The Legacy of Africa South of the Sahara

Music

Music has always played an important role in the daily life of Africa south of the Sahara. Characteristic of the music are its complex rhythms. Hand clapping, drums, and iron bells produce different rhythmic patterns. Over the years, the music of Africa south of the Sahara has influenced music around the world. Jazz, a popular type of music that began in the early 1900s in the United States, is based on a combination of European harmonies and African rhythms.

SUNSHINE STATE STANDARDS
Key Standard SS.A.3.3.1 The student understands ways in which cultural characteristics have been transmitted from one society to another (e.g., through art, architecture, language, other artifacts, traditions, beliefs, values, and behaviors).
FCAT LA.A.2.3.1 Reading: Identify Main Idea, Facts, and Details

Swahili Language

Swahili, also called Kiswahili, is a widespread language on the eastern coast of Africa. It evolved from the mixing of East African and Arab cultures. Swahili also includes words adapted from the English of British colonists, such as *penseli* (pencil), *basi* (bus), and *baiskeli* (bicycle). Today, it continues to be the language spoken in the business community and is one of the languages of Tanzania, Kenya, and Uganda.

Gold

For nearly 1,000 years, Africans south of the Sahara have used their prized possessions—gold and ivory—as signs of wealth and power. They have also traded these valuable materials for other commodities, such as glass, precious stones, and ceramics. Many European settlers came to South Africa to take part in the gold industry. Today, South Africa is the continent's largest gold producer.

Find Out More About It!

Study the text and photos on these pages to learn about inventions, creations, and contributions that have come from Africa south of the Sahara. Then choose the item that interests you the most and use the library or the Internet to learn more about it. Use the information you gather to write a short essay about how what you researched relates to you.

RESEARCH LINKS
CLASSZONE.COM

Coffee

More than 1,000 years ago, coffee trees grew in Ethiopia. Coffee beans were first used as a food. In the 1400s, coffee as a beverage was popular in Arabia, Egypt, and Turkey. In the following centuries, it was introduced to Europe and to North America. Today, coffee comes in many varieties and blends and is served as a hot or a cold beverage. It is also used to flavor ice cream and other treats.

Sculpture

The earliest evidence of African sculpture outside of Egypt dates from around 500 B.C. in Nok, located in what is now Nigeria. Archaeologists have found baked-clay heads and figures made by the Nok people. In the 1400s, sculptures of kings and thrones were created to show respect for royalty. They also represented the wealth of a region. Today, many African sculptures continue to be based on traditional themes. Artists create sculptures for religious and social purposes as well as for the retail and tourist trade.

Africa South of the Sahara 323

SECTION 2
Economies and Cultures

TERMS & NAMES
subsistence farming
cash crop
rite of passage

MAIN IDEA
The economies in Western and Central Africa are mostly a mix of traditional and market economies.

WHY IT MATTERS NOW
Economic development is one of the keys to sustaining democracy in Africa.

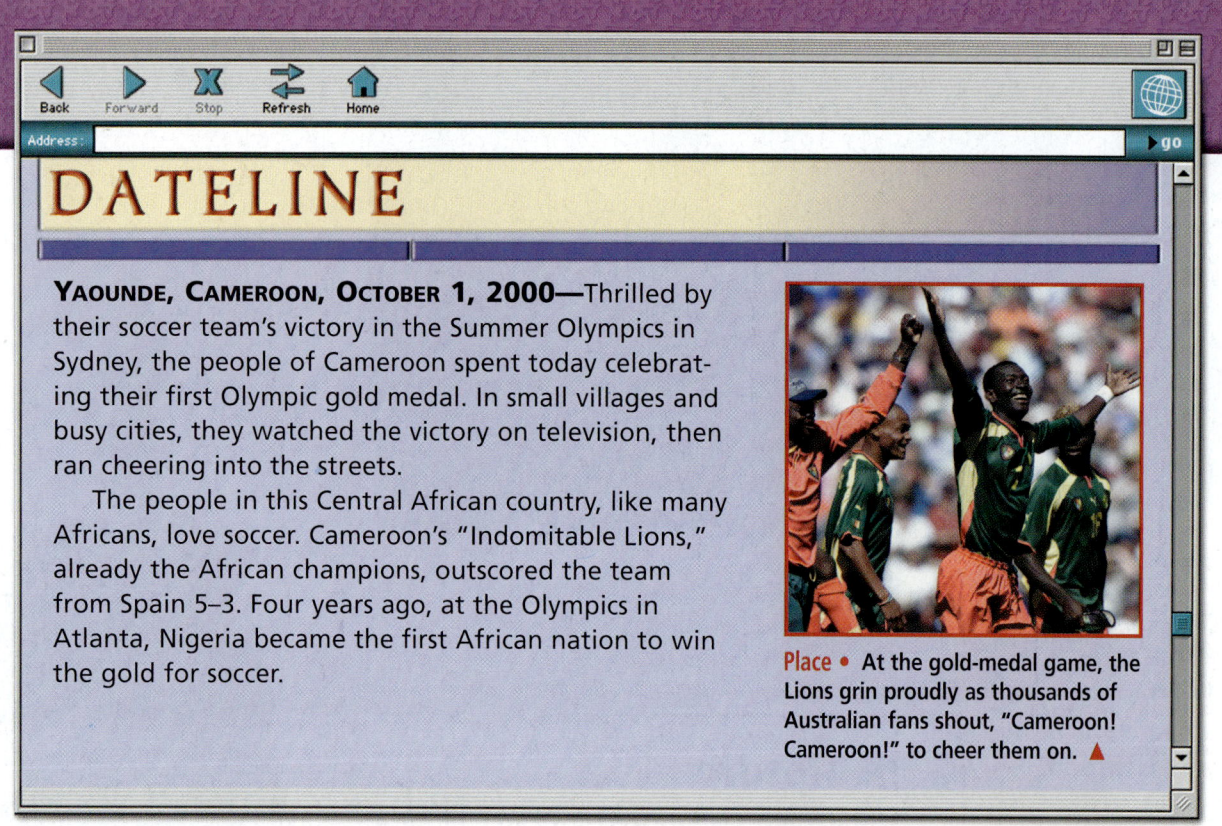

DATELINE

YAOUNDE, CAMEROON, OCTOBER 1, 2000—Thrilled by their soccer team's victory in the Summer Olympics in Sydney, the people of Cameroon spent today celebrating their first Olympic gold medal. In small villages and busy cities, they watched the victory on television, then ran cheering into the streets.

The people in this Central African country, like many Africans, love soccer. Cameroon's "Indomitable Lions," already the African champions, outscored the team from Spain 5–3. Four years ago, at the Olympics in Atlanta, Nigeria became the first African nation to win the gold for soccer.

Place • At the gold-medal game, the Lions grin proudly as thousands of Australian fans shout, "Cameroon! Cameroon!" to cheer them on. ▲

Economies of Western and Central Africa

Many Africans share not only a passion for soccer but also a common economic history. Most African countries once had traditional economies, which followed age-old trading customs. Colonial governments introduced market economies, in which goods were bought and sold. Government-controlled economies, or command economies, became common after independence. Today, most African countries again have market economies.

TAKING NOTES
Use your chart to take notes about Western and Central Africa.

Statements	My Inferences	Key Evidence
European colonial powers divided Africa...		
In most African countries, governments are...		

SUNSHINE STATE STANDARDS
Key Standard SS.D.2.3.1 The student understands ways production and distribution decisions are determined in the United States economy and how these decisions compare to those made in market, tradition-based, command, and mixed economic systems.
Other Standards SS.A.3.3.5, B.2.3.3
FCAT LA.A.2.3.1 Reading: Identify Main Idea, Facts, and Details

324 CHAPTER 11

Agriculture in Western and Central Africa

Most people in Western and Central Africa are farmers. Many practice **subsistence farming.** That is, they grow food, such as millet and sorghum, mainly to feed their own households. During the colonial era, European and African business owners started large plantations. They grew tropical crops—sugar cane, coffee, and cacao—for export. A crop grown only for sale is called a **cash crop.**

Reading Social Studies
A. Clarifying Is subsistence farming done for profit or need?

Edible Exports Have you eaten or used anything from Africa today? Chances are you have. Côte d'Ivoire (KOHT dee•VWAHR), formerly Ivory Coast, is the world's largest producer and exporter of cacao beans, which are used to make chocolate. Coastal West African countries also export coffee, bananas, pineapples, palm oil, peanuts, and kola nuts. Central African countries produce coffee, rubber, and cotton. These exports bring many African countries income for development, such as building roads and schools.

African Artisans

Although the majority of people are farmers, some have other jobs. Some people craft items out of metal, leather, or wood. These workers make things such as iron hoes, leather shoes, and beautiful pieces of art. Other people are entertainers and musicians. Musicians act as the historians in some traditional African societies. Their skills and stories are passed down from generation to generation.

Culture • Kente cloth, exported from West Africa, has become popular in many non-African countries. ▼

African Minerals

Almost every type of mineral in the world can be found somewhere in Africa. Valuable minerals exported from Central and Western Africa include diamonds, gold, petroleum, manganese, and uranium. Many Africans earn their living by working in mines.

Connections to Science

Disappearing Tusks Ivory from African elephant tusks has been used to make items such as piano keys, jewelry, and billiard balls. Many elephants have been killed for their tusks, which you can see below. To protect elephants, ivory products were banned internationally in the 1980s. However, the demand for ivory is still so great that people continue to hunt elephants illegally for their tusks.

Because elephants born without tusks are not hunted, they live and reproduce. Often their offspring are tuskless. Biologists have noted that about 30 percent of African elephants are now tuskless—an impressive increase from 1 percent in the 1930s.

Western and Central Africa

The Arms Trade in Western Africa, 2001

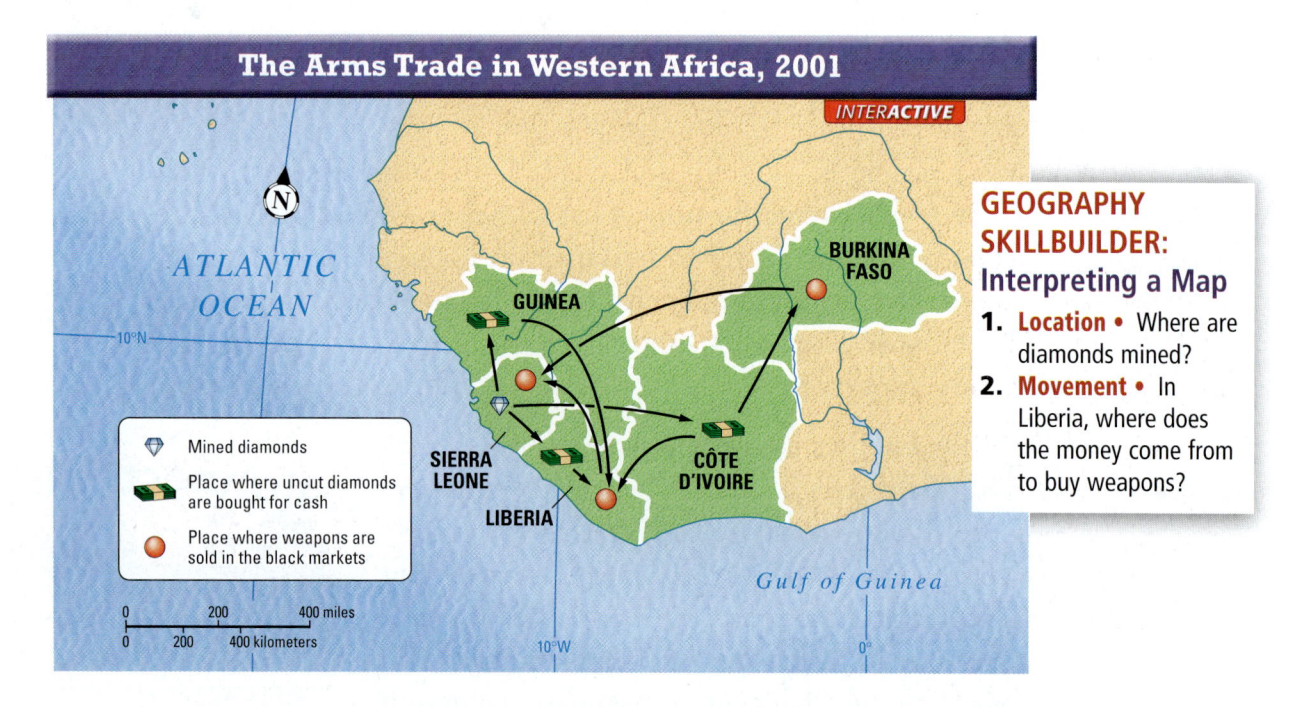

GEOGRAPHY SKILLBUILDER: Interpreting a Map
1. **Location** • Where are diamonds mined?
2. **Movement** • In Liberia, where does the money come from to buy weapons?

Diamonds for Weapons Africa's mineral wealth is sometimes used to help fund wars. During Angola's civil war, the government used income from oil exports to buy weapons, while rebel forces traded diamonds for guns. Diamonds have also been exported illegally to support brutal wars in Sierra Leone and the Democratic Republic of the Congo. In Sierra Leone, diamonds were smuggled out of the country in small envelopes and sold to buy weapons for rebel forces. World diamond markets are working to prevent the sale of "conflict diamonds."

Ways of Life in Western and Central Africa

In Western and Central Africa, hundreds of different ethnic groups speak more than 1,000 languages. People practice many different religions, including Islam and Christianity. Most Africans live in small villages, but more Africans are moving to large, crowded cities, such as Lagos, Nigeria, or Accra, Ghana. City living has put strains on traditional African family life and culture.

Family Structure Society in Western and Central Africa is based on extended families that include children, parents, grandparents, and other close relatives such as aunts and cousins. Some ethnic groups trace ancestry through the mother's family; others, through the father's family. People share both work and free time with their family.

Reading Social Studies

B. **Making Inferences** What aspects of city life do you think would put new strains on Africans from small villages?

Place • Many African extended families live in compounds such as this one. In addition to living areas, there are storage buildings and an open space for community life. ◀

Social Status

In many African societies, older people have higher status and more influence than younger ones. For example, when men of the Igbo people in Nigeria gather for discussions, they sit in order of age. The eldest men are served food and drink first. In some African communities, each age group has different responsibilities. Men of the most senior rank settle legal disputes and police the village. Female elders punish behavior that harms women, such as unfair treatment by husbands.

Spotlight on CULTURE

Seats of Art In Central and Western Africa, artists—not carpenters—make the most valued piece of household furniture: the stool. The Ashanti of Ghana believe that a person's spirit flows into a stool each time the person sits on it. Because of this, each individual in a household has his or her own stool. Nobody else is allowed to sit on the stool.

Each stool is decorated with special carvings that indicate the person's social status. The stools of the Luba people living in the Democratic Republic of the Congo reflect the importance the Luba place on their ancestors. Like the one at the right, most Luba stools feature a carving of an important ancestor of the owner.

THINKING CRITICALLY

1. **Recognizing Important Details**
   What do you think is the symbolism of the carved person holding up the seat of the stool?

2. **Drawing Conclusions**
   Why do you think the artist made this figure a woman?

For more on African art, go to

RESEARCH LINKS
CLASSZONE.COM

Western and Central Africa 327

Culture • These young boys of the Ituri forest in the Congo dance in outfits made of straw and woven cords during a rite of passage. ▶

Because age is so important, a special ceremony, which is called a **rite of passage**, marks the transition from one stage of life to another. A major rite of passage occurs when young men and women are recognized as adults. However, this tradition is dying out in parts of Africa. Some younger people are gaining higher status because they have skills that are needed. For example, as people move to cities, educated youths who can speak a European language are highly valued.

SECTION 2 ASSESSMENT

Terms & Names
1. Explain the significance of: (a) subsistence farming (b) cash crop (c) rite of passage

Using Graphics
2. Use a chart like this one to list characteristics of this region's economy and way of life. How might the economy affect how people live?

Economy	Way of Life

Main Ideas
3. (a) What types of economies are present in Western and Central Africa?
  (b) How is the use of Africa's mineral resources both beneficial and harmful to Africans?
  (c) How is African family structure similar to and different from American family structure?

Critical Thinking
4. **Drawing Conclusions**
  Do you think Africans will continue to have rites of passage in the future? Why or why not?

Think About
- how city life is affecting African societies
- other societies around the world

ACTIVITY -OPTION- Many Americans participate in rites of passage, such as baptisms, weddings, and funerals. Pretend you are studying American culture. Make a **poster** illustrating an American rite of passage.

SKILLBUILDER

Drawing Conclusions

SUNSHINE STATE STANDARDS
Key Standard SS.A.3.3.2 The student understands the historical events that have shaped the development of cultures throughout the world.
FCAT LA.A.2.3.1 Reading: Identify Main Idea, Facts, and Details

▶▶ Defining the Skill

You are drawing conclusions when you read carefully, analyze what you read, and form an opinion based on facts about the subject. Often you must use your own common sense, your experiences, and your previous knowledge of a subject to draw a conclusion.

▶▶ Applying the Skill

The passage to the right is about the years following independence in the Democratic Republic of the Congo. Use the following strategies to help you draw conclusions based on the passage.

How to Draw Conclusions

Strategy ❶ Read the passage carefully. Pay attention to the statements that can be proved to be true.

Strategy ❷ Locate the facts in the passage and list them in a diagram. Use your common sense, your experiences, and your previous knowledge to understand how the facts relate to one another.

Strategy ❸ Apply your common sense, experiences, and previous knowledge to the new facts from the passage, and then write a conclusion based on your gathered evidence.

Make a Diagram

A diagram is a way of organizing facts. The diagram to the right shows how to organize the facts and inferences from the passage above and a conclusion that could be drawn from them.

▶▶ Practicing the Skill

Turn to pages 325–326 and reread the passage entitled "African Minerals." Make a diagram like the one to the right to draw conclusions from the passage.

In 1960, the country then known as the Belgian Congo gained independence. Five years later, Mobutu Sese Seko seized power and renamed the country Zaire. Mobutu ruled Zaire until 1997. ❶ Even though this country has some of the richest resources in Africa—copper, gold, and diamonds—Mobutu led the country into greater poverty. ❶ He put much of the country's money into his personal bank accounts. ❶ Mobutu ruled like a dictator, requiring men who worked in the government to dress like him and allowing only his political party to have any power.

❶ In 1997, Laurent Kabila led a rebel army into Zaire from the east and took over the government of Zaire. ❶ He immediately renamed the country the Democratic Republic of the Congo. Many people in Congo hoped that Kabila would work to improve life there, but instead, he led the country into war with neighboring nations. ❶ When Kabila seized power, Mobutu fled to Morocco, where he died in 1997. ❶ At the time of his death, there was no mention on radio or television in Congo that he died.

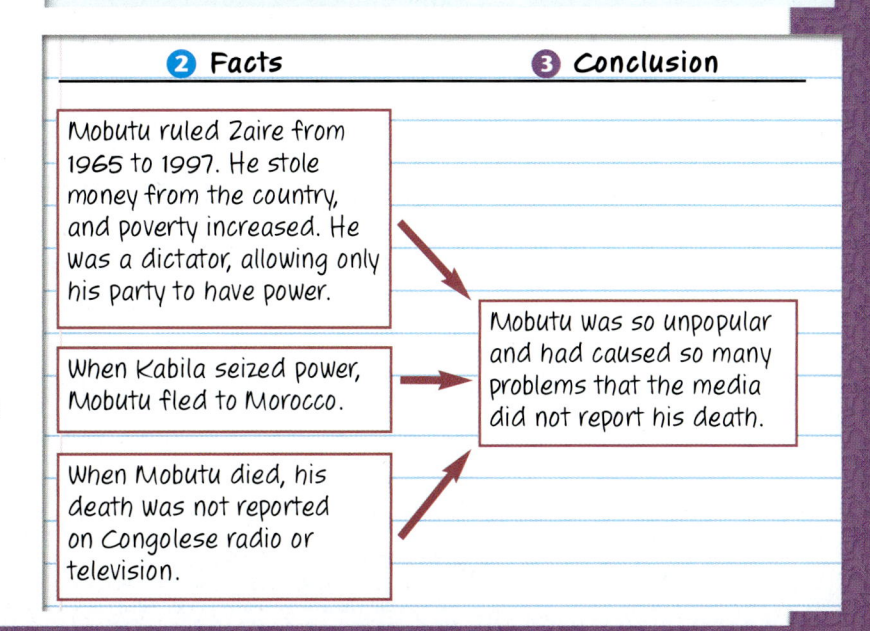

---

❷ Facts	❸ Conclusion
Mobutu ruled Zaire from 1965 to 1997. He stole money from the country, and poverty increased. He was a dictator, allowing only his party to have power.	Mobutu was so unpopular and had caused so many problems that the media did not report his death.
When Kabila seized power, Mobutu fled to Morocco.	
When Mobutu died, his death was not reported on Congolese radio or television.	

Western and Central Africa

SECTION 3

Nigeria Today

TERMS & NAMES
Yoruba
Igbo
Hausa
Wole Soyinka

MAIN IDEA
Nigeria has a rich diversity of peoples and resources.

WHY IT MATTERS NOW
Nigeria's diversity has caused civil war, from which the country is currently recovering.

DATELINE

ZAZZUA, HAUSALAND, ANCIENT NIGERIA, 1566—The Queen is dead! Long live the Queen! This week the peaceful and prosperous reign of Queen Bakwa came to an end. Her daughter, Amina, was crowned queen. Unlike her peace-loving mother, Queen Amina is a warrior in the Zazzua cavalry.

At her crowning, she announced her intention to force other West African rulers to honor her and allow Hausa traders to travel safely through their lands. She also intends to build earthen defense walls around all of Zazzua's towns. She will begin her first military campaign in three months' time.

Place • These earthen defense walls are known as *ganuwar Amina*, or "Amina's walls." ▲

A Look at Nigeria

Queen Amina's 16th-century military conquests helped make the present-day nation of Nigeria very diverse. Its land includes several types of environments, such as tropical rain forests, mangrove swamps, and savannas. Its people and cultures come from more than 250 ethnic groups. Nigeria has a long history and a rich artistic heritage. However, like other African countries, Nigeria faced violence on the way to becoming a modern democracy.

TAKING NOTES
Use your chart to take notes about Western and Central Africa.

Statements	My Inferences	Key Evidence
European colonial powers divided Africa...		
In most African countries, governments are...		

SUNSHINE STATE STANDARDS
Key Standard SS.A.3.3.5 The student understands the differences between institutions of Eastern and Western civilizations (e.g., differences in governments, social traditions and customs, economic systems and religious institutions).
Other Standards SS.A.3.3.1, B.1.3.3
FCAT LA.A.2.3.1 Reading: Identify Main Idea, Facts, and Details

History of Nigeria's People

The Nok people were one of the earliest known cultures in the land that is now Nigeria. By about 500 B.C., they occupied the central plateau. They were skilled in ironworking and weaving.

Today, about 60 percent of Nigerians belong to three major ethnic groups: the **Yoruba** (YAWR·uh·buh), the **Igbo**, and the **Hausa** (HOW·suh). The first Yoruba established their kingdom on the west bank of the Niger River. The Igbo were part of the Nri kingdom in the southeast, and the Hausa built cities in the northern savannas.

The Yoruba Most of the Yoruba today live in southwestern Nigeria. Before colonial rule, Yoruba society was organized around powerful city-states. Yoruba men grew yams, peanuts, millet, beans, and other crops on land around the cities. Artists and poets had great prestige in traditional Yoruba society. Yoruba women specialized in marketing and trade. Their businesses made some women wealthy and independent.

The Igbo For thousands of years, the Igbo have lived in the southeast region of Nigeria. Igbo villages are fairly democratic, with leaders being chosen rather than inheriting their position. They are known for their metalworking, weaving, and woodcarving. In British colonial times, many Igbo held jobs in business and government.

The Hausa The Hausa are the largest ethnic group in Nigeria. Almost all Hausa are Muslims. Most live in farming villages in northern Nigeria. Crafts such as leatherworking, weaving, and blacksmithing have been passed down through generations.

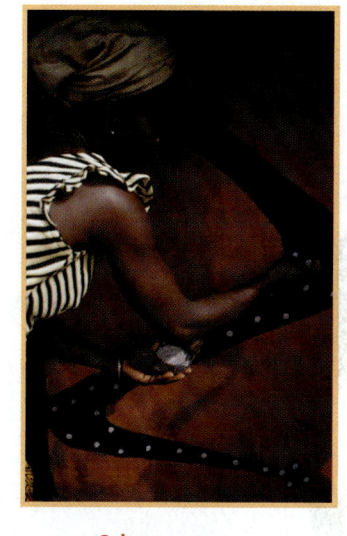

Culture • An Igbo woman paints a python on a house wall.

Reading Social Studies
A. Comparing How do the current locations of Nigeria's three ethnic groups compare with their original locations?

Ethnic Groups of Nigeria, 2001

GEOGRAPHY SKILLBUILDER: Interpreting a Map
1. **Culture** • Which of Nigeria's ethnic groups covers the largest area?
2. **Location** • Which ethnic groups live alongside Lake Chad?

Region • Cassava plants grow in Nigeria's tropical climate. Nigerians eat the cassava's starchy root, shown below. It must be prepared carefully, since it is poisonous if eaten raw. ▼

Becoming a Democracy

In the 1800s, the United Kingdom colonized the northern and southern areas of what is now Nigeria. English became the common language. The two regions were united in 1914. In the 1920s, Nigerians began to work toward separating from British rule. Nigeria finally gained independence in 1960.

When oil was found in eastern Nigeria, the Igbo people there declared their independence. They set up the Republic of Biafra (bee•AF•ruh). Civil war raged from 1966 to 1970, causing a million deaths from fighting or starvation. After the war, military rulers took over. People had little freedom. Sometimes elections were held, but leaders often ignored the results. Finally, in May 1999, Nigeria had a free election. Former military ruler Olusegun Obasanjo was elected president.

Reading Social Studies

B. Recognizing Important Details What event prompted the Igbo people to declare independence from Nigeria?

Nigeria's Economy

Nigeria has more than 123 million people—the largest population in Africa. More than half of Nigerians are farmers. Huge areas of the country have rubber, cacao, peanut, and palm oil plantations. The country has rich deposits of oil and natural gas. Oil is Nigeria's main export, supplying more than 90 percent of government income. Minerals, such as coal, iron ore, tin, lead, limestone, and zinc, are also important to the economy. Factories produce cars, cement, chemicals, clothing, and processed foods.

Biography

Wole Soyinka Wole Soyinka (WOH•leh shaw•YIHNG•kuh), a Yoruba man, was born in Abeokuta, Nigeria, in 1934. In 1986, Soyinka became the first black African to receive the Nobel Prize in literature. Soyinka (shown on the left) is best known for his plays, which combine African stories and European drama. He has also written novels, essays, and poetry. At the same time, he has been a voice for democracy, justice, and freedom of speech.

Soyinka's outspoken ideas got him into trouble with Nigeria's military rulers, and he was thrown into prison. After he was released, he left Nigeria. Soyinka lived in France and the United States for many years. He returned to Nigeria in 1998 to work for democratic reforms.

Nigerian Art and Literature

Nigeria's many cultures and ethnic groups have produced a rich mix of artistic styles. Yoruban artists have been making metal sculptures for about a thousand years. Yoruba also carve masks and figures out of wood. Decorated calabashes, or gourds, are another example of Nigerian art. Dried, hollow gourds are used as food containers or musical instruments. Baskets are made from local plants. Basket weavers turn practical containers into works of art.

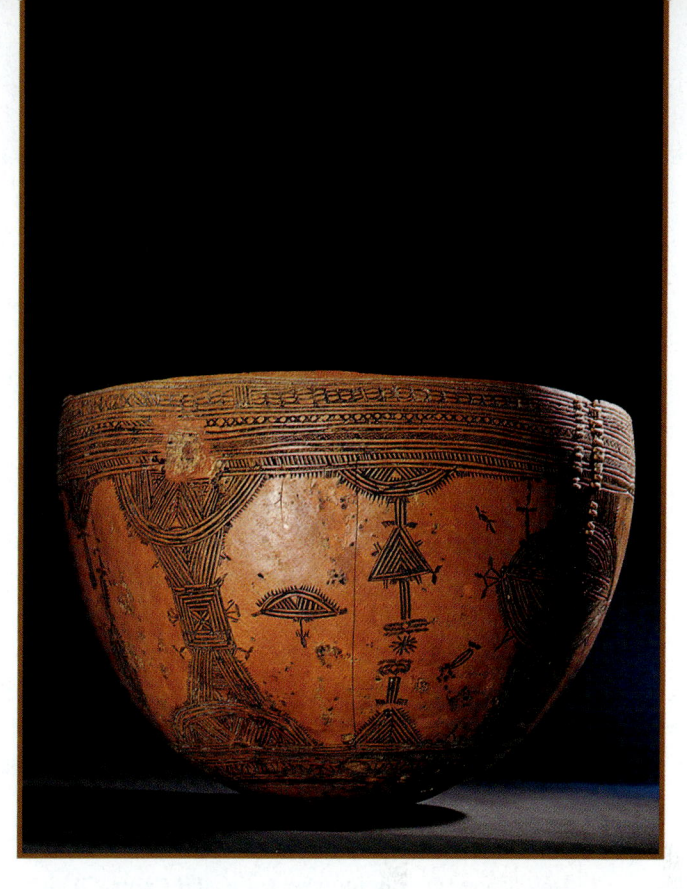

Nigerians are also famous for their literature. Nigerian writers such as Amos Tutuola, Ben Okri, and **Wole Soyinka** have used folktale themes. Their novels and plays combine these themes with modern-day concerns such as human rights.

Human-Environment Interaction • This decorated bowl was made from a calabash. ▲

SECTION 3 ASSESSMENT

Terms & Names
1. Explain the significance of: (a) Yoruba (b) Igbo (c) Hausa (d) Wole Soyinka

Using Graphics

2. Use a chart like this one to list the three major ethnic groups of Nigeria and give facts about each.

Group	Facts

Main Ideas

3. (a) How could a drought affect Nigeria's economy?
   (b) How did the discovery of oil affect Nigeria after it gained independence?
   (c) How are Nigeria's modern writers influenced by the past?

Critical Thinking

4. **Synthesizing**

   What relationship exists between Nigerian society and history and its art and literature?

   Think About
   - what modern Nigerian artists and writers are concerned about
   - how the past affects modern artists

ACTIVITY -OPTION- Make a **mask** inspired by Nigeria's history, economy, or peoples.

CHAPTER 11 ASSESSMENT

TERMS & NAMES

Explain the significance of each of the following:

1. coup d'état
2. mediate
3. ECOWAS
4. subsistence farming
5. cash crop
6. rite of passage
7. Yoruba
8. Igbo
9. Hausa
10. Wole Soyinka

REVIEW QUESTIONS

History and Political Change *(pages 317–321)*

1. What factors influenced the way in which European nations divided Western and Central Africa?
2. Describe the rule of Mobutu Sese Seko in the Democratic Republic of the Congo.
3. What were some positive and negative aspects of Nkrumah's leadership of Ghana?

Economies and Cultures *(pages 324–328)*

4. How do most people in Western and Central Africa earn a living?
5. What is the basis of society in most African countries? How is this changing?

Nigeria Today *(pages 330–333)*

6. Where does Nigeria's population rank in Africa?
7. What are the three major ethnic groups in Nigeria? In what region does each live?
8. What are some important resources and products of Nigeria's economy?

CRITICAL THINKING

Recognizing Effects

1. Using your completed diagram from Reading Social Studies, p. 316, summarize one of your inferences and the evidence you based it on.

Drawing Conclusions

2. How would the establishment of plantations growing cash crops affect a society used to subsistence farming? Try to think of both positive and negative effects.

Analyzing Issues

3. How does their ethnic diversity both help and hurt modern African nations?

Visual Summary

1 History and Political Change
- Colonial rule upset traditional forms of government and natural boundaries, causing problems for modern countries in Western and Central Africa.
- Ethnic violence, corrupt officials, and military rule have made it hard for many countries to establish stable, democratic governments.

2 Economies and Cultures
- Most people in Western and Central Africa are subsistence farmers, but cash crops and minerals are also important in the economy.
- The extended family is the basis of society in Africa south of the Sahara.

3 Nigeria Today
- Nigeria has a large population, valuable resources, and a rich cultural history, but it has faced problems since gaining independence.
- The Hausa, Yoruba, and Igbo are the largest of Nigeria's more than 250 ethnic groups.

STANDARDS-BASED ASSESSMENT

Use the map and your knowledge of world cultures and geography to answer questions 1 and 2.

Additional Test Practice, pp. S1–S33

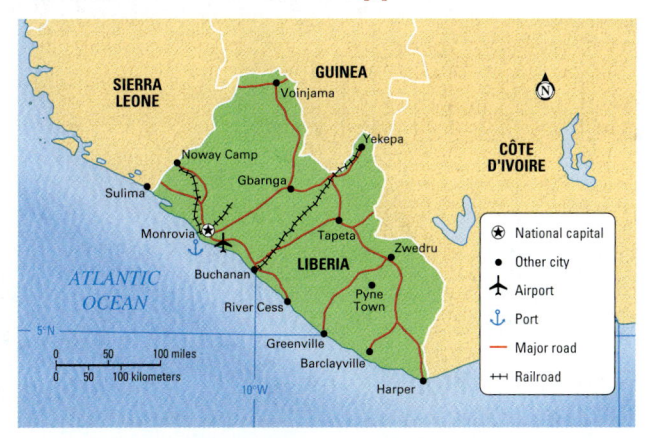

The Nigerian novelist Chinua Achebe gained fame for his novel about colonization, *Things Fall Apart*. In this passage, he discusses why his book is read all over the world. Use the quotation and your knowledge of world cultures and geography to answer question 3.

PRIMARY SOURCE

I knew I had a story, but how it fit into the story of the world—I really had no sense of that. Its meaning for the Igbo people was clear to me, but I didn't know how other people elsewhere would respond to it. Did it have any meaning . . . for them? I realized that it did when . . . the whole class of a girls' college in South Korea wrote to me, and each one expressed an opinion about the book. And then I learned something, which was that they had a history that was similar to the story of *Things Fall Apart*—the history of colonization.

CHINUA ACHEBE, interview in *Atlantic Monthly,* August 2, 2000

1. What form of transportation is available for someone traveling from Zwedru to Monrovia?
   A. airplane
   B. car
   C. boat
   D. train

2. Which two Liberian cities are connected by railroads?
   A. Buchanan and River Cess
   B. Buchanan and Norway Camp
   C. Buchanan and Yekepa
   D. Gbarnga and Monrovia

3. Why do other people besides the Igbo of Nigeria relate to Achebe's novel?
   A. Achebe is such a good writer that he made the story of the Igbo interesting.
   B. Achebe deliberately portrayed his story as part of the story of the world.
   C. People knew Achebe was a famous writer, so they wanted to read his book.
   D. Many countries have a colonial past, so their citizens can relate to the story.

TEST PRACTICE
CLASSZONE.COM

ALTERNATIVE ASSESSMENT

1. WRITING ABOUT HISTORY

Almost every type of mineral in the world can be found in Africa. Research what minerals are found in Western and Central Africa. How are they obtained? What minerals are exported? What are they used for? Write a report on your findings and share it with the class. Include a chart or a graph that provides additional information.

2. COOPERATIVE LEARNING

In a small group of classmates, divide the responsibilities of writing and producing a four-page newspaper about current events in Nigeria. Locate up-to-date information and photographs in the library or on the Internet to write articles about politics, economics, weather, human-interest stories, arts, and sports.

INTEGRATED TECHNOLOGY

Doing Internet Research

Choose a country in Western or Central Africa, other than Nigeria, as the subject of a country study. Then create a chart or poster summarizing your findings.

- Use the Internet to locate facts and information about that country's population, language, religion, government, ethnic groups, climate, important crops, and products.
- If possible, include a photograph from a Web site you used in your research.

For Internet links to support this activity, go to

RESEARCH LINKS
CLASSZONE.COM

CHAPTER 12
Eastern and Southern Africa

SECTION 1 History and Governments
SECTION 2 Economies and Cultures
SECTION 3 South Africa Today
SECTION 4 Kenya Today

Culture Tradition meets modern technology as two Masai girls in Masai Mara National Reserve in Kenya peer through the viewfinder of a long-range camera.

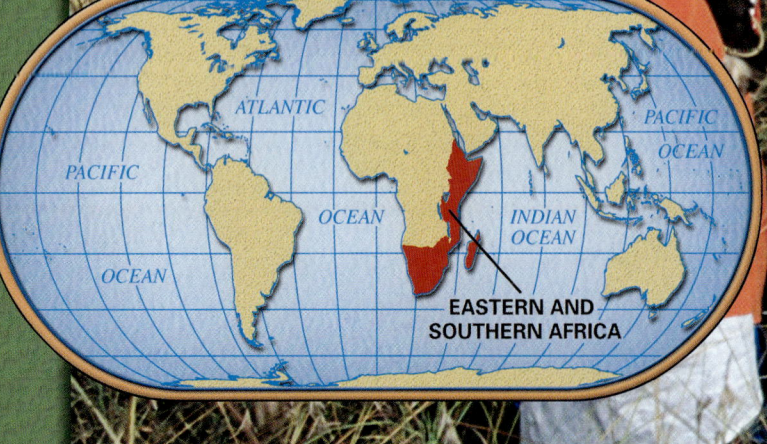

FOCUS ON GEOGRAPHY

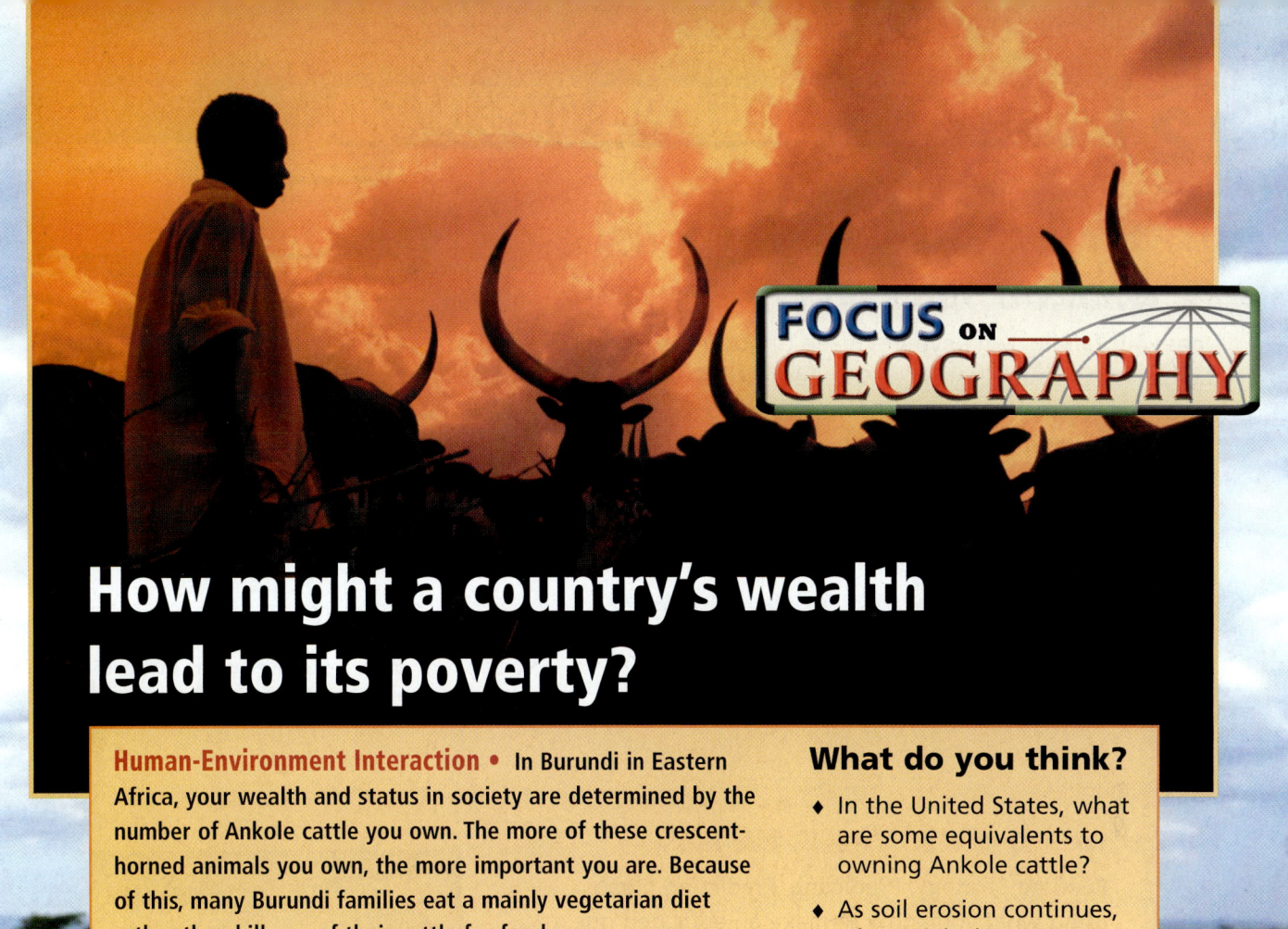

How might a country's wealth lead to its poverty?

Human-Environment Interaction • In Burundi in Eastern Africa, your wealth and status in society are determined by the number of Ankole cattle you own. The more of these crescent-horned animals you own, the more important you are. Because of this, many Burundi families eat a mainly vegetarian diet rather than kill one of their cattle for food.

Hundreds of thousands of Ankole cattle are overgrazing Burundi's limited grasslands. This leads to soil erosion and desertification. Many other herding societies in Eastern and Southern Africa are experiencing the same problem.

What do you think?
- In the United States, what are some equivalents to owning Ankole cattle?
- As soil erosion continues, what might happen to Burundi's Ankole cattle?

CHAPTER 12
READING SOCIAL STUDIES

BEFORE YOU READ

▶▶ What Do You Know?

Does your family own anything made of gold? If so, chances are that the gold came from Eastern or Southern Africa. What do you know about this region? What do you know about its people? What kinds of animals are found there? Recall what you read in Chapters 10 and 11, what you have learned in other classes, and what you have read or seen in the news about Kenya, South Africa, and the other countries of this region.

▶▶ What Do You Want to Know?

Decide what you know about Eastern and Southern Africa. In your notebook, record what you want to learn from this chapter.

Place • Mogadishu, the capital of Somalia, is one of many African cities devastated by civil war. ▲

READ AND TAKE NOTES

Reading Strategy: Predicting Predicting means using what you know to make an educated guess about what is going to happen. This is an important skill in social studies. Scholars look at the past and present to try to predict the future.

- Copy the chart into your notebook.
- As you read, record information about past and present situations in each category. If you find predictions about the future, record those also.
- After you read, review your information and use it to write your own predictions.

Place • Nairobi, Kenya, is a rapidly growing city with a population in 2000 of over 2 million. ▲

	Past	Present	Future
Government			
People			
Economy			
Culture			
South Africa			
Kenya			

SECTION 1

History and Governments

TERMS & NAMES
Great Zimbabwe
Masai
Zulu

MAIN IDEA
There is a great diversity of cultural groups in Eastern and Southern Africa.

WHY IT MATTERS NOW
This diversity has contributed to several conflicts as different countries work to establish stable democratic governments.

DATELINE EXTRA

HADAR, ETHIOPIA, NOVEMBER 1974

Three to three and a half million years ago, a humanlike being died beside a lake in Africa. This month, her remains were found by Donald Johanson and Maurice Taieb.

After studying the skeleton, scientists determined that the female had been approximately three and a half feet tall, and she might have walked on two legs. Humans and their ancestors are the only known mammals that walk on two legs rather than four.

Discoveries such as this skeleton are very rare. One of the discoverers said, "They're even harder to find than diamonds, but they're the key to understanding human origins."

Place • Scientists named the newly discovered skeleton "Lucy." Lucy's brain was about one-third the size of a modern human brain. ▶

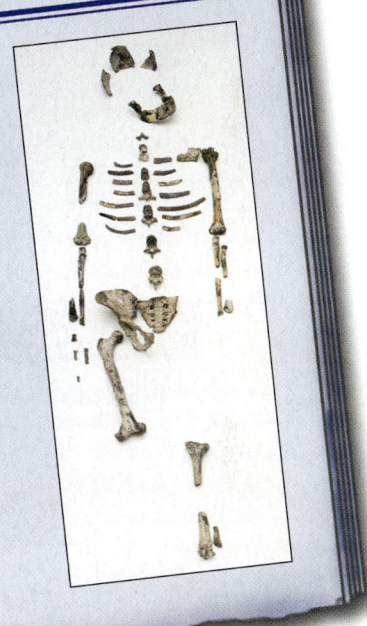

Early Humans in Eastern and Southern Africa

The oldest fossils of human ancestors have been found in African sites ranging from Ethiopia to South Africa. Tools of stone made about 2.5 million years ago have also been found in Eastern Africa. Slowly, early humans spread across Africa before migrating to other continents. The humans that remained in Africa became farmers and herders.

SUNSHINE STATE STANDARDS
Key Standard SS.A.3.3.5 The student understands the differences between institutions of Eastern and Western civilizations (e.g., differences in governments, social traditions and customs, economic systems and religious institutions).

Other Standards SS.A.2.3.2

FCAT LA.A.2.2.7 Reading: Recognize Compare and Contrast

TAKING NOTES
Use your chart to take notes about Eastern and Southern Africa.

	Past	Present	Future
Government			
People			
Economy			

Eastern and Southern Africa **339**

Early Eastern and Southern African Kingdoms

As the human population in Africa grew, societies became more complex. People began to trade with other regions. The income from trade helped build kingdoms.

The Aksum Empire Approximately 2,000 years ago, a great trading empire called Aksum (AHK•SOOM) developed in what is now Ethiopia. Find Aksum on the map below. Ships carried goods from Southern Africa, Arabia, Europe, and India to Aksum. About A.D. 350, King Ezana of Aksum became a Christian. Christianity spread throughout Ethiopia. When Islam came to Arabia, Aksum lost much of its trade because the Muslim Arabians preferred to trade with other Muslim nations.

Trade in Zimbabwe and Mozambique Around A.D. 700, trading empires arose in Southern Africa, in what are now Zimbabwe and Mozambique. These empires were rich in gold, copper, and iron. The mined metals were sent down the Zambezi River and then shipped across the Indian Ocean.

Human-Environment Interaction • Making stone tools is difficult. This symmetrical hand axe found in Tanzania had to be carefully chipped into shape. ▲

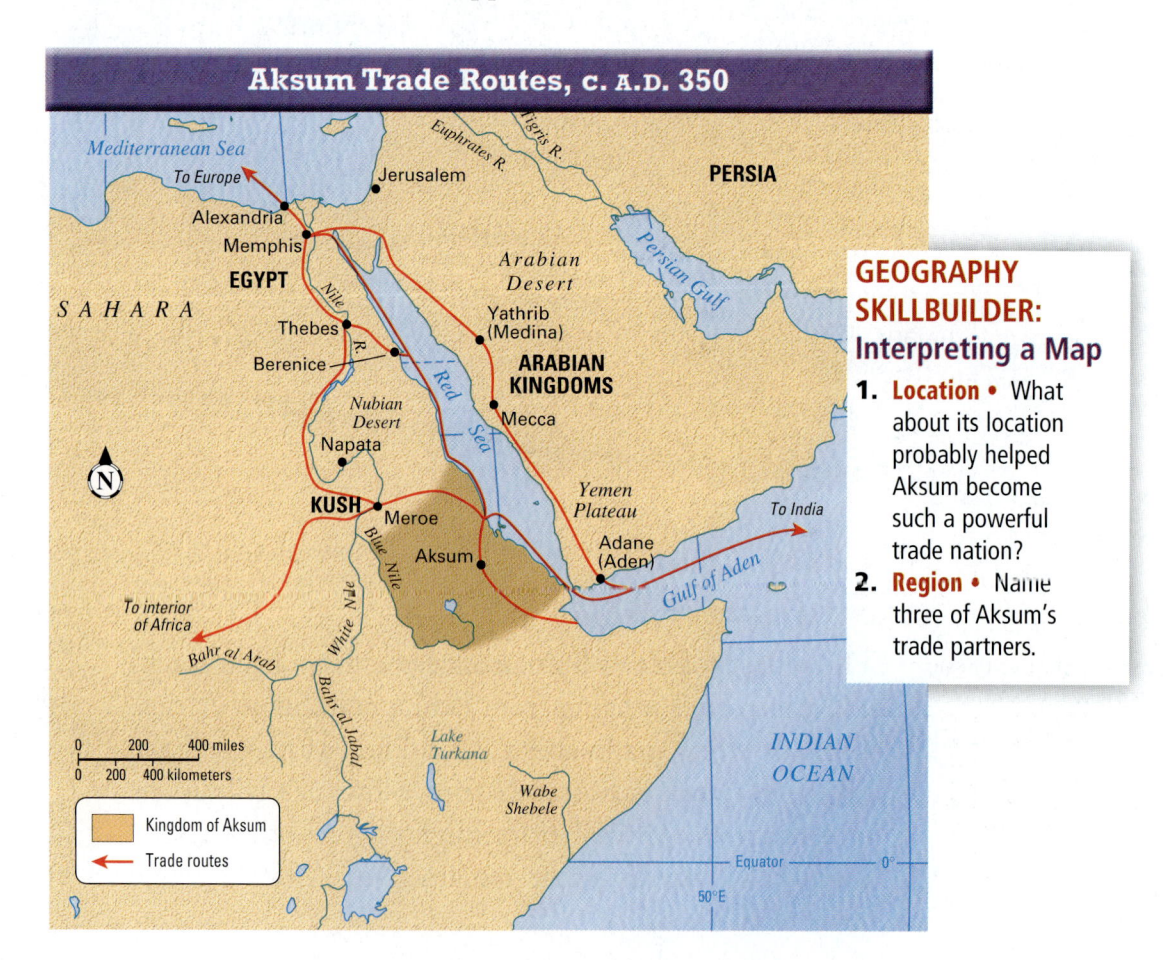

Aksum Trade Routes, c. A.D. 350

GEOGRAPHY SKILLBUILDER: Interpreting a Map

1. **Location •** What about its location probably helped Aksum become such a powerful trade nation?
2. **Region •** Name three of Aksum's trade partners.

340 CHAPTER 12

BACKGROUND

In the late 1800s, figurines of a bird were found in the ruins of the Great Zimbabwe. This Zimbabwe Bird is depicted on the flag of the present-day country of Zimbabwe, which you can see on page 286.

The Africans traded their precious metals for textiles and spices from India, and silk and porcelain from China. Porcelain is a hard, white, glasslike material first made by the Chinese.

The Shona was one of the great trading empires of the lower Zambezi River from about 1100 to 1500. Its people created walled stone structures. These stone enclosures were called *zimbabwes* (zihm·BAHB·weez). The **Great Zimbabwe** is a spectacular stone ruin of a city made up of three parts. The Great Enclosure is the largest single ancient structure in Africa south of the Sahara. The Hill Complex, begun in 900, is the oldest section. The Valley Ruins include remnants of earthen and mud brick buildings. This city was abandoned in the 1400s. (See page 311 for more about the Great Zimbabwe.)

Other Eastern and Southern African Societies

Eastern and Southern Africa had other societies besides the great trade kingdoms. Two of these societies were the Masai (mah·SY) and the Zulu (ZOO·loo).

The Masai and the Zulu

The **Masai** once lived in nearly all of Kenya and about half of what is now Tanzania in Eastern Africa. They raised grazing animals, especially cattle. The Masai were nomads who moved from place to place so their animals would have fresh land to graze. Land generally belonged to the whole group, not to one person or family. In the 1800s, the Masai began fighting among themselves over water and grazing rights. Many Masai warriors died in these wars. Long periods without rain followed, during which many Masai cattle died. The Masai society was weakened by these events.

Strange but TRUE

Floating Seeds Many sailors on trading vessels heading to and from the eastern coast of Africa saw huge seed pods floating on the ocean's surface. The seed pods were called *cocos de mer*, or coconuts of the sea.

It wasn't discovered until the late 1700s that the pods came from giant fan palm trees on the Seychelles Islands just north of Madagascar. The seeds of these trees are the largest in the world—some reaching 50 pounds in weight. It can take up to 10 years for a *coco de mer* to ripen.

Place • A typical Masai village is set up in a circle. This layout helps the Masai defend their villages from attack. ▼

Eastern and Southern Africa **341**

The **Zulu** migrated to Southern Africa about 1,800 years ago. They have traditionally lived in settled villages, grown grains, and raised cattle. In 1815, a man named Shaka Zulu became chief of the Zulu. He led his people in a series of wars to expand Zulu territory. As the Zulu conquered other peoples, they made them Zulu as well. Shaka Zulu held unlimited power. Anyone who disagreed with him could be killed. Shaka's half-brother assassinated him in 1828.

European Colonization Soon after the death of Shaka Zulu, the Zulu began losing land to European settlers. The British and Germans then invaded Masai territory in the 1880s and 1890s. The Masai, weakened by war and drought, were no longer powerful. The Europeans quickly took the lands they wanted. The Masai were forced to live on reserves—small territories set aside for them. By the late 1800s, the United Kingdom, Germany, and France had claimed most of Eastern and Southern Africa.

Region • The Zulu, like this warrior chief, were members of a highly organized military society. ▲

African Independence

World Wars I and II weakened Europe. After the wars, European nations began to lose control of their African colonies. This paved the way for the independence of African nations. Most of the countries of Eastern Africa, such as Kenya, Tanzania, Rwanda, and Burundi, became independent between 1960 and 1964. Most of the countries of Southern Africa achieved independence later. Almost all of the new African governments were democracies, but many of them were subsequently overthrown and became dictatorships. Today, many African nations are again turning toward democracy.

Place • These women and children in Mogadishu have struggled through years of brutal civil war in Somalia. ▼

Reading Social Studies

A. Clarifying What events in Europe enabled African nations to gain their independence?

Government in Somalia

From 1969 to 1991, Somalia was governed by a dictator, Siad Barre (SEE·ahd bah·RAY), who had unlimited power. In the 1980s, more than 100 leading citizens published an open letter criticizing the government. An open letter is a letter that is published in a newspaper. In the United States it is legal to publish letters criticizing leaders. In Somalia it was not. Forty-five of those who signed the open letter were arrested.

The arrests led to more protests. By 1990, fighting forced Barre to agree to reform his government. In 1991, he was driven from office. Since then, twelve clans have been fighting for control of the government.

Government in Rwanda

Through much of the 1900s, Rwandan women could not own land, hold jobs, or participate in government. In 1991, a new constitution was passed. It gave women the right to own property and hold jobs, but the new laws were not enforced. Then, in 1994, a civil war began in Rwanda. So many men were killed that women began taking over as heads of households. Finally, as a result of the deadly wars, women were able to claim their constitutional rights. Since the conflict, more laws benefiting women have been passed. Today, not only can a Rwandan woman own property, but she can inherit property as well.

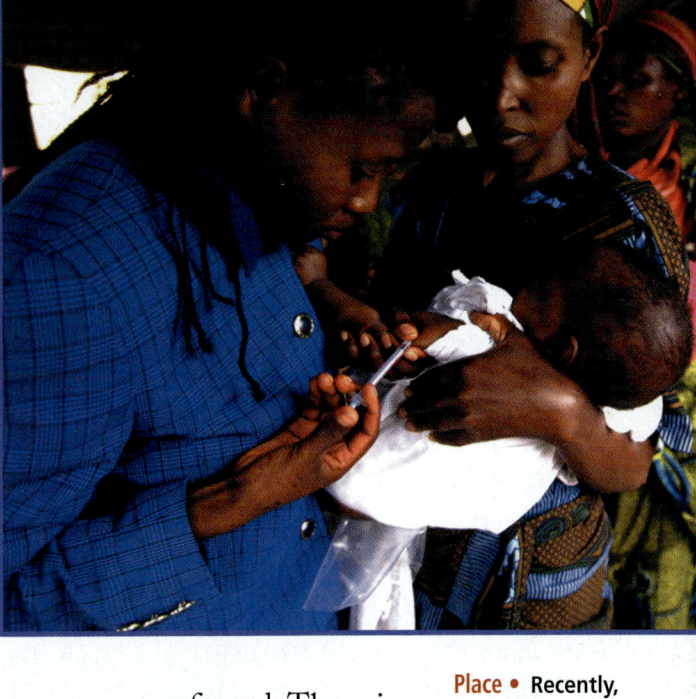

Place • Recently, Rwandan women have gained the right to own property and to work in fields such as medicine. ▲

Reading Social Studies

B. Analyzing Issues How did civil war in Rwanda lead to enforcement of women's rights?

SECTION 1 ASSESSMENT

Terms & Names
1. Explain the significance of: (a) Great Zimbabwe (b) Masai (c) Zulu

Using Graphics

2. Use a flow chart like this one to show the different societies that have flourished in Southern Africa.

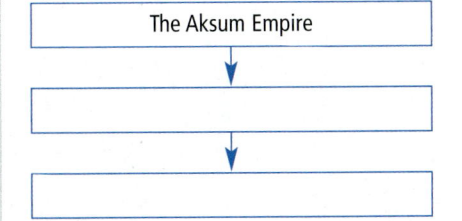

   [The Aksum Empire]
        ↓
   [   ]
        ↓
   [   ]

Main Ideas

3. (a) Explain how location helped build trade empires in ancient Ethiopia, Zimbabwe, and Mozambique.

   (b) What factors contributed to the weakening of the Masai society?

   (c) Describe how the lives of women in Rwanda have changed in recent years.

Critical Thinking

4. **Clarifying**

   What led to the downfall of Siad Barre in Somalia?

   Think About
   - how Barre ruled Somalia
   - the actions of the citizens

ACTIVITY -OPTION- Imagine you are a Rwandan woman in 1992. Write an **open letter** criticizing the government for not enforcing your constitutional rights.

Eastern and Southern Africa

Interdisciplinary Challenge

Discover the Source of the Nile

You are proud to be part of a daring expedition to the heart of Africa. The trip, which begins in 1856, is sponsored by the Royal Geographical Society. Its leaders are two of Britain's best-known explorers—John Hanning Speke (1827-1864) and Richard Burton (1821-1890). They are chasing a legend—that there is a great lake in the heart of Africa that is the source of the Nile—and you are the newest member of their team.

COOPERATIVE LEARNING On these pages are challenges your expedition will face as you search for the source of the Nile. Working with a small group of other explorers, decide which one of these challenges you will solve. Divide the work among group members. Look for helpful information in the Data File. Keep in mind that you will present your solution to the class.

SCIENCE CHALLENGE

"The African rain forest is full of hazards, from warring tribes to malaria to deadly snakes."

Exploring Africa is dangerous, especially in the mid-1800s. The African rain forest is full of hazards, from warring tribes to malaria to deadly snakes. While your expedition is deep in the jungle, you and your companions must be your own doctors. How can you keep yourself and others in the expedition healthy? Choose one of these options. Use the Data File for help.

ACTIVITIES

1. Research dangers and diseases you may encounter in the rain forest. Make a list of the safety equipment and medicines you will pack for the expedition.
2. Write a short manual on tropical diseases common in East Africa.

GEOGRAPHY CHALLENGE

". . . others are likely to challenge you."

Recently, Speke left the main expedition, and he now believes that he has found the Nile's source at Lake Ukerewe. He has renamed this huge lake Victoria, after the British queen. With him went a small group of people, and you are one of them. You are sure of your discoveries, but others are likely to challenge you. You need to demonstrate exactly how you found the source of the Nile. Choose one of these options. Use the Data File for help.

ACTIVITIES

1. Draw or trace a large map of East Africa that you can display on an easel. Make notes for a lecture-demonstration in which you will trace your route to show where the Nile begins.
2. Make a tabletop clay model of the lakes region of East Africa, including Lakes Victoria and Albert.

Activity Wrap-Up

As a group, review your solution to the challenge you selected. Then present your solution to the class.

DATA FILE

DISCOVERY TIME LINE

- **February 1858:** **Speke** and **Burton** are the first Europeans to reach Lake Tanganyika.
- **July 1858:** Speke breaks off from Burton, travels north, and finds and names **Lake Victoria**.
- **1860–1862:** Speke and **James Grant** map Lake Victoria. Speke finds and names **Ripon Falls,** where the Nile flows out of the lake. The explorers start to follow the Nile but are stopped by local warfare.
- **1863:** Speke passes on stories of another great lake to **Samuel W. Baker** and **Florence von Sass,** who find and name **Lake Albert.** It feeds into the White Nile.

AFRICA'S GREAT LAKES

- **Lake Victoria,** Uganda-Tanzania: area, 26,828 sq. mi.; length, 250 mi.; maximum depth, 270 ft.
- **Lake Tanganyika,** Tanzania-Congo: area, 12,700 sq. mi.; length, 420 mi.; maximum depth, 4,823 ft.
- **Lake Albert** (Mobuto), Congo-Uganda: area, 2,075 sq. mi.; length, 100 mi.; maximum depth, 168 ft.
- **Lake Turkana** (Rudolf), Kenya: area, 2,473 sq. mi.; length, 154 mi.; maximum depth, 240 ft.

SUNSHINE STATE STANDARDS
Key Standard SS.B.2.3.2 The student knows the human and physical characteristics of different places in the world and how these characteristics change over time.

FCAT LA.A.2.3.1 Reading: Identify Main Idea, Facts, and Details

To learn more about Nile exploration, go to

RESEARCH LINKS
CLASSZONE.COM

Africa South of the Sahara

SECTION 2

Economies and Cultures

TERMS & NAMES
pastoralism
overgrazing
kinship

MAIN IDEA
The economies of Eastern and Southern Africa are based primarily on agriculture.

WHY IT MATTERS NOW
Billions of dollars of U.S. aid goes to this region to boost its economy.

DATELINE

ETHIOPIA, 1985—Ethiopia has been experiencing a widespread famine for a year. In 1984, a drought hit Northern Ethiopia and other parts of Eastern Africa. Nearly all crops failed. Many nations sent food, but it was not enough. Almost one million Ethiopians have died of starvation.

The government has moved 600,000 people to Southern Ethiopia, where conditions are better. Another 100,000 went to Somalia, 10,000 to Djibouti, and 300,000 to Sudan. Currently, there is no end in sight to this tragedy.

Region • The drought has killed not only crops, but also many of Ethiopia's animals. ▲

Agriculture in Eastern and Southern Africa

Agriculture is the primary industry of countries in Eastern and Southern Africa, even though drought is a serious problem. An exception is the area around Lake Victoria, which tends to get enough rain to support many different kinds of crops. People in this area grow bananas, strawberries, sweet potatoes, and yams. Cash crops such as coffee and cotton are grown in parts of Kenya, Rwanda, Burundi, and Uganda.

SUNSHINE STATE STANDARDS
Key Standard SS.A.3.3.5
The student understands the differences between institutions of Eastern and Western civilizations (e.g., differences in governments, social traditions and customs, economic systems and religious institutions).
Other Standards SS.B.1.3.7, B.2.3.3
FCAT LA.A.2.2.7 Reading: Recognize Compare and Contrast

TAKING NOTES
Use your chart to take notes about Eastern and Southern Africa.

	Past	Present	Future
Government			
People			
Economy			

Political Boundaries of Eastern Africa, 2001

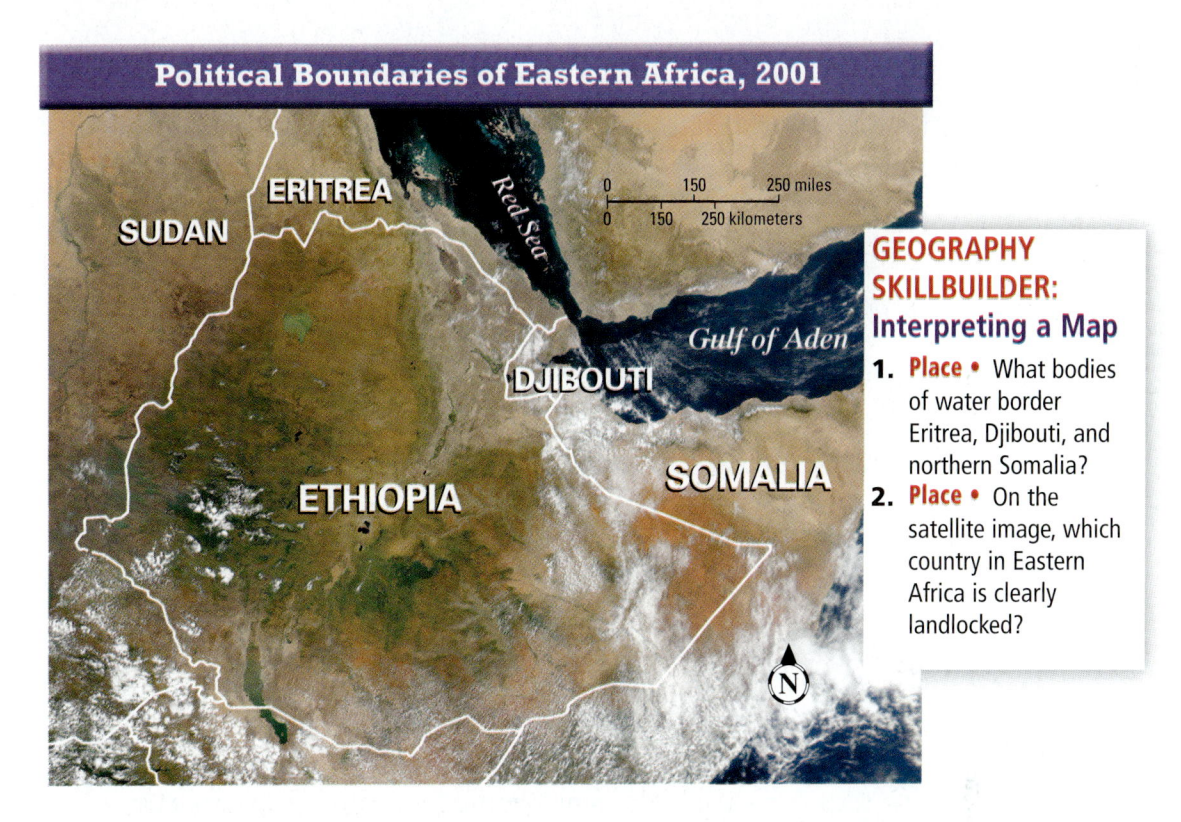

GEOGRAPHY SKILLBUILDER: Interpreting a Map

1. **Place** • What bodies of water border Eritrea, Djibouti, and northern Somalia?
2. **Place** • On the satellite image, which country in Eastern Africa is clearly landlocked?

Place • Sorghum is a cereal grain plant native to Africa. It is a mainstay in the diets of 500 million people in more than 30 countries. ▲

Pastoralism In some areas of Africa, there is not enough rain to grow any crops. Somalia and most of Kenya receive less than 20 inches of rain each year. People survive by raising grazing animals, such as cattle, sheep, or goats. This way of life is called **pastoralism**. Many pastoralists are nomads. Today, because of Africa's increasing population, there are fewer places for nomads to graze their animals. As a result, the land is suffering from **overgrazing**, or the process in which animals graze grass faster than it can grow back. Overgrazing is a cause of desertification in Africa.

Place • Tanzanian fishermen spread nets along the shore of Lake Victoria. This cichlid is one of the native fish threatened by the Nile perch in the lake. ▼

Fishing Africa's large lakes support commercial fishing. Lake Victoria was once home to almost 500 native species of fish. Most of these fish were too small to support a large fishing industry. The large Nile perch was then introduced into Lake Victoria. Since then, nearly all the native fish have disappeared. Today, commercial fishing of the Nile perch has brought many jobs to the area and provided an important export.

Eastern and Southern Africa **347**

GDP of Southern African Nations, 2000

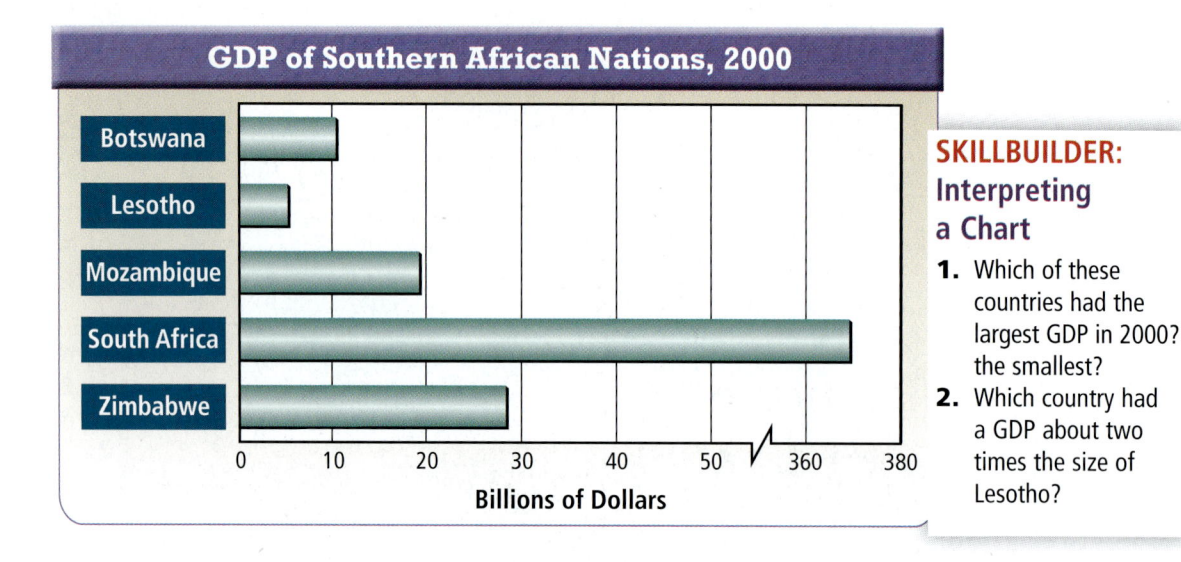

Country	Billions of Dollars
Botswana	~10
Lesotho	~5
Mozambique	~19
South Africa	~369
Zimbabwe	~28

SKILLBUILDER: Interpreting a Chart
1. Which of these countries had the largest GDP in 2000? the smallest?
2. Which country had a GDP about two times the size of Lesotho?

Africa's Economic Strength

Eastern Africa is the poorest region on the continent. Countries in Southern Africa have more diverse economies than do those in Eastern Africa. This means people have more ways to earn a living. For example, several countries in Southern Africa are rich in mineral resources, so there are jobs in mining. South Africa and Zimbabwe also have many manufacturing jobs. South Africa has by far the strongest economy in the region. In 2000 it had a gross domestic product, or GDP, of approximately $369 billion.

Reading Social Studies
A. Analyzing Causes What contributes to South Africa's strong economy?

Spotlight on CULTURE

The Beat Goes On People have made and played drums since at least 6000 B.C. In many African cultures, drums are more than musical instruments. The Yoruba used drums that imitate the pitch and pattern of human speech to transmit messages over many miles. These "talking" drums would, for example, send the message to an unpopular king that his people wanted him to resign. In Uganda, kettledrums were used to symbolize the king's power and offer him protection. Sacrifices of cattle were regularly made to the drums to give them a life force.

THINKING CRITICALLY

1. **Making Inferences**
   What status do you think drum players hold in African society? Why?
2. **Analyzing Motives**
   Why do you think the Yoruba people would use drums instead of a human messenger to send messages to their king?

For more on African music and culture, go to
RESEARCH LINKS CLASSZONE.COM

Reading Social Studies

B. Making Inferences Why do you think good transportation and communication will improve Southern Africa's economies?

Transportation and Communication The countries of Southern Africa work together to improve the economy of the region. This includes improving transportation and communication among countries. For example, the railway lines of Botswana, Namibia, Lesotho, South Africa, and Swaziland are linked. These lines carry goods from all areas of Southern Africa to major ports along the Atlantic and Indian coasts.

Cultures of Eastern and Southern Africa

Marriage and kinship are changing in Eastern and Southern Africa as people move to cities. **Kinship** means family relationships. Economic activity brings people together; as they trade goods, they trade ideas. Their behavior and attitudes change as well.

BACKGROUND

The Tumbuka healers of Malawi use special songs and dances to diagnose and cure their patients' diseases.

Music in Eastern and Southern Africa In Eastern and Southern Africa, musical traditions of many different cultural groups come together. One characteristic of Southern African music is repetition. The Shona people of Zimbabwe make *mbira* (ehm·BEER·uh) music. *Mbira* music forms patterns of repetition using different voices or instruments. In Zulu choral music, individual voices singing different parts enter a song at various points in a continuous cycle. This creates a rich and varied pattern of sound. Another traditional way of making music is called *hocketing*. Groups of musicians play flutes or trumpets. Each musician plays one note. Then they rotate, or take turns, playing one note after another to create a continuous, freeform song.

Culture • Joseph Shabalala, founder of the South African vocal group Ladysmith Black Mambazo, performs with women dancers in traditional Zulu dress. ▼

Connections to History

Ancient Churches Ethiopia adopted Christianity in the 500s. In the 1200s, King Lalibela of Ethiopia commissioned 11 churches to be built in the town of Roha. The town was later renamed after the emperor. All of the churches were carved from solid volcanic rock. A network of tunnels was built to connect the churches. Today, a community of approximately 1,000 monks presides over these ancient churches and the pilgrims who visit them.

Changing the Tune African musical traditions moved across North America, South America, and Europe because of the slave trade and European colonization. African musicians have added elements of European, West Asian, and American music to their own styles to create new types of music. *Jiti*, for example, is a type of Shona *mbira* music that follows the traditional *mbira* rhythms using an electric guitar.

Religion in Eastern and Southern Africa

Today, about 85 percent of Southern and Eastern Africans practice Islam or Christianity. Only 15 percent practice a traditional African religion. Many traditional African religions focus on the worship of sky gods, ancestors, or spirits of rivers and of Earth. However, like Islam and Christianity, African religions recognize one supreme creator. Many Africans practice a traditional African religion that is combined with another religion.

SECTION 2 ASSESSMENT

Terms & Names
1. Explain the significance of: (a) pastoralism (b) overgrazing (c) kinship

Using Graphics

2. Using a spider map like the one shown, fill in details that describe each type of economic activity. Add more lines as necessary.

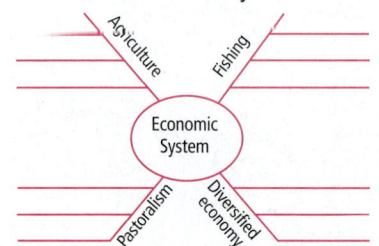

Main Ideas

3. (a) What geographic factors are responsible for the location of pastoralism in Eastern Africa?

   (b) How did cultural borrowing affect African music? How did it affect other types of music around the world?

   (c) What religious belief is common to all the major religions practiced by Africans?

Critical Thinking

4. **Recognizing Important Details**
   Describe unique characteristics of the music of some African peoples. What influence do they have in common?

   Think About
   - the variety of African music
   - how Africans incorporate European, West Asian, and American music

ACTIVITY -OPTION- Imagine you have moved from a community of nomads in Kenya to South Africa. Write a **letter** describing what your life was like as a nomad and what kind of job you might find in your new home.

SKILLBUILDER

Reading a Satellite Image

▶▶ Defining the Skill

A satellite image is a photograph taken from a satellite. Photographs taken from satellites can be of continents or neighborhoods. A satellite image of a large area shows water, land, and clouds. The color of the land indicates whether it is desert, forest, farmland, or mountains.

> **SUNSHINE STATE STANDARDS**
> **Key Standard SS.B.1.3.1** The student uses various map forms (including thematic maps) and other geographic representations, tools, and technologies to acquire, process, and report geographic information including patterns of land use, connections between places, and patterns and processes of migration and diffusion.
> **FCAT LA.A.2.3.1** Reading: Identify Main Idea, Facts, and Details

▶▶ Applying the Skill

This satellite image shows the continent of Africa. Use the strategies listed below to help you interpret the image.

How to Read a Satellite Image

Strategy ❶ Distinguish the land from the water. Water on a satellite image is blue or green. Notice the cloud formations, which appear as white on the image.

Strategy ❷ Look at the land. Areas that are desert are light tan. Mountainous areas are gray. Dark green areas show places where there is vegetation, or forests and farmland.

Strategy ❸ Compare the satellite image with the political map of Africa in the Unit Atlas on page 280. Use the chart below to match the regions on the satellite image as closely as possible with countries. Because of clouds, you cannot see the land in all parts of Africa.

Make a Chart

A chart will help you organize the information found on the satellite image and on the political map of Africa.

❸

Color on Satellite Map	Land Type	Countries
Light tan	Desert	Northern Africa
Orange	Semiarid	Sudan, Chad, Eastern Ethiopia, Namibia, Botswana
Dark green	Forest, farmland	Central Africa, Mozambique, Zimbabwe
Gray	Mountains	Ethiopia, Kenya

▶▶ Practicing the Skill

Turn to the satellite image shown on page 347. Compare that satellite image with the political map on page 280. Make a chart like the one shown above to organize the information found on the map and photo.

LITERATURE CONNECTIONS

MY FATHER'S FARM

NIGERIA, with over 123 million people, has the largest population of any country in Africa. More than half of all Nigerians live in rural villages. In this selection, the Nigerian writer Isaac Olaleye vividly describes his father's farm in a small village called Erin in western Nigeria. In the language of the Yoruba people, *erin* means "laughter."

In the heart of a great tropical forest
In space and solitude
Lies my father's farm.
In the acres of solitude
Grow rows of yams,[1]
White like sugar,
Their vines, mounting stakes,
Are clothed in pea green.

*

In the acres of solitude grow:
Rows of yams
The color of vanilla ice cream,
Rows of yams
Smooth as eggshells,
Rows of yams,
Gray like blueberries,
Rows of yams,
Yellow like lemons, and
Rows of yams,
Smooth and creamy as butter.

1. Throughout southern Nigeria, roots—especially yams, taro, and cassava—are the main crops grown on small farms.

Their vines, all mounting stakes,
And their leaves glowing green—
Yellowish green to emerald.
All the colorful rows delight me.
On my father's farm,
Where it is quiet enough to hear
Bees and flies as they buzz and hum
Through another busy day.

*

In the acres of solitude
Maize waves in the gentle wind.
Popondo beans hug one another.
Tomatoes sit on pumpkins.
The black-eyed peas climb the maize.
Sweet peas smother the okra
And while peppers flash
The color of danger,
White cotton balls
Laugh at them all.

SUNSHINE STATE STANDARDS
Key Standard SS.A.3.3.1 The student understands ways in which cultural characteristics have been transmitted from one society to another (e.g., through art, architecture, language, other artifacts, traditions, beliefs, values, and behaviors).
FCAT LA.E.2.3.1 Literature: Understand Character and Plot Development

Reading THE LITERATURE

What techniques does the poet use to describe the variety and texture of the yams growing in the fields of his father's farm? How does the poet use language, particularly verbs, to give the vegetables human traits?

Thinking About THE LITERATURE

At what time of year is this poem set? How can you tell? How might the images differ if the poem described the farm during another season of the year? during a drought?

Writing About THE LITERATURE

In the second stanza of "My Father's Farm," the poet uses repetition and similes. Do these devices enhance the poem? In what ways?

About the Author

Isaac Olaleye (b. 1941) was born and grew up in Nigeria. In addition to the poetry collection in which this poem appears, he has written several books for young people about Nigeria. As an adult he lived for several years in England before settling in the United States.

Further Reading "My Father's Farm" is one of 15 poems by Isaac Olaleye in the book *The Distant Talking Drum.* These poems capture daily life in a Nigerian village by treating such topics as a market day, a tropical rainstorm, and village weavers.

Africa South of the Sahara

SECTION 3
South Africa Today

TERMS & NAMES
veldt
Afrikaner
Boer
African National Congress
Nelson Mandela
sanction
Willem de Klerk

MAIN IDEA
South Africa is working to rebuild itself in the aftermath of apartheid.

WHY IT MATTERS NOW
Since the end of apartheid, South Africa has become a democracy.

DATELINE
EXTRA

WITWATERSRAND MAIN REEF, SOUTH AFRICA, 1896

Gold! Ten years ago, George Harrison, an Australian prospector, discovered gold in the Witwatersrand Main Reef. Most people, including Harrison, thought the find wasn't worth much. Harrison sold his claim for approximately $14. But many people were wrong.

The gold buried in the Witwatersrand is one of the biggest deposits in the world. Many expect these mines will soon produce 20 percent of the world's gold supply. Prospectors from all over the world are coming to the sleepy town of Johannesburg. Already, its population has passed 100,000.

Location • Johannesburg's growth is especially surprising considering that it is hundreds of miles from the nearest railroad, port, or major river. ▲

Geography of South Africa

Mineral-rich South Africa is located at the southern tip of Africa. The Witwatersrand, also called the Rand, remains the world's largest and richest gold field. It also contains diamonds, uranium, and platinum. Since South Africa is south of the Equator, winter is in July and summer is in January. Most of South Africa is on a plateau. Much of it is flat grassland called the **veldt** (vehlt), where farmers raise cattle, corn, fruit, potatoes, and wheat.

SUNSHINE STATE STANDARDS
Key Standard SS.B.2.3.2 The student knows the human and physical characteristics of different places in the world and how these characteristics change over time.
Other Standards SS.A.3.3.2, A.3.3.4
FCAT LA.A.2.3.1 Reading: Identify Main Idea, Facts, and Details

TAKING NOTES
Use your chart to take notes about Eastern and Southern Africa.

	Past	Present	Future
Government			
People			
Economy			

354 CHAPTER 12

Place • The Dutch landed at Table Bay and later established Cape Town nearby.

History of South Africa

South Africa was home to Khoisan and Bantu peoples for more than 1,500 years. The Khoisan were herders and hunters, and the Bantu were farmers.

European Settlers In 1652, the Dutch founded the Cape Town colony. Their descendents, called **Afrikaners,** make up more than half of modern South Africa's white population. Over time, Dutch settlers left Cape Town to become pastoral farmers. Known as **Boers,** they developed their own culture and fought with Africans over land.

German, French, and British settlers followed the Dutch during the 1700s and 1800s. The Cape Town colony came under British control in the early 1800s. Africans resisted British efforts to force them out of the region. Thousands of Boers established two independent states in the 1850s and followed a policy of apartheid.

Wealth and War The discovery of diamonds and gold in the second half of the 19th century renewed European interest in the area. It also attracted prospectors and settlers from Australia, the United States, and Eastern Europe. Between 1899 and 1902, the British and the Boers fought each other in the South African War. Africans supported the British in hopes of gaining some equal rights. The British won and the Boer states came under British rule. Black protest organizations were formed when their situation did not improve.

BACKGROUND
Cape Town later became the legislative capital of South Africa. The country also has an administrative capital in Pretoria and a judicial capital in Bloemfontein.

Reading Social Studies
A. Analyzing Motives What drew Europeans to South Africa?

Biography

Nelson Mandela (1918–)
Nelson Mandela, below, led the fight against apartheid. He continued to inspire his followers during his 26 years in prison for protest activities. In 1990, South African President Willem de Klerk helped obtain Mandela's release. In 1991, Mandela became president of the African National Congress. Amid escalating violence, Mandela and de Klerk worked to end apartheid. In 1993, they shared the Nobel Peace Prize for their efforts.

In 1994, Mandela became president of South Africa. His Truth and Reconciliation Commission investigated crimes committed under apartheid. He worked to improve the living standards of the black population and helped enact a new constitution.

Eastern and Southern Africa **355**

South Africans Today

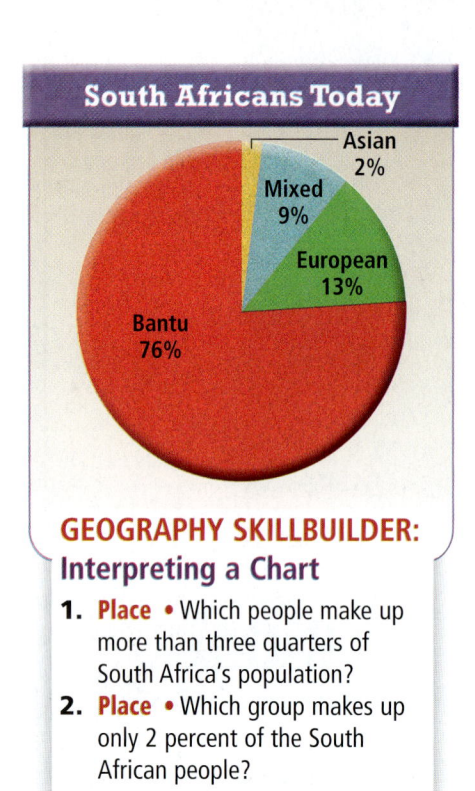

- Bantu 76%
- European 13%
- Mixed 9%
- Asian 2%

GEOGRAPHY SKILLBUILDER:
Interpreting a Chart
1. **Place** • Which people make up more than three quarters of South Africa's population?
2. **Place** • Which group makes up only 2 percent of the South African people?

A Nation of Apartheid

In 1910, the British colony became the Union of South Africa. Afrikaners retained a political voice in the new nation. Racial segregation or separation continued under several new laws. Nonwhites were discriminated against concerning where they could live and travel, what jobs they could hold, and whether they could attend school. Many were forced to leave their homes. Apartheid became the official policy of South Africa in 1948 under the rule of the Afrikaner Nationalist Party.

Reading Social Studies

B. Recognizing Important Details What were the main ways in which apartheid affected the lives of black South Africans?

The African National Congress

The ANC, or **African National Congress,** was a group of black Africans that opposed apartheid. When the government responded to their passive resistance during the 1950s with arrests and violence, the ANC became more aggressive in their protests. **Nelson Mandela** emerged as a leader of the ANC and the anti-apartheid movement. The fight continued for decades. Hundreds of demonstrators were killed, and thousands more were arrested.

Apartheid Ends

Strikes had a negative impact on the economy and forced the government to change some of the apartheid laws in the 1970s and again in the 1980s. In 1985, the United States and Great Britain agreed to impose economic sanctions against South Africa. A **sanction** is a measure taken by nations against a country violating international law. **Willem de Klerk,** a white South African who opposed apartheid, became president in 1989. He helped to repeal many apartheid laws and to release from jail those who had worked to eliminate the policy.

Provinces of South Africa, 2001

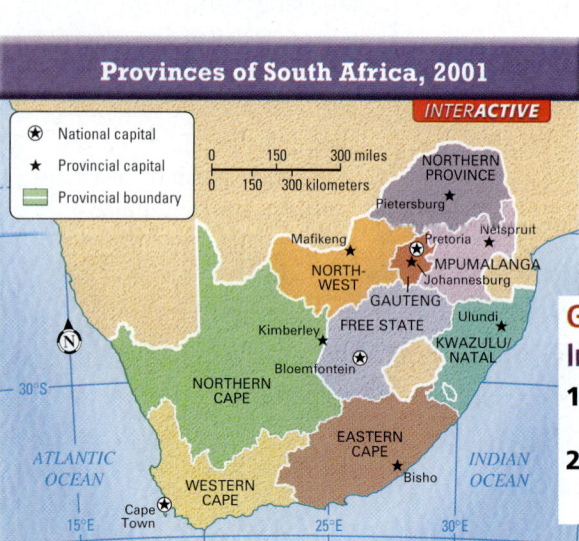

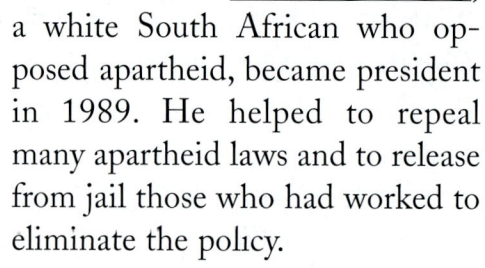

GEOGRAPHY SKILLBUILDER:
Interpreting a Map
1. **Place** • Name South Africa's three national capitals.
2. **Region** • How many provinces are there in South Africa?

In 1993, a new constitution gave all adults the right to vote. Nelson Mandela was elected president, served one five-year term, and retired in 1999. Thabo Mbeki (uhm·BAY·kee) then became president.

A New Era for South Africa

BACKGROUND
At the beginning of the 21st century, South Africa was conducting a new movement called "transformation." Transformation aimed at making every aspect of South African society available to every citizen.

Today, the constitution of South Africa guarantees the same rights to everyone in South Africa. However, most black South Africans remain very poor. The government is working to provide better housing and to bring electricity and water to communities without them. South Africa continues to have the strongest economy in Southern Africa.

Culture • South Africa's diverse cultures create a wide range of music and art. Zulu beadwork is one example. ▲

Cultures of South Africa Like its people, the cultures of South Africa are very diverse. For example, South Africa has 11 official languages. Although there are many official languages, English is understood by almost every South African because it is the language used in schools and universities. South African art and music are other examples of the country's diverse culture. Jazz and jive have combined with Zulu and Sotho rhythms to make a new, vibrant musical style.

SECTION 3 ASSESSMENT

Terms & Names

1. Explain the significance of:
   - (a) veldt
   - (b) Afrikaner
   - (c) Boer
   - (d) African National Congress
   - (e) Nelson Mandela
   - (f) sanction
   - (g) Willem de Klerk

Using Graphics

2. Use a chart like this one to list some of the reasons for conflicts between African and European groups during colonization.

European Group	Reason for Conflict

Main Ideas

3. (a) How have the veldt and the Witwatersrand contributed to South Africa's economy?
   (b) How did Nelson Mandela and the ANC influence South Africa's history?
   (c) How is apartheid related to South Africa's current political, social, and economic conditions?

Critical Thinking

4. Recognizing Effects

   What actions did South Africa and other nations take to change the policy of apartheid?

   Think About
   - the ANC's efforts
   - policies of the United States and Great Britain

ACTIVITY -OPTION- Create a **poster** urging South Africans to vote. List several reasons why voting is important.

SECTION 4

Kenya Today

TERMS & NAMES
multiparty system
Swahili
harambee

MAIN IDEA
Kenya is a beautiful land that has rich natural resources.

WHY IT MATTERS NOW
In the future, Kenya may become the engine for economic growth in Eastern Africa.

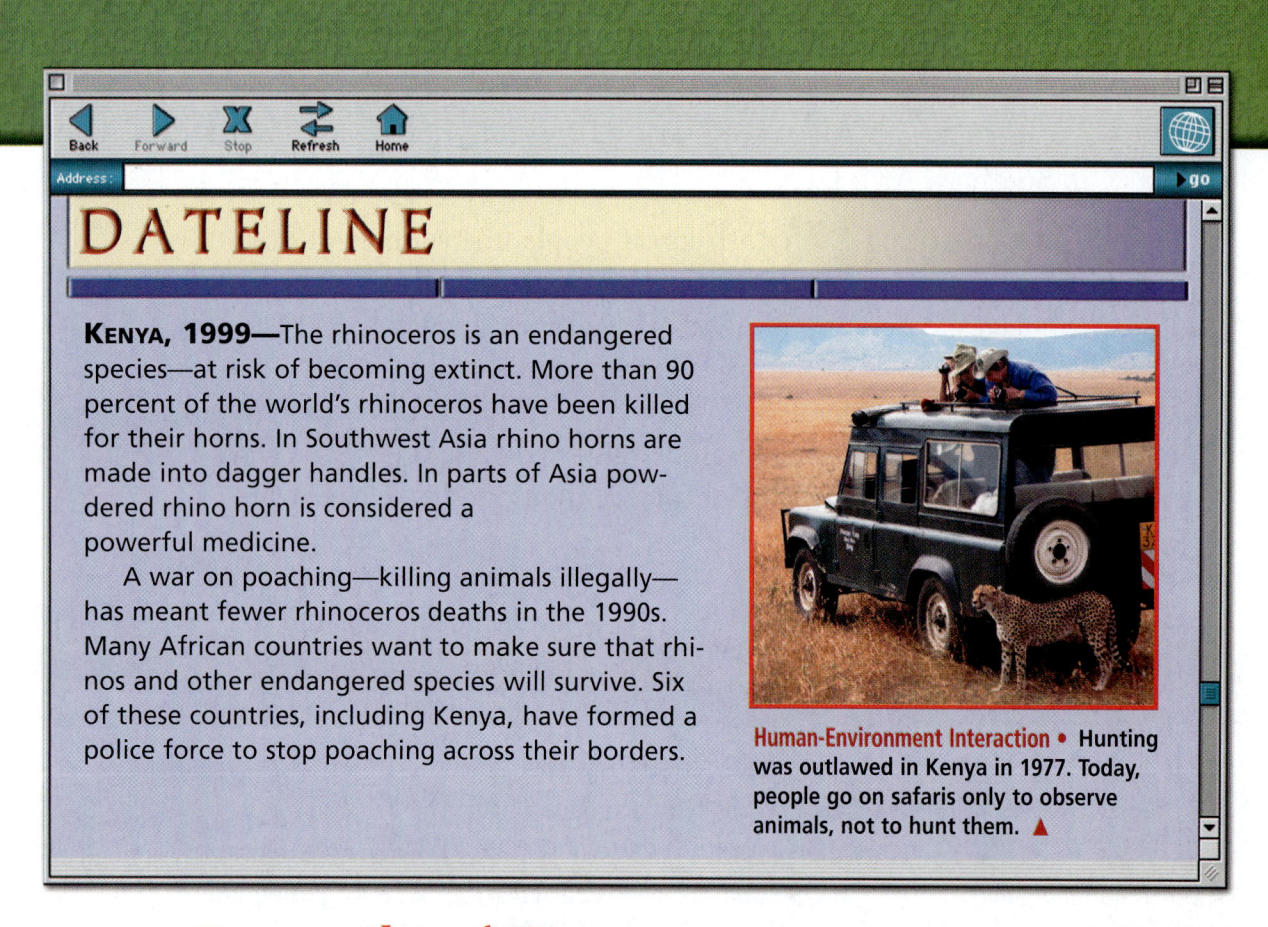

DATELINE

KENYA, 1999—The rhinoceros is an endangered species—at risk of becoming extinct. More than 90 percent of the world's rhinoceros have been killed for their horns. In Southwest Asia rhino horns are made into dagger handles. In parts of Asia powdered rhino horn is considered a powerful medicine.

A war on poaching—killing animals illegally—has meant fewer rhinoceros deaths in the 1990s. Many African countries want to make sure that rhinos and other endangered species will survive. Six of these countries, including Kenya, have formed a police force to stop poaching across their borders.

Human-Environment Interaction • Hunting was outlawed in Kenya in 1977. Today, people go on safaris only to observe animals, not to hunt them. ▲

Geography of Kenya

Kenya, on Africa's east coast, lies directly on the Equator. Its national park system is home to many threatened species, including rhinoceros, elephants, and cheetahs. Most of Kenya's human population lives in the highlands in the southwest, where there is rich soil and plenty of rain. Nairobi, the capital and largest city, and Mount Kenya are found here. Kenya's coast has tropical beaches and rain forests. The remaining three-quarters of Kenya are covered by a plain that is too dry for farming. Kenyans who live here are herders.

TAKING NOTES
Use your chart to take notes about Eastern and Southern Africa.

	Past	Present	Future
Government			
People			
Economy			

SUNSHINE STATE STANDARDS
Key Standard SS.B.2.3.2 The student knows the human and physical characteristics of different places in the world and how these characteristics change over time.
Other Standards SS.A.2.3.2, A.3.3.5
FCAT LA.A.2.3.1 Reading: Identify Main Idea, Facts, and Details

Kenya, 2001

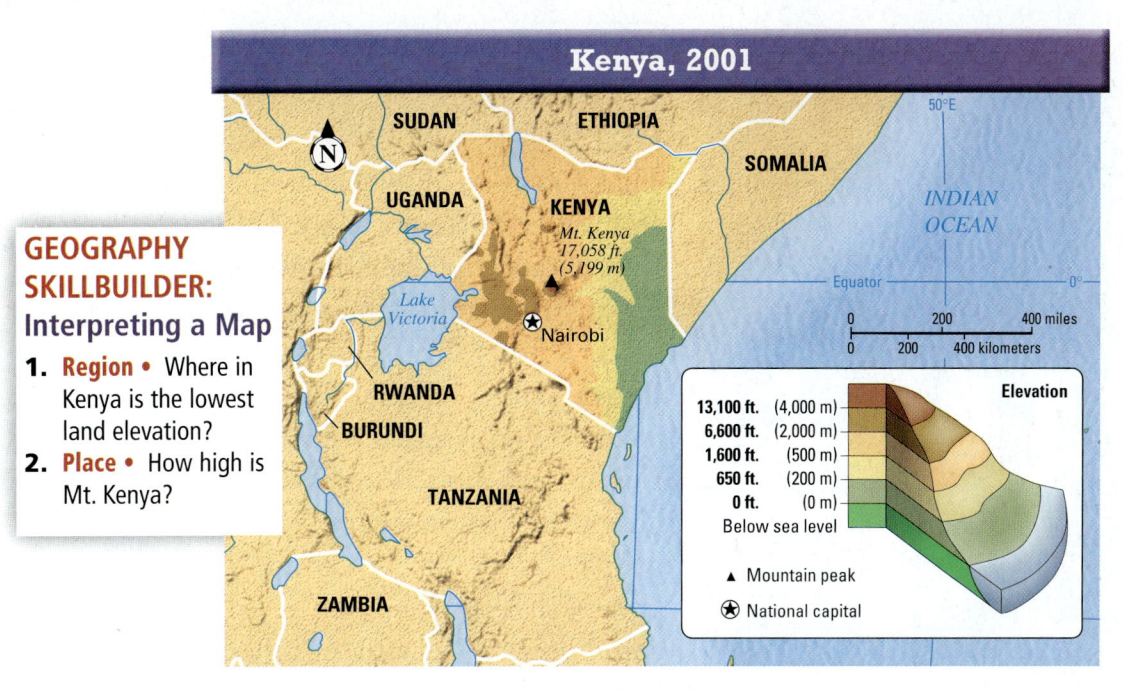

GEOGRAPHY SKILLBUILDER: Interpreting a Map
1. **Region •** Where in Kenya is the lowest land elevation?
2. **Place •** How high is Mt. Kenya?

Culture • The Masai people migrated to Kenya a few thousand years ago. Masai warriors carried leather shields such as this one to help defend themselves and their animals from attack. ▼

Early History of Kenya

The ancestors of modern Kenyans began arriving in Kenya approximately 3,000 years ago. They were farmers, herders, and hunters from other parts of Africa. Some were part of the Bantu migration. Others came from the northeast. Greek, Roman, and Arabian traders and sailors often visited Kenya's coast along the Indian Ocean. Arabs set up trading posts there about 1,200 years ago. Portuguese sailors arrived in the early 1500s and took control of these trading posts. In the late 1800s, Kenya became a British colony. It gained independence in 1963.

Government of Kenya

Kenya's first prime minister, Jomo Kenyatta, ruled from 1963 until 1978, when he died in office. Vice President Daniel arap Moi then became prime minister. Moi's party was the only political party. By the early 1990s, however, many Kenyans became dissatisfied with this political system. One problem was that Moi gave special favors to people of his own ethnic group, the Kalenjin. After Kenyans held violent demonstrations in 1991, Moi agreed to allow a **multiparty system.** This meant that other parties could offer ideas for new laws and policies that might be different from Moi's ideas. Despite the change, Moi remained in power. Some people believe that Moi won the 1992 and 1997 elections through fraud.

Culture • Prime Minister Moi takes this baton, a symbol of his authority, to every public function he attends. ▼

Eastern and Southern Africa **359**

Culture • Most Kenyans wear Western clothing, but a few rural groups still dress in their traditional native clothing. ▲

The People of Kenya

Thirty to forty different ethnic groups live in Kenya today. The Kikuyu are the largest group, making up approximately 20 percent of the population. Other large ethnic groups include the Kalenjin, Kamba, Luhya, and Luo. Most groups have their own language. Many people also know Swahili (swah·HEE·lee) and use it to communicate with other groups. **Swahili** is a Bantu language that includes many Arabic words. Swahili and English are the official languages of Kenya.

Education Education is very important to Kenyans. About 80 percent of Kenya's children go to elementary school. Government-run elementary schools are free, but students must pay tuition to attend high school. Most parts of Kenya have government-run schools. However, Kenyans value education so much that some have built their own schools in places where the government has not started them yet. These schools are called **harambee** schools. *Harambee* means "pulling together" in Swahili.

How Kenyans Earn a Living About 80 percent of Kenyans work in agriculture. The most profitable cash crops are coffee and tea. Farmers also grow bananas, corn, pineapples, and sugar cane. Tourism brings the most money into Kenya's economy. More than 500,000 tourists visit Kenya each year. Tourists come to visit the national parks to see the antelope, buffalo, elephants, giraffes, lions, and other native animals. Kenya protects these animals as an important natural resource.

Human-Environment Interaction • One of Kenya's most famous tourist attractions are the flamingos of Lake Nakuru. Unfortunately, their population is declining because the lake is polluted. ◀

Reading **Social Studies**
A. Drawing Conclusions Why do you think Swahili has Arabic influences?

BACKGROUND
The Masai Mara National Reserve in Kenya and the Serengeti National Park in Tanzania include a combined 6,345 square miles.

Place • Each month thousands of people move to Nairobi. The majority of newcomers are men. ▲

Nairobi

Nairobi is Kenya's capital. The city's name comes from a Masai word meaning "place of cool waters." With 2 million people, Nairobi is the biggest city in Eastern Africa. It has restaurants, bookstores, museums, and skyscrapers. Many foreign companies have offices in Nairobi. Every year, many Kenyans leave their rural homes to move to Nairobi. Not all of them find life in the city as easy as they had hoped. They are often unable to find work. Also, Nairobi suffers from water shortages and power outages. Despite these problems, many residents enjoy the big-city lifestyle that can be found in Nairobi.

Reading Social Studies

B. Identifying Problems What are the main problems Kenyans face after they move to Nairobi?

SECTION 4 ASSESSMENT

Terms & Names

1. Explain the significance of: (a) multiparty system   (b) Swahili   (c) *harambee*

Using Graphics

2. Use a time line like this one to document key events in Kenya's history.

   ┌─────────────────────────┐
   │ 1000 B.C., first Kenyans│
   └─────────────────────────┘
              ↓
   ┌─────────────────────────────┐
   │ A.D. 800s, first Arab trading posts │
   └─────────────────────────────┘
              ↓
   ┌─────────────────────────┐
   │   │
   └─────────────────────────┘

Main Ideas

3. (a) Why do most Kenyans live in the highlands?

   (b) Describe Kenya's government under Prime Minister Moi. How did it change in the 1990s?

   (c) How does the educational system of Kenya compare with that of the United States?

Critical Thinking

4. **Synthesizing**

   What problems might be caused by the system of languages in Kenya?

   Think About
   - the many ethnic groups
   - the use of Swahili and English

ACTIVITY -OPTION-   Imagine that you are on vacation in Kenya. Design a **postcard** to send home. Draw and write about some of the things you have seen on your visit.

Eastern and Southern Africa

CHAPTER 12 ASSESSMENT

TERMS & NAMES

Explain the significance of each of the following:

1. Zulu
2. pastoralism
3. overgrazing
4. kinship
5. veldt
6. Afrikaner
7. Nelson Mandela
8. sanction
9. multiparty system
10. *harambee*

REVIEW QUESTIONS

History and Governments *(pages 339–343)*
1. Why did the Masai and Zulu lose control of their own lands?
2. Explain how civil war in the recent histories of Somalia and Rwanda caused changes in each country.

Economies and Cultures *(pages 346–350)*
3. Why do so many people of Eastern Africa live as nomadic pastoralists?
4. How has the music of Eastern Africa changed?

South Africa Today *(pages 354–357)*
5. How have South Africa's rich natural resources affected events in its history?
6. How did apartheid limit the lives of nonwhites in South Africa?

Kenya Today *(pages 358–361)*
7. Why did Kenyans become dissatisfied with the government of Daniel arap Moi?
8. Describe the city of Nairobi.

CRITICAL THINKING

Forming and Supporting Opinions
1. Use your completed chart from Reading Social Studies, p. 338, to list three predictions for Africa's future. Explain your predictions.

Comparing
2. Compare the leadership shown by Somalia's Siad Barre, Kenya's Daniel arap Moi, and South Africa's Willem de Klerk.

Making Inferences
3. The Nobel Peace Prize is awarded to people who have done the most to create peace in the world. What did Nelson Mandela do to earn this award?

Visual Summary

1 History and Governments 
- The history of Eastern and Southern Africa spans millions of years and includes trading empires, European settlement, and independence.
- Nations of Eastern Africa have suffered under colonial governments and rulers with unlimited powers. They now are trying to achieve democracy and freedom.

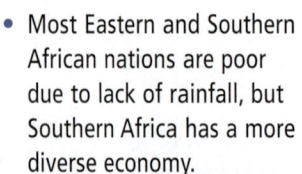

2 Economies and Cultures
- Most Eastern and Southern African nations are poor due to lack of rainfall, but Southern Africa has a more diverse economy.
- Eastern and Southern Africa have rich cultural heritages.

3 South Africa Today
- South Africa was first settled 2,000 years ago and was later colonized by the Dutch, French, Germans, and British.
- South Africa has the largest economy in Africa south of the Sahara.

4 Kenya Today
- Kenya has a varied geography, including beaches, plains, rain forests, and highlands that are home to many wild animals.
- Education is very important to Kenyans.

STANDARDS-BASED ASSESSMENT

Use the map and your knowledge of world cultures and geography to answer questions 1 and 2.

Additional Test Practice, pp. S1–S33

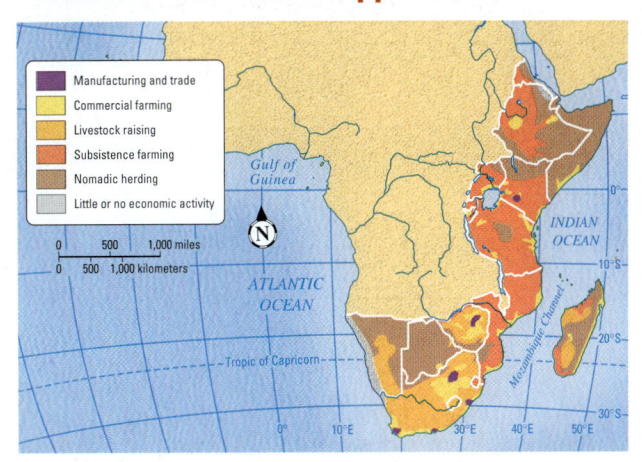

1. What is the least common use of land in both Southern and Eastern Africa?
   A. commercial farming
   B. livestock raising
   C. manufacturing and trade
   D. subsistence farming

2. What conclusion can you draw from this map?
   A. No manufacturing is done in either Eastern Africa or Southern Africa.
   B. Southern Africa has a more developed economy than Eastern Africa.
   C. Most people in Eastern and Southern Africa work on commercial farms.
   D. Large sections of Eastern and Southern Africa have no economic activity.

The following excerpt is from the speech that Nelson Mandela gave when he was released from prison. Use the quotation and your knowledge of world cultures and geography to answer question 3.

PRIMARY SOURCE

Today the majority of South Africans, black and white, recognize that apartheid has no future. It has to be ended by our own decisive mass action in order to build peace and security. The mass campaign of defiance and other actions of our organization and people can only culminate in the establishment of democracy. The destruction caused by apartheid on our sub-continent is in-calculable. The fabric of family life of millions of my people has been shattered. Millions are homeless and unemployed. Our economy lies in ruins and our people are embroiled in political strife.

NELSON MANDELA, speech of February 11, 1990

3. Why did Mandela believe that both black and white South Africans were ready to end apartheid?
   A. because apartheid had damaged family life and the South African economy
   B. because apartheid had caused a great leader like Mandela to be sent to prison
   C. because most South Africans were tired of world protests against apartheid
   D. because apartheid was a nationwide mass campaign of defiance and protest

TEST PRACTICE CLASSZONE.COM

ALTERNATIVE ASSESSMENT

1. WRITING ABOUT HISTORY

Many African countries are taking steps to ensure the survival of endangered animals. Research what animals are endangered in Eastern and Southern Africa. What are nations doing to help them survive? Is there any evidence that these efforts have been successful? Write a report on your findings and share it with the class.

2. COOPERATIVE LEARNING

With two or three other classmates, create a collage about the daily lives and culture of one ethnic group living in Eastern or Southern Africa. Decide on a group to research, then find out where and how the people live. Draw pictures and write poems or sentences that convey your findings. As a team, make a collage of your collective work.

INTEGRATED TECHNOLOGY

Doing Internet Research

Use the Internet to learn more about the climate and vegetation of one region of Eastern or Southern Africa. Write a report of your findings. List the Web sites you used to prepare your report.

- Find information about how the climate and vegetation affect people's lives.
- Create drawings, diagrams, or charts to present additional information.

For Internet links to support this activity, go to

RESEARCH LINKS CLASSZONE.COM

Eastern and Southern Africa

UNIT 5

Place The Grand Palace is the former residence of the king of Siam, the country now known as Thailand. The palace complex was constructed in 1782 in Bangkok, the national capital.

SOUTHERN ASIA

Chapter 13 Southern Asia: Place and Times

Chapter 14 India and Its Neighbors

Chapter 15 Southeast Asia Today

SOUTHERN ASIA

THE GRAND PALACE

ATLANTIC OCEAN
PACIFIC OCEAN
PACIFIC OCEAN
INDIAN OCEAN

INTEGRATED TECHNOLOGY

eEdition
- Interactive Maps
- Interactive Visuals

VIDEO
India: Renymol in India

INTERNET RESOURCES
Go to **classzone.com** for:
- Research Links
- Internet Activities
- Data Updates
- Unit Quiz
- Maps
- Test Practice
- Current Events
- Web Research Guide

Unit Atlas 5: Physical Geography

SUNSHINE STATE STANDARDS

Key Standard SS.B.1.3.1 The student uses various map forms (including thematic maps) and other geographic representations, tools, and technologies to acquire, process, and report geographic information including patterns of land use, connections between places, and patterns and processes of migration and diffusion.

Other Standards SS.B.1.3.3

FCAT LA.A.2.3.1 Reading: Identify Main Ideas, Facts, and Details

Southern Asia: Physical

Elevation
- 13,100 ft. (4,000 m)
- 6,600 ft. (2,000 m)
- 3,275 ft. (1,000 m)
- 650 ft. (200 m)
- 0 ft. (0 m)
- Below sea level
- ▲ Mountain peak

0 500 1,000 miles
0 500 1,000 kilometers

366 UNIT 7

Southern Asia

Precipitation in Southern Asia

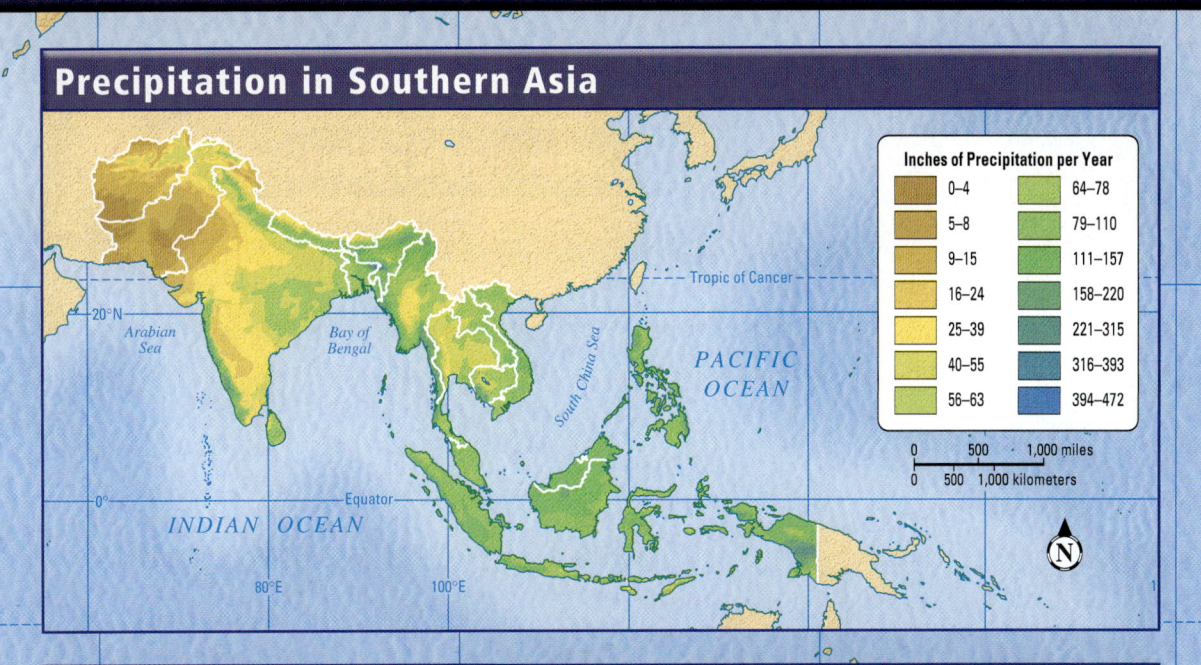

Inches of Precipitation per Year
- 0–4
- 5–8
- 9–15
- 16–24
- 25–39
- 40–55
- 56–63
- 64–78
- 79–110
- 111–157
- 158–220
- 221–315
- 316–393
- 394–472

Southern Asia–United States Landmass and Population

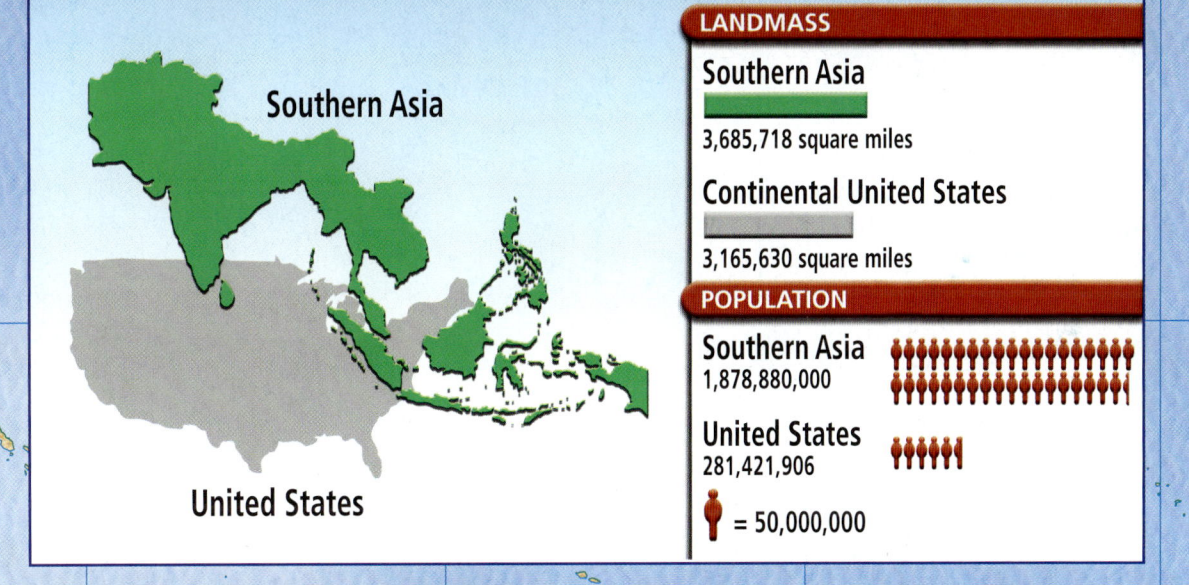

LANDMASS

Southern Asia
3,685,718 square miles

Continental United States
3,165,630 square miles

POPULATION

Southern Asia
1,878,880,000

United States
281,421,906

= 50,000,000

Fast Facts

✓ **MOST RAIN IN ONE MONTH:**
Meghalaya, India, July 1861, 366 in.

✓ **WORLD'S LARGEST RIVER DELTA:**
Ganges delta, Bangladesh

✓ **WORLD'S LARGEST ARCHIPELAGO:**
Indonesia, 3,231 mi., 17,000 islands

✓ **HUGE TSUNAMI:**
Java and Sumatra, 1883, 120-ft.-high wave

GEOGRAPHY SKILLBUILDER: Interpreting Maps and Visuals

1. **Location** • What mountain range lies in the north of India?
2. **Place** • Which two rivers form the Ganges delta?

UNIT 5 Atlas: Human Geography

Southern Asia: Political

Southern Asia

Religions of Southern Asia

Legend:
- Confucianism
- Christianity
- Buddhism
- Sunni Islam
- Traditional
- Sikhism
- Hinduism

Population Density of Southern Asia

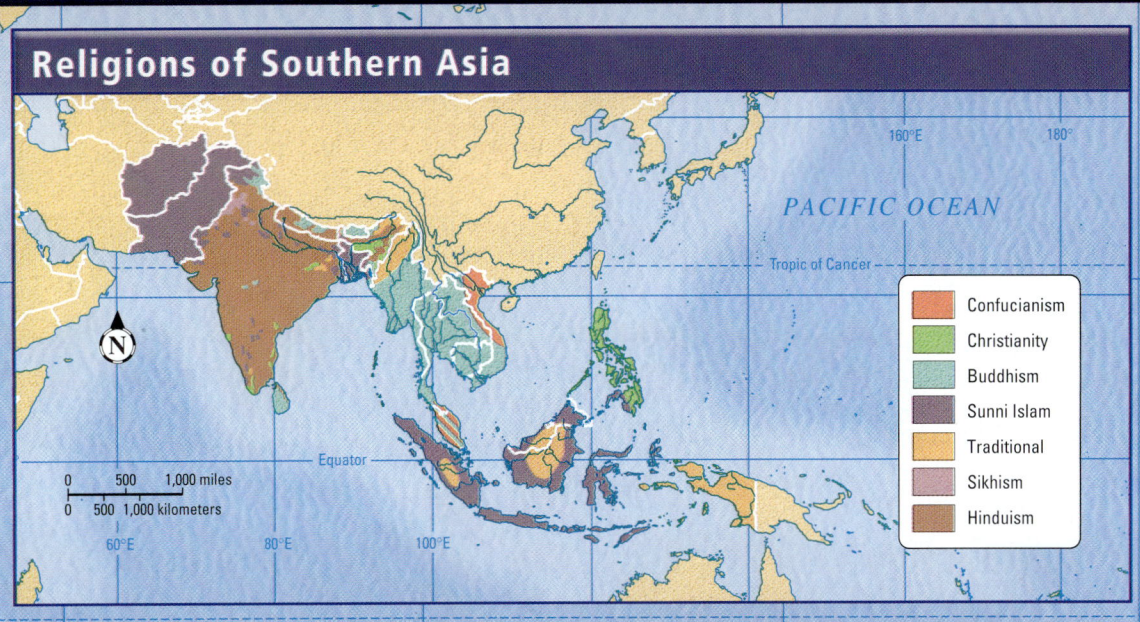

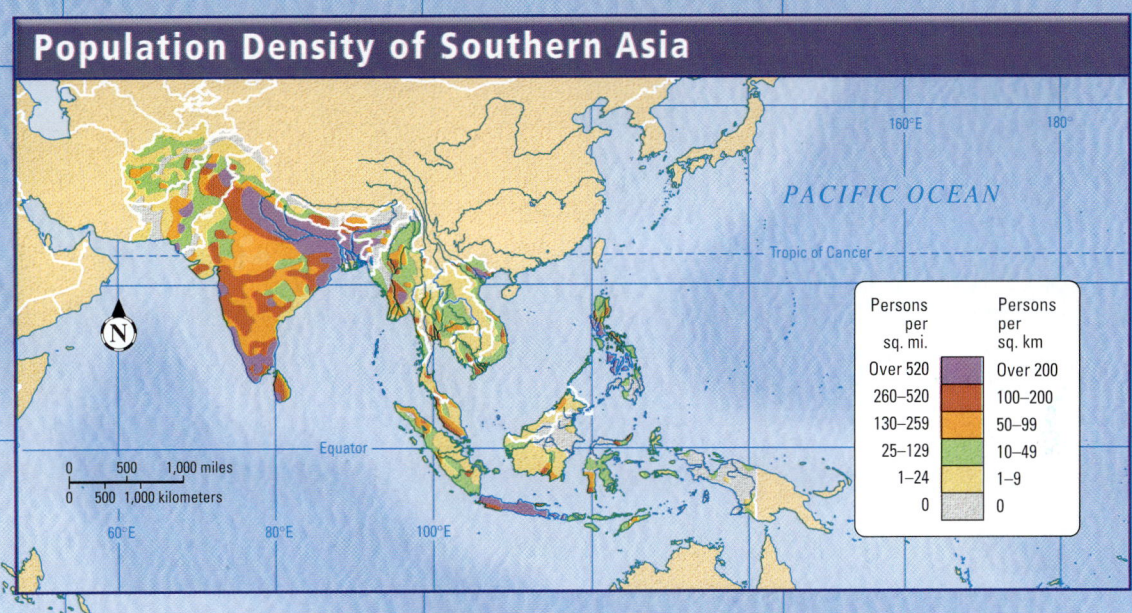

Persons per sq. mi.	Persons per sq. km
Over 520	Over 200
260–520	100–200
130–259	50–99
25–129	10–49
1–24	1–9
0	0

Fast Facts

✓ **WORLD'S SECOND LARGEST COUNTRY POPULATION:**
India, 1,002,142,000 (2000)

✓ **WORLD'S TALLEST BUILDING:**
Petronas Towers, Kuala Lumpur, Malaysia, 1,483 ft.

✓ **WORLD'S LARGEST PRODUCER OF TEA:**
Assam, India, 1,700,000 lbs. per yr.

✓ **SINKING CITY:**
Bangkok, Thailand, sinking at about 3 in. per yr.

GEOGRAPHY SKILLBUILDER: Interpreting Maps and Visuals

1. **Region** • What country has the largest Hindu population?
2. **Place** • Which country shares borders with India and Afghanistan?

Unit Atlas 5 Data File

For updates on these statistics, go to **DATA UPDATE CLASSZONE.COM**

Country Flag	Country/Capital	Currency	Population (2001) (estimate)	Life Expectancy (years) (2000)	Birthrate (per 1,000 pop.) (2000)
	Afghanistan Kabul	Afghani	26,813,000	46	43
	Bangladesh Dhaka	Taka	131,270,000	59	27
	Bhutan Thimphu	Ngultrum	2,049,000	66	40
	Brunei Bandar Seri Begawan	Dollar	344,000	71	25
	Cambodia Phnom Penh	Riel	12,492,000	56	38
	East Timor* Dili	Dollar	737,000	50	25
	India New Delhi	Rupee	1,029,991,000	61	27
	Indonesia Jakarta	Rupiah	228,438,000	64	24
	Laos Vientiane	Kip	5,636,000	51	41
	Malaysia Kuala Lumpur	Ringgit	22,229,000	73	25
	Maldives Male	Rufiyaa	311,000	71	35
	Myanmar Yangon	Kyat	41,995,000	54	30
	Nepal Kathmandu	Rupee	25,284,000	57	36
	Pakistan Islamabad	Rupee	144,617,000	58	39
	Philippines Manila	Peso	82,842,000	67	29
	Singapore Singapore	Dollar	4,300,000	78	13

*East Timor became an independent country on May 20, 2002.

Southern Asia

DATA FILE

Infant Mortality (per 1,000 live births) (2000)	Doctors (per 100,000 pop.) (1992–1999)	Literacy Rate (percentage) (1996–1999)	Passenger Cars (per 1,000 pop.) (1996–1999)	Total Area (square miles)	Map (not to scale)
149.8	11	32	2	250,775	
82.2	20	40	1	55,126	
70.7	16	42 (1995)	1	16,000	
24.0	85	88	441	2,226	
80.8	30	65 (1993)	1.2	69,898	
120.9	N.A.	48	23	5,641	
72.0	48	56	4	1,195,063	
45.7	16	84	12	779,675	
104.0	24	57	1.7	91,428	
7.9	66	84	143	128,727	
27.0	40	96	3	115	
82.5	30	83	0.7	261,789	
78.5	4	39	N/A	54,362	
91.0	57	44	8	310,403	
35.3	123	95	9	115,651	
3.2	163	91	95	225	

UNIT 5 Atlas

Data File

For updates on these statistics, go to
DATA UPDATE
CLASSZONE.COM

Country Flag	Country/Capital	Currency	Population (2000 estimate)	Life Expectancy (years) (2000)	Birthrate (per 1,000 pop.) (2000)
	Sri Lanka Colombo	Rupee	19,409,000	72	18
	Thailand Bangkok	Baht	61,798,000	73	16
	Vietnam Hanoi	Dong	79,939,000	66	20
	United States Washington, D.C.	Dollar	281,422,000	77	15

Mohandas Gandhi ▼

The Shwezigon Pagoda, a Buddhist temple in Myanmar ▲

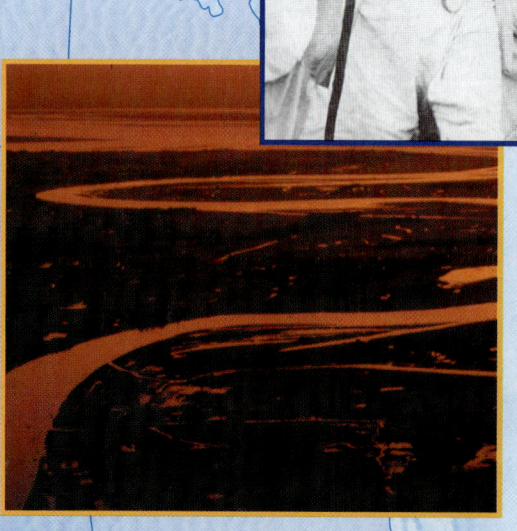

The Ganges River Valley ▲

372 UNIT 5

Southern Asia

DATA FILE

Infant Mortality (per 1,000 live births) (2000)	Doctors (per 100,000 pop.) (1992–1998)	Literacy Rate (percentage) (1996–1999)	Passenger Cars (per 1,000 pop.) (1996–1999)	Total Area (square miles)	Map (not to scale)
17.3	37	91	12	25,332	
22.4	24	94	25	198,455	
36.7	48	94	1	130,468	
7.0	251	97	489	3,787,319	

GEOGRAPHY SKILLBUILDER: Interpreting a Chart

1. **Place** • How much lower is Singapore's birthrate than India's?
2. **Region** • How much higher is the literacy rate in the Philippines than in Laos?

Dancer in Rasa Lila drama in India ▼

Boys in Indonesia studying the Qur'an ▲

Central Highlands in Sri Lanka ▲

Atlas 373

Chapter 13

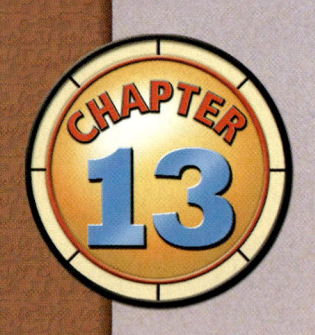

Southern Asia: Place and Times

Section 1   Physical Geography

Section 2   Ancient India

Section 3   Ancient Crossroads

Place The temple complex at Angkor Wat, Cambodia, is dedicated to the Hindu god Vishnu. Built in the 1100s, it covers almost one square mile.

FOCUS ON GEOGRAPHY

How did rivers contribute to the development of civilizations?

Human-Environment Interaction • The regular flooding of the Ganges River and other rivers during the rainy season deposits rich soil on the Northern Plains. This fertile soil has been farmed by the people of India for many centuries. A rich civilization known as the Gupta developed on these plains. The art, literature, philosophy, mathematics, and science developed during its golden age still influence the world.

What do you think?

- Why do complex civilizations depend on productive farmland?
- What might happen to a civilization if the climate changes and rivers dry up or change course?

CHAPTER 13 — READING SOCIAL STUDIES

BEFORE YOU READ

▶▶ What Do You Know?

Before you read the chapter, consider what you already know about Southern Asia. What stories have you read or heard about climbing the Himalayas, the highest mountains in the world? What do you know about explorers who have traveled the area's rain forests? What do you know about India? Have you read or heard about Hinduism or Buddhism, the major religions of Southern Asia? Reflect on what you have learned in other classes, what you have read, and what you may have seen in documentaries or news reports about the history of this region.

Culture • Shiva is one of the Hindu gods worshiped in Southern Asia.

Place • Mohenjo-Daro was once a thriving city in Southern Asia.

▶▶ What Do You Want to Know?

Decide what you know about Southern Asia. In your notebook, record what you hope to learn from this chapter.

READ AND TAKE NOTES

Reading Strategy: Categorizing Categorizing is a useful strategy for organizing information you read about in social studies. Categorizing means sorting things or ideas into groups. Use the chart at the right to categorize information about the geographic and human factors that shaped the ancient history of Southern Asia.

- Copy the chart into your notebook.
- As you read, look for information about geographic features and human civilization.
- When you reach the end of a section, record key details next to the appropriate headings.
- Note that the geography of Southeast Asia is discussed in Section 1 and Section 3.

Factors	Impact of Geography/ Contributions of Civilizations
South Asia	
Geography of Indian Subcontinent	
Indus River Civilization (about 2500–1700 B.C.)	
Aryans (1700 B.C.)	
Hinduism	
Buddhism (500 B.C.)	
Mauryan Dynasty (about 324–185 B.C.)	
Gupta Dynasty (A.D. 320–500)	
Southeast Asia	
Geography	
Location	
Early Advances	
Southeast Asian empires (6th century A.D.)	

SECTION 1

Physical Geography

TERMS & NAMES
subcontinent
Himalayas
Northern Plains
delta
sediment
Deccan Plateau
archipelago
monsoon

MAIN IDEA
Southern Asia's geography affects how the region's people live.

WHY IT MATTERS NOW
Studying the geography of Southern Asia will help you understand its history, economy, and customs.

DATELINE EXTRA

NEPAL, SOUTHERN ASIA, MAY 29, 1953

Today, New Zealander Sir Edmund Hillary and Sherpa tribesman Tenzing Norgay became the first people to reach the top of Mount Everest in the Himalayas. Using oxygen canisters and boots and clothing with special insulation, the two men overcame the tremendous cold, high winds, and thin air to reach their goal. "We didn't know if it was humanly possible to reach the top of Mount Everest," said Hillary of their adventure. "And even using oxygen as we were, if we did get to the top, we weren't at all sure whether we wouldn't drop dead or something of that nature." Hillary and Tenzing survived and will go down in history as the first people to stand atop the highest mountain in the world.

Human-Environment Interaction •
Tenzing Norgay (on the right) and Sir Edmund Hillary relax after their historic climb. ▲

The Variety of Southern Asia

The Unit Atlas maps on pages 366–367 show the great variety and contrasts in the geography of Southern Asia. There are the vast snow-capped mountain ranges, such as the Himalayas, and wet low-lying rain forests. Some people live in the mountains, while others live deep in the tropical rain forest or in the desert. Some places are dry, and others get plenty of water—some, in fact, get too much.

TAKING NOTES
Use your chart to take notes about Southern Asia.

Factors	Impact of Geography/ Contributions of Civilizations
SOUTH ASIA	
Geography...	
Indus River...	

SUNSHINE STATE STANDARDS
Key Standard SS.B.2.3.2 The student knows the human and physical characteristics of different places in the world and how these characteristics change over time.
FCAT LA.A.2.2.7 Reading: Recognize Compare and Contrast

Southern Asia: Place and Times 377

Southern Asia is divided into two regions, South Asia and Southeast Asia. South Asia includes Afghanistan, Bangladesh, Bhutan, India, the Maldives, Nepal, Pakistan, and Sri Lanka (sree LAHNG•kuh). The South Asian subcontinent includes the countries of India, Pakistan, Bangladesh, Nepal, and Bhutan. A **subcontinent** is a large landmass that is part of a continent, but is geographically separate from it. India is the largest country on the subcontinent and in Southern Asia. It is the second most populous country in the world, next to China.

Geographic Regions of South Asia

The subcontinent has three main geographic regions—the Northern Mountain Rim, the Northern Plains, and the Deccan (DEHK•uhn) Plateau. Just off the coast are two island countries, Sri Lanka and the Maldives. Each of these regions has distinctive landforms and climate that affect how people live.

The Northern Mountain Rim The Northern Mountain Rim is made up of several mountain ranges. The Hindu Kush Mountains are located to the west and the **Himalayas** to the east. The Karakoram Range lies between the two, extending along the northern border of Pakistan. These mountains form a wall that separates the subcontinent from the rest of Asia.

BACKGROUND
Geologists believe that the South Asian subcontinent was once part of the African continent. It broke away 200 million years ago. Forty million years ago, this subcontinent crashed into Asia and created the Himalayas.

Reading **Social Studies**

A. Making Inferences How might these mountains have made trade and travel by water important in ancient times?

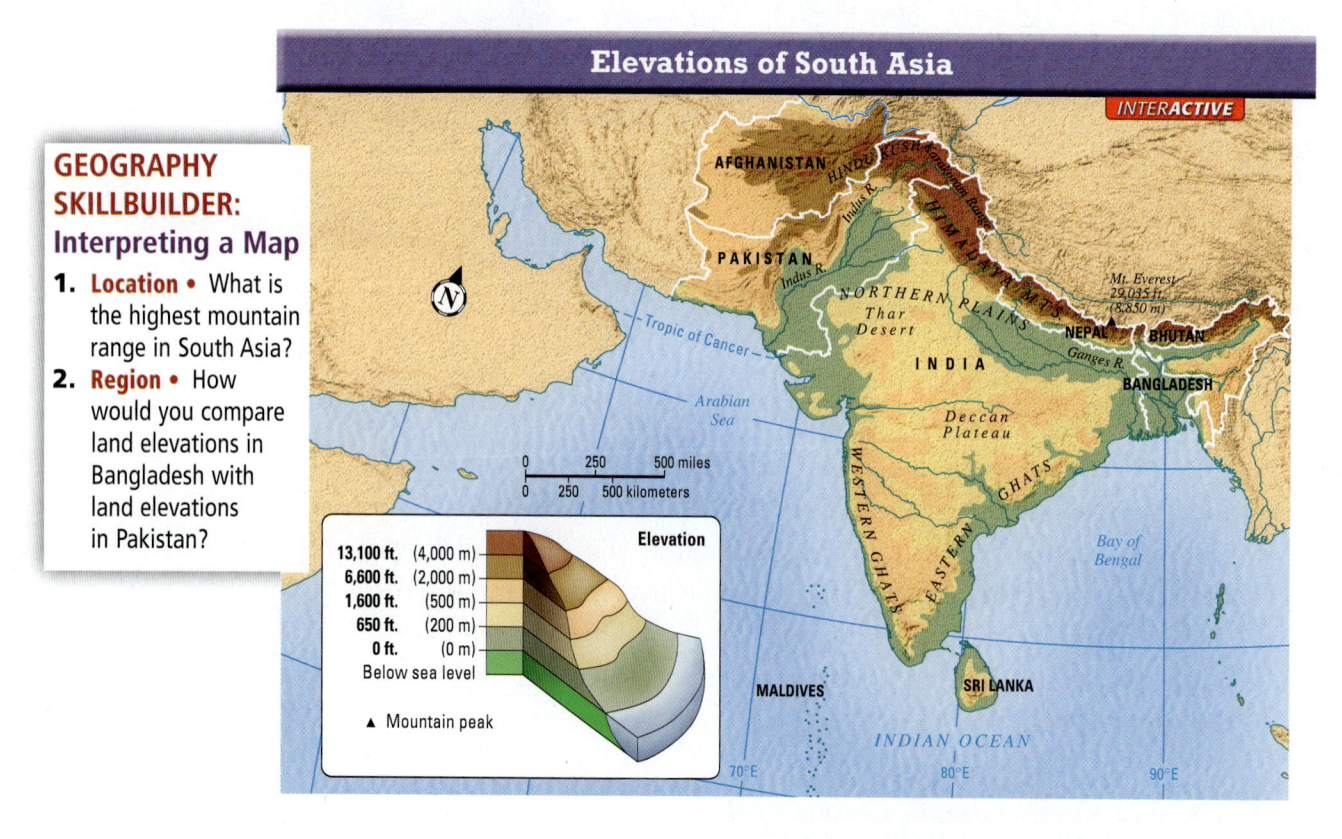

Elevations of South Asia

GEOGRAPHY SKILLBUILDER: Interpreting a Map

1. **Location** • What is the highest mountain range in South Asia?
2. **Region** • How would you compare land elevations in Bangladesh with land elevations in Pakistan?

Elevation
- 13,100 ft. (4,000 m)
- 6,600 ft. (2,000 m)
- 1,600 ft. (500 m)
- 650 ft. (200 m)
- 0 ft. (0 m)
- Below sea level
- ▲ Mountain peak

Mt. Everest 29,035 ft. (8,850 m)

However, there are some mountain passes that since ancient times have allowed travelers and invaders from Asia to get through the mountain barrier. The Khyber Pass, for example, connects the two modern-day countries of Pakistan and Afghanistan.

The Himalayas stretch for 1,500 miles across northern India and Nepal. They are 200 miles wide at some points, and many peaks are more than four and a half miles high. The tallest mountain in the world, Mount Everest, is almost five and a half miles high. This is taller than 23 Empire State Buildings stacked on top of one another. The terrain is rough in this region with few safe roads. It is also difficult to farm. As a result, fewer people live in this part of South Asia.

The Northern Plains The **Northern Plains** lie between the Himalayas and southern India. This region includes the Ganges (GAN·JEEZ) and Indus River valleys. The Ganges flows through Bangladesh and empties into the Bay of Bengal. The Indus River flows through Pakistan and empties into the Arabian Sea. The Indus and the Ganges rivers form large deltas where they empty into the sea. A **delta** is a triangular deposit of soil at the mouth of a river. The map on page 378 shows that the Ganges River delta is mostly within Bangladesh.

Human-Environment Interaction • People in heavily populated Bangladesh crowd aboard a Ganges River ferryboat. ▶

The Ganges River carries rich sediment from the Himalayas to the plains. **Sediment** includes minerals and debris that settle at the bottom of a river. During the rainy season, the Northern Plains flood, and the sediment from the Ganges River is deposited there. This makes the plains a fertile farming area.

Southern Asia: Place and Times

Reading Social Studies

B. Clarifying How could fertile soil lead to dense population?

Because of the fertile soil, parts of the Northern Plains are densely populated. In Bangladesh, for example, more than 130 million people live in an area smaller than the state of Wisconsin. In ancient times, the Indus River valley was also fertile and densely populated. Today, however, the valley is mostly desert, and few people live in this hot, dry region.

The Deccan Plateau As you can see from the map on page 378, the **Deccan Plateau** makes up most of southern India. The plateau has mineral deposits, as well as forests where elephants roam. Mountains border the plateau to the east and west—the Eastern and Western Ghats (gawts). The Western Ghats are the higher peaks, reaching 8,000 feet at the southern tip of India. A coastal plain runs between the mountains and the oceans on both coasts. Along these coastal plains the soil is fertile and water is plentiful. In the interior part of the plateau, between the mountain ranges, the soil is not as rich. People do farm there but water supplies are unreliable and it is hot year round. Fewer people live on the Deccan Plateau than in the Northern Plains.

Place • An elephant gets its tusks washed at an elephant training camp in Mudumalai National Park. ▲

Sri Lanka and the Maldives The islands of Sri Lanka and the Maldives lie south and southwest of India. Sri Lanka is a picturesque, mountainous island, 23 miles off the southern tip of India. Parts of it receive a great deal of rain.

The Maldives is a country made up of more than 1,200 low, flat coral islands called atolls. People live on only about 300 of these islands. The Maldives stretch south for 400 miles. The highest elevation in the entire chain is just over six feet above sea level.

BACKGROUND

If scientists' predictions about global warming are accurate, sea levels could rise dramatically. The Maldives would then disappear, or nearly disappear, under the sea.

Place • The central highlands of Sri Lanka have mountains that reach over 7,000 feet and offer some spectacular scenery. ◀

Place • Mount Merapi, called the Fire Mountain, is the most active volcano in Indonesia. ◀

Regions and Nations of Southeast Asia

Southeast Asia contains both a mainland region and many islands. The countries that make up Southeast Asia include Brunei, Cambodia, Indonesia, Laos, Malaysia, Myanmar (Burma), the Philippines, Singapore, Thailand, and Vietnam.

Mainland Southeast Asia
The mainland lies on two peninsulas—the Indochinese Peninsula and the Malay Peninsula. The countries of mainland Southeast Asia are Cambodia, Laos, Myanmar, Thailand, Vietnam, and part of Malaysia. The Mekong River drains more than 313,000 square miles of this region. It starts in the highlands of the Plateau of Tibet and ends in the South China Sea. It flows through Laos, central Cambodia, and into Vietnam. This area is a major rice-producing region and is densely populated.

Islands of Southeast Asia
The islands of Southeast Asia include Borneo, part of which belongs to the country of Malaysia, the island of Singapore, and the archipelagoes of Indonesia and the Philippines. An **archipelago** (AHR•kuh•PEHL•uh•GOH) is a group of islands.

Indonesia is the largest nation in Southeast Asia. It extends over an area about three times the size of Texas, and it has the fourth largest population in the world. Indonesia is made up of 17,000 islands that were formed by volcanoes.

Reading Social Studies

C. Making Inferences How do you think the Mekong River contributes to growing crops in this region?

Southern Asia: Place and Times

More than 6,000 of these islands are inhabited. The islands have a tropical climate with a lot of rain, but the soil is not very fertile. Still, more than half the people of Indonesia are farmers.

The 7,100 islands of the Philippines cover an area about the size of the state of Arizona. Only 800 of these islands are inhabited. Nearly half of the Philippine people are farmers.

Climate and Monsoons

Most of South Asia has three seasons—cool, hot, and rainy. The higher elevations are usually cooler. Much of India's weather is milder in the cool season. Sometimes frost forms on the Northern Plains. However, most of southern India is hot all year round.

Southeast Asia's climate has less variety. It is hot and rainy. Heavy seasonal winds and rains are common both to South Asia and Southeast Asia.

The Monsoon Cycle

The period from June through September marks the coming of the monsoon winds and the rainy season. A **monsoon** is a seasonal wind that blows over the northern part of the Indian Ocean. From April through October, the monsoon blows from the southwest, building up moisture over the ocean and bringing heavy rains to South Asia and Southeast Asia. From November through March, the monsoon blows from the northeast.

South Asia and Southeast Asia have different monsoon cycles. In South Asia, heavy monsoon rains fall from June through October. November through February is mostly cool and dry. Because March through late May is hot and humid, the monsoon rains in June bring great relief. In India, school starts in June, after the rains begin. Children take their main vacation during the spring, when it is too hot to study. The monsoon rains reach as far north as the Himalayas. However, there is very little rain in most of western Pakistan.

Strange but TRUE

The World's Most Destructive Volcano Krakatau (KRAK•uh•TOW), a volcanic island between Java and Sumatra in Indonesia, is pretty quiet these days (see below). In 1883, however, it erupted with explosions so loud they were heard in Australia and Japan, thousands of miles away. Krakatau's volcanic eruption caused tidal waves that killed 36,000 people. The eruption blew nearly 5 cubic miles of rock into the air and spewed out volcanic ash at least 17 miles high, throwing the region into darkness for days. This ash, blown around Earth for two years, caused amazing sunsets worldwide.

In Southeast Asia, there are two seasons. The summer monsoon lasts from April to September. During this time, there are heavy rains. The winter season from October through March is cool and dry.

Depending on Rain Agriculture depends on the timing of the monsoons. If the monsoons come too early, the farmers do not have time to plant their seeds. If the rains do not arrive or if they arrive too late, the crops fail. Sometimes the monsoons bring too much rain, resulting in severe flooding that ruins crops, damages property, and is dangerous to people.

Reading
Social Studies

D. Compare and Contrast How does this cycle of hot, cool, and rainy seasons compare with the cycle of seasons where you live?

Culture • These women in India are celebrating Teej, a festival for welcoming the coming of the monsoons. ▶

SECTION 1 ASSESSMENT

Terms & Names
1. Explain the significance of:　(a) subcontinent　(b) Himalayas　(c) Northern Plains　(d) delta
　(e) sediment　(f) Deccan Plateau　(g) archipelago　(h) monsoon

Using Graphics
2. Use a chart like this one to record important information about South Asia and Southeast Asia.

	South Asia	Southeast Asia
Countries		
Major Regions		
Major Rivers		
Monsoon Cycle		

Main Ideas
3. (a) Describe three distinctive regions of South Asia.
   (b) Where is the Mekong River? Which countries does it flow through?
   (c) Name two nations in Southeast Asia that are archipelagoes.

Critical Thinking
4. **Compare and Contrast**
   Compare the Northern Plains with the Deccan Plateau. How are they similar? How are they different?

   Think About
   ◆ location
   ◆ fertility of the soil and population density

ACTIVITY -OPTION- Photocopy a **map** of Southeast Asia. Using highlighter markers, spotlight the places you have learned about in Section 1. Share your map with the class.

Southern Asia: Place and Times

India and Its Neighbors, 2001

Legend:
- National boundary
- ★ National capital
- • Other city

GEOGRAPHY SKILLBUILDER: Interpreting a Map

1. **Location** • What country is both east and west of Bangladesh?
2. **Location** • What is the absolute location of the capital of Sri Lanka?

Ancient India

SECTION 2

TERMS & NAMES
Mohenjo-Daro
Aryan
Sanskrit
Hinduism
Vedas
caste
Ashoka

MAIN IDEA
The people of ancient India established social and cultural practices that became widespread throughout the region.

WHY IT MATTERS NOW
The scientific and cultural contributions of ancient India affect our lives today.

DATELINE

MAURYAN EMPIRE 232 B.C.—The great Emperor Ashoka died yesterday. He was dearly loved by his people, and millions will mourn his death. Horrified by the suffering and bloodshed he saw at the battle of Kalinga in 262 B.C., Ashoka embraced the teachings of Buddhism.

From that point on, he put his beliefs into action and ruled his people without violence. Who can possibly step forward to take the place of our great leader?

Place • Three lion figures top this pillar at Sarnath, one of many pillars Ashoka had erected during his reign. ▲

The Indus River Valley Civilization

Ashoka's empire was built on a civilization whose roots were more than 2,000 years old. Around 2500 B.C., a brilliant civilization developed in the Indus River valley. Sometimes called the Harappan civilization after one of its major cities, it flourished until about 1700 B.C. in an area that is mostly in present-day Pakistan. This civilization, which existed at the same time as ancient Egyptian civilization, stretched west to what is now Kabul, Afghanistan, and east to what is now Delhi, India. Its center was the rich farmland along the Indus River and its tributaries. The map on page 387 shows the extent of this civilization.

TAKING NOTES
Use your chart to take notes about Southern Asia.

Factors	Impact of Geography/ Contributions of Civilizations
SOUTH ASIA	
Geography...	
Indus River...	

SUNSHINE STATE STANDARDS
Key Standard SS.A.2.3.1 The student understands how language, ideas, and institutions of one culture can influence other (e.g., through trade, exploration, and immigration).
Other Standards SS.A.2.3.4, A.2.3.8
FCAT LA.A.2.3.1 Reading: Identify Main Ideas, Facts, and Details

Southern Asia: Place and Times 385

The civilization of the Indus River valley came to an end around 1700 B.C. No one knows for sure why the civilization ended. Some think the cause was a climate change—like a severe decrease in rainfall—while others think the urban centers were conquered and destroyed.

Hundreds of towns existed in the Indus River valley. There were two major cities: Harappa and **Mohenjo-Daro** (moh·HEHN·joh·DAHR·oh). Mohenjo-Daro was a large city with well-built homes and public buildings. Canals brought water from wells to farms outside the city walls.

Reading Social Studies

A. Making Inferences Why do you think this civilization developed in the Indus River valley rather than on the plains?

The Aryan Influence on South Asia

Around 1700 B.C., the **Aryans** (AIR·ee·uhnz) came to South Asia. These people migrated from southern Russia through passes in the Hindu Kush. The time of the Aryan arrival suggests that the Aryans played a role in the fall of the Harappan civilization, although there is no proof. Over time, the Aryan people and the people of the Indus River valley produced a new blend of culture in northern India.

A New People, a New Civilization The Aryans were different from the people of the Indus River valley. They spoke another language called **Sanskrit**.

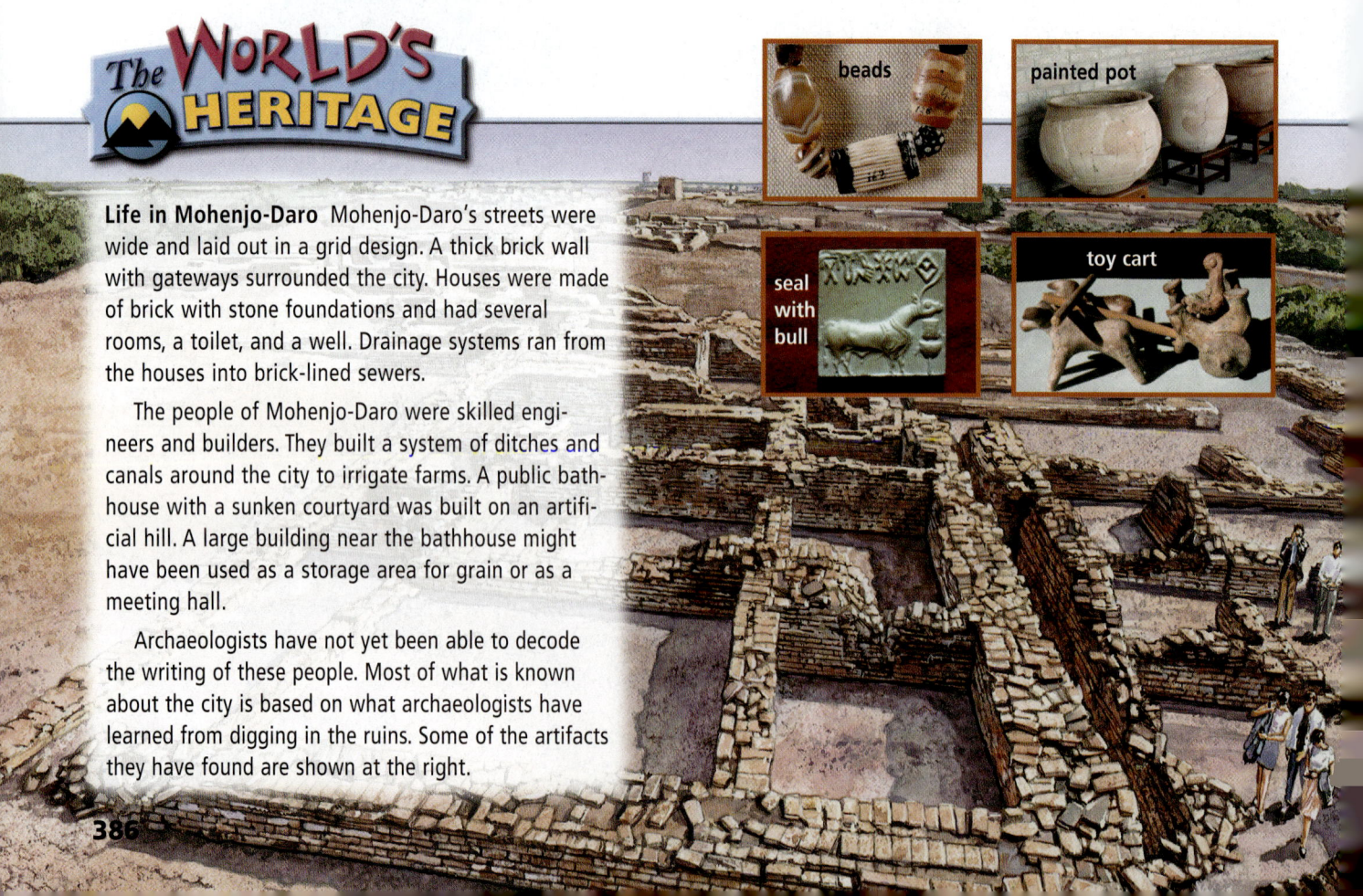

The World's Heritage

Life in Mohenjo-Daro Mohenjo-Daro's streets were wide and laid out in a grid design. A thick brick wall with gateways surrounded the city. Houses were made of brick with stone foundations and had several rooms, a toilet, and a well. Drainage systems ran from the houses into brick-lined sewers.

The people of Mohenjo-Daro were skilled engineers and builders. They built a system of ditches and canals around the city to irrigate farms. A public bathhouse with a sunken courtyard was built on an artificial hill. A large building near the bathhouse might have been used as a storage area for grain or as a meeting hall.

Archaeologists have not yet been able to decode the writing of these people. Most of what is known about the city is based on what archaeologists have learned from digging in the ruins. Some of the artifacts they have found are shown at the right.

- beads
- painted pot
- seal with bull
- toy cart

Indus River Valley Civilization, 1700 B.C.

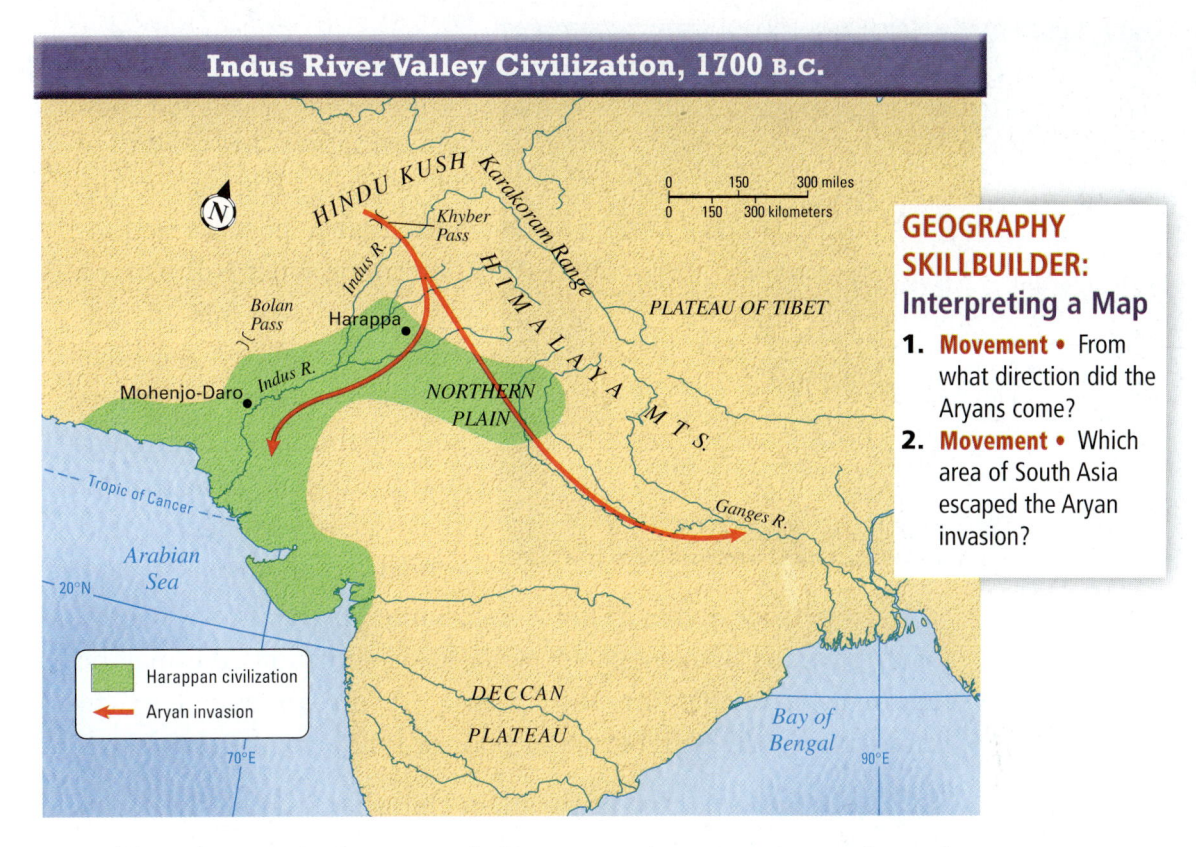

GEOGRAPHY SKILLBUILDER: Interpreting a Map
1. **Movement** • From what direction did the Aryans come?
2. **Movement** • Which area of South Asia escaped the Aryan invasion?

The Aryans had not settled in cities but were nomads and herders. Because the Aryans got their food and clothing from the animals they raised, they measured wealth by the number of cattle a person owned.

New Technology The Aryans brought new technology, animals, and ideas with them to South Asia. Sometime after 1000 B.C., the Aryans discovered iron ore in the Ganges River valley. Iron plows improved agriculture, and with the Aryan adoption of some local ways—like growing rice—they began to settle in towns. The Aryans also developed new iron weapons. These weapons were stronger than those of the Harappan people. Improved weapons and the introduction of the horse enabled the Aryans to rule northern India.

Reading Social Studies
B. Drawing Conclusions How did the Aryans' use of iron help them settle and control India?

Hinduism—A Way of Life

People of ancient India developed the religion of **Hinduism**, based on certain Aryan practices. Aryan priests chanted hymns in praise of their gods. For a long time, these hymns were passed down through oral tradition. Later, these hymns and other Aryan religious beliefs were written down and became part of the **Vedas** (VAY·duhz), or Books of Knowledge. The Vedas contain writings on prayers, hymns, religious rituals, and philosophy.

Southern Asia: Place and Times

Culture • The god Vishnu is said to take ten forms, including a fish, a tortoise, and a boar. Here, he is half man and half lion. ▲

Karma and Reincarnation

The ideas of karma and reincarnation are central to Hinduism. Karma is the idea that a person's actions determine what will happen after his or her death. Reincarnation is the idea that after death a person's soul is reborn into a different body. Hindus believe that the cycle of birth, death, and rebirth occurs many times.

Each person's status in life is determined by his or her behavior in previous lives. A person who leads a virtuous life may be reborn as a wealthy or wise person. A person who lives an immoral life may be reborn as a poor or sick person.

The Caste System

One of the main characteristics of Hinduism is the caste system. A **caste** is an inherited social class. Each person is born to a particular caste for his or her lifetime. Caste determines a person's job, marriage partner, and friends. The Hindu caste system was strongly influenced by the Aryan tribal social system, which was organized around the belief that people are not equal.

The Hindu caste system is based on four major classes—priests, warriors and princes, merchants and farmers, and laborers. Another group, once known as untouchables, has traditionally been considered inferior to the four major castes. Untouchables did the work that no one else wanted to do and were generally shunned by society. Today, the Hindu caste system is made up of thousands of castes and subcastes, but the four major castes are still the most important. The government and other groups are working to reduce the influence the caste system has on society.

Culture • The god Shiva may be represented in various forms. Here he is shown as the Lord of the Dance. ▶

BACKGROUND
Hindus worship many gods and goddesses. Most Hindu families have a shrine to a god or goddess set up in their homes.

Reading Social Studies
C. Analyzing Issues How do the caste system and the idea of reincarnation work together?

The Maurya and Gupta Dynasties

Two dynasties made important contributions to India. These dynasties were the Maurya and the Gupta. The contributions made by the people of these cultures still affect our lives today.

The Mauryan Empire

The first Indian empire was called the Maurya (324–185 B.C.). It was founded by the descendants of the Aryans who moved eastward from the region of the Indus River valley civilization. One of its emperors, **Ashoka,** created a unified government. He built a palace of stone and religious monuments. The Mauryans were known for their fine sculpture and sandstone carvings.

The Golden Age and the Gupta Dynasty

The Gupta Dynasty (A.D. 320–500) ruled during India's golden age in science, art, and literature. Most Gupta rulers were Hindus. However, both Hinduism and Buddhism were practiced throughout the empire at that time. Hindu and Buddhist beliefs inspired many artists. They created sculptures and paintings of Hindu gods and goddesses. Many temples were built that contained images of characters from Hindu mythology. Gupta architects hollowed out the solid stone of mountainside cliffs to create Buddhist temples. In the city of Ajanta, 30 Buddhist temples are carved into the side of a mountain.

Place • The Buddhist temples at Ajanta are carved into granite cliffs. The walls inside are covered with beautiful paintings. ▲

Biography

Ashoka Ashoka has been called one of the greatest emperors in world history. He ruled India's Mauryan Empire from 269 B.C. until his death in 232 B.C.

As a ruthless conqueror, Ashoka extended the Mauryan Empire over almost the entire subcontinent of South Asia. However, during one bloody battle, Ashoka became horrified at what he saw. He wrote, "150,000 persons were... carried away captive, 100,000 were [killed] and many times that number died." Ashoka vowed that this would be his last war, and he converted to the Buddhist religion.

He began to preach nonviolence and compassion for all living things and appointed "Officers of Righteousness" to relieve suffering among the people. Throughout the kingdom, the "principles for a just government" were carved in stone (shown at left) and displayed for all to see.

Southern Asia: Place and Times

Literature Sanskrit literature blossomed during the Gupta Dynasty. Kalidasa, who lived during the fifth century A.D., was the greatest poet and playwright of his age. His plays were used to teach moral principles and were filled with creativity and mystery.

Mathematics Gupta mathematicians made many important discoveries. They developed the concept of zero and the numerals that we use today. Centuries after the Gupta Empire fell, Europeans learned these numerals and the concept of zero from the Islamic civilizations of Southwest Asia. Europeans called this number system *Arabic*, the name still used today.

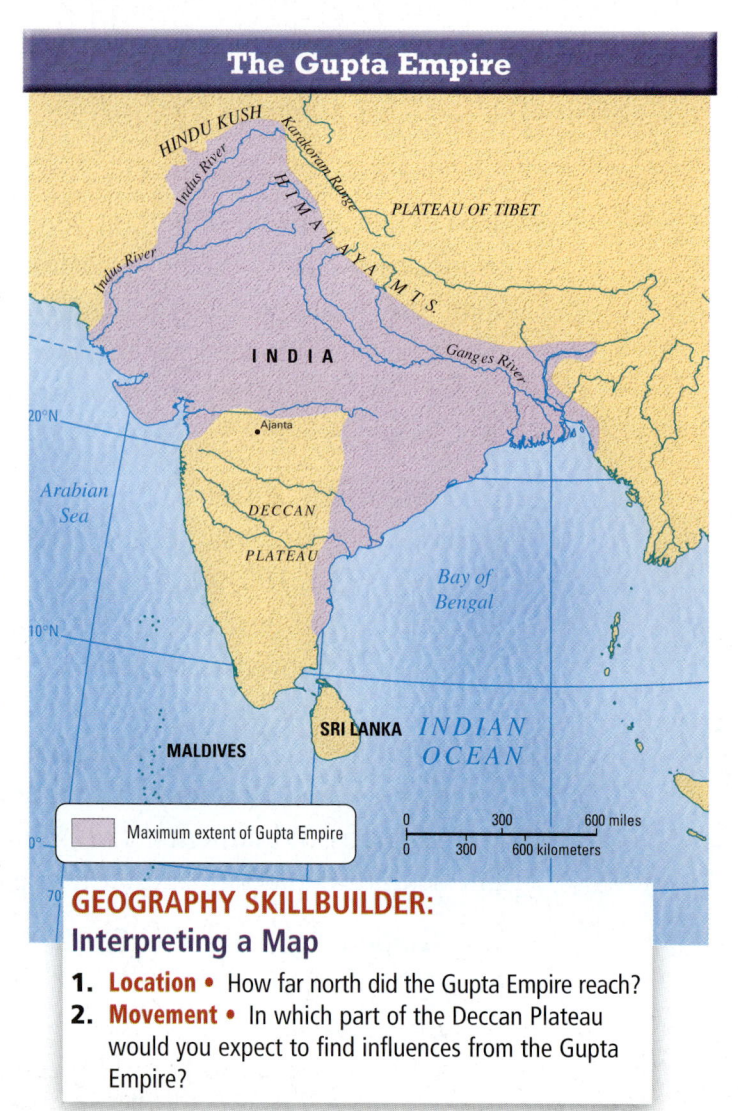

The Gupta Empire

Maximum extent of Gupta Empire

GEOGRAPHY SKILLBUILDER:
Interpreting a Map
1. **Location** • How far north did the Gupta Empire reach?
2. **Movement** • In which part of the Deccan Plateau would you expect to find influences from the Gupta Empire?

SECTION 2 ASSESSMENT

Terms & Names
1. Explain the significance of:
   (a) Mohenjo-Daro (b) Aryan (c) Sanskrit (d) Hinduism
   (e) Vedas (f) caste (g) Ashoka

Using Graphics
2. Use a spider map like the one below to record information about changes the Aryans brought to ancient India.

   (Aryans — Religion, Language, Weapons, Animals, Tools)

Main Ideas
3. (a) Describe the city of Mohenjo-Daro.
   (b) Describe three aspects of Hinduism.
   (c) Why is the Gupta Dynasty considered a golden age in science, art, and literature?

Critical Thinking
4. **Analyze**
   Why do you think the originally nomadic Aryans settled in India?

   Think About
   • where the Aryans came from and the geography of the subcontinent
   • the civilization the Aryans encountered
   • the discoveries the Aryans made in India

ACTIVITY -OPTION- Suppose you could go back in time to visit Mohenjo-Daro, the Mauryan Empire, or the Gupta Dynasty. Write a **paragraph** explaining which period you would visit and why.

390 CHAPTER 13

SKILLBUILDER

Reading an Elevation Map

▶▶ Defining the Skill

When you learn to read an elevation map, you will be able to tell how high above sea level the land in a region is. Land that is at sea level is at the same height, or level, as the sea. Land rises from that point. (In some inland areas, however, the land is actually below sea level.) The highest point above sea level on Earth is the peak of Mount Everest. It stands 29,028 feet above sea level. Elevation maps use color to show the height of the land. The key gives a color code for level of elevation. Usually, darker green areas are at or close to sea level. Light yellow or tan areas are the highest above sea level.

SUNSHINE STATE STANDARDS
Key Standard SS.B.1.3.1
The student uses various map forms (including thematic maps) and other geographic representations, tools, and technologies to acquire, process, and report geographic information including patterns of land use, connections between places, and patterns and processes of migration and diffusion.

FCAT LA.B.1.3.2 Writing: Draft and Revise

▶▶ Applying the Skill

The elevation map at the right shows the country of Pakistan. Pakistan, a country in southern Asia, has its southern border on the Arabian Sea. Its northern border is in the Hindu Kush mountain range and the Karakoram Range. Both ranges have mountain peaks higher than the highest peaks in the Rocky Mountains of the United States. Use the strategies below to help you read the elevation map.

Elevations of Pakistan

Elevation:
- 13,100 ft. (4,000 m)
- 6,600 ft. (2,000 m)
- 1,600 ft. (500 m)
- 650 ft. (200 m)
- 0 ft. (0 m)
- Below sea level

How to Read an Elevation Map

Strategy ❶ Read the key. Notice how land closest to sea level is a dark green. Land that is highest above sea level is dark brown.

Strategy ❷ Look at the map. Find each of the elevation regions indicated on the key.

Strategy ❸ Find the two highest mountain peaks. Follow the flow of the Indus River. Find the mountain pass. A pass is an opening in the mountain range where people have made roads or laid railroad lines because it is the easiest place to get from one side of the range to the other.

Write a Summary

A summary will help you understand the information found in the elevation map. The paragraph to the right summarizes the information found in the map of Pakistan.

> The southern border of Pakistan is on the Arabian Sea. Land along that border is at sea level and then rises dramatically to the northern regions of Pakistan, where some of the highest peaks on Earth can be found. The Indus River flows from an area of more than 6,600 feet through a region of less than 500 feet, until it reaches the sea. In the west of Pakistan are several mountain ranges that reach up to 5,000 feet. Pakistan is a country of great variety in elevation.

▶▶ Practicing the Skill

Turn to page 378 in Chapter 13, Section 1. Read the map, "Elevations of South Asia," and then write a paragraph summarizing the information found in that map.

Southern Asia: Place and Times

SECTION 3

Ancient Crossroads

TERMS & NAMES
Buddhism
Siddhartha Gautama
Four Noble Truths
Eightfold Path
Khmer
Angkor Wat

MAIN IDEA
The culture of ancient Southeast Asia was heavily influenced by traders and travelers from China, India, and other countries.

WHY IT MATTERS NOW
The culture of modern Southeast Asia still reflects the influence of ancient Indian and Chinese cultures.

DATELINE — EXTRA

THE RAIN FORESTS OF CAMBODIA, 1861

In the rain forests of Southeast Asia, a young French explorer has made a startling discovery. He stumbled onto what appears to be one of the largest and most impressive archaeological discoveries in history. "We hacked our way through the dense [rain forest]," said Henri Mouhot. "Suddenly the huge stone towers of an ancient city, some of them 200 feet high, appeared before us." Experts believe this city may have been built by the Khmer people, who ruled a vast empire in the region about 600 years ago.

Place • Henri Mouhot has discovered the extraordinary lost city of Angkor. ▲

Crossroads of Culture

The ancient city that Mouhot found was Angkor. It contains an impressive temple complex dating back to the time when the region was one of the crossroads of the ancient world. A crossroads is a place where people, goods, and ideas from many areas come together. In ancient times, travelers from India, China, and other countries came to Southeast Asian shores and made a lasting impression on the region.

TAKING NOTES
Use your chart to take notes about Southern Asia.

Factors	Impact of Geography/ Contributions of Civilizations
SOUTH ASIA	
Geography...	
Indus River...	

SUNSHINE STATE STANDARDS
Key Standard SS.A.2.3.1 The student understands how language, ideas, and institutions of one culture can influence other (e.g., through trade, exploration, and immigration).
Other Standards SS.B.2.3.8
FCAT LA.A.2.3.1 Reading: Identify Main Ideas, Facts, and Details

Trade Routes in Ancient Southern Asia

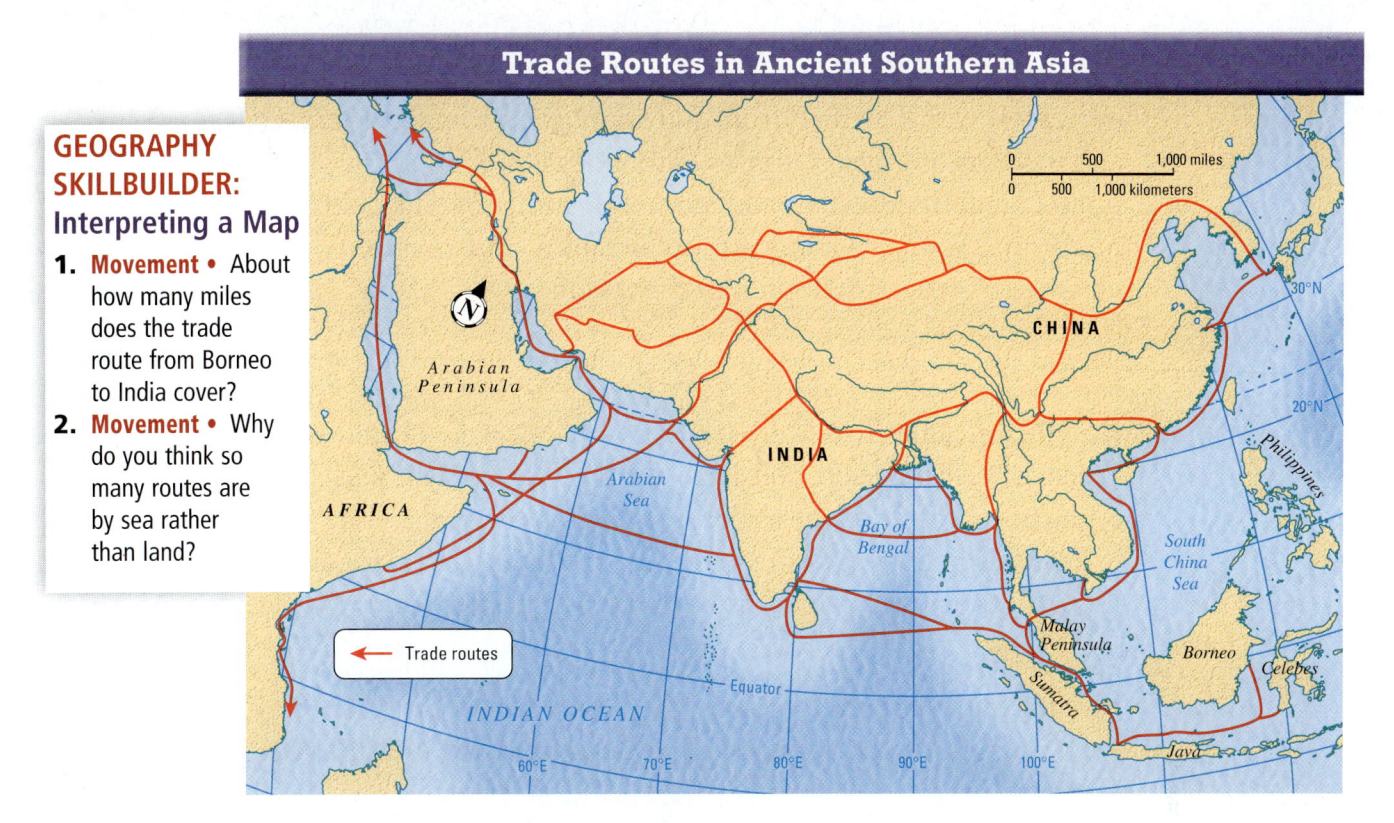

GEOGRAPHY SKILLBUILDER:
Interpreting a Map

1. **Movement** • About how many miles does the trade route from Borneo to India cover?
2. **Movement** • Why do you think so many routes are by sea rather than land?

BACKGROUND

Coastal traders used monsoon winds to sail their ships. They waited for favorable winds before sailing from India to Southeast Asia. When the winds shifted, the traders would sail back.

Reading Social Studies

A. Analyzing What effect did India have on Southeast Asia?

Early History Many important skills were developed in ancient Southeast Asia, including making tools from bronze, growing yams and rice, and sailing. In the past, historians thought that people from China or India brought these skills to the region. But now it seems clear that this knowledge was developed in Southeast Asia. Bronze Age items found in Thailand have been dated as far back as 3000 B.C. That is before bronze work was done in China. Eight to nine thousand years ago, rice was grown in Thailand. Yams and other roots were grown in Indonesia between 15,000 and 10,000 B.C. This is one of the earliest examples of agriculture ever found.

Trade and Travel Look at the map above. You can see that the central position of Southeast Asia made it a likely crossroads of trade for the area. Southeast Asia is in the center of the sea trading routes of the South Pacific and the Indian Ocean. Traders from India began to visit Southeast Asia around A.D. 100. Southeast Asian goods reached both India and China. From there, they traveled on to Southwest Asia and East Africa.

Southeast Asian trade goods included rice, tea, timber, and spices such as cloves, nutmeg, ginger, and pepper. Gold and other metals were also traded. Many ideas were shared as well. Religious ideas and knowledge spread. Skills such as farming and metalworking, as well as art forms and techniques, crossed to and from Southeast Asia.

Southern Asia: Place and Times

Influence of India Southeast Asia had a thriving culture of its own. However, it learned from and adopted customs from traders and travelers of other countries. Around A.D. 100, traders, Hindu priests, and Buddhist monks began to bring Indian culture to Southeast Asia, including art, architecture, and religion. These ideas were gradually adopted in the region.

Buddhism in Southeast Asia

Buddhism came from the same religious roots as Hinduism. It began in India around 500 B.C., although Hinduism and Islam eventually became more important religions in India. The ideas of Buddhism, however, spread to East and Southeast Asia, where it is still strong today. It is one of the major religions of the world.

The Signs of the Buddha The founder of Buddhism was **Siddhartha Gautama** (sih·DAHRTH·uh GAW·tuh·muh). He grew up as a wealthy prince and a member of the warrior class. Gautama lived in luxury in a palace with his wife and son.

One day, while out driving, he saw an old man. On other days, he saw a sick man, a corpse, and a holy man. Gautama interpreted these as signs to show him that life involves aging, sickness, and death. He believed that the holy man was a sign telling him to leave his family and seek the causes of human suffering.

For the next six years, Gautama was a wandering monk. He practiced self-denial and ate very little. However, he did not discover the cause of human suffering. One day, he decided to stop living a life of self-denial. He sat under a tree and began to meditate. Through meditation, Gautama gained enlightenment, or religious awakening. He now felt that he knew the reasons for human suffering and how to escape from it. News of his experience spread. People began to call him the Buddha, or the Enlightened One.

Buddhist Teachings The Buddha had once studied Hinduism. He was influenced by the Hindu beliefs in karma and reincarnation. These taught that life is a continuing cycle of death and rebirth. However, he did

Culture •
According to legend, the Buddha was sitting under a bodhi tree when he received enlightenment and the inspiration for his religious teachings. ▼

The Four Noble Truths and the Eightfold Path

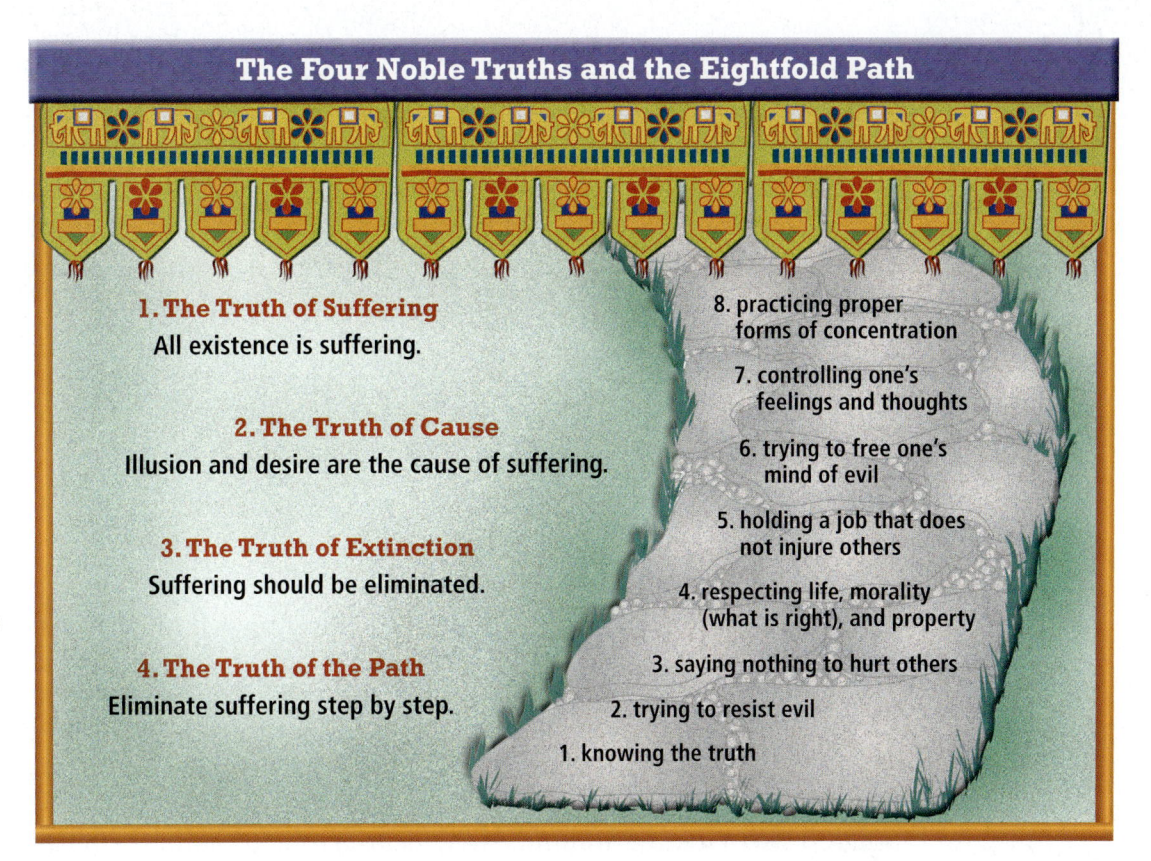

1. The Truth of Suffering
All existence is suffering.

2. The Truth of Cause
Illusion and desire are the cause of suffering.

3. The Truth of Extinction
Suffering should be eliminated.

4. The Truth of the Path
Eliminate suffering step by step.

8. practicing proper forms of concentration
7. controlling one's feelings and thoughts
6. trying to free one's mind of evil
5. holding a job that does not injure others
4. respecting life, morality (what is right), and property
3. saying nothing to hurt others
2. trying to resist evil
1. knowing the truth

Culture • People in many parts of the world today still try to follow the teachings of the Buddha. ▶

Reading Social Studies
B. Making Inferences What challenges might a person face in trying to follow the Eightfold Path?

not like the part of Hindu philosophy that was based on the Vedas, the ancient Aryan texts. In particular, he rejected the caste system and the role of priests.

The basic teachings of Buddhism are the **Four Noble Truths.** The first truth is that life is full of pain. The second truth is that suffering comes from the desire for possessions. The third truth explains that if people stop desiring these possessions, they will no longer suffer. The Buddha taught that the goal of life is to be free from desires and pain. Then one can progress to nirvana (neer·VAH·nuh), a state of happiness and peace.

The fourth truth says that people can escape suffering by following the Middle Way. The Middle Way is a set of guidelines called the **Eightfold Path.** These eight guidelines are as follows: right understanding, right purpose, right speech, right conduct, right means of livelihood, right effort, right awareness, and right meditation.

The Spread of Buddhism After the Buddha's death, his followers spread the new faith throughout southern India, Sri Lanka, and Southeast Asia. Buddhism also spread to Tibet, central Asia, China, Korea, and Japan. Buddhists organized schools and spiritual communities where monks and nuns could live and work.

Southern Asia: Place and Times

Indian Influence in Southeast Asia

As the influence of India spread, new images and religious art became part of Southeast Asian culture. Historians can trace these images from one country to another. Empires were founded on the beliefs of Hinduism, Buddhism, and, later, Islam. The success of empires often depended on the ongoing popularity of these beliefs.

Empire of the Khmer In the sixth century A.D., the **Khmer** (kmair) people established a great kingdom in present-day Cambodia. This kingdom was Hindu and very much influenced by Indian culture. The Khmer built great Hindu temples, including the huge complex, **Angkor Wat.** The Khmer kingdom spread through much of Southeast Asia. Then, as Buddhism grew in influence, the number of Hindu followers declined, and the Khmer lost power. The Khmer retreated south to the area near the city of Phnom Penh.

Indian influence in the form of Buddhism was also felt in the island nations of Southeast Asia. In Indonesia, a huge Buddhist temple called Borobudur was built in the sixth century. The builders used about 2 million cubic feet of stone to build the temple. It is shaped like a pyramid, with three terraces, or levels, which contain relief carvings. At the center, the temple is 103 feet high.

Reading Social Studies

C. Making Inferences How do you think Buddhism spread to other areas?

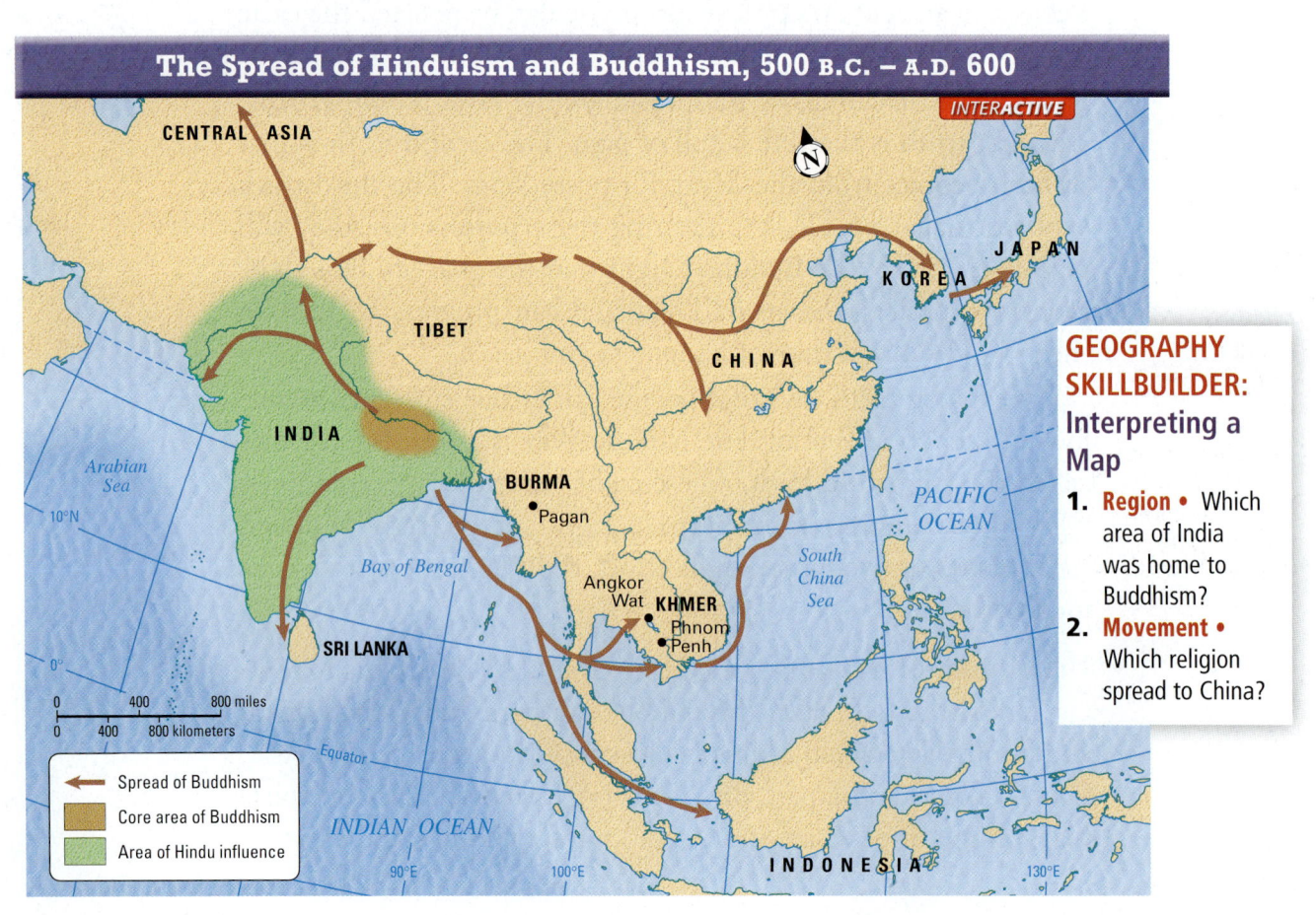

The Spread of Hinduism and Buddhism, 500 B.C. – A.D. 600

GEOGRAPHY SKILLBUILDER: Interpreting a Map

1. **Region** • Which area of India was home to Buddhism?
2. **Movement** • Which religion spread to China?

Legend:
- Spread of Buddhism
- Core area of Buddhism
- Area of Hindu influence

Place •
Borobudur is located in Indonesia on the large island of Java. The temple has three levels. Each represents a stage of spiritual perfection. ▲

Place • The Ananda temple is located at Pagan, the old capital city of Myanmar, which was an important Buddhist center. ▲

Indian culture also spread to Myanmar. There, Buddhism was firmly in place by the fifth and sixth centuries. In the 11th century, the powerful king Anawrahta established a strong Buddhist kingdom in the capital city of Pagan. There were soon thousands of Buddhist temples and buildings in the kingdom. The most famous is the Ananda temple.

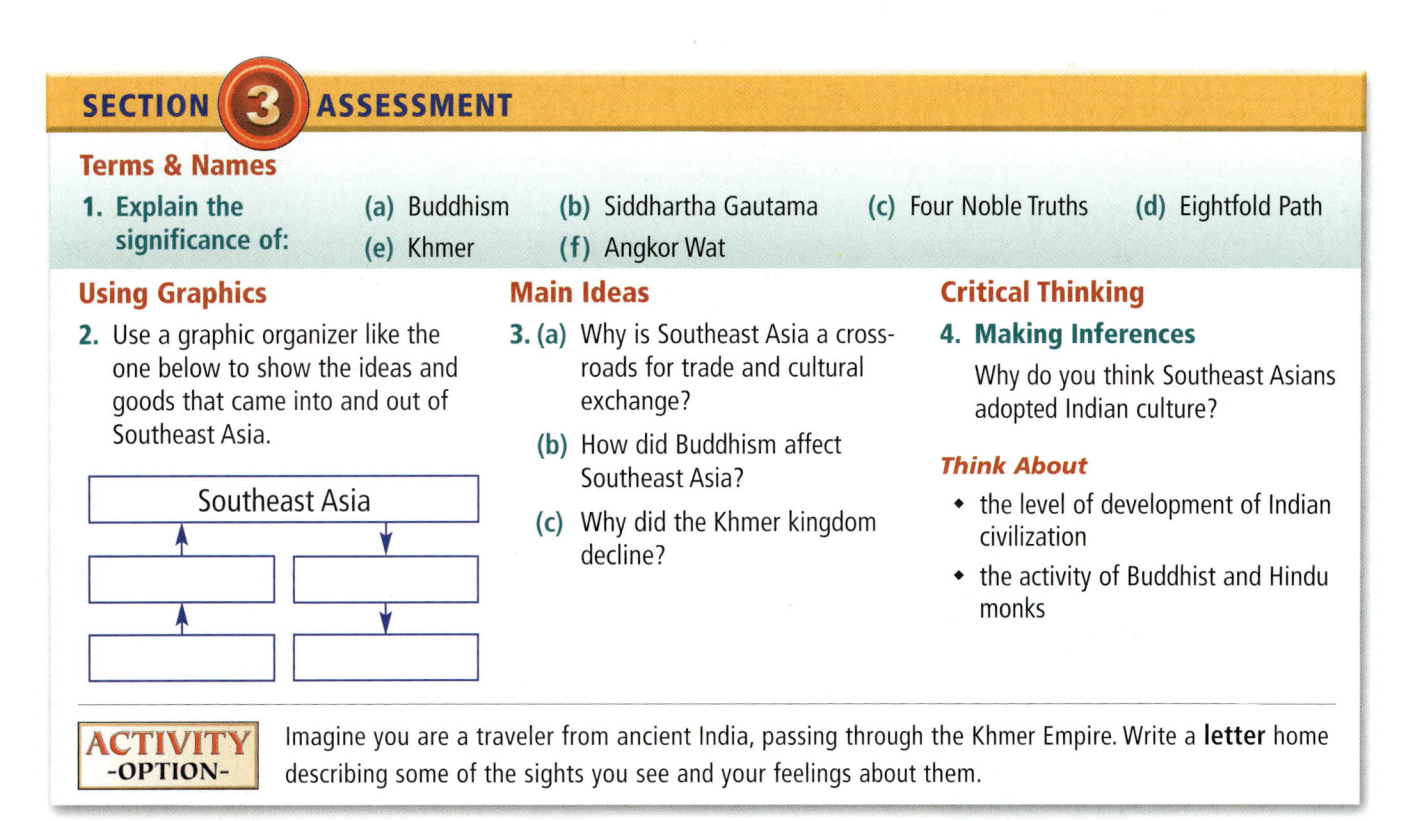

SECTION 3 ASSESSMENT

Terms & Names
1. Explain the significance of:
   - (a) Buddhism
   - (b) Siddhartha Gautama
   - (c) Four Noble Truths
   - (d) Eightfold Path
   - (e) Khmer
   - (f) Angkor Wat

Using Graphics
2. Use a graphic organizer like the one below to show the ideas and goods that came into and out of Southeast Asia.

[Southeast Asia diagram]

Main Ideas
3. (a) Why is Southeast Asia a crossroads for trade and cultural exchange?
   (b) How did Buddhism affect Southeast Asia?
   (c) Why did the Khmer kingdom decline?

Critical Thinking
4. **Making Inferences**

   Why do you think Southeast Asians adopted Indian culture?

   Think About
   - the level of development of Indian civilization
   - the activity of Buddhist and Hindu monks

ACTIVITY -OPTION- Imagine you are a traveler from ancient India, passing through the Khmer Empire. Write a **letter** home describing some of the sights you see and your feelings about them.

Southern Asia: Place and Times

CHAPTER 13 ASSESSMENT

TERMS & NAMES

Explain the significance of each of the following:

1. subcontinent
2. sediment
3. archipelago
4. monsoon
5. Aryan
6. Hinduism
7. caste
8. Buddhism
9. Siddhartha Gautama
10. Khmer

REVIEW QUESTIONS

Physical Geography (pages 377–383)
1. What are the three major geographical regions of South Asia?
2. How do the monsoons affect South Asia and Southeast Asia?

Ancient India (pages 385–390)
3. What did the Aryan people bring to the Indus Valley, and what did they learn from the civilization that was already in place?
4. What are the main beliefs and characteristics of Hinduism?
5. When did India's golden age occur, and what were its major contributions?

Ancient Crossroads (pages 392–397)
6. How did early travelers to Southeast Asia influence that region's culture?
7. How is Buddhism similar to and different from Hinduism?
8. How did Hindu and Buddhist beliefs affect the empires of Southeast Asia?

CRITICAL THINKING

Identifying Effects
1. Using your completed chart from Reading Social Studies, p. 376, write two or three sentences describing how Buddhism affected Southern Asia.

Making Inferences
2. If you were an archaeologist, what would you conclude about the people who inhabited Mohenjo-Daro, based on the evidence that currently exists?

Comparing and Contrasting
3. In what ways are Buddhism and Hinduism similar and different?

Visual Summary

1 Physical Geography
- The physical geography of South Asia and Southeast Asia includes mountains, plateaus, river deltas, and islands.
- Landforms and climate continue to influence where people settle and what they do for a living.

2 Ancient India
- Merging with the existing culture, the Aryan people influenced the development of social structure and religion in ancient India.
- Hinduism provided instruction for daily life as well as inspiration for artists and emperors.

3 Ancient Crossroads
- As a crossroads for trade and culture, ancient Southeast Asia shared goods and ideas with places as far away as India, China, and Africa.
- Hinduism and Buddhism became the foundation of several powerful empires in Southeast Asia.

STANDARDS-BASED ASSESSMENT

Use the map and your knowledge of world cultures and geography to answer questions 1 and 2.

Additional Test Practice, pp. S1–S33

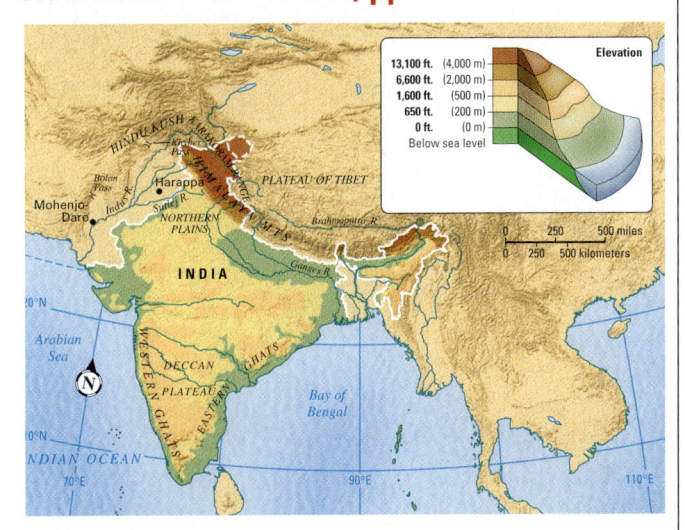

The following news report describes the effect of heavy monsoon rains in India. Use the quotation and your knowledge of world cultures and geography to answer question 3.

PRIMARY SOURCE

August 16, 2002 Monsoon rains have sent India's Brahmaputra River surging from its channel, swallowing up villages, drowning hundreds of people and leaving millions homeless. . . . Annual monsoon flooding has wreaked havoc across South Asia, killing more than 900 people in India, Bangladesh, and Nepal since June and displacing or trapping about 25 million more. In Bangladesh, the Flood Forecasting and Warning Center said Friday that heavy rains in parts of the Himalayas could cause the third flooding in the low-lying river delta since the monsoons began.

from MMII The Associated Press

1. Into what body of water does the Ganges River flow?
- **A.** Arabian Sea
- **B.** Bay of Bengal
- **C.** Brahmaputra River
- **D.** Indus River

2. Which region of India has the highest elevation?
- **A.** the eastern coast
- **B.** the western coast
- **C.** the northern tip
- **D.** the southern tip

3. What conclusion can you draw from this news report?
- **A.** No one should ever live in a region that experiences monsoons.
- **B.** The Indian government should change the course of the Brahmaputra River.
- **C.** The Flood Forecasting and Warning Center is doing a poor job.
- **D.** Heavy rains in mountains can cause floods in nearby lowlands.

TEST PRACTICE
CLASSZONE.COM

ALTERNATIVE ASSESSMENT

1. WRITING ABOUT HISTORY

Imagine you are a trader who has come to Southeast Asia from India around A.D. 100. Research what goods you might have brought to trade, what goods you hope to trade for, and what sites you have seen. Then write letter to a relative back home in India describing your experience. Share your letter with the class.

2. COOPERATIVE LEARNING

In a group with three or four other classmates, write a biographical sketch about one of the people in the chapter, such as Ashoka or Siddhartha Gautama. You might also want to invent a character such as an Indian trader, a Buddhist monk, or a Gupta or Khmer emperor. Discuss ideas about a situation in which the person you choose is trying to convince other people of his or her views and beliefs. Work together to write a script for a short play. Then divide the roles of the central character, supporters, and critics and perform the play for your class.

INTEGRATED TECHNOLOGY

Doing Internet Research

Use the Internet to research floods in the Ganges River valley. Then write a report about what you have learned. List the Web sites you used to prepare your report.

- Specifically try to find information about floods that have been caused by deforestation and soil erosion in Tibet.
- Include a map or chart that helps convey the information.

For Internet links to support this activity, go to

RESEARCH LINKS
CLASSZONE.COM

Southern Asia: Place and Times

CHAPTER 14

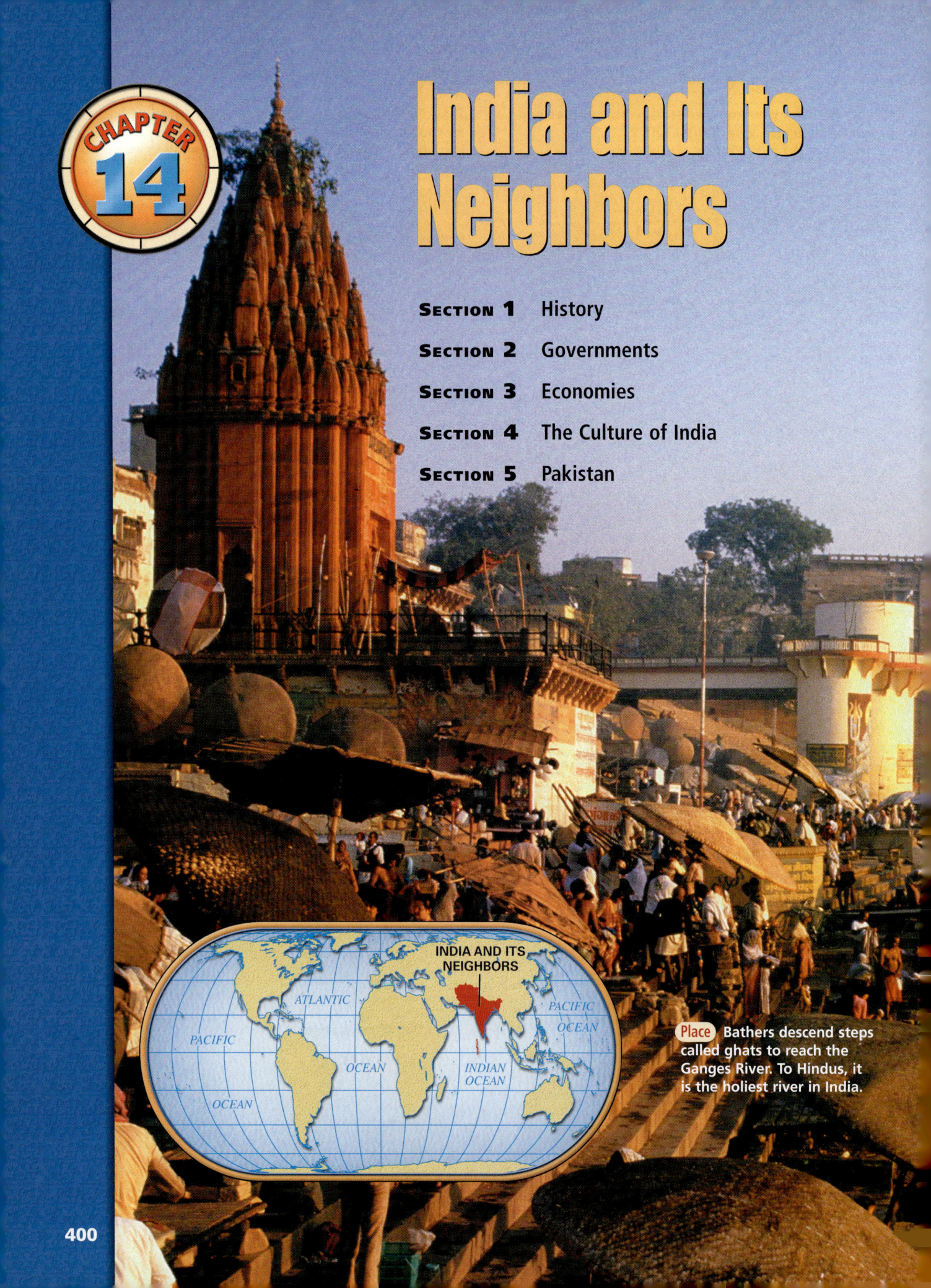

India and Its Neighbors

SECTION 1   History
SECTION 2   Governments
SECTION 3   Economies
SECTION 4   The Culture of India
SECTION 5   Pakistan

Place Bathers descend steps called ghats to reach the Ganges River. To Hindus, it is the holiest river in India.

FOCUS ON GEOGRAPHY

How has a sudden increase in population affected South Asia?

Place • By the beginning of the 21st century, South Asia had a population of well over 1 billion people. Its annual rate of growth is so high that it will soon have more people than China. Rapid population growth has put pressure on the region's resources and environment. There are not enough jobs for everyone. Many people live in poverty. India, which is the most heavily populated country in the region, struggles to feed its people. Farms are being overplanted in India. Its forests are disappearing as trees are cut down to create more farmland.

What do you think?

- Why is it important for countries to control population growth?
- How do you think continuing population growth will affect life in South Asia?

CHAPTER 14 READING SOCIAL STUDIES

BEFORE YOU READ

▶▶ What Do You Know?

Before you read the chapter, consider what you know about India and its neighbors. Who was Gandhi? Have you ever seen a Bengal tiger? How high is Mount Everest? What spices go into curry? Where do *The Jungle Books* take place? Reflect on what you read in Chapter 13 and what you have seen or heard in the news about India, Pakistan, and other countries in South Asia.

Place • Farmers in Afghanistan still use traditional methods. ▲

▶▶ What Do You Want to Know?

Decide what you know about India and its neighbors. In your notebook, record what you hope to learn from this chapter.

READ AND TAKE NOTES

Reading Strategy: Sequencing To sequence means to put events in the order in which they happened. Sequencing can help you understand how events lead to other events. Use the chart to the right to record key events in the histories of India and Pakistan and to note differences and similarities.

- Copy the chart into your notebook.
- As you read, look for dates and key events.
- In the top two boxes, record events and important details next to the dates.
- In the row of three boxes, record important details about India and Pakistan since 1947.

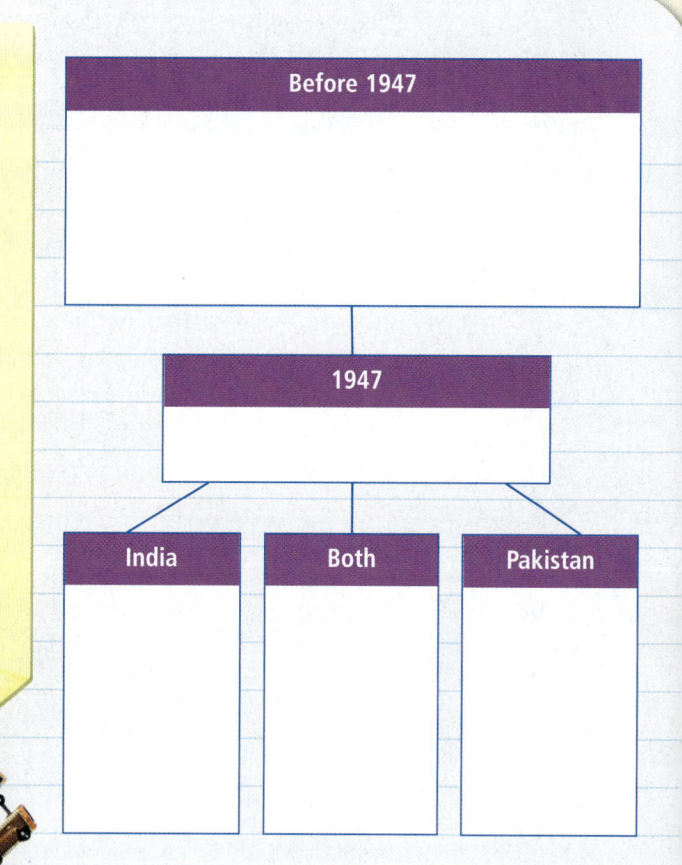

Before 1947

1947

| India | Both | Pakistan |

Place • The sitar is a popular instrument in India. ◀

402 CHAPTER 14

SECTION 1

History

TERMS & NAMES
Mughal Empire
Indian National Congress
Muslim League
Mohandas Gandhi

MAIN IDEA
The movements of people and ideas through the nations of South Asia have produced a varied and exciting history.

WHY IT MATTERS NOW
Similarities and differences among these nations have led to both development and conflict.

DATELINE EXTRA

RAMNURGER, NEAR BENARES ON THE GANGES RIVER, APRIL 19, 1796—A British ship anchored in the river yesterday after sailing many months from England. Today, boatmen and British sailors outfitted in our native cotton dress have been working madly to load the ship. They hope to sail before the monsoon winds and storms begin. Hundreds of boxes of tea, spices, and cotton fabric will travel back to England.

Movement • Despite great risk, ships from Great Britain, France, and Portugal sail to India and other parts of South Asia to carry back valuable spices, tea, and other goods. ▲

Islam Comes to India

The coast of India has been a site of trade for centuries. Arabs were trading along the coast of India a thousand years before the British arrived. Early in the eighth century A.D., Muslims from Arabia conquered northwest India. They converted many of the people of this region to their religion, Islam. Even today, the people of this region (what is now Afghanistan and Pakistan) are Muslim.

TAKING NOTES
Use your chart to take notes about India.

```
      Before 1947
         |
        1947
      /  |  \
  India Both Pakistan
```

SUNSHINE STATE STANDARDS
Key Standard SS.A.2.3.1 The student understands how language, ideas, and institutions of one culture can influence other (e.g., through trade, exploration, and immigration).
Other Standards SS.A.2.3.5
FCAT LA.A.2.3.1 Reading: Identify Main Ideas, Facts, and Details

India and Its Neighbors

Location •
The Hindu Kush Mountains in northern Pakistan helped to keep out invaders. ▲

Turks and Mongols Beginning in the 11th century A.D., Turkish Muslims from what is now Afghanistan attacked northwest India, replacing the Arabs. By 1206, the Turkish kingdom stretched south to the Deccan Plateau. The region was ruled from the city of Delhi by a sultan. During this time, Mongols from Central Asia began spreading west and south. Because of the mountains in the northeastern part of South Asia, the Mongols never invaded the region. Many people who were threatened by the Mongols fled across the mountains into South Asia. These artists, teachers, government officials, and religious leaders brought with them their culture and learning.

Vocabulary
sultan: emperor

The Mughal Empire

In the year 1526, Babur (BAH•buhr), a Mughal (moo•GUHL) ruler and a Muslim, invaded southward with his army. Eventually, his kingdom included northern India and land west into Afghanistan. Babur involved local leaders in his government and built trade routes, strengthening his rule. Babur's reign was the beginning of the great **Mughal Empire**.

Vocabulary
Mughal: Muslim Turks from what is now Turkistan

Culture • Akbar, shown here crossing the Ganges, had his life story told in words and pictures in the *Akbarnama*, or *The Memoirs of Akbar*. ▼

Akbar, Mughal Emperor The third Mughal emperor, Akbar, was a strong and intelligent leader who was careful to include both Hindus and Muslims in his government. His policies made India a place where both Hindus and Muslims could live in peace. He taxed people according to the size and value of their land, which meant that poor farmers were not taxed as heavily as they had been before. Akbar was a strong supporter of the arts. He provided studios for painters and gave awards to the best among them. He also created a position for the official Hindu poet of the nation.

End of the Empire During the period of the Mughal Empire, many new trade routes over land and water were established, making travel between regions easier. The trade routes also connected the empire with other parts of the world. In this way new ideas and inventions made their way into South Asia. Then, in the year 1707, with the death of the last Mughal emperor, the empire eventually collapsed.

Reading Social Studies
A. Drawing Conclusions How would trade routes help to strengthen an empire?

The Mughal Empire, 1524–1707

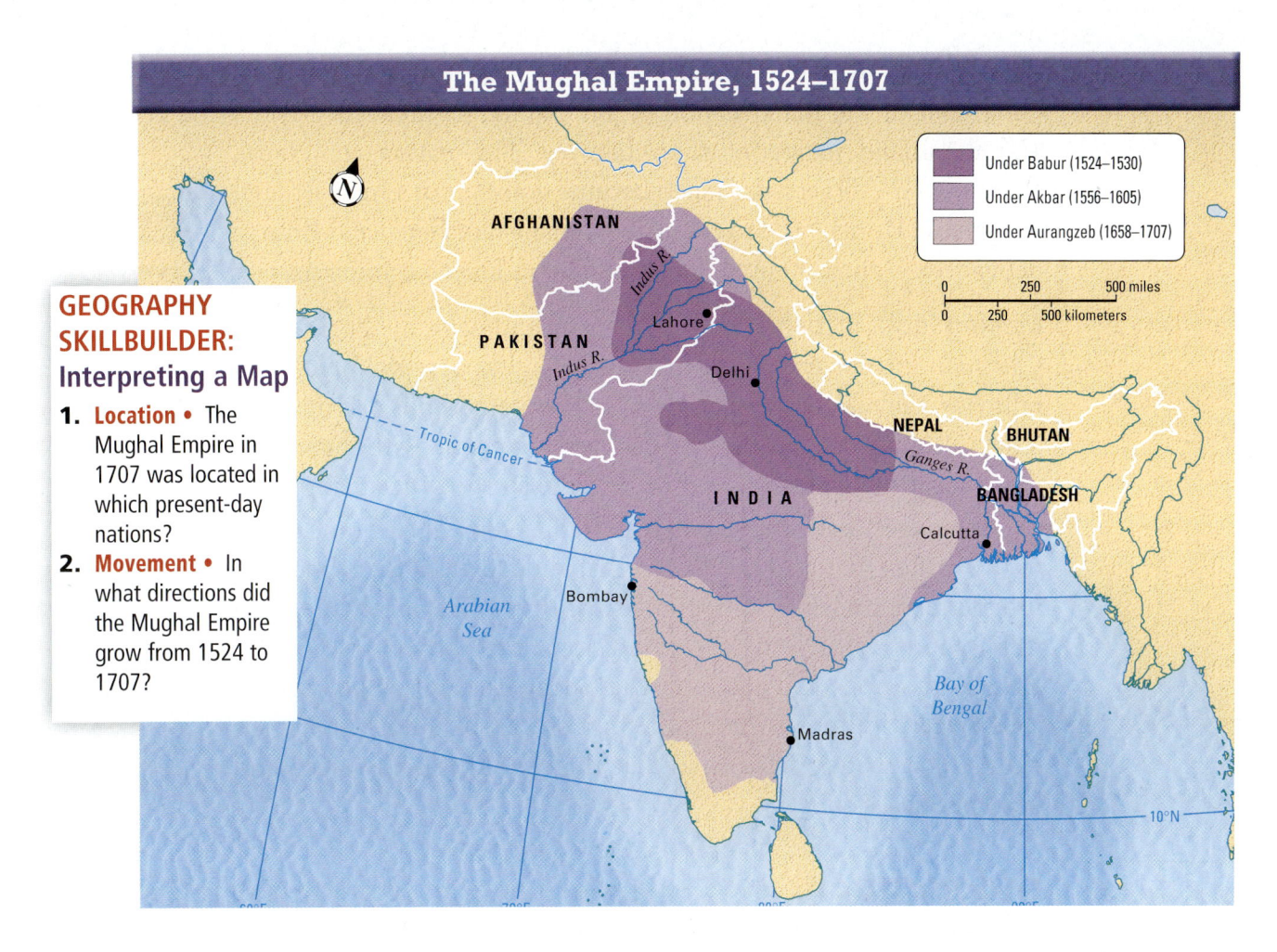

Legend:
- Under Babur (1524–1530)
- Under Akbar (1556–1605)
- Under Aurangzeb (1658–1707)

GEOGRAPHY SKILLBUILDER: Interpreting a Map

1. **Location •** The Mughal Empire in 1707 was located in which present-day nations?
2. **Movement •** In what directions did the Mughal Empire grow from 1524 to 1707?

Arrival of the British

In 1600, Queen Elizabeth I of England gave trade rights to the East India Company, an organization of English merchants, to trade in India and East and Southeast Asia. The Mughals agreed to let the British set up factories and trading centers. The East India Company shipped spices, tea, cotton, silk, indigo (used for dyeing), sugar, and saltpeter (used for gunpowder) to England. Gradually, the British increased their power. By 1818, after the Rajputs and other groups agreed to be ruled by the British, Great Britain's strength in the region was undeniable.

Movement • The British brought railroads to India, such as this steam train in Darjeeling, shown in 1930. ▼

India and Its Neighbors 405

India's Neighbors and Great Britain In 1796, Great Britain took possession of the island nation of Sri Lanka, then called Ceylon, and the island nation of the Maldives. The nations of Nepal, Bhutan, and Afghanistan never became colonies of Great Britain, though the British tried to colonize Afghanistan. Nepal and Bhutan depended on their mountainous frontiers to keep out foreigners.

Making India British The British army and navy, merchants, and Christian missionaries came to India, bringing new technology for railroads, the telegraph, steamships, and new methods of irrigation. They also introduced the British legal system, with new laws regarding landownership, and made English the official language.

Indians responded to the British in different ways. Some chose to live just as they had before the British arrived. Others chose to interact economically with the British by working for and with them while maintaining their traditions. Still others studied the British traditions and adopted what seemed useful while keeping their own traditions. Among the higher castes, parents sent their children to British schools so that they could learn English and become successful.

Reading Social Studies

B. Comparing Which changes brought by the British were cultural and which were technological?

Independence

In 1885, the **Indian National Congress** was formed to provide a forum where Indians could discuss their problems. Muslims formed the **Muslim League** in 1906. After World War I, Indians began to think of independence. They had a great leader in **Mohandas Gandhi**.

Biography

Mohandas Gandhi (GAHN•dee) Gandhi was born in India in 1869. He learned about discrimination when, as a young boy, he saw that no matter how wealthy and well educated Indians were, they were treated as second-class citizens by the British. Gandhi studied law in England and then spent the rest of his life working for justice for the Indian people.

He encouraged his followers to use nonviolence to resist the British and bring about social change. Gandhi believed that the forces of goodness and truth had powerful effects on people. As part of this belief, he went on hunger strikes and organized labor strikes and marches to force the British to grant India its independence.

The Indian people call Gandhi the *Mahatma*, which means "Great Soul." They honor him as the father of their nation. His ideas have influenced many people who have worked for justice around the world.

Vocabulary

monopoly: The sale of a good by only one company

BACKGROUND

On the Unit Atlas Map on page 368, find India, Pakistan, and Bangladesh. Before independence, this entire region was India.

Gandhi used nonviolence to impress upon the British the need for independence. He also wanted all Indians to be treated equally. He wanted women to have the same freedoms as men. He encouraged Hindus and Muslims to find peaceful ways to solve their problems. For example, to protest the British monopoly of salt, Gandhi led a 240-mile walk to the coast to gather sea salt.

Eventually, Great Britain realized that it would have to leave India, but the Indian National Congress and the Muslim League disagreed about how the new government would be formed. Muslims were afraid of losing power because Hindus were the majority in India. The solution was to divide India into two separate countries, India for the Hindus and Pakistan for the Muslims. The two countries were formed and granted independence in 1947. Sri Lanka became independent in 1948, and the Maldives in 1965.

Movement • Gandhi led his countrymen to the coast at Dandi to protest the British sale of salt. ▲

SECTION 1 ASSESSMENT

Terms & Names
1. Explain the significance of:
   (a) Mughal Empire
   (b) Indian National Congress
   (c) Muslim League
   (d) Mohandas Gandhi

Using Graphics

2. Use a Venn diagram like the one below to compare and contrast the rule of the Mughals and the British in India.

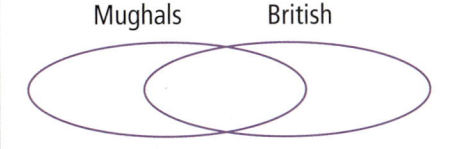

   Mughals   British

Main Ideas

3. (a) How did Islam reach India?
   (b) Name three achievements of the Mughal emperors.
   (c) Why did the British colonize India?

Critical Thinking

4. **Making Inferences**

   Do you think it was easier for rich Indians or poor Indians to live under British rule? Explain.

   Think About
   ◆ how Indians responded to British rule
   ◆ the opportunities for Indians of different castes

ACTIVITY -OPTION- Imagine being a reporter for an Indian newspaper and attending a speech given by Gandhi. Write a **short article** reporting on the speech and giving your reaction to it.

India and Its Neighbors

Technology: 750 B.C.

Qanats

Because much of their country has little or no rainfall, Iranians have relied on a system of collecting and transporting water that was developed more than 2,500 years ago. The ancient Iranians, known as Persians, dug 30-to-100-foot shafts at the feet of mountains to tap into the water table. They built underground tunnels called *qanat*s (KAH•NAHTS) that followed the slope of the land. These *qanat*s collect water that seeps into the ground from melting snow and from rivers and streams. Although they are expensive to build and difficult to maintain, the *qanat*s carry water to villages as much as 50 miles away for drinking and irrigating fields. They supply more than 75 percent of Iran's water.

SUNSHINE STATE STANDARDS
Key Standard SS.A.2.3.3 The student understands important technological developments and how they influenced human society
FCAT LA.A.2.3.1 Reading: Identify Main Ideas, Facts, and Details

INTERACTIVE

1 At the base of a mountain range, melting snow and rainwater collect underground on top of a layer of solid rock. The water table slopes downward farther and farther from the surface.

2 Workers dig a well as deep as 100 feet to reach the water table. This is called the mother well.

3 Shafts are dug at regular intervals so that villages can draw water and workers can maintain the tunnel.

4 Workers build a shaft and haul out soil. Then they use stone, soil, and existing mineral and salt deposits to line the tunnel.

Thinking Critically

1. Drawing Conclusions
What is a drawback of the *qanat* system?

2. Recognizing Effects
How would a drought affect the *qanat* system?

SECTION 2: Governments

TERMS & NAMES
Taliban
martial law
Dalit
Indira Gandhi
panchayat

MAIN IDEA
The countries of South Asia have different types of governments, but all face the challenges of economic growth and poverty.

WHY IT MATTERS NOW
As the nations of the world grow more and more connected, any individual nation's success becomes important to all.

DATELINE

NEW DELHI, INDIA, AUGUST 15, 1947—Jawaharal Nehru, India's first prime minister, has today solemnly declared India a free and independent nation. At 8:30 A.M. the new government was sworn in. Prime Minister Nehru then unfurled India's flag, the Tricolor, which flew for the first time from the Council House against a free sky.

In February, the British government had announced its willingness to grant India its independence. On June 3, Lord Mountbatten, viceroy of India, took to the airwaves to explain the method by which power would be transferred from one government to another. Yesterday, the nation waited breathlessly for midnight to arrive. After 300 years of colonial rule, India has won her freedom at last.

Place • Indians celebrate independence in the streets of Calcutta and other cities and towns throughout India. ▲

South Asia's Governments

Since independence, the nations of South Asia have chosen different forms of government. Some are republics. In a republic, the people elect leaders to represent them. Some countries, such as India, chose a parliamentary form of government. Others chose to be constitutional monarchies. In a constitutional monarchy, the king or queen serves a mostly ceremonial role, while the prime minister and cabinet actually run the government.

TAKING NOTES
Use your chart to take notes about India.

Before 1947

1947

India | Both | Pakistan

SUNSHINE STATE STANDARDS
Key Standard SS.A.3.3.5 The student understands the differences between institutions of Eastern and Western civilizations (e.g., differences in governments, social traditions and customs, economic systems and religious institutions).
Other Standards SS.C.2.3.6
FCAT LA.A.2.3.1 Reading: Identify Main Ideas, Facts, and Details

India and Its Neighbors

Afghanistan In 1964, a new constitution established a constitutional monarchy for Afghanistan. The monarchy collapsed in 1973 as the result of a coup. In 1979, the Soviet Union invaded Afghanistan and established a Communist government. A UN agreement forced Soviet troops to withdraw from Afghanistan in 1989, leaving behind an Afghani Communist government. This government was overturned and an Islamic republic was declared, but it did not have support from enough people and was too weak to maintain power.

A group of fundamentalist Muslims, the **Taliban,** took control of the government. Under the Taliban, people must follow strict rules. Women cannot go to school or hold jobs, nor can they go out in public without a male relative. Punishment for breaking rules includes being whipped or even executed.

The Taliban has been at war with opposing Muslim groups for many years. Although the Taliban has received help from a few other nations, such as Pakistan, most of the world has spoken out against the Taliban government. In 2001, the Taliban was accused of harboring terrorists responsible for the attacks on the United States made on September 11 of that year.

Culture • Bhutan is ruled by a king. This is King Jigme Dorji Wangchuk (JIHG•may DAWR•jee WAHNG•chook) in 1998. ▼

Bangladesh Bangladesh gained independence from Pakistan in 1971 and adopted its constitution in 1972. The constitution gives Bangladesh a parliamentary form of government, with a prime minister and a president. However, in 1975, and several times since, the military has taken over the government.

Bhutan For three centuries, Bhutan was ruled jointly by two types of leaders—one spiritual and the other political. In 1907, the spiritual ruler withdrew from public life, and since then Bhutan has had a king only. In 1953, an assembly, which meets twice a year to pass laws, was formed. Then, in 1968, a Council of Ministers was created to advise the king. The king appoints ministers, but the assembly must approve them.

The Maldives In 1965, the Maldives gained independence from Great Britain and became a republic three years later. The Citizens' Council has 48 members, 40 elected by the people and 8 appointed by the president. The president also appoints the judges, who follow Islamic law in making their judgments.

Nepal For centuries, Nepal was ruled exclusively by kings. The prime minister replaced the king as the country's ruling official. In 1962, Nepal became a constitutional monarchy and all political parties were banned. In the 1990s, the king allowed the formation of political parties. Soon, some had gained enough power to force a change in the government. The Nepalese wrote a new constitution and established a new parliamentary system.

Pakistan Pakistan gained independence from Great Britain in 1947. The constitution of 1947 gave Pakistan a parliamentary government. However, in 1958, **martial law** was declared. The military took control of the government and maintained power until 1988. Today, Pakistan is a republic, with a prime minister and a president, both of whom must be Muslim.

People in Pakistan have differing views about the role of Islam in the government. Some think Islam is what holds the people together as one nation. Others feel that Islam does not meet the needs of all the groups in the country and that it has actually pulled people apart.

Sri Lanka In 1948, Sri Lanka gained independence from Great Britain. Today, it is a democracy with a president as its leader. As in the United States, two political parties struggle for power in the government.

Reading Social Studies
A. Recognizing Important Details What two attitudes do Pakistanis have about the role of Islam in their government?

Culture • President Chandrika Kumaratunga (chan·DREE·kah kum·ruh·TUNG·ah), of Sri Lanka, opens the country's new Parliament in November 2000. ▲

The World's Largest Democracy

India is the world's largest democracy. Approximately 370 million Indians voted in the 1999 elections. The country's official head of state is the president. However, India's prime minister actually runs the government.

Place • The prime minister of Pakistan works in the Offices of Government in Islamabad, the capital. ▶

India's constitution went into effect in 1950, protecting Indians from being treated unfairly. According to the constitution, all Indians are assured the same basic rights. These include the rights of free speech and religion, which are protected in the courts.

The Changing Caste System India's new constitution stated that even the lowest and poorest classes could vote. The poor are also represented in the government. Special programs reserve jobs for people of the lower castes and secure places for them in schools. The **Dalits** (formerly called "untouchables") have gained political power. They were outside the caste system and considered even lower than the lowest caste. Today, they vote for leaders, though more changes are needed to ensure the Dalits have equal rights in the government and the economy.

Culture • An Indian woman has her finger marked before voting in a 1999 election in Gujarat.

Women in India After independence from Britain, Indian women gained many new rights. Finally, all women were granted the right to vote. It is now against the law in India to discriminate on the basis of gender.

Indian women began working at jobs that had been held only by men. Women became teachers and doctors. They were elected to public office. **Indira Gandhi** became India's first woman prime minister in 1966.

The World's Heritage

Nonviolence The Jain (JYN) religion was founded in India in the sixth century B.C. Its followers believe that people should never harm a living being, including the smallest insect. The Jain belief in nonviolence led to its use as a powerful political weapon.

Instead of leading an armed revolt, Gandhi used nonviolence as a tactic to drive the British out of India. The idea of nonviolence inspired American civil rights leader Martin Luther King, Jr. (shown at left below with his wife and Prime Minister Nehru). King used nonviolent methods, including marches and demonstrations, to fight against the discrimination of African Americans in the United States.

Village Life and Grass-roots Democracy

Since ancient times, small rural Indian villages have governed themselves. Today they are governed by the *panchayat* system. A ***panchayat*** is a village council. India's constitution allows these councils to govern themselves. The *panchayat* collects taxes for maintaining schools and hospitals. It builds roads and digs wells for drinking water. The councils also take care of primary school education in India.

Culture •
Traditionally, the *panchayat* meets under a banyan tree like this one. ▶

Reading Social Studies

B. Contrasting How are the three levels of *panchayats* different from one another?

Three Levels The *panchayat* works on three levels. The first level represents a village or a group of small villages. The second level is made up of *panchayat* chiefs from 100 villages. The third level represents an entire district. Some districts have as many as ten million people.

Today, there are over 3 million *panchayat* representatives in India. By law, one-third of them must be women. The constitution also makes room for the Dalits and other minorities to participate in the *panchayat* system.

SECTION 2 ASSESSMENT

Terms & Names
1. Explain the significance of: (a) Taliban   (b) martial law   (c) Dalit   (d) Indira Gandhi   (e) *panchayat*

Using Graphics
2. Use a chart like the one below to list the countries of South Asia and the features of their governments.

Country	Features of Government

Main Ideas
3. (a) Name three kinds of government found in South Asia.
   (b) What kind of government does India have?
   (c) Describe the responsibilities of the *panchayat*.

Critical Thinking
4. **Synthesizing**
   How did India's 1950 constitution change the lives of women and members of the lower castes?

   Think About
   ◆ the treatment of the lower castes and women before 1950
   ◆ what it means to live in a democracy

ACTIVITY -OPTION- Choose one of the following nations: Bhutan, Nepal, or Sri Lanka. Use the Internet to find a recent news story about it. **Summarize** the story for your class.

Interdisciplinary Challenge

Tour the Ganges River

You are a guide leading a group tour of the Ganges River in India and Bangladesh. Since ancient times, this great river has been central to Indian life and culture. The Ganges rises in an ice cave in the Himalayas and flows southeast across a wide plain into the Bay of Bengal. As it nears the coast, the river splits into many channels—the "Mouths of the Ganges"— which have built up a huge delta. You want your tour group to understand the river's importance over the centuries.

COOPERATIVE LEARNING On these pages are challenges you will encounter as you plan your tour of the Ganges. Working in a small group, choose one of these challenges. Divide the work among group members. Look in the Data File for helpful information. Keep in mind that you will present your solution to the class.

HISTORY CHALLENGE

"So much has happened in the Ganges region..."

To start your tour, give your group an overview of the Ganges and its place in history. So much has happened in the Ganges region; for centuries, cities and villages along the Ganges have been centers of trade, industry, and religion. How can you give your group a sense of place? What should the group learn from this trip? Choose one of these options. Use the Data File for help.

ACTIVITIES

1. Choose one city or region along the Ganges. Make a time line of major events that took place there, starting with its early history.
2. Design a travel brochure for a city in the Ganges Basin. Include a list of historical monuments and other attractions.

414 UNIT 5

SUNSHINE STATE STANDARDS
Key Standard SS.B.2.3.2 The student knows the human and physical characteristics of different places in the world and how these characteristics change over time.
FCAT LA.B.1.3.3 Writing: Edit Final Documents

MATH CHALLENGE

". . . plan a travel schedule . . . and keep to it."

Along the course of the Ganges are many historic cities and other attractions. One important part of a tour guide's job is to plan a travel schedule, or itinerary, and keep to it. Your trip is scheduled to take about four weeks. How will you plan your river journey? How will you divide your time? Choose one of these options to present information, using the map and the Data File for help.

ACTIVITIES

1. Prepare a four-week itinerary for the Ganges tour. List the places your group will visit and the time you will spend at each of them.

2. By riverboat, your trip from Kanpur to Allahabad—a distance of about 115 miles—takes about ten hours. After a stop for sightseeing, you leave Allahabad at 11:00 P.M. Your next stop is Varanasi, about 90 miles downriver. If you travel at the same speed as before, will you get to Varanasi in time for breakfast?

DATA FILE

THE GANGES
- **Length:** 1,557 mi.
- Headwaters in Himalayas: **Alaknanda** and **Bhagirathi** are main streams; other tributaries enter along river's course.
- Ganges Basin is one of the most densely populated areas in the world.

Major Tributaries
- **Yamuna:** flows from Himalayas past Delhi and Agra.
- **Brahmaputra** (also called Jamuna): joins Ganges in Bangladesh to form delta.

Important Sites in the Ganges Basin
- **Patna:** center of Asoka's empire (third century B.C.).
- **Agra:** on Yamuna River, site of **Taj Mahal;** once capital of Mogul Empire.
- **Allahabad:** at junction of Yamuna and Ganges rivers; a holy place to Hindus.
- **Varanasi** (Benares): Hindu holy city; pilgrims come to bathe in the river.
- **Delhi/New Delhi:** on Yamuna River, India's capital city; once a Mogul capital.
- **Kolkata (Calcutta):** on Hugli River, major channel of the Ganges; was capital of British India, now capital of West Bengal.
- **Dhaka:** capital of Bangladesh.

INDIA
Population: 1.01 billion; population density: 799/sq. mi.; 28 percent urban.
Area: about 1.3 million sq. mi.

BANGLADESH
Population: 129.2 million; population density: 2,324/sq. mi.; 24 percent urban.
Area: 55,600 sq. mi.

To learn more about the Ganges River, go to

RESEARCH LINKS
CLASSZONE.COM

Activity Wrap-Up
As a group, review your solution to the challenge you selected. Then present your solution to the class.

SECTION 3 Economies

TERMS & NAMES
jute
information technology
Green Revolution

MAIN IDEA
The countries of South Asia have economies that have changed and grown in the last century.

WHY IT MATTERS NOW
As the economies of South Asia's countries grow, these nations have more influence on the economies of their neighbors.

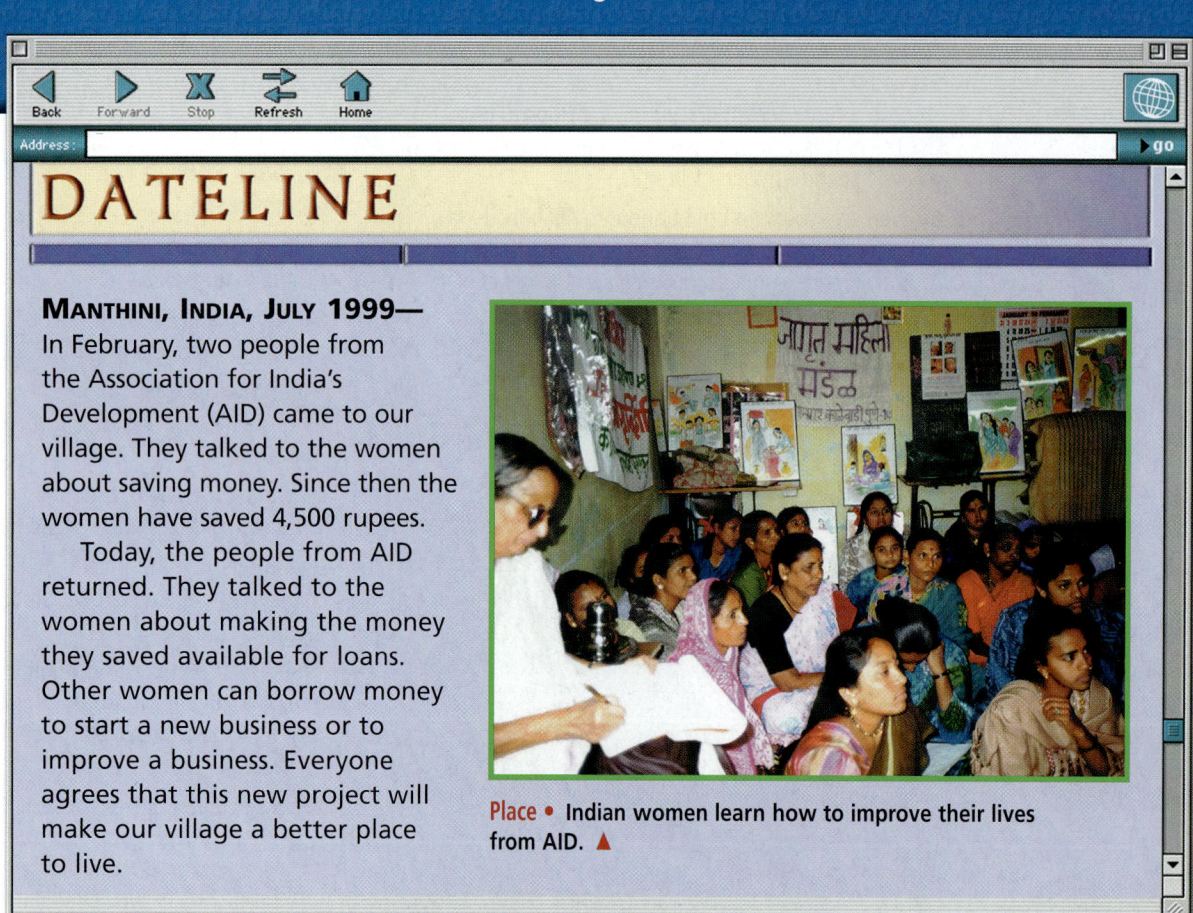

DATELINE

MANTHINI, INDIA, JULY 1999—In February, two people from the Association for India's Development (AID) came to our village. They talked to the women about saving money. Since then the women have saved 4,500 rupees.

Today, the people from AID returned. They talked to the women about making the money they saved available for loans. Other women can borrow money to start a new business or to improve a business. Everyone agrees that this new project will make our village a better place to live.

Place • Indian women learn how to improve their lives from AID. ▲

Developing Economies

Organizations like AID are helping the developing nations of South Asia to move from traditional economies to market economies. Most people in South Asia live in rural areas. They have low incomes and literacy levels and depend on traditional farming methods to survive. They are farmers, shepherds, and herders.

TAKING NOTES
Use your chart to take notes about India.

Before 1947
1947
India | Both | Pakistan

SUNSHINE STATE STANDARDS
Key Standard SS.D.2.3.1 The student understands ways production and distribution decisions are determined in the United States economy and how these decisions compare to those made in market, tradition-based, command, and mixed economic systems.
Other Standards SS.B.2.3.6
FCAT LA.A.2.3.1 Reading: Identify Main Ideas, Facts, and Details

416 CHAPTER 14

Human-Environment Interaction • This farmer in Afghanistan uses a plow and an ox, just as his ancestors did. ◄

Afghanistan In the 1960s and 1970s, Afghanistan worked to strengthen its economy. It built roads, dams, power plants, and factories. It provided education to more people and began irrigation projects. Then Afghanistan was invaded by the Soviet Union. The invasion was followed by civil war. Afghanistan has not returned to the improvement program of four decades ago. Today, Afghanistan is one of the poorest countries in the world. Most people work on farms, raising livestock. Only 12 percent of the land in Afghanistan is arable, and only half of that is cultivated in any year. Wheat is the chief crop, though cotton, fruits, and nuts are also grown.

Bangladesh Agriculture is a major part of the economy in Bangladesh. About three-fifths of the workers are farmers. The most important cash crops are rice, jute, and tea. Bangladesh supplies one-fifth of the world's **jute,** a fibrous plant used to make twine, bags, sacks, and burlap. Irrigation projects have reached many farms, but the monsoon rains bring floods and disaster to many farmers.

Bangladesh has almost no mineral resources, so its few industries are based on agricultural products, such as bamboo, which is made into paper at mills.

Bhutan and Nepal The economies of Bhutan and Nepal are similar. Until the 1950s and 1960s, both countries were largely isolated from the outside world. There were no highways or automobiles. Bhutan did not have a currency. People bartered for goods rather than using money. Since that time, with financial help from other countries and organizations, both countries have been working to modernize their economies. For example, they have built major roads allowing the transport of goods and people, especially tourists.

The Maldives The Maldives is one of the world's poorest nations. The majority of its workers fish or build or repair boats. Tourism has become an important industry as well. Nearly all the food people eat is imported, including rice, which is one of the main foods in people's diets.

Reading **Social Studies**
Making Inferences How might the monsoon season affect a subsistence farmer?

India and Its Neighbors

Human-Environment Interaction • Many people in the Maldives earn a living by fishing. ▲

Pakistan Pakistan is the richest country in South Asia. Half of its work force is employed in agriculture, forestry, and fishing. Pakistan is the third-largest exporter of rice in the world. Its important industries are fabric and clothing, sugar, paper, tobacco, and leather.

Sri Lanka Sri Lanka depends on agriculture and tourism. Its most important agricultural product is rice, followed by tea, rubber, and coconuts. Sri Lanka has not yet been able to benefit much economically from its many mineral resources.

India Although some regions of India have many valuable resources, millions of India's people are among the world's poorest. Most people work in agriculture. More than half of the farms are smaller than three acres. Farmers practice what is known as subsistence farming, which means they grow only enough food to live on. Rice and wheat are India's most important crops. Because many people do not eat meat, chickpeas and lentils are important sources of protein in the diet.

There is a growing information technology industry in India. **Information technology** includes computers, software, and the Internet. Since 1991, India's software exports have been doubling every year.

Human-Environment Interaction • Village women plant rice, one of the chief crops in India. They carry the new rice shoots to the fields in flat baskets, which they then place on their backs as protection from the sun. ▶

418 CHAPTER 14

South Asia Economic Activities and Resources, 2000

SKILLBUILDER:
Interpreting a Map
1. **Place** • Which countries contain gold?
2. **Place** • What is the main economic activity in Nepal?

The Green Revolution

In the 1960s, the **Green Revolution** introduced farmers to varieties of grain that were more productive, the widespread use of pesticides, and different methods for farming. In India, farmers grew more rice and wheat than they needed. Much of this surplus was set aside in case of a poor growing season. Some was exported. The Green Revolution had some negative results too. The use of chemicals damaged the land and polluted rivers.

The cost of such new methods is too high for some small farmers. As a result, many farmers in South Asia still use old farming techniques despite their governments' efforts to introduce reform.

SECTION 3 ASSESSMENT

Terms & Names
1. Explain the significance of: (a) jute (b) information technology (c) Green Revolution

Using Graphics
2. Use a chart like the one below to list the important economic activities of South Asian countries.

Country	Economic Activity

Main Ideas
3. (a) How do most people in the countries of South Asia make a living?
   (b) What new technology is becoming an important part of India's economy?
   (c) Why was the Green Revolution important in South Asia? What were its negative effects?

Critical Thinking
4. **Identifying Problems**
   What are the main problems faced by South Asian countries as they move from traditional economies to market economies?

   Think About
   - their natural resources
   - levels of economic development, including rates of poverty and literacy

ACTIVITY -OPTION- Choose a nation in South Asia. Imagine you are a government official applying to an international aid agency for help. Write a **letter** describing your economy and what it needs to develop further.

SECTION 4: The Culture of India

TERMS & NAMES
Taj Mahal
Mahabharata
dialect
Indo-Aryan
Dravidian
dowry

MAIN IDEA
India's rich cultural heritage has its roots in a long history and the influences of other cultures.

WHY IT MATTERS NOW
The languages, arts, and traditions of India, a country with over a billion people, have an international influence.

DATELINE

AGRA, NORTHERN INDIA, 1648—With tears in his eyes, Shah Jahan watched today as workers put the finishing touches on the Taj Mahal. The building is made of rare white marble and is decorated with semiprecious stones, such as lapis lazuli, crystal, and jade. The Taj Mahal is to be the tomb of Shah Jahan's wife, who died giving birth to their 14th child. "Some day, when I depart," Shah Jahan said, "we will lie here together forever."

Culture • The Taj Mahal has taken 20,000 workers 22 years to build. ▲

The Taj Mahal

The Mughal emperor Shah Jahan built the **Taj Mahal** for his beloved wife, Mumtaz Mahal. This white marble building with its onion-shaped domes and thin towers is one of the finest examples of Islamic architecture in the world. Today, it is India's most famous building and a symbol of India's rich artistic heritage.

TAKING NOTES
Use your chart to take notes about India.

| Before 1947 |
| 1947 |
| India | Both | Pakistan |

SUNSHINE STATE STANDARDS
Key Standard SS.A.3.3.1 The student understands ways in which cultural characteristics have been transmitted from one society to another (e.g., through art, architecture, language, other artifacts, traditions, beliefs, values, and behaviors).
Other Standards SS.A.2.3.7, A.3.3.5
FCAT LA.A.2.3.1 Reading: Identify Main Ideas, Facts, and Details

India and the Arts

Literature Two great works of world literature come from India. One, the **Mahabharata** (MAH·huh·BAH·ruh·tuh), is an epic poem, which means that it tells a lengthy story, in a grand style, of one or more heroes. The *Ramayana* is another famous epic poem. Both the *Mahabharata* and the *Ramayana* have influenced painters, dancers, and other writers in India. Both are important because they tell about the growth of Hinduism.

Culture • Long-necked stringed instruments, like the sitars (sih·TAHRS) shown here, are used to play North Indian classical music. ▲

Music and Film India has several styles of music, and each style is unique to a region of India. Music is played and sung in concerts, at parties, or in religious settings. Indians also love to see movies. India makes more films every year than any other country, including the United States. In rural areas, movie vans travel to villages to show films outdoors.

The Languages of India

The constitution of India now recognizes 18 official languages. However, Indians speak hundreds of other languages and dialects. A **dialect** is a regional variety of a language. Most languages in India come from one of two families: Indo-Aryan or Dravidian.

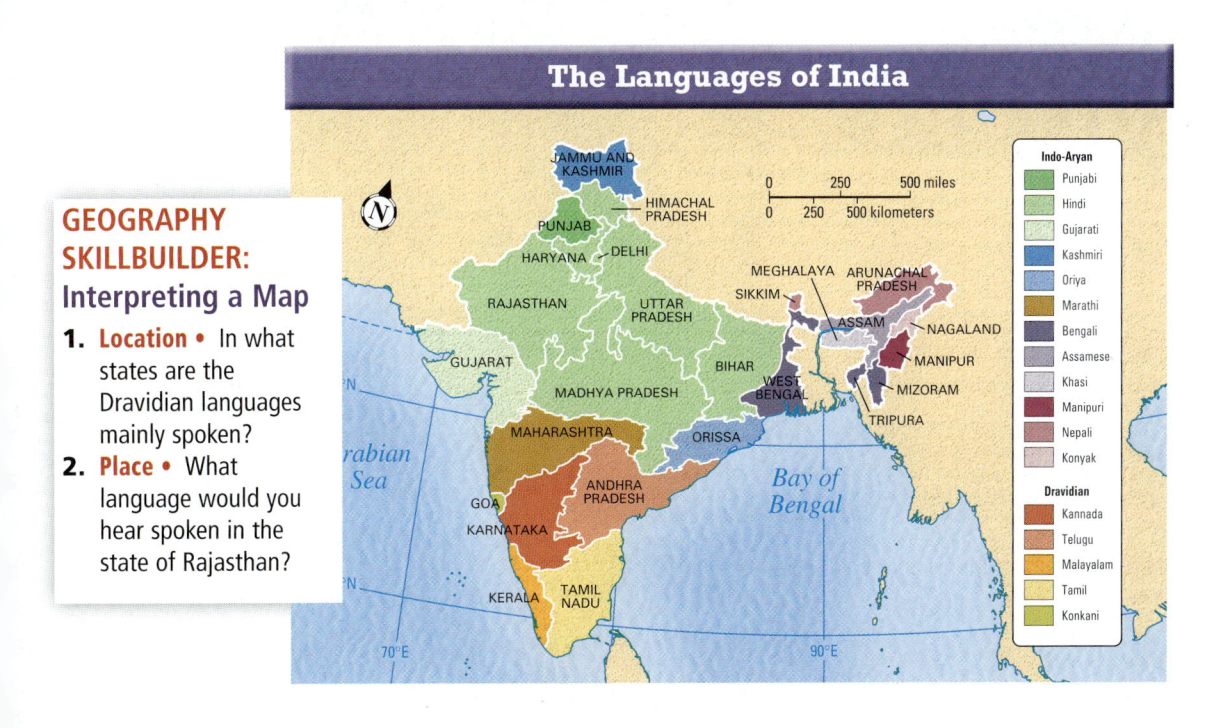

GEOGRAPHY SKILLBUILDER: Interpreting a Map

1. **Location •** In what states are the Dravidian languages mainly spoken?
2. **Place •** What language would you hear spoken in the state of Rajasthan?

The Languages of India

Indo-Aryan: Punjabi, Hindi, Gujarati, Kashmiri, Oriya, Marathi, Bengali, Assamese, Khasi, Manipuri, Nepali, Konyak

Dravidian: Kannada, Telugu, Malayalam, Tamil, Konkani

India and Its Neighbors 421

The Indo-Aryan Language Family **Indo-Aryan** languages are related to the Indo-European language family, which comes from the ancient Aryan language Sanskrit and includes almost all European languages. Today, about three-fourths of the people in northern and central India speak Indo-Aryan languages.

The Dravidian Language Family About one-fourth of all Indians speak Dravidian languages. **Dravidian** was the language spoken centuries ago in India. As invaders moved into the north, the speakers of Dravidian moved south.

English English, which came to India with British colonialism, is spoken by less than 5 percent of the population. However, because it is the language of business, government, and science, English is important in India.

Reading **Social Studies**

A. Drawing Conclusions What problems might exist when neighbors speak different languages?

Religion in Daily Life

Most people in India are Hindus. There are no rules dictating how Hinduism is practiced, nor is there one Hindu church. Many Hindus are vegetarians. Some Hindus perform daily rituals on behalf of their gods. The caste system, which is still in place in India, is less rigid than it once was.

Many Muslims who had been living in India moved to Pakistan and East Pakistan, now Bangladesh. Today, 14 percent of Indians are Muslim.

BACKGROUND Look back to Chapters 8 and 13 to review what you read about Islam and Hinduism.

Spotlight on CULTURE

The *Mahabharata* One of the greatest works of world literature comes from India. The epic poem the *Mahabharata* is the longest poem in the world. It was composed over a period of about 800 years, from about 400 B.C. to A.D. 400. The *Mahabharata* tells the story of two warring families, the five Pandava brothers (shown at right) and the Kauravas.

One famous section of the poem is called the *Bhagavad-Gita*. In this section, Arjuna, the leader of the Pandavas, receives good advice from his chariot driver, who is actually the god Krishna in disguise.

THINKING CRITICALLY

1. **Clarifying** How do you know that more than one person must have created the *Mahabharata*?
2. **Making Inferences** What do you think might happen to the events in a story created like the *Mahabharata*?

For more on the *Mahabharata*, go to

RESEARCH LINKS CLASSZONE.COM

The Family in India

Family is important to Indians. Often, several related families live together. Parents choose a bride or groom for their children from a family of the same caste. Parents may consider a potential mate's education, financial status, or even horoscope to help them make a decision.

Parents prefer sons to daughters, partly because men have more power in this society. Women who have male children have greater influence in their families. These attitudes are beginning to change. Also, when a woman marries, her parents must provide a **dowry**, money or property given by a bride to her new husband and his family. This can be expensive, especially for rural families. As India modernizes, this practice, too, is beginning to change.

Culture • A bride and groom circle a fire four times as part of a Hindu wedding ceremony. ▲

Family Meals

A typical meal varies from region to region in India. In the south and east, a meal usually includes rice. In the north and northwest, people eat a flat bread called a *chapati* (chuh•PAH•tee). Along with rice or *chapatis*, a meal may include beans or lentils, some vegetables, and maybe yogurt. Chili peppers and other spices like cardamom, cinnamon, and cumin give the food extra flavor. Meat is rarely eaten, either because it is forbidden by religion or because it is so expensive.

Reading Social Studies
B. Analyzing Motives Why might parents want to arrange their child's marriage?

SECTION 4 ASSESSMENT

Terms & Names
1. Explain the significance of:
   (a) Taj Mahal
   (b) *Mahabharata*
   (c) dialect
   (d) Indo-Aryan
   (e) Dravidian
   (f) dowry

Using Graphics
2. Use a spider map like the one below to list the unique traits of India's culture.

(Spider map: "India's unique culture" with branches: Religion, Arts and Recreation, Family, Languages)

Main Ideas
3. (a) Why are there so many official languages in India?
   (b) What religion plays the biggest role in Indian culture?
   (c) How is family an important part of Indian life?

Critical Thinking
4. Finding Causes
   Why do you think English is the language of business and government in India?

   Think About
   ◆ India's colonial history
   ◆ the country's cultural diversity

ACTIVITY -OPTION-
Develop a **plot** for an Indian movie. Describe it in a paragraph, and share your idea with a classmate.

SKILLBUILDER

Understanding Point of View

▶▶ Defining the Skill

The phrase *point of view* refers to the particular opinions or beliefs that a person holds. Education, religious beliefs, and life experiences all contribute to a person's point of view. Understanding point of view makes it possible to understand and explain a historical figure's opinions and actions.

SUNSHINE STATE STANDARDS
Key Standard SS.A.3.3.4 The student knows significant historical leaders who have influenced the course of events in Eastern and Western civilizations since the Renaissance.
FCAT LA.A.2.3.2 Reading: Identify Purpose and Point of View

▶▶ Applying the Skill

The passage to the right explains the differences and similarities between Mohandas Gandhi and Jawaharlal Nehru, who was the prime minister of India from 1947 until 1964. Use the strategies listed below to help you analyze their points of view.

How to Understand Point of View

Strategy ❶ Look for statements that reveal a person's point of view on a particular subject. Gandhi believed that government could not guarantee a person's rights. Nehru, on the other hand, had faith in the power of government.

Strategy ❷ Look for clues about why people hold the opinions they do. In these paragraphs you learn about Gandhi's and Nehru's childhoods, their educations, and their experiences as young men. How do these things influence their opinions?

Strategy ❸ Summarize the information given for each person that explains their opposing opinions.

Write a Summary

Writing a summary will help you understand differing points of view. The paragraph below and to the right summarizes the passage about Gandhi and Nehru.

▶▶ Practicing the Skill

Turn to page 419 in Section 3. Read "The Green Revolution." Then write a summary like the one on the right to understand the farmers' opposing points of view.

INDIAN INDEPENDENCE

Two of the men who led India in its struggle for independence from Great Britain, Mohandas Gandhi and Jawaharlal Nehru, had different ideas about how a fair and just society should be achieved.

❷ Gandhi grew up in a rural area of India, where he saw how difficult life was for many Indians. Through hard work and study he became a lawyer. Gandhi then lived in South Africa, a country that discriminated against people because of race. For 20 years he worked for the rights of Indian workers there. ❶ He saw how important it was for everyone in a country to have equal rights. At the same time, he did not trust that a government could provide people with those rights. He felt that each person individually had to seek ways to live in a fair and honorable manner.

❷ Nehru's father was a respected and wealthy lawyer, and Nehru had many privileges while growing up. Like Gandhi, Nehru went to England to study law. But when he finished his studies, he traveled around Europe, seeing other societies and learning about other governments. ❶ He came to believe that a government could be successful in granting its people equal rights and that it could do so by dividing up the land among all the people.

❸ Gandhi believed that government could not grant equal rights. He felt that each person, individually, could work for the good of the whole. Nehru, on the other hand, felt that government could grant equality by making sure that everyone had land.

SECTION 5

Pakistan

TERMS & NAMES
Mangla Dam
Tarbela Dam
Punjabi
Sindhi
Urdu

MAIN IDEA
Conflict between Muslims and Hindus in colonial times led to the creation of Pakistan.

WHY IT MATTERS NOW
Political and religious conflict continues to make this region unstable.

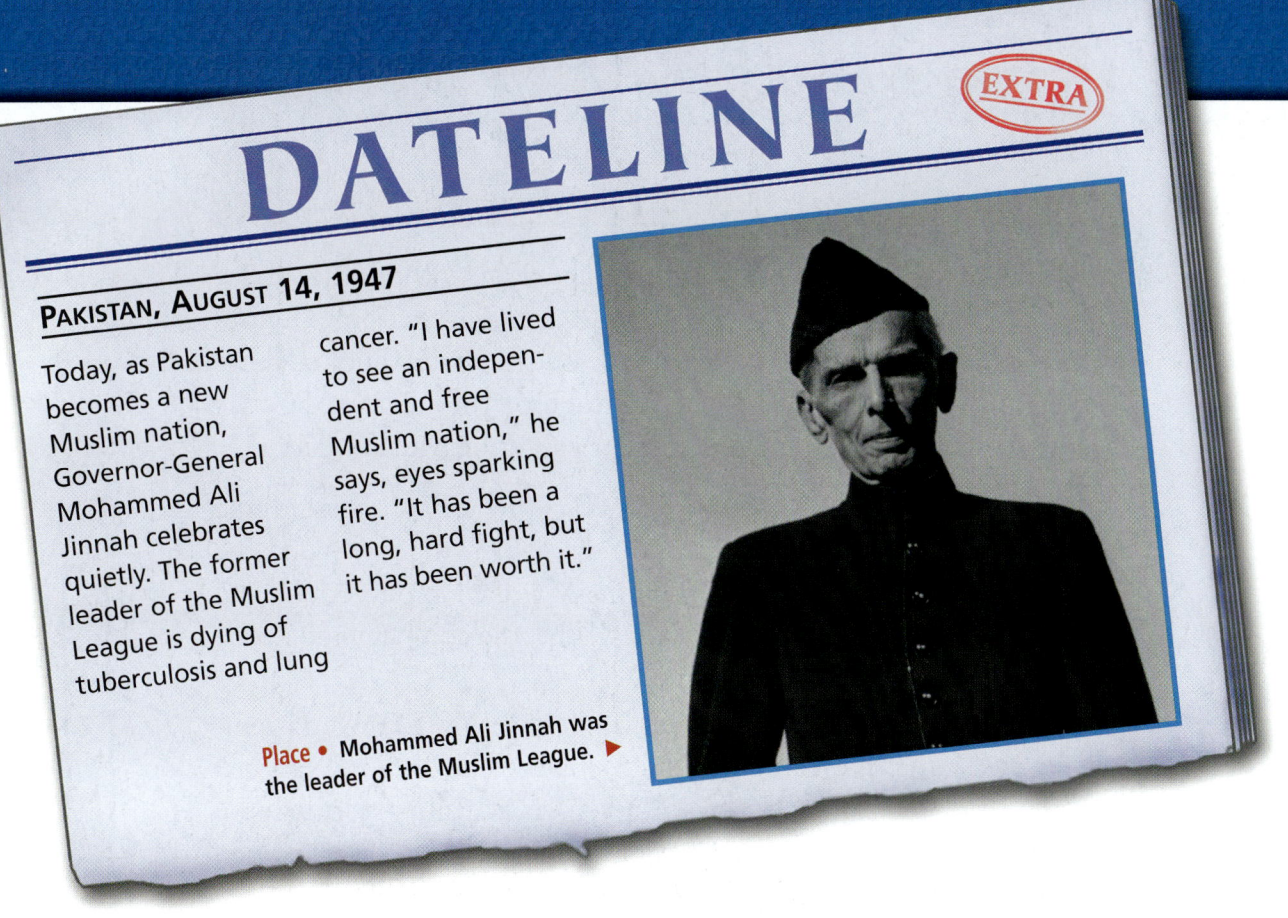

DATELINE

PAKISTAN, AUGUST 14, 1947—Today, as Pakistan becomes a new Muslim nation, Governor-General Mohammed Ali Jinnah celebrates quietly. The former leader of the Muslim League is dying of tuberculosis and lung cancer. "I have lived to see an independent and free Muslim nation," he says, eyes sparking fire. "It has been a long, hard fight, but it has been worth it."

Place • Mohammed Ali Jinnah was the leader of the Muslim League. ▶

History of Pakistan

Great Britain granted independence to Pakistan and India on the same day. Both South Asian countries have a long and sometimes common history. The Indus River flows through eastern Pakistan, from the mountains in the north to the Arabian Sea. This river valley was the site of one of the world's oldest civilizations. Over time, invaders and immigrants crossed the Himalayas and the Hindu Kush Mountains to reach this fertile area.

TAKING NOTES
Use your chart to take notes about India.

- Before 1947
- 1947
  - India
  - Both
  - Pakistan

SUNSHINE STATE STANDARDS
Key Standard SS.A.3.3.3 The student knows how physical and human geographic factors have influenced major historical events and movements.
Other Standards SS.A.3.3.5, B.2.3.5
FCAT LA.A.2.3.1 Reading: Identify Main Ideas, Facts, and Details

India and Its Neighbors 425

Culture •
The city of Mohenjo-Daro thrived over 4,000 years ago in the Indus River valley. ◄

In A.D. 712, Arab Muslims brought Islam to the Indus Valley region. Then, around the year 1000, Muslims from Central Asia built their own kingdom in the Indus River valley. Lahore (luh·HAWR), today one of the biggest cities in Pakistan, was the capital of their kingdom and a major center of Muslim culture.

The British Influence In the 1600s, the British East India Company set up trading posts in India, which then included the region that is now Pakistan. When the Mughal Empire, which had been ruling India, grew weak in the 1700s, the company took control of India.

With British rule, the Muslims lost power in the government, and over time, the Hindus gained power. The Indian National Congress was controlled by Hindus, so Muslims formed the Muslim League in 1906 as a way of keeping some political power. As India moved closer to independence from Great Britain, the Muslim League, led by Mohammed Ali Jinnah, called for an independent Muslim state.

Pakistan Becomes a Nation Differences between Hindus and Muslims led to violence. Neither the British nor the Indian National Congress could find a way to settle the differences between the two groups. So on August 14, 1947, at the same time that India gained independence, Pakistan was declared a separate Muslim nation. Millions of Muslims living in India moved to Pakistan, and Hindus in Pakistan moved to India.

Reading Social Studies

Using Maps Use the map below to find the locations of the four provinces of Pakistan.

Pakistan Divides When Pakistan became a nation, it included two regions—East Pakistan and West Pakistan—separated from each other by 1,000 miles. This distance made Pakistan a difficult country to rule. Although most people of East and West Pakistan were Muslim, they had many differences. Many East Pakistanis were angry that West Pakistan was in charge of the government. War broke out between East and West Pakistan. When the war ended, over a million people had lost their lives. In 1971, East Pakistan became the country of Bangladesh.

The Land of Pakistan

Pakistan (once West Pakistan) is divided into four provinces: Baluchistan, North-West Frontier, Punjab, and Sindh. Most Pakistanis live in the northeast province of Punjab.

BACKGROUND

The Indus River valley covers about 386,000 square miles. More than 150 million people live in this area. Sixty percent of the nation's farmable land is irrigated by the Indus River system.

Western and northern Pakistan are dry and mountainous, with few river valleys suitable for farming. The provinces of Sindh and Punjab are less mountainous, and although there is not much rain, the Indus River flows through them. About two-thirds of the people in Pakistan are farmers and herders who irrigate their land with water from the Indus River.

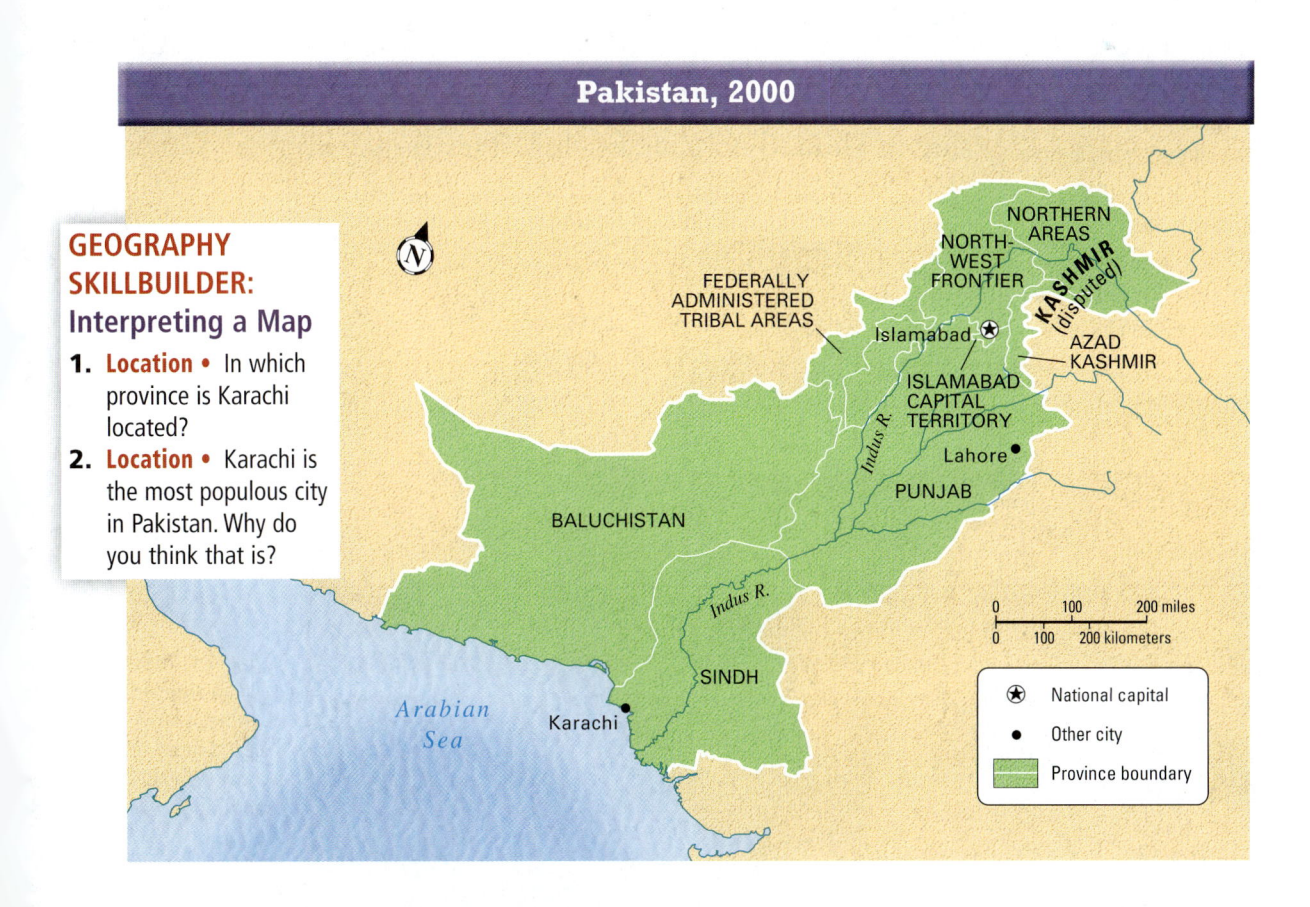

Pakistan, 2000

GEOGRAPHY SKILLBUILDER: Interpreting a Map

1. **Location** • In which province is Karachi located?
2. **Location** • Karachi is the most populous city in Pakistan. Why do you think that is?

India and Its Neighbors

River Power In 1967, Pakistan finished building the **Mangla Dam** on the Jhelum River in northeast Pakistan. The dam was built to control floodwaters and to provide hydroelectricity. In 1976, Pakistan opened one of the world's largest dams, the **Tarbela Dam.** Located on the Indus River, it is used for flood control and irrigation. In 1994, the Tarbela Dam began to produce hydroelectricity as well.

Connections to Technology

Drawbacks to Dams Dams can be useful for many things, such as irrigation and the production of electricity. Pakistan's Mangla Dam has stopped floods from destroying harvests (see below). Dams can also have negative effects. When a dam is built, hundreds of thousands of people may be forced to move because water that is held back by the dam covers nearby land and homes.

Fertile land can become unproductive because it becomes water-logged or because the salinity, or salt content, increases. Water has salt in it, and the salt stays behind in the soil. Over time, the salt content increases, and few plants will then grow in the soil. Wildlife suffers when rising waters disturb their natural habitats. In many countries, including Pakistan and India, there has been widespread opposition to dam building.

Language and Religion

Language divides the people of Pakistan, but the religion of Islam unites them. Each of Pakistan's four provinces has a unique culture with its own customs and languages.

Languages in Pakistan There are more than 20 languages spoken in Pakistan, of which **Punjabi** and **Sindhi** are the most common. Punjabi is spoken mostly in rural areas, and it is usually not written. **Urdu,** which is Pakistan's official language, is taught in schools. Students also learn their regional language. No single language is spoken by everyone in Pakistan, and in every province many different languages are spoken.

Movies made in Pakistan are usually in Punjabi or Urdu. The most popular newspapers are in Urdu, Sindhi, or English. This variety of languages has caused conflict among Pakistanis.

Culture • To read all the signs in Lahore, you would need to know several languages. ◀

Religion in Pakistan The country's official name is the Islamic Republic of Pakistan. More than 97 percent of Pakistanis are Muslim. Public schools base their teaching on Islam. Except in the homes of the wealthy and educated, women follow the rules of purdah.

Vocabulary
purdah: the practice of keeping women secluded

Modern Conflict in Pakistan

In 1947, when India and Pakistan became independent, each nation claimed the region of Kashmir. Find Kashmir on the map on page 633. This region is important to both nations because of its water resources. India and Pakistan have failed to reach an agreement about the future of Kashmir. Within South Asia, Hindus and Muslims have fought over whether Kashmir should join India or Pakistan or become independent.

Culture • Benazir Bhutto became the leader of Pakistan in 1988. She was the first Muslim woman ever elected to lead an Islamic state. ▲

Relations between Pakistan and India grew increasingly tense in 1998 when both nations tested nuclear weapons and then refused to sign a nuclear test-ban treaty. Since then, both nations have tested nuclear weapons and relations have not improved, though efforts continue to be made by Pakistan and India, with help from other nations.

SECTION 5 ASSESSMENT

Terms & Names
1. Explain the significance of:
   (a) Mangla Dam
   (b) Tarbela Dam
   (c) Punjabi
   (d) Sindhi
   (e) Urdu

Using Graphics
2. Use a chart like the one below to outline the history of Pakistan from its earliest beginnings to its creation as a modern nation in 1947.

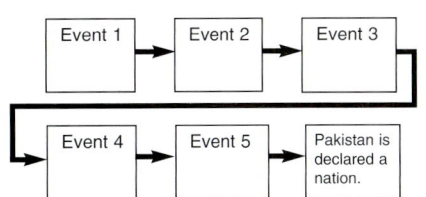

   Event 1 → Event 2 → Event 3
   Event 4 → Event 5 → Pakistan is declared a nation.

Main Ideas
3. (a) Why was Pakistan created in 1947?
   (b) Why are rivers an important natural resource in Pakistan?
   (c) What religion do most Pakistanis follow?

Critical Thinking
4. Drawing Conclusions
   Why do you think it is important for India and Pakistan to solve the problem of Kashmir peacefully?

   Think About
   • the results of conflicts between India and Pakistan
   • the reason relations between the two countries grew worse in 1998

ACTIVITY -OPTION- Draw a **political cartoon** that shows how the use of so many languages affects Pakistan.

India and Its Neighbors

CHAPTER 14 ASSESSMENT

TERMS & NAMES

Explain the significance of each of the following:

1. Mughal Empire
2. Mohandas Gandhi
3. Indira Gandhi
4. *panchayat*
5. jute
6. Green Revolution
7. dialect
8. dowry
9. Mangla Dam
10. Sindhi

REVIEW QUESTIONS

History (pages 403–407)
1. How did the East India Company influence India's history?
2. What was Mohandas Gandhi's contribution to India's independence?

Governments (pages 409–413)
3. What kinds of governments do the nations of South Asia have?
4. What rights did India's 1950 constitution give some people?

Economies (pages 416–419)
5. How are the economies of South Asian nations changing?
6. What is being done to improve the economies of South Asia?

The Culture of India (pages 420–423)
7. What languages are spoken in India and why?
8. What role does family play in the lives of most Indians?

Pakistan (pages 425–429)
9. What was the Muslim League, and what did it accomplish?
10. How has Pakistan taken advantage of its natural resources?

CRITICAL THINKING

Sequencing Events
1. Using your completed chart from "Reading Social Studies," p. 402, explain why India's independence was inevitable.

Evaluating Decisions
2. Based on what you know about India-Pakistan relations since 1947, was the partition of Pakistan a good idea?

Forming and Supporting Opinions
3. What is your opinion of Gandhi's philosophy of nonviolence?

Visual Summary

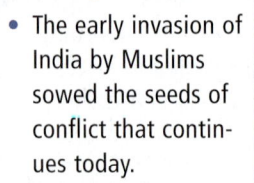

1 History
- The early invasion of India by Muslims sowed the seeds of conflict that continues today.
- Britain's influence in the region lasted from the 17th century until Indian independence in 1947.

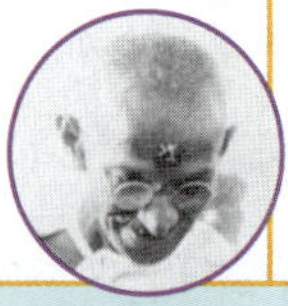

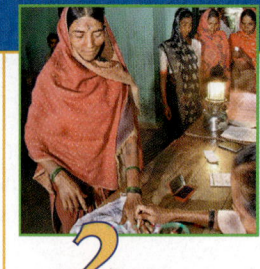

2 Governments
- Most South Asian countries are republics that became independent from British rule in the 20th century.

3 Economies
- The region's countries have traditional economies in which most people are farmers or market economies in which most people make money and buy what they need.

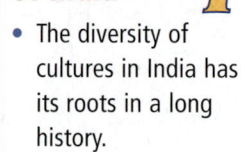

4 The Culture of India
- The diversity of cultures in India has its roots in a long history.
- Family plays an important role in the lives of most Indians.

5 Pakistan
- Pakistan is united by the common religion of Islam.
- Pakistan's history has been marked by conflict with other peoples in South Asia.

> STANDARDS-BASED ASSESSMENT

Use the map and your knowledge of world cultures and geography to answer questions 1 and 2.

Additional Test Practice, pp. S1–S33

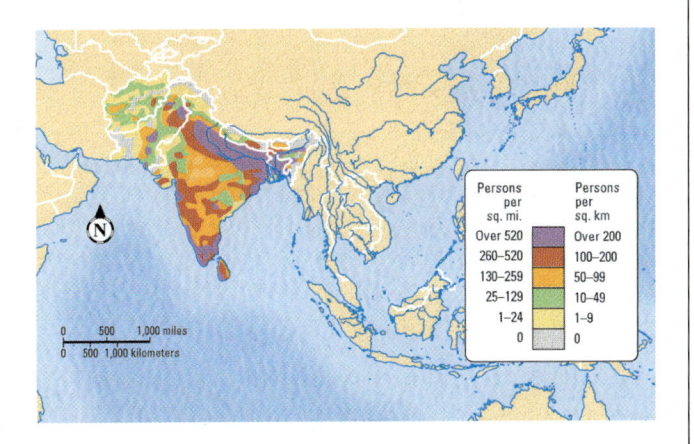

1. According to the map key, how many people per square mile live in the areas shaded in green?
   - A. 1–24
   - B. 25–129
   - C. 130–259
   - D. over 520

2. Which of the following areas of India has the greatest population density?
   - A. the eastern coast
   - B. the central plateau
   - C. the northwestern region
   - D. the northeastern region

The following passage is a well-known quotation by Indian leader Mohandas Gandhi. Use the quotation and your knowledge of world cultures and geography to answer question 3.

PRIMARY SOURCE

I do not want my house to be walled in on all sides and my windows to be stuffed. I want the cultures of all the lands to be blown about my house as freely as possible. But I refuse to be blown off my feet by any.

MOHANDAS GANDHI

3. Which of the following choices best restates Gandhi's opinion?
   - A. He believed that people of all nations should integrate, or mix, cultures.
   - B. He believed that it is dangerous for people to try to mix cultures.
   - C. He wanted to appreciate other cultures, yet he didn't want people of a foreign culture to rule him.
   - D. He wanted to keep elements of his culture in the privacy of his home, but not to display it in public.

TEST PRACTICE CLASSZONE.COM

ALTERNATIVE ASSESSMENT

1. WRITING ABOUT HISTORY

Mohandas Gandhi was responsible for bringing about social change in India and resisting British rule. His tactics were always nonviolent. Research the kinds of protests that Gandhi organized, such as hunger strikes, labor strikes, and marches. Then write a script for an interview in which he answers questions about his beliefs in general and about one specific protest of your choice. Share your written interview with the class.

2. COOPERATIVE LEARNING

In a group of three to five classmates, design a travel brochure for a traveler who is visiting South Asia for the first time. Include details about the region's history, geography, government, economies, and cultures, as well as information about the climate, transportation, and sites of interests. Divide the roles of editor, art director, and writers. Create a rough draft of the text, the layout, and ideas for photographs. Then display your completed brochure in your classroom.

INTEGRATED TECHNOLOGY

Doing Internet Research

Use the Internet to research the current leaders of India, Pakistan, and Afghanistan. These may be individuals or groups. Then write a report about what you have learned. List the Web sites you used to prepare your report.

- Focus on their beliefs and ideals—what they hope for their countries.
- Find a statement from each leader that you think best expresses these beliefs and ideals.
- Include a chart showing the leaders of each country.

For Internet links to support this activity, go to

RESEARCH LINKS CLASSZONE.COM

India and Its Neighbors

Literature Connections

The Sandstorm

IN SHABANU: DAUGHTER OF THE WIND, Suzanne Fisher Staples tells about 11-year-old Shabanu, the youngest child in a family of nomadic camel herders. Shabanu lives in the Cholistan Desert with her parents; her older sister, Phulan; her grandfather; and an aunt with two young children. She also has a camel named Mithoo and a pet dog named Sher Dil. In this hot and dry area of Pakistan, blinding sandstorms can strike without warning. When they do, they threaten the lives of the people who make the desert their home and of the camels they depend on for their livelihood.

One night Phulan shakes me awake in the middle of a deep sleep.

"Shabanu!" she shouts from such a great distance I can barely hear her.

She yanks the quilt away, and suddenly my skin is pierced by thousands of needles. The wind is howling around us. I can't see anything when I open my eyes, but I can tell by the sound and feel that it's a monstrous sandstorm, the kind few living things survive without protection. Phulan pulls me by the hand, but I yank away.

"Mithoo!" I stumble about the courtyard, tripping over huddled chickens, clay pots, and bundles of reeds that have broken away from the entrance. "Mithoo!"

Hands outstretched, I feel my way around the courtyard wall, where Mithoo normally sleeps. When I get to where the reeds were stacked on their stalks, lashed side by side and tied to cover the doorway, there is a gaping hole. Quickly I make my way around the courtyard again. Mithoo is gone.

1. A loose robe, worn by Islamic women, that covers the body and most of the face; also spelled *chador*.

2. A freshwater pond that serves as a water supply for desert nomads.

From SHABANU by Suzanne Fisher Staples, copyright © 1989 by Suzanne Fisher Staples. Used by permission of Alfred A. Knopf Children's Books, a division of Random House, Inc.

SUNSHINE STATE STANDARDS
Key Standard SS.B.2.3.7 The student knows how various human systems throughout the world have developed in response to conditions in the physical environment.
FCAT LA.E.2.3.1 Literature: Understand Character and Plot Development

"You can't find him without a light and something to put over your eyes!" Phulan shouts, pulling on my arm. Together we drag the bed through the doorway. Mama struggles to close the window shutters and Phulan and I manage to push the door shut and wedge the bed against it. Dadi lights a candle and swears softly as the light fills the room. Grandfather and Sher Dil are missing too.

"Where can he have gone?" Mama gasps, her eyes bright with fear. Grandfather had been sound asleep, and the storm must have wakened him.

Dadi uses the candle to light the kerosene storm lantern and pulls the bed away from the door. Mama throws a shawl around his shoulders. He pulls it over his head and I follow him out to the courtyard, where *khar* shrubs, their shallow roots torn from the dry sand, tumble and hurl themselves against the walls.

With my *chadr*[1] over my face, I can open my eyes enough to see the haze of the lantern in Dadi's hand, the light reflecting from the dust in a tight circle around him.

Auntie has already closed up her house, and Dadi pounds on the door for several minutes before she opens it again and we slip inside.

"Have you seen Grandfather?" asks Dadi.

"And Mithoo and Sher Dil?" I shout.

She stands in the center of her house, mouth open and speechless, her hands raised helplessly. My cousins stand behind her skirt, their eyes wide. From between her feet Sher Dil's black nose glistens in the lamplight. But no Grandfather and no Mithoo.

"Come to our house," Dadi orders her, handing me the lantern. "I'll close up here. Shabanu, come back for me," he says, bending to light Auntie's storm lantern.

When I return, Dadi holds the light so we can see each other.

"Mithoo will be fine," he says, and I know it is a warning not to ask to look for him. "When the wind has died and it's light, we'll find him standing near a tree by the *toba*."[2]

Reading THE LITERATURE

In this selection, the author draws on almost all of the five senses to help the reader understand what it might be like to live through a sandstorm. Find an example of how each sense is used to make the account more vivid.

Thinking About THE LITERATURE

What role does nature play in the lives of Shabanu and her family? How does the author make clear the challenges of living in the Cholistan Desert?

Writing About THE LITERATURE

In this story, Shabanu and her family work together to survive the sudden sandstorm. How do the members of the family help one another overcome the dangers of the storm?

About the Author

Suzanne Fisher Staples (b. 1945) has traveled widely as a reporter for a global news service. In 1979, she went to work in Southern Asia, covering such events as the civil war in Afghanistan. A 1985 trip to Pakistan, where she conducted a study of poor rural women, led her to write *Shabanu*. Staples currently lives in Florida.

Further Reading *The Land I Lost* by Huynh Quang Nhuong takes the reader to a tiny village in the central highlands of Vietnam, years before the Vietnam War. The book has won many awards, including selection as an ALA Notable Book.

CHAPTER 15

Southeast Asia Today

SECTION 1 History and Governments
SECTION 2 Economies and Cultures
SECTION 3 Vietnam Today

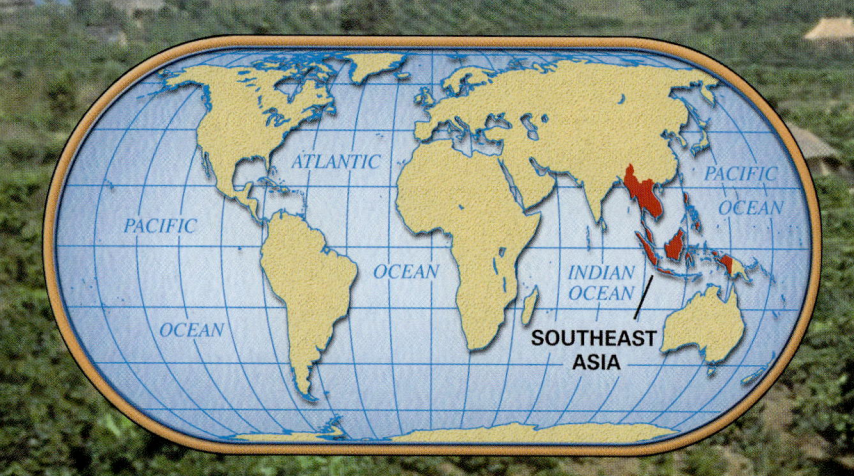

Human-Environment Interaction
People harvest tea leaves in a field near Bao Loc, Vietnam. Tea growing began in Southeast Asia when the Dutch brought seeds to Java from Japan.

FOCUS ON GEOGRAPHY

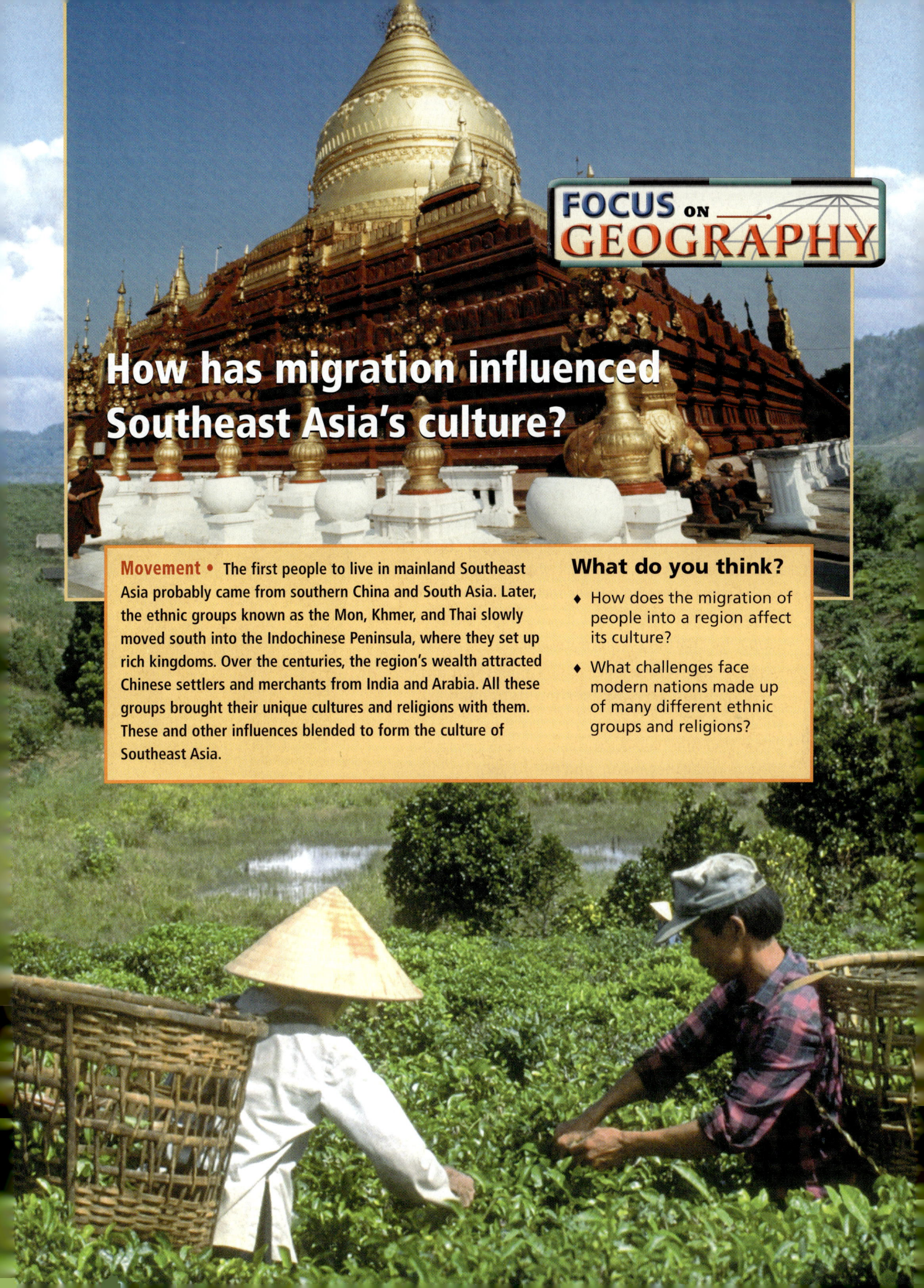

How has migration influenced Southeast Asia's culture?

Movement • The first people to live in mainland Southeast Asia probably came from southern China and South Asia. Later, the ethnic groups known as the Mon, Khmer, and Thai slowly moved south into the Indochinese Peninsula, where they set up rich kingdoms. Over the centuries, the region's wealth attracted Chinese settlers and merchants from India and Arabia. All these groups brought their unique cultures and religions with them. These and other influences blended to form the culture of Southeast Asia.

What do you think?

- How does the migration of people into a region affect its culture?
- What challenges face modern nations made up of many different ethnic groups and religions?

CHAPTER 15
READING SOCIAL STUDIES

BEFORE YOU READ

▶▶ What Do You Know?

Before you read the chapter, think about what you know about Southeast Asia. What countries make up this region? What do you know about the region's governments and economies? Have you ever seen a movie about the Vietnam War? What do you know about Vietnam today? Recall what you know from other classes, what you have read, and what you have seen on television.

Culture • Puppets made from water buffalo hides are used in the ancient art of shadow theater. ▼

▶▶ What Do You Want to Know?

In your notebook, record what you hope to learn from this chapter.

READ AND TAKE NOTES

Reading Strategy: Drawing Conclusions To draw conclusions, look at the facts and then use your common sense and experience to decide what the facts mean. Use the chart below to gather facts and draw conclusions about Southeast Asia.

- Copy the chart into your notebook.
- As you read, record facts and examples that answer each question. Look for specific information, as shown.
- After you read, review the facts and examples, decide what they mean, and record your conclusions.

Place • Singapore is a busy and wealthy city in Southeast Asia. ▲

	Facts/Examples	Conclusions
How are Southeast Asian nations linked to other countries?		
What forms of government are in the region?		
What factors affect economies in Southeast Asia today?		
What factors shape cultures in the region?		
What are the effects of the Vietnam War?		

SECTION 1

History and Governments

TERMS & NAMES
mandala
military dictatorship
East Timor

MAIN IDEA
Southeast Asia has experienced a variety of cultural and governmental influences throughout its history.

WHY IT MATTERS NOW
The current governments of the nations of Southeast Asia are relatively new and unstable.

DATELINE EXTRA

BURMA, 1274

Today, the famed traveler from Italy arrived. Marco Polo has come to Southeast Asia with his family. He is carrying important papers from a religious leader known as the Pope, but mostly he wants to see the land, the people, and the cultures. When he returns home, he plans to write a book about his adventures. Marco Polo marveled at our beautiful temples. He noted that they are "covered with gold, a full finger's breadth in thickness." Perhaps there is nothing quite so beautiful in Italy.

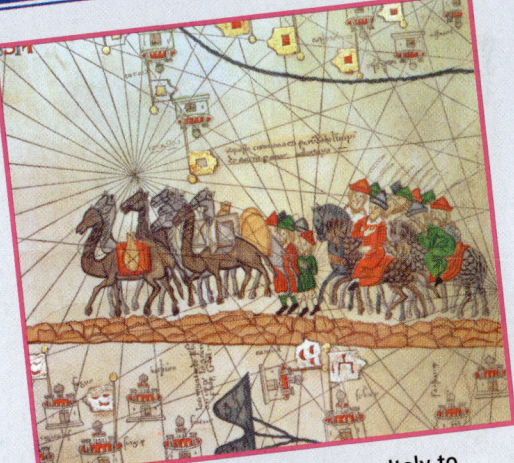

Culture • Marco Polo will return to Italy to share the wonders of the East. ▲

New Cultures in Southeast Asia

Seven hundred years before Marco Polo's visit, Southeast Asia had come under the influence of two stronger, more advanced cultures: China and India. China made Vietnam part of its empire. Vietnam was not able to gain its independence until A.D. 939. India never ruled any part of Southeast Asia, but its culture spread throughout the region and had a lasting influence.

TAKING NOTES
Use your chart to take notes about Southeast Asia.

	Facts/Examples	Conclusions
How are S.E. Asian nations linked...		
What forms of government are...		

SUNSHINE STATE STANDARDS
Key Standard SS.A.3.3.2 The student understands the historical events that have shaped the development of cultures throughout the world.
Other Standards SS.A.3.3.5
FCAT LA.A.2.2.7 Reading: Recognize Compare and Contrast

Southeast Asia Today **437**

Influences of China and India New religions—Hinduism, Buddhism, and Confucianism—came to Southeast Asia from China and India. So did writing systems, literature, and ideas about government and social class. Indian ideas about government were especially important.

Southeast Asian Governments Instead of states or nations, Southeast Asia was made up of mandalas. A **mandala** (MUHN·duh·luh) had at its center a ruler who worked to gain support from others. The ruler used trade and business to influence others and maintain power. Mandalas varied. Some were larger than others, some depended on agriculture, and some had more advanced technology. The mandala system stayed in place in many parts of Southeast Asia until the 19th century. One ancient mandala, called Oc Eo, was located in southern Vietnam. Ships from this port carried goods to and from places as far away as Rome. Over time, the mandalas developed into states, and the people began to think of themselves as belonging to these states. Because of trade and communication, new ideas were exchanged among the peoples of the region and between the region and other parts of the world. Each state took what it wanted from these new ideas and developed into a unique nation.

Human-Environment Interaction • For centuries, Southeast Asians have been trading by sea in ships like this one in Jakarta, Indonesia. ▼

Reading Social Studies
A. Summarizing How did nations develop out of mandalas?

The WORLD'S HERITAGE

Cambodia's Temple Treasures
Angkor (ANG·kawr) was an early civilization in northwestern Cambodia between the 9th and 15th centuries. Its capital, also called Angkor, contains temples that are among the world's greatest works of art and architecture.

One of these temples, Angkor Wat, is particularly splendid. It was built to honor the Hindu god Vishnu. This huge pyramid-shaped temple covers almost one square mile. Its stonework is covered with richly carved scenes from Hindu mythology. For centuries after the city and its magnificent temples were abandoned, jungle growth hid them until their rediscovery around 1860. Later, war kept admirers away. Today, efforts are under way to restore Angkor Wat as a world monument to Cambodian culture.

Culture • Today, most Indonesians, like these boys studying the Qur'an, are Muslims. ▲

Strange but TRUE

Dragons of Komodo On Komodo (kuh•MOH•doh) Island and a few other islands in Indonesia lives one of Earth's most fearsome creatures. Its body is covered with scales, and its tail is long and powerful. It has sharp teeth, long claws, and a yellow tongue that flicks in and out. If this description makes you think of a storybook dragon, you are not alone.

Hundreds of years ago, Chinese fishermen thought the same thing when they called this creature a dragon. Komodo dragons are really lizards. In fact, they're the largest living lizards in the world. Some Komodo dragons grow more than 10 feet long and weigh as much as 200 pounds. They're so strong that they can overpower and eat deer, wild pigs, and water buffalo. They have even been known to attack people.

New Religions Trade with other parts of the world also brought Christianity and Islam to Southeast Asia. In the ninth or tenth century, Muslim traders brought Islam to the region, especially to the islands of Sumatra and Java, part of what is now Indonesia. Islam spread gradually throughout the other islands of Indonesia and Malaysia.

In the early 1500s, Christian missionaries came to Southeast Asia from Portugal, France, and Spain. The Spanish missionaries met with success in the Philippines, where there was no organized religion to combat, although each group of Filipinos had its own set of beliefs. Today, about 90 percent of Filipinos are Christians. However, in the rest of Southeast Asia, the missionaries were not as successful. Buddhist monks worked to keep the missionaries from making converts.

European Colonialism

Europeans came to Southeast Asia as traders as well as missionaries. The Portuguese were the first to arrive, in 1509. The Spanish, the Dutch, the British, and the French all followed. These European traders came for wealth—spices, gems, and gold—not power. For the most part, the Europeans controlled port cities and nothing more for the first three centuries.

Southeast Asia, 2001

GEOGRAPHY SKILLBUILDER:
Interpreting a Map
1. **Location** • What bodies of water surround Southeast Asia?
2. **Region** • What nations of Southeast Asia are found on the mainland?

Then, in the 19th and early 20th centuries, these European nations began to colonize the nations of Southeast Asia. The Philippines was under Spanish rule until 1898, when it came under the rule of the United States. Cambodia, Laos, and Vietnam were all ruled by France. The British ruled Burma, most of Malaysia, and Singapore, and the Dutch ruled Indonesia. Only Thailand never became a colony.

During World War II, the Japanese pushed out most Europeans from the region. When the war ended in 1945, Cambodia, Vietnam, Laos, Malaysia, and Indonesia fought for independence. The Philippines won independence peacefully.

Culture • King Bhumibol Adulyadej (POO·mee·POHN ah·DOON·luh·DAYT) is the longest-reigning monarch in Thailand's history. His duties are mainly ceremonial. ▼

Contributions of the Europeans The Spanish learned of the chile pepper in North America and brought it to Southeast Asia. Immediately, the chile pepper became a familiar part of the diet in Southeast Asia. Coffee came to the region with the Dutch. Today, coffee is an important crop in Indonesia, Laos, and Vietnam.

After Independence

After gaining independence, many nations in Southeast Asia found themselves in turmoil. Political parties fought one another to gain power. In Vietnam, Myanmar, and Indonesia, the military eventually took control of the government. Over the next 20 years, the nations of Southeast Asia worked out their own unique government systems.

Reading Social Studies

B. Making Inferences How do you think the people of Myanmar might have felt about the overthrow of their elected government?

Governments Brunei, Malaysia, Cambodia, and Thailand are all constitutional monarchies. Indonesia, the Philippines, and Singapore are republics. Myanmar was also a republic, but in 1988, the military overthrew the government. Since then, it has been a **military dictatorship,** ruled by one man whose power comes from the military. Laos and Vietnam are both Communist states.

East Timor The island nation of **East Timor** declared its independence from Portugal in 1975. A month later, the neighboring country of Indonesia invaded and took over. The United Nations said the people of East Timor could decide their government for themselves. In 1999, they voted for independence.

However, Indonesia did not accept the people's ruling. The United Nations has accused the Indonesian army of killing and deporting people because of the vote. UN peacekeeping forces were stationed in East Timor. In August 2001, East Timor held its first democratic elections.

Citizenship IN ACTION

Aung San Suu Kyi (OWNG•SAHN•SOO•CHEE) Suu Kyi was born in Burma, now called Myanmar, in 1945. In 1988, she became the leader of a new national movement against the brutal military dictatorship that controlled Myanmar. She and millions of followers used peaceful methods to protest human rights abuses and to demand a democratic government. The military killed thousands of protesters. Suu Kyi was put under house arrest. In 1991, she won the Nobel Peace Prize.

SECTION 1 ASSESSMENT

Terms & Names
1. Explain the significance of: (a) mandala (b) military dictatorship (c) East Timor

Using Graphics

2. Use a cluster map like this one to take notes on ways the Chinese, Indian, European, and other cultures influenced Southeast Asian culture.

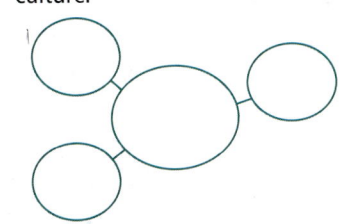

Main Ideas

3. (a) Who brought Islam and Christianity to Southeast Asia?
   (b) Why did European nations come to Southeast Asia?
   (c) How is the government of Thailand different from the government of the Philippines?

Critical Thinking

4. **Analyzing Causes**

   Why do you think many of the newly independent Southeast Asian nations came under the control of military dictators?

   Think About
   - the political and social confusion many countries find themselves in when their colonial rulers leave
   - the role of the military

ACTIVITY -OPTION- Make a **chart** showing the countries of Southeast Asia and each country's system of government.

Linking Past and Present

The Legacy of Southern Asia

Architecture

Even before the rise of Buddhism in the 5th century B.C., people in India made burial mounds for their dead. When the Buddha died, similar mound-shaped structures called stupas became symbols of his death and of Buddhism. Stupas became more elaborate over time. This architectural form spread throughout the Buddhist world and can be found in the pagodas—religious buildings—of Korea, Japan, and China, as well as in shrines in Sri Lanka and temples in Java.

Theater and Dance

In ancient times, theater and classical dance productions were held in the temples and royal courts of India. Spectators watched dancers act out stories of Hindu gods and myths, especially from famous epics. The two most famous epics are the *Ramayana* (ruh•MAH•yuh•nuh) and the *Mahabharata* (MAH•huh•BAH•ruh•tuh). Folk dancing, another dance form, was popular in rural areas. Modern dance in Southern Asia includes elements of both classical and folk dancing.

Cities

One of the first cities in the world, Mohenjo-Daro, was built along the Indus River in what is now Pakistan. After archaeologists discovered the 4,000-year-old city in 1922, they spent years excavating its ruins. What they unearthed was a city laid out in a grid pattern, with streets, houses, assembly halls, storerooms, public baths, and a sewer system. Many modern cities are laid out in grids, and some cities in India have public baths similar to the ones found in Mohenjo-Daro.

Find Out More About It!

Study the text and photos on these pages to learn about inventions, creations, and contributions that have come from Southern Asia. Then choose the item that interests you the most and use the library or the Internet to research the subject and learn more about it. Use the information you gather to create a diorama to share with the class.

RESEARCH LINKS
CLASSZONE.COM

SUNSHINE STATE STANDARDS
Key Standard SS.A.3.3.5 The student understands the differences between institutions of Eastern and Western civilizations (e.g., differences in governments, social traditions and customs, economic systems and religious institutions).

FCAT LA.A.2.3.7 Reading: Synthesize and Separate Information

Sanskrit Language

Sanskrit, the oldest written language of India, was first brought to India around 1500 B.C. The language has distinctive sounds, as well as complex grammar rules. Some of India's modern languages—Hindi, Bengali, and Punjabi—are based on Sanskrit. Though by 100 B.C. Sanskrit was no longer being spoken, it is still used in many Hindu ceremonies and in scholarly works and teachings.

Black Tea

Though tea bushes were found growing wild in Assam, India, in the 1820s, it was not until the mid-1880s that India began to export tea. Workers used a process that turned green leaves to a brownish black color to produce a blend known as black tea. Though tea had been grown in China for more than 3,000 years, by 1888 England was importing more tea from Southern Asia than from China. Today, some of the best black teas come from India.

Southern Asia   443

Economies and Cultures

SECTION 2

TERMS & NAMES
developing nation
Bahasa Indonesian
pagoda
thatch
batik

MAIN IDEA
The economically and culturally unique nations of Southeast Asia trade with most of the world.

WHY IT MATTERS NOW
Southeast Asia's successes contribute to the strength of other economies.

DATELINE

SURIN, THAILAND, NOVEMBER 17, 2001— One hundred elephants clashed today in a huge mock battle. Wooden weapons clattered and elephants trumpeted. Hundreds of tourists cheered during the Surin Elephant Round-Up. This yearly event reflects how important elephants have been to Thailand. Also featured was a tug of war with an elephant against men.

Place • A Thai man demonstrates his ease and skill with elephants. ▲

An Agricultural Economy

Events such as elephant roundups take place in rural areas, where three-fourths of the people in Southeast Asia live, many of them on small farms where they grow rice to feed their families, not to sell for profit. Many nations of Southeast Asia are **developing nations**. They are working to improve their economies and to help people live safe, healthy, successful lives.

TAKING NOTES
Use your chart to take notes about Southeast Asia.

	Facts/Examples	Conclusions
How are S.E. Asian nations linked...		
What forms of government are...		

SUNSHINE STATE STANDARDS
Key Standard SS.A.3.3.5 The student understands the differences between institutions of Eastern and Western civilizations (e.g., differences in governments, social traditions and customs, economic systems and religious institutions).
Other Standards SS.D.2.3.1
FCAT LA.A.2.3.1 Reading: Identify Main Ideas, Facts, and Details

Small Farms and Factories The Green Revolution and irrigation have helped some farmers grow more food. But many others have small plots of land and cannot afford to buy fertilizers, chemicals, and modern equipment. They must rely on good weather and hard work for successful harvests.

In the past 50 years, industry has become more important in Southeast Asia. Small factories that process crops, make clothing and fabric, and produce small electronic parts are the most common. Many people have moved into the larger cities looking for work.

Place • The people of Singapore enjoy a high standard of living. ▲

Singapore The small country of Singapore is an exception in Southeast Asia. Virtually everyone lives in the city, also called Singapore. Though small in size, Singapore is one of the richest nations in the world and has one of the busiest ports. The production of electronic goods is its most important industry, and more than half of these goods are exported.

The Cultures of Southeast Asia

The people of Southeast Asia live in widely differing geographical regions. In rural communities, people's lives have not changed much in the past century. In the big cities, however, history and tradition stand side by side with modern architecture, automobiles, and fast-food restaurants.

Languages In Indonesia, the Philippines, and Myanmar, where communities are separated by water, dense forests, or mountains, people speak many languages. However, most people from Indonesia also speak **Bahasa Indonesian** (bah·HAH·suh), the national language. In places where there is a large Chinese population, dialects are spoken. Indians who live in parts of Southeast Asia speak Hindi or Tamil.

Languages of Southeast Asia, 2002

Country	Official Language	Other Languages Spoken
Brunei	Malay	English, Chinese
Cambodia	Khmer	French, English
Indonesia	Bahasa Indonesian	English, Dutch, Javanese, local dialects
Laos	Lao	French, English, local languages
Malaysia	Bahasa Malay	English, Chinese dialects, Tamil, Hindi, Telugu, Malayalam, Punjabi, Thai, local languages
Myanmar	Burmese	Local languages
Philippines	Filipino, English	Local languages
Singapore	Mandarin Chinese, Malay, Tamil, English	
Thailand	Thai	English, local languages and dialects
Vietnam	Vietnamese	Chinese, English, French, Khmer, local languages

SKILLBUILDER: Reading a Chart
1. Which country has the most official languages? Why do you think that is?
2. Why do you think French is spoken in several countries?

Reading Social Studies

Drawing Conclusions
How can geography affect the languages of a nation?

Region • Buddhist temples are a common sight in Southeast Asia. ▶

Religions A form of Buddhism is the most common religion in mainland Southeast Asia. Islam, brought by Muslims who came to Southeast Asia several centuries ago, is practiced in Malaysia, the Philippines, Thailand, and Indonesia. Spanish and Portuguese missionaries spread the Catholic faith, which is most important today in southern Vietnam and the Philippines. Protestantism and Hinduism are also practiced in the region.

Architecture Statues of the Buddha can be seen in temples all over Southeast Asia. Often the temples consist of one or more **pagodas,** or towers, built in many levels, with sculptures or carvings of Buddha on each level. Houses, built of wood or bamboo, have roofs made of **thatch,** or woven palm fronds. In areas where there is flooding from monsoons, houses are built on stilts.

Spotlight on CULTURE

Wayang Kulit For over 1,000 years, shadow puppet theater has been a popular form of entertainment in Java, Bali, Thailand, and Cambodia. The most famous shadow theater is the Javanese *wayang kulit*. It tells ancient Hindu stories, such as the *Mahabharata*. To perform *wayang kulit*, the puppeteer sits behind a screen, moving the puppets (which are made from water buffalo hides) with rods connected to their bodies and arms. A light shines behind the puppets, casting shadows on the screen, and the audience sees only the shadows.

THINKING CRITICALLY

1. **Drawing Conclusions**
   What does the popularity of this art form tell you about Indonesian culture?

2. **Making Inferences**
   How do these puppets show the skill of Javanese craftspeople?

For more on *wayang kulit*, go to
RESEARCH LINKS
CLASSZONE.COM

Culture •
Weaving is an important part of Laotian culture. ▲

Culture • This Thai dance tells the story of the *Ramayana*. ▲

Dance Dancing is a popular art form in much of Southeast Asia. A dance might tell a story from history or the *Ramayana*, one of India's great epic poems. Dancers must train for years. They wear elaborate and beautiful costumes. The motions of their hands often tell the story.

Weaving Weavers in Southeast Asia use available resources. In the Philippines, fabrics are sometimes made of pineapple fiber. In Indonesia, weavers make cotton **batik** (buh·TEEK), using wax and dye to make intricate patterns on fabric. In Laos, they weave cotton and silk from fibers that are grown in Laos.

SECTION 2 ASSESSMENT

Terms & Names
1. Explain the significance of: **(a)** developing nation **(b)** Bahasa Indonesian **(c)** pagoda **(d)** thatch **(e)** batik

Using Graphics
2. Use a chart like this one to list important characteristics of the economies and cultures of Southeast Asia.

Economic Characteristics	Cultural Characteristics

Main Ideas
3. **(a)** Where do most of the people in Southeast Asia live?
   (b) How have the economies of Southeast Asia changed in the past 50 years?
   (c) What are the three main religions in Southeast Asia?

Critical Thinking
4. **Synthesizing**

   Why are so many languages spoken in Southeast Asia?

   Think About
   - the region's varied history and cultural influences
   - how geography contributes to the development of different ethnic groups and their languages

ACTIVITY -OPTION- Trace a **map** of Southeast Asia from the Unit Atlas on page 366. Draw arrows and write labels to show the paths of cultural influences.

Southeast Asia Today **447**

SKILLBUILDER

Distinguishing Fact from Opinion

▶▶ **Defining the Skill**

A fact is a piece of information that can be proved to be true. Statements, statistics, and dates all may be facts. An opinion, on the other hand, is a belief, feeling, or judgment that is expressed by someone. An opinion cannot be proved to be true. Being able to distinguish fact from opinion is one part of critical thinking. It helps you know whether to trust an argument or to change your own opinion when someone is trying to influence you.

SUNSHINE STATE STANDARDS
Key Standard SS.A.3.3.5
The student understands the differences between institutions of Eastern and Western civilizations (e.g., differences in governments, social traditions and customs, economic systems and religious institutions).
FCAT LA.A.2.3.8 Reading: Validate Information

▶▶ **Applying the Skill**

The passage to the right tells about an unusual law in the country of Singapore. Use the strategies below to help you distinguish fact from opinion.

How to Distinguish Fact from Opinion

Strategy ❶ Look for facts, or information that can be proved to be true.

Strategy ❷ Look for statements that express a person's opinion, judgment, or feeling.

Strategy ❸ Think about how the facts in the passage could be checked for accuracy. Where might you look to see if they are true? Identify the facts and opinions expressed in the passage. List the facts and opinions in a chart. Also list where you could look to prove a fact.

> **A SINGAPORE LAW**
>
> ❶ In 1992, Singapore began a program to stop littering. People caught tossing litter have to put on bright yellow vests and spend 12 hours sweeping up garbage. They may also be fined up to $2,940. And if they are caught several times, they have to attend a meeting where they learn about the costs of pollution. The punishment seems to be working. One woman who was sweeping garbage said, ❷ "Anyway, it is very embarrassing."

Make a Chart

The chart below lists some of the statements from the passage and shows whether they are facts or opinions.

Statement	❸ Can It Be Proved?	Fact or Opinion?
In 1992, Singapore began a program to stop littering.	Yes. Check a newspaper story or the laws in Singapore.	Fact
People caught littering have to sweep garbage for up to 12 hours.	Yes. Check a newspaper story or a magazine article.	Fact
"Anyway, it is very embarrassing."	No. This statement expresses a person's feelings.	Opinion

▶▶ **Practicing the Skill**

Turn to page 437 in Chapter 15, Section 1, and read the Dateline. Make a chart like the one above in which you list key statements and then determine whether they are facts or opinions.

SECTION 3

Vietnam Today

TERMS & NAMES
Ho Chi Minh
Politburo
doi moi
supply and demand
Tet

MAIN IDEA
Vietnam has struggled for centuries to be a unified nation.

WHY IT MATTERS NOW
The United States and other countries have established new trade relations with a unified Vietnam.

DATELINE

SAIGON, SOUTH VIETNAM, APRIL 30, 1975—At last the war between North and South Vietnam is over. Saigon, the capital of South Vietnam, has fallen. Few thought this day would ever come. At this moment, North Vietnamese citizens and soldiers march victoriously toward Saigon.

Hundreds of South Vietnamese fought to climb aboard the last helicopters lifting Americans off the roof of the United States embassy. The thousands left behind worry about what will happen to them now.

Place • Helicopters evacuate Americans and some Vietnamese from defeated South Vietnam. ▲

A History of Struggle

The Vietnam War was only the latest in a series of wars and invasions that the people of Vietnam had endured. China ruled Vietnam for more than a millennium, until A.D. 939. During this time, the Chinese built roads and waterways. They introduced the use of metal plows, farm animals, and improved methods of irrigation. Though China strongly influenced life in Vietnam, the Vietnamese protected their own culture and traditions.

TAKING NOTES
Use your chart to take notes about Southeast Asia.

	Facts/Examples	Conclusions
How are S.E. Asian nations linked...		
What forms of government are...		

SUNSHINE STATE STANDARDS
Key Standard SS.A.3.3.2 The student understands the historical events that have shaped the development of cultures throughout the world.
Other Standards SS.A.3.3.5
FCAT LA.A.2.3.1 Reading: Identify Main Ideas, Facts, and Details

Southeast Asia Today **449**

China invaded Vietnam again in 1407, but in 1428, after ten years of fighting, the Vietnamese were able to force out the Chinese. For a time, Vietnam enjoyed peace and prosperity. But during the 1500s and again in the 1600s, Vietnam was disrupted by civil wars. It has not enjoyed a long period of peace and growth like the one in the 1400s since.

French Rule In 1858, Napoleon III, the ruler of France, invaded Vietnam. He wanted to increase the size of his empire and benefit from more trade in Southeast Asia. Gradually, over the next 25 years, France took control of all of Vietnam, Cambodia, and Laos.

The French transported natural resources such as rice, coal, gems, and rubber out of Vietnam. They exported French goods to Vietnam, making the Vietnamese buy them at higher prices than they would have paid for goods made in neighboring countries. The French failed to bring health care and education to the people of Vietnam. Because of irrigation, there was more land to farm, but most farmers could not afford the land. During the first half of the 20th century, 3 percent of landowners in southern Vietnam owned 45 percent of the land. Peasants, who made up 70 percent of the landowners, owned only about 15 percent of the land.

War

Over time, the Vietnamese organized against the French. Some people, especially in northern Vietnam, also looked to China for help. **Ho Chi Minh** (HOH CHEE MIHN), who studied Communism in the Soviet Union and China, became a leader in Vietnam's independence movement.

North and South Vietnam France tried to maintain its rule over Vietnam, but Ho Chi Minh and his government began fighting the French. He received support from the Communist government in China. The United States government, worried that Communism would spread to Vietnam and other parts of the world, sent money and weapons to the French.

In 1954, an agreement was signed that again divided Vietnam into two parts: Communist North Vietnam and U.S.-supported South Vietnam. In South Vietnam, no government was able to rule successfully, and soon the Vietminh began looking for ways to overthrow South Vietnam's government and unite all of Vietnam as a Communist nation.

Place • Ho Chi Minh was president of North Vietnam from 1954 to 1969. ▲

BACKGROUND
The organization that led Vietnam's independence movement was called the Vietminh.

Reading Social Studies
A. Analyzing Motives Why did the Vietnamese want to be independent from France?

Movement • Over 500,000 U.S. troops were in Vietnam in the late 1960s. ▼

Place • Many people in the United States protested the war in Vietnam. ▲

The United States Intervenes Not wanting South Vietnam to fall to Communism, the United States provided it with military support. In 1965, the United States went a step further and began bombing North Vietnam. By 1973, however, opposition to the war by citizens in the United States led to the withdrawal of troops. North Vietnam overwhelmed South Vietnam, and the war ended in 1975. Three million Vietnamese died during the war, and four million were wounded. Bombs and chemical weapons destroyed much of Vietnam, leaving more than half the people homeless. The country reunited in 1976 as the Socialist Republic of Vietnam. Several hundred thousand South Vietnamese fled to the United States and other nations.

Vietnam Divided, 1973

> **GEOGRAPHY SKILLBUILDER:**
> **Interpreting a Map**
> 1. **Movement •** What body of water does the Red River flow into?
> 2. **Location •** Why might the capital city of Hanoi be located where it is?

Southeast Asia Today **451**

Vietnam Today

Vietnam is now a communist nation. People elect representatives to the National Assembly, which then chooses the prime minister. A group called the **Politburo** (PAHL·iht·BYUR·oh) heads the only political party, the Communist Party. The Communist Party and especially the Politburo have a major role in the government.

The Government and the Economy
In a Communist nation, the government owns and runs industries and services. The government makes almost all decisions about the economy. After the Vietnam War, many people lived in poverty, while many educated people left the country. It was a difficult time for the new government. In an effort to improve the economy, the government restricted trade with other nations. Instead, this made the economic situation worse.

In 1986, the government began a policy called *doi moi* (doy moy), or "change for the new." Under *doi moi,* individuals gain more control of some industries. The state still owns the land, but farmers decide how to work it. Businesses can control prices, which rise and fall according to **supply and demand**. The price of a good goes up or down depending on how many people want it and how much of that good is available.

Farming and Industry
Most of the farmland in Vietnam is in the deltas of the Red and Mekong rivers. Almost four-fifths of the farmland is planted with rice, the main staple of the Vietnamese diet. There are also plantations for growing rubber, bananas, coffee, and tea. The most profitable industry in Vietnam is food processing. Seafood is frozen or canned and then exported to nations such as Japan, Germany, and the United States. Also important is silk, which is produced in Vietnam, woven into textiles, and exported around the world.

Place • People live in houseboats on the Saigon River in Ho Chi Minh City. ▲

Opening Doors
Perhaps the biggest boost to the Vietnamese economy occurred when Vietnam opened up trade with the rest of the world. Foreigners started businesses and invested in Vietnam, bringing money and modern technology with them.

In 1994, the United States began trading again with Vietnam. This is when the two nations reopened diplomatic relations. The governments now communicate and work together.

Reading **Social Studies**
B. Recognizing Effects Why might it have taken so long for diplomatic relations between Vietnam and the United States to be reopened?

Culture • During the three days of Tet, people celebrate the New Year. ▲

Living in Vietnam

In the large cities of Vietnam, many people live in apartment buildings. One apartment may house children, their parents, and their grandparents. In the country, families live in stone houses in the north and in houses built of bamboo and wood in the warmer south. Many people do not have electricity or running water, and get their water from wells or creeks.

Along the Mekong River, many people live in houseboats or in houses built on stilts to be safe from floods. In the mountains, people may live in longhouses (long, narrow buildings that hold up to 30 or 40 people). A fireplace in the middle of the house is used for cooking and warmth. A hole in the roof lets out the smoke.

Holidays The most important holiday is **Tet**, the Vietnamese New Year. This three-day festival includes parades, feasts, dances, and family gatherings. Tet marks the beginning of spring. People bring tree buds indoors to blossom. Fireworks light up the skies. Families feast on dried fruit, pickled vegetables, candy, and fish, duck, or meat in rice cakes. To start the New Year, people wear new clothes, pay debts, and settle old arguments. Children may receive gifts of money wrapped in red rice paper.

SECTION 3 ASSESSMENT

Terms & Names
1. Explain the significance of: (a) Ho Chi Minh   (b) Politburo   (c) *doi moi*   (d) supply and demand   (e) Tet

Using Graphics

2. Use a sequence chart like this one to list the main events that led to the reunification of Vietnam in 1976.

   1858: Napoleon III invades Vietnam
   ↓
   ↓
   ↓
   ↓
   1976: Vietnam reunited

Main Ideas

3. (a) Why did Ho Chi Minh want independence from France?
   (b) Why did the United States wage war against North Vietnam?
   (c) How is Vietnam governed today?

Critical Thinking

4. **Contrasting**

   Contrast the effects of Chinese and French rule on Vietnam.

   Think About
   - the contributions of China to the culture of Vietnam
   - the reasons foreign powers wanted to rule Vietnam
   - the response of the Vietnamese to French rule

ACTIVITY -OPTION- How do former enemies learn to get along? Think of a way to encourage good relations between the United States and Vietnam. Share your **idea** with your classmates.

Southeast Asia Today **453**

CHAPTER 15 ASSESSMENT

TERMS & NAMES

Explain the significance of each of the following:
1. mandala
2. military dictatorship
3. East Timor
4. Bahasa Indonesian
5. batik
6. Ho Chi Minh
7. Politburo
8. *doi moi*
9. supply and demand
10. Tet

REVIEW QUESTIONS

History and Governments (pages 437–441)
1. In what ways was the culture of Southeast Asia shaped by other cultures?
2. How did World War II and the end of colonialism affect Southeast Asia?

Economies and Cultures (pages 444–447)
3. How do most of the people in Southeast Asia make a living?
4. In what ways are people in Southeast Asia culturally different from one another?

Vietnam Today (pages 449–453)
5. Why were Ho Chi Minh and the Vietminh trying to overthrow the government of South Vietnam?
6. What two government policies contributed to Vietnam's growing economy?

CRITICAL THINKING

Drawing Conclusions
1. Using your completed chart from Reading Social Studies, p. 436, decide whether or not it is in the best interests of Southeast Asian countries to develop industries that will enable them to increase their international trade. List the facts and examples that support your conclusion.

Clarifying
2. Why do you think Southeast Asian nations were in political turmoil after the colonial powers withdrew?

Forming and Supporting Opinions
3. What personal qualities did Ho Chi Minh need to possess in order to lead Vietnam's independence movement?

Visual Summary

1 History and Governments
- India and China greatly influenced the culture of Southeast Asia.
- When European colonialism ended, Southeast Asian nations established their own governments including constitutional monarchies, republics, military dictatorships, and Communist states.

2 Economies and Cultures
- Most of the people in Southeast Asia make their living by farming, but industry is growing.
- Language, religion, and art in Southeast Asia are a blend of local and foreign influences.

3 Vietnam Today
- Vietnam struggled against France, China, the United States, and itself before being reunited as a single, independent country in 1976.
- Today Vietnam is a Communist nation that encourages world trade, including trade with the United States.

STANDARDS-BASED ASSESSMENT

Use the map and your knowledge of world cultures and geography to answer questions 1 and 2.

Additional Test Practice, pp. S1–S33

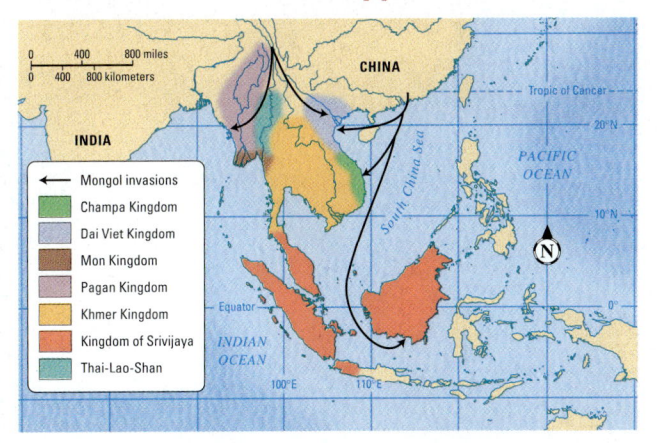

The following statement by former Secretary of State Henry Kissinger summarizes the impact of the Vietnam War. Use the quotation and your knowledge of world cultures and geography to answer question 3.

PRIMARY SOURCE

Vietnam is still with us. It has created doubts about American judgment, about American credibility, and about American power—not only at home, but throughout the world. It has poisoned our domestic debate. So we paid an exorbitant price for the decisions that were made in good faith and for good purpose.

HENRY KISSINGER quoted in *Vietnam: A History* by Stanley Karnow

1. Which of the following phrases best describes the overall direction of the Mongol invasions shown on the map?

   A. east from India
   B. south from China
   C. north from Srivijaya
   D. west from Champa

2. Which of the following kingdoms did the Mongols reach by sea travel?

   A. Khmer
   B. Pagan
   C. Srivijaya
   D. Thai-Lao-Shan

3. According to Kissinger, what was the long-term effect of the Vietnam War?

   A. As time passed, people began to see the war as a noble, successful effort.
   B. He came to believe the decision to fight in Vietnam was made from bad motives.
   C. The war made people in other countries feel more positively about American power.
   D. The war created negative feelings about America both at home and abroad.

TEST PRACTICE CLASSZONE.COM

ALTERNATIVE ASSESSMENT

1. WRITING ABOUT HISTORY

The most important holiday in Vietnam is Tet. Research what a Vietnamese family would do to celebrate this three-day festival. How would they prepare? What would they eat and wear? What activities would they participate in? What rules would they follow? Write a report on your findings and share it with the class.

2. COOPERATIVE LEARNING

In a group of three to five classmates, create a television or radio newscast about a significant event described in the chapter. For example, you might focus on the withdrawal of Europeans from Southeast Asia, the invasion of East Timor by Indonesia, or the Vietnam War. After deciding on a topic, divide the tasks of researching the information and assuming the roles of director, writers, and anchor. Work on a rough draft of the report and practice delivering the broadcast. Then perform the final version for the class.

INTEGRATED TECHNOLOGY

Doing Internet Research

Use the Internet to research education in Southeast Asia. Write a report about your findings. List the Web sites you used to prepare your report.

- Choose one country and find out as much information as you can about how children are educated, how many years they go to school, and what it's like to be a student in that country.
- Include photographs or drawings to illustrate your information.

For Internet links to support this activity, go to

RESEARCH LINKS CLASSZONE.COM

UNIT 6

Place The Great Wall of China stretches for thousands of miles. Built to defend China from foreign invaders, the Great Wall was constructed in stages from the 7th century B.C. to the 15th century A.D.

EAST ASIA, AUSTRALIA, OCEANIA, AND ANTARCTICA

Chapter 16 East Asia, Australia, and Oceania: Land and History

Chapter 17 China and Its Neighbors

Chapter 18 Australia, New Zealand, Oceania, and Antarctica

INTEGRATED TECHNOLOGY

eEdition
- Interactive Maps
- Interactive Visuals

VIDEO
Japan: Shuntsuke in Japan

INTERNET RESOURCES
Go to **classzone.com** for:
- Research Links
- Internet Activities
- Data Updates
- Unit Quiz
- Maps
- Test Practice
- Current Events
- Web Research Guide

457

UNIT 6 Atlas: Physical Geography

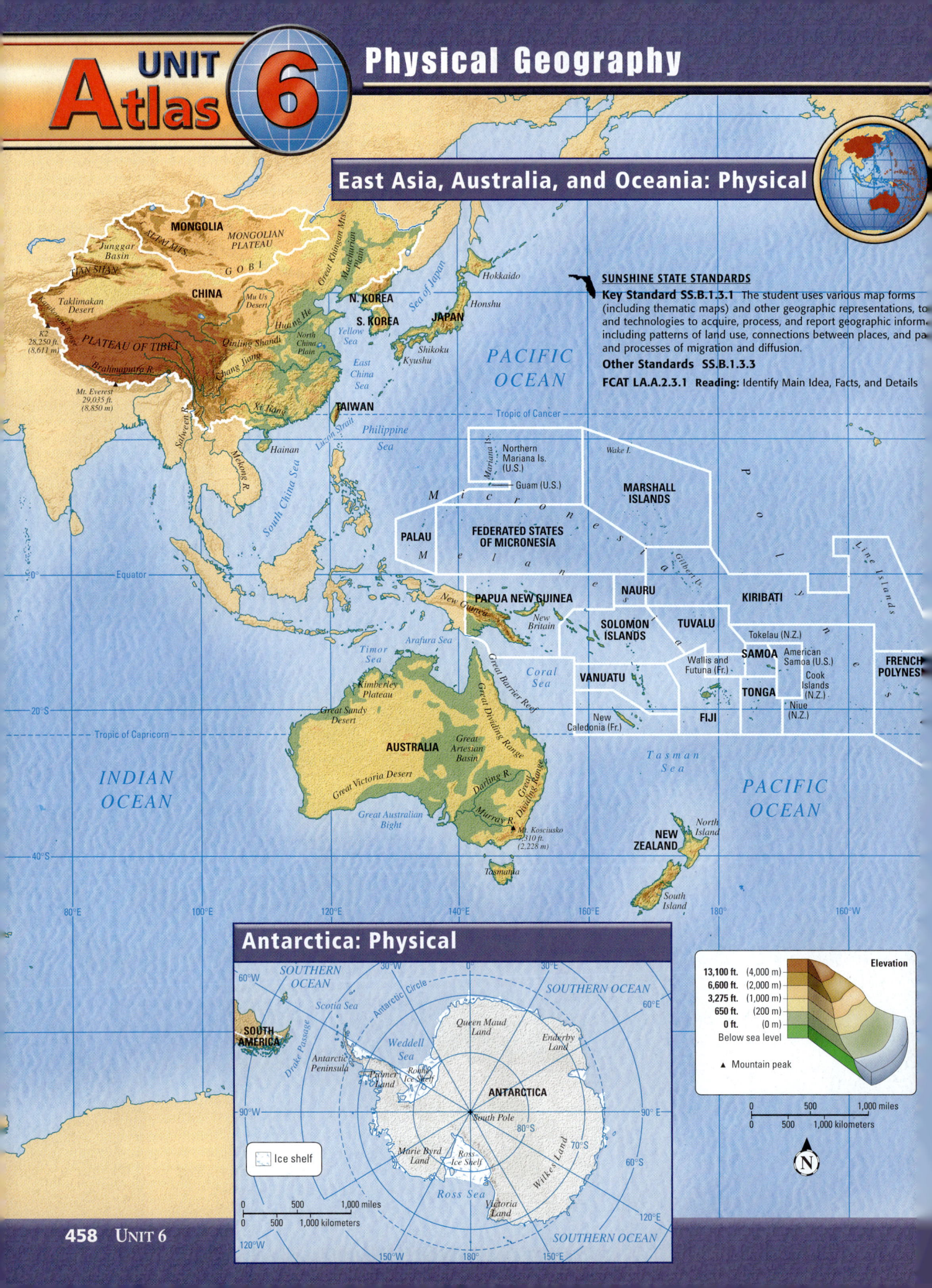

East Asia, Australia, and Oceania: Physical

SUNSHINE STATE STANDARDS
Key Standard SS.B.1.3.1 The student uses various map forms (including thematic maps) and other geographic representations, to and technologies to acquire, process, and report geographic inform including patterns of land use, connections between places, and pa and processes of migration and diffusion.
Other Standards SS.B.1.3.3
FCAT LA.A.2.3.1 Reading: Identify Main Idea, Facts, and Details

Antarctica: Physical

Elevation
- 13,100 ft. (4,000 m)
- 6,600 ft. (2,000 m)
- 3,275 ft. (1,000 m)
- 650 ft. (200 m)
- 0 ft. (0 m)
- Below sea level
- ▲ Mountain peak

Ice shelf

East Asia, Australia, Oceania, and Antarctica

Vegetation of East Asia, Australia, and Oceania

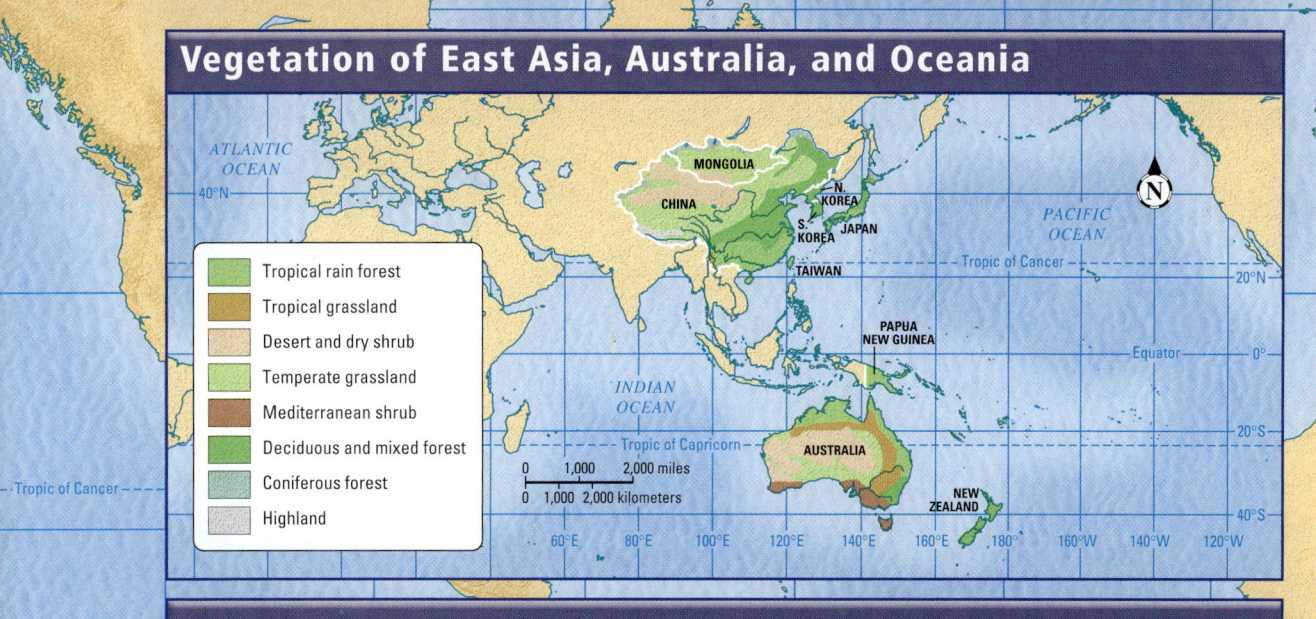

Legend:
- Tropical rain forest
- Tropical grassland
- Desert and dry shrub
- Temperate grassland
- Mediterranean shrub
- Deciduous and mixed forest
- Coniferous forest
- Highland

East Asia, Australia, and Oceania–United States Landmass and Population

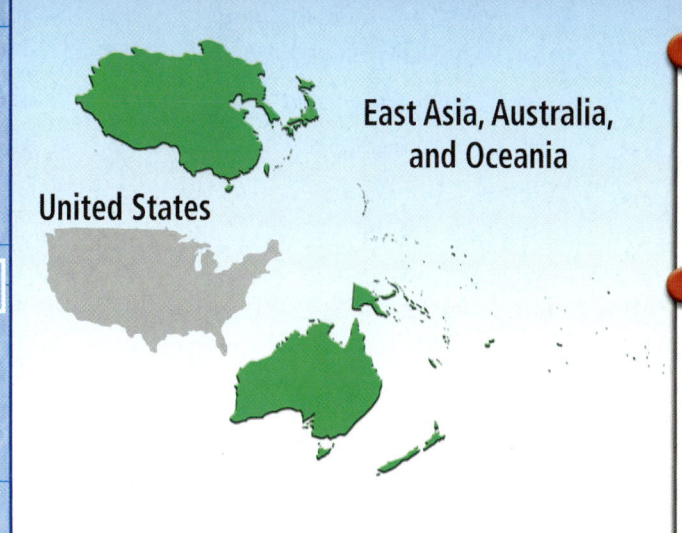

LANDMASS
- East Asia, Australia, and Oceania: 7,837,975 square miles
- Continental United States: 3,165,630 square miles

POPULATION
- East Asia, Australia, and Oceania: 1,515,889,363
- United States: 281,421,906
- ♦ = 50,000,000

Fast Facts

- **HIGHEST MOUNTAIN IN THE WORLD:** Mt. Everest, 29,035 ft.
- **LONGEST RIVER:** Chang Jiang, 3,915 mi.
- **WORLD'S GREATEST VOLCANIC ERUPTION:** Taupo Volcano, New Zealand, around A.D. 130; 33 billion tons of debris from the eruption covered 20,000 sq. mi.
- **ONLY IN AUSTRALIA:** Kangaroos, koalas, and platypuses are found in the wild only in Australia.

GEOGRAPHY SKILLBUILDER: Interpreting Maps and Visuals
1. **Location** • Name three rivers in East Asia.
2. **Place** • Which country in the region has tropical grassland?

Unit 6 Atlas

Human Geography

East Asia, Australia, and Oceania: Political

- ★ National capital
- • Other city

Antarctica: Political

East Asia, Australia, Oceania, and Antarctica

The International Date Line

Religions of East Asia, Australia, and Oceania

Legend:
- Protestant
- Muslim (Sunni)
- Shinto
- Buddhist
- Confucian
- Hindu
- Other

FAST FACTS

✓ **LARGEST POPULATION IN THE WORLD:**
China, 1,273,111,000 (2001 estimate)

✓ **SPARSEST POPULATION IN THE WORLD:**
Mongolia, 4.4 people per sq. mi.

✓ **LARGEST CITY IN THE WORLD:**
Tokyo, 26,444,000 (2000)

GEOGRAPHY SKILLBUILDER: Interpreting Maps and Visuals

1. **Place** • Which country in this region has no coast?
2. **Location** • Name an island in this region that is on the other side of the International Date Line from Vanuatu.

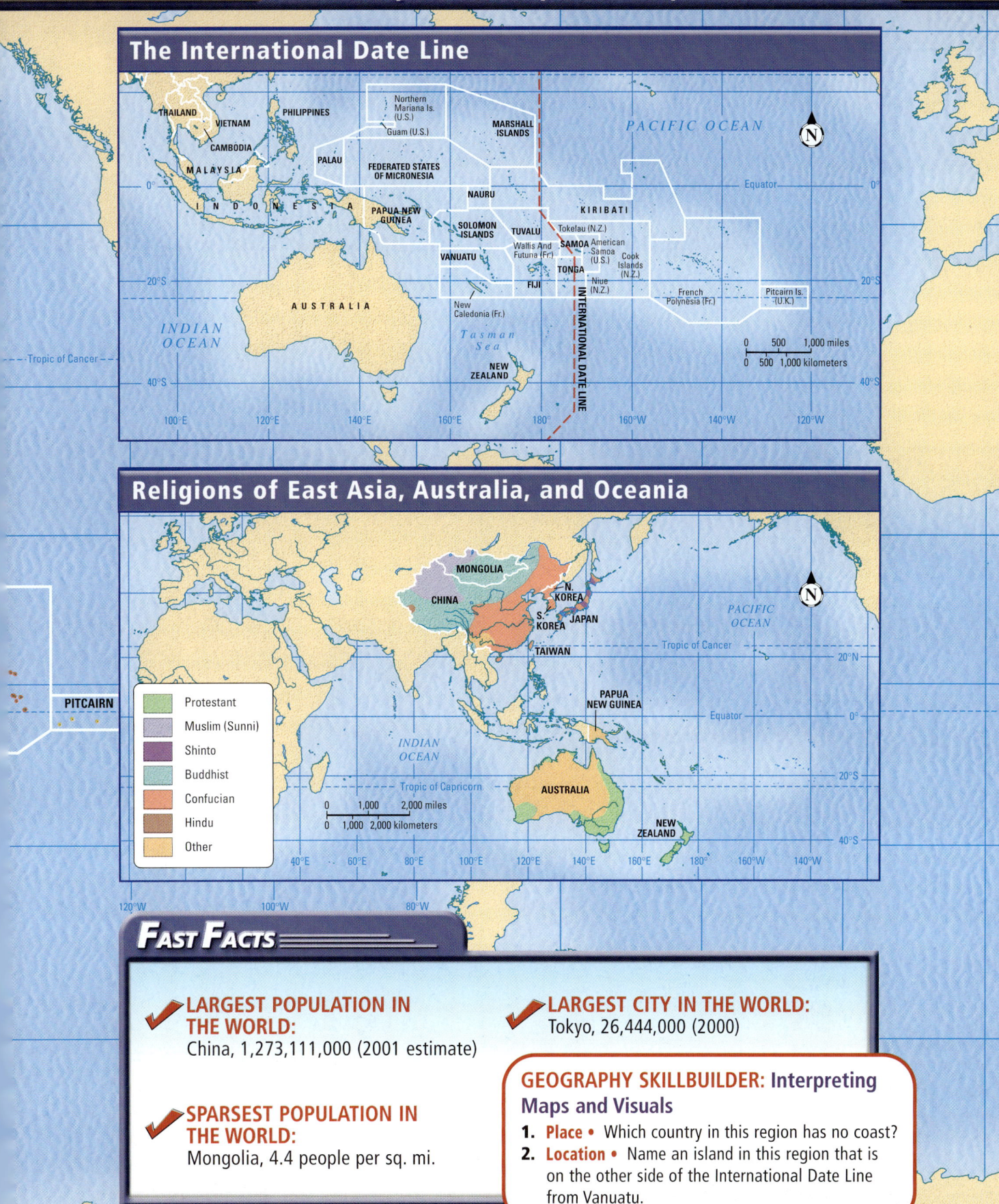

Unit Atlas 6 Data File

For updates on these statistics, go to **DATA UPDATE** CLASSZONE.COM

Country Flag	Country/Capital	Currency	Population (2001 estimate)	Life Expectancy (years)	Birthrate (per 1,000 pop.) (2000 estimate)
	Australia Canberra	Australian Dollar	19,358,000	79	13
	China Beijing	Renminbi	1,273,111,000	71	15
	Fiji Suva	Dollar	844,000	67	22
	Japan Tokyo	Yen	126,772,000	80	9
	Kiribati Tawara	Australian Dollar	94,000	62	33
	Marshall Islands Majuro	U.S. Dollar	71,000	65	26
	Micronesia, Fed. States of Palikir	U.S. Dollar	135,000	66	33
	Mongolia Ulaanbaatar	Tugrik	2,655,000	63	20
	Nauru Yaren Administrative Center	Australian Dollar	12,000	61	19
	New Zealand Wellington	New Zealand Dollar	3,864,000	77	15
	North Korea Pyongyang	Won	21,968,000	70	21
	Palau Koror	U.S. Dollar	19,000	67	18
	Papua New Guinea Port Moresby	Kina	5,049,000	56	34
	Samoa Apia	Tala	179,000	68	31
	Solomon Islands Honiara	Dollar	480,000	71	37
	South Korea Seoul	Won	47,904,000	74	14
	Taiwan Taipei	New Taiwan Dollar	22,370,000	75	13

East Asia, Australia, Oceania, and Antarctica

DATA FILE

Infant Mortality (per 1,000 live births) (2000)	Doctors (per 100,000 pop.) (1994–1999)	Literacy Rate (percentage) (1996–1998)	Passenger Cars (per 1,000 pop.) (1996–1997)	Total Area (square miles)	Map (not to scale)
5.3	240.0	100	453	2,967,909	
31.4	161.7	82	4	3,704,427	
12.9	48.0	92	37	7,055	
3.5	193.2	99	367	143,619	
62.0	30.0	90	N/A	277	
30.5	42.0	93	N/A	70	
46.0	57.0	90	N/A	1,055	
34.1	243.3	83	8	604,247	
25.0	157.0	99	N/A	8.2	
5.5	217.0	100	391	103,736	
26.0	297.0	99	N/A	46,609	
19.2	110.0	98	N/A	191	
77.0	7.0	72	5	178,260	
25.0	34.0	98	7	1,209	
25.3	14.0	54	N/A	11,500	
11.0	136.1	98	2	38,022	
6.6	100.0	94	198	13,887	

Atlas 463

Unit Atlas 6 Data File

For updates on these statistics, go to
DATA UPDATE CLASSZONE.COM

Country Flag	Country/Capital	Currency	Population (2000 estimate)	Life Expectancy (years)	Birthrate (per 1,000 pop.) (2000 estimate)
	Tonga Nuku'alofa	Pa'anga	104,000	71	27
	Tuvalu Fongafale	Australian Dollar	11,000	64	22
	Vanuatu Port-Vila	Vatu	193,000	65	35
	United States Washington, D.C.	Dollar	281,422,000	77	15

An Aborigine artist ▼

Easter Island stone heads ▼

Science station in Antarctica ▼

East Asia, Australia, Oceania, and Antarctica

DATA FILE

Infant Mortality (per 1,000 live births) (2000)	Doctors (per 100,000 pop.) (1994–1999)	Literacy Rate (percentage) (1996–1998)	Passenger Cars (per 1,000 pop.) (1996–1997)	Total Area (square miles)	Map (not to scale)
19.0	44	93	31	270	
24.8	30	95	N/A	9	
39.0	12	36	21	5,700	
7.0	251	97	489	3,787,319	

GEOGRAPHY SKILLBUILDER: Interpreting a Chart
1. **Place** • How much lower is Vanuatu's literacy rate than New Zealand's?
2. **Place** • How much larger is Australia's population than Kiribati's?

Terraced rice fields in China ▼

A Chinese family ▼

A Shinto archway in Japan ▲

Atlas 465

CHAPTER 16

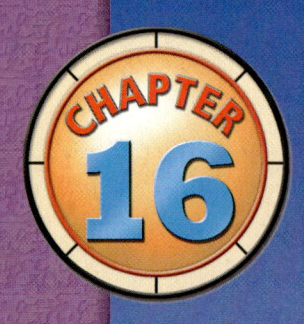

East Asia, Australia, and Oceania: Land and History

SECTION 1 Physical Geography
SECTION 2 Ancient China
SECTION 3 Ancient Japan

Place Mount Uluru, also called Ayers Rock, stands out against the flat desert of Australia's Red Center, the vast interior part of Australia. Uluru is the largest single rock in the world.

FOCUS ON GEOGRAPHY

Does land area have any influence on population?

Place • With more than 1.2 billion people in 2000, China (shown above) has the largest population in the world. It is also larger in area than most countries, with 3.6 million square miles of land.

Australia, on the other hand, is home to 19 million—a population that is 63 times smaller than China's. However, Australia's land area, at 2.9 million square miles, is only slightly smaller than China's. In effect, the two countries are similar in land area, but their population sizes are dramatically different.

What do you think?

- If a country is large in size, will it necessarily have a large population? What other factors contribute to population size? Think about natural resources, social conditions, and climate.

- How do the physical features of a country affect where people can or will live? Does harsh physical geography in some parts of a country affect the overall population, or just the population density?

CHAPTER 16 READING SOCIAL STUDIES

BEFORE YOU READ

▶▶ What Do You Know?

Before you read the chapter, consider what you already know about East Asia, Australia, and Oceania. What are the geographic features of these areas? Have you seen a television program about the Ring of Fire or about Australia's Outback? You may have learned about ancient China and ancient Japan in other classes. Do you know who Confucius was or who the Japanese samurai warriors were? Do you know anyone who has visited the Great Wall of China, which is the world's longest wall?

▶▶ What Do You Want to Know?

Decide what else you want to know about East Asia, Australia, and Oceania. In your notebook, record what you hope to learn from this chapter.

Place • China's emperors lived in the Forbidden City, which still stands in the capital, Beijing. ▲

READ AND TAKE NOTES

Reading Strategy: Comparing and Contrasting
Comparing and contrasting places helps you understand more about each one. Comparing means looking for similarities, while contrasting means looking for differences. Making a comparing and contrasting chart for the countries in this chapter will help you better understand them.

- Copy the chart into your notebook.
- As you read the chapter, look for information about the geography and civilizations of ancient China and ancient Japan.
- Record key details under the appropriate headings in the chart.

Culture • Japanese warriors called samurai wore intricate suits of armor. ◀

	Ancient China	Ancient Japan
Geography		
Government		
Religion/Philosophy		
Discoveries/Inventions		
Trade/International Relations		

SECTION 1

Physical Geography

TERMS & NAMES
Mount Everest
Mount Fuji
Ring of Fire
typhoon
outback
Great Barrier Reef

MAIN IDEA
The physical features of East Asia, Australia, and Oceania are the result of different geological processes.

WHY IT MATTERS NOW
Understanding these countries' physical features helps us to understand their political and economic roles in the world.

DATELINE

YOKOHAMA, JAPAN, SEPTEMBER 1, 1923—Today, as thousands of people in Tokyo and in Yokohama were preparing to have lunch, a powerful earthquake struck. Walls bulged and buildings lurched as though made of cardboard.

Hundreds of thousands of houses completely collapsed, trapping unknown numbers of victims. The ground heaved and tossed, and in one area the earth was lifted 24 feet high. The massive uplifting of the ground caused thousands of landslides.

Some of the worst damage was caused by the fires that followed the quake. When the tremors began, people were cooking on stoves. Within minutes, kitchen fires sprang up throughout the cities. Many people who survived the quake died in the fires. As night falls, the entire city of Tokyo is in flames.

Human-Environment Interaction • It will take many people a long time to clean up the wreckage from the earthquake. ▲

The Lands of the Region

Japan is one among many countries in the region of East Asia, Australia, and Oceania, which you can see on page 460 of the Unit Atlas. East Asia includes China, Japan, North Korea, South Korea, Mongolia, and Taiwan. Australia is an island, a nation, and a continent all its own, with New Zealand as a nearby neighbor. The thousands of islands in Oceania are grouped into three subregions—Melanesia, Micronesia, and Polynesia.

TAKING NOTES
Use your chart to take notes about East Asia, Australia, and Oceania.

	Ancient China	Ancient Japan
Geography		
Government		

SUNSHINE STATE STANDARDS
Key Standard SS.B.2.3.2 The student knows the human and physical characteristics of different places in the world and how these characteristics change over time.
FCAT LA.A.2.3.1 Reading: Identify Main Idea, Facts, and Details

East Asia, Australia, and Oceania: Land and History **469**

China

Look at the map below. Notice that the geography within China's boundaries varies greatly. Over much of China's area, mountains rise to great heights. Rivers and plains cover the eastern part of China. To the southwest, the land rises to high plateaus, and to the northwest, it stretches out in long, dry deserts.

Region • The Himalayas loom in the distance beyond this family. ▲

China's Mountains
Look again at the map. You can see that China's highest mountains are in the west. The Himalayas run along China's southwestern border, dividing China from Nepal. The highest peak in the Himalayas—and in the world—is **Mount Everest**, at 29,035 feet. Notice also the Plateau of Tibet. It spreads across one-fourth of China's land and is the highest plateau on Earth, earning it the nickname "roof of the world."

China's Great Rivers
China's three great rivers are the Huang He (hwahng huh), the Chang Jiang (chahng jyahng), and the Xi Jiang (shee jyahng). They all start in the highlands and flow east. The southernmost is the Xi Jiang, as you can see on the map.

BACKGROUND
The Chang Jiang is known in the West as the Yangtze (yang•see).

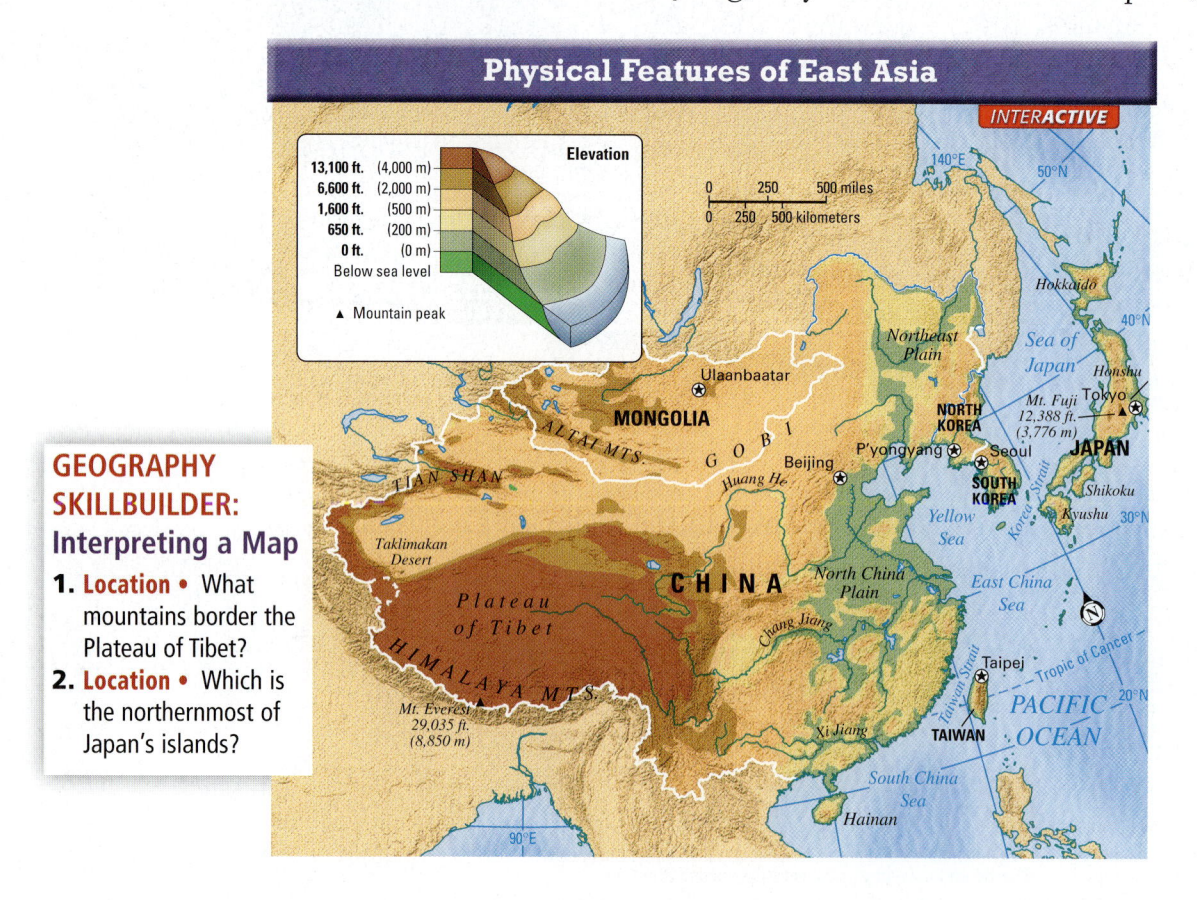

Physical Features of East Asia

GEOGRAPHY SKILLBUILDER:
Interpreting a Map
1. **Location •** What mountains border the Plateau of Tibet?
2. **Location •** Which is the northernmost of Japan's islands?

470 CHAPTER 16

North of it, the Chang Jiang winds across China. At over 3,400 miles, this is China's longest river.

The northernmost river is the Huang He, or Yellow River. Its name comes from the color of the fine silt that covers the plains along parts of the river. You can see that the Huang He begins in the Plateau of Tibet. On its course east through the North China Plain, it often overflows. Because of the thousands of lives lost in its floods, the Chinese often call the river "China's Sorrow."

Vocabulary
silt: windblown material similar to clay

China's Deserts Two large deserts span China's northern lands. You can see on the map that the Taklimakan (TAH·kluh·muh·KAHN) covers northwestern China. With an east-west length of about 600 miles, it is one of the world's largest sandy deserts. During the spring, dust storms with the strength of hurricanes occur frequently, lifting the desert's dust as high as 13,000 feet in the air.

East of the Taklimakan, in central northern China, sprawls the Gobi (GOH·bee). In Mongolian, *gobi* means "waterless place." The Gobi's dryness is harsh, and so are its temperatures. In the summer, the Gobi's temperature can rise to 113°F. In the winter, it may get down to -40°F.

Japan

Japan is a country of islands that stretch for 1,500 miles across the Pacific Ocean. Look at the map on page 458 to see the four main islands—Hokkaido (hah·KY·doh), Honshu (HAHN·shoo), Shikoku (shee·KAW·koo), and Kyushu (kee·OO·shoo). Honshu is the largest, as well as the home of Japan's capital, Tokyo.

Japan sits atop two tectonic plates that often sink below a third plate. Because of this, Japan is more likely to have volcanic eruptions and earthquakes than are many places on Earth.

Place •
Much of the Gobi is made of rock rather than sand. ▲

Reading Social Studies
A. Drawing Conclusions Why do you think the Japanese built Tokyo where they did?

Mountains and Volcanoes Mountains cover more than 80 percent of Japan's land. Instead of forming ranges, these mountains are blocks separated by lowlands. This formation results from faults, or cracks in the rock, that cause the land either to lift up into a mountain or to drop down into lowlands. The largest stretch of lowlands is the Kanto Plain, where Tokyo lies.

East Asia, Australia, and Oceania: Land and History

Japan's tallest mountain, **Mount Fuji,** is an active volcano. Volcanic eruptions are common in Japan, which is part of the **Ring of Fire**—an area of volcanic activity along the borders of the Pacific Ocean. This is where most of the world's earthquakes and volcanoes occur.

Earthquakes Japan records as many as 1,500 minor earthquakes each year. In 1923, a major earthquake hit Tokyo and its surrounding regions, which you read about on page 469. After 1923, Japan became a world leader in constructing buildings able to withstand the shock of frequent earthquakes.

Human-Environment Interaction • More than 100,000 people a year climb Mount Fuji, which is considered sacred in Japan. ▲

Climate Japan's climate is largely controlled by monsoons. In the winter, the monsoons bring cold rain and snow to Japan's western coast. In the summer, they bring warm rains to the south and east. During the summer and early fall, storms called typhoons also occur often. A **typhoon** is a hurricane that occurs in the western Pacific.

BACKGROUND
Even with their top-notch construction, more than 100,000 buildings were destroyed in 1995 by another major earthquake in Kobe (KOH•BEE).

The Koreas

North and South Korea lie on the mountainous Korean Peninsula, which you can see on the map on page 470. North Korea is a land filled with mountains and valleys. Its major rivers, the Yalu and Tumen, mark the border with China. Its climate is temperate, with cold, dry winters and hot, humid summers.

The Ring of Fire

GEOGRAPHY SKILLBUILDER: Interpreting a Map
1. **Location** • Which continents border the Ring of Fire?
2. **Place** • Is Mount Fuji the only volcano in Japan?

472 CHAPTER 16

Most of the rain each year falls between June and September, brought on by the monsoons of the Pacific. South Korea is a mix of rugged mountain ranges, coastal plains, and river valleys. Its main rivers are the Han, the Kum, and the Naktong.

Australia

Australia is one of the largest countries on Earth, though it is the smallest continent. Its landscape is unique in that it has not changed dramatically for more than 250 million years. In other continents, such as Europe and North America, major landscape changes have occurred even in just the past 25,000 years.

Flat and Dry Australia

Look at the map below. Notice the Great Dividing Range that runs along Australia's eastern coast. This chain is the largest in Australia, but none of these mountains rise higher than 5,000 feet. To their west, vast plains extend across most of Australia. Australians call this huge stretch of interior land the **outback.**

Australia is the flattest continent on Earth, and it is also extremely dry. Deserts cover one-third of the country. The majority of people live along the northern and eastern coasts, where much of Australia's fresh water is found.

Reading Social Studies

B. Contrasting Contrast the influence of physical features on settlement patterns in Japan and Australia.

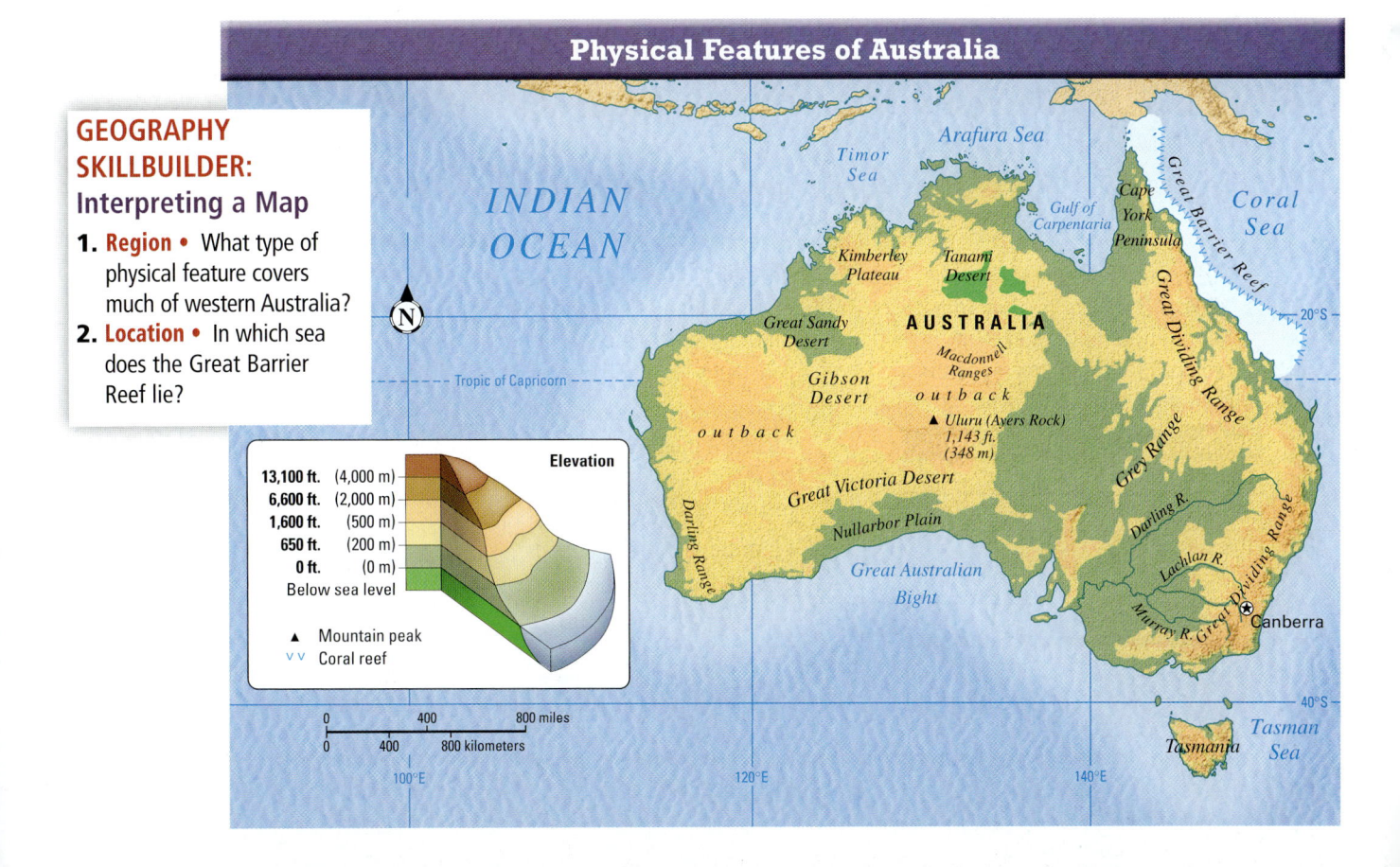

Place• Australia is home to many animals that are native only to that continent, such as the kangaroo. ▲

Physical Features of Australia

GEOGRAPHY SKILLBUILDER: Interpreting a Map
1. **Region** • What type of physical feature covers much of western Australia?
2. **Location** • In which sea does the Great Barrier Reef lie?

The Great Barrier Reef Off Australia's northeastern coast stretches the world's largest coral reef system, called the <u>Great Barrier Reef</u>. Made of more than 2,500 individual reefs and islands, the Great Barrier Reef extends 1,250 miles through the Pacific Ocean. Some of the reefs, called fringing reefs, run along coastlines. Others exist as far as 100 miles from shore. Over 400 species of coral and other ocean life call the reef home.

New Zealand and Other Pacific Islands

Thousands of islands dot the Pacific to the north and east of Australia. On the map on page 458 of the Unit Atlas, you can see that New Zealand's two main islands, which sit about 1,000 miles east of Australia, are among the largest. Most of the others are tiny in comparison.

The roughly 20,000 islands of Oceania are of three types: continental islands, high oceanic islands, and low oceanic islands. Continental islands, such as New Guinea (GIHN·ee) and New Zealand, are parts of Earth's crust that sit above the surface of the water. They often have active volcanoes, even though they were not formed by volcanic activity. High oceanic islands, such as Tahiti (tuh·HEE·tee), are mountainous islands formed by volcanic activity. Most of the islands of Oceania are low oceanic islands, which formed from coral reefs.

SECTION 1 ASSESSMENT

Terms & Names
1. Explain the significance of:
   (a) Mount Everest
   (b) Mount Fuji
   (c) Ring of Fire
   (d) typhoon
   (e) outback
   (f) Great Barrier Reef

Using Graphics

2. Make a chart like this one to note the physical features in each region. You can list more features than the ones shown here.

Region	Rivers	Deserts
China		
Japan		
The Koreas		
Australia		
Oceania		

Main Ideas

3. (a) How is Japan affected by the three tectonic plates on which its islands rest?
   (b) Why are some regions of Australia much more suitable for living than others? Which regions are suitable?
   (c) What three types of islands exist in the Pacific?

Critical Thinking

4. **Drawing Conclusions**
   Considering China's geographic features, which areas do you think have large populations? Which have small populations?

Think About
- physical features that encourage population settlement
- physical features that would be hard to live in or near

ACTIVITY -OPTION- Make a **diagram** that shows how high oceanic islands and low oceanic islands form.

SECTION 2

Ancient China

TERMS & NAMES
dynasty
Genghis Khan
Kublai Khan
Confucius
bureaucracy
Taoism
Lao Tzu

MAIN IDEA
The ancient Chinese developed a civilization that has lasted longer than any other on Earth.

WHY IT MATTERS NOW
China's very long and relatively stable existence has helped it to become one of the most powerful countries in the world.

DATELINE

THE IMPERIAL PALACE, CHINA, 2700 B.C.—Our 14-year-old Empress Si Ling-chi has made an amazing discovery. While walking in the palace gardens, she noticed that caterpillars, which just a few days before were eating mulberry tree leaves, had spun themselves into cocoons. These cocoons hung from branches, within easy reach of our empress, who plucked one and took it home to examine. When she dropped it into boiling water, it unraveled into a tangle of threads.

The empress immediately sent her maids to gather more cocoons. Soon she had enough thread for weaving, and she produced a shining fabric she called silk. Plans are now underway to begin manufacturing huge quantities of this wondrous fabric.

Human-Environment Interaction • Many Chinese women will work to twist the thin silk strands together to make thread thick enough for weaving. ▲

Foundations of Chinese Civilization

Silk is just one of the many inventions for which the ancient Chinese are known. Over the course of thousands of years, the Chinese have built the longest-lasting culture in the world.

As early as 5000 B.C., Chinese people lived in the fertile river valley of the Huang He. Sometime in the 1700s B.C., their lives changed drastically when invaders, called the Shang (shahng), entered their valley. These invaders established China's first permanent, organized civilization.

SUNSHINE STATE STANDARDS
Key Standard SS.A.2.3.8 The student knows the political, social, and economic institutions that characterized the significant aspects of Eastern and Western civilizations.
Other Standards SS.A.2.3.1, A.2.3.3
FCAT LA.A.2.3.1 Reading: Identify Main Idea, Facts, and Details

TAKING NOTES
Use your chart to take notes about East Asia, Australia, and Oceania.

	Ancient China	Ancient Japan
Geography		
Government		

East Asia, Australia, and Oceania: Land and History 475

For most of China's history since the Shang takeover, the country was ruled by **dynasties**, or families of rulers. Dynasties rose and fell in succession—some lasting only 15 years, others continuing for hundreds of years. Look at the chart to the right to learn the names and dates of each dynasty.

The Dynasties of China	
Dynasty	Dates
Shang	1700s–1122 B.C.
Zhou	1122–221 B.C.
Qin	221–206 B.C.
Han	206 B.C.–A.D. 220
Sui	A.D. 581–618
Tang	A.D. 618–907
Song	A.D. 960–1279
Yuan	A.D. 1279–1368
Ming	A.D. 1368–1644
Qing	A.D. 1644–1911

SKILLBUILDER: Interpreting a Chart
1. Which dynasty ruled China in A.D. 1?
2. Which was the last dynasty to rule China?

Mongol Rule In the A.D. 1200s, China's greatest fear came to pass—foreign invaders conquered China. In 1211, the Mongols invaded China. They were led by **Genghis Khan** and later by his grandson **Kublai Khan**. In 1279, Kublai Khan conquered China's Song (sung) Dynasty. In its place, he founded the Yuan Dynasty. He also established a capital at Ta-tu.

The Ming Dynasty Warfare eventually broke out among the Mongol leaders, weakening the Yuan Dynasty significantly. The dynasty that took over was called the Ming. Because of his great military success, Ming founder Zhu Yuanzhang (joo yoo•ahn•jang) was called the Hongwu emperor—meaning "vast military power." In his battles, he won from the Mongols the Yunnan province. With this piece of land in his charge, he unified the region that is China today.

Reading Social Studies
A. Making Inferences How might life in China have changed when foreigners took over?

Strange but TRUE

The Tomb of Shih Huang-ti In 1974, farmers near Xi'an (shee•ahn) made a spectacular discovery. While digging a new well, their shovels hit some broken bits of pottery. Digging deeper, they found not water but a headless clay body. What they had uncovered was the tomb of China's Qin emperor Shih Huang-ti (sheer•hwahng•dee)—filled with an army of about 8,000 life-sized clay soldiers and horses (shown at right).

The foot soldiers, charioteers, and archers were buried 22 centuries ago to guard the emperor in death just as his real soldiers had in life. Although the soldiers' heads and bodies are all similar, their eyes, ears, noses, lips, and hairstyles vary. Among the 8,000 soldiers, no two faces are the same.

When the Hongwu emperor died, one of his grandsons took power, naming himself the Yongle emperor—meaning "eternal contentment." He is famous for rebuilding the Yuan capital, which he renamed Beijing (bay·jihng). He ordered a huge palace complex to be constructed in the capital. This was called the Forbidden City because only the emperor, his family, and some of his officials could enter it.

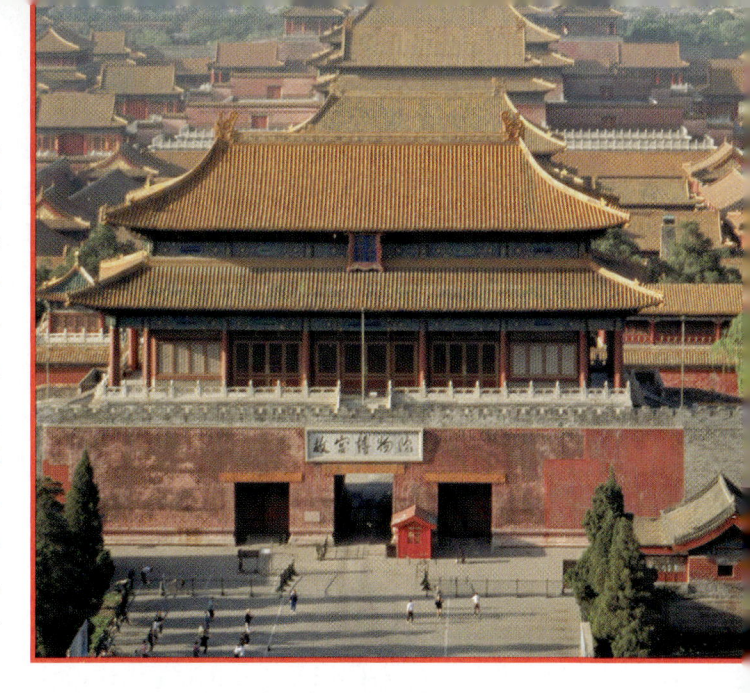

The Ming Dynasty came to an end in 1644 at the hands of invaders from northeastern China, called the Manchu (MAN·choo). These attackers established China's last dynasty, the Qing (chihng), which ruled China until 1911.

Location •
The Forbidden City is the largest complex of buildings of its age in the world. ▲

Religion and Philosophy

China's dynasties are known for particular achievements—some military, some artistic, some technological, and some spiritual. Several of the world's most influential philosophies and religions arose during the thousands of years of Chinese history.

Confucianism Toward the end of the Zhou Dynasty, a man named Kongfuzi—later called **Confucius** (kuhn·FYOO·shuhs) by Europeans—developed a new philosophy. Confucius taught the importance of moral character and of individuals taking responsibility for the state of their society. He also taught that a ruler, like a good father, should take care of his people and be kind to them.

> **A VOICE FROM CHINA**
>
> If you are personally upright, things get done without any orders being given. If you are not personally upright, no one will obey even if you do give orders.
>
> *Confucius*

Reading Social Studies

B. Forming and Supporting Opinions What do you think of Confucius' opinion of how a successful ruler should behave?

The teachings of Confucius were not widely known during his lifetime. Only after his death did his students succeed in spreading his philosophy.

East Asia, Australia, and Oceania: Land and History

The Impact of Confucianism In 121 B.C., the Han emperor Wudi established Confucianism as the official philosophy guiding the Chinese bureaucracy. **Bureaucracy** is the administration of a government through departments, called bureaus. The appointed officials that staff the bureaus are called bureaucrats. The Han called their bureaucracy the civil service and staffed it with scholars of Confucianism. The civil service gave the government capable officials and contributed to the stability of the culture.

Vocabulary
scholar: specialist in a given subject

Taoism The Zhou period also gave rise to **Taoism** (DOW·IHZ·uhm). This philosophy was developed in the 500s B.C. by **Lao Tzu** (low dzuh), who wrote the main Taoist book—the *Tao-te Ching* (DOW· duh JIHNG). Lao Tzu described a force that guides the universe, though it cannot be seen or named. He called this force the *Tao*, which means "way of nature." The greatest achievement for any person, in Taoist belief, is to find harmony with the Tao and, therefore, with nature.

Buddhism in China During the A.D. 200s, while the Han Dynasty was beginning to collapse, Buddhism made its way to China through traders from India and other areas in Asia. During the Tang Dynasty, Buddhist teachings of how to escape suffering appealed to many Chinese. However, Buddhism did not replace Confucianism or Taoism in China. The Chinese belief system today includes elements of all three philosophies.

Culture •
This statue shows Taoism's founder, Lao Tzu. ▲

Connections to Technology

Gunpowder One Chinese invention had an explosive impact on the world—gunpowder. The Chinese had invented the first gunpowder, called black powder, by A.D. 1000. They used it originally not in guns (which were invented in Southwest Asia in the 1300s), but in fireworks used in warfare.

By the 1300s, people in the West were using gunpowder to power weapons, such as guns and the medieval Belgian cannon shown below. By the 1600s, Europeans also began using it for more peaceful tasks like mining and road construction.

Achievements of the Dynasties

China has also given the world some important inventions. Around 2700 B.C., the Chinese invented silk cloth and a new system of writing. In the first two centuries A.D., the Chinese invented paper and a type of pottery called porcelain. In the A.D. 1200s, Chinese navigators began using the compass. These inventions helped shape the civilizations of Asia and, through trade, Europe.

Silk The ancient Chinese were able to keep the secret of how to manufacture silk from foreigners for centuries, although others did eventually learn the Chinese method.

As long as no one else understood the process, however, China earned all the profits of the silk trade. Caravans carried the precious fabric for thousands of miles to cities in Europe and Southwest Asia, along a trade route named for the fabric—the Silk Road.

Movement •
Porcelain was an important trade item that the Chinese carried along the Silk Road. ▼

The Silk Road The first records of travel and trade along the Silk Road date to the Han Dynasty, around 114 B.C. On the map below, you can see the route of the 4,000-mile long Silk Road. Along it, the Chinese carried not only silk but also much-desired items such as porcelain, tea, incense, and spices. Travelers on the Silk Road faced many natural hazards—extreme heat, lack of water, sandstorms in the desert, and blizzards and altitude sickness in the mountains. Also, robbers lurked on the trade routes. Nevertheless, the Silk Road stayed in use until sea routes to Asia proved safer and until the Ming Dynasty decided to limit foreign trade.

Reading Social Studies
C. Clarifying If the Silk Road was so dangerous, why did the Chinese continue to use it?

Porcelain People often refer to fine pottery as china. The term actually refers to porcelain, a delicate but strong type of ceramic that the Chinese made from a kind of clay called kaolin (KAY•uh•lihn). When fired in a kiln, the clay changes into a hard, glassy substance. As with silk, the Chinese kept the method for producing porcelain secret for many years after its invention during the Tang Dynasty.

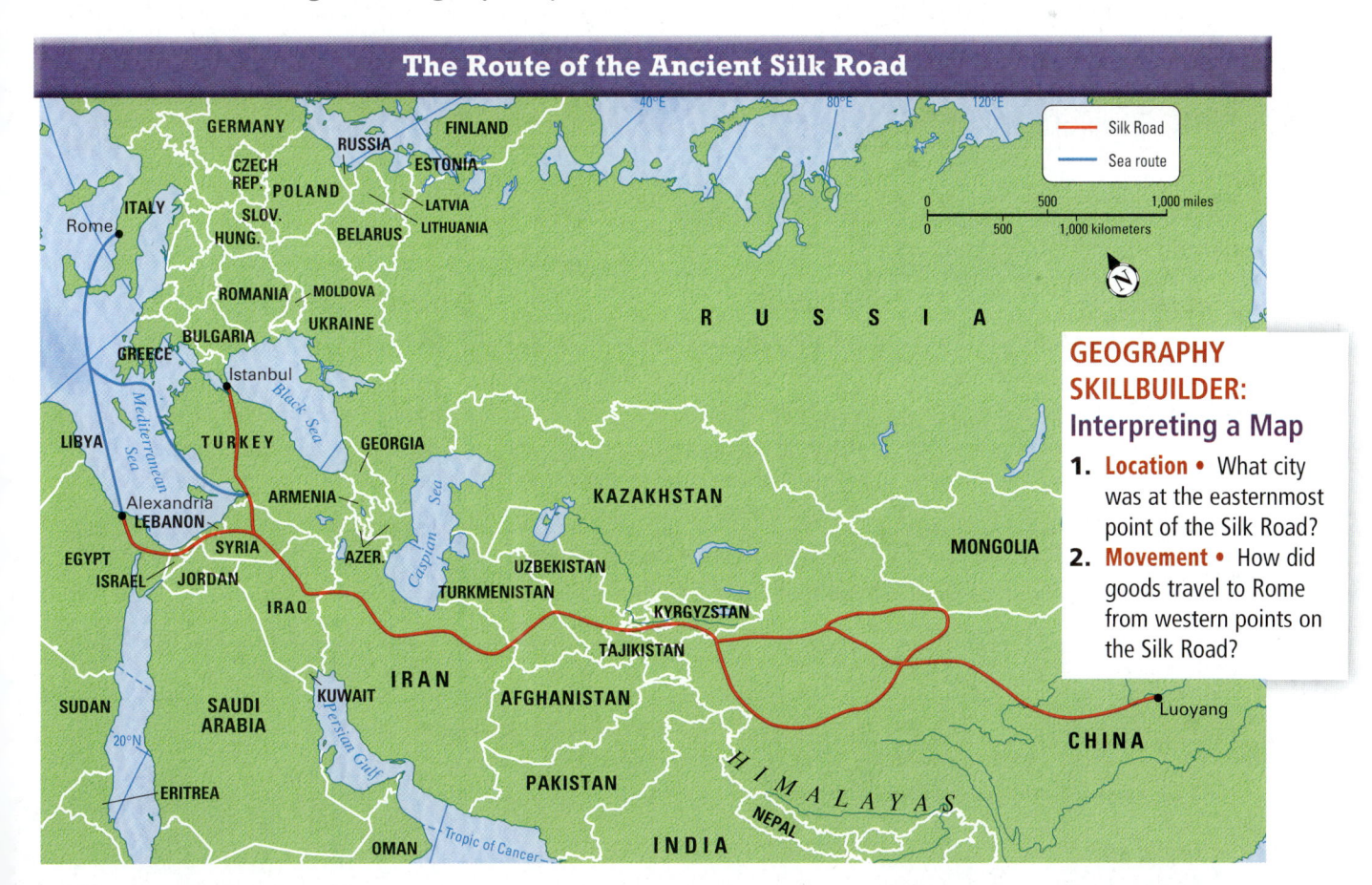

Vocabulary
kiln: high-temperature oven used to bake clay until it hardens

The Route of the Ancient Silk Road

GEOGRAPHY SKILLBUILDER: Interpreting a Map
1. **Location •** What city was at the easternmost point of the Silk Road?
2. **Movement •** How did goods travel to Rome from western points on the Silk Road?

Writing During the Shang Dynasty, the Chinese developed a written language. As in cuneiform, the Chinese system at first used pictograms to represent objects or ideas. Later, they simplified the pictograms into symbols, called characters, that do not look exactly like what they represent. About 50,000 characters exist in the Chinese written language. Most words are made up of compound graphs—two or more characters used together. Both the Japanese and Koreans use Chinese characters in their writing systems.

Culture • Chinese characters like these are drawn with brushes dipped in ink. ▲

The Great Builders The ancient Chinese built large construction projects like the Great Wall. Many emperors ordered the building of canals. The most important of these was the Grand Canal, which allowed grain from fertile river valleys to be carried more easily to the cities. Construction began on the first segment of the canal in the 600s B.C. Today, it extends for more than 1,000 miles to connect the northern city of Beijing with the southern city of Hangzhou (hahng·joh).

The WORLD'S HERITAGE

The Longest Wall Stretching for about 1,500 miles across northern China, the Great Wall is the world's longest structure. Construction began in the 600s B.C. with a number of fortified walls to keep out invaders. Later, a series of emperors ordered the walls to be connected. In the 1400s, damaged sections were rebuilt and new portions were added, giving the Great Wall its present form.

Building the Great Wall required the labor of thousands of workers using pounded earth, bricks, and stones. When the wall was finished, over a million soldiers stood guard in its watchtowers. Today, tourists from around the world come to see the Great Wall, which symbolizes China's long history. (See photograph on pages 456–457.)

SECTION 2 ASSESSMENT

Terms & Names

1. Explain the significance of:
   - (a) dynasty
   - (b) Genghis Khan
   - (c) Kublai Khan
   - (d) Confucius
   - (e) bureaucracy
   - (f) Taoism
   - (g) Lao Tzu

Using Graphics

2. Make a time line like the one below to show the dates of Chinese inventions.

   [2640 B.C. INVENTION OF SILK]

Main Ideas

3. (a) How did the Chinese incorporate Confucianism into their government?

   (b) Why did the Chinese try to keep their process for making silk secret?

   (c) In the Chinese writing system, what do characters stand for?

Critical Thinking

4. Drawing Conclusions

   More than just goods for trade traveled along the Silk Road. What else did the Silk Road bring to the people living along it?

   Think About
   - the different cultures that existed along the Silk Road
   - the people and ideas that traveled along the Silk Road

ACTIVITY -OPTION- Imagine you lived in ancient China. Write a **journal entry** describing your experience with one of the religions that developed in China.

SKILLBUILDER

Creating a Database

> **SUNSHINE STATE STANDARDS**
> **Key Standard SS.B.2.3.1** The student understands the patterns and processes of migration and diffusion throughout the world.
> **FCAT LA.B.1.3.1 Writing:** Organize for Type and Purpose

▶▶ Defining the Skill

A database is a collection of information, or data, that is organized so that you can find and retrieve information on a certain topic quickly and easily. Once you set up a database on the computer, you can search for specific information without going through the entire database. Learning how to use a database will help you to create your own.

▶▶ Applying the Skill

The screen below shows a database for the history of settlement in Melanesia. Use the strategies listed below to help you understand and use the database.

How to Create a Database

Strategy ❶ Read the title to identify the topic of the database. In this title, the most important words, or keywords, are "history," "settlement," and "Melanesia." These keywords were used to begin the research for this database.

Strategy ❷ Identify the kind of data you need to enter in your database. These will become the column headings of your database. In this case, the key words "country," "settlement," "colonization," and "independence" were chosen to focus the research.

Strategy ❸ Identify the entries included under each heading.

Strategy ❹ Use the database to help you find information quickly. For example, if this database were on a computer, you could search for "United Kingdom" to find out which of these countries were colonized by the United Kingdom.

❶ History of the Settlement of Melanesia

❷ Country	First Settlement	Colonization	Independence
Fiji ❸	3,500 years ago	1874 by United Kingdom ❹	1970
New Caledonia	3,000 years ago	1853 by France	not independent
Papua New Guinea	50,000 years ago	1793 by United Kingdom ❹ 1828 by Holland ❹ 1885 by United Kingdom and Germany 1921 by Australia	1975
Solomon Islands	4,000 years ago	1886 by Germany and United Kingdom ❹	1978
Vanuatu	3,300 years ago	1906 by United Kingdom and France ❹	1980

▶▶ Practicing the Skill

Turn to page 475 in Chapter 16, Section 2, "Foundations of Chinese Civilization." Create a database about the dynasties of China. Use the information in the section to provide the data. Use a format like the one above for your database.

East Asia, Australia, and Oceania: Land and History

LITERATURE CONNECTIONS

WAR WOUNDS

BASED VERY CLOSELY on the life of its author, Sook Nyul Choi, *Echoes of the White Giraffe* is the story of a 15-year-old Korean girl, Sookan. As the war between North Korea and South Korea rages, Sookan, her mother, and her younger brother, Inchun, are forced to flee their home in Seoul. They become separated from Sookan's father and older brothers. Sookan, her mother, and Inchun find shelter at a settlement for war refugees in Pusan, a city in southern Korea. There, Sookan slowly begins to make friends, including Junho, a boy who sings with her in a church choir.

"Is that a picture of your dog?" Junho asked, looking at the pencil sketch of Luxy that rested on top of the bookcase. "You must miss it very much...."

"Oh that," I said, flustered and surprised. "Yes, that's my boxer, Luxy." I missed my dog, but I hadn't talked about her with anyone since we left Seoul.... I frequently thought of how Luxy used to wait eagerly at the top of the stone steps in front of our house for me to come home from school. Then, at night, she would sleep at the foot of my bed. But I never talked of Luxy, for I was afraid that people might think I was childish and insensitive to mourn the loss of my dog when so many people were dead or missing. Junho was different, though ... sharing my sadness.... I stared at Luxy's picture, and I imagined how scared she must have felt when we all abandoned her. Suddenly the acrid[1] smell of bombs and sweeping fires filled my lungs, and the sound of sirens and planes flying low overhead buzzed in my ears. My mind raced back to that horrible day in late June when the dark airplanes roared through the skies and dropped a shower of dark, egg-shaped bombs from their bellies.... I shook my head and swallowed hard....

"What is it, Sookan? What are you thinking about?" Junho said, looking very concerned.

"Oh, Junho, I was remembering the first bombing of Seoul. It was horrible.... All I could do was stand by the window and watch the bombs explode. Hyunchun, my third brother,

1. Harsh; foul.

came rushing into my room, shouting, '... Come on. Those planes will be right on top of us next. Let's go.'"

"Did you all get out safely?" Junho asked anxiously....

"Oh, yes. We put thick blankets over our heads and joined the throngs of people headed up Namsan Mountain. We stayed up on the mountain all night and watched the bombs erupt into flames in the city below.... As we were sitting there, I realized my brother Jaechun was holding a large bundle in his arms, which he rocked back and forth like a baby. I instantly realized it was Luxy wrapped in that bundle.... It was a good thing that Luxy was bundled up to look like an infant, for other people on the mountain would have been afraid if they knew a dog was with them. They would have panicked, fearing that a dog would go crazy with the noise and the crowds and might bite them...

"The bombing finally stopped at dawn and we began making our way back home. We found our house half bombed and smoldering. We were hungry, and exhausted, and didn't know what we would do next. We ... started to unwrap poor Luxy. When we uncovered her, she gave such a loud, joyous bark.... She made us laugh and forget that we were sitting in the middle of a bombed city."

Junho's face brightened.... "Luxy was lucky to be so well loved and cared for."

"Well, ... Things got worse. About six months after that, we had to leave Seoul. I left her all alone. I don't know what happened to her. ... There were more bombs, and we had to run and follow the retreating South Korean and U.N. soldiers going south.... Mother, Inchun and I were separated from my father and my three older brothers. The three of us, along with thousands of other refugees, walked the whole day in the bitter cold snow to Inchon harbor. I was terribly cold and scared.... It was only once we were on the ship that I even thought of my Luxy.... I felt so guilty and ashamed that I never mentioned Luxy to Mother or to Inchun....

"... Each time I see a dog or hear a dog bark, I feel guilty that I did not love Luxy enough to save her; she, my dog, who depended on me. I had thought only of myself...."

Junho listened intently.... "You couldn't have walked with her in that cold snow. She may still be alive in Seoul. You shouldn't feel bad."

Reading THE LITERATURE

How does the author show how much Sookan misses her pet? What are some of the reasons Sookan doesn't want to think or talk about her dog? Why does Sookan decide to share her feelings about her dog with Junho?

Thinking About THE LITERATURE

How does the life of Sookan and her family change as a result of the war? Besides missing her pet, what other emotions does the loss of Luxy bring out in Sookan?

Writing About THE LITERATURE

The title "War Wounds" has two meanings, one literal—the words mean exactly what they say—and the other figurative—the words have a symbolic meaning. What do you think are the literal and figurative meanings of the title of this selection?

About the Author

Sook Nyul Choi (b. 1937) was born in Pyongyang, Korea, and spent two and a half years as a refugee during the Korean War. She later emigrated to the United States, where she attended college and then taught school. She now lives in Cambridge, Massachusetts.

Further Reading The first book by Sook Nyul Choi was *Year of Impossible Goodbyes*. It is a moving fictionalized account of Choi's last months in Pyongyang under Japanese rule.

SECTION 3
Ancient Japan

TERMS & NAMES
Shinto
clan
Heian Age
The Tale of Genji
Zen
samurai
shogun

MAIN IDEA
For hundreds of years, Japan developed its unique culture with influence from only its closest neighbors, China and Korea.

WHY IT MATTERS NOW
Japan continues to follow an independent path in world affairs.

DATELINE EXTRA

THE COAST OF JAPAN, A.D. 1281

Fifty-three days ago, our people were horrified to see a fleet of ships carrying 140,000 Mongol invaders approaching our shores. The Mongol emperor of China, Kublai Khan, sent the ships to conquer our country. Our brave samurai fought valiantly, but the Mongols had powerful crossbows and catapults that hurled terrifying missiles. Our warriors were near defeat.

Then, out of nowhere, a typhoon arose on the water. Mongol ships were smashed and sunk by the furious storm. Our people will always remember this *kamikaze*—the "divine wind"—that saved our country.

Culture • Japanese samurai prepare to battle the Mongols. ▲

Early Japan

Long before the *kamikaze* (KAH•mih•KAH•zee) saved Japan from Mongol defeat, people inhabited its islands. From 10,000 to 300 B.C., hunters, gatherers, and skilled fishermen lived along Japan's eastern coast. Toward the end of this period, the Japanese began practicing a religion called **Shinto**, which means "the way of the gods." Shinto teaches that supernatural beings, called kami (KAH•mih), live in all objects and forces of nature.

TAKING NOTES
Use your chart to take notes about East Asia, Australia, and Oceania.

	Ancient China	Ancient Japan
Geography		
Government		

SUNSHINE STATE STANDARDS
Key Standard SS.A.2.3.8 The student knows the political, social, and economic institutions that characterized the significant aspects of Eastern and Western civilizations.

FCAT LA.A.2.3.1 Reading: Identify Main Idea, Facts, and Details

The early Japanese lived in kingdoms organized around clans. A **clan** is a group of families who trace their descent from a common ancestor. Clans in Japan were each led by a chief who inherited the position. Around A.D. 250, the Yamato clan emerged as the most powerful, and it established a government that ruled Japan for hundreds of years.

Place • This gateway standing in the sea is the entrance to the Itsukushima Shrine, one of Japan's most famous places of Shinto worship. ▲

Outside Influences

Around the time that the Yamato clan took power, Japan began using new ideas and practices from its neighbors, Korea and China. From Korea, the Japanese gained knowledge of how to use bronze and iron technology to make tools and weapons, as well as how to grow an important crop—rice. Japanese religious life also changed significantly when the Koreans introduced Buddhism into Japan. This religion was one of many ideas and customs that originated in China and were brought to Japan by Koreans. In the A.D. 500s, China began to influence Japan's culture directly, as well.

Prince Shotoku At that time, Japanese rulers believed an understanding of Chinese civilization would help them gain political power in East Asia. Japan's Prince Shotoku Taishi (shoh·TOH·koo tay·EE·shee) became a Buddhist and a student of Chinese literature and culture. He established diplomatic relations with China and sent priests and students there to study its culture. Through this exchange, the Japanese adopted China's writing system, calendar, and system of centralized government.

The Heian Age In A.D. 794, the emperor Kammu built a new capital called Heian-kyo (HAY·ahn·KYOH). The period from that year to 1185 is called the **Heian Age** and is considered Japan's golden age. During this period, Japanese culture flourished. A bustling population of 100,000 made up of aristocrats, servants, and artisans lived in Heian-kyo.

Reading Social Studies

A. Recognizing Effects What does Japan's experience with learning from its neighbors tell you about the importance of cultural exchange?

Vocabulary
artisan: craftsperson

Citizenship IN ACTION

Tokyo National Research Institute for Cultural Properties Keeping the rich cultural heritage of Japan alive is the mission of the Tokyo National Research Institute for Cultural Properties. The Institute's scientists, researchers, art historians, and other experts are dedicated to preserving Japan's art, artifacts, ancient monuments, and historic sites, such as Buddhist temples (see below).

In 1995, the Institute opened the Japan Center for International Cooperation in Conservation. The Japan Center works across national borders to help preserve ancient sites throughout the world.

East Asia, Australia, and Oceania: Land and History

Members of the royal court lived in luxury and high style. Many aristocratic women wrote diaries, letters, and novels about life in the imperial court. Lady Murasaki Shikibu (MOO‑rah‑SAH‑kee SHEE‑kee‑BOO) wrote the world's first novel, called *The Tale of Genji*. In the novel, Lady Murasaki described life at Heian‑kyo's imperial court.

Zen Buddhism After first being established at the Heian‑kyo court, Buddhism became a national religion. One branch of Buddhism, called **Zen**, was the most influential in Japan. Zen emphasizes that people can achieve enlightenment suddenly, rather than through many years of painful study. Zen teaches that to reach enlightenment, a person must focus intensely to understand certain concepts, called koans (KOH‑AHNZ). Koans are statements or questions that seem to make little sense. However, if someone concentrates very hard to understand one of them, then he or she might reach enlightenment.

Culture • In this illustration, Lady Murasaki sits under the moon, planning *The Tale of Genji*. ▲

Vocabulary
imperial: relating to an empire or emperor

BACKGROUND
This is one of the most famous koans: "What is the sound of one hand clapping?"

Feudal Japan

By the 1100s, the Heian‑kyo aristocracy lost control of the country to powerful lords. The strongest lords enlisted warriors to fight rival lords. Japan began to develop a feudal system similar to that of medieval Europe, with the country divided into huge estates.

The Samurai While the aristocracy at the Heian‑kyo court lived lavishly, disorder and violence spread throughout the rest of the country. Lords needed protection against outlaws and bandits. They relied on warriors called **samurai** (SAM‑uh‑RY) to protect their estates.

Human‑Environment Interaction •
Zen Buddhists take pride in creating peaceful gardens as settings for meditation. ▼

Reading Social Studies

B. Recognizing Important Details How did the use of samurai differ from the use of an army?

BACKGROUND

In a shogunate, the emperor and his court carried out merely ceremonial roles.

As with European knights, the samurai each pledged to serve a particular lord. They provided him with military and bureaucratic services. By law and privilege, samurai and their families became a distinct social class.

The Kamakura Shogunate During the 1100s, Japan was torn by a murderous war between two clans battling for power. After 30 years of fighting, the Minamoto clan claimed victory. In 1192 in Kamakura, the clan's leader, Yoritomo, established a new kind of warrior government called a shogunate (SHOH·guh·niht). He took on the role of **shogun**—or the emperor's chief general—and held most of the country's power.

In 1274 and again in 1281, the shoguns faced their greatest challenge—Kublai Khan attempted to invade and conquer Japan. On page 484, you read about the events of the second battle. The Kamakura shogunate defeated the Mongols, but at a great cost. The war drained the treasury, and the shogun was unable to pay the samurai. They turned back to individual lords for support, and many years of fighting among lords followed.

Tokugawa Shogunate

Finally, in the 1560s, the fighting began to settle down. The lord Tokugawa Ieyasu (TOH·koo·GAH·wah ee·yeh·YAH·soo) defeated his rivals and became shogun in 1603. In that year, he moved the capital to Edo.

Spotlight on CULTURE

Fine Protection Samurai, who fought hand to hand against their enemies, wore finely made suits of armor and helmets for protection. Low-ranking samurai wore lightweight armor made of small metal panels. The highest-ranking samurai sported much fancier armor, such as the suit shown here. Made of iron panels that were laced or pinned together, it could also include panels of thick leather or linked pieces of metal called chain mail.

The armor was often intricately decorated. The entire suit could weigh as much as 40 pounds. At celebrations, to add to the finery, a samurai wore over his armor a long, loose tunic made of brightly dyed silk and embroidered with his family symbol.

THINKING CRITICALLY

1. **Drawing Conclusions** What does this suit of armor tell you about the rank of the warrior who wore it?
2. **Clarifying** For what purpose did samurai wear beautiful tunics over their armor?

For more on Japanese culture, go to

RESEARCH LINKS
CLASSZONE.COM

The First Europeans in Japan In 1543, just before the Tokugawa Shogunate began, the first Europeans arrived in Japan. They brought firearms and other goods to trade for gold and silver. In 1549, Catholic missionaries arrived in Japan and began converting many Japanese. By 1614, 300,000 Japanese had become Catholics, including many peasants.

The Closing Door By the 1630s, Tokugawa Ieyasu was worried about foreigners in Japan. He got word that the Spanish had established a settlement in the Philippines. To avoid such a situation in Japan, he ordered all Christians to leave the country. He also declared that any Japanese who left the country would be put to death upon their return. He banned most European trade, finalizing his decision to free Japan of European influences. This situation continued for 200 years, during which Japan isolated itself from most outside contact.

Place • Today, Edo is called Tokyo and is still Japan's capital. ▲

SECTION 3 ASSESSMENT

Terms & Names
1. Explain the significance of:
   (a) Shinto
   (b) clan
   (c) Heian Age
   (d) *The Tale of Genji*
   (e) Zen
   (f) samurai
   (g) shogun

Using Graphics
2. Use a spider map like this one to list important facts about the development of Japan's culture.

- Early Japan
- Outside Influences
- Ancient Japan
- Feudal Japan
- Tokugawa Shogunate

Main Ideas
3. (a) How did the Chinese and the Koreans influence Japan's culture?
   (b) What services did samurai provide, and to whom?
   (c) Under the shogunates, who held more power—the emperor or the shogun?

Critical Thinking
4. Evaluating Decisions
   Do you think Tokugawa Ieyasu was right to isolate Japan from European influence? Explain.

   Think About
   • the period before Tokugawa Ieyasu gained control of Japan
   • European influence elsewhere
   • effects of Japan's isolation

ACTIVITY -OPTION- Write a **short story** from the perspective of a samurai, a shogun, or a lord about life in feudal Japan.

Technology: 2009

SUNSHINE STATE STANDARDS
Key Standard SS.B.2.3.6 The student understands the environmental consequences of people changing the physical environment in various world locations.
FCAT LA.A.2.3.1 Reading: Identify Main Idea, Facts, and Details

INTERACTIVE

Three Gorges Dam

Rising in the Kunlun Mountains of Tibet, the Chang Jiang winds for more than 3,400 miles. It flows through some of China's most fertile agricultural land before emptying into the East China Sea at Shanghai. A stretch of the Chang Jiang known as the Three Gorges includes some of the world's most beautiful scenery. It is also an area rich in archaeological treasures dating back thousands of years. At this site, the Chinese government is building the world's largest dam. With an estimated completion date of 2009, the dam will help control floods and generate much-needed electricity. At the same time, however, construction of the dam will destroy archaeological sites and much of the region's natural beauty while forcing between 1 and 2 million people to relocate.

Three Gorges Dam Facts
- **Height:** 600 ft. (181 m)
- **Width:** 1.5 mi. (2.415 km)
- **Reservoir:** 370 mi. (595.7 km) long
- **Cost:** $25 billion
- **Workers:** 40,000
- **Years to Complete:** 17

CHINA

Area to be flooded

Three Gorges Dam
Sandouping
Wuhan
Shanghai
Chongqing
Jialing R.
Chang Jiang (Yangtze R.)

A series of locks will enable ocean-going ships to travel as far as Chongqing, at the far end of the new reservoir. This is expected to greatly improve the economy of Chongqing.

The dam will control flooding. However, it may also affect fishing and create other environmental problems.

Water-driven turbines will generate as much electricity as 18 nuclear reactors. This hydroelectric power, one of the cleanest forms of energy, will reduce air pollution. That is important in China because the Chinese burn so much coal.

When the Three Gorges reservoir is filled in 2009, it will be less than 1 mile wide but 370 miles long—about the distance from Los Angeles to San Francisco.

Thinking Critically

1. Analyzing Motives
How will the Three Gorges Dam benefit China? What are the drawbacks of the dam?

2. Recognizing Effects
The construction of the dam will cause the flooding of about 1,300 archaeological sites. How will this affect China's cultural heritage?

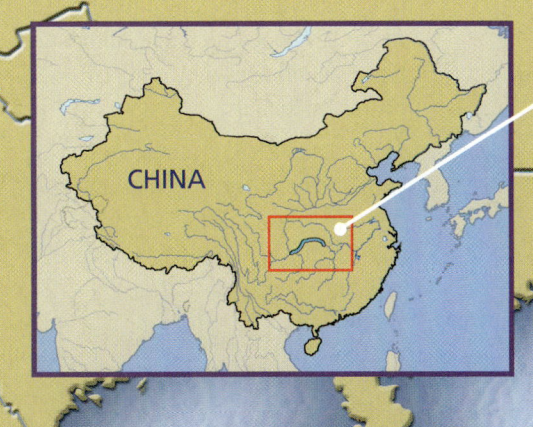

UNIT 6 *East Asia, Australia, Oceania, and Antarctica*

CHAPTER 16 ASSESSMENT

TERMS & NAMES

Explain the significance of each of the following:

1. Mount Everest
2. Ring of Fire
3. outback
4. dynasty
5. Confucius
6. bureaucracy
7. clan
8. *The Tale of Genji*
9. Zen
10. shogun

REVIEW QUESTIONS

Physical Geography *(pages 469–474)*

1. Why do the Chinese often call the Huang He "China's Sorrow"?
2. Where do most of the world's earthquakes and volcanic eruptions occur?
3. How does Australia's landscape differ from that of the world's other continents?

Ancient China *(pages 475–480)*

4. How did the Forbidden City get its name?
5. What are some important inventions from China?
6. Describe the three philosophies that were popular in ancient China.

Ancient Japan *(pages 484–488)*

7. How did Japanese culture show influences from both China and Korea?
8. What roles did the emperors, the lords, and the samurai play in feudal Japan?
9. How did the Japanese respond to Europeans arriving in Japan?

CRITICAL THINKING

Comparing and Contrasting

1. Using your completed chart from Reading Social Studies, p. 468, describe important similarities and differences between ancient China and ancient Japan.

Making Inferences

2. How do you think China's dynasties helped establish and maintain a stable government?

Drawing Conclusions

3. Why did the shogun Tokugawa Ieyasu feel that isolating Japan from Europe was a good idea?

Visual Summary

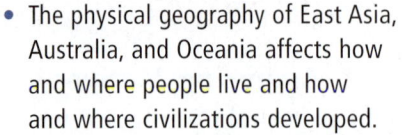

1. Physical Geography

- The physical geography of East Asia, Australia, and Oceania affects how and where people live and how and where civilizations developed.
- Japan and Oceania are particularly vulnerable to earthquakes and volcanic eruptions.

2. Ancient China

- The ancient Chinese developed the longest-lasting civilization in history. It has existed for 4,000 years.
- Chinese civilization produced inventions and ideas that influenced both Asia and Europe.

3. Ancient Japan

- Over hundreds of years, ancient Japan developed a unique culture that was influenced by only its nearest neighbors.
- Japan established a feudal system with lords and warriors. Eventually, the country established a central military government, which lasted into the 1800s.

STANDARDS-BASED ASSESSMENT

Use the map and your knowledge of world cultures and geography to answer questions 1 and 2.

Additional Test Practice, pp. S1–S33

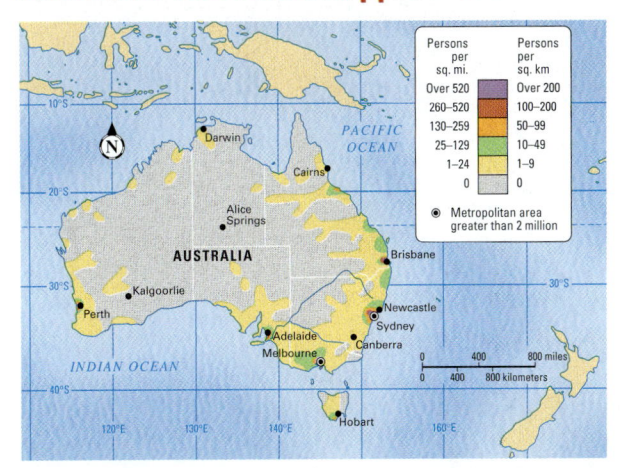

The following passage from the travel account of Marco Polo describes the Gobi Desert. Use the quotation and your knowledge of world cultures and geography to answer question 3.

PRIMARY SOURCE

[Travelers] who intend to cross the desert usually halt for a considerable time . . . to make the necessary preparations for their further journey. . . . The stock of provisions [supplies] should be laid in for a month, that time being required for crossing the desert in the narrowest part. To travel it in the direction of its length would prove a vain [useless] attempt, as little less than a year must be consumed.

MARCO POLO, *The Travels of Marco Polo*

1. What is the population density in most of Australia?
   A. 0 persons per sq. mile
   B. 1–24 persons per sq. mile
   C. 25–129 persons per sq. mile
   D. 130–259 persons per sq. mile

2. In which region are most of Australia's major cites located?
   A. in the north
   B. in the west
   C. on the coast
   D. in the interior

3. Why did Marco Polo warn travelers against crossing the desert at its longest point?
   A. People found better scenery when they traveled the shorter route.
   B. The longer route took a year and required too many supplies.
   C. On the shorter route, travelers had less chance of sandstorms.
   D. The longer route crossed a desert, while the shorter route avoided it.

TEST PRACTICE
CLASSZONE.COM

ALTERNATIVE ASSESSMENT

1. WRITING ABOUT HISTORY

The world's largest coral reef system, the Great Barrier Reef, lies off the coast of Australia. Research this reef. Then find out what species of coral and sea life can be found there. What are the major environmental dangers to the reef? Write a report on your findings. Share your report with the class.

2. COOPERATIVE LEARNING

The Silk Road was a hazardous trade route. In a group of three to five classmates, create a talk show about travel on the Silk Road around 114 B.C. Research the kinds of people and animals that traveled along the route, the terrain they passed through on the journey, the hazards they faced, and the cargo they carried. Have each group member take on a role such as talk-show host, traveler, or trader. Then write scripts for each role. Conduct your talk show in front of the class.

INTEGRATED TECHNOLOGY

Doing Internet Research

Use the Internet to do research about an earthquake or volcanic eruption that occurred in the Ring of Fire. Write a report of your findings. List the Web sites you used to prepare your report

- Focus on its location and physical features, and explain why it is so unusual.
- Include pictures showing the event or its aftermath.

For Internet links to support this activity, go to

RESEARCH LINKS
CLASSZONE.COM

East Asia, Australia, and Oceania: Land and History

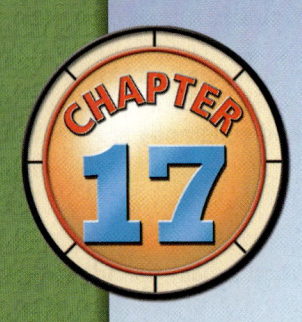

CHAPTER 17
China and Its Neighbors

SECTION 1 Establishing Modern China

SECTION 2 The Governments of East Asia

SECTION 3 The Economies of East Asia

SECTION 4 The Cultures of East Asia

SECTION 5 Establishing Modern Japan

FOCUS ON GEOGRAPHY

How does exchanging ideas affect a region's development?

Movement • The cultures of East Asia have been shaped by the exchange of ideas among them. Chinese merchants and soldiers crossed mountains, rivers, and seas to reach the Koreas and Japan. They brought with them Chinese influences that soon became part of the other cultures of East Asia.

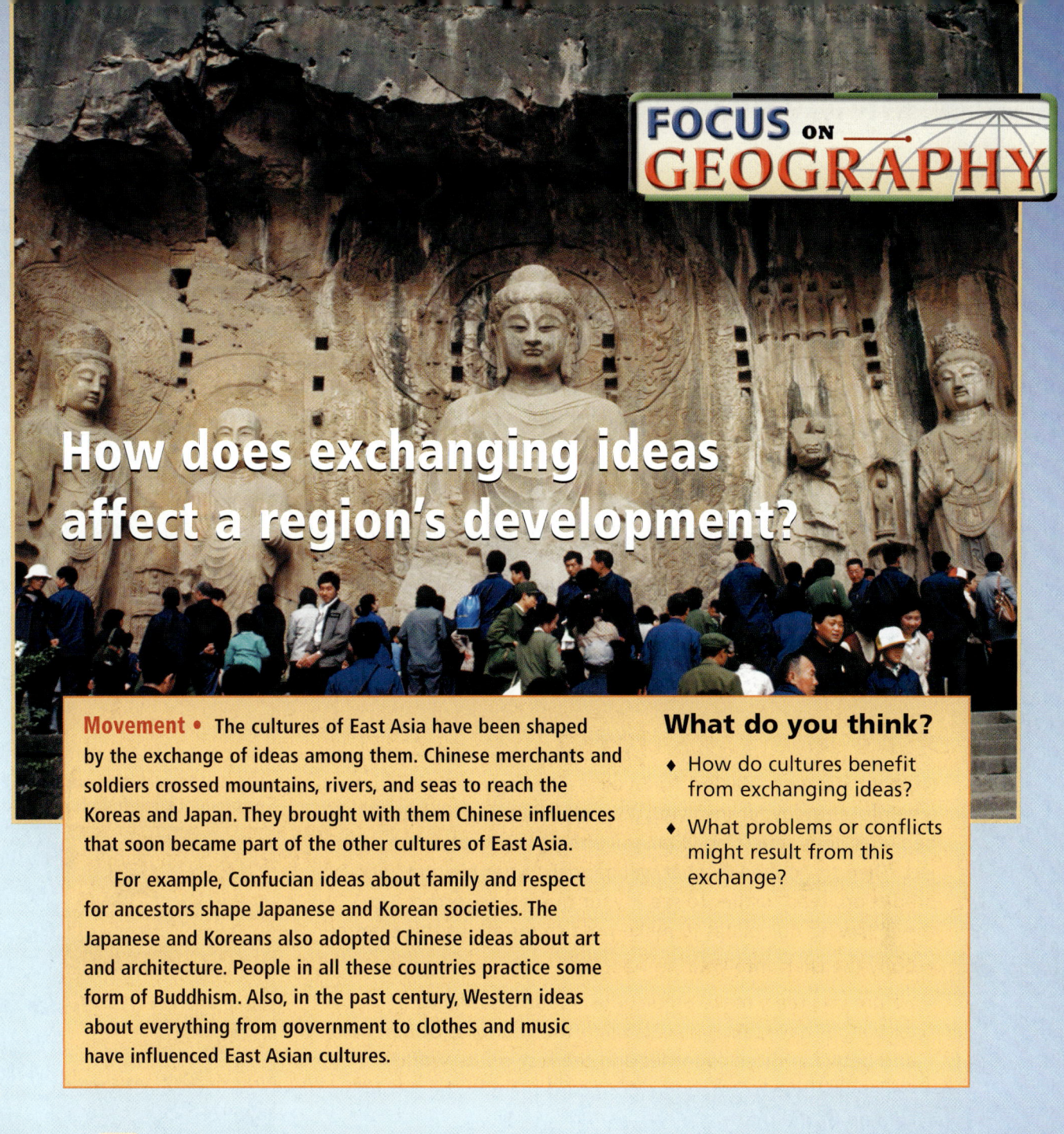

For example, Confucian ideas about family and respect for ancestors shape Japanese and Korean societies. The Japanese and Koreans also adopted Chinese ideas about art and architecture. People in all these countries practice some form of Buddhism. Also, in the past century, Western ideas about everything from government to clothes and music have influenced East Asian cultures.

What do you think?
- How do cultures benefit from exchanging ideas?
- What problems or conflicts might result from this exchange?

Place Millions of people in China use bicycles as their main form of transportation. This bicycle parking lot in Shanghai is filled to capacity.

CHAPTER 17 READING SOCIAL STUDIES

BEFORE YOU READ

▶▶ What Do You Know?

Before you read the chapter, consider what you already know about East Asia. Recall what you learned in Chapter 16 about ancient China and ancient Japan. Have you seen or tried the martial art tae kwon do? Do you know why sumo wrestlers are so honored in Japan? Reflect on what you have learned in other classes, what you have read in books or magazines, and what you have heard in the news about recent events in these countries.

▶▶ What Do You Want to Know?

Decide what else you want to know about East Asia. In your notebook, record what you hope to learn from this chapter.

Place • Many children in China take part in activities led by the Chinese Communist Party. ▲

READ AND TAKE NOTES

Reading Strategy: Making Predictions Making predictions is a helpful strategy for involving yourself in what you read. As you begin reading, reflect on what you already know about the subject. Then try to predict what will happen. After making your prediction, read further to see if your guess was correct. Use the following guidelines to make predictions about this chapter.

- Copy the chart into your notebook.
- Before you read, make predictions about what kinds of exchanges have taken place among the countries of East Asia and between those countries and the rest of the world. Organize these by category and record them in the second column of the chart.
- In the third column, list facts from the chapter that tell you whether your predictions were correct or incorrect.

Culture • Chinese-American actor Bruce Lee brought kung fu to Hollywood. ▼

Category	Predictions	Correct or Incorrect
Economy		
Religion		
Government		
Culture		

SECTION 1

Establishing Modern China

TERMS & NAMES
Opium War
Taiping Rebellion
Boxer Rebellion
Sun Yat-sen
Chiang Kai-shek
Mao Zedong
Great Leap Forward
Cultural Revolution

MAIN IDEA

After the end of China's last dynasty and decades of conflict, a Communist government took control of China in 1949.

WHY IT MATTERS NOW

Because China is a large country with a huge population, its influence politically and economically is felt around the world.

DATELINE

THE FORBIDDEN CITY, BEIJING, CHINA, FEBRUARY 12, 1912 — Word has just been received that Pu Yi, the six-year-old boy emperor, has given up China's throne. The Qing emperor, whose royal name is Xuantong, will probably be China's last emperor. Under a recent agreement, China will now be a republic led by a president. The age of dynasties has ended.

No one yet knows what will become of this last emperor, who once was called "The Son of Heaven." For the time being, he will be allowed to remain in the Imperial Palace of the Forbidden City. But his future, like China's, is uncertain.

Culture • Pu Yi is shown here, standing next to his father and brother. ▲

China's Last Dynasty

In 1644, the Manchus established the Qing Dynasty—China's last and largest empire. The Qing drew both the southwestern region of Tibet and the island of Taiwan into China. However, by the mid-1800s, China's population had more than tripled, straining the country's ability to produce enough food. Shortages, famines, and wars overwhelmed Qing rulers, helping to bring their empire to an end.

TAKING NOTES
Use your chart to take notes about China and its neighbors.

Category	Predictions	Correct or Incorrect
Economy		
Religion		

SUNSHINE STATE STANDARDS
Key Standard SS.A.3.3.2 The student understands the historical events that have shaped the development of cultures throughout the world.
Other Standards SS.A.3.3.4
FCAT LA.A.2.3.1 Reading: Identify Main Idea, Facts, and Details

China and Its Neighbors 495

Place • This monument in Tiananmen Square shows the Chinese seizing the British opium in Canton. ▲

The Opium War The Qing rulers faced turmoil early on because of a drug called opium. They tried several times to prohibit the sale of opium in China but were not successful. In the late 1700s, the British began smuggling opium from India into China. They used opium, rather than money, to buy Chinese goods, which hurt China's economy.

In 1839, the Chinese government seized all the opium the British had stored in the Chinese port of Canton. The British responded with an attack, and the first **Opium War** began. Because Qing rule was weak, the British overpowered the Chinese. The Opium War ended in 1842 with the signing of the Treaty of Nanking. This treaty forced the Chinese to pay Great Britain money, hand over Hong Kong to British control, and allow British traders into more Chinese ports.

The Rise of Nationalism Angered by the Treaty of Nanking, peasants rebelled around China. The greatest revolt, the **Taiping Rebellion** (ty•PIHNG), raged for 14 years and took 20 million lives. Peasants demanded equality for women, the end of private property, and the division of surplus harvest among the neediest. The Chinese military, with help from other nations, finally crushed the last of the rebellion in 1868.

In 1900, another rebel group, called the Boxers, rose up in the **Boxer Rebellion**. The Boxers hoped to defeat the Qing Dynasty and force all foreigners out of China. British, French, Russian, Japanese, and American troops joined together to defeat the Boxers, leaving China's government in turmoil.

A New Republic Many Western-educated Chinese wanted a new government. One ambitious leader, **Sun Yat-sen** (sun yaht•sehn), had long hoped China would become a democracy. He founded the Chinese Nationalist Party, which in 1911 toppled the Qing Dynasty. The next year, China became a republic. Sun Yat-sen was named the first provisional president. For political reasons, he gave up the first presidency to Yuan Shigai (yoo•AHN shee•ky).

Reading Social Studies

A. Recognizing Important Details Why would the Treaty of Nanking have angered the Chinese?

BACKGROUND

The Boxers called themselves the "Righteous and Harmonious Fists." The British called this group the Boxers because they practiced a kind of boxing that they thought made them safe from bullets.

Over the next 16 years, China was in turmoil. Yuan struggled with rebels for power, and before and during World War I, China fought against Japan. During this time, the Nationalist Party gained more members. The Chinese Communist Party also formed. By the end of 1925, the Nationalist Party had about 200,000 members, and the Communist Party had about 10,000.

The Fight for Control In 1927, the two parties joined forces, and **Chiang Kai-shek** (chang ky·shehk), one of Sun Yat-sen's military commanders, became the leader of China. Soon, Chiang turned against the Communists, and the two parties began a long fight for power. In 1934, because the Nationalists seemed close to victory, the Communists retreated on what is known as the Long March. About 100,000 Communists marched more than 6,000 miles north to escape the Nationalist forces.

Chiang Kai-shek maintained control of China until 1949. During this time, the government improved transportation, provided education to more people, and encouraged industry. The lives of peasants and workers were not improved. Gradually many of these people turned to the Communist Party for help.

Communist Revolution

By the end of the Long March, a leader emerged in the Communist Party—**Mao Zedong** (mow dzuh·dahng). When World War II began and Japan invaded China, Chiang Kai-shek turned to Mao and the Communist Red Army for help. At the end of the war in 1945, China's two parties again turned on each other. In 1949, the Communists defeated the Nationalists, forcing Chiang Kai-shek to flee to Taiwan. On October 1, Mao declared China a Communist state called the People's Republic of China.

Biography

Sun Yat-sen (1866–1925) Sun Yat-sen grew up in a poor farmer's family in northern China. In 1879, his older brother, who had been working in Hawaii, brought Sun to Honolulu. Sun learned about Western ways and became interested in Christianity. This troubled his brother, who sent him back to China after four years.

Sun studied medicine and became a doctor, but he had bigger ideas. He thought that China needed to move ahead, to leave some of its traditional ways behind and overcome the past political humiliations. After many struggles, Sun helped China to become a republic. Today, he is known as the Father of Modern China.

Culture • Chiang Kai-shek waved his hat at a celebration of the founding of the Nationalist Party. ▼

China and Its Neighbors

The Long March, 1934

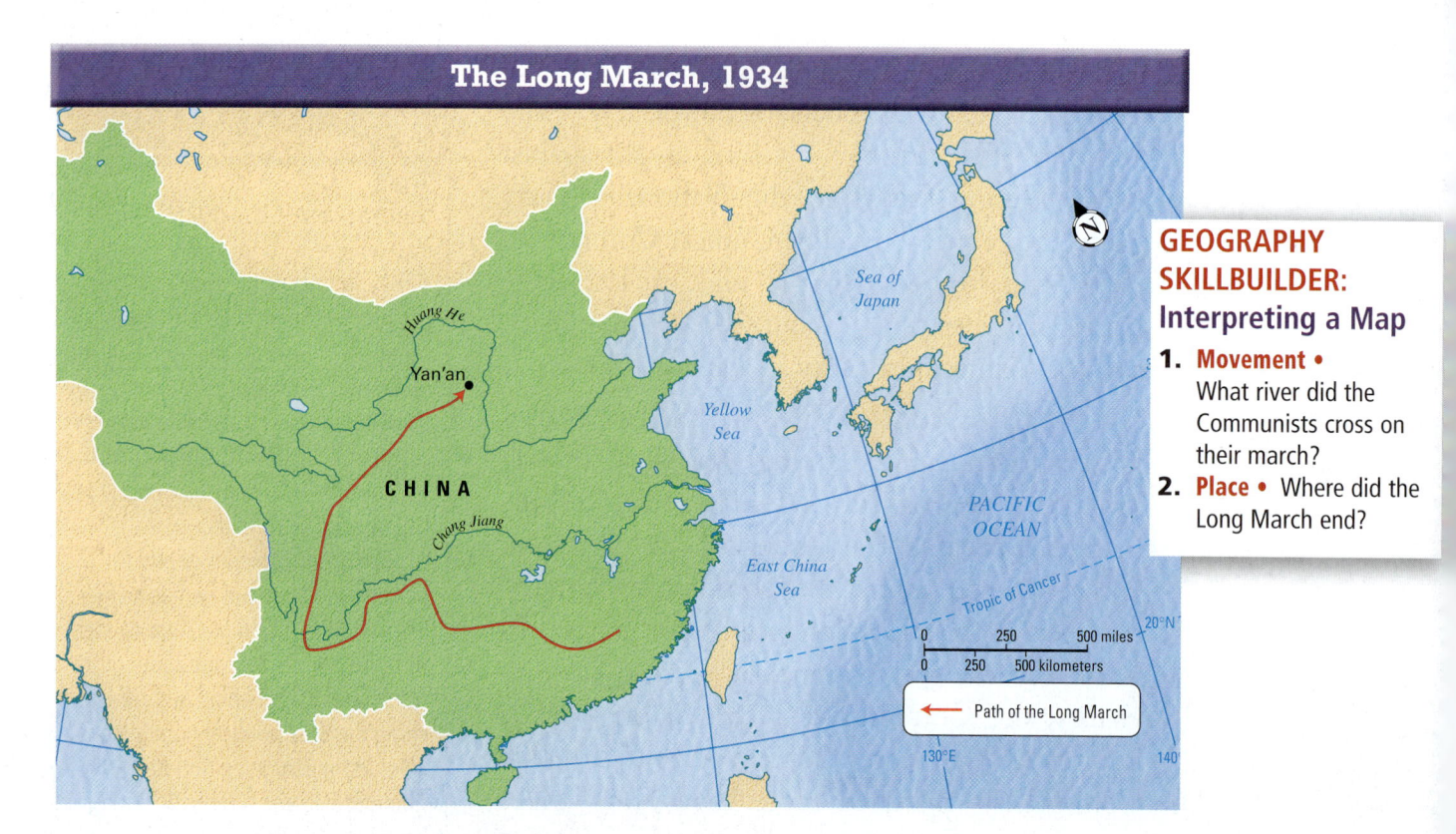

GEOGRAPHY SKILLBUILDER: Interpreting a Map

1. **Movement** • What river did the Communists cross on their march?
2. **Place** • Where did the Long March end?

Reform and Revolution

Mao Zedong became head of the Chinese Communist Party and China's government. The party set policy and the government carried it out, giving Chairman Mao nearly absolute power.

Chairman Mao's Reforms The Communists instituted many reforms. They seized land from the wealthy and gave it to the peasants. They also established a five-year plan that brought China's industry under government control. As in the Soviet Union, peasants combined their land into collective farms and worked together to grow food.

In 1958, Mao Zedong launched a program, called the **Great Leap Forward,** to speed up economic development. Collective farms became huge communes of 25,000 people. The communes grew crops, ran small industries, and provided education and health care for their members. In one year, this program shattered China's economy.

Reading Social Studies

B. Synthesizing How do you think Mao expected communes to help economic development?

Place • This famous portrait of Mao Zedong hangs in Tiananmen Square. ◄

498 CHAPTER 17

Poor agricultural production, droughts, and floods caused one of the worst famines in history. From 1958 to 1960, as many as 20 million people starved, while millions more died of disease. China then abandoned the Great Leap Forward, and Mao's influence wavered.

The Cultural Revolution After the Great Leap Forward, many people in government called for reform. Mao feared that they wanted to make China a capitalist country. In 1966, Mao launched a movement called the **Cultural Revolution,** which aimed to remove opposition to the Communist Party. Mao's new supporters were called the Red Guards. They sought out and punished people who spoke against Mao's principles or who had contact with Western people or ideas. China fell into chaos once again.

During this time, the economy weakened and the government was unable to carry out many of its duties. Goods and services, such as health care and transportation, were not made available to the people. Many Chinese began calling for reform.

Culture • These Red Guards at a rally waved copies of the "Little Red Book," a collection of Mao's sayings. ▼

SECTION 1 ASSESSMENT

Terms & Names
1. Explain the significance of:
   - (a) Opium War
   - (b) Taiping Rebellion
   - (c) Boxer Rebellion
   - (d) Sun Yat-sen
   - (e) Chiang Kai-shek
   - (f) Mao Zedong
   - (g) Great Leap Forward
   - (h) Cultural Revolution

Using Graphics
2. Use a sequence map like this one to list the events that led to the establishment of the People's Republic of China.

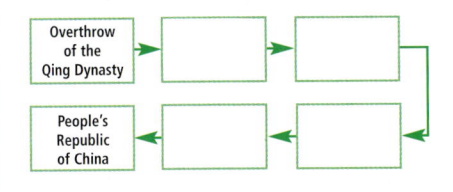

   Overthrow of the Qing Dynasty → □ → □
   People's Republic of China ← □ ← □

Main Ideas
3. (a) Who fought in the Opium War, and why?
   (b) What role did the Nationalist Party play in China?
   (c) What reforms did Mao Zedong make?

Critical Thinking
4. **Recognizing Effects**

   How do you think European actions in China contributed to feelings of discontent among China's peasants?

   Think About
   - European involvement in China during the 1900s
   - the different goals of Europeans and the Chinese

ACTIVITY -OPTION- Imagine you are a journalist. Make a **list of questions** you would like to ask a person who lived during the Cultural Revolution.

China and Its Neighbors

Interdisciplinary Challenge

Visit the Forbidden City

For centuries, only members of the emperor's household could pass through the gates of China's famous Forbidden City. Today, however, *you* are there to plan a TV feature about the palace complex. This collection of massive buildings with curving, golden-tiled roofs is actually a city within a city within a city. The Forbidden City is a square within the larger Imperial City, which is at the center of Beijing's Inner City district. The first things you see are huge buildings and broad, open squares. Stone carvings and fantastic animal figures decorate pillars and gateways.

COOPERATIVE LEARNING On these pages are challenges you will encounter as you visit the Forbidden City. Working with a small group, choose one of these challenges to meet. Divide the work among group members. You will find helpful information in the Data File. Keep in mind that you will present your solution to the class.

ARTS CHALLENGE

". . . China's greatest artists used all their skills."

China's Ming emperors built the Forbidden City as the heart of their vast empire. To please the Ming and later Qing (Ch'ing) emperors, China's greatest artists used all their skills. They decorated palaces with elaborate statues and paintings. Many are animal figures, which are important symbols in Chinese mythology. What aspects of art and architecture do you want to include? How will you present them? Choose one of these options. Look for information in the Data File.

ACTIVITIES
1. Design a home page for a museum exhibit and virtual tour, focusing on the arts of the Ming Dynasty and the Forbidden City.
2. Sketch one of the fantastic animals used in Chinese art and architecture, such as the dragon. Research what it symbolizes and write a short caption for your drawing.

DATA FILE

FORBIDDEN CITY

- Completed in **1420** by the **Yung-lo** emperor of the Ming dynasty, who moved the capital to Beijing. Buildings have been rebuilt.

- Major buildings in Beijing's Outer City and Inner City are built along a straight, north-south, 1.7-mile axis. The axis passes across **Tiananmen Square** through large parks to the gates of the Forbidden City. The city is surrounded by a moat and a wall.

- The **entrance** is through the **Meridian Gate**, which leads to marble bridges over the moat. Across the bridges is a great open square that leads to the **Gate of Supreme Harmony**. Through the Gate of Supreme Harmony lie the three state halls of the Forbidden City.

- **Outer Court:** three great halls of state—the **Hall of Supreme Harmony,** the **Hall of Complete Harmony,** and the **Hall of Preserving Harmony**—stand one behind another on a marble platform.

- **Inner Court:** palaces, courtyards, and pavilions where the emperor, his family, and the palace staff lived.

MING DYNASTY (1368–1644)

- **Restored Chinese rule** after conquest and rule by Mongols.

QING (CH'ING) DYNASTY (1644–1911)

- **Last emperors** of China; dynasty **overthrown by revolution.**

SUNSHINE STATE STANDARDS
Key Standard SS.A.2.3.7 The student knows significant achievements in art and architecture in various urban areas and communities to the time of the Renaissance (e.g., the Hanging Gardens of Babylon, pyramids in Egypt, temples in ancient Greece, bridges and aqueducts in ancient Rome, changes in European art and architecture between the Middle Ages and the High Renaissance).

FCAT LA.A.2.3.5 Reading: Locate, Organize, Interpret Information

To learn more about the Forbidden City, go to

RESEARCH LINKS
CLASSZONE.COM

HISTORY CHALLENGE

". . . palaces and courtyards where the emperor's family . . . lived."

As you approach the Forbidden City, you pass through three great state halls, one behind another on a marble platform. Official receptions and banquets were held here. Behind the halls are palaces and courtyards where the emperor's family and the men and women who served them lived. How can you show the importance of what took place within these walls? Use one of these options to present information. Look in the Data File for help.

ACTIVITIES

1. Make an annotated map of the Forbidden City. Include captions to explain the events that took place in major palaces and halls.
2. Make a time line of the Ming and Qing (Ch'ing) rulers who built and occupied the Forbidden City.

Activity Wrap-Up

As a group, review your solution to the challenge you selected. Then present your solution to the class.

East Asia, Australia, Oceania, and Antarctica

SECTION 2

The Governments of East Asia

TERMS & NAMES
Deng Xiaoping
human rights
Tiananmen Square
Diet

MAIN IDEA
The nations of China and North Korea have Communist governments. The other nations of East Asia are republics.

WHY IT MATTERS NOW
Many people in China and North Korea would like to see change in their governments and are turning to other nations for help.

DATELINE

SEOUL, SOUTH KOREA, DECEMBER 10, 2000— South Koreans are throwing a huge party today. President Kim Dae-jung has received the Nobel Peace Prize, a prize that is given annually to honor someone who has worked for peace.

Since 1947, when North and South Korea officially proclaimed themselves as separate nations, the relationship between the two countries has been tense. Just this year, for the first time, the presidents of North and South Korea met to discuss ways to reunite their divided countries. President Kim said that his goal was "to realize peace on the Korean peninsula, and to develop exchange [and] cooperation between both Koreas."

Culture • President Kim Dae-jung (on the right) received his Nobel Prize today in Oslo, Norway. ▲

Working Toward Change

North Korea and China are Communist nations, and both have seen war and conflict in the past 50 years. Through efforts from within and from organizations and nations around the world, both nations are working to improve the lives of their people. They are also gradually becoming a part of the world market.

TAKING NOTES
Use your chart to take notes about China and its neighbors.

Category	Predictions	Correct or Incorrect
Economy		
Religion		

SUNSHINE STATE STANDARDS
Key Standard SS.C.2.3.7 The student understands current issues involving rights that affect local, national, or international political, social, and economic systems.
Other Standards SS.A.3.3.4, A.3.3.5
FCAT LA.A.2.3.1 Reading: Identify Main Idea, Facts, and Details

China's Government Today

When Mao Zedong died in 1976, the Cultural Revolution ended. Moderates who wanted to restore order and economic growth took power in 1977. Their leader was **Deng Xiaoping** (duhng show•pihng).

Under Deng, the Chinese government established diplomatic relations with the United States and increased trade with other countries. It also made reforms, such as allowing farmers to own land. It released many political prisoners and reduced the police force's power. However, the government was not willing to give up any of its basic control.

The Chinese Communist Party Officially, China's highest government authority is the National People's Congress. In practice, the Chinese Communist Party holds the real power. It controls what happens locally. The government allows only churches and temples that are closely linked to this party to operate.

Place • The Chinese Communist Party sponsors activities for children, such as playing in a marching band. ▲

The Fight for Human Rights

China's Communist government has a history of repressing criticism of its policies. Such actions often lead to the violation of **human rights,** which are rights to which every person is entitled. They include the freedom to say or write what you think, to worship as you believe, to be safe from physical harm and political persecution, and to have enough to eat.

Reading Social Studies
A. Making Inferences What other rights would you include on a list of human rights?

Tiananmen Square In 1989, the Chinese military denied citizens a basic human right—freedom of speech—when it attacked protesters calling for democracy in **Tiananmen Square** (tyahn•ahn•mehn). For weeks, protesters occupied this 100-acre square in Beijing. Demonstrations soon occurred in other Chinese cities. The military killed hundreds and wounded thousands in their attempts to end the protests. As the events of 1989 unfolded, people around the world spoke up against the Chinese government. Since then, efforts have been made to help the people of China in their struggle for human rights.

China and Its Neighbors

Culture • The protesters in Tiananmen Square included students, workers, and government employees. ▲

China's Neighbors

China's neighbors have different kinds of governments. Some are republics, while others are Communist.

Japan The United States occupied Japan after it was defeated in World War II. U.S. general Douglas MacArthur helped set up a constitutional monarchy with a parliamentary government and a separate judiciary. The parliament is called the **Diet,** and the House of Representatives holds most of the power. The Diet chooses the country's prime minister, who is then officially appointed by the emperor.

The constitution states that the emperor's position is symbolic. Thus the emperor has had limited power, though many people regard the emperor as partly divine. The constitution also gives the Japanese people rights and responsibilities similar to those of Americans.

North and South Korea Korea used to be one country, but it was divided after World War II. The Soviet Union helped set up a Communist dictatorship in the north, and the United States helped set up a democratic republic in the south. Each government thought it should govern the whole of the Korean Peninsula.

Reading **Social Studies**

B. Hypothesizing Why do you think Japan has an emperor, if the position is only symbolic?

North and South Korea, 2001

GEOGRAPHY SKILLBUILDER: Interpreting a Map
1. **Location •** Why do you think the capitals of North and South Korea are located on rivers?
2. **Movement •** Measure the distance between South Korea and Japan. What can you conclude about trade between these two nations?

504 CHAPTER 17

In 1950, North Korea invaded South Korea. For three years the two fought the Korean War, but the borders did not change. In June of 2000, the two nations started talking about reuniting.

North Korea, or the Democratic People's Republic of Korea, is still a Communist state. Although there is a president and a cabinet, the Korean Workers' Party holds power. The people have little freedom, and the legislature—the Supreme People's Assembly—has little power.

South Korea, or the Republic of Korea, is a republic with a government similar to that of the United States. Power is divided among legislative, executive, and judiciary branches. People vote for the president as well as the legislature—the National Assembly. The government guarantees its citizens freedom of the press and of religion.

Mongolia One of the world's oldest countries, Mongolia was under either Chinese or Russian domination for years. It has been an independent republic since 1991 and has a constitution that guarantees its citizens certain basic rights. However, there is still a strong element of Communist party control in the government.

Taiwan Also a republic, Taiwan has a multiparty democratic system. For years it was a Chinese colony, but since 1949, the Chinese Nationalist government has been based there. The question of whether Taiwan and China will unify under one government has long caused conflict.

SECTION 2 ASSESSMENT

Terms & Names
1. Explain the significance of: (a) Deng Xiaoping (b) human rights (c) Tiananmen Square (d) Diet

Using Graphics
2. Use a chart like this one to list and compare the major characteristics of East Asia's governments.

Country	Characteristics of Government
China	
Japan	
North Korea	
South Korea	
Mongolia	
Taiwan	

Main Ideas
3. (a) Who holds the power in China's government?
   (b) Which East Asian countries have governments similar to China's?
   (c) How do the governments of North Korea and South Korea differ?

Critical Thinking
4. Hypothesizing
   Why do you think the Chinese government has taken actions that repress human rights?

   Think About
   • China's political stance
   • the goals of China's dissidents

ACTIVITY -OPTION- Write a **news story** that describes the events that helped establish the government of Japan, North Korea, or South Korea.

SECTION 3
The Economies of East Asia

TERMS & NAMES
tungsten
antimony
textile
cooperative

MAIN IDEA
East Asian economies have changed, some drastically, since World War II.

WHY IT MATTERS NOW
As these economies grow stronger, they play a larger role in global markets and have a larger influence on the economies of other nations.

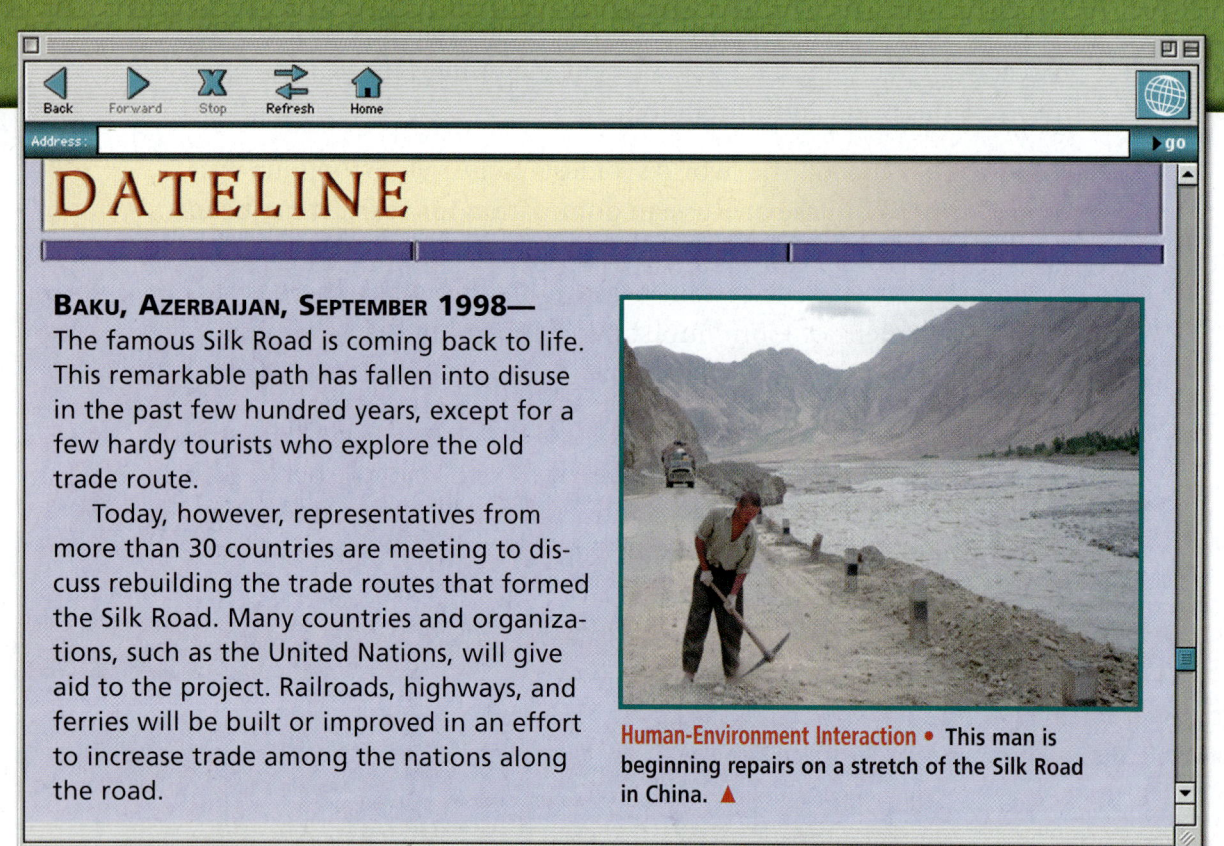

DATELINE

BAKU, AZERBAIJAN, SEPTEMBER 1998— The famous Silk Road is coming back to life. This remarkable path has fallen into disuse in the past few hundred years, except for a few hardy tourists who explore the old trade route.

Today, however, representatives from more than 30 countries are meeting to discuss rebuilding the trade routes that formed the Silk Road. Many countries and organizations, such as the United Nations, will give aid to the project. Railroads, highways, and ferries will be built or improved in an effort to increase trade among the nations along the road.

Human-Environment Interaction • This man is beginning repairs on a stretch of the Silk Road in China. ▲

Economies of the Region

Since World War II, East Asia's countries have grown more active in the world market. Today, Japan has one of the strongest economies in the world. Consumers in the United States regularly purchase goods made in China, Japan, Taiwan, and South Korea. However, wars, droughts, and internal conflicts have made economic growth difficult for some countries, such as North Korea.

TAKING NOTES
Use your chart to take notes about China and its neighbors.

Category	Predictions	Correct or Incorrect
Economy		
Religion		

SUNSHINE STATE STANDARDS
Key Standard SS.D.2.3.1 The student understands ways production and distribution decisions are determined in the United States economy and how these decisions compare to those made in market, tradition-based, command, and mixed economic systems.

FCAT LA.A.2.3.1 Reading: Identify Main Idea, Facts, and Details

Place • Located on China's south coast, Hong Kong is a major port and financial center for East Asia. ◀

China's Economy

Although this has begun to change, China's government controls most of its economy. It owns all financial institutions, such as banks, and the larger industrial firms. The government also sets the prices on goods and plans the quantity of goods each worker should produce.

Industry China has put a strong emphasis on improving its industry. It has become one of the world's largest producers of cotton cloth and of two metals—**tungsten** and **antimony**. The industries that have seen the most growth are machine building, metal production, and the making of chemical fertilizers and clothing.

Farming Many people in China live in the countryside and make a living by farming. They use traditional methods, such as plowing with oxen, rather than using farm machinery. Much of the land in China—in the deserts and mountainous regions—cannot be farmed. Nevertheless, China is the world's largest producer of rice. It is also a major source of wheat, corn, soybeans, peanuts, cotton, and tobacco.

Human-Environment Interaction • Much of China's rice is produced on terraced gardens like these. ▼

Human-Environment Interaction • Chinese villagers in Yunnan work in the rice terraces. ▲

China and Its Neighbors

Other East Asian Economies

Taiwan Taiwan has a growing market economy that relies heavily on manufacturing and foreign trade. Since 1988, Taiwanese businesses have invested billions of dollars in mainland China, significantly contributing to China's fast-growing economy.

North Korea Like China's, North Korea's government controls the economy. Also like China, North Korea has emphasized the growth of industry. Iron, steel, machinery, chemical, and textile production are the main industries in North Korea. A **textile** is a cloth manufactured by weaving or knitting.

Many people in North Korea are farmers. They work on large **cooperatives,** where some 300 families share the farming work. These farms have become more productive as improvements in irrigation, fertilizers, and equipment have been made.

For most of the 20th century, North Korea traded with other Communist nations. Since the fall of the Soviet Union, North Korea has opened its borders to investment and trade with other countries.

South Korea The economy of South Korea has changed dramatically since the early 1960s. At that time, it was a poor nation of subsistence farmers. Since then, however, the government has supported the expansion of the textile industry and the building of factories that make electronics, small appliances, and equipment. The government also helped develop iron, steel, and chemical industries. Today, South Korea has one of the world's strongest economies. It is a major producer of automobiles and electronics and trades with many countries.

Japan The government of Japan does not control its economy in the way the governments of China and North Korea control theirs. However, it does oversee and advise all aspects of the economy, including trade, investment, banking, and production.

Like South Korea's, Japan's economy has grown significantly since the mid-20th century. Japan is a small nation with few natural resources and little farmland. Industry and a skilled, educated work force are vitally important to Japan's economy.

Place • This is one of many new ships manufactured by South Korea's shipbuilding industry. ▲

Reading **Social Studies**
A. Evaluating Decisions Do you think it makes sense for so many farmers to share their work?

Reading **Social Studies**
B. Synthesizing What is the benefit of having the government control the economy?

Industry in East Asia, 2000

Map legend:
- Automobile manufacturing
- Chemicals
- Food processing
- Electronics/High-tech
- Engineering
- Gas
- Iron and steel
- Textiles

GEOGRAPHY SKILLBUILDER: Interpreting a Map

1. **Place** • Name three cities in which food processing is an industry.
2. **Place** • What industries exist in Taiwan?

The country imports the raw materials it needs and transforms them into goods for export. Ships, automobiles, steel, plastics, machinery, cameras, and electronics are Japan's major exports. The United States is Japan's biggest customer, although Japan also exports goods around the world. It is currently one of the world's largest economic powers.

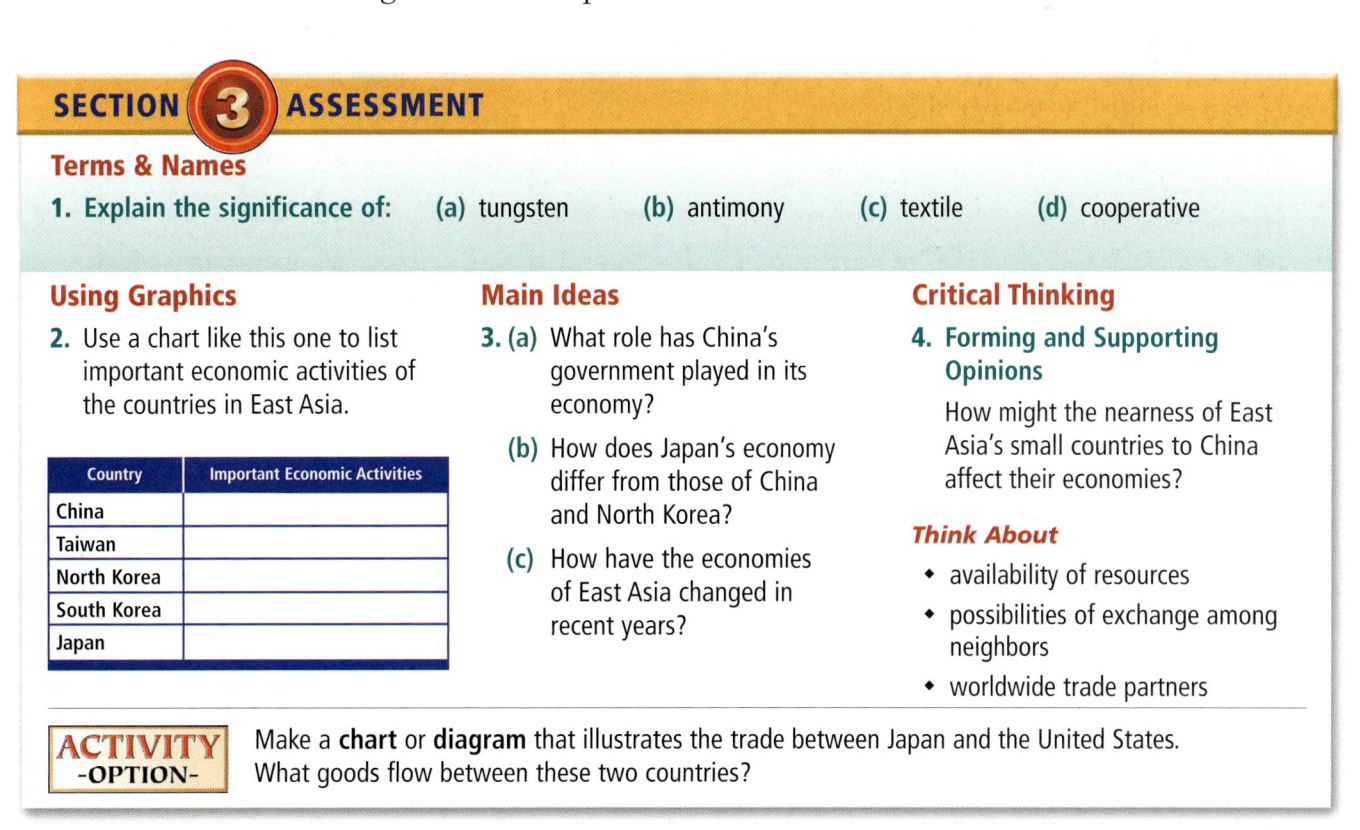

SECTION 3 ASSESSMENT

Terms & Names

1. Explain the significance of: (a) tungsten (b) antimony (c) textile (d) cooperative

Using Graphics

2. Use a chart like this one to list important economic activities of the countries in East Asia.

Country	Important Economic Activities
China	
Taiwan	
North Korea	
South Korea	
Japan	

Main Ideas

3. (a) What role has China's government played in its economy?
   (b) How does Japan's economy differ from those of China and North Korea?
   (c) How have the economies of East Asia changed in recent years?

Critical Thinking

4. **Forming and Supporting Opinions**

   How might the nearness of East Asia's small countries to China affect their economies?

   Think About
   - availability of resources
   - possibilities of exchange among neighbors
   - worldwide trade partners

ACTIVITY -OPTION- Make a **chart** or **diagram** that illustrates the trade between Japan and the United States. What goods flow between these two countries?

China and Its Neighbors

SECTION 4

The Cultures of East Asia

TERMS & NAMES
zither
haiku
Han

MAIN IDEA
The cultures of the nations of East Asia share much in common because of years of cultural exchange.

WHY IT MATTERS NOW
As East Asians are introduced to Western culture, they are careful not to forget their own cultural heritage.

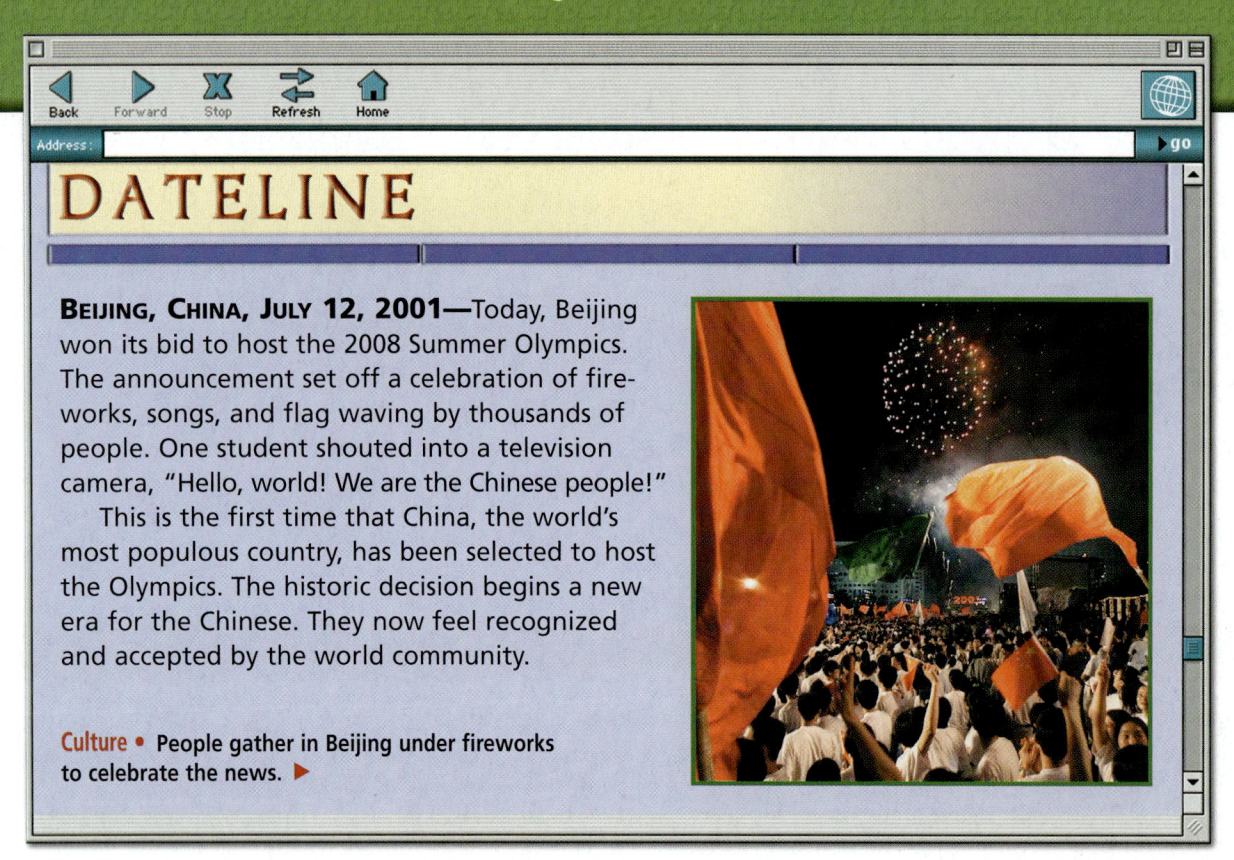

DATELINE

BEIJING, CHINA, JULY 12, 2001—Today, Beijing won its bid to host the 2008 Summer Olympics. The announcement set off a celebration of fireworks, songs, and flag waving by thousands of people. One student shouted into a television camera, "Hello, world! We are the Chinese people!"

This is the first time that China, the world's most populous country, has been selected to host the Olympics. The historic decision begins a new era for the Chinese. They now feel recognized and accepted by the world community.

Culture • People gather in Beijing under fireworks to celebrate the news. ▶

Cultural Exchange

Cultural exchange has occurred for centuries among the countries of East Asia. In recent decades, these countries have been influenced by Western culture as well. At the same time, aspects of East Asian cultures have spread outside the region. International events like the Olympics are sure to generate more awareness of the region around the world.

TAKING NOTES
Use your chart to take notes about China and its neighbors.

Category	Predictions	Correct or Incorrect
Economy		
Religion		

SUNSHINE STATE STANDARDS
Key Standard SS.A.3.3.1 The student understands ways in which cultural characteristics have been transmitted from one society to another (e.g., through art, architecture, language, other artifacts, traditions, beliefs, values, and behaviors).
Other Standards SS.A.2.3.7, A.3.3.5
FCAT LA.A.2.3.1 Reading: Identify Main Idea, Facts, and Details

Exchange Within East Asia

East Asian cultures have much in common because of cultural exchange. Many of the shared aspects of culture originated in China, whose civilization has already existed for 4,000 years. For example, the Japanese and Koreans adapted the Chinese writing system to their own languages. The Japanese also adopted Chinese ideas about centralized government, urban planning, and painting techniques. Similarly, the Koreans picked up Chinese printing techniques and methods of government administration.

Place • This Buddhist temple in China stretches across a peaceful pond. ◀

Reading Social Studies
A. Making Inferences By what means do you think the countries of East Asia passed their culture on to one another?

Religion The religions of East Asia are strong indicators of cultural exchange within the region. Buddhism, for example, originated in India. The Chinese learned about the religion around 1,700 years ago. They then passed on their understanding of it to the Koreans, who later transmitted their knowledge to the Japanese. Some of the elements of Buddhism that the Japanese adopted were incorporated into their native Shinto religion. The Koreans and Japanese also developed interest in Confucianism. It, too, spread from China to their countries.

Culture • Many Taoists practice tai chi, a form of exercise meant to relieve the body of stress and worry. ▼

Practices Today Throughout East Asia, many people still practice Buddhism and Confucianism. They also practice other religions, such as Christianity and Taoism. The Communist government of North Korea discourages religious freedom. South Koreans, however, practice Buddhism and Christianity. Mongolians practice Tibetan Buddhism. Taiwan's dominant religion is based on Buddhism, Confucianism, and Taoism. Japan's two major religions are Zen Buddhism and Shinto.

Cultural Exchange with East Asia Throughout History

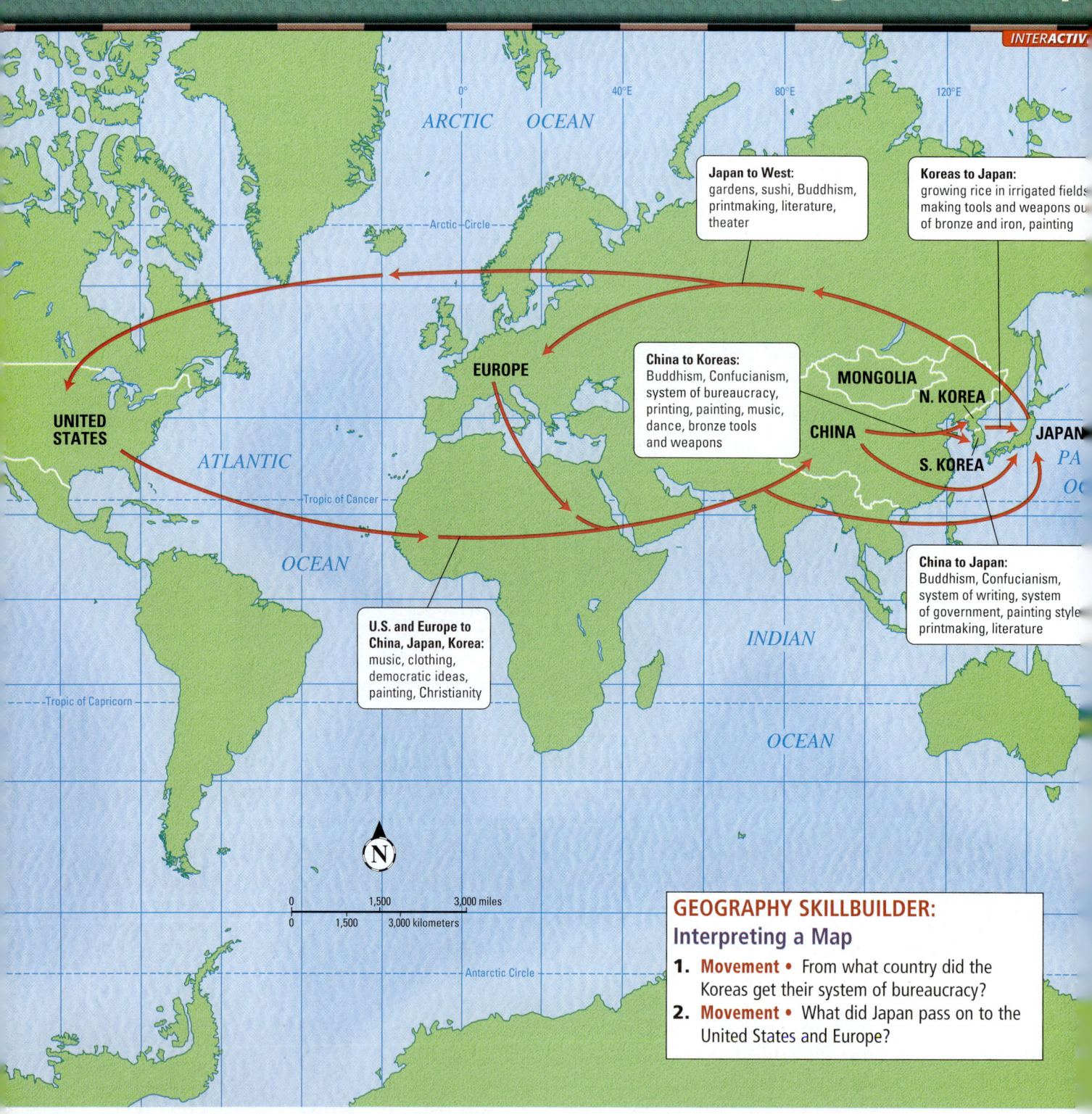

Japan to West: gardens, sushi, Buddhism, printmaking, literature, theater

Koreas to Japan: growing rice in irrigated fields, making tools and weapons out of bronze and iron, painting

China to Koreas: Buddhism, Confucianism, system of bureaucracy, printing, painting, music, dance, bronze tools and weapons

China to Japan: Buddhism, Confucianism, system of writing, system of government, painting style, printmaking, literature

U.S. and Europe to China, Japan, Korea: music, clothing, democratic ideas, painting, Christianity

GEOGRAPHY SKILLBUILDER: Interpreting a Map

1. **Movement** • From what country did the Koreas get their system of bureaucracy?
2. **Movement** • What did Japan pass on to the United States and Europe?

Arts Past and Present

Like the religions, the art forms of East Asia's countries reflect cultural exchange. For example, similar methods of painting and making pottery are used throughout the region. However, each country also boasts unique artistic traditions.

Art in China Chinese art forms date back thousands of years. The art of bronze casting was developed around 1100 B.C. Music and dance are also ancient art forms in China. Many different kinds of instruments have been found in ancient tombs. Bells, flutes, drums, and a stringed instrument called a **zither** are all still played in China.

Fine porcelain dishes and vases are among China's greatest art treasures. The scenes, designs, and words that decorate them have also helped historians understand the cultural life of ancient China.

Today, theater is a popular art form in China. There are at least 300 forms of traditional opera in China. At the Beijing Opera, actors wear elaborate costumes to perform dramas based on Chinese stories, folklore, and history.

Art in Japan Buddhist ideas have influenced the arts in Japan. Artists consider simplicity, delicacy, and tradition to be important in their artwork. Painting, printing, dance, music, and theater all reflect these ideals. In literature, the **haiku** (HY·koo) is a world-famous form of Japanese poetry. Each haiku uses only 17 syllables. The goal of the form is to suggest, in a short description, much more than is stated. Many Japanese poets, such as Basho (1644–1694), have written haiku since the form was developed hundreds of years ago.

Some artists in Japan are working to preserve traditional crafts. Potters and weavers, in particular, receive money from the Japanese government so that they can continue their work and teach others. These artists are considered living treasures.

Reading Social Studies
B. Clarifying What importance does the Japanese government give to traditional arts?

Culture • *Bunraku* puppetry is a famous Japanese art form. The puppets are nearly life-size. Each one is manipulated by three puppeteers, who control different parts of it. ▼

Bunraku Puppetry

Omozukai
Chief manipulator
• holds puppet
• moves puppet's head, body, and right hand

Ningyo
Bunraku puppet

Ashizukai
Third manipulator
• moves puppet's legs

Hidarizukai
Second manipulator
• moves puppet's left hand

Culture and Communism

Communism has significantly affected some of East Asia's cultures. In North Korea and China, the Communists repressed artistic freedom. During the Cultural Revolution in China, artwork was frequently damaged or destroyed. Writers were forced to create propaganda instead of expressing their own ideas. Even Mao wrote poetry, but his poems only concerned Communist ideals. Playwrights and painters who created work that reflected Communist ideals were allowed to continue their work. Artists who used their art to criticize the government were punished.

In North Korea today, the government still controls the work of artists. The Chinese government has shown greater willingness to allow artists to pursue their own ideas.

Reading Social Studies
C. Drawing Conclusions Why do you think the Communists worried about allowing artistic freedom?

The Chinese People

China contains about one-fifth of the world's population. Most people in China belong to an ethnic group called the **Han**. In addition, there are about 55 minority groups in China. Each has its own spoken language, and some also have their own written language. In school, students often speak their native language, and Mandarin Chinese is taught as the official language.

Spotlight on CULTURE

The Martial Arts The martial arts are a unique form of fighting. Karate originated in Japan and involves striking and kicking with hands and feet. The Koreans practice a similar martial art called tae kwon do (ty kwahn doh). The Japanese also developed other forms, such as judo (JOO•doh) and aikido (EYE•kee•DOH), that involve throwing or blocking an attack.

The Chinese call their fighting style kung fu, and for centuries, they shared it only with other Chinese. In the mid-1800s, however, Chinese laborers introduced their martial arts to the United States. In the 1960s, a young Chinese American, Bruce Lee (shown at right), began teaching kung fu's fantastic flying leaps and spin-kicks to Hollywood stars. He soon became an international action-movie star.

THINKING CRITICALLY

1. **Making Inferences** What advantage might a kung fu fighter have over a fighter with no knowledge of this martial art?
2. **Drawing Conclusions** How might Hollywood have contributed to kung fu's popularity?

For more on martial arts, go to
RESEARCH LINKS
CLASSZONE.COM

Changes to the Family The Chinese have traditionally lived in large, extended families. To slow down population growth, the Chinese government decreed in the 1980s that each married couple in a city may have only one child. Rural families may be allowed to have a second child, and families in ethnic minorities may have more than one child. Most Chinese households today are made up of small family units that may include the grandparents.

Family members in China depend on one another and follow traditional patterns. In a family, elders are greatly respected. Children, because there are so few, are given lots of attention. In the past, marriages were arranged by the parents, but that is no longer common. In present-day China, most parents work outside the home, so grandparents often care for the children.

Place • As is typical in China, this couple has only one child. ▲

SECTION 4 ASSESSMENT

Terms & Names
1. Explain the significance of: (a) zither   (b) haiku   (c) Han

Using Graphics

2. Use a diagram like this one to list aspects of culture that East Asian countries have exchanged with each other.

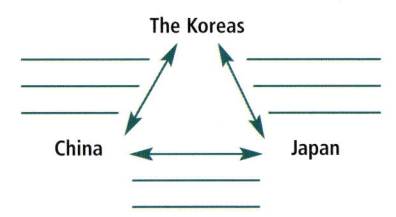

   The Koreas
   China   Japan

Main Ideas

3. (a) What is the goal of Japan's living treasures?
   (b) How has the government affected religion and art in China and North Korea?
   (c) What led the Chinese government to place restrictions on family size?

Critical Thinking

4. **Drawing Conclusions**
   What factors do you think encourage cultural exchange?

   Think About
   - migration patterns
   - geographic features
   - speaking related languages

ACTIVITY -OPTION- Make a **list** of five questions that you would like to ask a Chinese teenager about his or her life.

China and Its Neighbors

SECTION 5
Establishing Modern Japan

TERMS & NAMES
Meiji Restoration
Hiroshima
Nagasaki
homogeneous
Ainu

MAIN IDEA
After World War II, the Japanese built a modern industrial economy that is one of the largest in the world.

WHY IT MATTERS NOW
One challenge for Japan is to protect its unique identity even as it welcomes influences from the rest of the world.

DATELINE EXTRA

TOKYO, JAPAN, MAY 3, 1947

Today, Japan celebrated its rebirth as a new nation. Less than two years after its surrender at the end of World War II, Japan has a Western-style constitution.

Emperor Hirohito conducted a solemn ceremony to celebrate the occasion. The government issued a pocket-sized pamphlet to every Japanese family. The new constitution is printed inside. It expresses the hopes of the Japanese for a peaceful future.

Culture • Emperor Hirohito stands before a crowd of 20,000 people celebrating the new constitution. ▲

History

The people of Japan have seen remarkable changes in the past century, not just in their country's government, but also in its economy and its relations with the rest of the world. From the mid-1600s to the 1800s, Japan was a fairly isolated nation. It traded with China but was unaffected by the rest of the world.

TAKING NOTES
Use your chart to take notes about China and its neighbors.

Category	Predictions	Correct or Incorrect
Economy		
Religion		

SUNSHINE STATE STANDARDS
Key Standard SS.A.3.3.5 The student understands the differences between institutions of Eastern and Western civilizations (e.g., differences in governments, social traditions and customs, economic systems and religious institutions).
Other Standards SS.A.3.3.2
FCAT LA.A.2.3.1 Reading: Identify Main Idea, Facts, and Details

The Meiji Restoration Japan's location made it a convenient place for ships sailing from the United States to stop and replenish supplies of food and fuel. In 1853, American naval vessels commanded by Commodore Matthew C. Perry landed in Japan. Perry used a show of force to open Japan to Western contact, ending nearly 200 years of Japanese isolation.

In 1867, a group of samurai overthrew the ruling Tokugawa Shogunate and restored the emperor as head of government. The period that followed, from 1868 through 1911, became known as the **Meiji Restoration**, because the new emperor was called Meiji (MAY·JEE). During this time, the Japanese people built modern industries and developed the economy. Japan became wealthy and powerful. Following a series of wars, Japan assumed control of Taiwan, Korea, and Manchuria.

Culture •
A Japanese artist painted this scene of Commodore Perry in Japan in 1853. ▲

Reading Social Studies
A. Summarizing What factors contributed to instability in Japan in the early 1900s?

In the Early 1900s Japan, allied with the United States, Britain, and France, defeated Germany in World War I and thus was able to expand its holdings of ex-German colonies in the Pacific. The Great Kanto Earthquake in 1923 hurt Japan's economy, and like much of the world, Japan was affected by the Great Depression. During the 1930s, the military took control of Japan's government. In 1937, Japan invaded China and became involved in a long war there. Also at this time, Japan developed closer relations with Nazi Germany and Fascist Italy. As a result, the United States stopped selling oil to Japan. In 1941, Japan bombed the U.S. naval base at Pearl Harbor in Hawaii, bringing the United States into World War II.

World War II By 1942, the Japanese military had won many victories in East Asia and the South Pacific. But in June 1942, Japan lost the Battle of Midway; and in February 1943, it lost a battle on Guadalcanal Island. These defeats turned the tide of the war.

China and Its Neighbors

Place • This scene of Nagasaki after the bombing shows only a few buildings still standing. ▲

In 1945, the United States dropped atomic bombs on two Japanese cities—**Hiroshima** (HEER•uh•SHEE•muh) and **Nagasaki** (NAH•guh•SAH•kee). Emperor Hirohito then agreed to surrender, putting an end to the war.

Economy and Government

After World War II, Japan's economy and government were in shambles. Its cities had been bombed. Many Japanese were homeless and without jobs.

Economy The Japanese values of hard work and saving money helped to rebuild the economy. The United States also gave Japan help through loans and advice. By the mid-1950s, Japanese industrial production matched its prewar levels. Today, Japan has one of the most powerful economies in the world.

Culture • Many Japanese women, like this one, hold jobs in business and industry. ▼

Like the United States, Japan encourages free enterprise. This type of system can motivate people to develop new ideas as well as to expand their businesses with little government interference.

Women and the Economy Women's participation in the work force has grown since World War II. However, discrimination exists, and long-held ideas about women's roles as mother and housekeeper are changing very slowly. Approximately two-fifths of Japanese women hold jobs, but many of these jobs are temporary or part-time. Few women hold management positions.

Government After World War II, the United States occupied Japan until 1952. It helped set up a new government. Under the new constitution, the rights and responsibilities of the Japanese are similar to those of Americans.

Today, Japan has a constitutional monarchy with a parliamentary government. The Diet is the highest law-making body in the country. Before 1945, Japan's emperor was the head of the government. He is now a symbolic head of state.

Culture

Japan's population is **homogeneous,** or largely the same. Most of its people are descended from the Mongolian people who settled Japan thousands of years ago. The exception is the approximately 15,000 Ainu (EYE·noo) people. Scholars believe that the **Ainu** came to Japan from Europe well before the other settlers arrived.

Social Behavior In Western culture, especially in the United States, people think of themselves first as individuals. In Japan, as in most of Asia, people think of themselves first as part of a group. Social behavior in Japan is governed by an idea the Japanese call *on* (ohn). This value is based on Confucian principles about proper relationships. The Japanese take the relationship between children and their elders particularly seriously. People always display respectful behavior toward their parents and elders. They also put the needs of their parents and elders before their own needs. Japanese people also seriously consider an elder's judgment when making important decisions.

Urban Living More than 90 percent of Japanese families live in urban areas. Many people live in apartment buildings, in part because there is not much space for single-family homes; because of this, owning a home is very expensive.

Reading Social Studies

B. Forming and Supporting Opinions What is your opinion of putting the group ahead of the individual? What are the pros and cons of it?

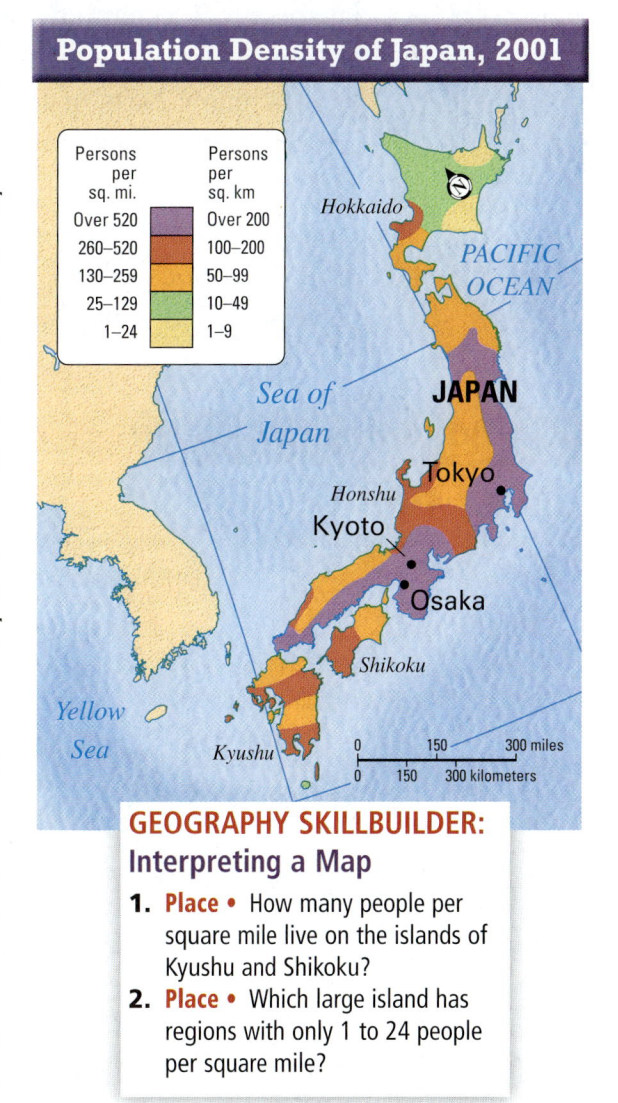

Population Density of Japan, 2001

Persons per sq. mi.	Persons per sq. km
Over 520	Over 200
260–520	100–200
130–259	50–99
25–129	10–49
1–24	1–9

GEOGRAPHY SKILLBUILDER:
Interpreting a Map
1. **Place** • How many people per square mile live on the islands of Kyushu and Shikoku?
2. **Place** • Which large island has regions with only 1 to 24 people per square mile?

China and Its Neighbors

Culture • Excited fans release balloons before a baseball game at the Fukuoka Dome on the island of Kyushu. ▲

Many people commute to their jobs or to school. Most major cities have subway systems. During rush hour, these trains are packed with people traveling to and from work. High-speed commuter trains connect many of the big cities. The fastest trains reach speeds of 160 miles an hour. Railway tunnels also connect the islands. The world's first undersea railway tunnel was built to connect the islands of Kyushu and Honshu.

Cultural Exchange Some aspects of Japanese culture have gained popularity in the United States in recent years. These include the Japanese tea ceremony, sushi, and Japanese flower arranging. Japanese gardens, which stress simplicity in design, have been built in many parts of the world. Bonsai (bahn•SY)—the art of growing tiny, elegant plants and trees—has also gained popularity.

Two sports are wildly popular in Japan, both having come to Japan from other parts of the world. Baseball and soccer games draw enormous crowds. Today, several of Japan's top baseball players, such as Ichiro Suzuki, play on U.S. teams.

SECTION 5 ASSESSMENT

Terms & Names

1. Explain the significance of:
   (a) Meiji Restoration
   (b) Hiroshima
   (c) Nagasaki
   (d) homogeneous
   (e) Ainu

Using Graphics

2. Use a sequence chart like this one to list the events leading to the growth of Japan's modern economy.

   Perry arrives in Japan → ☐ → ☐

   Japan creates strong economy ← ☐ ← ☐

Main Ideas

3. (a) How did World War II affect Japan's economy?
   (b) What effect has Confucianism had on the daily lives of the Japanese?
   (c) How has Japan been influenced by other cultures?

Critical Thinking

4. **Analyzing Causes**
   Why do you think Japan is such a densely populated country?

   Think About
   - Japan's land area and geographic features
   - social and cultural beliefs
   - standard of living

ACTIVITY -OPTION- Plan the **schedule** of a Japanese Culture Day. Think about what activities you might have, what speakers you could invite, and what you would want participants to learn about Japan.

520 CHAPTER 17

SKILLBUILDER

Reading a Population Density Map

▶▶ Defining the Skill

A population density map allows you to compare the population densities of different regions. It shows how many people live in each square mile or square kilometer.

▶▶ Applying the Skill

The map below shows the population density of North Korea, South Korea, and Japan. Use the strategies listed below to help you read the map.

SUNSHINE STATE STANDARDS
Key Standard SS.B.1.3.1
The student uses various map forms (including thematic maps) and other geographic representations, tools, and technologies to acquire, process, and report geographic information including patterns of land use, connections between places, and patterns and processes of migration and diffusion.

FCAT LA.A.2.3.1 Reading: Identify Main Idea, Facts, and Details

How to Read a Population Density Map

Strategy ❶ Read the map key. This key uses color to show population density. Areas with very dense population are purple. Areas with sparse population are pale yellow.

Strategy ❷ Look at the map. Find the areas on the map that are most densely populated. Then locate areas that are less densely populated.

Strategy ❸ Read the labels on the map. Notice that the major cities of these countries are in very densely populated areas. Look at the islands of Japan and notice which ones are the least populated.

Strategy ❹ Summarize the information given in the map. Use the key to help you remember which areas are more densely populated than others.

Write a Summary

Write a summary that will help you understand the information given in the map. The paragraph below and to the right summarizes the information from the map.

▶▶ Practicing the Skill

Turn to page 519 in Chapter 17, Section 5, "Culture." Look at the map titled "Population Density of Japan, 2001" and write a paragraph summarizing what you learned from it.

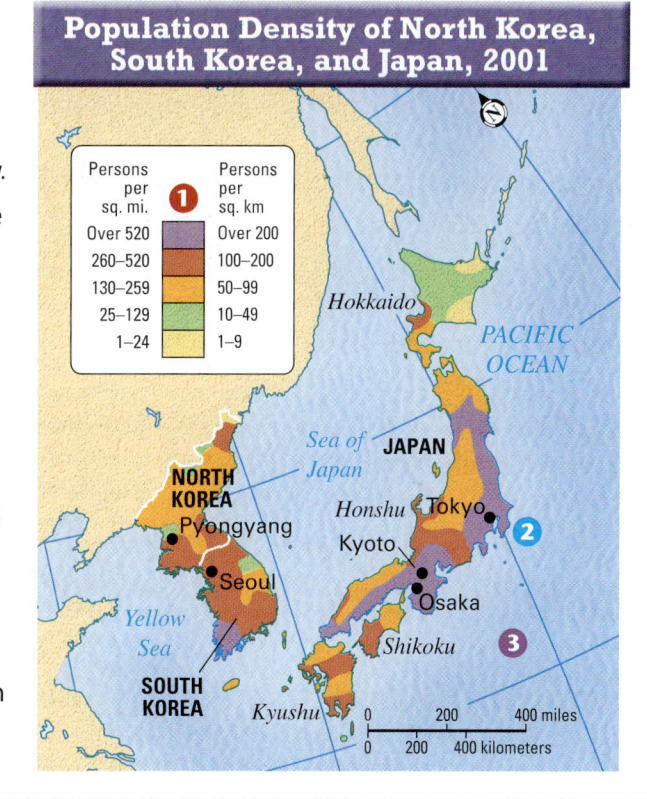

Population Density of North Korea, South Korea, and Japan, 2001

Persons per sq. mi.	Persons per sq. km
Over 520	Over 200
260–520	100–200
130–259	50–99
25–129	10–49
1–24	1–9

❹ All three of these East Asian countries are densely populated. Japan is the most densely populated of the three. The areas around Japan's cities are more densely populated than those around the cities of the Koreas. In all three countries, the cities are in very densely populated areas, as would be expected. Of the larger islands of Japan, Hokkaido is the least populated. North Korea is slightly less populated than South Korea.

China and Its Neighbors

CHAPTER 17 ASSESSMENT

TERMS & NAMES

Explain the significance of each of the following:
1. Sun Yat-sen
2. Mao Zedong
3. Cultural Revolution
4. human rights
5. Diet
6. cooperative
7. haiku
8. Han
9. homogeneous
10. Ainu

REVIEW QUESTIONS

Establishing Modern China *(pages 495–499)*
1. Describe two rebellions under the Qing Dynasty.
2. What change did the Communists make in China in 1949?

The Governments of East Asia *(pages 502–505)*
3. What changes occurred in the Chinese government at the end of the Cultural Revolution?
4. How has the Chinese government repressed freedom?

The Economies of East Asia *(pages 506–509)*
5. Who controls China's economy?
6. What are some important East Asian products?

The Cultures of East Asia *(pages 510–515)*
7. Give two examples of cultural exchange in East Asia.
8. What changes did Communism bring to the arts in China?

Establishing Modern Japan *(pages 516–520)*
9. What changes occurred during the Meiji Restoration?
10. How do the Japanese regard their elders?

CRITICAL THINKING

Hypothesizing
1. Using your completed chart from Reading Social Studies, p. 494, explain which of your predictions proved correct.

Drawing Conclusions
2. Why do you think Mao Zedong was successful in winning the civil war against the Nationalists?

Forming and Supporting Opinions
3. What is your opinion of the dissidents who demonstrated in Tiananmen Square? Should they have been more obedient to their government?

Visual Summary

1. Establishing Modern China
- The Nationalists toppled China's Qing Dynasty in 1911.
- Mao Zedong declared China Communist in 1949.

2. The Governments of East Asia
- China and North Korea are the only Communist countries in East Asia.
- China's government continues to repress people's freedom, but less so than in the past.

3. The Economies of East Asia
- Though they have faced challenges, East Asia's economies have grown strong.

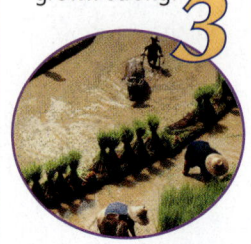

4. The Cultures of East Asia
- Over the years, much cultural exchange has occurred in East Asia.
- Communism has changed Chinese culture, but traditions such as the arts still thrive.

5. Establishing Modern Japan
- After the devastating destruction of World War II, the Japanese rebuilt their economy to be one of the strongest in the world.

> STANDARDS-BASED ASSESSMENT

Use the map and your knowledge of world cultures and geography to answer questions 1 and 2.

Additional Test Practice, pp. S1–S33

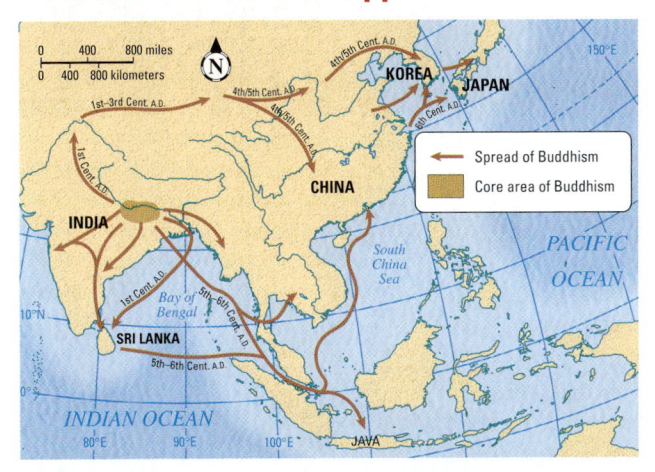

The following passage is from a news report about the government response to protests in Tiananmen Square. Use the quotation and your knowledge of world cultures and geography to answer question 3.

PRIMARY SOURCE

Several hundred civilians have been shot dead by the Chinese army during a bloody military operation to crush a democratic uprising in [Beijing's] Tiananmen Square. Tanks rumbled through the capital's streets late on 3 June as the army moved into the square from several directions, randomly firing on unarmed protesters. The injured were rushed to hospital on bicycle rickshaws by frantic residents shocked by the army's sudden and extreme response to the peaceful mass protest.

BBC News, June 4, 1989

1. In what country did Buddhism originate?
   A. China
   B. India
   C. Japan
   D. Sri Lanka

2. During which time period did Buddhism spread to Sri Lanka?
   A. 1st century A.D.
   B. 1st–3rd century A.D.
   C. 4th–5th century A.D.
   D. 5th–6th century A.D.

3. What were the student demonstrators demanding?
   A. changes to the class schedule
   B. democratic reform
   C. labor unions
   D. the release of political prisoners

TEST PRACTICE
CLASSZONE.COM

ALTERNATIVE ASSESSMENT

1. WRITING ABOUT HISTORY

Since the 1980s, the Chinese government has decreed that most Chinese families may have only one child. Research the effectiveness of this rule over the past 20 years. Has the birth rate decreased in China? What is the general public opinion concerning the rule? How well are people obeying the rule? Write a report on your findings. Include a chart or a graph. Share your report with the class.

2. COOPERATIVE LEARNING

Work in a small group of classmates to create a visual presentation about Japan's living treasures, artists who practice ancient Japanese crafts or art forms. Make a list of the living treasures, then assign one to each group member. Individually, research and write reports about each artist. The reports should include pictures of the art being practiced. As a group, give a presentation to the class.

INTEGRATED TECHNOLOGY

Doing Internet Research

Use the Internet to do research about the Long March. Write a report of your findings. List the Web sites you used to prepare your report.

- Look for details about the climate and the terrain the marchers had to endure along the route of the march.
- Explain what hardships the marchers probably faced because of these factors.
- If possible, include a quotation by someone who made the Long March.

For Internet links to support this activity, go to

RESEARCH LINKS
CLASSZONE.COM

China and Its Neighbors 523

CHAPTER 18
Australia, New Zealand, Oceania, and Antarctica

Section 1 History and Governments
Section 2 Economies and Cultures
Section 3 Antarctica

Place Two main islands and several smaller islands make up New Zealand, whose capital, Wellington, encircles this harbor on North Island.

How can people affect a region's environment?

FOCUS ON GEOGRAPHY

Human-Environment Interaction • When Europeans first came to Australia, New Zealand, and Oceania, the landscape had been largely unchanged for tens of thousands of years. In Australia and New Zealand, the settlers cleared the forests to provide land for farming and housing.

This human activity has had some unexpected consequences on the environment. In Australia, for example, more than 40 percent of the country's forests have been destroyed. Over-cultivation of this land has depleted the soil of valuable nutrients. Over-irrigation has resulted in too high a level of salt in the soil. As you can see above, very few plants are able to grow in salty soil.

What do you think?

♦ What do immigrants risk by changing an environment too quickly after settling in it?

♦ How might the people of Australia, New Zealand, and Oceania have benefited if the settlers had balanced development with environmental concerns?

CHAPTER 18 READING SOCIAL STUDIES

BEFORE YOU READ

▶▶ What Do You Know?
Before you read the chapter, think about what you already know about Australia, New Zealand, Oceania, and Antarctica. If you have been to this region, look back at your journal or photos and reflect on your experiences there.

▶▶ What Do You Want to Know?
Decide what else you want to know about this region. In your notebook, record what you hope to learn from this chapter.

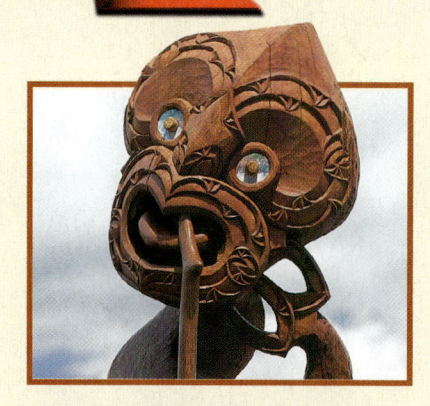

Culture • Wood carvings like this are made by native people throughout New Zealand. ▲

READ AND TAKE NOTES

Reading Strategy: Making Inferences Making inferences means figuring out what a writer has suggested but not directly stated. It requires studying what is stated and using common sense and previous knowledge.

Use the chart below to gather facts about Australia, New Zealand, Oceania, and Antarctica. Then make inferences about Hawaii from them.

- Copy the chart in your notebook.
- As you read the chapter, record facts about each place.
- After you read, review the facts and make inferences based on those facts.

Culture • Australian athlete Cathy Freeman lit the Olympic torch in the summer of 2000. ▲

	Place	Stated Facts	Inferences About Hawaii
Population	Australia		
	New Zealand		
	Oceania		
	Antarctica		
Government	Australia		
	New Zealand		
	Oceania		
	Antarctica		
Economy	Australia		
	New Zealand		
	Oceania		
	Antarctica		
Culture	Australia		
	New Zealand		
	Oceania		
	Antarctica		

SECTION 1

History and Governments

TERMS & NAMES
Maori
Aborigine
Melanesia
Micronesia
Polynesia
Commonwealth of Nations

MAIN IDEA
The nations of this region were first settled by people from nearby and later colonized by European nations.

WHY IT MATTERS NOW
In many nations today, different groups struggle for their rights and for the opportunity to rule.

DATELINE

WAITANGI, NEW ZEALAND, 1940—One hundred years after it was signed, the Treaty of Waitangi can finally be seen by the public. On February 6, 1840, this historic treaty was signed by Lieutenant Governor William Hobson, several other Englishmen living in New Zealand, and about 45 Maori chiefs.

Long, heated arguments occurred between the English and the Maori chiefs about the treaty, which described how the British would rule New Zealand. The Maori chiefs were concerned that their people's rights would not be protected.

Many Maori today feel that the treaty has not been upheld and that their rights have not been protected. According to the treaty, lands, forests, and fisheries owned by Maori would remain theirs. Today, however, Maori citizens own only 5 percent of New Zealand's land.

Culture • This painting shows William Hobson and a Maori chief signing the treaty in 1840. ▲

History of the Region

Long before the British arrived in New Zealand, the country's first settlers—the **Maori** (MOW•ree)—lived there. In fact, people inhabited many of the islands in the Pacific and Indian oceans for thousands of years before any Europeans arrived. Today, we know this region as Australia, New Zealand, and Oceania.

TAKING NOTES
Use your chart to take notes about Australia, Oceania, New Zealand, and Antarctica.

	Places	Facts	Inferences
Population	Australia		
	New Zealand		
	Oceania		
	Antarctica		

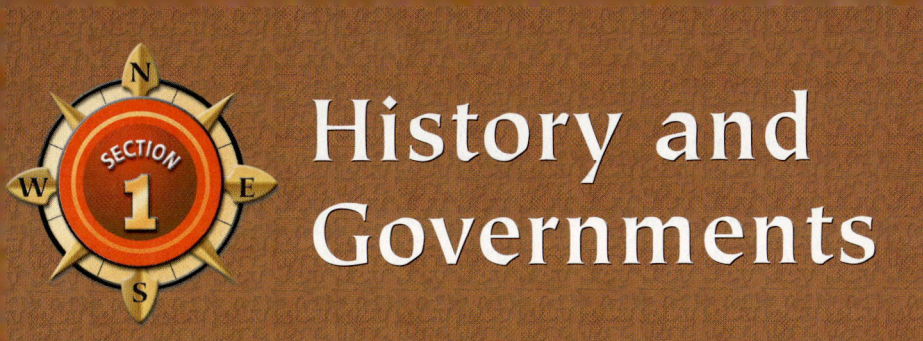

SUNSHINE STATE STANDARDS
Key Standard SS.B.1.3.3 The student knows the social, political, and economic divisions on Earth's surface.
Other Standards SS.A.2.3.6, A.3.3.5
FCAT LA.A.2.3.1 Reading: Identify Main Idea, Facts, and Details

Australia, New Zealand, Oceania, and Antarctica 527

People of the Region

Australia's first inhabitants migrated there from Southeast Asia at least 40,000 years ago. Their descendants are called **Aborigines** (AB•uh•RIHJ•uh•neez). Settlers from Southeast Asia arrived in Oceania about 33,000 years ago. On the map on page 529, you can see the three regional groups of the Pacific—**Melanesia, Micronesia,** and **Polynesia.** Southeast Asians migrated first to Melanesia, then spread into Micronesia and finally Polynesia. About 1,000 years ago, Polynesians settled New Zealand. These settlers were the Maori.

Reading Social Studies

A. **Using Maps** Look at the maps on pages 460 and 529. Why do you think Southeast Asians settled the islands in the order they did?

Island Life Geography influenced which islands people settled. If an island had fresh water, wildlife, and vegetation, people settled there. If an island was too dry or too small, or lacked sources of food, it remained unpopulated.

Most of the early islanders fished or farmed. They also traded with nearby islanders. Because of the vast expanses of ocean, however, distinct languages and cultures developed over time.

Europeans in the Pacific In the 1500s, Europeans explored the Pacific for spices. In the 1600s and 1700s, missionaries and other settlers arrived. Some of them carried diseases, such as smallpox.

Culture • This Aborigine artist displays one of the paintings on tree bark for which his people are famous. ▲

Spotlight on CULTURE

Maori Carvings The Maori have a long history of carving wood, stone, and bone. Many of the carvings are of human figures—either ancestors, gods, or characters from myths. Often, the carvings are found on items like canoes, weapons, and jewelry, though many also stand alone.

The most distinctive features of Maori carvings are the spiral patterns and seashells that decorate them, both of which you can see on the carvings shown here.

For more on the Maori, go to

RESEARCH LINKS CLASSZONE.COM

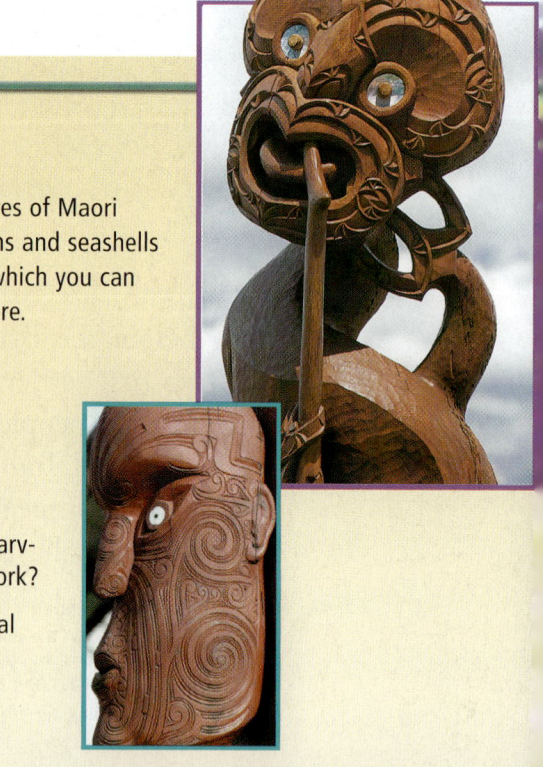

THINKING CRITICALLY

1. **Making Inferences** Think about the materials the Maori use in their carvings. How do you think these materials have helped to preserve their artwork?

2. **Hypothesizing** What do you think might be the inspiration for the spiral patterns that the Maori use on their carvings?

The Island Groups of the Pacific

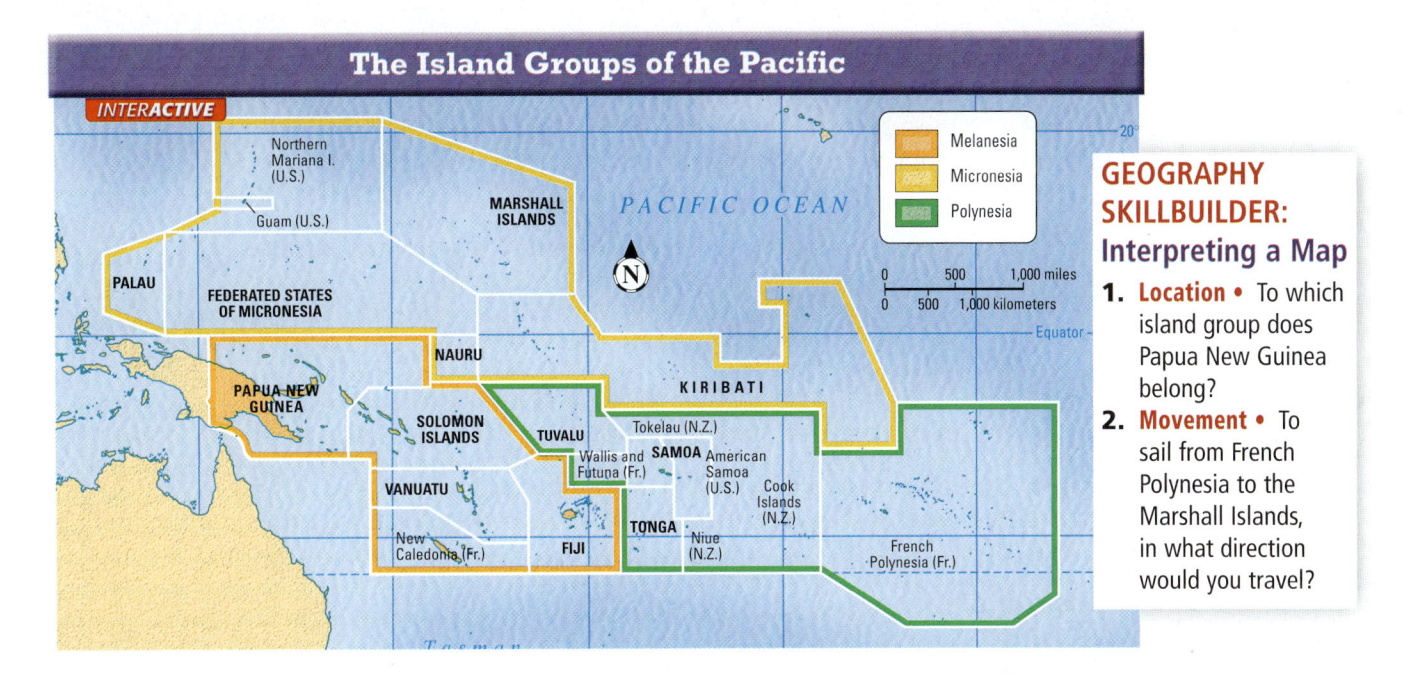

GEOGRAPHY SKILLBUILDER: Interpreting a Map

1. **Location** • To which island group does Papua New Guinea belong?
2. **Movement** • To sail from French Polynesia to the Marshall Islands, in what direction would you travel?

Many of the native islanders died from these diseases. Some settlers also brought hardship upon the islanders by enslaving them.

Britain, France, Germany, Spain, the United States, and later Japan all established colonies in the Pacific. Since 1962, many islands have gained independence. Others are still colonies. For example, France governs New Caledonia, and the United States controls Guam.

Europeans in Australia and New Zealand In the 1700s, Great Britain sent many people to Australia. Some were convicts who labored on farms, and others were free colonists. By 1859, six British colonies made up Australia. In 1901, these colonies became states of the Commonwealth of Australia.

In the 1790s, New Zealand was settled by whale hunters and traders from Great Britain, the United States, and France, as well as European missionaries and colonists. In 1840, the Maori and the British signed the Treaty of Waitangi, which gave control of New Zealand to Britain. New Zealand did not become a self-governing country until 1907.

Strange but TRUE

Mysterious Stone Statues Far out in the Pacific, along the slopes of Easter Island, stands a strange sight. Giant stone heads peer out across the landscape. Hundreds more lie knocked down all across the island.

The island's early inhabitants carved these statues (shown below), which weigh up to 90 tons, out of the side of a volcano. How they moved the statues many miles to their present locations, however, is a mystery that may never be solved.

Impact of European Settlement When Europeans first came to Australia, as many as 750,000 Aborigines populated the continent. As more settlers arrived, Aborigines were forced into the country's interior. Today, only 1 percent of Australia's population is of Aborigine descent. Similarly, in New Zealand, only about 14 percent of the population today is of Maori descent.

Reading Social Studies
B. Drawing Conclusions What factors could explain why Aborigines are now such a small minority in Australia?

Governments

The governments of Australia, New Zealand, and the nations of Oceania are quite varied. Some are democracies, some are monarchies, and some are ruled by other nations. Many countries have governments that resemble those of the nations that colonized them.

Australia and New Zealand Australia and New Zealand belong to the **Commonwealth of Nations.** This is a group of countries that were once British colonies and share a heritage of British law and government. Great Britain's monarch is their head of state but has no real power.

Oceania A few islands of Oceania still have official ties to various countries. For example, the United States is responsible for the defense of the Federated States of Micronesia, while the French Polynesians vote in French elections. Other islands rule themselves, such as Tonga, which is a constitutional monarchy.

Region •
This photo shows a selection of flags from Oceania. ▼

SECTION 1 ASSESSMENT

Terms & Names
1. Explain the significance of:
   (a) Maori
   (b) Aborigine
   (c) Melanesia
   (d) Micronesia
   (e) Polynesia
   (f) Commonwealth of Nations

Using Graphics
2. Use a chart like this one to list and compare important details of the history of Australia, New Zealand, and Oceania.

	Australia	New Zealand	Oceania
Early Inhabitants			
European Settlement			
Government Today			

Main Ideas
3. (a) Where did the earliest settlers of Australia and Oceania come from?
   (b) List three reasons Europeans traveled to the region's islands.
   (c) What do the governments of Australia and New Zealand have in common?

Critical Thinking
4. Summarizing
   How did geography affect the region's settlement patterns?

Think About
- which islands the original settlers inhabited
- how the arrival of Europeans affected native populations

ACTIVITY -OPTION- Imagine that you were a Maori inhabitant of New Zealand. Write a **dialogue** between you and one of the European settlers.

Economies and Cultures

SECTION 2

TERMS & NAMES
copra
matrilineal society
patrilineal society

MAIN IDEA
There is great diversity among the economies and cultures of the nations of the Pacific.

WHY IT MATTERS NOW
Modern communication and transportation have brought this once isolated region into closer contact with the rest of the world.

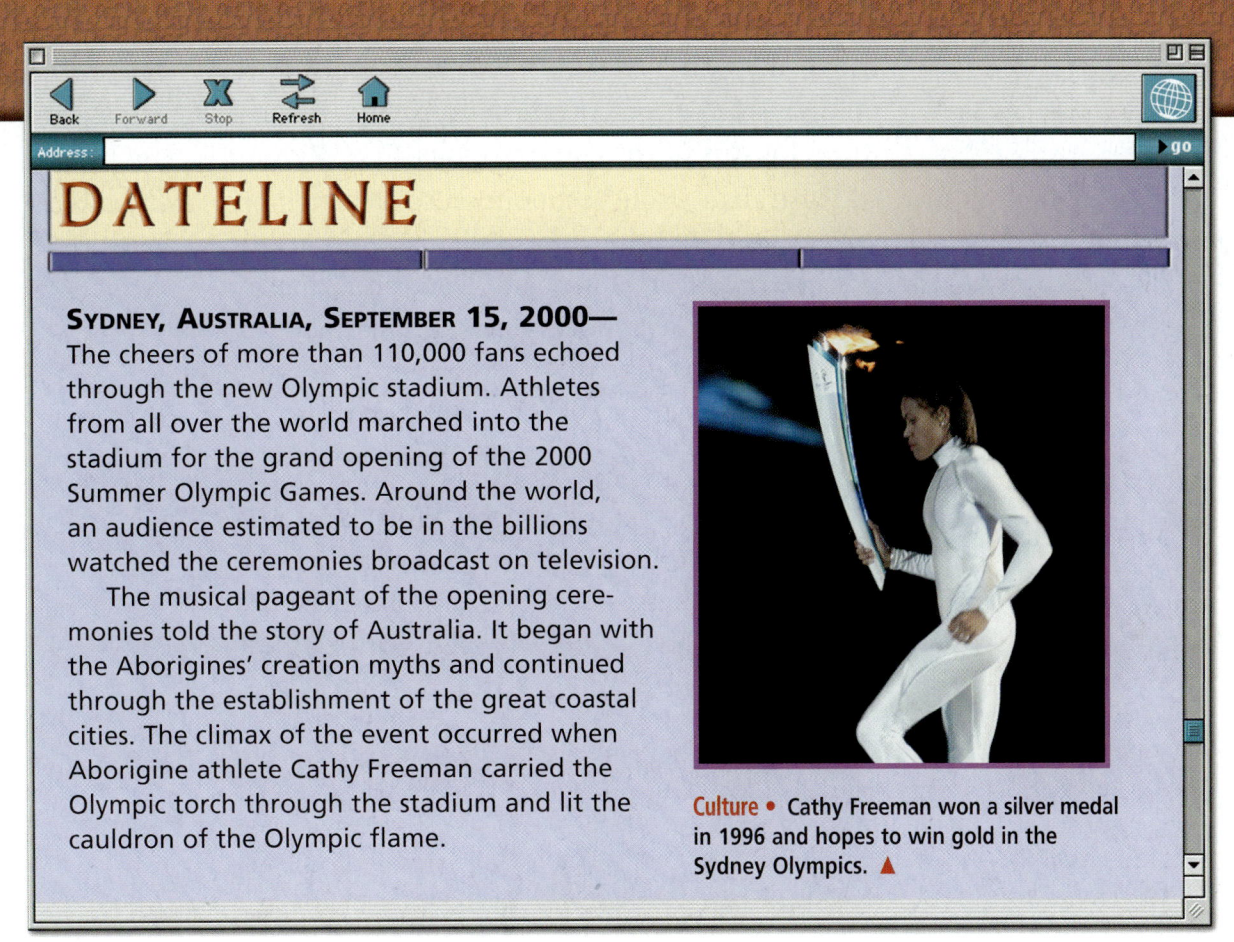

DATELINE

SYDNEY, AUSTRALIA, SEPTEMBER 15, 2000— The cheers of more than 110,000 fans echoed through the new Olympic stadium. Athletes from all over the world marched into the stadium for the grand opening of the 2000 Summer Olympic Games. Around the world, an audience estimated to be in the billions watched the ceremonies broadcast on television.

The musical pageant of the opening ceremonies told the story of Australia. It began with the Aborigines' creation myths and continued through the establishment of the great coastal cities. The climax of the event occurred when Aborigine athlete Cathy Freeman carried the Olympic torch through the stadium and lit the cauldron of the Olympic flame.

Culture • Cathy Freeman won a silver medal in 1996 and hopes to win gold in the Sydney Olympics. ▲

SUNSHINE STATE STANDARDS
Key Standard SS.A.3.3.5
The student understands the differences between institutions of Eastern and Western civilizations (e.g., differences in governments, social traditions and customs, economic systems and religious institutions).
Other Standards
SS.D.2.3.1
FCAT LA.A.2.3.1
Reading: Identify Main Idea, Facts, and Details

Resources and Economies

The economies of Australia, New Zealand, and Oceania have various foundations. On the one hand, tourists travel to the region to enjoy its beaches, mountains, fjords, and unusual plant and animal life. Thousands also came to Australia for the 2000 Summer Olympic Games. On the other hand, agriculture is the traditional base of the region's economies. Australia and New Zealand still depend more on farming than do most other developed countries.

TAKING NOTES
Use your chart to take notes about Australia, Oceania, New Zealand, and Antarctica.

Population	Places	Facts	Inferences
	Australia		
	New Zealand		
	Oceania		
	Antarctica		

Australia, New Zealand, Oceania, and Antarctica

Connections to Technology

TV in Tuvalu The Polynesian island nation Tuvalu (too·VUH·loo) has poor soil and few natural resources. Its most valuable possession may be its Web address: ".tv." Television organizations hoped to use those letters in their own Web addresses.

In 1998, Tuvalu sold the rights for ".tv" to a Canadian company. The government has since used the money from the sale to make life better for the people of Tuvalu.

Oceania's Economies Most people who live in Oceania fish, grow their own food, and build their own homes. However, some commercial agriculture does exist on the islands. **Copra** (KOH·pruh)—dried coconut meat—and coconut oil are important agricultural exports. Tourism also contributes significantly to the economies of some islands, such as Tahiti.

Australia's Economy Australia has a strong market economy and relatively free trade with other nations, especially Japan. Service industries—including health care, tourism, news media, and transportation—provide nearly three-fourths of the country's jobs.

Australia's strong economy also depends on mining and farming. Australia is the world's leading producer of bauxite, lead, and zinc. It has also developed vast fields of natural gas. Wheat is Australia's most important cash crop, and about 80 percent of the harvest is exported. Sugar cane is also an important cash crop.

Trade During colonial times, Australia and New Zealand mostly traded with Great Britain. Today, Australia's main trading partners are Japan and the United States, while New Zealand's main trading partner is Australia.

Reading Social Studies

A. Synthesizing List some factors that might have allowed Australia to have a stronger economy than the islands of Oceania have.

Products of Australia, 2001

Map legend: Bauxite, Cattle, Lead, Natural gas, Sheep, Uranium, Zinc

GEOGRAPHY SKILLBUILDER: Interpreting a Map

1. **Location** • Where is most of the uranium in Australia found?
2. **Region** • Locate the sheep-ranching areas. What other products come from these areas?

532 CHAPTER 18

Asian countries are also playing a bigger role in New Zealand's economy. In 1983, Australia and New Zealand signed a free-trade agreement to boost the trade between them.

Cultures and Change

Despite their remote locations, the islands of the region have attracted immigrants from around the world. Modernization and tradition both play strong roles in the region.

Oceania Modernization has affected life in parts of Oceania. For example, modernization has clearly changed modes of transportation. For short trips, villagers take canoes just as they always have. However, for longer trips, they outfit canoes with modern outboard motors or travel by ship or airplane.

Tradition continues to be strong, especially in art forms and family structures. For example, matrilineal societies are less common than patrilineal societies, but they are still found in parts of Oceania, such as Papua New Guinea. In **matrilineal societies,** ancestry is traced through the mother's side of the family. In **patrilineal societies,** ancestry is traced through the father's side.

Reading Social Studies
B. Hypothesizing What else about life in Oceania could modernization affect?

Place • In Papua New Guinea, people still perform traditional dances. ▼

Biography

Charlie Perkins Charlie Perkins (shown above, center) grew up in Australia's outback near Alice Springs. Perkins was the first Aborigine in Australia to graduate from college. He also played professional soccer in England. However, he is best known for his struggle against discrimination.

In 1965, Perkins led "freedom rides" throughout Australia to teach people about equal rights for Aborigines. On these rides, he met with clubs and organizations to discuss discrimination. He also led activities such as taking Aborigine children swimming in pools where only white children were allowed to swim.

Perkins has been compared to Martin Luther King, Jr. When Perkins died in October 2000, Australia's prime minister said, "Charlie was a tireless fighter for the cause of his people."

Australia and New Zealand Australia has a diverse population. For example, people worship in mosques, churches, synagogues, and Buddhist temples. In the past 50 years, immigrants have come from many parts of the world, such as Cambodia, Laos, and Vietnam. Some of them came from places where there was war or other danger. In a memoir, writer Barbara Marie Brewster described her pleasant surprise at Australia's diversity.

> **A VOICE FROM AUSTRALIA**
>
> As we drove home, I was struck by the extraordinary mixture Australia represented. Here were two Americans, a German, a Hungarian, and a Malay girl from Brunei, and we'd been talking with an Englishman who was a Buddhist monk in a monastery in Australia, founded and funded by Thais and run by an Italian abbot. I liked it.
>
> **Barbara Marie Brewster**

In New Zealand, over half a million people are Maori. Most others are descendants of Scottish, English, Irish, and Welsh settlers. Many Asians also live in the cities, such as the capital, Wellington, and the largest city, Auckland.

SECTION 2 ASSESSMENT

Terms & Names
1. Explain the significance of: (a) copra (b) matrilineal society (c) patrilineal society

Using Graphics

2. Use a diagram like this one to organize the important economic activities of Australia, New Zealand, and Oceania.

Economic Activities		
Australia	New Zealand	Oceania

Main Ideas

3. (a) How do the economies of Oceania and Australia benefit from the region's physical geography?
   (b) How do Australia and New Zealand cooperate economically?
   (c) What is the relationship between modernization and tradition in Oceania?

Critical Thinking

4. **Drawing Conclusions**
   In what ways do you think Australia's ethnic diversity affects its culture and politics?

   Think About
   - the various ethnic groups in Australia and how long each has lived there
   - how different ethnic groups contribute to diversity in other countries

ACTIVITY -OPTION- Make up an **advertising slogan** to promote tourism in Australia, Oceania, or New Zealand.

SKILLBUILDER

Using Primary Sources

▶▶ Defining the Skill

Primary sources are materials written by people who lived during historical events. They include letters, diaries, articles, videotapes, speeches, eyewitness accounts, and photographs. Secondary sources, such as social studies books, are materials designed to discuss or teach about an event. When you research a topic, look for useful primary sources. Include these in your writing if you want to illustrate or prove an important point.

SUNSHINE STATE STANDARDS
Key Standard SS.A.1.3.2
The student knows the relative value of primary and secondary sources and uses this information to draw conclusions from historical sources such as data in charts, tables, graphs.
FCAT LA.A.2.3.6 Reading: Use Variety of Reference Materials

▶▶ Applying the Skill

The passage to the right is an example of an essay about Captain James Cook's first voyage to the Pacific. Use the strategies listed below to help you determine when and how to use a primary source in your own writing.

How to Use Primary Sources

Strategy ❶ Choose a primary source that gives key information about your subject. Be sure that the material is from a primary source and not a secondary source.

Strategy ❷ Analyze the primary source and consider what the document was supposed to achieve and who would read it. Ask yourself how the primary source can help prove your point.

Strategy ❸ Quote the primary source exactly as it is written. Some primary sources, such as this letter, will have different language, spelling, capitalization, and punctuation than modern sources.

Make a Chart

Making a chart will help you determine when and how to use a primary source. The chart to the right explains the use of the primary source in the passage (above, right).

> Captain James Cook made three trips from England to the South Pacific. The seeming purpose of his first trip in 1768 was to observe the movements of the planet Venus. ❶ As this letter from the king clearly shows, however, Britain's true purpose was to find and claim the southern continent:
>
> ❸ Whereas the making Discoverys of Countries hitherto unknown, and the Attaining a Knowledge of distant Parts ... will redound greatly to the Honour of this Nation as a Maritime Power, as well as to the Dignity of the Crown of Great Britain, and may tend greatly to the advancement of the Trade and Navigation thereof; ... You are therefore in Pursuance of His Majesty's Pleasure hereby requir'd and directed to put to Sea with the Bark you Command so soon as the Observation of the Transit of the Planet Venus shall be finished ....

Subject	Primary Source	Reason for Quoting the Primary Source
Captain Cook's first voyage to the South Pacific in 1768	The secret instructions given to Captain Cook	To prove that the true purpose of the voyage was different from the stated purpose

▶▶ Practicing the Skill

Turn to page 534 in Chapter 18, Section 2. Read the quotation from a primary source found there. Make a chart like the one above to determine how and why the primary source was used.

Australia, New Zealand, Oceania, and Antarctica

SECTION 3
Antarctica

TERMS & NAMES
ice shelf

MAIN IDEA
Antarctica is an ice-covered continent where scientific research is the main activity.

WHY IT MATTERS NOW
Research in Antarctica provides information about climate change and other scientific subjects.

DATELINE

SOUTH POLE, ANTARCTICA, DECEMBER 14, 1911—Today Norwegian explorer Roald Amundsen beat British explorer Robert Falcon Scott in their race to reach the South Pole.

At first, Amundsen had planned an attempt on the North Pole. However, after American explorer Robert Peary reached the North Pole in 1909, Amundsen secretly changed his plans. Amundsen's decision to try for the South Pole brought him into competition with Scott. Scott had been planning a journey to the South Pole for some time.

Amundsen and his four-man crew set off for the South Pole after the Antarctic spring arrived in October 1911. They skied over snow, ice, and mountains with 52 dogs pulling four sleds of supplies. Two months later Amundsen became the first person to reach the South Pole.

Movement • Roald Amundsen reaches the South Pole. ▲

The Continent of Antarctica

Antarctica was the last continent on Earth to be explored. It is also the coldest, iciest, windiest, and driest continent on Earth. Unlike other continents, Antarctica has no permanent population.

Antarctica is the southernmost region on Earth. It is also the fifth largest continent, covering more than five million square miles in area.

TAKING NOTES
Use your chart to take notes about Australia, Oceania, New Zealand, and Antarctica.

	Places	Facts	Inferences
	Australia		
Population	New Zealand		
	Oceania		
	Antarctica		

SUNSHINE STATE STANDARDS
Key Standard SS.B.2.3.9 The student understands ways the interaction between physical and human systems affects current conditions on Earth.
Other Standards SS.B.2.3.1, B.2.3.2, B.2.3.8
FCAT LA.A.2.3.1 Reading: Identify Main Idea, Facts, and Details

Land and Climate

An icecap, a thick layer of ice and snow, covers 98 percent of Antarctica. The icecap holds about 70 percent of the world's fresh water. Under it lie mountains, plateaus, and valleys.

Land Regions The Transantarctic Mountains divide the continent into East Antarctica and West Antarctica. A high plateau covers the central part of East Antarctica. The South Pole, the southernmost point on Earth, is located on this plateau.

Much of West Antarctica is below sea level. If the icecap melted, this region would consist mainly of mountainous islands and the large Antarctic Peninsula.

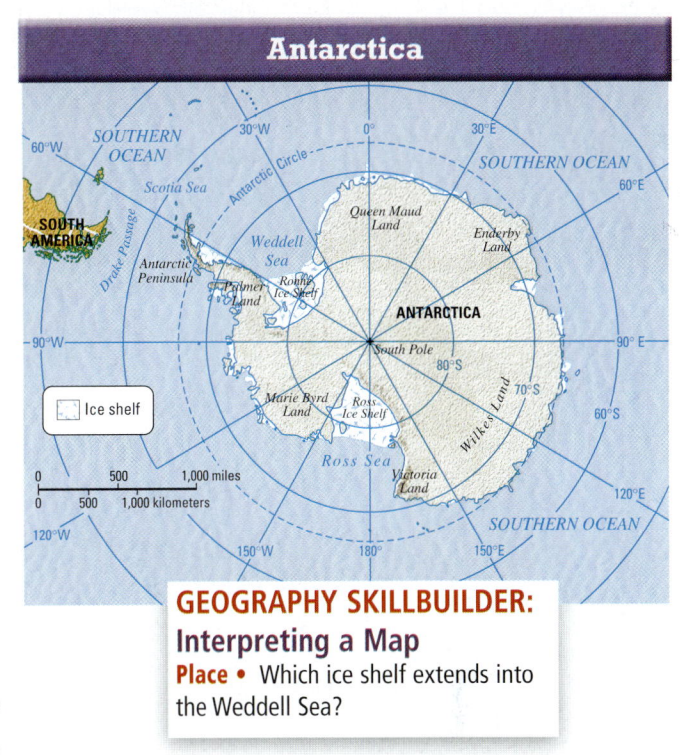

GEOGRAPHY SKILLBUILDER:
Interpreting a Map
Place • Which ice shelf extends into the Weddell Sea?

Climate Antarctica's climate is so cold and dry that the continent is called a polar desert. Inland areas are colder and drier than coastal areas. In winter, which lasts from May through August, inland temperatures can drop to more than 100° F below zero. Inland areas receive no rain and just a few inches of snowfall a year.

The Southern Ocean The Atlantic, Indian, and Pacific oceans meet around Antarctica to form the Southern Ocean. Almost 60 percent of the Antarctic coastline consists of glaciers and ice shelves. An **ice shelf** is a sheet of ice that floats on water but connects to land on one side.

History of Exploration

Since ancient times, people had suspected that a continent existed in the far south. For centuries sea captains and navigators searched for this southern continent. Norwegian whalers had landed on the continent by the 1890s.

Australia, New Zealand, Oceania, and Antarctica

Biography

Robert Falcon Scott (1868–1912)
Robert Falcon Scott wanted to be the first man to reach the South Pole. However, he took a longer route than Roald Amundsen and arrived there 34 days after Amundsen. Scott relied partly on ponies to carry supplies. The ponies were not suited to the harsh conditions, and Scott and his four-man crew had to haul supplies themselves. Their return trip ended in tragedy. The entire party of five died from a combination of injuries, starvation, and exposure. The frozen bodies of Scott and two other members of his party were found just 11 miles from a supply station.

The exploration of Antarctica began in the early 1900s. The British explorers Robert Falcon Scott and Ernest Shackleton led expeditions into the interior of the continent. This period is called the "heroic age" because explorers braved such harsh conditions. Some, like Robert Scott, even sacrificed their lives.

Exploration of Antarctica by airplane began in the 1920s. American naval officer Richard Byrd became the first person to fly over the South Pole in 1929. Photographs taken from planes and later satellites gave more information about Antarctica's geography.

As time passed, scientific interest in Antarctica grew. By the 1950s, 12 nations had set up more than 50 research stations there.

Reading Social Studies
A. Drawing Conclusions Why do you think Antarctica remained undiscovered for so long?

Resources

Antarctica's cold, dry interior supports just a small variety of plants and animals, including lichens, mosses, and insects. The Southern Ocean has abundant wildlife, including whales that eat small, shrimplike animals called krill. Large numbers of birds, penguins, and seals nest along the coast and feed in the ocean.

Antarctica has deposits of coal as well as iron and other minerals. These resources would be costly to mine, however.

The Antarctic Treaty Some nations have claimed parts of Antarctica, but the claims have not been recognized. In 1959, 12 nations signed the Antarctic Treaty, agreeing to reserve the continent for scientific research and to share the results. Since 1959, more than 30 other countries have signed the treaty.

The Scientific Community

As a result of the Antarctic Treaty, scientists from more than 25 countries are the main inhabitants of Antarctica. In the summer, as many as 20,000 scientists, support staff, and tourists come to the continent. Only about 1,000 remain through the winter. The scientists conduct research on many subjects, including wildlife, glaciers, and stars.

Global Warming Scientists in Antarctica also study climate change. The icecap preserves evidence of temperature changes throughout history. From studying ice samples, scientists have learned that temperatures in the Antarctic Peninsula have risen by 4.5°F over the last 50 years. Some scientists believe this data supports the theory of global warming, but others disagree. Global warming is a theory that worldwide temperatures are rising because of human activity and the burning of fossil fuels.

Many scientists do agree that warmer temperatures caused the rapid collapse of an ice shelf on the Antarctic Peninsula in early 2002. This ice shelf was larger than Rhode Island.

Strange but TRUE

Gondwana the Supercontinent
Hundreds of millions of years ago, Antarctica had a warmer climate. Scientists have found fossils in Antarctica of trees and plants that also grew in South America, Africa, India, and Australia. In fact, Antarctica was joined to these lands, forming a giant continent that scientists call Gondwana. Over millions of years, Gondwana broke up, and the lands slowly drifted to their present locations.

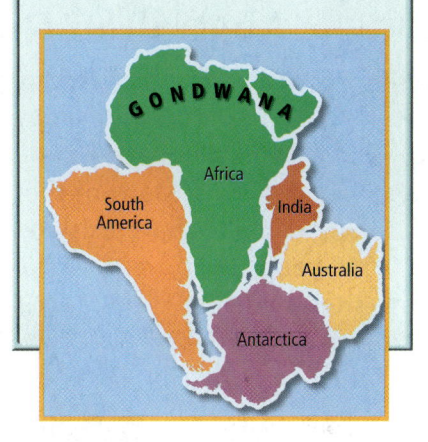

3

Terms & Names
1. Explain the significance of: (a) ice shelf

Using Graphics
2. Use a chart like this one to list important geographic details about Antarctica.

Size of Continent	Location	Land Regions	Inland Climate

Main Ideas
3. (a) What are the main characteristics of Antarctica's landscape and climate?
   (b) What was the outcome of Amundsen and Scott's historic race to the South Pole?
   (c) How did the Antarctic Treaty affect the development of Antarctica?

Critical Thinking
4. **Synthesizing**
   In what ways does Antarctica differ from all other continents?

Think About
 • its physical geography
 • its climate
 • its exploration and settlement

ACTIVITY -OPTION- Imagine that you are a scientist who has been invited to live in Antarctica for a year to conduct research. Write a letter in which you accept or turn down the invitation and give your reasons.

Australia, New Zealand, Oceania, and Antarctica

Linking Past and Present

The Legacy of East Asia, Australia, and Oceania

SUNSHINE STATE STANDARDS
Key Standard SS.A.3.3.5 The student understands the differences between institutions of Eastern and Western civilizations (e.g., differences in governments, social traditions and customs, economic systems and religious institutions).
FCAT LA.A.2.3.1 Reading: Identify Main Idea, Facts, and Details

Australian Rock Art

There are thousands of sites in Australia where rocks are engraved and painted with silhouettes of humans and animals. Many of these rock-art sites have existed for almost 10,000 years. Every year, visitors tour these sites and learn about the early people of Australia.

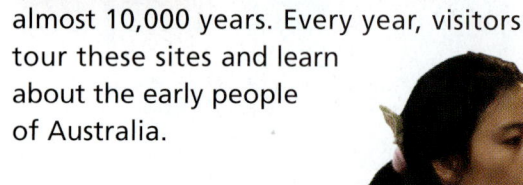

Soybeans

Although the origin of the soybean plant is unknown, soybeans were being grown in China around 1200 B.C. They were introduced into the United States in 1804 and today are used as a vegetable and as a source of soymilk and tofu.

Martial Arts

Martial arts are forms of self-defense, many of them weaponless. In ancient times, people developed martial arts in China, India, and Tibet in the belief that they allowed peaceful energy, called *chi*, to flow through one's body. Today, people around the world practice martial arts for self-defense, sport, exercise, and spiritual development and as a means of reducing stress and lowering blood pressure.

Find Out More About It!

Study the text and photos on these pages to learn about inventions, creations, and contributions that have come from East Asia, Australia, and Oceania. Then choose the item that interests you the most and do research in the library or on the Internet to learn more about it. Use the information you gather to write an article for your school or local newspaper that tells more about the contribution.

RESEARCH LINKS
CLASSZONE.COM

Origami

Origami, the art of folding paper into artistic objects, most likely originated from *gohei*, the art of folding cloth offerings in the Shinto religion of Japan. In origami, paper is folded to create figures of birds, animals, flowers, and people. Some origami figures actually have moving parts. Hundreds of books and courses on origami are available throughout the world.

Boomerangs

A boomerang is a curved, flat stick that is thrown either as a weapon or as a toy. Although boomerangs have been found in many parts of the world, they are most often associated with Australia and its native people, the Aborigines. Most Aboriginal boomerangs were "nonreturning"—that is, they did not return after they were thrown. A correctly thrown returning boomerang, on the other hand, will fly out, loop around, and return to the person who threw it. Returning boomerangs are used mainly for sport and as children's toys.

CHAPTER 18 ASSESSMENT

TERMS & NAMES

Explain the significance of each of the following:

1. Maori
2. Aborigine
3. Melanesia
4. Micronesia
5. Polynesia
6. Commonwealth of Nations
7. copra
8. matrilinial society
9. patrilineal society
10. ice shelf

REVIEW QUESTIONS

History and Governments *(pages 527–530)*

1. How did the isolation of the islands of Oceania affect the languages and cultures that developed there?
2. Describe two ways in which European settlers brought hardship to the people of Oceania.
3. Do Aborigines and Maori represent a large or small part of their countries' populations?

Economies and Cultures *(pages 531–534)*

4. Name two crops that are beneficial to the economies of Oceania.
5. What type of industry provides the majority of jobs in Australia?
6. How has modern life transformed transportation in Oceania?

Antarctica *(pages 536–539)*

7. What covers most of the land of Antarctica?
8. Why has Antarctica been called a polar desert?
9. What is the main human activity in Antarctica?

CRITICAL THINKING

Analyzing Motives

1. Using your completed chart from Reading Social Studies, p. 526, explain why you think Australia continues to attract immigrants from such a variety of cultures.

Making Inferences

2. Why do you think Great Britain is no longer the main trading partner of Australia and New Zealand?

Drawing Conclusions

3. Why is there no permanent population in Antarctica?

Visual Summary

1 History and Governments

- People from Southeast Asia settled Australia, New Zealand, and Oceania and developed their own cultures long before the Europeans arrived.
- Europeans, Americans, and Japanese later colonized the region, which now has many forms of government.

2 Economies and Cultures

- Australia's economy is more developed that those of Oceania.
- The diverse populations of Australia and New Zealand are descended from early settlers, colonists, and immigrants.

3 Antarctica

- Antarctica's extreme cold and remote location prevented exploration for centuries.
- Scientific research is the main activity in Antarctica today.

STANDARDS-BASED ASSESSMENT

Use the map and your knowledge of world cultures and geography to answer questions 1 and 2.

Additional Test Practice, pp. S1–S33

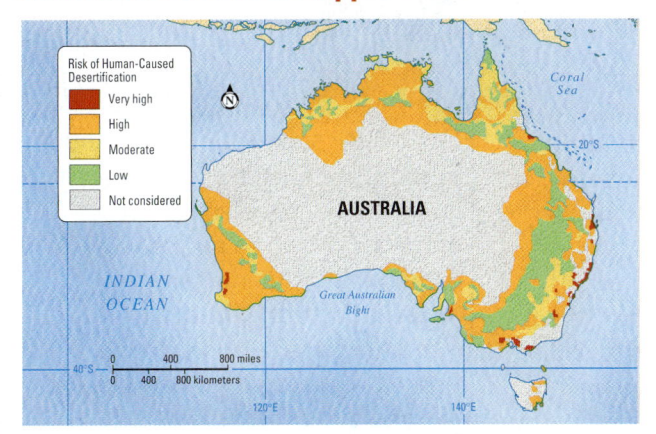

In this passage from his diary, Robert Scott discusses one of his men. Use the quotation and your knowledge of world cultures and geography to answer question 3.

PRIMARY SOURCE

Friday, March 16 or Saturday 17 Lost track of dates, but think the last correct. Tragedy all along the line. At lunch, the day before yesterday, poor Titus Oates said he couldn't go on; he proposed we should leave him in his sleeping-bag. That we could not do. . . .

This was the end. He slept through the night before last, hoping not to wake; but he woke in the morning — yesterday. It was blowing a blizzard. He said, "I am just going outside and may be some time." He went out into the blizzard and we have not seen him since.

ROBERT SCOTT, *Scott's Last Expedition: the Journals*

1. Where are the regions most at risk for desertification?
- **A.** central Australia
- **B.** along the coasts
- **C.** the northwest
- **D.** islands off the east coast

2. About what proportion of the country is at some risk for desertification?
- **A.** 5 percent
- **B.** 30 percent
- **C.** 80 percent
- **D.** 100 percent

3. The passage supports which of the following observations?
- **A.** Robert Scott was a cruel leader who pushed his men to the limit.
- **B.** The men on Scott's expedition were in high spirits, even in the face of danger.
- **C.** Scott was a selfish man who cared only about his own survival.
- **D.** Scott was concerned about his men and wanted them to survive.

TEST PRACTICE
CLASSZONE.COM

ALTERNATIVE ASSESSMENT

1. WRITING ABOUT HISTORY

The first Maori to arrive in New Zealand found an uninhabited land, with plants and animals they had never seen before. Research these plants and animals, such as the moa. Then find out how the Maori changed the land. What new things did they bring? What animals faced extinction after their arrival? Write a report on your findings. Share your report with the class.

2. COOPERATIVE LEARNING

The first settlers of Australia and Oceania came from Southeast Asia. In a group of three to five classmates, create an illustrated map with arrows showing the paths of migration. List the approximate dates of each migration. Illustrate the map with pictures or drawings of the people and items from their cultures. Divide the tasks of research, drawing, and writing among members of the group, assigning one or two members to each task.

INTEGRATED TECHNOLOGY

Doing Internet Research

Use the Internet to research Antarctica's Lake Vostok. Then, write a report of your findings. List the Web sites you used to prepare your report.

- Focus on its location and physical features, and explain why it is so unusual.
- Include a chart that summarizes the key facts about the lake.

For Internet links to support this activity, go to

RESEARCH LINKS
CLASSZONE.COM

Australia, New Zealand, Oceania, and Antarctica

SPECIAL REPORT: Terrorism and the War in Iraq

The Attack: September 11, 2001

Terrorism is the use of violence against people or property to force changes in societies or governments. Acts of terrorism are not new. Throughout history, individuals and groups have used terror tactics to achieve political or social goals.

In recent decades, however, terrorist groups have carried out increasingly destructive and high-profile attacks. The growing threat of terrorism has caused many people to feel vulnerable and afraid. However, it also has prompted action from many nations, including the United States.

Many of the terrorist activities of the late 20th century occurred far from U.S. soil. As a result, most Americans felt safe from such violence. All that changed, however, on the morning of September 11, 2001.

A Surprise Strike

As the nation began another workday, 19 terrorists hijacked four airplanes heading from East Coast airports to California. The hijackers crashed two of the jets into the twin towers of the World Trade Center in New York City. They slammed a third plane into the Pentagon outside Washington, D.C. The fourth plane crashed into an empty field in Pennsylvania after passengers apparently fought the hijackers.

The attacks destroyed the World Trade Center and badly damaged a section of the Pentagon. In all, some 3,000 people died. Life for Americans would never be the same after that day. Before, most U.S. citizens viewed terrorism as something that happened in other countries. Now they knew it could happen on their soil as well.

Officials soon learned that those responsible for the attacks were part of a largely Islamic terrorist network known as al-Qaeda. Observers, including many Muslims, accuse al-Qaeda of preaching a false and extreme form of Islam. Its members believe, among other things, that the United States and other Western nations are evil.

U.S. president George W. Bush vowed to hunt down all those responsible for the attacks. In addition, he called for a greater international effort to combat global terrorism. "This battle will take time and resolve," the president declared. "But make no mistake about it: we will win."

Securing the Nation

As the Bush Administration began its campaign against terrorism, it

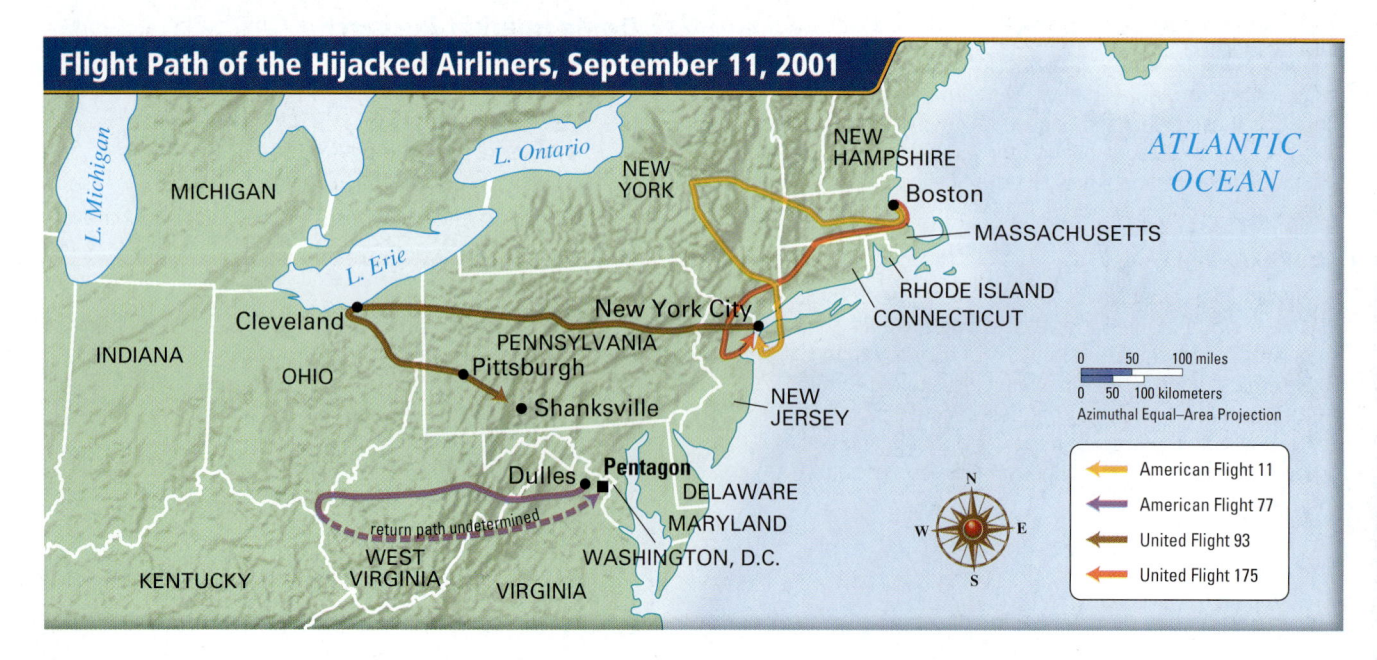

Flight Path of the Hijacked Airliners, September 11, 2001

SUNSHINE STATE STANDARDS
Key Standard SS.A.5.3.2 The student understands ways that significant individuals and events influenced economic, social, and political systems in the United States after 1880.
FCAT LA.A.2.3.1 Reading: Identify Main Idea, Facts, and Details

also sought to prevent any further attacks on America. In October 2001, the president signed into law the USA Patriot Act. The law gave the federal government a broad range of new powers to strengthen national security.

The new law enabled officials to detain foreigners suspected of terrorism for up to seven days without charging them with a crime. Officials could also monitor all phone and Internet use by suspects, and prosecute terrorist crimes without any time restrictions or limitations.

In addition, the government created a new cabinet position, the Department of Homeland Security, to coordinate national efforts against terrorism. President Bush named former Pennsylvania governor Tom Ridge as the first Secretary of Homeland Security.

Underneath a U.S. flag posted amid the rubble of the World Trade Center, rescue workers search for survivors of the attack.

Some critics charged that a number of the government's new anti-terrorism measures violated people's civil rights. Supporters countered that occasionally limiting some civil liberties was justified in the name of greater national security.

The federal government also stepped in to ensure greater security at the nation's airports. The September 11 attacks had originated at several airports, with four hijackings occurring at nearly the same time. In November 2001, President Bush signed the Aviation and Transportation Security Act into law. The law put the federal government in charge of airport security. Before, individual airports had been responsible for security. The new law created a federal security force to inspect passengers and carry-on bags. It also required the screening of checked baggage.

While the September 11 attacks shook the United States, they also strengthened the nation's unity and resolve. In 2003, officials approved plans to rebuild on the World Trade Center site and construct a memorial. Meanwhile, the country has grown more unified as Americans recognize the need to stand together against terrorism.

Stunned bystanders look on as smoke billows from the twin towers of the World Trade Center moments after an airplane slammed into each one.

SPECIAL REPORT: Terrorism and the War in Iraq

Fighting Back

The attack against the United States on September 11, 2001, represented the single most deadly act of terrorism in modern history. By that time, however, few regions of the world had been spared from terrorist attacks. Today, America and other nations are responding to terrorism in a variety of ways.

The Rise of Terrorism

The problem of modern international terrorism first gained world attention during the 1972 Summer Olympic Games in Munich, Germany. Members of a Palestinian terrorist group killed two Israeli athletes and took nine others hostage. Five of the terrorists, all the hostages, and a police officer were later killed in a bloody gun battle.

Since then, terrorist activities have occurred across the globe. In Europe, the Irish Republican Army (IRA) used terrorist tactics for decades against Britain. The IRA has long opposed British control of Northern Ireland. Since 1998, the two sides have been working toward a peaceful solution to their conflict. In South America, a group known as the Shining Path terrorized the residents of Peru throughout the late 20th century. The group sought to overthrow the government and establish a Communist state.

Africa, too, has seen its share of terrorism. Groups belonging to the al-Qaeda terrorist organization operated in many African countries. Indeed, officials have linked several major attacks against U.S. facilities in Africa to al-Qaeda. In 1998, for example, bombings at the U.S. embassies in Kenya and Tanzania left more than 200 dead and 5,000 injured.

Most terrorists work in a similar way: targeting high profile events or crowded places where people normally feel safe. They include such places as subway stations, bus stops, restaurants, or shopping malls. Terrorists choose these spots carefully in order to gain the most attention and to achieve the highest level of intimidation.

Terrorists use bullets and bombs as their main weapons. In recent years, however, some terrorist groups have used biological and chemical agents in their attacks. These actions involve the release of bacteria or poisonous gas into the air. Gas was the weapon of choice for a radical Japanese religious cult, Aum Shinrikyo. In 1995, cult members released sarin, a deadly nerve gas, in subway stations in Tokyo. Twelve people were killed and more than 5,700 injured. The possibility of this type of terrorism is particularly worrisome, because biochemical agents are relatively easy to acquire.

Terrorism: A Global Problem

PLACE	YEAR	EVENT
Munich, Germany	1972	Palestinians take Israeli hostages at Summer Olympics; hostages and terrorists die in gun battle with police
Beirut, Lebanon	1983	Terrorists detonate truck bomb at U.S. marine barracks, killing 241
Tokyo, Japan	1995	Religious extremists release lethal gas into subway stations, killing 12 and injuring thousands
Omagh, Northern Ireland	1998	Faction of Irish Republican Army sets off car bomb, killing 29
Moscow, Russia	2002	Rebels from Chechnya seize a crowded theater; rescue effort leaves more than 100 hostages and all the terrorists dead

Hunting Down Terrorists

Most governments have adopted an aggressive approach to tracking down and punishing terrorist groups. This approach includes spying on the groups to gather information on membership and future plans. It also includes striking back harshly after a terrorist attack, even to the point of assassinating known terrorist leaders.

Another approach that governments use is to make it more difficult for terrorists to act. This involves eliminating a terrorist group's source of funding. President Bush issued an executive order freezing the U.S. assets of alleged terrorist organizations as well as various groups accused of supporting terrorism. President Bush asked other nations to freeze such assets as well. By the spring of 2002, the White House reported, the United States and other countries had blocked nearly $80 million in alleged terrorist assets.

Battling al-Qaeda

In one of the more aggressive responses to terrorism, the United States quickly took military action against those it held responsible for the September 11 attacks.

U.S. officials had determined that members of the al-Qaeda terrorist group had carried out the assault under the direction of the group's leader, Osama bin Laden. Bin Laden was a Saudi Arabian millionaire who lived in Afghanistan. He directed his terrorist activities under the protection of the country's extreme Islamic government, known as the Taliban.

The United States demanded that the Taliban turn over bin Laden. The Taliban refused. In October 2001, U.S. forces began bombing Taliban air defenses, airfields, and command centers. They also struck numerous al-Qaeda training camps. On the ground, the United States provided assistance to rebel groups opposed to the Taliban. By December, the United States had driven the Taliban from power and severely weakened the al-Qaeda network. However, as of 2003, Osama bin Laden was still believed to be at large.

Osama bin Laden delivers a videotaped message from a hidden location shortly after the U.S.-led strikes against Afghanistan began.

Troops battling the Taliban in Afghanistan await transport by helicopter.

SPECIAL REPORT: Terrorism and the War in Iraq

The War in Iraq

In the ongoing battle against terrorism, the United States confronted the leader of Iraq, Saddam Hussein. The longtime dictator had concerned the world community for years. During the 1980s, Hussein had used chemical weapons to put down a rebellion in his own country. In 1990, he had invaded neighboring Kuwait—only to be pushed back by a U.S.-led military effort. In light of such history, many viewed Hussein as an increasing threat to peace and stability in the world. As a result, the Bush Administration led an effort in early 2003 to remove Hussein from power.

The Path to War

One of the main concerns about Saddam Hussein was his possible development of so-called weapons of mass destruction. These are weapons that can kill large numbers of people. They include chemical and biological agents as well as nuclear devices.

Bowing to world pressure, Hussein allowed inspectors from the United Nations to search Iraq for such outlawed weapons. Some investigators, however, insisted that the Iraqis were not fully cooperating with the inspections.

U.S. and British officials soon threatened to use to force to disarm Iraq. During his State of the Union address in January 2003, President Bush declared Hussein too great a threat to ignore in an age of increased terrorism. Reminding Americans of the September 11 attacks, Bush stated, "Imagine those 19 hijackers with other weapons and other plans—this time armed by Saddam Hussein. It would take one vial, one canister, one crate slipped into this country to bring a day of horror like none we have ever known. We will do everything in our power to make sure that day never comes."

Operation Iraqi Freedom

In the months that followed, the UN Security Council debated what action to take. Some countries, such as France and Germany, called for letting the inspectors continue searching for weapons. British prime minister Tony Blair, however, accused the Iraqis of "deception and evasion" and insisted inspections would never work.

On March 17, President Bush gave Saddam Hussein and his top aides 48 hours to leave the country or face a military strike. The Iraqi leader refused. On March 19, a coalition led by the United States and Britain launched air strikes in and around the Iraqi capital, Baghdad. The next day, coalition forces marched into Iraq though Kuwait. The invasion of Iraq to remove Saddam Hussein, known as Operation Iraqi Freedom, had begun.

The military operation met with strong opposition from numerous countries. Russian president Vladimir Putin claimed the invasion could "in no way be justified." He and others criticized the policy of attacking a nation to prevent it from future misdeeds. U.S. and British officials, however, argued that they would not wait for Hussein to strike first.

As coalition troops marched north to Baghdad, they met pockets of stiff resistance and engaged in fierce fighting in several southern cities. Meanwhile, coalition forces parachuted into northern Iraq and began moving south toward the capital city. By early April, Baghdad had fallen and the regime of Saddam Hussein had collapsed. After less than four weeks of fighting, the coalition had won the war.

U.S. Army Specialist Shoshana Johnson was one of several Americans held prisoner and eventually released during the war in Iraq.

As the regime of Saddam Hussein collapsed, statues of the dictator toppled.

established their own interim government several months after the war. The new governing body went to work creating a constitution and planning democratic elections.

Meanwhile, numerous U.S. troops had to remain behind to help maintain order and battle pockets of fighters loyal to Saddam Hussein. As for the defeated dictator, intelligence officials searched for clues of his whereabouts. The former Iraqi leader disappeared toward the end of the war, and it was unclear whether he had died or escaped.

Finally, the United States and Britain came under increasing fire for failing to find any weapons of mass destruction in the months after the conflict ended. U.S. and British officials insisted that it would be only a matter of time before they found Hussein's deadly arsenal.

Despite the unresolved issues, coalition leaders declared the defeat of Saddam Hussein to be a victory for global security. In a post-war speech to U.S. troops aboard the aircraft carrier *USS Abraham Lincoln*, President Bush urged the world community to keep moving forward in its battle against terrorism. "We do not know the day of final victory, but we have seen the turning of the tide," declared the president. "No act of the terrorists will change our purpose, or weaken our resolve, or alter their fate. Their cause is lost. Free nations will press on to victory."

President George W. Bush and British prime minister Tony Blair stood together throughout the war.

The Struggle Continues

Despite the coalition victory, much work remained in Iraq. The United States installed a civil administrator, retired diplomat L. Paul Bremer, to help oversee the rebuilding of the nation. With the help of Bremer and others, the Iraqis

---

Special Report Assessment

1. Main Ideas
a. What steps did the U.S. government take to make the nation more secure after the attacks on September 11, 2001?
b. Why did the United States take military action against the Taliban in Afghanistan?
c. What was the result of Operation Iraqi Freedom?

2. Critical Thinking
Analyzing Issues Is it important for the U.S. government to respect people's civil rights as it wages a war against terrorism? Why or why not?

THINK ABOUT
- what steps are necessary to protect the nation
- a government that grows too powerful

Reference Section

World Cultures AND Geography

SKILLBUILDER HANDBOOK
Skills for reading, thinking, and researching   **R2**

GLOSSARY AND SPANISH GLOSSARY
Important terms and definitions   **R24**
Important terms and definitions translated into Spanish   **R35**

INDEX
Index of all topics in textbook   **R47**

Skillbuilder Handbook

Table of Contents

Reading and Communication Skills

1.1	Summarizing	R2
1.2	Taking Notes	R3
1.3	Sequencing Events	R4
1.4	Finding Main Ideas	R5
1.5	Categorizing	R6
1.6	Making Public Speeches	R7

Critical Thinking Skills

2.1	Analyzing Points of View	R8
2.2	Comparing and Contrasting	R9
2.3	Analyzing Causes; Recognizing Effects	R10
2.4	Making Inferences	R11
2.5	Making Decisions	R12
2.6	Recognizing Propaganda	R13
2.7	Identifying Facts and Opinions	R14
2.8	Forming and Supporting Opinions	R15
2.9	Identifying and Solving Problems	R16
2.10	Evaluating	R17
2.11	Making Generalizations	R18

Print and Visual Sources

3.1	Interpreting Time Lines	R19

Technology Sources

4.1	Using an Electronic Card Catalog	R20
4.2	Creating a Database	R21
4.3	Using the Internet	R22
4.4	Creating a Multimedia Presentation	R23

1.1 Summarizing

Defining the Skill
When you **summarize,** you restate a paragraph, passage, or chapter in fewer words. You include only the main ideas and most important details. It is important to use your own words when summarizing.

Applying the Skill
The passage below discusses the economic importance of the Indian Ocean in global trade. Use the strategies listed below to help you summarize the passage.

How to Summarize

Strategy ❶ Look for topic sentences stating the main idea or ideas. These are often at the beginning or end of a section or paragraph. Briefly restate each main idea—in your own words.

Strategy ❷ Include key facts and any names, locations, dates, numbers, amounts, or percentages from the text.

Strategy ❸ After writing your summary, review it to see that you have included only the most important details.

THE INDIAN OCEAN

❶ The Indian Ocean is of great economic importance to southern Asia, the Middle East, northern Africa, and southern Europe. The southern tip of India divides the Indian Ocean into the Bay of Bengal to the east and the Arabian Sea to the west. The Arabian Sea feeds directly into the Persian Gulf and also the Red Sea. ❷ Much oil leaves the Middle East by traveling through the Persian Gulf into the Arabian Sea.

❷ In 1869, the Suez Canal opened, linking the Mediterranean and Red seas. This made it possible to sail between the Indian Ocean and the Mediterranean Sea without going around Africa.

❷ Ships used the Indian Ocean to sail between ports in Asia and Eastern Africa and ports in southern Europe. Trade among the regions increased.

Write a Summary
You should be able to write your summary in a short paragraph. The paragraph at right summarizes the passage you just read.

❸ *The Indian Ocean is of great economic importance to southern Asia, the Middle East, northern Africa, and southern Europe. Since the opening of the Suez Canal in 1869, the Indian Ocean has more directly connected African and Asian ports to those in southern Europe.*

Practicing the Skill
Turn to Chapter 13, Section 1, "Physical Geography." Read "The Northern Plains" and write a paragraph summarizing the passage.

1.2 Taking Notes

Defining the Skill
When you **take notes,** you write down the important ideas and details of a paragraph, passage, or chapter. A chart or an outline can help you organize your notes to use in the future.

Applying the Skill
The following passage describes several different types of bodies of water. Use the strategies listed below to help you take notes on the passage.

How to Take and Organize Notes

Strategy ❶ Look at the title to find the main topic of the passage.

Strategy ❷ Identify the main ideas and details of the passage. Then summarize the main idea and details in your notes.

Strategy ❸ Identify key terms and define them. The term *hydrosphere* is shown in boldface type and underlined; both techniques signal that it is a key term.

Strategy ❹ In your notes, use abbreviations to save time and space. You can abbreviate words such as *gulf (g.), river (r.)* and *lake (l.)*, as long as you write the proper name of the body of water with the abbreviation.

> ❶ **BODIES OF WATER**
>
> ❷ All the bodies of water on Earth form what is called ❸ the **hydrosphere**. The world's ❷ oceans make up the largest part of the hydrosphere. Oceans have smaller regions. ❷ Gulfs such as the Gulf of Tonkin and seas such as the Sea of Japan are extensions of oceans. Land partially encloses these waters.
>
> ❷ Oceans and seas contain salt water, but most lakes and rivers contain fresh water. The water in rivers, such as the ❷ Nile River in Africa, flows down a channel in one direction. This movement is the current. Lake water, such as that found in ❷ Lake Victoria in Tanzania, can have currents too, even though the water is surrounded by land. Some lakes feed into rivers, and some rivers supply water to lakes.

Make a Chart
Making a chart can help you take notes on a passage. The chart below contains notes from the passage you just read.

❷ Item	Notes
1. ❸ hydrosphere	all water on Earth
a. oceans	salt water; largest part of hydrosphere
b. gulfs and seas	❹ G. of Tonkin; ❹ S. of Japan part of ocean
c. lakes and rivers	usually fresh water; ❹ Nile R. flows; ❹ L. Victoria surrounded by land

Practicing the Skill
Turn to Chapter 1, Section 1, "The World at Your Fingertips." Read "History and Geography" and use a chart to take notes on the passage.

1.3 Sequencing Events

Defining the Skill

Sequence is the order in which events occur. Learning to follow the sequence of events through history will help you to better understand how events relate to one another.

Applying the Skill

The following passage gives a short history of Vietnam's struggles with foreign invaders. Use the strategies listed below to help you follow the sequence of events.

How to Find the Sequence of Events

Strategy ① Look for specific dates provided in the text. The dates may not always read from earliest to latest, so be sure to match an event with the date.

Strategy ② Look for clues about time that allow you to order events according to sequence. Words such as *later, before, today, then, until, years ago,* and different tenses such as *are, were,* or *would be* may help to sequence the events.

A HISTORY OF CONFLICT

Vietnam has a history of invasions and wars. Beginning ① in 1858, France conquered Vietnam and controlled it ② until World War II began ① in 1939. During the war, Japanese forces occupied Vietnam. The war ended ① in 1945 with Japan's defeat. The French ② then tried to regain power in Vietnam, but the Vietnamese resisted and drove out the French ① in 1954.

② At the time, Vietnam was divided: A Communist government ruled North Vietnam, and a U.S.-backed government ruled South Vietnam. ① During the 1960s and early 1970s, North and South Vietnam fought each other. The United States sent troops to aid the South. Unable to win, U.S. forces pulled out ① in 1973. ① In 1975, North Vietnam conquered the South.

Make a Time Line

Making a time line can help you sequence events. The time line below shows the sequence of events in the passage you just read.

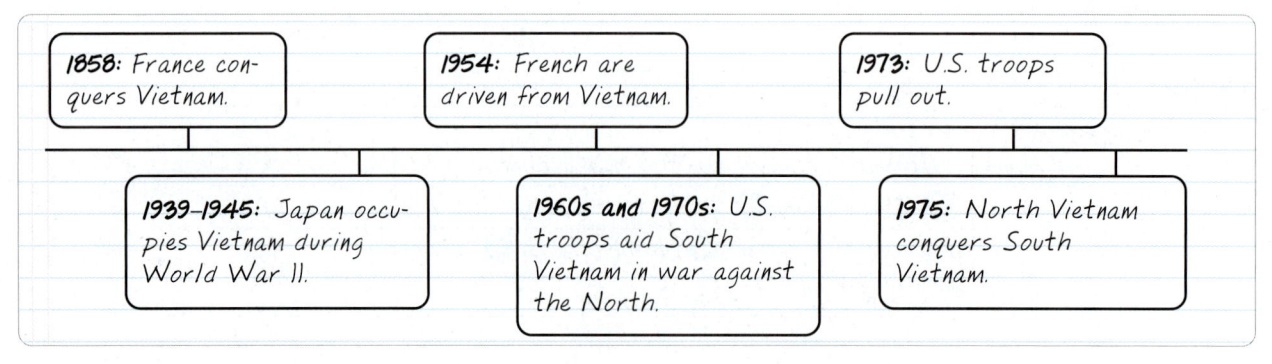

- **1858:** France conquers Vietnam.
- **1939–1945:** Japan occupies Vietnam during World War II.
- **1954:** French are driven from Vietnam.
- **1960s and 1970s:** U.S. troops aid South Vietnam in war against the North.
- **1973:** U.S. troops pull out.
- **1975:** North Vietnam conquers South Vietnam.

Practicing the Skill

Turn to Chapter 14, Section 1, "History." Read "Arrival of the British" and "Independence." Make a time line showing the sequence of events from the passages.

1.4 Finding Main Ideas

Defining the Skill
The **main idea** is a statement that summarizes the subject of a speech, an article, a section of a book, or a paragraph. Main ideas can be stated or unstated. The main idea of a paragraph is often stated in the first or last sentence. If it is the first sentence, it is followed by sentences that support that main idea. If it is the last sentence, the details build up to the main idea. To find an unstated idea, use the details of the paragraph as clues.

Applying the Skill
The following paragraph provides reasons why Japan and Australia make such good trading partners. Use the strategies listed below to help you identify the main idea.

How to Find the Main Idea

Strategy ❶ Identify what you think may be the stated main idea. Check the first and last sentences of the paragraph to see if either could be the stated main idea.

Strategy ❷ Identify details that support the main idea. Some details explain that idea. Others give examples of what is stated in the main idea.

> **TRADING PARTNERS**
>
> Australia is an island. Japan is also an island, though not nearly as large as Australia. Australia is not nearly as densely populated as Japan is. ❷ In Japan, an average of 867 people live in each square mile. In Australia, an average of 6 people live in each square mile. ❷ Australia has wide-open lands available for agriculture, ranching, and mining. ❷ Japan buys wool from Australian ranches, wheat from Australian farms, and iron ore from Australian mines. To provide jobs for its many workers, ❷ Japan has developed industries. Those industries ❷ sell electronics and cars to Australia. ❶ Australia and Japan are major trading partners because each has something the other needs.

Make a Chart
Making a chart can help you identify the main idea and details in a passage or paragraph. The chart below identifies the main idea and details in the paragraph you just read.

> **Main Idea:** Australia and Japan are good trading partners because each supplies something the other needs.
> **Detail:** Japan's population density is 867 people per square mile; Australia's is 6 per square mile.
> **Detail:** Australia has land, natural resources, and agricultural products.
> **Detail:** Japan buys wool, wheat, and iron from Australia.
> **Detail:** Japan has many industries.
> **Detail:** Australia buys electronics and cars from Japanese industries.

Practicing the Skill
Turn to Chapter 15, Section 2, "Economies and Cultures." Read "An Agricultural Economy" and create a chart that identifies the main idea and the supporting details.

1.5 Categorizing

Defining the Skill
To **categorize** is to sort people, objects, ideas, or other information into groups, called categories. Historians categorize information to help them identify and understand patterns in historical events.

Applying the Skill
The following passage examines several aspects of life in the neighboring countries of India and Pakistan. Use the strategies listed below to help you categorize information.

How to Categorize

Strategy ❶ First, decide what kind of information needs to be categorized. Decide what the passage is about and how that information can be sorted into categories. For example, this passage discusses differences between India and Pakistan.

Strategy ❷ Then find out what the categories will be. Look for general words that could be category headings, such as *languages* or *religion*.

Strategy ❸ Once you have chosen the categories, sort information into them. What are the languages, religions, and economic activities associated with each country?

INDIA AND PAKISTAN

❶Although India and Pakistan are neighbors, the two countries differ in many ways. Most people in India ❷ work in agriculture. However, a growing number of Indians work in the information technology industry. ❷ In Pakistan, about half the workforce is employed in agriculture, forestry, and fishing.

India has 18 official ❷ languages. The most widely spoken are Hindi, Bengali, Telugu, Marathi, and Tamil. ❷ Urdu is Pakistan's official language and is taught in schools. However, Punjabi and Sindhi are the most widely spoken languages.

In the area of ❷ religion, about 97 percent of Pakistanis practice Islam. ❷ In India, more than 80 percent of the people practice Hinduism.

Make a Chart
Making a chart can help you categorize information. Sometimes your main categories can be further divided into smaller, or sub-categories. You should have one more column than you have categories. The chart below shows how the information from the passage you just read can be categorized.

❸ Country	Economic Activity	Major Languages	Main Religion
India	Agriculture; information technology	Hindi, Bengali, Telugu, Marathi, Tamil	Hinduism
Pakistan	Agriculture; forestry; fishing	Punjabi, Sindhi, Urdu	Islam

Practicing the Skill
Turn to Chapter 16, Section 2, "Ancient China." Read "Achievements of the Dynasties." Then make a chart in which you categorize the accomplishments of Chinese dynasties.

1.6 Making Public Speeches

Defining the Skill
A speech is a talk given in public to an audience. Some speeches are given to persuade the audience to think or act in a certain way, or to support a cause. You can learn how to **make public speeches** effectively by analyzing great speeches in history.

Applying the Skill
The following is from a speech that British suffragette Emmeline Pankhurst gave to explain why women were using forceful tactics to gain the vote. Use the strategies listed below to help you analyze Pankhurst's speech and prepare a speech of your own.

How to Analyze and Prepare a Speech

Strategy ❶ Choose one central idea or theme and organize your speech to support it. Pankhurst organized her speech around the idea that a thing worth having is worth fighting for.

Strategy ❷ Use words or images that will win over your audience. Pankhurst asked her audience to put themselves in women's place by using such phrases as "if the situation were reversed."

Strategy ❸ Repeat words or images to drive home your main point—as if it is the "hook" of a pop song. Pankhurst repeats the phrase *You know perfectly well* to urge male listeners to consider how it would feel to suffer the injustices that women faced.

WHY WE ARE MILITANT

❶ Now, gentlemen, . . . you know perfectly well that there never was a thing worth having that was not worth fighting for. ❸ You know perfectly well that ❷ if the situation were reversed, if you had no constitutional rights and we had all of them, if you had the duty of paying and obeying and trying to look as pleasant, and we were the proud citizens who could decide our fate and yours, because we knew what was good for you better than you knew yourselves, ❸ you know perfectly well ❷ that you wouldn't stand for it a single day, and you would be perfectly justified in rebelling against such intolerable conditions.

Make an Outline
Making an outline like the one to the right will help you make an effective public speech.

Practicing the Skill
Turn to Chapter 10, Section 4, "The Road to Independence." Read the section, especially the quote from the Pan-African Congress on page 308, and use the quote as the subject for your speech. First, make an outline like the one to the right to organize your ideas. Then write your speech. Next, practice giving your speech. Make it a three-minute speech.

Title: Why We Are Militant

I. *Introduce Theme:* There never was a thing worth having that was not worth fighting for.

II. *Repeat theme:* You know perfectly well that if the situation were reversed, you wouldn't stand it for a single day.
   A. if men had no constitutional rights and women had all of them
   B. if men had to act obedient and pleasant all the time
   C. if women could decide men's fates and had the power to say what was good for them

III. *Conclude:* You would be perfectly justified in rebelling against such intolerable conditions.

2.1 Analyzing Points of View

Defining the Skill

Analyzing points of view means looking closely at a person's arguments to understand the reasons behind that person's beliefs. The goal of analyzing a point of view is to understand different historical viewpoints about a topic.

Applying the Skill

The following passage discusses two views about imperialism in Africa and southwest Asia at the turn of the 20th century. Use the strategies below to help you analyze the points of view.

How to Analyze Points of View

Strategy ❶ Look for statements that demonstrate a particular point of view on an issue. For example, Cecil Rhodes expresses a pro-imperialist view, while Sayyid Jamal al-Din al-Afghani opposes imperialism.

Strategy ❷ Think about why different people or groups might take the positions they do. Why might Rhodes support imperialism while al-Afghani oppose it?

Strategy ❸ Write a summary that explains why different people might take different positions on this issue.

IMPERIALISM

During the late 1890s and early 1900s, many lands in Africa and southwest Asia became colonies. European nations seized these lands to gain power and prestige, as well as to gain access to raw materials. Many Europeans also felt that they were bringing a better way of life to conquered lands. ❶ "The more of the world we inhabit," declared the British businessman Cecil Rhodes, "the better it is for the human race." Not everyone agreed. In Persia, the nationalist leader Sayyid Jamal al-Din al-Afghani was angry about the Persian ruler's cooperation with British imperialists. ❶ "This criminal has offered the provinces of Persia to auction to the Powers," he stated, "and is selling the realms of Islam and abodes of Muhammad and his household to foreigners."

Make a Diagram

Using a diagram can help you analyze points of view. The diagram below analyzes the different points of view regarding imperialism in Africa and Southwest Asia.

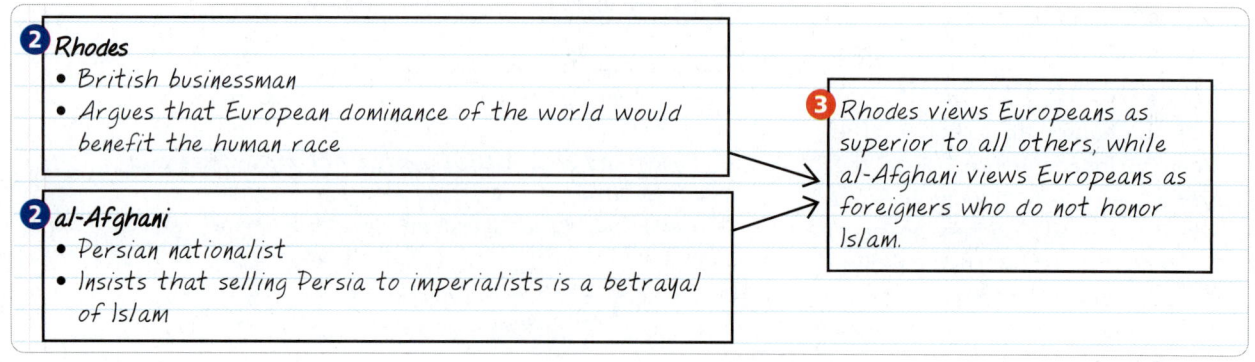

❷ Rhodes
- British businessman
- Argues that European dominance of the world would benefit the human race

❷ al-Afghani
- Persian nationalist
- Insists that selling Persia to imperialists is a betrayal of Islam

❸ Rhodes views Europeans as superior to all others, while al-Afghani views Europeans as foreigners who do not honor Islam.

Practicing the Skill

Turn to Section 3 of Chapter 15, "Southeast Asia Today." Read the passage entitled "War" and make a chart to analyze the different points of view about the Vietnam War.

2.2 Comparing and Contrasting

Defining the Skill
Comparing means looking at the similarities and differences between two or more things. **Contrasting** means examining only the differences between them. Historians compare and contrast events, personalities, behaviors, beliefs, and situations in order to understand them.

Applying the Skill
The following passage describes the Dead Sea in southwest Asia and the Red Sea located between northeast Africa and southwest Asia. Use the strategies below to help you compare and contrast these two bodies of water.

How to Compare and Contrast

Strategy ❶ Look for two aspects of the subject that can be compared and contrasted. This passage compares the Red Sea and the Dead Sea, two extremely salty bodies of water that are close to one another.

Strategy ❷ To find similarities, look for clue words indicating that two things are alike. Clue words include *both, together, similarly*.

Strategy ❸ To contrast, look for clue words that show how two things differ. Clue words include *however, but, on the other hand,* and *yet*.

SALTY SEAS

❶ According to the Bible, God parted the Red Sea so Moses could lead his people across it. The Bible also mentions the Dead Sea, calling it the Salt Sea. This is because the Dead Sea is the saltiest body of water in the world. ❷ *Similarly*, the Red Sea also has a high salt content. Many observers argue that the Dead Sea is not really a sea at all. It is more of a lake since it is fed by the River Jordan and is surrounded by land on all four sides. ❸ *On the other hand*, the Indian Ocean feeds the Red Sea. The Red Sea is also the larger of the two seas. It is 174,000 square miles, while the Dead Sea is only 400 square miles. ❷ *Both* bodies of water provide minerals for commercial use, especially salt.

Make a Venn Diagram

Making a Venn diagram will help you identify similarities and differences between two things. In the overlapping area, list characteristics shared by both subjects. Then, in the separate ovals, list the characteristics of each subject not shared by the other. This Venn diagram compares and contrasts the Red Sea and the Dead Sea.

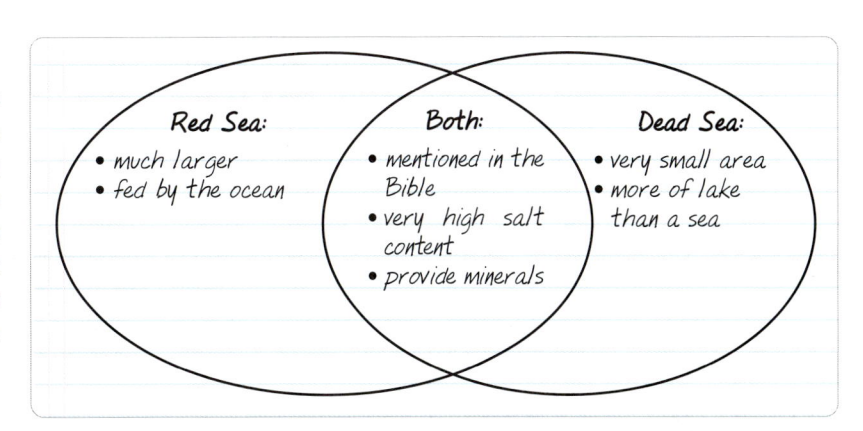

Red Sea:
- much larger
- fed by the ocean

Both:
- mentioned in the Bible
- very high salt content
- provide minerals

Dead Sea:
- very small area
- more of lake than a sea

Practicing the Skill
Turn to Chapter 8, Section 4, "Birthplace of Three Religions." Read "Abraham and the Origin of Judaism" and "Jesus and the Birth of Christianity." Then make a Venn diagram showing similarities and differences between the religions of Judaism and Christianity.

2.3 Analyzing Causes; Recognizing Effects

Defining the Skill
A **cause** is an action in history that makes something happen. An **effect** is the historical event that is the result of the cause. A single event may have several causes. It is also possible for one cause to result in several effects. Historians identify cause-and-effect relationships to help them understand why historical events took place.

Applying the Skill
The following paragraph describes changes in the government of China. Use the strategies below to help you identify the cause-and-effect relationships.

How to Analyze Causes and Recognize Effects

Strategy ❶ Ask why an action took place. Ask yourself a question about the title, such as, "Why did China undergo political change?"

Strategy ❷ Look for effects. Ask yourself, "What happened?" (the effect). Then ask, "Why did it happen?" (the cause). For example, "Why did China become a Communist state?"

Strategy ❸ Look for clue words that signal causes, such as *because, as a result,* and *led to.*

---

❶ POLITICAL CHANGE IN CHINA

❷ In 1949, China became a Communist state. For years, China's Communists had been battling the nation's ruling party, the Nationalists. The Nationalists had improved transportation and encouraged industry. Yet, they did little to improve the live of peasants and workers. ❸ This *led* many peasants to support the Communist Party, which promised to help the poor.

In 1949, the Communists defeated the Nationalists. ❸ *As a result,* ❷ the Communists took control of China. They set up a one-party rule in which their leader, Mao Zedong, held nearly total power. The Communists punished those who spoke out against the government.

Make a Diagram
Using a diagram can help you understand causes and effects. The diagram below shows two causes and an effect for the passage you just read.

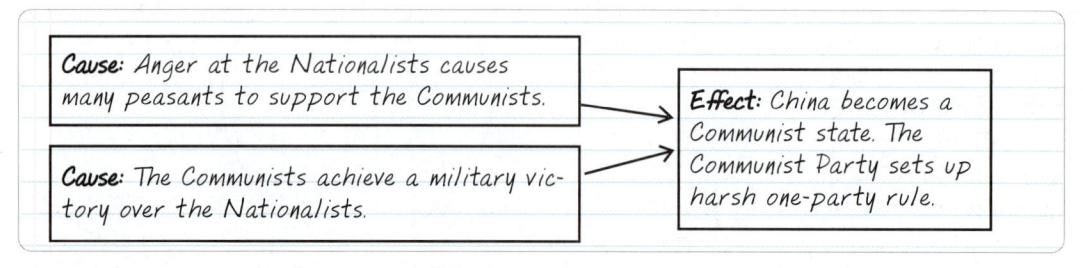

Cause: Anger at the Nationalists causes many peasants to support the Communists. → *Effect:* China becomes a Communist state. The Communist Party sets up harsh one-party rule.

Cause: The Communists achieve a military victory over the Nationalists.

Practicing the Skill
Turn to Chapter 16, Section 3, "Ancient Japan." Read "Feudal Japan" and make a diagram about the causes and effects of the civil conflict in early Japan.

2.4 Making Inferences

Defining the Skill
Inferences are ideas that the author has not directly stated. **Making inferences** involves reading between the lines to interpret the information you read. You can make inferences by studying what is stated and using your common sense and previous knowledge.

Applying the Skill
The passage below examines the great pyramids of ancient Egypt. Use the strategies below to help you make inferences from the passage.

How to Make Inferences

Strategy ❶ Read to find statements of facts and ideas. Knowing the facts will give you a good basis for making inferences.

Strategy ❷ Use your knowledge, logic, and common sense to make inferences that are based on facts. Ask yourself, "What does the author want me to understand?" For example, from the facts about the pyramids' purpose, you can make the inference that the Egyptians believed in life after death. See other inferences in the chart below.

THE PYRAMIDS OF EGYPT

One reason that ancient Egypt is famous is for its giant pyramids. ❶ The Egyptians built these magnificent monuments for their kings, or pharaohs. Each pyramid was a resting place where an Egyptian pharaoh planned to spend the afterlife. The pharaoh appointed a leader to organize the construction project. ❶ The leader of the project assembled a staff that managed the workers and tracked the supplies. A single pyramid might contain 92 million cubic feet of stone, enough to fill a large sports stadium. ❶ Workers built these long-lasting structures with none of the modern cutting tools and machines that we have today.

Make a Chart

Making a chart will help you organize information and make logical inferences. The chart below organizes information from the passage you just read.

❶ Stated Facts and Ideas	❷ Inferences
Egyptians built their pyramids as resting places for their pharaohs in the afterlife.	Egyptians believed in life after death
A staff oversaw construction of the project.	Pyramid building was a complicated task that required organization.
The Egyptians built the pyramids without modern equipment.	The Egyptians were skilled engineers and hard workers.

Practicing the Skill
Turn to Chapter 15, Section 2, "Ancient Mesopotamia and the Fertile Crescent." Read "A Culture Based on Writing" and use a chart like the one above to make inferences about scribes in Mesopotamia.

2.5 Making Decisions

Defining the Skill

Making decisions involves choosing between two or more options, or courses of action. In most cases, decisions have consequences, or results. Sometimes decisions may lead to new problems. By understanding how historical figures made decisions, you can learn how to improve your own decision-making skills.

Applying the Skill

The following passage shows some decisions made by Mongol leader Kublai Khan after his armies conquered China. Use the strategies below to analyze his decisions.

How to Make Decisions

Strategy ❶ Identify a decision that needs to be made. Think about what factors make the decision difficult.

Strategy ❷ Identify possible consequences of the decision. Remember that there can be more than one consequence to a decision.

Strategy ❸ Identify the decision that was made.

Strategy ❹ Identify actual consequences that resulted from the decision.

CONTROLLING AN EMPIRE

Upon taking control of China, Kublai Khan had a decision to make. ❶ He could allow Chinese officials to continuing running the country or bring in people from his other lands to lead the government. ❷ He worried that if he gave the Chinese too much power, they would try to take back their country. ❷ However, he feared that foreign rulers would have difficulty understanding Chinese culture. In addition, their presence would cause widespread resentment among the Chinese. ❸ In the end, Kublai Khan entrusted the government to foreigners. ❹ The Chinese did indeed resent the presence of foreign rulers. Such resentment played a key role in the eventual collapse of Mongol rule in China.

Make a Flow Chart

A flow chart can help you identify the process of making a decision. The flow chart below shows the decision-making process in the passage you just read.

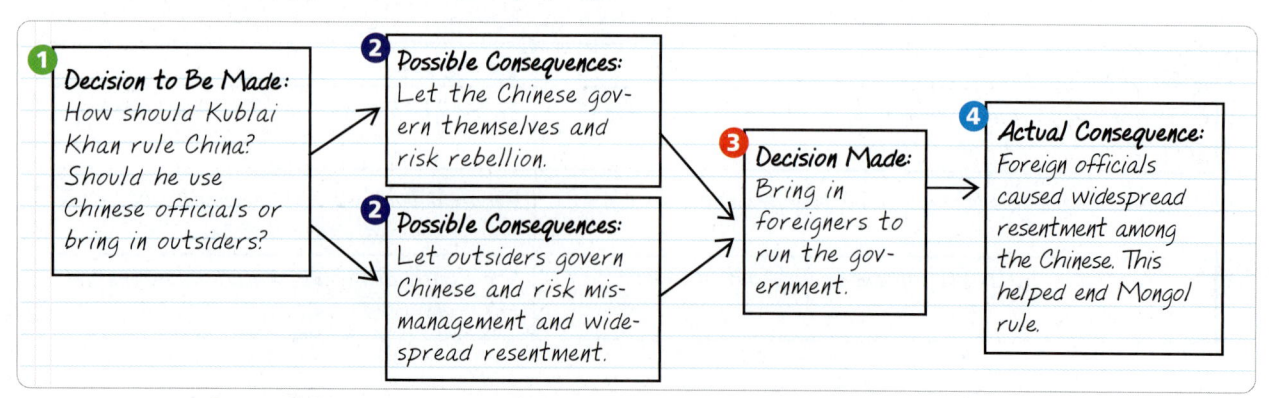

❶ **Decision to Be Made:** How should Kublai Khan rule China? Should he use Chinese officials or bring in outsiders?

❷ **Possible Consequences:** Let the Chinese govern themselves and risk rebellion.

❷ **Possible Consequences:** Let outsiders govern Chinese and risk mismanagement and widespread resentment.

❸ **Decision Made:** Bring in foreigners to run the government.

❹ **Actual Consequence:** Foreign officials caused widespread resentment among the Chinese. This helped end Mongol rule.

Practicing the Skill

Turn to Chapter 6, Section 2, "Eastern Europe and Russia." Read "The Breakup of the Soviet Union" and make a flow chart to identify Gorbachev's decision and its consequences.

2.6 Recognizing Propaganda

Defining the Skill

Propaganda is communication that aims to influence people's opinions, emotions, or actions. Propaganda is not always factual. Rather, it uses one-sided language or striking symbols to sway people's emotions. Modern advertising often uses propaganda. By thinking critically, you will avoid being swayed by propaganda.

Applying the Skill

The photograph below shows Chinese workers in 1950 celebrating the first anniversary of the founding of the People's Republic of China. Use the strategies listed below to help you understand how the photograph works as propaganda.

How to Recognize Propaganda

Strategy ❶ Identify the aim, or purpose, of the photograph. Point out the subject and explain the point of view.

Strategy ❷ Identify those images in the photograph that viewers might respond to emotionally and identify the emotions.

Strategy ❸ Think critically about the image. What facts have been ignored or omitted?

Make a Chart

Making a chart will help you think critically about a piece of propaganda. The chart below summarizes the information from the pro-Chinese government photograph.

❶	Identify Purpose	The photograph aims to show that the Chinese people support their ruler Mao Zedong.
❷	Identify Emotions	The image of so many people carrying posters of Mao gives the impression of widespread support for the Chinese leader. The fact that the marchers appear to be workers is meant to demonstrate Mao's popularity among the working class.
❸	Think Critically	The image ignores the fact that China under the Communists was a one-party state that allowed no protests. So one might wonder whether the marchers in the photo truly support Mao or were forced to carry the posters.

Practicing the Skill

Turn to Chapter 6, Section 1, "Eastern Europe Under Communism." Read "Soviet Culture," paying special attention to the photograph on page 354. Use a chart like the one above to think critically about the statue shown in the photograph as an example of propaganda.

2.7 Identifying Facts and Opinions

Defining the Skill

Facts are events, dates, statistics, or statements that can be proved to be true. **Opinions** are judgments, beliefs, and feelings. By identifying facts and opinions, you will be able to think critically when a person is trying to influence your own opinion.

Applying the Skill

The following passage touches on life for Indian under British rule. Use the strategies listed below to help you distinguish facts from opinions.

How to Recognize Facts and Opinions

Strategy ❶ Look for specific information that can be proved or checked for accuracy.

Strategy ❷ Look for assertions, claims, and judgments that express opinions. In this case, one speaker's opinion is expressed in a direct quote.

Strategy ❸ Think about whether statements can be checked for accuracy. Then, identify the facts and opinions in a chart.

INDIA UNDER BRITISH RULE

❶ By 1850, nearly all of the Indian subcontinent had come under British control. India both benefited from and suffered under British colonialism. ❶ On the positive side, the British built the world's third largest railroad network across India. The railroad enabled India to develop a modern economy and to unite its different regions. On the negative side, the British considered Indians an inferior race and suppressed many of their rights. ❷ As one British officer remarked, "However well educated and clever a native may be, . . . no rank we can bestow on him would cause him to be considered an equal of the British officer."

Make a Chart

The chart below analyzes the facts and opinions from the passage above.

Statement	❸ Can It Be Proved?	❸ Fact or Opinion
The British controlled most of the Indian subcontinent by 1850.	Yes. Check history books and maps.	Fact
The British laid the world's third largest railroad at that time across India.	Yes. Check railroads of that time to compare lengths.	Fact
A member of the Indian military could never hope to be the equal of a British officer.	No. This cannot be proved. It is what one speaker believes.	Opinion

Practicing the Skill

Turn to Chapter 9, Section 4, "Israel Today." Read "Life on a Kibbutz" and then make a chart in which you analyze key statements in the passage to determine whether they are facts or opinions.

SKILLBUILDER HANDBOOK

2.8 Forming and Supporting Opinions

Defining the Skill
When you **form opinions,** you interpret and judge the importance of events and people in history. You should always **support your opinions** with facts, examples, and quotations.

Applying the Skill
The following passage describes the impact of apartheid on South Africa. Use the strategies listed below to form and support an opinion about the policy.

How to Recognize Facts and Opinions

Strategy ❶ Look for important information about the subject. Information can include facts, quotations, and examples.

Strategy ❷ Form an opinion about the subject by asking yourself questions about the information. For example, how important was the subject? How does it relate to similar subjects in your own experience?

Strategy ❸ Support your opinions with facts, quotations, and examples. If the facts do not support the opinion, then rewrite your opinion so that it is supported by the facts.

THE POLICY OF APARTHEID

From the mid- to late-twentieth century, South Africa had a policy called apartheid, which separated whites and nonwhites. ❶ Nonwhites faced discrimination concerning where they could live, what jobs they could hold, and whether they could attend school. Many were forced to leave their homes and relocate in less desirable regions. Many nonwhites protested these policies, leading to years of conflict. A number of nations also criticized apartheid. ❶ In 1985, the United States and Great Britain restricted trade with South Africa. In 1989, Willem de Klerk became president of South Africa. He opposed apartheid. His efforts helped to end the country's policy of segregation.

Make a Chart
Making a chart can help you organize your opinions and supporting facts. The following chart summarizes one possible opinion about the policy of apartheid in South Africa.

❷ Opinion	The policy of apartheid oppressed many South Africans and hurt the nation's economy.	
❸ Facts	Nonwhites faced discrimination concerning where they could live, what jobs they could hold, and whether they could attend school.	
	Many nonwhites were forced to relocate in less desirable regions.	
	Nations opposed to apartheid restricted trade with South Africa.	

Practicing the Skill
Turn to Chapter 11, Section 1, "History and Political Change." Read "Government in Ghana," and form your own opinion about the independent government in Ghana. Make a chart like the one above to summarize your opinion and the supporting facts and examples.

2.9 Identifying and Solving Problems

Defining the Skill

Identifying problems means finding and understanding the difficulties faced by a particular group of people during a certain time. **Solving problems** means understanding how people tried to remedy those problems. By studying how people solved problems in the past, you can learn ways to solve problems today.

Applying the Skill

The following paragraph describes the problems that resulted from the return of Hong Kong to Chinese rule after 99 years under British control. Use the strategies listed below to help you see how the Chinese and British governments tried to solve these problems.

How to Identify Problems and Solutions

Strategy ❶ Look for the difficulties or problems caused by the situation.

Strategy ❷ Consider how the problem affected people or groups with different points of view. For example, the main problem described here is what to do about Hong Kong's government and economy.

Strategy ❸ Look for the solutions people or groups tried to deal with the problem. Think about whether the solution was a good one for people or groups with differing points of view.

HONG KONG'S RETURN

Britain took control of Hong Kong in 1842 after defeating China in a war. In 1898, the two nations signed an agreement allowing Britain to rule Hong Kong until 1997. Hong Kong's economy flourished. ❶ As British rule neared its end, concerns arose about Hong Kong's future. ❷ Hong Kong wanted to maintain its capitalist economy and democratic ways. However, it would soon become part of China, which was now Communist. ❷ China wanted to control Hong Kong but did not want to scare off the industries that made the island profitable. ❸ As a result, Chinese and British leaders reached an agreement allowing Hong Kong to maintain much of its government and free-enterprise economy.

Make a Chart

Making a chart will help you identify and organize information about problems and solutions. The chart below shows problems and solutions included in the passage you just read.

❶ Problem	❷ Differing Points of View	❸ Solution
Hong Kong had to return to Chinese rule, but China was Communist and Hong Kong was not.	Hong Kong wanted to maintain its government and economic system. China wanted to rule Hong Kong but not scare off profitable industries.	The Chinese and British agreed to keep much of Hong Kong's government and economic system intact.

Practicing the Skill

Turn to Chapter 12, Section 3, "South Africa Today." Read "A Nation of Apartheid." Then make a chart that summarizes the problems that South Africa faced after independence and how it solved those problems.

2.10 Evaluating

Defining the Skill
To **evaluate** is to make a judgment about something. Historians evaluate the actions of people in history. One way to do this is to examine both the positives and the negatives of a historical action, then decide which is stronger—the positive or the negative.

Applying the Skill
The following passage examines the rule of Mustafa Kemal of Turkey. Use the strategies listed below to evaluate the success of his reforms.

How to Evaluate

Strategy ❶ Before you evaluate a person's actions, first determine what that person was trying to do. In this case, think about what Kemal wanted to accomplish.

Strategy ❷ Look for statements that show the positive, or successful, results of his actions. For example, did he achieve his goals?

Strategy ❸ Also look for statements that show the negative, or unsuccessful, results of his actions. Did he fail to achieve something he tried to do?

Strategy ❹ Write an overall evaluation of the person's actions.

> **KEMAL RULES TURKEY**
>
> In 1923, Turkey became an independent republic. Mustafa Kemal became Turkey's first president. ❶ Kemal wanted Turkey to resemble European countries rather than its Islamic neighbors. Kemal quickly got rid of Turkey's Islamic government and replaced it with a secular, or non-religious, system. He also replaced the Arabic language and calendar with Western versions of each. ❸ Kemal's actions drew protests from many traditionalists. ❷ However, Kemal's moves helped to modernize Turkey. ❷ They also benefited women, who had lived with many restrictions under Islamic law. Women now had greater social freedom. They also could vote and run for political office.

Make a Diagram for Evaluating

Using a diagram can help you evaluate. List the positives and negatives of the historical person's actions and decisions. Then make an overall judgment. The diagram below shows how the information from the passage you just read can be diagrammed.

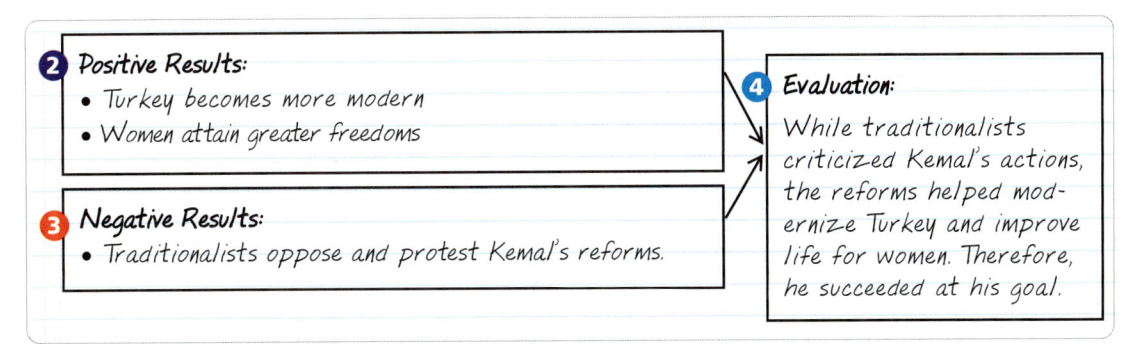

❷ **Positive Results:**
- Turkey becomes more modern
- Women attain greater freedoms

❸ **Negative Results:**
- Traditionalists oppose and protest Kemal's reforms.

❹ **Evaluation:**
While traditionalists criticized Kemal's actions, the reforms helped modernize Turkey and improve life for women. Therefore, he succeeded at his goal.

Practicing the Skill
Turn to Chapter 12, Section 2, "Economies and Cultures." Read "Fishing" under "Agriculture in Eastern and Southern Africa," and make a diagram in which you evaluate the decision to introduce the Nile Perch to Lake Victoria.

2.11 Making Generalizations

Defining the Skill
To **make generalizations** means to make broad judgments based on information. When you make generalizations, you should gather information from several sources.

Applying the Skill
The following passages describe the immigrant groups who have come into Australia. Use the strategies listed below to make a generalization about Australia and its people.

How to Make Generalizations

Strategy ❶ Look for information that the sources have in common. These three sources all look at immigration to Australia and the mix of foreign people.

Strategy ❷ Form a generalization that describes Australia in a way that all three sources would agree with. State your generalization in a sentence.

COMING TO AUSTRALIA

After World War II ended in 1945, . . . ❶ Europeans left homeless by the war [moved] to Australia . . . Australia also accepts refugees from other lands, especially Southeast Asia.
—*World Book Encyclopedia*

❶ The number of settlers arriving in Australia between July 2001 and June 2002 totaled 88,900. They came from more than 150 countries. Most were born either in New Zealand, the United Kingdom, China, South Africa, India, or Indonesia.
—*Australian Immigration Fact Sheet* (government Web site)

❶ I was struck by the extraordinary mixture Australia represented. Here were two Americans, a German, a Hungarian, and a Malay girl from Brunei.
—*Barbara Marie Brewster*

Make a Chart
Using a chart can help you make generalizations. The chart below shows how the information you just read can be used to generalize about the population of Australia.

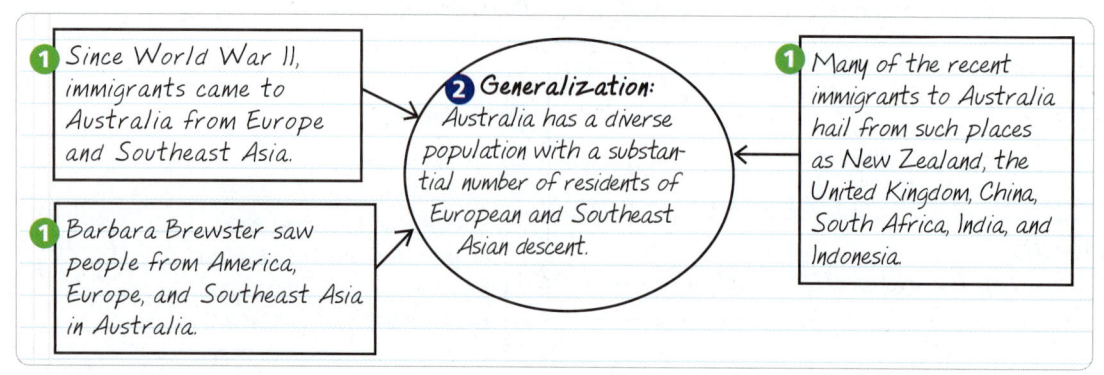

- ❶ Since World War II, immigrants came to Australia from Europe and Southeast Asia.
- ❶ Barbara Brewster saw people from America, Europe, and Southeast Asia in Australia.
- ❶ Many of the recent immigrants to Australia hail from such places as New Zealand, the United Kingdom, China, South Africa, India, and Indonesia.

❷ **Generalization:** Australia has a diverse population with a substantial number of residents of European and Southeast Asian descent.

Practicing the Skill
Turn to Chapter 11, Section 3, "Nigeria Today." Read Section 3 and the Biography of Wole Soyinka on page 332. Also read "My father's Farm" on page 352. Then use a chart like the one above to make a generalization about life and art in Nigeria.

3.1 Interpreting Time Lines

Defining the Skill

A **time line** is a visual list of events and dates shown in the order in which they occurred. Time lines can be horizontal or vertical. On horizontal time lines, the earliest date is on the left. On vertical time lines, the earliest date is often at the top.

Applying the Skill

The time line below lists dates and events associated with the invention of the first systems of writing. Use the strategies listed below to help you interpret the information.

How to Read a Time Line

Strategy ❶ Read the dates at the beginning and end of the time line. These will show the period of history that is covered. The time line to the right is a horizontal time line. It shows the sequence of events from left to right instead of from top to bottom.

Strategy ❷ Read the dates and events in sequential order, beginning with the earliest one. Pay particular attention to how the entries relate to each other. Think about whether earlier events influenced later events.

Strategy ❸ Summarize the focus, or main idea, of the time line. Try to write a main idea sentence that describes the time line.

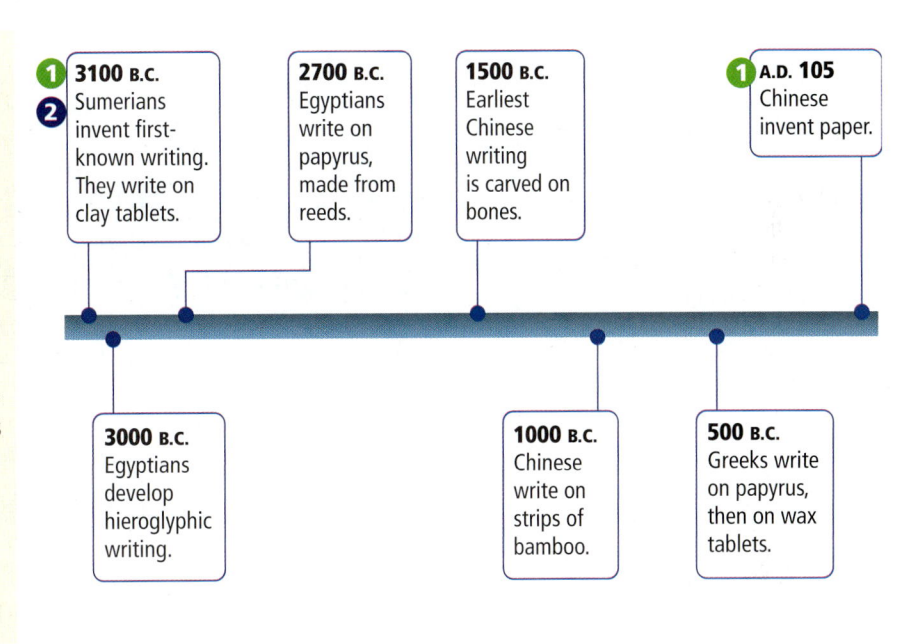

❶❷ **3100 B.C.** Sumerians invent first-known writing. They write on clay tablets.

2700 B.C. Egyptians write on papyrus, made from reeds.

1500 B.C. Earliest Chinese writing is carved on bones.

❶ **A.D. 105** Chinese invent paper.

3000 B.C. Egyptians develop hieroglyphic writing.

1000 B.C. Chinese write on strips of bamboo.

500 B.C. Greeks write on papyrus, then on wax tablets.

Write a Summary

Writing a summary can help you understand information shown on a time line. The summary to the right states the main idea of the time line and tells how the events are related.

❸ *Different groups developed writing at different times, beginning with the Sumerians in 3100 B.C. At first, people used available resources such as clay, papyrus, and bone for writing materials. The paper we use today was invented in A.D. 105.*

Practicing the Skill

Turn to pages S24–S25, and write a summary of the information shown on one of the time lines.

4.1 Using an Electronic Card Catalog

Defining the Skill

An **electronic card catalog** is a library's computerized search program that will help you locate books and other materials in the library. You can search the catalog by entering a book title, an author's name, or a subject of interest to you. The electronic card catalog also provides basic information about each book (author, title, publisher, and date of publication). You can use an electronic card catalog to create a bibliography (a list of books) on any topic that interests you.

Applying the Skill

The screen shown below is from an electronic search for information about the Congo River. Use the strategies listed below to help you use the information on the screen.

How to Use an Electronic Card Catalog

Strategy ❶ Begin searching by choosing either subject, title, or author, depending on the topic of your search. For this search, the user chose "Subject" and typed in the words "Congo River."

Strategy ❷ Once you have selected a book from the results of your search, identify the author, title, city, publisher, and date of publication.

Strategy ❸ Look for any special features in the book. This book includes maps and four pages of notes.

Strategy ❹ Locate the call number for the book. The call number indicates the section in the library where you will find the book. The card catalog should indicate whether or not the book is available in the library you are using. If not, it may be in another library in the network.

```
Search Request:
❶ Subject        Title          Author

  Find  Options  Locations  Backup  Startover  Help

❷ Winternitz, Helen. East Along the Equator: A
  Journey up the Congo and into Zaire. New York:
  Atlantic Monthly Press, 1987.
     ❷ AUTHOR:     Winternitz, Helen
     ❷   TITLE:    East Along the Equator: A Journey
                   up the Congo and into Zaire/Helen
                   Winternitz.
     ❷ PUBLISHED:  New York: Atlantic Monthly Press,
                   1987.
     ❸ PAGING:     xi, 274p.: map; 23 cm.
       SERIES:     Traveler
     ❸ NOTES:      p. 271–274
     ❹ CALL NUMBER: 916.751043 Wi
```

Practicing the Skill

Turn to Chapter 13, "Southern Asia: Place and Times," and find a topic that interests you, such as active volcanoes, the history of the Gupta Dynasty, the teachings of Buddhism, or conquering Mount Everest. Use the SUBJECT search on an electronic card catalog to find books about your topic. Make a bibliography of books about the subject. Be sure to include the author, title, city, publisher, and date of publication for all the books in your bibliography.

4.2 Creating a Database

Defining the Skill
A **database** is a collection of data, or information, that is organized so that you can find and retrieve information on a specific topic quickly and easily. Once a computerized database is set up, you can search it to find specific information without going through the entire database. The database will provide a list of all information in the database related to your topic. Learning how to use a database will help you learn how to create one.

Applying the Skill
The chart below is a database for famous mountains in the Eastern Hemisphere. Use the strategies listed below to help you understand and use the database.

How to Create a Database

Strategy ❶ Identify the topic of the database. The keywords, or most important words, in this title are "Mountains" and "Eastern Hemisphere." These words were used to begin the research for this database.

Strategy ❷ Identify the kind of data you need to enter in your database. These will be the column headings of your database. The key words "Mountain," "Location," "Height," and "Interesting Facts" were chosen to focus the research.

Strategy ❸ Identify the entries included under each heading.

Strategy ❹ Use the database to help you find information quickly. For example, in this database you could search for "Mountains over 28,000 feet" to find a list of famous mountains that are more than 28,000 feet tall.

❶ FAMOUS MOUNTAINS OF THE EASTERN HEMISPHERE			
❷ MOUNTAIN	LOCATION	HEIGHT ABOVE SEA LEVEL (FEET)	INTERESTING FACTS
❸ Dhaulagiri	Nepal	26,810	Name means "White Mountain"
Everest	Border of Nepal and China	❹ 29,035	Tallest mountain in the world
Fuji	Japan	12,388	Considered sacred by many Japanese
K2	Pakistan	❹ 28,250	Second tallest mountain in the world
Khan-Tengri	Border of China and Kyrgyzstan	22,940	Pyramid-shaped mountain known as "Lord of the Sky"
Xixabangma Feng (formerly Gosainthan)	China	26,291	Related to many Hindu myths of Shiva

Practicing the Skill
Create a database of Southern and Southeast Asian countries that shows the name of each country, its location, its land area, and its population. Use the information on pages 370–373, "Data File" to provide the data. Use a format like the one above for your database.

4.3 Using the Internet

Defining the Skill

The **Internet** is a computer network that connects to universities, libraries, news organizations, government agencies, businesses, and private individuals throughout the world. Each location on the Internet has a home page with its own address, or URL (Universal Resource Locator). With a computer connected to the Internet, you can reach the home pages of many organizations and services. The international collection of home pages, known as the World Wide Web, is a good source of up-to-date information about current events as well as research on subjects in geography.

Applying the Skill

The Web page below shows helpful links for Unit 1 of *World Cultures and Geography*. Use the strategies listed below to help you understand how to use the Web page.

How to Use the Internet

Strategy ❶ Go directly to a Web page. For example, type http://www.classzone.com/books/wc_survey/ in the box at the top of the screen and press ENTER (or RETURN). The Web page will appear on your screen. Then click on the link for Unit 1. A new web page will appear. Find the link for research links. Click on it and you will go to a third web page. Finally, click on the link for *Web sites on the world* and it will take you to the screen shown here.

Strategy ❷ Explore the links on the right side of the screen. Click on any one of the links to find out more about a specific subject. These links take you to other pages on this Web site. Some pages include links to related information that can be found at other places on the Internet.

Strategy ❸ When using the Internet for research, you should confirm the information you find. Web sites set up by universities, government agencies, and reputable news sources are more reliable than other sources. You can often find information about the creator of a site by looking for copyright information.

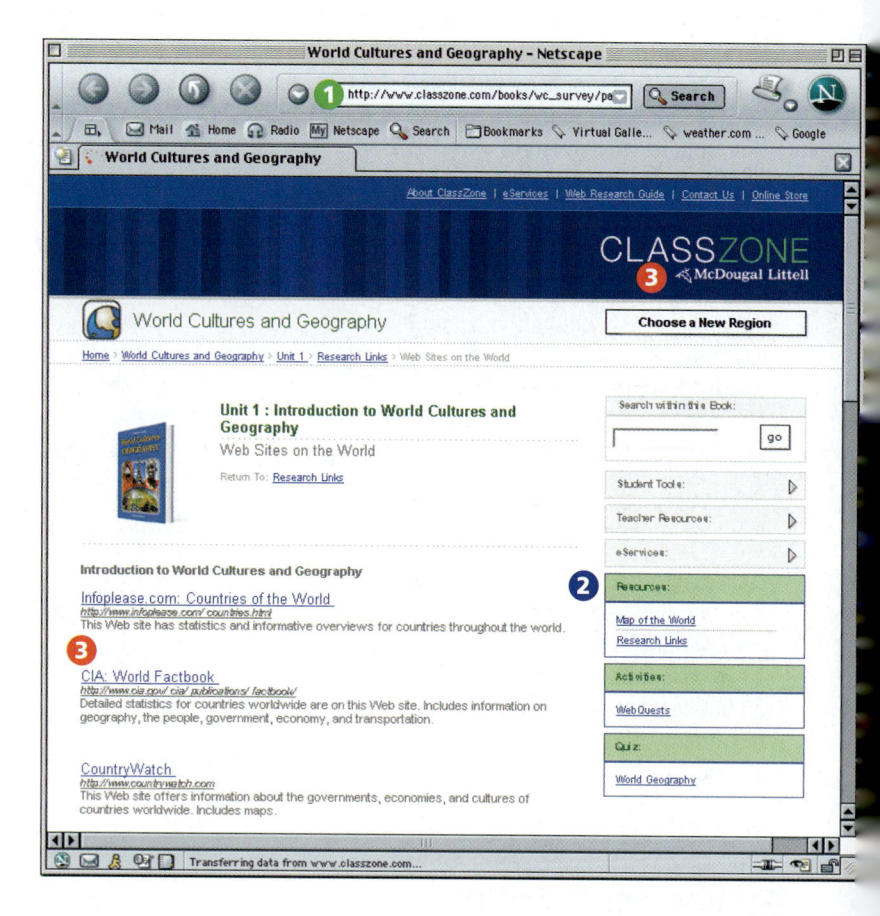

Practicing the Skill

Turn to Chapter 16, Section 1, "Physical Geography." Read the section and make a list of thematic maps you would like to research. If you have Internet access, go to classzone.com. There you will find links that provide more information about the topics in the section.

R22 SKILLBUILDER HANDBOOK

4.4 Creating a Multimedia Presentation

Defining the Skill
Movies, CD-ROMs, television, and computer software are different kinds of media. To **create a multimedia presentation,** you need to collect information in different media and organize them into one presentation.

Applying the Skill
The illustration below shows students using computers to create a multimedia presentation. Use the strategies listed below to help you create your own multimedia presentation.

How to Create a Multimedia Presentation

Strategy ❶ Identify the topic of your presentation and decide which media are best for an effective presentation. For example, you may want to use video or photographic images to show the dry character of a desert. Or, you may want to use CDs or audio tapes to provide music or to make sounds that go with your presentations, like the sounds of a camel.

Strategy ❷ Research the topic in a variety of sources. Images, text, props, and background music should reflect the region and the historical period of your topic.

Strategy ❸ Write the script for the presentation and then record it using a microphone and audiotape. You could use a narrator and characters' voices to tell the story. Primary sources are an excellent source for script material.

Strategy ❹ Videotape the presentation or create it on your computer. Having the presentation as a file on your computer will preserve it for future viewing and allow you to show it to different groups of people.

Practicing the Skill
Turn to Chapter 18, "Australia, New Zealand, Oceania, and Antarctica." Choose a topic from the chapter and use the strategies listed above to create a multimedia presentation about it.

Glossary

A

Aborigine (AB•uh•RIHJ•uh•nee) *n.* one of Australia's first inhabitants or their descendants. (p. 528)

absolute location *n.* the exact spot on Earth where a place is found. (p. 36)

acid rain *n.* rain or snow that carries air pollutants to Earth. (p. 180)

Aegean (ih•JEE•uhn) **Sea** *n.* a branch of the Mediterranean Sea that is located between Greece and Turkey. (p. 73)

African National Congress (ANC) *n.* a group of black Africans opposed to apartheid. (p. 356)

Afrikaner *n.* a descendant of the Dutch settlers of South Africa. (p. 355)

Ainu (EYE•noo) *n.* the descendants of Japan's early settlers from Europe. (p. 519)

alliance (uh•LY•uhns) *n.* an agreement among people or nations to unite for a common cause and to help any alliance member that is attacked. (p. 128)

Angkor Wat *n.* a Hindu temple in Cambodia, built by the Khmer people. (p. 396)

antimony *n.* a type of metal. (p. 507)

apartheid (uh•PAHRT•HYT) *n.* an official policy of racial separation formerly practiced in South Africa. (p. 310)

Arab-Israeli Wars *n.* a series of wars between 1948 and 1973 that were fought between Israel and the Arab countries of Iraq, Syria, Egypt, Jordan, and Lebanon. (p. 244)

archipelago (AHR•kuh•PEHL•uh•GOH) *n.* a group of islands. (p. 381)

armed neutrality *n.* a policy by which a country maintains military forces but does not take sides in the conflicts of other nations. (p. 179)

Aryan (AIR•ee•uhn) *n.* a member of an ethnic group that migrated from what is now southern Russia through central Asia, settling in India. (p. 386)

Aswan High Dam *n.* a dam built in 1956 by the Egyptian leader Gamal Abdel Nasser to control the flooding of the Nile River. (p. 257)

Athens *n.* the capital of Greece and once one of the most important ancient Greek city-states. (p. 74)

Austria-Hungary *n.* in the 1900s, a dual monarchy in which the Hapsburg emperor ruled both Austria and Hungary. (p. 126)

B

Bahasa (bah•HAH•suh) **Indonesian** *n.* the national language of Indonesia. (p. 445)

Bantu migration *n.* the gradual spreading of the Bantu across Africa over 2,000 years. (p. 297)

batik (buh•TEEK) *n.* a method of dyeing fabric in which any parts of the fabric not intended to be dyed are covered with wax that is later removed. (p. 447)

Berlin Wall *n.* a wire-and-concrete wall that divided Germany's East Berlin and West Berlin from 1961 to 1989. (p. 189)

Boer *n.* one of a group of Dutch colonists in South Africa or one of their descendants. (p. 355)

Boxer Rebellion *n.* a rebellion led by a group called the Boxers in China in 1900. (p. 496)

Buddhism *n.* a religion founded by Siddhartha Gautama in India in the 500s B.C. (p. 394)

bureaucracy *n.* the administration of a government through departments called bureaus. (p. 478)

C

caliph (KAY•lihf) *n.* the title used by rulers of the Muslim community from 632 until 1924. (p. 235)

capitalism *n.* an economic system in which the factories and businesses that make and sell goods are privately owned and the owners make the decisions about what goods to produce. (p. 109)

cartographer *n.* a person who makes maps. (p. 45)

cash crop *n.* a crop grown for sale. (p. 325)

caste *n.* an inherited social class of traditional Hindu society that separates people from other classes by birth, occupation, or wealth. (p. 388)

censorship *n.* the outlawing of materials that contain certain information. (p. 197)

Christianity *n.* a religion that developed out of Judaism and that is based on the life and teachings of Jesus. (p. 231)

circumnavigate *v.* to sail completely around. (p. 104)

citizen *n.* a legal member of a country. (p. 20)

city-state *n.* a central city and its surrounding villages, which together follow the same law, have one form of government, and share language, religious beliefs, and ways of life. (p. 73)

clan *n.* a group of families who trace their descent from a common ancestor. (p. 485)

class system *n.* a system in which society is divided into different social groups. (p. 219)

coalition government *n.* a government formed by political parties joining together. (p. 156)

Cold War *n.* after World War II, a period of political noncooperation between the members of NATO and the Warsaw Pact nations, during which these countries refused to trade or cooperate with each other. (p. 141)

collective farm *n.* a government-owned farm that employs large numbers of workers, often in Communist countries. (p. 139)

colonialism *n.* a system by which a country maintains colonies outside its borders. (p. 125)

Commonwealth of Nations *n.* a group of countries, including Australia and New Zealand, that were once British colonies and that share a heritage of British law and government. (p. 530)

Constantinople *n.* the capital of the Ottoman Empire, now called Istanbul. (p. 236)

continent *n.* a landmass above water on earth. (p. 35)

cooperative *n.* a large farm on which hundreds of families work. (p. 508)

copra (KOH•pruh) *n.* dried coconut meat. (p. 532)

coup d'état (KOO day•TAH) *n.* an overthrow of a government by force. (p. 319)

Court of Human Rights *n.* the Council of Europe's court that protects the rights of all citizens in whichever of its member countries they live. (p. 164)

Crusades *n.* a series of military expeditions led by Western European Christians in the 11th, 12th, and 13th centuries to reclaim control of the Holy Lands from the Muslims. (p. 95)

Cultural Revolution *n.* a movement that Mao Zedong began in China in 1966 in an attempt to remove opposition to the Communist Party. (p. 499)

culture *n.* the beliefs, customs, laws, art, and ways of living that a group of people share. (p. 21)

culture region *n.* an area of the world in which many people share similar beliefs, history, and languages. (p. 24)

culture trait *n.* the food, clothing, technology, beliefs, language, and tools that the people of a culture share. (p. 21)

cuneiform (KYOO•nee•uh•FAWRM) *n.* a Sumerian system of writing, in which wedge-shaped symbols were used. (p. 220)

currency *n.* money used as a form of exchange. (p. 163)

czar (zahr) *n.* in Russia, an emperor. (p. 113)

D

Dalit *n.* a member of a group of people in India, formerly known as untouchables, who were outside the caste system, were considered lower than the lowest caste, and have gained some rights under India's new constitution. (p. 412)

Deccan Plateau *n.* a plateau that makes up most of southern India. (p. 380)

delta *n.* a triangular deposit of soil at the mouth of a river. (p. 379)

deposed *v.* removed from power. (p. 150)

desertification *n.* the process by which land that can be farmed or lived on turns into desert. (p. 294)

détente (day•TAHNT) *n.* a relaxing of tensions between nations. (p. 151)

developing nation *n.* a newly industrialized nation. (p. 444)

dialect *n.* a regional variety of a language. (p. 521)

Diet *n.* Japan's parliament. (p. 504)

dissident *n.* a person who openly disagrees with a government's policies. (p. 197)

diversity *n.* variety of cultures and viewpoints. (p. 309)

doi moi (doy moy) *n.* the name of a Vietnamese policy, meaning "change for the new." (p. 452)

dowry *n.* money or property given by a bride's family to her new husband and his family. (p. 423)

Dravidian *n.* an Indian language. (p. 422)

drought *n.* a long period of time without rain. (p. 294)

dual monarchy *n.* a form of government in which one ruler governs two nations. (p. 126)

Duma (DOO•muh) *n.* one of the two houses of the Russian legislature. (p. 158)

dynasty *n.* a family of rulers. (p. 476)

E

East Timor *n.* an island nation in Southeast Asia. (p. 441)

economics *n.* the study of how resources are managed in the production, exchange, and use of goods and services. (p. 20)

ECOWAS *n.* the Economic Community of West African States, formed in 1975 to improve trade within Western Africa and with countries outside the region. (p. 321)

Eightfold Path *n.* in Buddhism, a set of guidelines for how to escape suffering. (p. 395)

empire *n.* a nation or group of territories ruled by an emperor. (p. 81)

ethnic cleansing *n.* the organized killing of members of an ethnic group or groups. (p. 157)

euro *n.* the common unit of currency used by European Union countries. (p. 163)

European Community *n.* an association developed after World War II to promote economic unity among the countries of Western Europe. (p. 186)

European Union (EU) *n.* an economic and political grouping of countries in Western Europe. (p. 162)

F

fascism (FASH•IHZ•uhm) *n.* a political philosophy that promotes a strong, central government controlled by the military and led by a powerful dictator. (p. 130)

fellahin (FEHL•uh•HEEN) *n.* peasant farmers in Egypt. (p. 259)

fertile *adj.* rich in resources and nutrients. (p. 213)

Fertile Crescent *n.* a region consisting of what is now Iraq, northeast Syria, and part of southeast Turkey, shaped like a crescent and having fertile soil. (p. 217)

feudalism *n.* in medieval Europe, a political and economic system in which lords gave land to less powerful nobles, called vassals, in return for which the vassals agreed to provide various services to the lords. (p. 86)

Five Pillars of Islam *n.* in Islam, the most important teachings of Muhammad. (p. 234)

fjord (fyawrd) *n.* a long, narrow, deep inlet of the sea located between steep cliffs. (p. 68)

Florence *n.* a city in Italy that was a bustling center of banking, trade, and manufacturing during the 14th century. (p. 96)

Four Noble Truths *n.* the central teachings of Buddhism. (p. 395)

French Resistance *n.* an anti-German movement in France during World War II. (p. 184)

French Revolution *n.* a revolution that began on July 14, 1789, and that led to France's becoming a republic. (p. 110)

G

geography *n.* the study of people, places, and the environment. (p. 18)

Good Friday Accord *n.* an agreement signed in 1998 by Ireland's Protestants and Catholics that established the Northern Ireland Assembly to represent voters from both groups. (p. 175)

government *n.* the people and groups within a society that have the authority to make laws, to make sure they are carried out, and to settle disagreements about them. (p. 19)

Grand National Assembly *n.* Turkey's legislature. (p. 271)

Great Barrier Reef *n.* world's largest coral reef system, located off Australia's northeastern coast. (p. 474)

Great Leap Forward *n.* a program that Mao Zedong began in China in 1958 to speed up economic development. (p. 498)

Great Rift Valley *n.* a series of broad, steep-walled valleys that stretch from the Red Sea to Mozambique. (p. 293)

Great Zimbabwe *n.* a stone city built by the Shona people, beginning in the A.D. 900s, in the area that is today Zimbabwe. (p. 341)

Green Revolution *n.* a movement that began in the late 1960s, through which genetically improved grains, pesticides, and new farming methods were introduced to farmers in developing nations. (p. 419)

guild *n.* a business association created by people working in the same industry to protect their common interests and maintain standards within the industry. (p. 88)

H

haiku (HY•koo) *n.* a Japanese form of poetry that contains only 17 syllables. (p. 513)

haj *n.* a pilgrimage to Mecca that most Muslims try to make at least once in a lifetime (p. 251)

Han *n.* the majority ethnic group in China. (p. 514)

harambee *adj.* a Swahili term that means "pulling together" and that is used in reference to Kenyan schools built by Kenyan people rather than by the government. (p. 360)

Hausa (HOW•suh) *n.* the largest ethnic group in Nigeria. (p. 331)

Heian Age *n.* the golden age of Japanese culture, from 794 to 1185. (p. 485)

hieroglyphics *n.* a writing system in which pictures and symbols are used to represent words and sounds. (p. 225)

Himalayas *n.* a mountain range that stretches about 1,500 miles across south-central Asia. (p. 378)

Hinduism *n.* a religion developed in ancient India. (p. 387)

Hiroshima (HEER•uh•SHEE•muh) *n.* a Japanese city on which the United States dropped an atomic bomb in 1945. (p. 518)

history *n.* a record of the past. (p. 18)

Holocaust *n.* the organized killing of European Jews and others by the Nazis during World War II. (p. 130)

homogeneous *adj.* mostly the same. (p. 519)

human right *n.* a right to which every person is entitled. (p. 503)

hunter-gatherer *n.* a person who finds food by hunting, fishing, and gathering wild grains, fruits, and nuts. (p. 214)

Hutu *n.* the ethnic majority of Rwanda-Burundi. (p. 305)

hydroelectricity *n.* electrical power generated by water. (p. 180)

I

ice shelf *n.* a sheet of ice that floats on water but connects to land on one side. (p. 537)

Igbo *n.* an ethnic group in southeastern Nigeria. (p. 331)

imperialism *n.* the practice of one country's controlling the government and economy of another country or territory. (p. 104)

impressionism *n.* a style of art that creates an impression of a scene rather than a strictly realistic picture. (p. 187)

Indian National Congress *n.* in India, a congress formed in 1885 to provide a forum for Indians to discuss their problems. (p. 406)

Indo-Aryan *adj.* related to the family of languages that includes almost all European and many Indian languages. (p. 422)

Industrial Revolution *n.* a period of change beginning in the late 18th century, during which goods began to be manufactured by power-driven machines. (p. 108)

information technology *n.* technology, including computers, software, and the Internet, that helps us process and use information. (p. 418)

interdependence *n.* the economic, political, and social dependence of culture regions on one another. (p. 26)

Iron Curtain *n.* a political barrier that isolated the peoples of Eastern Europe after World War II, restricting their ability to travel outside the region. (p. 136)

irrigation *n.* the process of bringing water to dry land. (p. 215)

Islam *n.* a religion that teaches that there is one god and that Muhammad is his prophet. (p. 232)

J

Janissary *n.* one of a group of soldiers loyal to the sultan of the Ottoman Empire. (p. 237)

Judaism *n.* the monotheistic religion founded by Abraham and whose followers are called Jews. (p. 230)

jute *n.* a fibrous plant used to make twine, bags, sacks, and burlap. (p. 417)

K

Khmer (KMAIR) *n.* an ancient ethnic group in Cambodia. (p. 396)

kibbutz (ki•BOOTS) *n.* a Jewish farming village in Palestine (or present-day Israel) whose members own everything in common, sharing labor, income, and expenses. (p. 265)

kinship *n.* family relationships. (p. 349)

Kurd *n.* a member of a group of mountain people who live in Armenia, Georgia, Iran, Iraq, Lebanon, Syria, and Turkey. (p. 246)

L

labor force *n.* a pool of available workers. (p. 109)

latitude *n.* a measure of distance north or south of the equator. (p. 36)

Law of Return *n.* a law enacted in 1950 in Israel, granting Jews anywhere in the world permission to move to Israel and become citizens. (p. 266)

London *n.* the capital of England. (p. 173)

longitude *n.* a measure of distance east or west of a line called the prime meridian. (p. 36)

M

Magna Carta (MAG•nuh KAHR•tuh) *n.* a document signed by England's King John in 1215 that guaranteed English people basic rights. (p. 89)

Mahabharata (MAH•huh•BAH•ruh•tuh) *n.* an epic poem about the growth of Hinduism. (p. 421)

mandala (MUHN•duh•luh) *n.* in Southeast Asia, a political system in which a central ruler worked to gain support from others and used trade and business to influence others and maintain power. (p. 438)

mandate *n.* a country placed under the control of another power by international agreement. (p. 244)

Mangla Dam *n.* a dam built on the Jhelum River in northeast Pakistan to control floodwaters and to provide hydroelectricity. (p. 428)

manorialism *n.* a social system in which peasants worked on a lord's land and supplied him with food in exchange for his protection of them. (p. 87)

Maori (MOW•ree) *n.* the first inhabitants of New Zealand. (p. 527)

map projection *n.* one of the different ways of showing Earth's curved surface on a flat map. (p. 47)

martial law *n.* temporary military rule during a time of war or a time when the normal government has broken down. (p. 411)

Masai (mah•SY) *n.* an ethnic group in Africa. (p. 341)

matrilineal society *n.* a society in which ancestry is traced through the mother's side of the family. (p. 533)

mediate *v.* to help find a peaceful solution. (p. 321)

medieval (MEE•dee•EE•vuhl) *adj.* relating to the period of history between the fall of the Roman Empire and the beginning of the modern world, often dated from 476 to 1453. (p. 85)

Mediterranean Sea *n.* an inland sea that borders Europe, Southwest Asia, and Africa. (p. 68)

Meiji Restoration *n.* in Japan, the period from 1868 to 1911, during which the country was again ruled by an emperor after hundreds of years of military rule. (p. 517)

Melanesia *n.* one of three regional island groups into which the Pacific Islands are divided. (p. 528)

Micronesia *n.* one of three regional island groups into which the Pacific Islands are divided. (p. 528)

migrate *v.* to move from one area in order to settle in another. (p. 38)

military dictatorship *n.* a government ruled by a person in the military. (p. 441)

missionary *n.* a person who goes to another country to do religious and social work. (p. 303)

Mohenjo-Daro (moh•HEHN•joh•DAHR•oh) *n.* a large ancient city in the Indus River valley. (p. 386)

monsoon *n.* a seasonal wind that brings great amounts of rain. (p. 382)

Mount Everest *n.* the highest mountain peak in the world, located in the Himalayas on the border of China and Nepal. (p. 470)

Mount Fuji *n.* the tallest mountain and an active volcano in Japan. (p. 472)

Mughal Empire *n.* an empire, lasting from 1526 to 1707, that covered most of the subcontinent of India. (p. 404)

multiparty system *n.* a political system in which two or more parties exist. (p. 359)

Muslim *n.* a follower of the religion Islam. (p. 232)

Muslim Brotherhood *n.* a fundamentalist Muslim group that believes that Egypt should be governed solely by Islamic law in order to be true to the principles of Islam. (p. 258)

Muslim League *n.* a group formed by Muslims in India in 1906 to protect their rights. (p. 406)

N

Nagasaki (NAH•guh•SAH•kee) *n.* a Japanese city on which the United States dropped an atomic bomb in 1945. (p. 518)

nationalism *n.* strong pride in one's nation or ethnic group. (p. 123)

NATO (NAY•toh) *n.* the North Atlantic Treaty Organization, a defense alliance formed in 1949, with the countries of Western Europe, Canada, and the United States agreeing to defend one another if attacked. (p. 131)

nonrenewable resource *n.* a resource that cannot be replaced or that can be replaced only over millions of years. (p. 295)

Northern Plains *n.* plains that lie between the Himalaya Mountains and southern India. (p. 379)

O

OAU *n.* the Organization of African Unity, an organization formed in 1963 to promote unity among all Africans. (p. 321)

oligarchy (AHL•ih•GAHR•kee) *n.* a government in which a few powerful individuals rule. (p. 74)

ombudsman *n.* a Swedish official who protects citizens' rights and ensures that the courts and civil service follow the law. (p. 179)

one-party system *n.* a system in which there is only one political party and only one candidate to choose from for each government position. (p. 316)

OPEC *n.* the Organization of Petroleum Exporting Countries, which decides the price and amount of oil produced each year in Iraq, Iran, Saudi Arabia, Kuwait, Venezuela, and other countries. (p. 250)

Opium War *n.* a war over the trade of the drug opium, which was fought between the Chinese and the British from 1839 to 1842. (p. 496)

Orthodox Jew *n.* a Jew who strictly follows Jewish law. (p. 267)

Ottoman Empire *n.* a Muslim empire that lasted from the early 1400s until after World War I. (p. 236)

outback *n.* the vast, flat plain that extends across most of central Australia. (p. 473)

overgrazing *n.* a process in which animals graze grass faster than it can grow back. (p. 347)

P

pagoda *n.* a Buddhist tower built in many levels, with sculptures or carvings of Buddha on each level. (p. 446)

paleontologist *n.* a scientist who studies fossils. (p. 296)

Palestine *n.* a Southwest Asian region often called the Holy Land. (p. 244)

panchayat *n.* a village council in India. (p. 412)

papyrus (puh•PY•ruhs) *n.* a paperlike material made from a reed. (p. 224)

parliamentary republic *n.* a republic whose head of government, usually a prime minister, is the leader of the political party that has the most members in the parliament. (p. 155)

pastoralism *n.* a way of life in which people raise cattle, sheep, or goats as their primary economic activity. (p. 347)

patrician (puh•TRIHSH•uhn) *n.* in ancient Rome, a member of a wealthy, landowning family that claimed to be able to trace its roots back to the founding of Rome. (p. 79)

patrilineal society *n.* a society in which ancestry is traced through the father's side of the family. (p. 533)

peninsula *n.* a body of land surrounded by water on three sides. (p. 68)

Persian Gulf War *n.* a 1991 war between the United States and Iraq. (p. 247)

petrochemical *n.* a product made from petroleum or natural gas. (p. 251)

pharaoh (FAIR•oh) *n.* a king of ancient Egypt. (p. 225)

philosopher *n.* a person who studies and thinks about why the world is the way it is. (p. 75)

plain *n.* a large flat area of land that usually does not have many trees. (p. 69)

plateau *n.* a raised area of relatively level land. (p. 292)

plebeian (plih•BEE•uhn) *n.* a common citizen of ancient Rome. (p. 79)

polis *n.* the central city of a city-state. (p. 73)

Politburo (PAHL•iht•BYUR•oh) *n.* the group that heads a Communist party. (p. 452)

Polynesia *n.* one of three island groups into which the Pacific Islands are divided. (p. 528)

primary product *n.* a raw material used to manufacture other products. (p. 250)

private property rights *n.* the right of individuals to own land or industry. (p. 149)

propaganda (PRAHP•uh•GAN•duh) *n.* material designed to spread certain beliefs. (p. 148)

Protestant *n.* a member of a Christian church based on the principles of the Reformation. (p. 100)

Punjabi *n.* one of two most commonly spoken languages in Pakistan. (p. 428)

puppet government *n.* a government that is controlled by an outside force. (p. 137)

pyramid *n.* a structure with four triangular sides that rise from a rectangular base to meet at a point on top. (p. 225)

Q

Qur'an (kuh•RAN) *n.* the sacred text of Islam. (p. 232)

R

racism *n.* the belief that one race is inferior to another. (p. 308)

Ramadan (RAM•uh•DAHN) *n.* the ninth month of the Islamic year. (p. 251)

Reformation *n.* a 16th-century movement to change practices within the Roman Catholic Church. (p. 99)

Reign of Terror *n.* the period between 1793 and 1794 during which France's new leaders executed thousands of its citizens. (p. 111)

relative location *n.* the location of one place in relation to other places. (p. 37)

Renaissance *n.* an era of creativity and learning in Western Europe from the 14th century to the 16th century. (p. 96)

renewable resource *n.* a resource that can be used and replaced over a relatively short time period. (p. 295)

republic *n.* a form of government in which people rule through elected representatives. (p. 79)

reunification *n.* the uniting again of parts. (p. 190)

Riksdag (RIHKS•DAHG) *n.* Sweden's parliament. (p. 178)

Ring of Fire *n.* an area of volcanic activity along the borders of the Pacific Ocean. (p. 472)

rite of passage *n.* a special ceremony that marks the transition from one stage of life to another. (p. 328)

Rosh Hashanah (RAWSH huh•SHAW•nuh) *n.* the Jewish New Year. (p. 267)

Russian Revolution *n.* the 1917 revolution that removed the Russian monarchy from power after it had ruled for 400 years. (p. 116)

S

Sahel (suh•HAYL) *n.* a semiarid region south of the Sahara Desert. (p. 294)

samurai (SAM•uh•RY) *n.* a Japanese warrior who pledged to serve a particular lord and protect his estate. (p. 486)

sanction *n.* a penalty imposed upon a nation that is violating international law. (p. 356)

Sanskrit *n.* the classical language of India and Hinduism. (p. 386)

savanna *n.* a flat grassland in a tropical or subtropical region with scattered trees and shrubs. (p. 294)

scarcity *n.* a word economists use to describe the conflict between people's desires and limited resources. (p. 20)

Scientific Revolution *n.* a period of great scientific change and discovery during the 16th and 17th centuries. (p. 108)

scribe *n.* a professional record keeper or copier of documents. (p. 220)

secede *v.* to withdraw from a political union, such as a nation. (p. 175)

secondary product *n.* a product manufactured from raw materials. (p. 250)

secular *adj.* not specifically relating to religion. (p. 267)

sediment *n.* small fragments of rock or other materials that can be moved around by wind, water, or ice. (p. 379)

Senate *n.* the assembly of elected representatives that was the most powerful ruling body of the Roman Republic. (p. 79)

Shinto *n.* a Japanese religion that developed around 300 B.C. (p. 484)

shogun *n.* in feudal Japan, the emperor's chief general, who held most of the country's power. (p. 487)

Sindhi *n.* a language spoken in Pakistan. (p. 428)

skerry *n.* a small island. (p. 181)

socialism *n.* an economic system in which businesses and industries are owned collectively or by the government. (p. 186)

Solidarity *n.* a trade union in Poland that originally aimed to increase pay and improve working conditions and that later opposed Communism. (p. 194)

standard of living *n.* a measure of quality of life. (p. 163)

subcontinent *n.* a large landmass that is part of a continent but that has its own geographic identity. (p. 378)

subsistence farming *n.* a method of farming in which people grow food mainly to feed their households rather than to sell. (p. 325)

Sumerian *n.* one of the first inhabitants of Mesopotamia. (p. 218)

supply and demand *n.* an economic concept that states that the price of a good rises or falls depending on how many people want it (demand) and depending on how much of the good is available (supply). (p. 452)

Swahili (swah•HEE•lee) *n.* a Bantu language spoken in Africa. (p. 360)

T

Taiping (ty•PIHNG) **Rebellion** *n.* the greatest of the peasant revolts that occurred in China in response to the signing of the Treaty of Nanking. (p. 496)

Taj Mahal *n.* the most famous building in India, built by the Mughal emperor Shah Jahan in the A.D. 1640s. (p. 420)

Taliban *n.* a group of fundamentalist Muslims who took control of Afghanistan's government in 1996. (p. 410)

Taoism (DOW•ihz•uhm) *n.* a Chinese philosophy founded in the 200s B.C. by Lao Tzu. (p. 478)

Tarbela Dam *n.* a dam built on the Indus River to improve irrigation and flood control. (p. 428)

tariff *n.* a fee imposed by a government on imported or exported goods. (p. 163)

Tet *n.* the Vietnamese New Year. (p. 453)

textile *n.* cloth manufactured by weaving or knitting. (p. 508)

thatch *n.* woven palm fronds, reeds, or straw used to build roofs. (p. 446)

The Tale of Genji *n.* the world's first novel, written by Lady Muraskai Shikibu of Japan in the 11th century/ (p. 486)

thematic map *n.* a map that focuses on a specific idea or theme. (p. 46)

theocracy (thee•AHK•ruh•see) *n.* a government ruled by a religious leader. (p. 235)

Tiananmen (tyahn•ahn•mehn) **Square** *n.* a square in Beijing, China, where thousands of protesters gathered in demonstration and were injured or killed by the military in 1989. (p. 503)

tradeoff *n.* an exchange of one benefit for another. (p. 258)

tungsten *n.* a type of metal. (p. 507)

Tutsi *n.* the ethnic minority of Rwanda-Burundi. (p. 305)

typhoon *n.* a hurricane that occurs in the western Pacific Ocean. (p. 472)

U

Ural (YUR•uhl) **Mountains** *n.* a mountain range that divides Europe from Asia. (p. 69)

Urdu *n.* the official language of Pakistan. (p. 428)

V

Vedas (VAY•duhz) *n.* the Books of Knowledge of the ancient Aryans, which were the basis of Hinduism. (p. 387)

veldt (vehlt) *n.* the flat grassland of Southern Africa. (p. 354)

W

Warsaw Pact *n.* a treaty signed in 1955 that established an alliance among the Soviet Union, Albania, Bulgaria, Czechoslovakia, East Germany, Hungary, Poland, and Romania. (p. 141)

World War I *n.* a war fought from 1914 to 1918 between the Allies (Russia, France, the United Kingdom, Italy, and the United States) and the Central Powers (Austria-Hungary, Germany, Turkey, and Bulgaria). (p. 127)

World War II *n.* a war fought from 1939 to 1945 between the Axis powers (Germany Italy, and Japan) and the Allies (the United Kingdom, France, the Soviet Union, and the United States). (p. 130)

Y

Yom Kippur (YAWM KIHP•uhr) *n.* in Judaism, the Day of Atonement. (p. 267)

Yoruba (YAWR•uh•buh) *n.* an ethnic group in southwestern Nigeria. (p. 331)

Z

Zen *n.* a branch of Buddhism practiced in Japan, which emphasizes that people can achieve enlightenment suddenly. (p. 486)

ziggurat *n.* a Mesopotamian terraced pyramid in which each terrace is smaller than the one below it. (p. 218)

Zionism *n.* a movement that encouraged Jews to return to Palestine, the Jewish homeland, which many Jews call Zion. (p. 264)

zither *n.* a type of stringed instrument. (p. 513)

Zulu (ZOO•loo) *n.* an ethnic group in Africa. (p. 342)

Spanish Glossary

A

Aborigine (AB•uh•RIHJ•uh•nee) [aborigen australiano] *s.* los primeros pobladores de Australia o uno de sus descendientes. (pág. 528)

absolute location [ubicación absoluta] *s.* lugar exacto donde se halla un lugar en la Tierra. (pág. 36)

acid rain [lluvia ácida] *s.* lluvia o nieve que lleva sustancias contaminantes a la Tierra. (pág. 180)

Aegean (ih•JEE•uhn) **Sea** [mar Egeo] *s.* parte del Mar Mediterráneo ubicada entre Grecia y Turquía. (pág. 73)

African National Congress [Congreso Nacional Africano] *s.* grupo de africanos negros que se oponen al apartheid. (pág. 356)

Afrikaner [afrikander] *s.* descendiente de los primeros colonos holandeses en Sudáfrica. (pág. 355)

Ainu [ainu] *s.* descendientes de los primeros pobladores de Japón provenientes de Europa. (pág. 519)

alliance (uh•LY•uhns) [alianza] *s.* acuerdo de unión entre pueblos o naciones por una causa común y de ayuda mutua en caso de que uno sea atacado. (pág. 128)

Angkor Wat [Angkor Wat] *s.* templo hindú en Camboya construido por el pueblo khemer. (pág. 396)

antimony [antimonio] *s.* tipo de metal. (pág. 507)

apartheid (uh•PAHRT•HYT) [apartheid] *s.* política oficial de segregación racial que se llevó a cabo anteriormente en Sudáfrica. (pág. 310)

Arab-Israeli Wars [guerras árabe-israelíes] *s.* guerras del período comprendido entre 1948 y 1973, entre Israel y los países árabes de Irak, Siria, Egipto, Jordania y el Líbano. (pág. 244)

archipelago (AHR•kuh•PEHL•uh•GOH) [archipiélago] *s.* grupo de islas. (pág. 381)

armed neutrality [neutralidad armada] *s.* política mediante la cual un país mantiene fuerzas armadas pero no participa en conflictos de otras naciones. (pág. 179)

Aryan [ario] *s.* miembro de un grupo étnico que emigró de lo que hoy es el sur de Rusia y se estableció en la India, pasando por Asia central. (pág. 386)

Aswan High Dam [presa de Aswán] *s.* dique construido en 1956 por el líder egipcio Gamal Abdel Nasser con el fin de controlar las inundaciones del río Nilo. (pág. 257)

Athens [Atenas] *s.* capital de Grecia y una de las ciudades-estado más importantes de la antigua Grecia. (pág. 74)

Austria-Hungary [Austria-Hungría] *s.* monarquía dual mediante la cual a comienzos del siglo XX el emperador de la dinastía de los Hasburgo gobernó Austria y Hungría. (pág. 126)

B

Bahasa (bah•HAH•suh) **Indonesian** [bahasa indonesia] *s.* lengua nacional de Indonesia. (pág. 445)

Bantu migration [emigración bantú] *s.* difusión gradual de los bantú por África durante más de 2000 años. (pág. 297)

batik (buh•TEEK) [batik] *s.* método de teñido mediante el cual las partes de la tela que no se deben teñir son cubiertas con cera que luego se remueve. (pág. 447)

Berlin Wall [Muro de Berlín] *s.* pared de cemento y alambre que desde 1961 a 1989 dividía la parte este de Berlín de la parte oeste. (pág. 189)

Boer [boer] *s.* miembro de un grupo de colonos holandeses o sus descendientes establecidos en Sudáfrica. (pág. 355)

Boxer Rebellion [Rebelión Bóxer] *s.* rebelión llevada a cabo en 1900 por un grupo denominado Bóxer en la China. (pág. 496)

Buddhism [budismo] *s.* religión fundada por Siddhartha Gautama en la India en el siglo VI a. de C. (pág. 394)

bureaucracy [burocracia] *s.* administración de un gobierno que se divide en departamentos o ministerios. (pág. 478)

C

caliph (KAY•lihf) [califa] *s.* título que recibían los gobernantes de las sociedades musulmanas desde el año 632 hasta 1924. (pág. 235)

capitalism [capitalismo] *s.* sistema económico en el cual las empresas y comercios que fabrican y venden productos y mercancías son de propiedad privada; los dueños de dichas empresas y comercios deciden lo que desean producir y vender. (pág. 109)

cartographer [cartógrafo] *s.* persona que hace mapas. (pág. 45)

cash crop [cultivo industrial] *s.* cultivo que se produce para la venta. (pág. 325)

caste [casta] *s.* clase social heredada que separa a las personas de otras clases por motivos de nacimiento, ocupación o riqueza. (pág. 388)

censorship [censura] *s.* prohibición de materiales que contienen cierta información. (pág. 197)

Christianity [cristianaismo] *s.* religión derivada del judaísmo, basada en la vida y las enseñanzas de Jesús. (pág. 231)

circumnavigate [circunnavegar] *v.* dar la vuelta alrededor de algo en una nave. (pág. 104)

citizen [ciudadano] *s.* habitante legal de un país. (pág. 20)

city-state [ciudad estado] *s.* ciudad central y sus aldeas aledañas que acatan las mismas leyes, tienen una sola forma de gobierno y comparten una lengua, creencias religiosas y estilos de vida. (pág. 73)

clan [clan] *s.* grupo de personas con lazos familiares que tienen en común los mismos ancestros. (pág. 485)

class system [sistema de clases] *s.* sistema mediante el cual se divide la sociedad en diferentes grupos sociales. (pág. 219)

coalition government [gobierno de coalición] *s.* gobierno formado por la unión de partidos políticos. (pág. 156)

Cold War [Guerra Fría] *s.* período político posterior a la Segunda Guerra Mundial, caracterizado por la falta de cooperación y relaciones comerciales entre los países miembros de la OTAN y las naciones del Pacto de Varsovia. (pág. 141)

collective farm [granja colectiva] *s.* granja que pertenece al gobierno, que emplea a gran número de trabajadores generalmente en países comunistas. (pág. 139)

colonialism [colonialismo] *s.* sistema mediante el cual un país mantiene colonias en otras partes del mundo. (pág. 125)

Commonwealth of Nations [Mancomunidad Británica de Naciones] *s.* grupo de países, que incluye Australia y Nueva Zelandia, que fueron colonias británicas y que en la actualidad comparten la herencia británica en el campo jurídico y de gobierno. (pág. 530)

Constantinople [Constantinopla] *s.* capital de Turquía durante Del Imperio otomano, ahora llamada Estambul. (pág. 236)

continent [continente] *s.* masa continental sobre agua en la Tierra. (pág. 35)

cooperative [cooperativa] *s.* grande establecimiento agrícola donde trabajan centenares de familias. (pág. 508)

copra (KOH•pruh) [medula de coco] *s.* substancia seca que forma parte del coco de la palma. (pág. 532)

coup d'état (KOO day•TAH) [golpe de estado] s. acción de derrocar o hacer caer un gobierno por la fuerza. (pág. 319)

Court of Human Rights [Corte de Derechos Humanos] s. corte que protege los derechos de ciudadanos que habitan en países miembros. (pág. 164)

Crusades [las cruzadas] s. serie de expediciones militares dirigidas por cristianos de Europa occidental en los siglos XI, XII y XIII, para apoderarse de nuevo de las Tierras Santas, en poder de los musulmanes. (pág. 95)

Cultural Revolution [Revolución Cultural proletaria] s. movimiento iniciado en 1966 por Mao Tse Tung en China, en un intento de eliminar la oposición del Partido Comunista. (pág. 499)

culture [cultura] s. conjunto de creencias, costumbres, leyes, formas artísticas y de vida compartidas por un grupo de personas. (pág. 21)

culture region [región cultural] s. territorio donde muchas personas comparten creencias, historia y lenguas similares. (pág. 24)

culture trait [característica culturale] s. alimento, vestimenta, tecnología, creencia, lengua u otro elemento compartido por un pueblo o cultura. (pág. 21)

cuneiform (KYOO•nee•uh•FAWRM) [escritura cuneiforme] s. sistema sumerio de escritura que usa símbolos con forma de cuña. (pág. 220)

currency [moneda] s. sistema que sirve para medir el valor de las cosas que se intercambian. (pág. 163)

czar (zahr) [zar] s. emperador ruso. (pág. 113)

D

Dalit [dalit] s. miembro de un grupo de personas en la India, también conocidas como los "intocables", fuera del sistema de castas y considerados por debajo de la casta inferior, que adquirieron algunos derechos bajo la nueva constitución de la India. (pág. 412)

Deccan Plateau [meseta de Dekán] s. meseta que ocupa casi todo el sur de la India. (pág. 380)

delta [delta] s. depósito de tierra de forma triangular en la boca de un río. (pág. 379)

deposed [depuesto] v. removido del poder. (pág. 150)

desertification [desertificación] s. proceso mediante el cual la tierra que antes podía cultivarse o era habitable se convierte en un desierto. (pág. 294)

détente (day•TAHNT) [distensión] s. disminución de la tensión entre países. (pág. 151)

developing nation [nación en vías de desarrollo] s. nación recién industrializada. (pág. 444)

dialect [dialecto] s. forma regional de una lengua. (pág. 521)

Diet [Dieta] s. nombre que recibe el parlamento de Japón. (pág. 504)

dissident [disidente] s. persona que abiertamente muestra desacuerdo con la política de un gobierno. (pág. 197)

diversity [diversidad] s. variedad de culturas y puntos de vista. (pág. 309)

doi moi (doy moy) [doi moi] s. nombre que recibe una política de renovación y reforma llevada a cabo en Vietnam. (pág. 452)

dowry [dote] s. dinero o propiedad que entrega la familia de la novia a su futuro esposo y su familia. (pág. 423)

Dravidian [lengua drávida] s. lengua india. (pág. 422)

drought [sequía] s. período largo de falta de lluvia. (pág. 294)

dual monarchy [monarquía dual] s. gobierno en que un solo jefe gobierna dos naciones. (pág. 126)

Duma (DOO•muh) [Duma] s. una de las dos cámaras de la legislatura rusa. (pág. 158)

dynasty [dinastía] s. familia de soberanos. (pág. 476)

E

East Timor [Timor Oriental] s. nación situada en una isla en el sudeste asiático. (pág. 441)

economics [economía] s. estudio del uso de los recursos naturales y del modo de producción, intercambio y utilización de los productos, mercaderías y servicios. (pág. 20)

ECOWAS [CEDEAO, Comunidad Económica de los Estados de África Occidental] s. comunidad económica formada por los estados de África occidental en 1975 para mejorar el comercio en la región del África occidental y con países fuera de la región. (pág. 321)

Eightfold Path [Óctuple Sendero] s. conjunto de reglas en la religión budista que enseñan cómo escapar del sufrimiento. (pág. 395)

empire [imperio] s. nación o conjunto de territorios gobernados por un emperador. (pág. 81)

ethnic cleansing [limpieza étnica] s. matanza sistemática (genocidio) de uno o varios grupos étnicos que conforman una minoría. (pág. 157)

euro [euro] s. unidad monetaria de los países miembros de la Unión Europea. (pág. 163)

European Community [Comunidad Europea] s. asociación creada después de la Segunda Guerra Mundial para promover la unidad económica entre los países de Europa occidental. (pág. 186)

European Union [Unión Europea] s. asociación económica y política de países de Europa occidental. (pág. 162)

F

fascism (FASH•IHZ•uhm) [fascismo] s. filosofía que promueve un gobierno centralista fuerte, controlado por el ejército y dirigido por un dictador poderoso. (pág. 130)

fellahin (FEHL•uh•HEEN) [fellahín] s. nombre que recibe un agricultor en Egipto. (pág. 259)

fertile [fértil] adj. abundante en recursos y nutrientes. (pág. 213)

Fertile Crescent [Media Luna Fértil] s. región comprendida entre lo que hoy es Irak, el nordeste de Siria y parte del sudeste de Turquía, que tiene la forma de un creciente o medialuna y que posee tierras fértiles. (pág. 217)

feudalism [feudalismo] s. sistema político y económico de la Europa medieval en el que los señores feudales repartían tierras a miembros de la nobleza menos poderosos, llamados vasallos, quienes, a cambio de éstas, se comprometían a brindar varios servicios a los señores feudales. (pág. 86)

Five Pillars of Islam [los cinco pilares del Islam] s. las enseñanzas más importantes de Mahoma en la religión musulmana. (pág. 234)

fjord (fyawrd) [fiordo] s. entrada larga y estrecha del mar formada entre acantilados abruptos. (pág. 68)

Florence [Florencia] s. ciudad italiana que durante el siglo XIV mantuvo una dinámica actividad bancaria, comercial y manufacturera. (pág. 96)

Four Noble Truths [las cuatro nobles verdades] s. las enseñanzas más importantes del budismo. (pág. 395)

French Resistance [Resistencia francesa] s. en Francia, un movimiento antialemán durante la Segunda Guerra Mundial. (pág. 184)

French Revolution [Revolución francesa] s. revolución que comenzó el 14 de julio de 1789 y tuvo como resultado la conversión de Francia en una república. (pág. 110)

G

geography [geografía] s. estudio de los pueblos, lugares y el medio ambiente. (pág. 18)

Good Friday Accord [Acuerdo del Viernes Santo] s. acuerdo firmado por los protestantes y católicos de Irlanda del Norte que estableció la Asamblea de Irlanda del Norte, asamblea esta que representa a los votantes de ambos grupos. (pág. 175)

government [gobierno] s. los individuos y grupos en una sociedad que tienen la autoridad de crear leyes y hacerlas cumplir, y de resolver desacuerdos que puedan surgir con respecto a ellas. (pág. 19)

Grand National Assembly [Gran Asamblea Nacional] s. poder legislativo de Turquía. (pág. 271)

Great Barrier Reef [Gran Barrera de Arrecife/Coral] s. arrecife de coral más grande del mundo, ubicado al noreste de la costa australiana. (pág. 474)

Great Leap Forward [Gran Salto Adelante] s. programa llevado a cabo por Mao Zedong en China en 1958 para acelerar el desarrollo económico. (pág. 498)

Great Rift Valley [Valle de la Gran Depresión] s. sucesión de extensos valles profundos que se extienden desde el Mar Rojo hasta Mozambique. (pág. 293)

Great Zimbabwe [Gran Zimbabue] s. ciudad en Zimbabue construida por los shona a principios del siglo X a. de C. y hecha de piedra. (pág. 341)

Green Revolution [revolución verde] s. movimiento que empezó a fines de la década de los 60 y que introdujo granos mejorados con ingeniería genética en la agricultura de naciones en vías de desarrollo. (pág. 419)

guild [gremio] s. asociación creada por personas que trabajan en una misma industria, con el fin de proteger sus intereses comunes y mantener ciertos criterios y principios aplicables a la industria. (pág. 88)

H

haiku (HY•koo) [haiku] s. forma de poesía japonesa que tiene sólo 17 sílabas. (pág. 513)

haj [haj] s. peregrinación a la Meca que la mayoría de los musulmanes intenta hacer por lo menos una vez en su vida. (pág. 251)

Han [han] s. etnia principal en China. (pág. 514)

harambee [harambee] adj. término en swahili que significa cooperar, que se usa para referirse a las escuelas construidas por los kenianos y no por el gobierno de Kenia. (pág. 360)

Hausa (HOW•suh) [hausa] s. etnia más numerosa en Nigeria. (pág. 331)

Heian Age [Período de Heian] s. época de oro de la cultura japonesa, desde 794 hasta 1185. (pág. 485)

hieroglyphics [jeroglíficos] s. sistema de escritura que utiliza dibujos y símbolos para representar palabras y sonidos. (pág. 225)

Himalayas [El Himalaya] s. cadena montañosa cuya extensión es de aproximadamente 1500 millas en el sur de Asia. (pág. 378)

Hinduism [hinduismo] s. religión desarrollada en la antigua India. (pág. 387)

Hiroshima (HEER•uh•SHEE•muh) [Hiroshima] s. ciudad japonesa en donde Estados Unidos arrojó una bomba atómica en 1945. (pág. 518)

history [historia] s. un registro de los acontecimientos del pasado. (pág. 18)

Holocuast [Holocausto] s. matanza sistemática (genocidio) de los judíos europeos y otros por el partido nazi durante la Segunda Guerra Mundial. (pág. 130)

homogeneous [homogéneo] adj. sin diferencias en la mayor parte. (pág. 519)

human right [derecho humano] s. derecho que pertenece a toda persona. (pág. 503)

hunter gatherer [cazador y recolector] s. persona que procura alimentos mediante la caza y la recolección de granos y frutas salvajes. (pág. 214)

Hutu [hutu] s. mayoría étnica de Rwanda-Burundi. (pág. 305)

hydroelectricity [electricidad hidráulica] s. energía eléctrica producida por el agua. (pág. 180)

I

ice shelf [plataforma de hielo] s. extensión de hielo que flota en el agua pero tiene un lado conectado a la tierra. (pág. 537)

Igbo [igbo] s. grupo étnico del sudeste de Nigeria. (pág. 331)

imperialism [imperialismo] s. práctica mediante la cual un país controla el gobierno y la economía de otro país o territorio. (pág. 104)

impressionism [impresionismo] s. estilo de arte que crea una impresión de algo en lugar de una obra con características concretas. (pág. 187)

Indian National Congress [Congreso Nacional Indio] s. congreso formado en 1885 en la India, donde los habitantes podían debatir sus problemas. (pág. 406)

Indo-Aryan [indoario] adj. que pertenece a la familia de lenguas que incluye a todas las lenguas europeas y muchas lenguas indias. (pág. 422)

Industrial Revolution [Revolución industrial] s. período de cambio en el siglo XVIII que dio lugar a la fabricación de productos por máquinas. (pág. 108)

information technology [tecnología informática] s. tecnología como computadoras, software y la Internet, que sirve para procesar y usar la información. (pág. 418)

interdependence [interdependencia] s. dependencia económica, política y social que mantienen las sociedades de diversas regiones culturales. (pág. 26)

Iron Curtain [Cortina de Hierro] s. barrera política que aisló los países de Europa del Este luego de la Segunda Guerra Mundial, limitando la capacidad de movimiento y tránsito fuera de esta región. (pág. 136)

irrigation [irrigación] s. proceso mediante el cual se riega el terreno seco. (pág. 215)

Islam [Islam] s. religión que enseña que hay un dios y que Mahoma es su profeta. (pág. 232)

J

Janissary [jenízaro] s. miembro del grupo de soldados leales al sultán del Imperio otomano. (pág. 237)

Judaism [judaísmo] s. primera religión monoteísta fundada por Abraham y cuyos seguidores se denominan judíos. (pág. 230)

jute [yute] s. planta fibrosa que se usa para hacer cordel, bolsas, sacos y arpillera. (pág. 417)

K

Khmer (KMAIR) [khmer] s. antigua etnia en Camboya. (pág. 396)

kibbutz (ki•BŎŎTS) [kibutz] s. pueblo o comunidad judía de agricultores en Palestina (o lo que hoy es Israel), cuyos miembros poseen todo en forma colectiva y comparten la labor agrícola, el ingreso y los gastos. (pág. 265)

kinship [parentesco] s. relación entre miembros de una familia. (pág. 349)

Kurd [kurdo] s. habitante que vive en las montañas de Armenia, Georgia, Irán, Irak, Líbano, Siria y Turquía. (pág. 246)

L

labor force [fuerza laboral] s. trabajadores disponibles. (pág. 109)

latitude [latitud] s. distancia norte-sur con relación al ecuador, de la superficie terrestre. (pág. 36)

Law of Return [Ley de Retorno] s. ley sancionada en 1950 mediante la cual se otorga permiso a los judíos de cualquier parte del mundo para inmigrar a Israel y convertirse en ciudadanos. (pág. 266)

London [Londres] s. capital de Inglaterra. (pág. 173)

longitude [longitud] *s.* distancia este-oeste de un punto de la Tierra, a partir de la línea inicial llamada primer meridiano (meridiano de Greenwich). (pág. 36)

M

Magna Carta (MAG•nuh KAHR•tuh) [Carta Magna] *s.* documento firmado por el rey Juan de Inglaterra en 1215 que garantizó los derechos básicos de las personas en ese país. (pág. 89)

Mahabharata (MAH•huh•BAH•ruh•tuh) [*Mahabharata*] *s.* poema épico sobre la expansión del hinduismo. (pág. 421)

mandala (MUHN•duh•luh) [mandala] *s.* sistema político en el sudeste de Asia en el que el gobernante con poder central intento obtener apoyo de otros y recurrío al comercio para ejercer influencia y mantener el poder. (pág. 438)

mandate [protectorado] *s.* país puesto bajo el control de otro por medio de un acuerdo internacional. (pág. 244)

Mangla Dam [presa Mangla] *s.* dique construido en el río Jhelum en el nordeste de Pakistán con el fin de controlar las aguas y proveer energía hidroeléctrica. (pág. 428)

manorialism [régimen señorial] *s.* sistema social en el que campesinos trabajan las tierras de un señor, a cambio de protección y seguridad. (pág. 87)

Maori (MOW•ree) [maorí] *s.* los primeros pobladores de Nueva Zelandia. (pág. 527)

map projection [proyección cartografía] *s.* una de las diversas maneras de mostrar la curvatura de la Tierra en una superficie plana. (pág. 47)

martial law [ley marcial] *s.* sistema temporal de gobierno militar durante tiempos de guerra o cuando el gobierno está en crisis. (pág. 411)

Masai (mah•SY) [masai] *s.* grupo étnico en África. (pág. 341)

matrilineal society [sociedad matrilineal] *s.* sociedad en la que sólo la línea materna se tiene en cuenta para determinar el árbol genealógico. (pág. 533)

mediate [mediar] *v.* ayudar en un conflicto para encontrar soluciones de paz. (pág. 321)

medieval (MEE•dee•EE•vuhl) [medieval] *adj.* que pertenece al período de la historia comprendido entre la caída del Imperio romano y el comienzo del mundo moderno, aproximadamente desde 476 a 1453. (pág. 85)

Mediterranean Sea [mar Mediterráneo] *s.* mar interno que bordea Europa, el sudoeste de Asia y África. (pág. 68)

Meiji Restoration [Restauración Meiji] *s.* período japonés comprendido entre 1868 y 1911 durante el cual Japón fue gobernado nuevamente por un emperador después de siglos de gobierno militar. (pág. 517)

Melanesia [Melanesia] *s.* uno de los tres grupos regionales de islas en el océano Pacífico. (pág. 528)

Micronesia [Micronesia] *s.* uno de los tres grupos regionales de islas en el océano Pacífico. (pág. 528)

migrate [migrar] *v.* irse de un área para establecerse en otra. (pág. 38)

military dictatorship [dictadura militar] *s.* gobierno de una persona militar. (pág. 441)

missionary [misionero] *s.* persona que va a otro país para transmitir enseñanzas religiosas y realizar obras de bien. (pág. 303)

Mohenjo-Daro (moh•HEHN•joh•DAHR•oh) [Mohenjo-Daro] *s.* ciudad antigua de gran tamaño ubicada en el valle del río Indo. (pág. 386)

monsoon [monzón] *s.* viento de estación que trae gran cantidad de lluvias. (pág. 382)

Mount Everest [monte Everest] *s.* pico más alto del Himalaya y en el mundo, ubicado en las fronteras de China y Nepal. (pág. 470)

Mount Fuji [monte Fuji] *s.* montaña más alta en Japón. (pág. 472)

Mughal Empire [Imperio mogol] *s.* imperio que duró de 1526 hasta 1707 y que comprendió la mayor parte del subcontinente de la India. (pág. 404)

multiparty system [sistema pluripartidista] *s.* sistema político en donde existe dos o más partidos. (pág. 359)

Muslim [musulmán] *s.* seguidor de la religión islámica. (pág. 232)

Muslim Brotherhood [Hermandad Musulmana] *s.* grupo musulmán fundamentalista que cree que Egipto debe ser gobernado solamente por la ley islámica para cumplir con los principios del Islam. (pág. 258)

Muslim League [Liga Musulmana] *s.* grupo formado por musulmanes en la India en 1906, establecido para proteger sus derechos. (pág. 406)

N

Nagasaki (NAH•guh•SAH•kee) [Nagasaki] *s.* ciudad japonesa en donde Estados Unidos arrojó una bomba atómica en 1945. (pág. 518)

nationalism [nacionalismo] *s.* intenso orgullo por el país o grupo étnico propio. (pág. 123)

NATO (NAY•toh) [OTAN, Organización del Tratado del Atlántico Norte] *s.* alianza de defensa que agrupa a los países de Europa occidental, Canadá y Estados Unidos, que acuerdan la defensa común en caso de ataque. (pág. 131)

nonrenewable resource [recurso no renovables] *s.* recurso que no se puede sustituir o que se puede sustituir sólo tras miles o millones de años. (pág. 295)

Northern Plains [llanuras del a norte] *s.* llanuras que se extienden entre el sistema montañoso del Himalaya y el sur de la India. (pág. 379)

O

OAU [OUA, Organización de la Unidad Africana] *s.* organización formada en 1963 para promover la unidad entre todos los africanos. (pág. 321)

oligarchy (AHL•ih•GAHR•kee) [oligarquía] *s.* gobierno de sólo unos pocos individuos poderosos. (pág. 74)

ombudsman [defensor del pueblo] *s.* funcionario del gobierno sueco que protege los derechos de los ciudadanos y asegura que los tribunales y la administración pública cumplan con la ley. (pág. 179)

one-party system [sistema monopartidista] *s.* sistema donde sólo se puede votar por un partido político y por un candidato para cada puesto de gobierno. (pág. 316)

OPEC [OPEP, Organización de Países Exportadores de Petróleo] *s.* organización que determina el precio y la cantidad de petróleo que se deberá producir cada año en Irak, Irán, Arabia Saudita, Kuwait y Venezuela. (pág. 250)

Opium War [Guerra del Opio] *s.* guerra por el control del comercio del opio entre China y Gran Bretaña desde 1839 a 1842. (pág. 496)

Orthodox Jew [judío ortodoxo] *s.* judío que cumple estrictamente con la ley judía. (pág. 267)

Ottoman Empire [Imperio otomano] *s.* imperio musulmán, desde comienzos del siglo XV hasta la década de 1920. (pág. 236)

outback [llanura desértica] *s.* vasta superficie plana que se extiende por casi toda la zona central de Australia. (pág. 473)

overgrazing [pastoreo excesivo] *s.* proceso mediante el cual se lleva a pastar demasiado ganado sin permitir que la tierra recupere su vegetación. (pág. 347)

P

pagoda [pagoda] *s.* torre budista de muchos niveles, con esculturas o imágenes del Buda talladas en cada nivel. (pág. 446)

paleontologist [paleontólogo] s. científico que estudia los fósiles. (pág. 296)

Palestine [Palestina] s. región en el sudoeste de Asia, comúnmente llamada Tierra Santa. (pág. 244)

panchayat [panchayati] s. consejo rural en India. (pág. 412)

papyrus (puh•PY•ruhs) [papiro] s. material semejante al papel, hecho de un junco. (pág. 224)

parliamentary republic [república parlamentaria] s. república cuyo jefe de estado, en general un primer ministro, es el líder del partido político que tiene la mayoría de representantes en el parlamento. (pág. 155)

pastoralism [pastoreo] s. forma de subsistencia mediante la cría de ganado, ovejas o cabras. (pág. 347)

patrician (puh•TRIHSH•uhn) [patricio] s. miembro de familia adinerada y hacendada en la antigua Roma, que afirmaba que sus orígenes se remontan a la época de la fundación de Roma. (pág. 79)

patrilineal society [sociedad patrilineal] s. sociedad en las que sólo la línea paterna se tiene en cuenta para determinar el árbol genealógico. (pág. 533)

peninsula [península] s. territorio rodeado de agua en tres de sus lados. (pág. 68)

Persian Gulf War [Guerra del Golfo Pérsico] s. guerra entre Estados Unidos e Irak, en 1991. (pág. 247)

petrochemical [producto petroquímico] s. producto derivado del petróleo crudo y gas natural. (pág. 251)

pharaoh (FAIR•oh) [faraón] s. antiguo rey egipcio. (pág. 225)

philosopher [filósofo] s. persona que estudia y piensa sobre el mundo y su naturaleza. (pág. 75)

plain [llanura] s. superficie extensa y plana que suele no tener muchos árboles. (pág. 69)

plateau [meseta] s. área plana situada a cierta altura sobre el nivel del mar. (pág. 292)

plebeian (plih•BEE•uhn) [plebeyo] s. ciudadano corriente (sin título de nobleza) en la antigua Roma. (pág. 79)

polis [polis] s. ciudad central de una ciudad estado. (pág. 73)

Politburo (PAHL•iht•BYUR•oh) [Politburo] s. grupo que encabeza un partido comunista. (pág. 452)

Polynesia [Polinesia] s. uno de los tres grupos regionales de islas en océano Pacífico. (pág. 528)

primary product [producto primario] s. materia prima. (pág. 250)

private property rights [derechos de propiedad privada] s. derechos individuales de ser propietario de bienes raíces, campos o industrias. (pág. 149)

propaganda (PRAHP•uh•GAN•duh) [propaganda] s. material cuyo objetivo es difundir ciertas creencias. (pág. 148)

Protestant [protestante] s. miembro de una iglesia cristiana fundada de acuerdo a los principis de la Reforma. (pág. 100)

Punjabi [punjabí] s. lengua hablada en Pakistán. (pág. 428)

puppet government [gobierno títere] s. gobierno que hace lo que le indica un poder exterior. (pág. 137)

pyramid [pirámide] s. estructura con cuatro lados triangulares que se erige de una base rectangular y se junta con un vértice común en la parte superior. (pág. 225)

Q

Qur'an (kuh•RAN) [Corán] s. texto sagrado del Islam. (pág. 232)

R

racism [racismo] s. creencia de que una raza es inferior a otra. (pág. 308)

Ramadan (RAM•uh•DAHN) [Ramadán] s. noveno mes del año islámico. (pág. 251)

Reformation [Reforma] *s.* movimiento del siglo XVI que se propuso cambiar las prácticas de la Iglesia Católica. (pág. 99)

Reign of Terror [reino del Terror] *s.* período comprendido entre 1793 y 1794 durante el cual las nuevas autoridades en Francia ejecutaron miles de ciudadanos. (pág. 111)

relative location [ubicación relativa] *s.* ubicación de un lugar en relación con otros. (pág. 37)

Renaissance *s.* período de creatividad y de aprendizaje en Europa occidental entre los siglos XIV y XVI. (pág. 96)

renewable resource [recurso renovable] *s.* recurso que puede usarse y reemplazarse luego de un relativamente corto período. (pág. 295)

republic [república] *s.* forma de gobierno controlado por sus cuidadanos a través de representantes elegidos por los cuidadanos. (pág. 79)

reunification [reunificación] *s.* acción de unificar nuevamente las partes. (pág. 190)

Riksdag (RIHKS•DAHG) *s.* parlamento sueco. (pág. 178)

Ring of Fire [Cinturón de Fuego del Pacífico] *s.* área de actividad volcánica en el océano Pacífico. (pág. 472)

rite of passage [rito de paso] *s.* ceremonia especial que marca la transición de una etapa de la vida a otra. (pág. 328)

Rosh Hashanah (RAWSH huh•SHAW•nuh) [Rosh Hashana] *s.* año nuevo judío. (pág. 267)

Russian Revolution [Revolución rusa] *s.* revolución de 1917 que eliminó la monarquía rusa del poder luego de 400 años de vigencia. (pág. 116)

S

Sahel (suh•HAYL) [Sahel] *s.* región semiárida en el sur del Sahara. (pág. 294)

samurai (SAM•uh•RY) [samurai] *s.* guerrero japonés que mediante juramento presta servicio a un señor particular, protegiendo su propiedad. (pág. 486)

sanction [sanción] *s.* multas impuestas en un país que viola la ley internacional. (pág. 356)

Sanskrit [sánscrito] *s.* lengua clásica de la India y del hinduismo. (pág. 356)

savanna [sabana] *s.* llanura de regiones tropicales y subtropicales con escasos árboles y vegetación. (pág. 294)

scarcity [escasez] *s.* palabra usada por los economistas para describir el conflicto que existe entre el deseo de los seres humanos y los recursos limitados para satisfacerlo. (pág. 20)

Scientific Revolution [Revolución científica] *s.* período de grandes cambios científicos y descubrimientos durante los siglos XVI y XVII. (pág. 108)

scribe [escriba] *s.* profesional que se encarga de archivar o copiar documentos. (pág. 220)

secede [separarse] *v.* independizarse de una unidad política, como una nación. (pág. 175)

secondary product [producto secundario] *s.* producto manufacturado con materias primas. (pág. 250)

secular [secular] *adj.* no relacionado con ninguna religión. (pág. 267)

sediment [sedimento] *s.* pequeños fragmentos de roca que son movidos por el viento, el agua o el hielo. (pág. 379)

Senate [Senado] *s.* asamblea más poderosa de la República romana, cuyos representantes eran elegidos. (pág. 79)

Shinto [shinto] *s.* religión japonesa que se desarrolló alrededor de 300 a. de C. (pág. 484)

shogun [shogun] *s.* jefe militar del emperador japonés, en la época feudal, que ejercía el mayor poder. (pág. 487)

Sindhi [sindhi] *s.* lengua que se habla en Pakistán. (pág. 428)

skerry [arrecife] *s.* islote. (pág. 181)

socialism [socialismo] *s.* sistema económico en donde algunos negocios e industrias le pertenecen a una cooperativa o al gobierno. (pág. 186)

Solidarity [Solidaridad] *s.* sindicato polaco cuya finalidad inicial fue aumentar el salario, mejorar las condiciones laborales de los trabajadores y luego oponerse al Comunismo. (pág. 194)

standard of living [nivel de vida] *s.* forma de medir la calidad de vida. (pág. 163)

subcontinent [subcontinente] *s.* gran masa territorial que es parte de un continente pero que posee su propia identidad geográfica. (pág. 378)

subsistence farming [agricultura de subsistencia] *s.* método de agricultura mediante el cual los agricultores cultivan alimentos principalmente para alimentar a sus familias en vez de venderlos. (pág. 325)

Sumerian [sumerio] *s.* uno de los primeros pobladores de la Mesopotamia. (pág. 218)

supply and demand [oferta y demanda] *s.* concepto económico que establece que el precio de un producto sube o baja según la cantidad de personas que lo deseen (demanda) y según la disponibilidad del mismo (oferta). (pág. 452)

Swahili (swah•HEE•lee) [swahili] *s.* lengua bantú africana. (pág. 360)

T

Taiping (ty•PIHNG) **Rebellion** [rebelión Taiping] *s.* la mayor insurrección campesina que ocurrió en China a raíz de la firma del Tratado de Nanking. (pág. 496)

Taj Mahal [Taj Majal] *s.* la construcción más famosa de la India, construida por el emperador mogol Sha Jahan, en la década de 1640. (pág. 420)

Tale of Genji, The [*Cuento de Genji*] *s.* primera novela de la literatura universal, escrita por la japonesa Murasaki Shikibu en el siglo XI. (pág. 486)

Taliban [talibán] *s.* grupo musulmán fundamentalista que tomó el poder en Afganistán en 1996. (pág. 410)

Taoism (DOW•IHZ•uhm) [taoísmo] *s.* filosofía china fundada en el siglo III a. de C. por Lao Tzu. (pág. 478)

Tarbela Dam [presa de Tarbela] *s.* dique construido en el río Indo para el control de aguas e irrigación. (pág. 428)

tariff [arancel aduanero] *s.* tarifa o suma de dinero impuesto por el gobierno en productos que se importan o exportan. (pág. 163)

Tet [Tet] *s.* año nuevo vietnamita. (pág. 453)

textile [textil] *s.* material que se produce mediante el tejido de fibras. (pág. 508)

thatch [techo de paja] *s.* hojas de palmeras, cañas o paja que se usan para construir techos. (pág. 446)

thematic map [mapa temático] *s.* mapa que se centra en una idea o tema particular. (pág. 46)

theocracy (thee•AHK•ruh•see) [teocracia] *s.* gobierno encabezado por una autoridad religiosa. (pág. 235)

Tiananmen (tyahn•ahn•mehn) **Square** [Plaza de Tiananmen] *s.* plaza en Beijing, China, donde miles de manifestantes fueron heridos o matados por el ejército en 1989. (pág. 503)

tradeoff [contrapartida] *s.* la renuncia de ciertos beneficios a cambio de otros. (pág. 258)

tungsten [tungsteno] *s.* un metal. (pág. 507)

Tutsi [tutsi] *s.* etnia minoritaria en Rwanda-Burundi. (pág. 305)

typhoon [tifón] *s.* huracán muy frecuente del océano Pacífico occidental. (pág. 472)

U

Ural (YUR•uhl) **Mountains** [Montes Urales] *s.* cadena montañosa que divide Europa de Asia. (pág. 69)

Urdu [urdu] *s.* lengua oficial en Pakistán. (pág. 428)

V

Vedas (VAY•duhz) [Vedas] *s.* libros sagrados que contienen el conocimiento de los antiguos arios y en los cuales se basa el hinduismo. (pág. 387)

veldt (vehlt) [estepa meridional africana] *s.* pradera del sur de África. (pág. 354)

W

Warsaw Pact [Pacto de Varsovia] *s.* tratado firmado en 1955 que estableció una alianza entre la Unión Soviética, Albania, Bulgaria, Checoslovaquia, Alemania Oriental, Hungría, Polonia y Rumania. (pág. 141)

World War I [Primera Guerra Mundial] *s.* guerra de 1914 a 1918 entre los aliados (Rusia, Francia, el Reino Unido, Italia y los Estados Unidos) y las potencias centrales (Imperio autro-húngaro, Alemania, Turquía y Bulgaria). (pág. 127)

World War II [Segunda Guerra Mundial] *s.* guerra de 1939 a 1945 entre las potencias del Eje (Alemania, Italia y Japón) y los aliados (el Reino Unido, Francia, la Unión Soviética y los Estados Unidos). (pág. 130)

Y

Yom Kippur (YAWM KIHP•uhr) [Yom Kippur] *s.* Día de la Expiación (purificación) en la religión judía. (pág. 267)

Yoruba (YAWR•uh•buh) [yoruba] *s.* grupo étnico en el sudoeste de Nigeria. (pág. 331)

Z

Zen [zen] *s.* rama del budismo que se practica en Japón, que hace hincapié en el hecho de que el ser humano puede alcanzar el iluminismo repentinamente. (pág. 486)

ziggurat [zigurat] *s.* pirámide de la región mesopotámica, formada por terrazas, cada una de las cuales es más pequeña que la de abajo. (pág. 218)

Zionism [sionismo] *s.* movimiento que fomenta el deseo de los judíos de volver a Palestina, la tierra natal judía, que muchos judíos llaman Sión. (pág. 264)

zither [cítara] *s.* instrumento de cuerda. (pág. 513)

Zulu (ZOO•loo) [zulú] *s.* grupo étnico africano. (pág. 342)

Index

An *i* preceding a page reference in italics indicates that there is an illustration, and usually text information as well, on that page. An *m* or a *c* preceding an italic page reference indicates a map or a chart, as well as text information on that page.

A

Abeokuta, Nigeria, *i332*
Aborigines, *i528*, 530, *i533*, 539
Abraham, *i230*
absolute location, 36
Aburi, *i309*
Accra, Ghana, *i320*
acid rain, 180
Acropolis, *i75*
adaptation, 40
Adulyadej, Bhumidol, *i440*
Aegean Sea, *m73*
Aeneid, 82
Aeschylus, 63
Affonso, King, 301
Afghanistan, 378, *i402*, 410, *i417*
   terrorists and, 547
   U.S. military action in, 547
Africa, *i210–211*, 288–363
   political systems, *m308*
African National Congress (ANC), *i355*, 356
African Union, 321
African Woman Food Farmer Initiative, *i294*
Afrikaners, 355–356
afterlife, 225, 227
Agra, *i420*
agriculture, *m169*
Aida, *i256*
aikido, 514
Ainu, 519
airplanes
   hijacking of, 544, *m544*
Ajanta, *i389*
Akbar, 404
Akbarnama, *i404*
Aksum empire, 340
Alexander II, 115
Alexander Nevsky, *i140*
Alexander the Great, *i76*
Alexandria, 46
Alhambra, *i236*
alliances, 128, 272
Allies, 128–129, 130, *i184*

Alps, 58, 68
al-Qaeda, 544, 546, 547
Altaic peoples, *m149*
Amina, Queen, 330
Amundsen, Roald, *i536*
Ananda temple, *i397*
Anawrahta, 397
Angkor, 392, *i438*
Angkor Wat, *i374–375*, *m396*, *i438*
Anglo–Iranian Oil Company, *i249*
Ankole cattle, *i337*
Annan, Kofi, 320
Antalya, Turkey, *i246*
Antarctic Treaty, 538
Antarctica, 47, 536–539
antimony, 507
apartheid, *i310*, *i355*, 356
aqueduct, *i64–65*, *i82*
Arabian Sea, 379
Arabic, *i242*, *i246*
Arab-Israeli Wars, *i229*, 244, *m245*, *i266*
Arc de Triomphe, *i184*
archaeologists, *i18*
archipelago, 36, 381
Arctic Circle, *m47*
arctic climate region, *c38*
Aristophanes, 75
Aristotle, *i76*
Arjuna, *i422*
armed neutrality, 179
arms trade, *m326*
artifacts, *i18*
Aryans, 386, 395
Ashanti, *i327*
Ashoka, *i385*, *i389*
Assamese, *m421*
Association for India's Development (AID), *i416*
astrolabe, *i43*, *i94*, *i104*
Aswan, 46, *m257*
Aswan High Dam, *i257*
Atatürk, 271
Athena, *i75*
Athens, Greece, *i72*
Auckland, 534

Augustan Age, 81–82
Augustus, Caesar, *i81*
Aurangzeb, *m405*
Australia, *m36*, *i466–467*, *m473*, 474, 527–530, 531–532, 534
Austria, as member of EU, *c162*
Austria-Hungary, *m126*, 127–128, 130
Axis powers, 130, 140
Ayatollah/Khomeini. *See* Khomeini, Ayatollah.
Ayers Rock, *i466–467*

B

Babur, 404
Babylonia, *i45*, *i217*
Baghdad, Iraq, 548
Bahai, 251
Bahasa Indonesian, *c445*
Bahasa Melayu, *c445*
Baku, Azerbaijan, *i506*
Bali, *i446*
Balkan states, *m157*
Ballets Russes, *i125*
Balthus, 187
Baltic states, 157
Baluchistan, *i427*
Banani, *i288–289*
Bangladesh, 378, *i379*, 410, 417, 422
Bantu, *i296*, 359, 360
banyan tree, *i413*
Bao Loc, Vietnam, *i434–435*
baptize, 231
Barcelona, *i173*
Barre, Siad, 342
Barry, Charles, *i175*
baseball, 520
Basho, 513
Bastille, *i110*
batik, 447
Battleship Potemkin, *i140*
Baule gold masks, *i290*
bauxite, *m532*
Bawka, Queen, 330
Bayeux Tapestry, *i86*
Beatles, *i176*

R47

Beauvoir, Simone de, 187
Beethoven, Ludwig van, *i190*
Begin, Menachem, *i258*
Beijing, *i468*, 477, 480, *i495*, 503, *i510*
Beijing Opera, 513
Belgian Congo, 319
Belgium, as member of EU, *c162*
Belka, 148
Bengal, Bay of, 379
Bengali, *m421*
Ben-Gurion, David, 265
Benin, *c306*
Bergman, Ingmar, 181
Berlin, *i120–121*, *i131*, *i188*
Berlin Wall, *i141*, 188–189
Bethlehem, Palestine, 230
Bhagavad-Gita, *i422*
Bhutan, 378, 406, 410, 417
Bhutto, Benazir, *i429*
Biafra, 310, 332
Big Ben, *i175*
bin Laden, Osama, 547
Biography (feature), *i76*, *i97*, *i131*, *i190*, *i226*, *i258*, *i332*, *i355*, *i389*, *i406*, *i497*, *i533*, *i538*
biological weapons, 546, 548
Black Death, 93
black powder, *i278*
Blair, Tony, *i549*
Bloody Sunday, 115
Blue Mosque, *i200–201*
bodhi tree, *i394*
Boers, 355
Bonaparte, Napoleon, *i111*
Bonnard, Pierre, 187
bonsai, 520
Book of the Dead, *i224*
Borneo, 381
Borobudur, 396, *i397*
Bosnia and Herzegovina, 157, 158
Botswana, *c348*
Brandenburg Gate, *i141*
Bremer, L. Paul, 549
Breuil, Henri, 185
Brewster, Barbara Marie, 534
British Empire, *i125*
bronze, 393
Brunei, 381, 441, *c445*
Brunelleschi, Filippo, 97
bubonic plague, 93
Bucephalus, *i76*
Buddha, 446

Buddhism, *i385*, *i389*, 394, *i394*, *i397*, *i446*, 478, *i485*, *i511*, 534
bureaucracy, 278
Burma, 381. See also Myanmar.
Burmese, *c445*
Burundi, *i337*
Bush, George W.
   antiterrorism measures and, 544–545, 547
   war against terrorism and, 544, 547
   War with Iraq and, 247, 548–549, *i549*
Bushmen, 297
Byrd, Richard, 538

C

Cabot, John, *m105*
Caesar, Julius, *i80*, 81
Cairo, Egypt, *i223*, *i242*, *i256*, *m256*, *m257*, 260, *i260*, *i261*
calabash, *i333*
Calcutta, *i409*
calendar, 232, 251
caliph, 237
Cambodia, *i374–375*, 381, *i438*, *i446*, 534
camels, *i298*
Cameroon, 297, *i316*, *i324*
Camus, Albert, 187
Canton, China, *i496*
Cape Town, *i355*
capitalism, 109, 499
capital resources, 20
caravans, 298
carpets, *i252*
Carthage, 79
cartographers, 45. See also mapmakers.
carving, *i528*, *i529*
cassava, *i332*
caste system, 388, 395, 422
castles, *i87*
Catherine the Great, 113, *i114*
Catholic Action for Street Children, *i320*
Catholic Church, 446, 488
cattle, *m532*
Caucasian peoples, *m149*
causes, analyzing, R10
cave paintings, *i185*
censorship, *i150*, 197
Cézanne, Paul, 187
chador, *i253*

Champa kingdom, *m455*
Chang Jiang, *m470*
chapati, 423
Charlemagne, 85
Charles, Prince, of Denmark, *i123*
charts
   interpreting, *c244*, *c306*, *c348*
   reading, *c294*
Chechnya, 158
cheetah, *c335*
chemical weapons, 546
chess, 158
Chiang Kai-shek, *i497*
China, *i456–457*, 470–471, *i470*, *m470*, 475–480, *i475*, *c476*, 489, *i492-493*, *i494*, 495–499, 514, 515
   creation myths, 28–29
Chinese Communist Party, *i494*, 497–499, *i503*
Chinese Nationalist Party, 496–497, 505
Christianity, 66, 83, 85–86, 89, 95, 99–100, 104, *i158*, *i180*, *i229*, 230–231, *i350*, 439, 488, 511
Christmas Carol, A, 176
Chronicles of Narnia, The, 177
chronometer, *i43*
Chunnel, *i67*
Chutter Munzil Palace, *i24*
cichlid, *i347*
Ciller, Tansu, *i271*
circumference of Earth, *i46*
circumnavigation, 104
citizen rights, *i16*
citizenship, 20,
   naturalization and, 20
Citizenship in Action, *i21*, *i39*, *i225*, *i294*, *i320*, *i441*, *i485*
city-states, 73, 96–97
civil rights and antiterrorism measures, 545
clan, 485
class system, 219
cliffside dwellings, *i288–289*
climate map, *m216*, *m222*
Clinton, Bill, *i271*
coal, 70, *m159*, *m169*, *m250*
coalition government, 156
coconut, *i341*, 532
coco de mer, *i341*
coelacanth, *i295*
coffee, 360

Cold War, 140–141, 150, *i154*
collective farms, *i139*, 498
colonial empires, 124–125
colonialism, 125, 303–305, 439–440
Colosseum, 39, *i52–53*
Columbus, Christopher, 103, *m105*
Comaneci, Nadia, *i149*
command economy, 20–21
Commonwealth of Nations, 530
communes, 498
communication system, 17
Communism, 137, *i188*, *i193*, 194–195, 197, 450, 451, 452, 497–499, 502–503, 504, 514
Communist Party, 452, *i494*, 497
compass, *i42*, 278
compound graphs, 480
concentration camp, *i131*
conclusions, drawing, *i329*
Confucianism, 511, 519
Confucius, 477
Congo, Democratic Republic of the, 318
Congo River, *i292*, *i317*, *m318*
Connections to Citizenship, *i266*
Connections to Economics, *i88*, *i163*
Connections to History, *i86–87*, *i185*, *i350*
Connections to Language, *i73*, *i159*
Connections to Literature, *i272*
Connections to Math, *i46*, *i98*
Connections to Science, *i18*, *i103*, *i157*, *i325*
Connections to Technology, *i428*, *i278*, *i532*
Constantine, *i83*
Constantinople, *i200–201*, 236
constitutional monarchy, 124, 441, 519, 530
continents, *i35*, *i539*
convents, 86
Cook, James, *c535*
cool forest, *c38*
cool grassland, *c38*
cooperatives, 508
copper, *m250*
copra, 532
corn, *m169*, *m250*
Côte d'Ivoire, 325
cotton, *m250*, 259
Counter Reformation, 100
coup d'état, 155, 319
Court of Human Rights, 164

Cousteau, Jacques, 199
Crimean War, 115
Croatia, *i152*, 157,
Croats, 157, 158
Crusades, *i95*
Cultural Revolution, 499, 503, 514
culture, 21
   region, 24–26
   traits, 21
cuneiform, *i45*, *i220*
Curie, Marie, 192
currency, 163, *i319*
Cyrillic alphabet, *i159*
czar, 113
Czechoslovak Communist Party, 151

D

D'Arcy, William Knox, 249
Dai Viet Kingdom, *m455*
dairy, *m169*
Dalits, 412
Dandi, *i407*
Danube River, 68
Darjeeling, *i405*
database, creating, *i481*, R21
Dead Sea, *i215*
Deccan Plateau, 378, 380, 404
delta, 37, 379
democracy, 19, 167, 342
Deng Xiaoping, 503
Denmark, as member of EU, *c162*
Department of Defense, U.S., 43
Department of Homeland Security, U.S., 545
desert, *i37*, *c38*, *m159*
desertification, *i291*, 294
détente, 151–152
developing countries, 21
developing nations, 444
Diaghilev, Sergey, *i125*
dialect, 421
diamonds, *i295*, *m326*
Dias, Bartolomeu, 103
Dickens, Charles, 176
dictatorships, 319, 342, 441, 504
Diet, 504, 519
disciple, 231
disease, 104, 109, 349, 528
dissident, 197
diversity, 309
Djibouti, *i346*

dogs
   in space, 148
   in World War I, 129
doi moi, 452
Dome of the Rock, *i229*
domes, *i112*
dowry, 423
Doyle, Sir Arthur Conan, 176
Draa Valley, *i215*
Dravidian languages, 422, *m466*
Dresden, Germany, *i107*
drip irrigation, 265
drought, 294, *i346*
drums, *i348*
dual monarchy, 126
Dubček, Alexander, 151
Dubrovnik, Croatia, *i152*
Duma, 158
Duomo (Florence), *i96*
dynamite, *i178*
dynasties, *c476*, *i495*

E

Earth
   measuring, *i46*
   physical features, 37
   as unified system, 39
Earth Observing System (EOS), 33
earthquake, 35, *i469*, 472, 517
Easter Island, *i529*
Eastern Ghats, 380
East India Company, 405
East Timor, 441
Echoes of the White Giraffe, 482–483
Economic Community of West African States (ECOWAS), 321
Economic Cooperation Act of 1948, 132
economics, 20–21
   development, 20–21
Edo, 487, 488
effects, recognizing, R10
Egypt, 46, 256–261
   ancient, 223–227, *i254–255*
Eightfold Path, *i395*
Eisenstein, Sergey, *i140*
elections, 19
electronic card catalog, using, *i153*, R20
elephants, *i276–277*, *i325*, *i444*
elevation maps, reading, *m391*
Elmina, 301
embargo, 247, *i250*

emigration, 38
emperor, 113
empire, 81
endangered animals, c335, i358
Endeavour, i44
English Channel, i67
English language, i242, i246, 422, c445
environmental change, 33
epidemic, 93
equator, 36, i41
Erasmus, Desiderius, 98
Eratosthenes, i46
Essy, Amara, 321
Estonia, 157
Ethiopia, i339, i346, i350
ethnic cleansing, 157, 158
ethnic group, 246
Euphrates River, i213, 214
Euripides, 75
euro, i146, i161, 163
Europe, 67–71, 127–132
European Central Bank, i162
European Union (EU), 161-164, 186, 273
Eurostar trains, i67
Everest, Mount, i377, 379, 470
execution, 111
exile, 230
Ezana, King, 229

F

fact from opinion, distinguishing, c448, R14
factories, i109
famine, i346, 495
farmland, m159
Farouk, King, 257, i258
fascism, 130
federal government, of U.S., aviation security and, 545
Federated States of Micronesia, 530
fellahin, i259
Fertile Crescent, 217, m218
feudalism, 86
fief, 86
Fifth Republic, 185
Filipino language, c445
Filipinos, 439
Finland, as member of EU, c162
Fire Mountain, i381
fish, m159, m169, m250, i295, i347, i418, i527
fjord, 68

flags, i174, 341, i409
flamingos, i360
Flemings, 164
flood, i16
Florence, Italy, 96, 182–183
Focus on Geography, i15, i33, i65, i93, i121, i145, i171, i211, i241, i289, i315, i337, i375, i401, i435, i467, i493, i525
food
    shortages, 20
Forbidden City, i468, i477, i500–501
forest, m159, i160
fossils, 339
Four Noble Truths, i395
France, 184–187
    as member of EU, c162
Frank, Anne, i131
Frankfurt, Germany, i162
Franz Ferdinand, i127
freedom
    of religion, 503
    of speech, 332, 503
freedom rides, i533
Freeman, Cathy, i526, i531
free trade, 533
French Polynesians, 530
French Resistance, 184
French Revolution, 110–111
fringing reefs, 474
Fuji, Mount, i472
Fukoaka Dome, i520
fundamentalism, 252, 410

G

Gagarin, Yuri, i147, i148
Galápagos Islands, 39
Galbraith, John Kenneth, 431
Galilee, 230
Galilei, Galileo, i108
Gama, Vasco da, 103
Gambia River, i318
Gandhi, Indira, 412
Gandhi, Mohandas, i406, i407, 412, 424
Ganges River, i37, i375, i379, m387, i400–401, i403
ganuwar Amina, i330
Gaul, 80
Gaulle, Charles de, 184, 185
Gdańsk, Poland, i193
Genghis Khan, 476
generalization, making, 91, R18

geography, 18–19, 35–40
geometry, i46
Germany, 188–191
    as member of EU, c162
Ghana, 299, c306, 327
ghats, i606–607
Ghats, 380, i400–401
Gilgamesh, i221
glaciers, 37, 537
gladiators, i52–53
Global Positioning System, i43, 45
global warming, 380, 539
globe, i46
Globe Theater, i176
Gobi Desert, i471
gold, m159, 299, 354, 393
Gondwana, m539
Good Friday Accord, 175
Good Hope, Cape of, 103
Gorbachev, Mikhail, 154, i154
gorilla, c335
Gospels, 230
government, 19
Grand Canal, 480
Grand National Assembly, 271
granite, 255
Grass, Günter, 191
grassland, c38, m159
Great Barrier Reef, 474
Great Britain, 173–177
    War with Iraq and, 549
Great Depression, 517
Great Enclosure, 341
Great European Plain, 69, 71
Great Kanto Earthquake, 517
Great Leap Forward, 498–499
Great Rift Valley, 293
Great Sphinx, i260
Great Wall of China, i456–457, 480
Great Zimbabwe, 341
Greece
    ancient, 72–76
    as member of EU, c162
Green Revolution, 419, 445
Greenwich, England, 27, 41
gross domestic product (GDP), c348
Guadalcanal Island, 517
Guam, 529
guilds, 88
guillotine, 111
Gujarati, m421
Gulf Stream, m91

R50

gunpowder, 405, *i278*
Gupta Dynasty, 375, 389, *m390*
Gutenberg, Johannes, *i99, i166*

H

Hadar, Ethiopia, *i339*
Haifa, Israel, 251
haiku, 513
haj, i251
half-timber architecture, *i191*
Hammurabi, *i217*
Han, 473, 514
Han Dynasty, *c476,* 479
Hangzhou, China, 480
harambee schools, 360
Harappan civilization, 385
Harrison, George (Australian prospector), *i354*
Harrison, John, 43
Hatshepsut, *i226*
Hausa, *i330, m331*
Hawaiian Creole, 25
health care, 160, 498
Hebrew, 230, *i242,* 246
Heian Age, 485–486
Heian-kyo, 485
helicopter, 94
Henry the Navigator, Prince, 93, *i101,* 102
Heraclitus, 75
Hermitage Museum, *i115*
Herodotus, 223
hieroglyphs, 225
hijacking. *See* airplanes, hijacking of.
Hillary, Sir Edmund, *i377*
Hill Complex, 341
Himalayas, 377, 378, 379
Hindi, *m421*
Hinduism, 24, *i374–375, i376,* 387–388, 394, *i400–401,* 404, 407, 422, *i423,* 438, 446
Hindu Kush Mountains, 378, *i404,* 425
Hirohito, Emperor, *i516,* 518
Hiroshima, Japan, 518
historical maps, reading, *m248*
Hitler, Adolf, 130
Ho Chi Minh, *i450*
Ho Chi Minh City, Vietnam, *i452*
Hobson, William, *i527*
hocketing, 349
Hokkaido, 471
Holy Land, *i95*

Holy Sepulcher, Church of the, *i229, i231*
Homeland Security. *See* Department of Homeland Security, U.S.
Hong Kong, 496, *i507*
Hongwu emperor, 476–477
Honshu, 471, 520
Horus, 226
House of Commons, British, 174, *i175*
House of Lords, *i175*
Huang He, *m470–471,* 475
human resources, 20
human rights, 333, 503
Hunger Project, *i294*
hunter-gatherers, *i214*
Hussein, Saddam, 246–247, 548–549
Hutu, *i305*
hydroelectric power, *m169,* 180

I

Iberian Peninsula, 68
Ibo, *i309*
icons, *i158*
Id al-Fitr, 251
Igbo, 327, *m331,* 332
Iliad, i272
immigration, 17, 19, 38
imperialism, 104
impressionism, *i187*
India, *i24,* 378, 403–409
Indian National Congress, 406, 407, 426
Indian Ocean, 393
indigo, 405
Indo-Aryan, *m421,* 422
Indochinese Peninsula, 381
Indo-European
 languages, 422
 peoples, *m149*
Indonesia, *i381, m440, c445*
Indus River, 379, 385–386, *m387, m427*
industrialization, 109
industrial revolution, 108
infant mortality, *c59, c61, c63, c207, c209, c283, c285, c287, c371, c373, c463, c465*
information technology, 418
Institute for the Study and Implementation of Graphic Heritage Techniques (INSIGHT), *i225*
interdependence, 26

Interdisciplinary Challenge, *i22–23, i182–183, i254–255, i344–345, i442–443, i500–501*
interferometry, 44
International Date Line, *m27*
international trade, 17
Internet, researching topics on, *i106,* R22
Iran, Shah of, *i249*
Iran-Iraq War, 246
Iraq, War with. *See* War with Iraq.
Ireland, as member of EU, *c162*
Irish Catholic nationalists, 175
Irish Protestants, 175
iron, *m159, m169, m250*
Iron Curtain, 138, *m139,* 141
irrigation, 19, 215, 445, 449, 450
 tools, *i215*
Isabella, Queen, 103
Isis, *i227*
Islam, 25, 232, 236–237, 246, 251, 350, 403–404, 446, 544. *See also* Muslims.
 Five Pillars of, 234, *i235, i237*
Islamabad, Pakistan, *i411,* 427
Ismail Pasha, 256
Israel, 19, 230, 264–267
Israel Defense Forces (IDF), 265
Istanbul, Turkey, *i240–241, i273*
Italy, as member of EU, *c162*
Ivan IV, Czar, 112, 113
ivory, *i325*
Ivory Coast, 309, 325

J

Jaffa, *i264*
Jahan, Shah, *i420*
Jainism, 412
Jakarta, Indonesia, *i438, m440*
Janissaries, *i237*
Japan, 469, 471–472, 484–488, 504, 506, 508, 516–520, *m521*
Japan Center for International Cooperation in Conservation, *i485*
Java, *i397, i446*
Jemison, Mae, *i21*
Jemison Institute for Advancing Technology in Developing Countries, *i21*
Jerusalem, *i229,* 230–231, *m233*
Jesuits, 100
Jesus Christ, *i229*

R51

Jigme Singye Wangchuk, King, *i410*
jiti, 350
Johannesburg, South Africa, *i354*
Johanson, Don, *i339*
John Paul II, Pope, *i197*
John the Baptist, 231
Judaism, 130, 229, 230, 264–267, 534
judo, *i514*
jute, 417

K

Kabila, Joseph, 319
Kabila, Laurent Désiré, 319
Kaiser Wilhelm Memorial Church, *i120–121*, *i131*
Kalahari Desert, 293, *c294*
Kalenjin, 359, 360
Kalidasa, 390
Kamakura Shogunate, 487
Kamba, 360
kami, *i484*
kamikaze, 484
kangaroo, *i473*
Kannada, *m421*
Kanto Plain, 471
Karakoram Range, 378
karate, *i514*
karma, 388
Kashmir, 429
Kashmiri language, *m421*
Kazakhstan, 155
Kazan, 112
Kemal, Mustafa, *i270–271*
Kente cloth, *i316*, *i325*
Kenya, *i307*, *i336–337*, *i358*, 359–361
Kenya, Mount, *i292*, 358
Kenyatta, Jomo, *i307*
kettledrums, *i348*
Khafre, *i254–255*, *i260*
Khasi, *m421*
Khmer, 396, 435, *c445*, *m455*
Khomeini, Ayatollah, 246
Khrushchev, Nikita, 150, *i151*
Khufu, *i254–255*
Khuzistan province, Persia, *i249*
Khyber Pass, 379
kibbutz, *i265*, 265
Kilimanjaro, Mount, 292
kiln, 479
Kim Dae-jung, *i502*
King, Martin Luther, Jr., *i412*
kinship, 349

Klerk, Willem de, *i355*, 356
Knesset, 265
koan, 486
Kofti Yeebwa, King, *i309*
Komodo dragon, *i439*
Kongfuzi, 477
Kongo, *i301*
Konkani, *m421*
Konyak, *m421*
Korea, 472, 485, 504–505
Korean Peninsula, 472, *i502*, *m504*, 505
Korean War, 505
Korean Workers' Party, 505
Kosciusko, Thaddeus, 196
Krakatau, *i382*
Kremlin, *i147*, *i154*
Krishna, *i422*
Kublai Khan, 476, *i484*, 487
Kum, 473
Kumaratunga, Chandrika, *i411*
kung fu, *i494*, *i514*
Kurds, 246, 272
Kuwait, 247
Kyrgyzstan, *m155*
Kyushu, 471, *i520*

L

La Belle Ferronnière, *i98*
Ladysmith Black Mambazo, *i349*
Lahore, Pakistan, 426, *i428*
Laika, *i148*
Lailibela, Emperor, *i350*
Lao, *c445*
Laos, 381, 441, *i447*
Lao Tzu, *i278*
Lascaux cave paintings, *i185*
Last Supper, The, *i231*
Latin America, 25
latitude, 6, 36, *i41*
Latvia, 157
Law of Return, 266
law of supply and demand, 452
Law of the Twelve Tables, *i79*
lead, *m159*, *m250*, *m532*
League of Nations, 17
Lee, Bruce, *i494*, *i514*
Leeuwenhoek, Antoni van, 108
Leipzig, Germany, *i107*
Leipzig-Dresden railway, *i107*
Lenin, Vladimir, 138
Leonardo da Vinci, 94, 98, *i231*
Leopold, King, 318

Lesotho, GDP, *c348*
Lewis, C. S., 177
Liberia, *c306*
life expectancy, 21, *m48*, *c58*, *c60*, *c62*, *c206*, *c208*, *c282*, *c284*, *c286*, *c370*, *c372*, *c462*, *c464*
limestone, 255
limited government, 19
linear perspective, *i98*
Linking Past and Present, *i42–43*, *i166–167*, *i268–269*, *i322–323*, *i414–415*, *i536–537*
Linnaeus, Carolus, 108
literacy, 21
Literature Connections, *i28–29*, *i134–135*, *i262–263*, *i352–353*, *i432–433*, *i482–483*
Lithuania, 157
"Little Red Book," *i499*
lizards, *i439*
lodestone, 42
London, England, 67, 164
longitude, 6, 36, *i41*, 43
Long March, 497, *m498*
Louis IX, *i95*
Louis XVI, 110
Luba, 327
Lucknow, *i24*
Lucy, *i339*
Luhya, 360
Luo, 360
Luther, Martin, 99, *i100*
Lutheran Church, 180
Luxembourg, as member of EU, *c162*
Luycx, Luc, *i161*
Lyceum, *i76*

M

Mabovitz, Golda, 264
MacArthur, Douglas, 504
Mac Cumhail, Fionn, 134–135
Macedonia, 157
Madagascar, *i341*
Magellan, Ferdinand, 103, *m105*
Magna Carta, *i89*
magnetic compass, *i42*
Mahabharata, 421, *i422*, *i446*
Mahatma, *i406*
main idea, finding, R5
Malawi, 349
Malayalam, *m421*, *c445*,
Malay Peninsula, 381

Malaysia, 381, c445
Maldives, 378, 380, 406, 407, 410, 417
Mali, i288–289, i291, 299, c306
Mamelukes, 257
Manchester United, i173
Manchuria, 517
Manchus, 495
mandala, 438
Mandarin Chinese, c445
Mandarins, The, 187
mandate, 244
Mandela, Nelson, i355, 356–357
Manet, Edouard, i187
Mangla Dam, i428
Manipuri, m421
Mann, Thomas, 191
manor, 86
manorialism, 87
Mansa Musa, King, i300
Manthini, i416
manufacturing, i137–138, i475
Maori, i527, i528, 530, 534
Mao Zedong, 497, i498, 499, 503, 514
mapmakers, 4, 45, 47
mapmaking technology, 42–43
map projections, 7, 47
maps, 45–47
    Africa, m304, m326, m347
    African slave trade, m302
    Antarctica, m537, m543
    Arctic Circle, m126
    Aswan High Dam, m257
    Babylonian world, m45
    Balkan states, m157
    Bantu migration, m297
    Belize, i119
    Brazil, m498, m523
    climate, m216, m222
    comparing, i222
    culture regions, m25
    East Asia, m509, m512
    Europe, m57, m71, m129, m132
    European colonial possessions, m124
    Fertile Crescent, m218
    France, m185
    Germany, m189
    Greek colonization, m73
    Gulf Stream, m91
    India, m366, m384, i399
    interpreting, m25, m36, m47, m48, m55, m57, m71, m80, m81, m96, m102, m105, m114, m124, m126, m129, m132, m138, m149, m155, m157, m159, m179, m185, m189, m194, m203, m205, m216, m218, m233, m250, m257, m259, m279, m281, m297, m302, m304, m308, m318, m326, m331, m347, m359, m367, m369, m378, m384, m387, m390, m405, m419, m427, m440, m451, m459, m461, m470, m472, m479, m498, m504, m509, m512, m519, m529, m532
    Israel, m19
    Italy, m96
    Japan, m519
    Kenya, m359
    Korea, m504
    life expectancy, m48
    Mediterranean, m19
    Mercator, m47
    Nigeria, m331
    Nile River, m257, m259
    North Island, New Zealand, m46, m50
    Oceania, m529
    physical, m56, m204, m280, m368, m378, m391, m399, m460, m470, m473
    Poland, m194
    political, m54, m96, m124, m155, m174, m179, m189, m194, m202, m245, m248, m278, m296, m304, m313, m347, m359, m366, m384, m390, m405, m427, m440, m451, m455, m458
    population, m48, m143, m149, m259, m431, m491, m519, m521, m523
    Portuguese explorers, m102
    Rand McNally Atlas, A1–A37
    reading, m31, m248, m275, m391, m399, m521
    Ring of Fire, m472
    road, m46
    Rome, m80, m81
    Russia, m114, m159
    Southeast Asia, m440
    Sweden, m179
    time zone, m27, m31
    United Kingdom, m174
    vegetation zone,
    Vietnam, m451
    world, m30
Marathi, m421
marble, 82
Marie Antoinette, 110
market economy, 20–21
Marshall Plan, 132
martial arts, i514
martial law, 411
Masai, i336–337, i341, i359, 361
Masai Mara National Reserve, i336–337, 360
math, 390
matrilineal societies, 533
Maurya, 389
mbira, 349, 350
McCullough, David, 18
Mecca, 231–232, i251, 300
mediation, 321
Medici family, i97
medieval period. *See* Middle Ages.
Medina, 232
Mediterranean Sea, m54, 68
Mediterranean vegetation region, c38
Mehmed V, Sultan, 237
Meiji Restoration, 517
Meir, Golda, 264, 266
Mekong River, 381, 453
Melanesia, 469, 528
Melbourne, Australia, 36
Memoirs of Akbar, The, i404
Menkaure, i254–255
Merapi, Mount, i381
Mercator, Gerardus, 47
Mercator projection, i47
meridians, i41
Mesopotamia, i213, i219, 221, i228, 230
messiah, 231
metalworking, 393
metropolis, 73
Micronesia, 469, 528
Middle Ages, 84–89
middle class, 88
Middle East
    Israeli-Palestinian conflict in, 244–245
Middle Way, 395
Midway, Battle of, 517
migration, 38, m39
military dictatorship, i441
Milošević, Slobodan, 157
Milosz, Czeslaw, 196–197
Minamoto clan, 487
minerals, 70, i354
Ming Dynasty, c476, 477, 479

missionaries, 303, 439, 446, 488, 528, 529
Mobutu, Joseph Désiré, 319
Mogadishu, Somalia, *i338, i342*
Mohenjo-Daro, *i376, i386, i426*
Moi, Daniel arap, *i359*
monarchy, 174, 178, 530
monasteries, 85–86
Monet, Claude, *i187*
Mongolia, 505
Mongol invasions, *m455, i484*, 487
Mongols, 112, 404, 476, 511
Mon kingdom, *m455*
monks, 85–86, 99, 166
Monnet, Jean, 185
monopoly, 407
monotheism, 229–229
Mons, 435
monsoon, 382, *i383*, 393, 472, 473
moon, *i32*
Morocco, *i215*
Moscow, Russia, *i112*
Mouhot, Henri, *i392*
Mountbatten, Lord, 409
movable type, *i94, i166*
movement, 18, 19, 38, 39
Mozambique, 340
 GDP, *c348*
Mughal Empire, 404, *m405*, 420, 426
Muhammad, 229, 231–232, 234–235
multiculturalism, 25
multiparty system, 359
mummies, *i227*
Mumtaz Mahal, 420
Murasaki Shikibu, *i486*
Muslim Brotherhood, 258
Muslim League, 406, 407, *i425*
Muslims, 24, 155, 157, 158, 229, 231–232, 236, 251, 300, 331, 403, 404, 407, 410, 422, 426, 439, 446, 544
Mussolini, Benito, 130
Myanmar, 381, *i397, m440*, 441, *c445*
Myerson, Morris, 264

N

Nagasaki, Japan, *i518*, 518
Nairobi, Kenya, *i338*, 358, *i361*
Naktong, 473
Nakuru, Lake, *i360*
Namib Desert, *c294*
Nanking, Treaty of, 496
Napoleon III, 450
Napoleonic Wars, 111
Nasser, Gamal Abdel, *i257*, 258
National Aeronautics and Space Administration (NASA), 33
National Assembly (France), 185
National Assembly (South Korea), 505
nationalism, 111, 123–125
National People's Congress, 503
natural disasters, 33
natural gas, *m159, m250, m532*
naturalization, 20
natural regions, *c38*
natural resources, 20
nautical map, 46
navigation, 39, *i42–43*
Nazi Party, 130
Nehru, Jawaharlal, 409, *i412*, 424
Nepal, *i377*, 378, 411, 417
Nepali language, *m421*
Netherlands, The, as member of EU, *c162*
Neve Shalom/Wahat al-Salem, *i266*
New Caledonia, 529
New Delhi, India, *i409*
New Guinea, 474
New York City. *See* September 11 terrorist attack.
New Zealand, 469, 474, 527–530, 531–534
Nicholas II, Czar, 116
Niger, *c306*
Nigeria, *c306, c309*, 330–333
Niger River Valley, 299
Nile River, 214, *i223*, 224, *m257, m259*, 293
9-11 terrorist attack. *See* September 11 terrorist attack.
Ninth Symphony (Beethoven), 190
nitroglycerin, 166
Nkrumah, Kwame, *i319*, 320
Nobel, Alfred, *i166, i178*
Nobel Prize, *i378, i178*
 economics, *i20*
 literature, 191, 197, *i332*
 peace, *i258, i502*
 physics, *i192*
nobles, 114–115
Nok, *i331*
nomads, 253
nonrenewable resources, 295
nonviolence, *i412*
Norgay, Tenzing, *i377*
North Atlantic Treaty Organization (NATO), 131, 151, 156, 157–158, 272
Northern Ireland, 175
Northern Plains, 378, 379–380
North Island, New Zealand, *m46, m50, i524–525*
North Korea, *i502, m504*, 505, 506, 508, 514, *m521*
North Pole, *i41*
North-West Frontier, 427
Norway, *i123*
Notre Dame Cathedral, *i184*
Nubia, 225
nuclear energy generation, *c186*
nuns, 85–86, 99
Nyasa, Lake, *c313*

O

Oceania, 469, 474, 527–530, 531–533
Octavian, 81
Odyssey, *i272*
oil, *m159, i249*, 250–251, *m275*, 332
Okavango River, 293
Okri, Ben, 333
Olaleye, Isaac, *i352–353*
Old City, Jerusalem, *m229*
oligarchy, 74
Oliver Twist, 176
Olympics, *i316, i324, i510, i514, i531*
ombudsmen, 179
on, 519
one-party system, 137
opium, *i496*
Opium War, 496
Organization of African Unity (OAU), *i321*
Organization of Petroleum Exporting Countries (OPEC), 250
Oriya, *m421*
Orthodox Jews, 267
Orwell, George, 177
Osama bin Laden. *See* bin Laden, Osama.
Osiris, *i227*
Oslo, Norway, *i502*
Ottoman Empire, 236–237, *i243, m248*
Outback, 473
outline, making, *i183, i192*
overgrazing, 347

P

Pagan, *i397*
pagodas, 446
Pakistan, 378, *m391*, 411, 418, 422, *i425*, 426–429
Palazzo Medici, *i97*
paleontologists, 296
Palestine, 230, 244
Palestine Liberation Organization (PLO), 245
Pan-Africanism, 308
panchayat, 412–413
Pandavas, *i422*
Pangaea, *i35*, 291
paper, 224, 278
Papua New Guinea, *i533*
papyrus, *i224*
Paris, France, *i184*
Parliament, British, 174, *i175*
parliamentary republic, 155–156, 185, 195
Parthenon, *i75*
pastoralism, 347
patrician, 79
patrilineal societies, 533
peninsulas, 68
Pentagon
    September 11 terrorist attack on, 544
Pericles, 74
Perkins, Charlie, *i533*
Perry, Commodore Matthew C., *i517*
Persian Gulf War, 247
Peter the Great, *i113*, 114
Petra, Jordan, *i39*
petrochemicals, 251
petroleum, *m169*, *i241*, *m250*
pharaoh, *i223*, 225
Philip, Prince, *i307*
Philip II, King, *i76*
Philippines, 381, 439, *c445*
philosopher, 75, 477
Phnom Penh, 396
phosphate, *m250*
Piccadilly Circus, *i170–171*
Pippi Longstocking, 181
place, 37
plague, 93
plain, 69
plateaus, 292
Plato, 75, *i76*
plebeian, 79
plow, *i214*, *i417*
poaching, *i358*
point of view, understanding, 424, R8
Poland, 193–197
polis, 73
Politburo, 452
political cartoon, interpreting, *i128*, *i133*
pollution, 109, *i157*, *i360*
Polo, Marco, *i437*
Polynesia, 469, 528
polytheism, 229
pope, *i197*, *i437*
population, *m48*, *c306*
    of Greece, *i60*
    Latin American, *c49*
population density maps, reading, *m521*
porcelain, 278, 479, 513
Porsche, Ferdinand, *i190*
portolan charts, *i42*
Portugal, *c162*
potsherds, *i228*
pottery, *i228*, *i296*, *i476*, 278, 512, 513
Prague Spring, 151
precipitation, 71
Pretoria, South Africa, 355
priests, 218–219
primary product, 250
primary sources, using, *i535*
Prime Meridian, *i27*, 36
Princip, Gavrilo, 127
printing, 511
    press, *i99*, *i166*
private property rights, 149–150
propaganda, *i148*, 514
prospecting, *i354*
protest, *i193*, 504
    of Viet Nam War, *i451*
Protestant, 100, 446
Proust, Marcel, 187
Provence, 165
pull factors of migration, 38
Punjab, 427
Punjabi language, *m421*, 428
puppet government, 137
puppets, *i436*, *i446*
push factors of migration, 38
Pu Yi, *i495*
Pygmies, 297
pyramids
    in Egypt, 39, 225, 227, *i254–255*, *i260*
Pyrenees mountains, 68

Q

Qin Dynasty, *c476*
Qing Dynasty, *c476*, *i495*, 496
Qinling Range, 28
Qur'an, *i232*, *i439*

R

railroads, *i107*, 159, 349, *i506*
    high-speed, *i144–145*, 520
rain forest
    Amazon, *i392*
Rajputs, 405
Ramadan, 251
Ramayana, 421, *i447*
Rasputin, *i116*
Rawlings, Jerry John, *i320*
Re, 226
Red Guards, *i499*
Reed, Walter, *i216*
Reformation, 99
region, 37–38
Regional Data Files, 58–63, 206–209, 282–287, 370–373, 462–465
Reichstag, *i188*, 190
Reign of Terror, 111
reincarnation, 388
relative location, 37
Remembrance of Things Past, 187
remote sensing, 33, 45
Renaissance, 96
renewable resources, 295
Renoir, Pierre, 187
republic, 79, *i495*
resources, 20
    capital, 20
    human, 20
    natural, 20
reunification, 188–190
Rhine River, 68
rhinoceros, *c335*, *i358*
rice, 393, *i418*, *i507*
Ridge, Tom, 545
rift, 293
Righteous and Harmonious Fists, 496

rights
  women's, 252, *i258*
Riksdag, 178–179
Rilke, Rainer Maria, 191
Ring of Fire, 472
rite of passage, 328
rivers,
  and settlement patterns, 15
road map, *m46*
Robinson projection, *m47*
Roman Catholic Church. *See* Catholic Church.
Roman Empire, *i52–53*
Romanov family, 116
Roman Peace, 82
Roman Republic, 79–81
Rome, 78–83
Rosh Hashanah, 267
Rowling, J. K., *i177*
Rublev, Andrei, *i158*
Ruhr Valley, 58, 70
rupees, *i416*
Russia, 112–116, 137
  language, 159
Russian Revolution, 116
Rwanda, *i343*

S

Sadat, Anwar, *i258*
safaris, *i358*
Sagarmatha National Park, 36
Sagres, Portugal, *i101*
Sahara, *i210–211, i291, c294*
Sahel, 294
Saigon, South Vietnam, *i449*
St. Basil, Cathedral of, *i112*
St. Lucia's Day, *i180*
St. Petersburg, Russia, 113
St. Vincent, Cape of, 93
salt as currency, 298
saltpeter, 405
samurai, *i484*, 486, *i487*, 517
sanction, 356
sand dunes, *i291*
Sans, 297
Sanskrit, 386, 422
Sarajevo, Bosnia and Herzegovina, *i127*
satellite images, reading, *i351*
satellites, *i33, i351*
  telecommunications, *i21*
  view of Earth, *i51*
savannas, 294

Scandinavian Peninsula, *i68*
scarcity, 20
Schliemann, Heinrich, 272
scientific revolution, 108
Scott, Robert Falcon, 536, *i538*
scribes, 220–221
scuba, 199
secession, 175
secondary product, 250
secret police, 140
sediment, 379
Segovia, Spain, *i64*
self-defense, *i514*
Sen, Amartya, *i20*
Senate
  French, 185
  Roman, 79
Seoul, South Korea, *i502*
September 11 terrorist attack, 544–545, *m544*
sequencing events, R4
Serbia, *m157*
Serbs, 157, 158
Serengeti National Park, *i276–277, i303*, 360
serfs, 87, 115
settlement patterns and transportation, 15
Seuss, Dr., *i143*
Seven Wonders of the Ancient World, *i255*
Sèvres, France, *i243*
sextant, *i43*
Seychelles Islands, *i341*
Shaanxi province, 28
Shabalala, Joseph, *i349*
Shabanu: Daughter of the Wind, 432–433
shadoof, *i215*
shadow theater, *i436, i446*
Shaka Zulu, 342
Shakespeare, William, 98, *i176*
Shamash, *i217*
Shang, 475–476
  Dynasty, *c476*
Shanghai, China, *i492–493*
sheep, *i259, m532*
Shelley, Mary, 176
Shensi province, 28
Sherpa, 36, *i377*
Shih Huang-ti, 476
Shi'ites, 246

Shikoku, 471
Shinto, 484, 511
shipbuilding, *i508*
Shiva, *i376, i388*
shogun, 487
Shona, 341, 349
Shotoku, Prince, 485
Shuttle Radar Topography Mission (SRTM), 44
Siddhartha Gautama, 394
Sierra Leone, 326
silk, *i475*, 278–479
Silk Road, *m479, i506*
silt, 224
Sinan, 238
Sindh, 427
Sindhi, 428
Singapore, *i15*, 381, *i436, i445, c448*
sitar, *i402, i421*
skerries, 181
Skillbuilders
  analyzing points of view, R8
  analyzing causes; recognizing effects, R10
  categorizing, R6
  comparing and contrasting, R9
  comparing maps, *i222*
  creating database, *i481, iR21*
  creating multimedia presentation, *iR23*
  distinguishing fact from opinion, *c448*
  drawing conclusions, *i329*
  evaluating, R17
  finding main ideas, R5
  forming and supporting opinions, R15
  identifying and solving problems, R16
  identifying facts and opinions, R14
  interpreting chart, *c38, c244, c306, c348*
  interpreting map, *m25, m36, m47, m48, m71, m80, m81, m96, m102, m105, m114, m124, m126, m129, m132, m138, m149, m155, m157, m159, m179, m185, m189, m194, m216, m218, m233, m250, m257, m259, m297, m302, m304, m308, m318, m326, m331, m347, m359, m378, m384, m387, m390, m405, m419, m427, m440, m451, m470, m472, m473, m479, m498, m504,*

  m509, m512, m519, m529, m532, m537
  interpreting political cartoon, *i128, i133, i143*
  interpreting time lines, R19
  making decisions, R12
  making generalizations, *c77,* R18
  making inferences, R11
  making outline, *i192*
  making public speeches, R7
  reading chart, *c294*
  reading elevation map, *m391*
  reading historical map, *m248*
  reading latitude and longitude, *i41*
  reading political cartoon, *i133*
  reading population density map, *m519, m521*
  reading satellite image, *i351*
  reading time-zone map, 27
  recognizing propaganda, R13
  researching topics on Internet, *i106*
  sequencing events, R4
  summarizing, R2
  taking notes, R3
  understanding point of view, 424
  using electronic card catalog, *i153, iR20*
  using primary sources, *i535*
  using the Internet, *iR22*
slave labor, in Soviet Union, 140, 150
slavery, 105
slave trade, *i301, m302,* 309
Slavic languages, *i159*
Slovenia, 157
smallpox, 528
smuggling, 496
snow leopard, *i36*
soccer, *i173, i316,* 324, 520
socialism, 186
Socrates, 75
Solidarity, *i194–195*
Solomon's Temple, *i230*
Solzhenitsyn, Aleksandr, *i150*
Somalia, *i338, i342, i346*
Song Dynasty, *c476*
Songhai, 300
Sophocles, 75
sorghum, *i347*
South Africa, GDP, *c348*
South African War, 355
South America, 229–63

South Korea, *i502, m504,* 505, 506, 517, *m521*
South Pole, *i41,* 536
Southern Ocean, 537
Soviet Air Force, *i147*
Soviet Union, *i122, i137*
Soyinka, Wole, *i332,* 333
space shuttle, *i44*
Spain,
  as member of EU, *c162*
Sparta, Greece, *i74*
spices, 102, 341, 393, *i403*
Spotlight on Culture, *i47, i82, i99, i115, i125, i140, i150, i156, i220, i252, i309, i327, i348, i420, i446, i487, i514, i528*
Sputnik 2, i148
Sri Lanka, 378, *i380,* 406, 411, 418
Srivijaya, *m455*
Stalin, Joseph, *i138*
standard of living, 163
status quo, 320
steam locomotive, *i107*
Stephenson, George, *i107*
Stockholm, Sweden, *i178*
stone tools, *i340*
Strange but True, *i25, i74, i79, i116, i129, i148, i215, i295, i341, i382, i439, i476, i529, i539*
Stranger, The, 187
Street Girls Aid, *i320*
Strelka, *i148*
strike, *i193*
Strindberg, August, 181
subcontinent, 378
subsistence farming, 325
Sudan, *i346*
Suez Canal, *i256*
Sui Dynasty, *c476*
Suleiman I, 236, *i236*
sultan, *i232, i239,* 404
Sumerians, 218, *i220, i228*
sumo, 494
Sundiata, 299
Sunnis, 246
Sun Yat-Sen, 496
supercontinent theory, 35
supply and demand, 452
Supreme People's Assembly, 505
Surin, Thailand, *i444*
Surin Elephant Round-Up, *i444*

Suu Kyi, Aung San, *i441*
Suzuki, Ichiro, 520
Swahili, 297, 307, 360
Sweden, *i123,* 178–181
  as member of EU, *c162*
Sydney, Australia, *i531*
Syene, *i46*
Syria, *i243,* 246

T

Table Bay, *i355*
tae kwon do, 494, *i514*
Tahiti, 532
tai-chi, i511
Taieb, Maurice, *i339*
Taiping Rebellion, 496
Taiwan, 495, 505, 508, 517
Tajikistan, 155
Taj Mahal, *i420*
Taklimakan Desert, 471
Tale of Genji, The, i486
Taliban, 410, 547
talking drums, *i348*
Tamil, *m421, c445*
Tanganyika, Lake, 293, *c313*
Tang Dynasty, *c476,* 278, 479
tanka, 491
Tanzania, *i276–277, i340*
Taoism, 278, 511
Tao-te Ching, 278
Tatars, *i112*
Ta-tu, 476
taxes, *i160*
tea, 393, *i403, i434–435*
technology, 20
Technology, (feature) *i44, i117, i228, i311, i408, i489*
tectonic plates, 35,
Teej, i383
Tel Aviv, Israel, *i264*
Tellem tribe, *i288–289*
Telugu, *m421*
temperate forest, *c38*
Terra, i33
terrorism,
  definition of, 546
  effects of, 546
  international, *c546*
  reasons for, 546
  tactics of, 546

R57

terrorist attacks. *See also* September 11 terrorist attack.
   in Beirut, *c546*
   in Kenya, 546
   in Moscow, *c546*
   in Munich, 546, *c546*
   in Northern Ireland, 546, *c546*
   in Peru, 546
   in Tanzania, 546
   in Tokyo, 546, *c546*
Tet, *i453*
textiles, 508
Thailand, 381, 440, *c445*, *i446*
Thais, 435
Thames River, *i175*
thatch, 446
theater, 513
thematic maps, 46
theocracy, 235
Thomas, Lewis, 32
Thutmose II, *i226*
Thutmose III, *i223*, *i226*
Tiananmen Square, *i496*, 503, *i504*
Tiber River, 78
Tibet, 495
   Plateau of, 471
Tibetan Buddhism, 511
Tigris River, 214
timber, 393
Timbuktu, 300
time line, *c247*, *cRI 9*
time zone, *m27*
Tin Drum, The, 191
Tito, Marshal, 157
toba, 432–433
Tokugawa Ieyasu, 487, 488
Tokugawa Shogunate, 488, 517
Tokyo, Japan, 471, 472, *i488*, *i516*
Tokyo National Research Institute for Cultural Properties, *i485*
Tonga, 530
totalitarian government, 19
totalitarianism, 19
tradeoff, 258
Transantarctic Mountains, 743
transformation, 357
travel, 15
Tricolor, *i409*
Trojan War, *i272*
Troy, *i272*
Truth and Reconciliation Commission, *i355*

Tsingling Mountains, 28
Tumbuka, 349
Tumen, 472
tundra, *c38*, *m159*
tungsten, 507
tunnels, *i350*, 520
Turkana, Lake, *c313*
Turkey, *m216*, 270–273
Turkmenistan, 155
Tuscany, 165
Tutankhamen, *i225*
Tutsi, *i305*
Tutuola, Amos, 333
Tuvalu, *i532*
typhoid, 109
typhoon, 472

U

Uganda, 346, *i348*
Ukraine, 114, *i156*
Uluru, Mount, *i466–467*
Underground (London), *i170–171*
Union of Soviet Socialist Republics (USSR). *See* Soviet Union.
Unit Atlases, 54–63, 202–209, 278–287, 366–373, 458–465
United Kingdom of Great Britain and Northern Ireland, 173–177
   as member of EU, *c162*
United Nations, *i17*, 158, 247, *i291*, 441, *i506*
United Nations Educational, Scientific, and Cultural Organization (UNESCO), 39
United States, 19, *c306*
   in Vietnam, 450–451
unlimited government, 19
untouchables, 412
Ur, 230
Uralic and Altaic peoples, *m149*
Ural Mountains, 69
uranium, *m532*
urban planning, 511
Urdu, 428
USA Patriot Act, 545
Uzbekistan, 155

V

Valley of the Tombs of the Kings, *i225*
Valley Ruins, 341
vassal, 86

Vedas, 387, 395
vegetation
   climate and, 222
   zones, *c38*
veil, *i270*
veldt, 354
Versailles, Treaty of, 129–130
Via Appia, *i78*
Victoria, Lake, *i293*, *c313*, 346
Victoria Falls, 293
Vietnam, 381, 437, 438, *c445*
Vietnamese, *c445*
Virgil, 82
Vishnu, *i374–375*, *i388*, *i438*
Visigoths, *i84*
volcanic rock, *i350*
volcano, *i292*, *i381*, *i382*, 471, *i529*
Volga River, 68
Vostok I, *i147*

W

Wagner, Richard, 190
Wailing Wall, *i230*
Waitangi, Treaty of, *i527*, 529
Walesa, Lech, *i194*
Walloons, 164
war, 495. *See also* World War I; World War II; war against terrorism; War with Iraq.
   use of dogs in, *i129*
war against terrorism
   Bush administration and, 547
   in Afghanistan, *i547*
War with Iraq, 247, 548–549
Warsaw, Poland, *m194*
Watt, James, *i117*
wayang kulit, *i446*
weapons of mass destruction, 548–549
weaving, *i447*, 513
   silk, *i475*
Wellington, New Zealand, *i524–525*, 534
Western Ghats, 380
westernization, 252
Westminster Hall, *i175*
wheat, *m250*
White House, *i166*
Wilhelm, Kaiser, *i120–121*
William the Conqueror, *i86*
Winter Palace, *i115*
Witwatersrand, *i354*

women
  in Islam, 252
wood carvings, Maori, *i526, i528*
Woolf, Virginia, 177
World's Heritage Sites, 39
World's Heritage, *i36, i75, i108, i158, i175, i214, i260, i303, i386, i412, i438,* 480
World Trade Center, 544–545, *i546* See also September 11 terrorist attack.
World War I, *i122,* 127–130, 342
World War II, 130–132, 185, 193, 308, 342, *i516,* 517

X

Xi'an, *i476*
Xi Jiang, *m470*
Xuantong, 495

Y

Yahweh, 230
Yalu, 472
yam, *i309*
Yamato clan, 485
Yangtze River, *m470*
Yellow River, 471
Yokohama, Japan, *i469*
Yoritomo, 487
Yoruba, *m331,* 333, *i348*
Yuan Dynasty, *c476*
Yuan Shigai, 496
Yugoslavia, *i152,* 157
Yunnan province, 476, *i507*

Z

Zaire, 319
Zaire River, *i292*
Zambezi River, 293
Zazzua, *i330*
Zen Buddhism, 486, 511
Zhou Dynasty, *c476,* 477
Zhu Yuanzhang, 476
ziggurat, *i218*
Zimbabwe, 340–341
  GDP, *c348*
Zionism, 264–265
zither, 513
Zulu, 297, 341–342, *i349, i357*

Acknowledgments

Text Credits

Chapter 3, page 75: Quote by Herakleitos, translated by Guy Davenport, from *7 Greeks,* copyright © 1995 by Guy Davenport. Reprinted by Sales Territory: U.S./Canadian rights only.

Chapter 4, page 134: "The Giant's Causeway" from *Irish Fairy Tales and Legends* retold by Una Leavy. Copyright © 1996 by The Watts Publishing Group Ltd.

Chapter 5, page 143: Excerpt from *Blood, Toil, Tears and Sweat* by Winston Churchill. Reproduced with permission of Curtis Brown Ltd., London, on behalf of the Estate of Sir Winston S. Churchill. Copyright © the Estate of Sir Winston S. Churchill.

Chapter 7, page 199: Excerpt from "Presentation Speech" by Egil Aarvik. Copyright © The Nobel Foundation. Reprinted by permission of The Nobel Foundation.

Chapter 8, page 221: Quote from *Everyday Life in Babylonia and Assyria* by H. W. F. Saggs. Copyright © 1965 by B. T. Batsford.

Chapter 9, page 262: "Thread by Thread" by Bracha Serri, translated by Shlomit Yaacobi and Nava Mizrahi, from *The Space Between Our Footsteps: Poems and Paintings from the Middle East,* selected by Naomi Shihab Nye. Copyright © 1998.

Chapter 12, page 352: "My Father's Farm" text copyright © 1995 by Isaac Olaleye from *The Distant Talking Drum: Poems from Nigeria* by Isaac Olaleye. Published by Wordsong/Boyds Mills Press, Inc. Reprinted by permission.

Chapter 13, page 399: Excerpt from "Monsoons Leave Millions Homeless" Associated Press, August 16, 2002. Copyright © 2002 The Associated Press. Reprinted by permission.

Chapter 16, page 477: Quote from "Analects", page 57 from *The Essential Confucius,* translated by Thomas Cleary. Copyright © 1992 by Thomas Cleary. Reprinted by permission of HarperCollins Publishers Inc.

page 482: From *Echoes of the White Giraffe* by Sook Nyul Choi. Copyright © 1993 by Sook Nyul Choi. Reprinted by permission of Houghton Mifflin Company. All rights reserved.

Art Credits

Beverly Doyle 28; Ken Goldammer 12; Nenad Jakesevic 175, 198, 228, 408; Rich McMahon 44, 117; Gary Overacre 134–135; Matthew Pippin xiv, 214, 225, 254, 311, 344, 386, 500, 513. All other artwork created by Publicom, Inc.

Map Credits

This product contains proprietary property of MAPQUEST.COM. Unauthorized use, including copying, of this product is expressly prohibited.

Photography Credits

Cover *Clockwise from top left* Copyright © Art Wolfe/Stone/GettyImages; Copyright © Superstock, Inc., Copyright © Bill Cardoni/Bruce Coleman, Inc.; **ii–iii** Copyright © Stone/GettyImages; **ii** *top left* Copyright © Art Wolfe/Stone/GettyImages; *top right* Copyright © Superstock, Inc.; **iii** *top* Copyright © Bill Cardoni/Bruce Coleman, Inc.; **vi** *bottom* NASA; *children* (See page 14 for full credits); **vii** *top left* Erich Lessing/Art Resource, New York; *bottom left* Dave Bartruff/Corbis; *bottom right* Hulton|Archive/Getty Images; *top* Erich Lessing/Art Resource, New York; *top right* Reunion des Musées Nationaux/ Art Resource, New York; *center right* Scott Gilchrist/Archivision.com; **viii** *top left* S. Bavister/Robert Harding Picture Library; *bottom left* John Noble/Corbis; *bottom* John Launois/Black Star Publishing/PictureQuest; *bottom right* AFP/Corbis; *top* Copyright © Brannhage/Premium/Panoramic Images; **ix** *bottom left* Archivo Iconografico, S. A./ Corbis; *bottom* Copyright © IFA/Bruce Coleman; *top center* Carmen Redondo/Corbis; *top right* Ashmolean Museum, Oxford, England/The Bridgeman Art Library; **x** *top left* John Noble/ Corbis; *center left* Charles and Josette Lenars/Corbis; *bottom left* Copyright © Boyd Norton/The Image Works; *top right* Giraudon/Art Resource, New York; **xi** *center left* Brian A. Vikander/Corbis; *bottom* Wolfgang Kaehler/Corbis; *center right* Caroline Penn/Corbis; *top right* Paul Almasy/Corbis; **xii** *top* Reunion des Musées Nationaux/Art Resource, New York; *bottom* N. Blythe/ Robert Harding Picture Library; **xiii** *top* Quadrillion/Corbis; *center* James L. Amos/Corbis; *bottom* Eric Crichton/ Bruce Coleman/PictureQuest; *bottom right* Michael S. Yamashita/Corbis; **S12** Reprinted with the permission of the *St. Louis Post Dispatch,* 2002; **S13** The Granger Collection/New York; **S26** Hulton|Archive/Getty Images; **S30** Victoria & Albert Museum, London/Art Resource, New York; **S32** Mary Evans Picture Library.

UNIT ONE

2–3 NASA; **4** *bottom right* NOAA; *left* Copyright © Owen Franken/Stock Boston/PictureQuest; *top right* Science Museum/ Science and Society Picture Library, London.

Chapter 1

14 *top left* Brian A. Vikander/Corbis; *top center* Owen Franken/Corbis; *bottom left* Tim Thompson/Corbis; *center left* Kevin Schafer/Corbis; *bottom center* Maria Taglienti/The Image Bank/GettyImages; *center right* James A. Sugar/Corbis; *bottom right* Nicholas deVore III/Photographers Aspen/PictureQuest; *top right* Dean Conger/Corbis; **15** *top* © Steve Vidler/eStock Photo -- All rights reserved; *bottom left* The Purcell Team/Corbis; *center left* Helen Norman/Corbis; *center* Nik Wheeler/Corbis; *bottom center* Dennis Degnan/Corbis; *center right* Neil Rabinowitz/Corbis; *bottom right* Martin Rogers/Corbis; **16** *top* Copyright © Jim West; *bottom* K. Gilham/Robert Harding Picture Library; **17** *top* Picture Finders/eStock Photography/PictureQuest; *bottom* The Military Picture Library/Corbis; **18** *bottom* Thomas Hoepker/Magnum/PictureQuest; *top* Copyright © Ellen Senisi/The Image Works; **19** *left* Oliver Benn/Stone/GettyImages; *right* Copyright © Alon Reininger/Contact Press Images; *center* Copyright © Alex Farnsworth/The Image Works; **20** *top right* Copyright © Jim West; *bottom left* Richard Drew/AP/ Wide World Photos; **21** NASA/Roger Ressmeyer/Corbis; **22** Copyright © Angus McIntyre 1987-2001; **23** *bottom* © Rich Iwasaki/Stock Connection/Picture Quest; *top* Photo: comstock.com; **24** *right* Hulton|Archive/Getty Images; *left* Lindsay Hebberd/Corbis; **26** *left* Dean Conger/Corbis; *right* K. Gilham/ Robert Harding Picture Library; *center* Chris Andrews Publications/Corbis; **30** *bottom left* Picture Finders/eStock Photography/PictureQuest.

Chapter 2

32–33 Copyright © SuperStock; **33** *top* NASA; **34** *top* Christopher Morris/Black Star Publishing/PictureQuest; *bottom* © Wolfgang Kaehler; **35** *left* The Granger Collection, New York; **36** © Tom Brakefield/Corbis; **37** *top* Christopher Morris/Black Star Publishing/PictureQuest; *bottom* World Perspectives/Stone/ GettyImages; **38** Copyright © Eastcott-Momatiuk/The Image Works; **39** © Wolfgang Kaehler; **42** *top left* Ethnic Art Institute of Micronesia; *top right* National Maritime Museum Picture Library, London; *bottom right* Royalty Free/Corbis; **43** *bottom* Austrian Archives/Corbis; *center right, top* National Maritime Museum Picture Library, London; *center left* Reproduced with permission of Garmin Corporation; **45** *right* The Granger Collection, New York; **46** Illustration © Bill Cigliano; **47** The Newberry Library/The Granger Collection, New York; **50** David S. Boyer/National Geographic.

UNIT TWO

52–53 Stuart Dee/The Image Bank/GettyImages.

Chapter 3

64–65 Copyright © James L. Stanfield/National Geographic Society Image Collection; **65** *top* Robert Harding Picture Library; **66** *top* Sef/Art Resource, New York; *bottom left, bottom right* Erich Lessing/Art Resource, New York; **67** Bill Ross/Corbis; **68** Arnulf Husmo/Stone/GettyImages; **69** Walter Bibikow/Index Stock Imagery/PictureQuest; **70** *top left* Jonathan Blair/Corbis; *top right* Eye Ubiquitous/Corbis; *bottom* Johan Elzenga/Stone/GettyImages; **72** *all* Greek Culture Ministry/AP/Wide World Photos; **73** HorreeZirkzee Produk/Corbis; **74** Foto Marburg/ Art Resource, New York; **75** Sef/Art Resource, New York; **76** *left* Nimatallah/Art Resource, New York; *right* Scala Art Resource, New York; **78** Copyright © Macduff Everton/The Image Works; **79** Erich Lessing/Art Resource, New York; **80** Giraudon/Art Resource, New York; **81** Erich Lessing/Art Resource, New York; **82** *top left* Jeff Rotman; *center* Scala/Art Resource, New York; *bottom right* O. Alamany and E. Vicens/Corbis; *bottom center* Bettmann/Corbis; **83** Erich Lessing/Art Resource, New York; **84** Art Resource, New York; **85** Reunion des Musées Nationaux/Art Resource, New York; **86** Catherine Karnow/Corbis; *spread* Musée de la Tapisserre, Bayoux, France/The Bridgeman Art Library; **87** *top* Jose Fuste Raga/eStockPhotography/PictureQuest; **88** Erich Lessing/Art Resource, New York; **89** *right* Dept. of the Environment, London/The Bridgeman Art Library; *left* The Granger Collection, New York; **90** *top left* Sef/Art Resource, New York; *bottom* Erich Lessing/Art Resource, New York; *top right* Jose Fuste Raga/eStockPhotography/PictureQuest.

Chapter 4

92–93 Bruno Barbey/Magnum/PictureQuest; **93** *top* The Granger Collection, New York; *center* Leonard L. T. Phodes/Animals Animals; **94** *center* Mary Evans Picture Library; *top* Reunion des Musées Nationaux/Art Resource, New York; *bottom* The Pierpont Morgan Library/Art Resource, New York; **95** The Granger Collection, New York; **96** Alinari/Art Resource, New York; **97** *top* Scott Gilchrist/Archivision.com; *bottom* Palazzo Medici-Riccardi, Florence, Italy/The Bridgeman Art Library; **98** *bottom* Scala/Art Resource, New York; *top* Reunion des Musées Nationaux/Art Resource, New York; **99** The Pierpont Morgan Library/Art Resource, New York; **100** Corbis; **101** Giraudon/Art Resource, New York; **103** North Wind Pictures; **104** Reunion des Musées Nationaux/Art Resource, New York; **107** AKG London; **108** *center* Scala/Art Resource, New York; *top* NASA; *bottom* Copyright © Will & Deni McIntyre/Photo Researchers; **109** The Granger Collection, New York; **110** Hulton-Deutsch Collection/Corbis; **111** Victoria & Albert Museum, London/Art Resource, New York; **112** *right* © Courtesy of the Estate of Ruskin Spear/Private Collection/Phillips, Fine Art Auctioneers, New York/The Bridgeman Art Library; *left* Giraudon/Art Resource, New York; **113** *top* Scala/Art Resource, New York; *bottom* Roger Tidman/Corbis; **114** Erich Lessing/Art Resource, New York; **115** Chuck Nacke/Woodfin Camp/PictureQuest; **116** Hulton-Deutsch Collection/Corbis; **118** *top left* North Wind Pictures; *bottom left* Alinari/Art Resource, New York; *bottom right* Hulton-Deutsch Collection/Corbis; *top right* © Courtesy of the Estate of Ruskin Spear/Private Collection/Phillips, Fine Art Auctioneers, New York/The Bridgeman Art Library; **119** The Library of Congress Website.

Chapter 5

120–121 Michael S. Yamashita/Corbis; **121** *top* Owen Franken/Corbis; **122** *top* Ralph White/Corbis; *bottom* Hulton|Archive/Getty Images; **123** Hulton|Archive/Getty Images; **125** *bottom* Hulton|Archive/Getty Images; *center* Gianni Dagli Orti/Corbis; *top* Mark Rykoff/Rykoff Collection/Corbis; **127** *right* Bettmann/Corbis; *left* Hulton|Archive/Getty Images; **128** *top* Hulton|Archive/Getty Images; *bottom* Art Young; **129** Hulton| Archive/ Getty Images; **131** *bottom* Hulton|Archive/Getty Images; *top* Hulton-Deutsch Collection/Corbis; **133** Reprinted with the permission of the *St. Louis Post Dispatch*, 2002; **136** Paul Almasy/Corbis; **137** *bottom* Sovfoto/Eastfoto/PictureQuest; *top* Ralph White/ Corbis; **138** *bottom* Hulton|Archive/Getty Images; *top* Sovfoto/Eastfoto/PictureQuest; **139** Culver Pictures; **140** *bottom* Hulton|Archive/Getty Images; *center* The Kobal Collection; **141** Dave Bartruff/Corbis; **142** *right* Sovfoto/Eastfoto/PictureQuest; *left* Hulton|Archive/Getty Images; *center* Hulton-Deutsch Collection/Corbis; **143** Mandeville Special Collections at UCSD.

Chapter 6

144–145 Copyright © Brannhage/Premium/Panoramic Images; **145** *top* Sovfoto/Eastfoto; **146** *top* Premium Stock/Corbis; *bottom* Craig Aurness/Corbis; **147** Mark Rykoff/Corbis; **148** *left* NASA/AP/Wide World Photos; *right* Sovfoto/Eastfoto; **149** Copyright © Giuliano Bevilacqua/TimePix; **150** Bryn Colton/Corbis; **151** *top* Bettmann/Corbis; *bottom* AP/Wide World Photos; **152** Bojan Brecelj/Corbis; **154** David and Peter Turnley/Corbis; **156** Craig Aurness/Corbis; **157** Copyright © Bios (F. Gilson)/Peter Arnold; **158** Scala/Art Resource, New York; **160** Sovfoto/Eastfoto/PictureQuest; **161** *bottom* Hoa Qui/Index Stock Imagery/PictureQuest; *top* Premium Stock/Corbis; **162** AFP/Corbis; **163** Mike Mazzaschi/Stock Boston/PictureQuest; **164** S. Bavister/Robert Harding Picture Library; **165** Copyright © Malcolm S. Kirk/Peter Arnold; **166** *bottom* John Neubauer/Photo Edit/PictureQuest; *top right* Underwood & Underwood/Corbis; *top left* Bettmann/Corbis; **167** *top* Wolfgang Kaehler/Corbis; *left* Paul A. Souders/Corbis; *center* Roger Ressmeyer/Corbis; *bottom right* Academy of Natural Sciences of Philadelphia/Corbis; **168** *left* Bettmann/Corbis; *right* Premium Stock/Corbis; *center* David and Peter Turnley/Corbis.

Chapter 7

170–171 Alan Thornton/Stone/GettyImages; **171** *top* Mark A. Leman/Stone/GettyImages; **172** *top* Ted Spiegel/Corbis; *bottom* www.carpix.net; **173** *bottom right* Michael Neveux/Corbis; *center* AFP/Corbis; **176** *bottom* John Launois/Black Star Publishing/PictureQuest; *top* Copyright © Julian Nieman/Collections; **177** AFP/Corbis; **178** *right* Nik Wheeler/Corbis; *left* Ted Spiegel/Corbis; **179** Hans T. Dahlskog/Pressens Bild; **180** *bottom* AFP/Corbis; *top* Alex Farnsworth/The Image Works; **181** John Noble/Corbis; **182–183** Museo de Firenze Com'era, Florence, Italy/The Bridgeman Art Library; **184** *right* Bettmann/Corbis; *left* Corbis; **185** Bettmann/Corbis; **186** Robert Estall/Corbis; **187** Art Resource, New York; **188** *right* AFP/Corbis; *left* Thomas Hoepker/Magnum/PictureQuest; **190** *bottom center* Erich Lessing/Art Resource, New York; *top* www.carpix.net; *bottom right* Josef Karl Stieler/Archivo Iconografico, S. A./Corbis; **191** Carmen Redondo/Corbis; **193** Chuck Fishman/Contact Press Images/PictureQuest; **194** Bettmann/Corbis; **195** Dennis Chamberlain/Black Star Publishing/PictureQuest; **196** Steven Weinberg/Stone/GettyImages; **197** Vittoriano Rastelli/Corbis; **198** *top left* Copyright © Alex Farnsworth/The Image Works; *top right* Thomas Hoepker/Magnum/PictureQuest; *bottom right* Bettmann/Corbis; *center* Corbis.

UNIT THREE

200–201 Copyright © IFA/Bruce Coleman; **208** *center* Richard T. Nowitz/Corbis; *right* Dagli Orti/Egyptian Museum Cairo/The Art Archive; *left* Copyright © IFA/Bruce Coleman; **209** *left* Copyright © Floyd Norgaard/Ric Ergenbright Photography; *center* Copyright © Hubertus Kanus/Photo Researchers; *right* Copyright © ANAX/IMAPRESS/The Image Works.

Chapter 8

210–211 Erv. Schowengerdt; **211** *top* Copyright © SuperStock; **212** *top* Roger Wood/Corbis; *bottom* Bojon Brecelj/Corbis; **213** *right* Copyright © Ingeborg Lippman/Peter Arnold; *left* Musée du Louvre, Paris/The Bridgeman Art Library; **215** *top right* Copyright © Robert Fried Photography; *top left* Copyright © Floyd Norgaard/Ric Ergenbright Photography; *bottom right* Richard T. Nowitz/Corbis; **217** Erich Lessing/Art Resource, New York; **218** Roger Wood/Corbis; **219** *bottom* Erich Lessing/Art Resource, New York; *top* Ancient Art and Architecture Collection, London; **220** *bottom right* Ashmolean Museum, Oxford, England/The Bridgeman Art Library; *center* Bettmann/Corbis; **221** Erich Lessing/Art Resource, New York; **223** *right* Dagli Orti/Egyptian Museum Cairo/The Art Archive; *left* Dagli Orti/Luxor Museum, Egypt/The Art Archive; **224** *center* Wolfgang Kaehler/Corbis; *top* Erich Lessing/Art Resource, New York; **225** Kevin Cain, Institute for Study and Intergration of Graphical Heritage Techniques, www.pelleas.org; **226** *left* Dagli Orti/Egyptian Museum Cairo/The Art Archive; *right* Scala/Art Resource, New York; **227** *right* Charles Lenars/Corbis; *left* Philip De Bay/Historical Picture Archive/Corbis; **230** *top* The Jewish Museum, New York/Art Resource, New York; *bottom* Copyright © Fred Bruemmer/Peter Arnold; **231** *top* Scala/Art Resource, New York; *bottom* Carmen Redondo/Corbis; **232** Bojon Brecelj/Corbis; **234** Philip De Bay/Historical Picture Archive/Corbis; **236** *top* Copyright © Kevin Schafer/Peter Arnold; *bottom* Dagli Orti/Egyptian Museum Cairo/The Art Archive; **237** Mary Evans Picture Library; **238** *top left* Copyright © Robert Fried Photography; *top center* Erich Lessing/Art Resource, New York; *center* Erich Lessing/Art Resource, New York; *top right* Copyright © Fred Bruemmer/Peter Arnold; *bottom right* Philip De Bay/Historical Picture Archive/Corbis.

Chapter 9

240–241 Grant V. Faint/The Image Bank/GettyImages; 241 *top* Hubertus Kanus/Photo Researchers; 242 *top* Laura Zitc; *bottom* © Robert Holmes/Corbis; 243 Bettmann/Corbis; 246 © Robert Holmes/Corbis;247 © Reuters NewMedia Inc./Corbis; 249 *all* Hulton|Archive/Getty Images; 250 *right* Lambert/Hulton|Archive/Getty Images; *left* Copyright © Mark Antman/The Image Works; 251 Copyright © Kazuyoshi Nomachi/HAGA/The Image Works; 252 Chrisite and Apos's Images/Corbis; 253 Copyright © Margot Granitsas/The Image Works; 256 Bettmann/Corbis; 257 *top* Bettmann/Corbis; *bottom* Sean Saxton/Corbis; 258 *bottom* Corbis; *top* Bettmann/Corbis; 259 Copyright © O. Louis Mazzatenta/NGS Image Collection; 260 Copyright © Richard T. Nowitz; 261 *top* Robert Holmes; *center* Laura Zitc; 262–263 David and Peter Turnley/Corbis; Paul A. Souders/Corbis; Richard T. Nowitz/Corbis; Moshe Shai/Corbis; *all others* Cory Langley; 264 *right* Hulton|Archive/ Getty Images; 264 *left* AP/Wide World Photos; 265 Copyright © Richard T. Nowitz; 266 *top* Copyright © Richard T. Nowitz; *bottom* © Milner Moshe/Corbis Sygma; 267 Rina Castelnuovo/PictureQuest; 268 *top* Robert Frerck/Woodfin Camp/PictureQuest; *bottom* Archivo Iconografico, S. A./Corbis; 269 *bottom* Copyright © Elan Sun Star/Index Stock; *center* Elio Ciol/Corbis; *top* David Young-Wolff/Photo Edit/PictureQuest; 270 *right* Culver Pictures; 271 *top* The Granger Collection, New York; *bottom* Copyright © Diana Walker/TimePix; 272 Ruggero Vanni/Corbis; 273 Adam Woolfitt/Corbis; 274 *top left* Copyright © Tannenbaum/The Image Works; *bottom left* Copyright © Kazuyoshi Nomachi/HAGA/The Image Works; *center* Sean Saxton/Corbis; *top right* Copyright © Richard T. Nowitz; *bottom right* Adam Woolfitt/Corbis.

UNIT FOUR

276–277 W. Perry Conway/Corbis.

Chapter 10

288–289 Copyright © Wolfgang Kaehhler; 289 *top* The Granger Collection, New York; 290 *top* Giraudon/Art Resource, New York; *bottom* Copyright © Syracuse Newspapers/The Image Works; 291 Copyright © Still Pictures (Schytte)/Peter Arnold; 292 *center left* Dave G. Houser/Corbis; *center right* John Noble/Corbis; 292–293 Corbis; 293 *bottom right* Peter Johnson/Corbis; 294 David and Peter Turnley/Corbis; 295 *left* D. Boone/Corbis; *right* Bettmann/Corbis; 296–297 Charles and Josette Lenars/Corbis; 298 Patrick Ward/Corbis; 299 *top* Werner Forman/Corbis; *bottom* Copyright © Bob Burch/Index Stock; 300 John Webb/The Art Archive; 301 *right* The Granger Collection, New York; *left* Adam Woolfitt/Corbis; 303 *left* Copyright © Boyd Norton/The Image Works; *right* Ann and Carl Purcell/Words and Pictures/PictureQuest; 305 Howard Davies/Corbis; 307 *right* Copyright © Marc and Evelyne Bernheim/Woodfin Camp; *left* Betty Press/Woodfin Camp/PictureQuest; 309 *center* Copyright © Gerald Buthaud; *bottom* Gerald Buthaud/Cosmos/Woodfin Camp; 310 Alon Reininger/Contact Press Images/PictureQuest; 311 I. Vanderharst/Robert Harding Picture Library; 312 *bottom left* Corbis; *bottom center* Copyright © Bob Burch/Index Stock; *top center* Adam Woolfitt/Corbis; *bottom right* Copyright © Marc and Evelyne Bernheim/Woodfin Camp.

Chapter 11

314–315 Jason Lauré; 315 *top* Copyright © Robert Caputo/Aurora; 316 *top* Reuters NewMedia Inc./Corbis; *bottom* Owen Franken/Corbis; 317 *bottom* Bettmann/Corbis; *top* The Granger Collection, New York; 318 Hulton|Archive/Getty Images; 319 *bottom* Copyright © Griffith J. Davis/TimePix; 320 *top* Copyright © Kwaku Sakyi-Addo/Reuters/TimePix; *bottom* Jason Lauré; 321 AFP/Corbis; 322 *right* Edward R. Degginger/Bruce Coleman/PictureQuest; *left* Tony Wilson-Bligh/Papilio/Corbis; 323 *top left* Kennan Ward/Corbis; *top center* Julian Calder/Corbis; *bottom right* Werner Forman Archive/Art Resource, New York; 324 *right* Reuters NewMedia Inc./Corbis; *left* AFP/Corbis; 325 *left* Owen Franken/Corbis; *right* Steve Jackson/Black Star Publishing/PictureQuest; 327 *bottom* Bonhams, London/The Bridgeman Art Library; *top* Jose Azel/Aurora/PictureQuest; 328 Chris Barton; 330 Werner Forman Archive/Art Resource, New York; 331 *right* Margaret Courtney-Clarke/Corbis; *left* AFP/Corbis; 332 *bottom* AFP/Corbis; *top* Wolfgang Kaehler/Corbis; *center* Richard A. Cooke/Corbis; 333 Werner Forman/Archive/Art Resource, New York; 334 *left* Copyright © Kwaku Sakyi-Addo/Reuters/TimePix; *center* Jose Azel/Aurora/ PictureQuest; *right* AFP/Corbis.

Chapter 12

336–337 Jim Zuckerman/Corbis; 337 *top* The Durcell Team/Corbis; 338 *top* David and Peter Turnley/Corbis; *bottom* Thierry Geenen/Liaison/GettyImages; 339 Copyright © John Reader/Science Photo Library/Photo Researchers; 340 Courtesy, Kathy Schick & Nicholas Toth. Artwork by R. Freyman & N. Toth based on a drawing by Mary Leakey; 341 *right* Wolfgang Kaehler/Corbis; *left* Yann Arthus-Bertrand/Corbis; 342 *top* Bettmann/Corbis; *bottom* David and Peter Turnley/Corbis; 343 Copyright © Betty Press/Woodfin Camp/PictureQuest; 346 AFP/Corbis; 347 *left* Copyright © Grant Heilman/Grant Heilman Photography; *center top* Frank Lane Picture Agency/Corbis; *bottom right* Yann Arthus-Bertrand/Corbis; 348 David Samuel Robbins/Corbis; 349 Nubar Alexanian/Corbis; 350 Carmen Redondo/Corbis; 351 NASA; 352–353 Betty Press/Woodfin Camp/PictureQuest; 354 *bottom right* Lee Foster/Words and Pictures/ PictureQuest; *top Photographs of South Africa* (Cape Town, 1894). Reprinted from Photo Publishing Co.; 355 *bottom* AFP/Corbis; *top* The Granger Collection, New York; 357 Pictor International/PictureQuest; 358 Michele Burgess/Index Stock Imagery/PictureQuest; 359 *right* Corbis; *left* Copyright © William F. Campbell/TimePix; 3610 *top* Yann Arthus-Bertrand/Corbis; *bottom* Charles and Josette Lenars/Corbis; 361 Thierry Geenen/Liaison/GettyImages; 362 *top left* Courtesy, Kathy Schick & Nicholas Toth. Artwork by R. Freyman & N. Toth based on a drawing by Mary Leakey; *top right* AFP/Corbis; *bottom left* Nubar Alexanian/Corbis; *bottom right* Charles and Josette Lenars/Corbis; 363 NASA.

UNIT FIVE

364–365 John Lamb/Stone/GettyImages; **372** *left* Ann and Carl Purcell/PictureQuest; *center* Bettmann/Corbis; *right* Alison Wright/Corbis; **373** *center* James Strachan/Stone/GettyImages; *left* Lindsay Hebberd/Corbis; *right* AFP/Corbis.

Chapter 13

374–375 John Elk/Stone/GettyImages; **375** *top* Ann and Carl Purcell/PictureQuest; **376** *top* Reunion des Musées Nationaux/Art Resource, New York; *bottom* Corbis; **377** Hulton-Deutsch Collection/Corbis; **379** Copyright © RafiQur Rahman/Reuters/TimePix; **380** *bottom* James Strachan/Stone/GettyImages; *top* Ted Wood/Black Star Publishing/PictureQuest; **381** Paul Almasy/Corbis; **382** Charles O'Rear/Corbis; **383** Lindsay Hebberd/Corbis; **385** Sarnath, Uttar Pradesh, India/The Bridgeman Art Library; **386** *top center* Archivo Iconografico, S. A./Corbis; *top right* Paul Almasy/Corbis; *bottom center* Charles and Josette Lenars/Corbis; *bottom right* Corbis; **388** *all* Reunion des Musées Nationaux/Art Resource, New York; **389** *bottom* The Granger Collection, New York; *top* Chris Lisle/Corbis; **392** The Granger Collection, New York; **394** Jeremy Homer/Corbis; **397** *top right* Eye Ubiquitous/Corbis; *all others* Charles and Josette Lenars/Corbis; **398** *center* The Granger Collection, New York; *right* Jeremy Homer/Corbis; *left* James Strachan/Stone/GettyImages.

Chapter 14

400–401 David Sutherland/Stone/GettyImages; **401** *top* Catherine Karnow/Corbis; **402** *top* Caroline Penn/Corbis; *bottom* Amma Clopet/Corbis; **403** Christie's Images, London/The Bridgeman Art Library; **404** *top* Ric Ergenbright/Corbis; *bottom* Victoria & Albert Museum, London/The Bridgeman Art Library; **405** Hulton-Deutsch Collection/Corbis; **406–407** Bettmann/Corbis; **409** Hulton|Archive/Getty Images; **410** Copyright © Robert Nickelsberg/TimePix; **411** *bottom* Corbis; *top* Sena Vidanagama/AFP/Corbis; **412** *top* Sebastian D'Souza/AFP/Corbis; *bottom* Bettmann/Corbis; **413** Copyright © D. Banerjee/Dinodia Picture Agency; **414** *center* Lindsay Hebberd/Corbis; *top left* Baron/Hulton-Deutsch Collection/Corbis; *top right* Chris Lisle/Corbis; *bottom right* Richard Bickel/Corbis; **415** *center* Jeremy Homer/Corbis; *top* Diego Lezama Orezzoli/Corbis; *bottom* Victoria & Albert Museum, London/The Bridgeman Art Library; **416** Courtesy of AID; **417** Caroline Penn/Corbis; **418** *top* Adam Woolfitt/Corbis; *bottom* Lindsay Hebberd/Corbis; **420** Cris Haigh/Stone/GettyImages; **421** Amma Clopet/Corbis; **422** Surya Temple, Somnath, Bombay, India/Dinodia Picture Agency, Bombay India/Bridgeman Art Library; **423** Earl & Nazima Kowall/Corbis; **425** Bettmann/Corbis; **426** Paul Almasy/Corbis; **428** *left* Bettmann/Corbis; *right* Nik Wheeler/Corbis; **429** *left* Saeed Khan/AFP/Corbis; **430** *bottom left* Bettmann/Corbis; *top left* Sebastian D'Souza/AFP/ Corbis; *top right* Earl & Nazima Kowall/Corbis; *center* Lindsay Hebberd/Corbis; *bottom right* Nik Wheeler/Corbis; **432** Ric Ergenbright/Corbis; **433** Dave Bartruff/Corbis.

Chapter 15

434–435 Wolfgang Kaehler/Corbis; **435** *top* Alison Wright/Corbis; **436** *bottom* Ted Streshinsky/Photo 20-20/PictureQuest; *top* Copyright © Walter H. Hodge/Peter Arnold; **437** The British Library, London/The Bridgeman Art Library; **438** *left* Nik Wheeler/Corbis; *right* Copyright © TomPix/Peter Arnold; **439** *left* AFP/Corbis; *right* Copyright © Jose Azel/Woodfin Camp; **440** Hulton|Archive/Getty Images; **441** AFP/Corbis; **442** *bottom left* Brian A. Vikander/Corbis; *bottom right* David Samuel Robbins/Corbis; **443** Brian A. Vikander/Corbis; **444** Hulton|Archive/Getty Images; **445** Ted Streshinsky/Photo 20-20/PictureQuest; **446** *top* Pictor International/PictureQuest; *bottom* Copyright © Walter H. Hodge/Peter Arnold; **447** *right* Kevin R. Morris/Corbis; *left* Chris Rainier/Corbis; **449** Bettmann/Corbis; **450** Charles Bonnay/Black Star Publishing/PictureQuest; **451** *left* Bettmann/Corbis; *right* Dennis Brack/Black Star Publishing/PictureQuest; **452** Copyright © Dan Gair/Index Stock; **453** Hulton|Archive/Getty Images; **454** *left* Hulton|Archive/Getty Images; *center* Chris Rainier/Corbis; *right* Hulton|Archive/Getty Images.

UNIT SIX

456–457 Copyright © Panoramic Images; **464** *left* Penny Tweedie/Corbis; *center* James L. Amos/Corbis; *right* © Galen Rowell/Corbis; **465** *left* Keren Su/Stone/GettyImages; *center* Copyright © Bill Lai/The Image Works; *right* Christopher Arnesen/Stone/GettyImages.

Chapter 16

466–467 Copyright © Eric Crichton/Bruce Coleman/PictureQuest; **467** *top* Liu Liqun/Corbis; **468** *bottom* Scala/Art Resource, New York; *top* Dallas and John Heaton/Corbis; **469** Bettmann/Corbis; **470** David Samuel Robbins/Corbis; **471** Dean Conger/Corbis; **472** Charles Rotkin/Corbis; **473** Michael S. Yamashita/Corbis; **475** Giraudon/Art Resource, New York; **476** Erich Lessing/Art Resource, New York; **477** Dallas and John Heaton/Corbis; **478** *right* Reunion des Musées Nationaux/Art Resource, New York; *left* NorthWind Pictures; **479** Reunion des Musées Nationaux/Art Resource, New York; **480** Reunion des Musées Nationaux/Art Resource, New York; **482–483** Corbis; **482** *bottom* Robert Pearcy/Animals Animals; *spread* Corbis; **484** Culver Pictures; **485** *top* Copyright © Bill Lai/The Image Works; *bottom* Craig Lovell/Corbis; **486** *top* Tsukioka Yoshitoshi/ Asian Art and Archaeology, Inc./*bottom* Michael S. Yamashita/Corbis; **487** Scala/Art Resource, New York; **488** N. Blythe/Robert Harding Picture Library; **490** *left* Charles Rotkin/Corbis; *center* Reunion des Musées Nationaux/Art Resource, New York; *right* Copyright © Bill Lai/The Image Works.

Chapter 17

492–493 Paul W. Liebhardt/Corbis; **493** *top* Wolfgang Kaehler/Corbis; **494** *bottom* Bettmann/Corbis; *top* Jay Dickman/Corbis; **495** Bettmann/Corbis; **496** Wolfgang Kaehler/Corbis; **497** *all* Bettmann/Corbis; **498** Roger Ressmeyer/Corbis; **499** Sovfoto/Eastfoto/PictureQuest; **500** John Wang/PhotoDisc/GettyImages; **502** AFP/Corbis; **503** Jay Dickman/Corbis; **504** David and Peter Turnley/Corbis; **506** David Samuel Robbins/Corbis; **507** *bottom left* Keren Su/Stone/GettyImages; *top* Travelpix/FPG/GettyImages; *bottom right* Yann Layma/Stone/GettyImages; **508** Vito Palmisano/Stone/GettyImages; **510** Reuters NewMedia Inc./Corbis; **511** *top* Brian A. Vikander/Corbis; *bottom* Vince Streano/Corbis; **514** Bettmann/Corbis; **515** Christopher Arnesen/Stone/GettyImages; **516** Bettmann/Corbis; **517** Courtesy of the U.S. Naval Academy Museum; **518** *top* Corbis; *bottom* Jed & Kaoru Share/Corbis; **520** Michael S. Yamashita/Corbis; **522** *bottom left* Roger Ressmeyer/Corbis; *bottom center* Jay Dickman/Corbis; *center* Keren Su/Stone/GettyImages; *top* Christopher Arnesen/Stone/GettyImages; *bottom right* Michael S. Yamashita/Corbis.

Chapter 18

524–525 Copyright © John Eastcott/YVA Momatiuk/The Image Works; **525** *top* Penny Tweedie/Corbis; **526** *top* Daniel Aubry; *bottom* Reuters NewMedia Inc./Corbis; **527** Alexander Turnbull Library, Wellington, N. Z./The Bridgeman Art Library; **528** *center* Daniel Aubry; *top* Penny Tweedie/Corbis; *bottom* Werner Forman/Corbis; **529** James L. Amos/Corbis; **530** Royalty Free/Corbis; **531** Reuters NewMedia Inc./Corbis; **533** *top* Penny Tweedie/Corbis; *bottom* Quadrillion/Corbis; **536** *top right* © Bettmann/Corbis; **537** *bottom* © Wolfgang Kaehler/Corbis; **538** © Hulton-Deutsch Collection/Corbis **542** *left* James L. Amos/Corbis; *center* Quadrillion/Corbis; *right* © Wolfgang Kaehler/Corbis.

Special Report

545 *top* AP/Wide World Photos; *bottom* AP/Wide World Photos; **547** *top* AP/Wide World Photos; *bottom* AP/Wide World Photos; **548** AP/Wide World Photos; **549** *left* © Mario Tama/Getty Images; *right* © Reuters NewMedia Inc./Corbis.

McDougal Littell Inc. has made every effort to locate the copyright holders for the images used in this book and to make full acknowledgment for their use. Omissions brought to our attention will be corrected in subsequent editions.